P9-DMI-127

HEART OF THE COUNTRY
RAVES FOR THE BRILLIANT NEW NOVEL

"A remarkable work, rich and compelling."
—ALFRED COPPEL
author of *THE MARBURG CHRONICLES*

"Mr. Matthews has written a book that pulsates with life, its characters and events so compelling and harsh that the novel is difficult to set aside. . . . A triumphant and captivating novel."
—*KANSAS CITY STAR*

"Pure realism so ingeniously crafted that a reader can believe that the people are real and that it all happened as Matthews wrote it."
—*CHICAGO TRIBUNE BOOKWORLD*

"Fascinating . . . a page-turner"
—*NEW YORK TIMES BOOK REVIEW*

"(A) remarkable historical novel . . . Matthews has taken huge risks of subject matter and style and emerged triumphant. . . . A stunning, mesmerizing performance."
—*NEWSWEEK*

"Harsh . . . Vivid . . . *HEART OF THE COUNTRY* succeeds in a way in which few novels of the American West have done."
—*CHRISTIAN SCIENCE MONITOR*

"By far, it's the best book I've read in a long, long time. It's America with all our Americanisms unfolding . . . Matthews' prose has made exquisite music in this buffalo-world of the prairies."
—CHARLES SULLIVAN
PROVIDENCE JOURNAL-BULLETIN

"This gothic western . . . is a bold and blasphemous story that questions our beliefs and ideas about the Old West. And yet, in showing the dark underside of our heroic myths, it enhances the breadth of life on the frontier by adding a new dimension to that experience; it does not diminish it."
—*LOS ANGELES TIMES*

HEART
OF THE
COUNTRY

GREG MATTHEWS

PINNACLE BOOKS
KENSINGTON PUBLISHING CORP.
http://www.pinnaclebooks.com

PINNACLE BOOKS are published by

Kensington Publishing Corp.
850 Third Avenue
New York, NY 10022

Pinnacle and the P logo Reg. U.S. Pat. & TM Off.

First Zebra Printing: January, 1988

First Pinnacle Printing: December, 1997
10 9 8 7

Printed in the United States of America

CONTENTS

for Jane—again

PART ONE
THE CUCKOO

CHAPTER ONE

In Kansas there is a town called Valley Forge.

Its origins are obscure. It is generally believed that in 1854 a lone farmer *en route* to California by ox-drawn wagon lost heart for the journey in this place, dug a shallow pit for shelter against the wind, roofed it with planks torn from his vehicle and declared himself the first citizen of what he believed would surely become a thriving township. It is also said the man had a supply of whiskey with him, and on his first night inside the pit, alone with a howling westerly and his bottles, he declared himself mayor in perpetuity. In the slowly unwinding hours before dawn it occurred to the mayor that his projected community should bear a name, and in the whiskey-grip of patriotism he emerged from his hole in the ground to the open and uncaring prairie.

Raising his hands, one still in possession of a near-empty bottle, he turned clumsily until he faced the east with its first flush of light. Intoning the name of George Washington, continuing with a stumbling eulogy to that father of the nation, he conferred upon the featureless grassland the name it would retain until such times as the sun cease to climb into the heavens and water cease to flow and American hearts turn from God. His declaration was borne away on the wind, but remained echoing grandly in his fuddled brain. Vastly pleased with his work, the founder of Valley Forge drained the last mouthful from his bottle and flung it away into the dark with a yell of exultation. Thrown off balance by his impulsive gesture he fell, and returned on hands and knees to his home. There, huddled in blankets against a wall of soil, he slept the deep sleep of accomplishment.

With the return of sobriety some twelve hours later, the mayor gave consideration to his future and that of his creation. That the two were inextricably linked he had no doubt. Emerging for the second time from his dugout he was greeted by the dull bellowing of his oxen; beset by thirst, they awaited relief. The mayor scouted the locality and discovered a creek with a meagre trickle of water meandering nearby. While his oxen drank he scanned the horizon. To eyes now undimmed by whiskey the landscape was drear indeed. Not one tree, not so much as a stunted bush presented itself. The land rolled away with the monotonous dip and swell of a languid ocean. Turning slowly, the mayor experienced a momentary lapse of euphoria as the emptiness, the sheer absence of feature impressed itself upon him. Completing a three-quarter circle, he noted with gratitude a low ridge to the northwest, perhaps two or three miles distant, its welcome, if barely perceptible, prominence graced with the unmistakable darkness of foliage.

Leaving his team to graze, the mayor walked to the ridge, his spirits considerably revived. Here was that rare commodity of the prairie—timber. The ridge ran north to south for almost a mile and was at least forty feet high along its spine. The eastern slope, protected from the prevailing winds, provided shelter for blackjack, elm, ash, cottonwood and box elder—a small cornucopia of lumber with which to build a town. The mayor rubbed his hands in anticipation; God had directed him to the right place. He briefly considered relocating his home in the lee of the ridge, then decided against it. His choice of settlement had been arbitrary, made at dusk when the ridge was an indefinable smudge on the horizon, beyond recognition as natural shelter; if the Lord had wanted him to abandon his trek to California close by the ridge He would have revealed it while daylight allowed. No, it was divine will that had determined the location of the dugout, and as such it was not to be contravened. The ridge was close enough; Valley Forge would expand to enfold it in due time. The mayor was content.

For several days he laboured harder than ever before in his life. A dugout is an inappropriate domicile for one elected to high office; the mayor therefore carefully spaded up blocks of prairie earth and built for himself a pioneer home of sod, raising the walls layer by layer until he could build them no higher without the aid of a stool or ladder. He drove his oxen to the ridge and returned with several choice timbers for use as roof beams; the trimmed branches he wove between the beams in a rough lattice. He removed the canvas from his wagon and tied it into place, a gently billowing ceiling, then covered this with more sod, grass side up, to form a living roof.

The mayor surveyed his home with pride. A log cabin of more substantial mien would follow, but for the moment the dictates of the season required that a crop be sown with all haste. He had come equipped with two sacks of seed, one wheat and one rye, and a plough. With these rudiments of agricultural enterprise the mayor began to farm. The task was arduous and drove him to his earthen bed at night numbed with exhaustion. Before his eyes closed he repeated the name "Valley Forge" to himself several times, and drew strength and succour from its talismanic intonation.

One morning the mayor awoke to the sound of muted thunder, yet the sky was clear. The invisible storm seemed to originate from the direction of the ridge. Having heard improbable tales of freakish weather in the west, the mayor decided to witness this meteorological marvel, if such it was, for himself. Climbing through the trees to the top of the ridge he found his expectations both rewarded and confounded. Below him, from the base of the ridge there stretched a violently undulating sea of buffalo. The mayor recognised the creatures from newspaper illustrations, yet was awed by their numbers. The earth beneath his boots quaked at the pounding of their million hoofs, the air choked him with the dust of their passing. Their massive tufted humps and domed heads bobbed with frantic, almost comical haste as they thundered by, the furthest reaches of the herd lost along a horizon shrouded in dust and distance. Recovering his senses, the mayor's first thoughts were for his home. Moving along the ridge to its southernmost point, in which direction the buffalo were travelling with such urgency, he saw that Valley Forge and its environs were to be spared destruction; beyond the ridge's extremity lay a hitherto unnoticed feature of the landscape, a subsidence of the plain flanked on its eastern boundary by a sloping crescent or secondary ridge which served to channel the edges of the herd away to the south-west. The mayor breathed a hasty prayer of thanks; God surely was looking after His chosen place.

The mayor estimated the herd at tens of thousands. After watching it pass with unabated speed and volume for half an hour he revised this figure to hundreds of thousands. He awaited the end of the herd. When it had not arrived after another half hour he abandoned estimates in favour of practical action; he ran to the sod house, checked the load in his cap and ball rifle and staggered back to the ridge, lungs afire with the effort, legs trembling. He need not have hurried; the herd continued to slide past as before. Surely, he thought, they exist in their millions! He aimed, fired, but no buffalo fell. He reloaded, took careful aim, squeezed the trigger in the approved manner. The detonation of cap and powder was lost in the general tumult, and so, it seemed, was the ball, for the target merely swerved fractionally and kept on. Realising his small bore weapon was useless against adult animals, he chose for his third attempt a gangling calf, and succeeded in bringing it down. It lay in a splay-legged heap at the base of the ridge, occasionally trampled upon by its seniors. While he waited patiently to collect his supper the mayor pondered on the possible causes of this titanic stampede—wolves, perhaps, or some thunderstorm too far away to be seen or heard from Valley Forge. No lesser thing

14

could have served to frighten so great a number; there were enough buffalo to encircle the globe.

Around noon the herd dwindled and died away to a scant few beasts, footsore and dazed, rag-tag tail-enders limping forlornly after their speedier fellows. While the mayor descended from the ridge and sank his knife inexpertly into the calf's belly, the answer to his idle question was some fifteen miles away, performing the same task with considerably greater skill.

That night the mayor feasted royally. He celebrated his acquisition of fresh meat with the broaching of a bottle, his first since the founding of the community. He slept soundly, belly rumbling with contentment, the interior of the sod house gradually succumbing to an effluvium of flatus.

In the morning he opened his door to be confronted by a dozen or so Indians. The illustrated newspapers had prepared the mayor for such an encounter, but the raw physicality of their presence sent an uncomfortable flutter through his already strained bowels. Their hair was so long and black, their skin so brown, so greasy, their seminakedness so utterly alien to anything the mayor had known in the east. They squatted before him like idols, their ponies grazing unconcernedly behind. He matched their basilisk stares, knowing that to reveal fear would bring them to their feet in an instant, hatchets poised to crush his skull. The mayor stood his ground and considered his chances. Should he step backwards into the sod house and return with rifle in hand? Perhaps he should simply close the door and wait for them to depart.

One of the Indians stood. The mayor's bowels churned with alarm. He knew the choice that lay before him: to die with clean breeches or to die befouled. A God-fearing man could not present himself to St. Peter bow-legged and beshat. He strode away from his home, away from the Indians, head high, buttocks clenched. The Indians watched with interest as the mayor unhitched his suspenders, squatted and found instant relief. His action provoked a brief conversation among them. He returned and presented himself at arm's reach from the standing Indian, hands on hips, chest thrust forward defiantly. Now they could kill him; purged of supper and self doubt, the mayor awaited his tragic yet manly demise. The Indian raised a hand, his fingers curved. He threw back his head and produced a gargling sound. This was not the bloodcurdling war cry the mayor had read of. The Indian repeated his action and the mayor understood at last. Whiskey! His guests wanted whiskey! He hastened to satisfy their need. Presented with a bottle, the Indian grasped it without a smile and tipped a prodigious quantity into his throat. His companions rose and accepted the liquor in turn. The mayor noticed for the first time that three of their number were women, and felt overwhelming embarrassment at having defecated within sight of them. He consoled himself with the thought that among these children of nature the bodily functions were perhaps not surrounded by the conventions of privacy. The women did not drink. The emptied bottle dropped to the prairie with a forlorn thud. The Indians waited patiently for another. Divining their need, the mayor provided.

Halfway through this second bottle the drinkers began to reel and utter hearty whoops of approval. Their leader clasped his benefactor warmly by the shoulders in a gesture of appreciation and friendship before sliding gently to the ground, where several of the others had already taken their ease. The squaws sat stoically by their ponies. One gave suck to an infant. When the third bottle was broached the mayor became uneasy. Who knew what crimes Indians under the influence might commit? They would almost certainly develop violent tendencies. He strolled into the sod house, loaded his rifle in readiness then hid it under a blanket. He returned to the drinkers and wished them gone; his land required attention and already much of the morning had been wasted. The Indians continued to drink, then fell asleep, snoring without restraint. The mayor sat by his doorway and smoked his pipe, damning the intrusion. He dared not leave them, for he had heard Indians were notorious thieves. The squaws shared dried meat from a buckskin bag among themselves. None was offered to the mayor.

The slanting rays of a westering sun revived the men. Their leader demanded yet more whiskey. The mayor handed over his last two bottles and retired for the night. A mayor ought not to be a drinking man anyway; it eroded public confidence in his ability. He watched between the planks of his door as the Indians built a fire and became raucously drunk all over again. He sat facing the door with the loaded rifle across his knees, waiting for the inevitable attack. Fear kept him awake until the small hours before dawn, when the threat of aggression seemed unlikely; communal snoring came to him on the night air, soothing as a lullaby.

Awakened in mid morning by the rifle sliding from his lap, the mayor stepped cautiously outside. Indians and ponies, all were gone. Five empty bottles and a pile of cold ashes graced what he liked to imagine was his front yard. He rounded a corner of the sod house to ensure his oxen had not been stolen or butchered. They stared back at him with bovine placidity, chewing their everlasting cud. A squaw sat with her back to the sod wall, watching him. He looked around for her pony. There was none. Had they abandoned her? This new development was disquieting. The mayor wanted no involvement with redskins, yet here was one squatting by his home with no apparent intention of leaving. His hospitality had been sorely abused by Indian overindulgence, and now this squaw had been left behind to plague him! The mayor swore, surprising himself with profanity he would not normally have used before men, let alone a woman. He pointed emphatically at the horizon and told her to be gone. The squaw ignored him. He came closer and inspected her. He did not find her attractive. The nature of Indian gratitude slowly wormed its way behind his anger, and the mayor's jaw dropped with comprehension. Whiskey had bought him a wife! He stared at the sky and wondered how best to cope with the gift that had been so unexpectedly thrust upon him.

While he pondered, he ploughed. Perhaps if he paid her no attention the squaw would wander off. He went nowhere near the house all day. In the evening, his irritation fuelled by hunger, he returned to find her cooking remnants of buffalo calf over a fire of dried buffalo dung. He ate in silence. The squaw waited until he had finished before feeding herself. The mayor lit an oil lamp and studied her. She was plump, with no discernible waist. Her face was without expression or pleasing contour, a flat face with black, unblinking eyes. She stared back. He would have preferred that she lower her gaze to indicate maidenly modesty, but the concept was apparently foreign to her.

The mayor lit his pipe. A woman to tend his needs was not an unappealing prospect. True, she was not the girl of his dreams, but she appeared to be young. He squinted through the dim lamplight at her shapeless deerhide smock; her breasts appeared to be full and the mayor cheered up somewhat. He was not a man of wide experience with women, but was sufficiently acquainted with the delights to be had from the female body to regard this interloper with a less jaundiced eye than before. His loins reacted to this train of thought, causing him to shift and squirm uncomfortably. He smiled for the first time at his new-found companion and bedfellow. The smile was not returned, but the mayor was by now in a state of pleasant anticipation and took no offence. He introduced himself, pointing to his chest, then pointed to the squaw. She tapped herself between the breasts and spoke a name unintelligible to the mayor's ears. This would not do; her name henceforth would be Millie. He impressed this fact upon her by repetition. She mastered the word with surprising ease, despite a tendency to stress the second syllable. The mayor congratulated himself on his ability to instruct a simple heathen. He regarded her with the benevolence a man would bestow upon a favourite hound, pride of ownership reflected in his smile.

CHAPTER TWO

In time other settlers joined the mayor at Valley Forge. Timber was taken from the ridge, homes built, farms established. Sensing the imminent fruition of his plans, the mayor took it upon himself to survey a townsite. With infinite care he set aside an area of land as yet unclaimed by the ploughs of his neighbours and laid out a grid ten blocks square with streets wide enough to turn a wagon. His ready tongue convinced all that Valley Forge should be the name of this yet-to-be-realised community. The mayor was looked upon with some indulgence. Respect was owed him as the first man to set down roots in the area but he was, after all, a squawman. Behind his back they called him "the King of Nowhere County" and "the Mayor of Mudville", and smiled.

They allowed him to pace off the town blocks and knock stakes into the soil; someone had to do it, and he performed his self-appointed task well. He raised the first building on a street in Valley Forge and declared it a general store, then rode to the nearest town, some seventy miles distant, to place an order for supplies. Four months later, in the bitter cold of winter, the goods arrived. By now the town boasted a blacksmith, a livery stable and a saloon, and was included in not one, but two stage routes. The mayor began to feel he lived at the hub of the earth. He applied to the territorial government for permission to open a post office at the store. Permission was granted, one more step taken toward the realisation of his dream of elected office.

His aspirations were no secret. A gregarious man, he lectured anyone within hearing on the need to consolidate the foothold the people of Valley Forge had established in the

19

wilderness, to grow streets and buildings as they had grown grain and cattle on the land, to build and populate with all haste, to create a cluster of humanity that would one day achieve the size necessary for official recognition as a township. When the great day arrived work would begin on that hallowed edifice, a town hall. This crowning glory raised its walls in the mayor's imagination even while Valley Forge consisted of half a dozen ramshackle dwellings. The hall would be of quarried stone, not lumber, and the mayoral office would be panelled with polished walnut. Old Glory would stand beside a desk of solid teak, and His Honour the Mayor would conduct municipal business from the comfort of a stuffed leather throne. Stained glass windows depicting the march of progress westward across the plains would cast a mellow light across the features of he whose dream had become reality, the founding father of the community, the man in whose honour a statue was erected in the town square, hands firmly grasping bronze lapels, the personification of manifest destiny.

This vision lay behind the mayor's eyes through every waking moment; it haunted the hours spent on his farm and while he managed the store and post office; it dictated glowing eulogies to Valley Forge for publication in eastern newspapers, extravagant phrases worthy of this land of milk and honey that wanted only people, more people, to realise its potential as harbinger of civilisation in the glorious territory of Kansas. And for the future? Would not a town, guided by the wisest head, eventually become a city? City Hall! The notion left him breathless, left him quivering with purpose, straining to summon the world to his door.

Reality, like a leaden weight, will bring the grandest vision to earth. A neighbour finally took pity on the mayor and defined its shape; no citizen, no matter how civic minded, no matter how suited by temperament and ability, could ever hope to achieve recognition in public office while sharing his home with a squaw. It was that simple. Even if the mayor chose to sanctify his union with Millie by way of a Christian marriage the result would be the same: defeat at the polls. The neighbour advised an early solution to the problem, now, while Valley Forge was still the merest hamlet. Newcomers were arriving almost every week to swell the population; the fewer who were acquainted with the mayor's unfortunate choice of domestic partner the greater his chances of election on that distant but fast approaching day.

The mayor saw sense in this line of reasoning, yet was loath to act upon it. The presence of Millie in his life and home had become an accepted fact. His meals were prepared promptly, the fare monotonous but filling, his house swept free of dust each day. The memory of Millie's first encounter with a broom and its function brought a smile to his face. True, their conversation on any day seldom exceeded the dozen or so words of English she had mastered, but there had been no real need to teach her more; the entire community was available to the mayor for lengthy discussion on weighty matters. Not least to be taken into consideration was her willingness to engage in coitus. Her body, plump and warm and yielding, afforded him a measure of delight beyond his expectations. Through the winter she had shielded him from the melancholy that will descend on a man snowbound and alone. She did not often smile, but not once had he seen her frown. She was not prone to sulking or laziness. He could not be sure of her contentment, but she appeared not to begrudge her lot. In all, she had brought to him a quiet happiness, a sense of well-being on which to base his grandiose schemes. But with her by his side he would not be elected mayor.

For several days he agonised. Unable to perform the act of love, he convinced himself he no longer found her desirable. The ample weight of her body beside him, silent, compliant, irritated him. How could a man sleep without room to stretch? He ordered her to sleep on the floor. Given the least opportunity, expedience will bend morality and principle to its will. Mere selfishness will accomplish radical changes in perception; against political ambition Millie stood no chance. His decision made, the mayor purchased a ticket for her on a stage route south. There, the government had set aside land deemed suitable for the Indian population ousted from Kansas and other territories by the influx of white settlers. The mayor did not know to which tribe Millie belonged, nor did he know which tribes were to be found herded together on the government reservation. Millie was an Indian and would be with her own kind. It was only fitting and just, he assured himself.

He drove her to the stage depot. Millie proved to be the only passenger departing from Valley Forge that day. The depot clerk, divining the mayor's plan, respecting the delicacy of his emotions, spoke to him only of the weather and the prospect of a fine crop this year. The mayor was grateful for this display of tact, and made a mental note to elevate the clerk to a position of municipal authority at some future date. The stagecoach from the north pulled in, trailing a plume of dust. The passengers climbed stiffly down to stretch their legs while a fresh team was put into harness. Proudly wearing a new calico dress she did not realise was a parting gift, Millie admired the horses. The mayor looked at the street, at the sky, anywhere but at Millie. The call to board came. Believing the mayor was taking her on a journey, Millie entered the coach with mild excitement. She had in her hand a small tote bag, also new and containing ten dollars. Settling herself among the other passengers, she waited for the mayor to join her.

The driver's whip cracked, the team leaned into their collars and the stage began to move. Puzzled, Millie put her head through the open window and saw the man who had been hers for as many moons as there were fingers on her hand walking away from the depot, back straight, head high. She was not alarmed, for every seat was occupied; her man would have to follow in his wagon. But if that were so, she asked herself, why had he placed her in the stagecoach at all? Why did they not travel together in the wagon, as husband and wife should? Peering through the window again, she could see no wagon following behind. Doubt took root inside her and grew into a knot that tightened with the passing of every mile. The passengers talked among themselves and stared at her with unfriendly eyes. Alone among strangers, Millie knew fear.

When Valley Forge at last disappeared behind a low rise the driver halted the stage and stepped down. He informed Millie her proper place was not inside, but on top with the baggage. Realising she did not understand, he opened the door and beckoned her out. Millie stood in the road, confused. Was she to wait here for her man to arrive? Losing patience, the driver pointed to the roof. Millie climbed awkwardly from the wheel up to the driver's box, and was assisted on to the roof by another passenger travelling beside the driver. She sat crosslegged among the tied-down valises and chests, facing the rear of the coach; perhaps her man would come into sight at any moment. Both men found her position amusing, and agreed that Indians were contrary animals at the best of times. The stage began to roll.

Millie watched the empty road unwind, two ruts worn into the prairie sod, straight as the horizon. Swaying left and right, secured to her perch only by the strength of her fingers, she felt the cold wind of betrayal whisper through her veins. Rides-Two-Horses had left her with the white man as punishment for her failure to conceive sons; even the curse of daughters had not been placed in her belly. "Empty Pot", he had called her, and traded her for the drink that makes men fall down. Her new man had treated her kindly, had not laughed scornfully in her face nor been rough with her body. She had known happiness in his house of earth. As her contentment had grown, so, too, had a bud of flesh in her womb. A small voice came from the cradle of her hips, a male voice, and Millie's heart had sung to the tiny swelling maleness within her, encouraging him, building strength in his limbs.

When the sickness of new life came upon her she crept from the sod house early each morning to vomit; her son needed much room inside her, and with the insistence of a man pushed the food of yesterday from her mouth as he grew. The father of her son must not witness these moments

23

of filth and pain. In time he would see how her belly fattened and would link his joy with hers. He would know pride when a man child dropped from her loins, and would hold her gift in his arms.

But he had not noticed the change in her, for as she ate to feed her son her own body grew big, hiding him behind swathes of flesh. Her neck and face expanded, her very fingers became plump. She attempted to share the secret with her man by pointing to her belly. He poured a measure of bad tasting fluid down her throat which made her bowels flow. She did not risk repeating this unpleasantness; when her son made his appearance into the light of the world her man's surprise would double his joy and pride. Millie nursed her secret and smiled inwardly, waiting for the great moment of birth. That time grew nearer and still her man knew nothing. He knew nothing when he drove her to town in his wagon and gave her to strangers. Like Rides-Two-Horses he believed her to be empty. Had he known the truth he would not have done this bad thing. Like all men he was without patience, and had removed her from his home.

Millie did not associate the ticket in her bag with any destination. She believed herself the property of the man holding the reins, the one who had ordered her on to the roof to be near him; a careful man kept that which he owned close by. She did not want to be his, for he had shown no respect, laughing at her as she levered her bulk up on to the roof. She wished to be back with the father of her son, to make him see how he had wronged her. He would take her back once he knew, of that she was certain. When the coach stopped she would get down and walk home. Bounced and buffeted, covered with dust, Millie hung on grimly to the baggage.

Late in the afternoon the first way-station on the road south was reached, a sod house standing in isolation on the prairie. A lone cow munched feed along with a dozen horses in the corral. While the lathered team was changed the passengers entered the station for coffee and week-old biscuits, or sought relief over a trench screened from view by a sod wall. A hollow-ribbed dog lifted its leg by the stage and splashed a rear wheel. The driver disappeared to share a drink with the station manager. The ostlers paid Millie no attention. Now was the time for her to descend and begin walking.

She eased her cramped legs from beneath her and was instantly struck by pain. It began in her belly and lanced through her heart. She attempted to crawl backwards to the driver's box but could not move for the wrenching agony it provoked. Sweat flooded her body; she panted for breath, then tried again. This time the pain punished her severely. Her vision swam, her brain turned inside her skull, bees droned in her ears. The smell of horse sweat and dung brought bile to her throat, plugging the scream that fought to escape. She held herself still, controlling her body, then slowly, with infinite care, eased herself back into her former position. The pain subsided to a dull aching deep within her. She sat for fifteen minutes, breathing steadily, reassuring her son he would come to no harm.

The passengers resumed their seats. Jokes were made about the fat squaw on the roof and the possibility of her crashing through if the road become any rougher. The driver whipped up his fresh team and the way-station dwindled to insignificance. Millie felt panic crawl down her spine; every turn of the wheels took her further from the place she wished to be. She must get off before the distance to be walked grew too great. She turned her head; the driver and passenger beside him were watching the road, talking loudly above the din of hoofs and squealing wood and leather and iron. Grasping the baggage ropes, she hauled herself forward on to her knees. The pain flared briefly in protest, then settled. She edged toward the canvas slope of the luggage boot at the rear and turned to ease her legs down its thrumming surface. Her feet found the tailgate while her hands still held the roof rail. She paused to gain strength, belly throbbing, sweat drenching her sides. The road unrolled six feet below her shoes. She could move neither up nor down. A whimper of despair rose in Millie's throat. She released her grip on the rail. The tarpaulin offered no hold; her bulk slid back and forth across it with every lurching movement of the stage for half a mile before the wheels on the left side rolled into a deeper than usual rut. The entire vehicle tilted, and Millie slid from canvas to air. Her impact with the ground drove breath and consciousness from her body. The window blinds had been drawn down against dust and heat. No one saw her fall.

Millie lay on her side in the road while the afternoon sun lowered itself toward the horizon and bled its light across the plains. Her eyes opened. Her hand swam into view, the two outer fingers scraped and raw, bent backwards. She asked her son if he lived but received no reply; perhaps he slept to shield himself from the pain surrounding him. She ordered her limbs to raise her from the ground. Her belly burned with a fierce, insistent fire. Millie lifted her shoulders with trembling arms, gathered her legs beneath her and forced herself to stand. The scream that burst from her sent prairie dogs scuttling to their holes. Blood thundered in her ears, the red and gold sky reeled. Millie swayed ponderously, made her quivering legs turn in the direction of Valley Forge. She began to walk. Each halting step taken fanned the dark flame inside her, little by little consuming her strength.

Dusk gathered around Millie as she walked, chiding herself for her pain. Her brothers had plunged their arms into beehives to prove their manhood and endured the agony that followed without flinching. For her son she would do the same. Her pain, coiling and clenching around his bed of flesh, would make him strong. From her suffering would come a man for whom suffering was a gentle rain to be shrugged off and forgotten, a man whose face would reveal no hurt to the world, man of fire-hardened wood, warrior of stone.

The stage ruts ran before her, dark and straight and never-ending, the surrounding prairie washed in moonlight. A shadow marched at Millie's feet. She came within sight of a lamp burning in the waystation's window. Should she beg for help, make them understand her pain? No, her pride would not allow it. She would be remembered as the fat one on top of the coach; they would mock her. She left the road to circle around the building and corral, fearing the dog would scent her. The pain had settled into rhythm with Millie's footsteps. She walked with arms folded tightly across her belly, the little tote-bag swinging at her wrist, broken fingers throbbing in unison with the greater pain within.

Her shadow shifted with the rising moon as Millie trudged north, her pace gradually slowing. She no longer thought of her man at Valley Forge and the great mistake he had made. Even her son was edged from her mind by the weariness that fought for attention against the pain. Millie's eyes began to play cunning tricks; the road, which she knew to be straight, would suddenly veer sideways, trying to deceive her feet into losing their way. Twice she had to walk in a circle to find the ruts again. Finally the road tired of supporting her weight and guiding her way; before Millie's eyes it sank into the prairie, simply vanished from sight, as if white men with their wheels had never crossed the land and left the scars of their passing. She walked on, her head growing heavy. Now the moon played mischievous games, turning in ever-widening circles above her. Earth and sky conspired to keep Millie from her objective, yet on she walked with jaw set firm, determined that no magic should defeat her.

The prairie rose up to meet her knees, then her belly and face. Millie grunted with surprise, issued a command to her body and rolled slowly on to her back. The tiny campfires of the sky people glimmered and shone above her, as many as there were blades of grass in all the world. They would not see her, for she had no fire. The moon lay somewhere behind her head, tired of its spinning. Millie watched the campfires closely, allowing them to draw her away from the agony of her flesh. The sky people carried fire upon their heads as they moved across their limitless black plain, searching, always searching for the sky buffalo. Millie knew

27

the greatest number were gathered in a herd that stretched across all the sky, for most of the fires were there also. Pain drove Millie into the sky to join them, but no matter how high she flew the fires remained far away. Millie dreamed of shining people who carried fire in bowls atop their shining faces. A shining one approached her. Millie recognised the face of her mother and smiled. Her mother drove the fire into her belly.

Millie screamed, but no sound would come. The sky above her was blue. Her body convulsed; her son of stone fought to be free of her. His limbs flexed and thrashed. Millie's thighs flooded with blood and water. A monstrous horned and bearded head lowered itself to her face, its shaggy brow casting a cool shadow across her eyes. Mucus-slimed nostrils huffed and dilated at the scent of blood; a thick purple tongue snaked out to lick the salt sweat from her brow. A massive hump bulked at the edge of her vision as a second buffalo nuzzled her legs. Millie breathed the rank animal smell, her face and neck spattered with saliva. She was not afraid. The sky buffalo had come to be with her, to lend their strength. They crowded around her in their hundreds, their thousands, mighty heads lowered to graze.

Her body began to split. Her son was a buffalo calf gouging at her with his horns, scrabbling with sharp hoofs toward the light. She was gutted with an axe, her belly was turned inside out and raked with thorns, her spine bent like a bow until it snapped. Her horned son pushed his swollen head from her thighs and bellowed. Startled, the buffalo retreated, heads swaying with alarm, leaving Millie and her child in a perfect circle of clear ground. The sound dwindled to a hacking wail that spiralled into the cloudless sky and was lost. The herd lowered its collective head to resume grazing. Millie felt the warm and wet lump of flesh plastered to her thighs, felt its quivering cries travel through the cord binding them together, up into her tortured belly and into her heart, which shattered into a thousand shards of stone.

Delivered of her son, attended by beasts, Millie surrendered herself to death.

All morning and into the afternoon the herd slowly grazed its way past the body in the calico dress. Flies gathered to feast on the bloody afterbirth. They crawled over the small membranous creature with its tightly shut eyes and open mouth and twitching, kicking limbs. Its frenetic wailing ceased as the sun's heat penetrated the cloth. The last few buffalo meandered past, and on a low rise overlooking the tail end of the herd two horsemen appeared. One dismounted, drew a rifle from its scabbard and rested it across the saddle. A shot boomed, a buffalo staggered and fell. The rifleman remounted and the two men, a relief driver and an ostler from the way-station, ambled toward their kill, in no particular hurry to begin the dirty work of skinning and gutting.

They saw Millie's body and rode closer, believing the darkened heap to be a dead calf. Dismounting, they walked to the fly-infested mass and stared. A boot nudged Millie's thigh. A cloud of flies rose at the intrusion and a thin wail came from beneath the dusty calico. The cloth was pulled back with a rifle barrel. The two men looked at Millie's son and at each other. The ostler knelt and drew his knife, severed the flyblown cord and lifted the child.

"Shouldn't be alive," said the driver. "Take a look in her purse." Millie's ticket and ten dollars were found.

The following day a feed wagon rolled into Valley Forge and stopped by the stage depot. Millie's blanket-wrapped body lay in the wagon bed, accompanied by a shovel. The ostler told his story. The depot clerk stared at the blanket and at the baby swaddled in a rawhide jacket on the driver's seat, then sent a boy to fetch the mayor from his store. By the time he arrived at least twenty people, most of the permanent population of Valley Forge, were gathered around the wagon. The blanket was drawn from Millie's face. The baby howled. The mayor swayed on his feet with shock, encircled by eyes. The silence of the townspeople pressed against him, heavy with accusation.

"I didn't know. . . ." He floundered for escape. "She said she wanted to leave. . . ."

"How'd she do that?" asked a woman. "She never spoke but a handful of words."

"There was no sign of a child. . . . I didn't know. . . ." The words strangled him. The crowd waited for more, disbelieving. The ostler noted their reaction; these people were primed for a verdict of guilty, had already condemned the little man in their midst. Stammering his excuses, searching for a sympathetic face, he would never be allowed to live this down, even if the dead woman was only an Indian. The ostler enjoyed the novelty of watching a man drown in air; they would eat up this story back at the way-station. Boys, he'd say, today I saw a man strung up without a rope.

The mayor's shoulders slumped. The stony faces around him bore down on his dreams of elected office and crushed them to dust. He saw they had been waiting for this, the chance to let him know they considered him nothing but a strutting rooster, crowing for the dawn as though he alone had created it.

"Best get her buried," said the ostler, taking charge. The crowd, he knew, would stand there till kingdom come, just staring at the little squaw-man and cutting him to pieces with their eyes, enjoying themselves. He climbed on to the feed wagon and took up the reins. "Which way's your place, mister?" The mayor looked up. Pity in the ostler's eyes drew him on to the wagon seat beside the baby.

The mayor stared straight ahead as they left Valley Forge. His hands lay in his lap like rag dolls, his jaw hung slack. The ostler studied him from the corner of his eye. "Lucky for you we got a cow at the station. We gave the kid some milk and he took to it. I brung some along." He reached below the seat and hauled up two whiskey-bottles by their necks, incongruously white, stoppered with cloth teats. "You better find a wet nurse pretty fast, though." The mayor nodded dumbly, the demon of humiliation howling in his ears.

They reached the mayor's sod house and stopped. The mayor spoke, his voice toneless, distant. "She should be in the shade. . . ." He pointed to the ridge and the wagon moved on, bumping across the prairie.

Millie was laid to rest under a cottonwood tree. The ostler maintained it was only fair he should keep the ten dollars from Millie's purse; he'd gone to a power of trouble over mother and baby both. The mayor made no reply and was left at the ridge, alone with his son and his thoughts beneath the noon sky.

It was finished. All his aspirations had been dashed to pieces by this one error of judgement, the taking into his home of a squaw. The people of Valley Forge had tolerated the arrangement only because they needed him to organise for them, to plan the townsite and petition the government, to be the humming, driving catalyst who had created around himself a community with which to define and complement his existence. Now, having barely begun, the dream was over. The mayor could not mistake the look on those faces. He had fallen. A man who drove his woman out to give birth and die on the prairie could never hold his head up again, not here.

He smothered the guilt for his inadvertent crime, pushed it away from him, thought of the future. He was still young; there were other towns struggling for existence in the west, needing him. He would seek a place already established, far from Valley Forge, a hamlet waiting only for a man of his abilities to speed its progress. He would first return home to Indiana and borrow money from his brother, then start for the new territories to begin again. He would marry a respectable woman, someone chaste, demure, worthy of him. The marriage, already an accomplished event in his mind, would be a firm base on which to build a career. He would become a family man, a solid citizen. His sons would enjoy all the advantages his position could provide. He must not allow his confidence to be undermined by this unfortunate episode. Having cast himself as victim of fate in the first act of his personal drama, the mayor prepared for his entrance upon a new and unsullied stage before an audience eagerly awaiting his performance. He would not disappoint them, whoever they were. He must leave immediately; a shrewd man cut his losses and built anew with all haste.

A cry from his son scattered the comforting vision. He looked at the creature lying naked and fretful at his side and frowned. A nameless half-breed bastard had no place in the life the mayor planned. He found himself wishing it had died along with its mother, and guiltily expunged the thought. Without taking the baby in his arms he tilted a whiskey-bottle, plugged the squalling mouth with a rag teat and welcomed the silence.

By the following noon the mayor's arrangements had been made. For an absurdly low price he sold his store and farm to Lucius Croft, the neighbour who had advised ridding himself of Millie. The irony did not escape him, but Croft was the only man in town who could afford even this meagre sum. He drove his wagon with a single chest of possessions, his son and a gallon of milk along the main street, heading east. No one raised a hand in farewell or asked his destination. The townspeople watched with satisfaction as the mayor passed from their lives.

CHAPTER THREE

Dr. Cobden's sole moment of relaxation on any day was to stroll through the streets of St. Louis at twilight. He generally restricted his regimen to the area around his home on DeWitte Street. The houses here were grand, the brick sidewalks overshadowed by splendid trees. He took particular pleasure in the soft lamplight flowing from windows as he passed, in the muted sounds of domestic clatter and discord reaching the street through curtains opened to catch the evening breeze. He walked slowly, savouring the air, appreciating the last flush of gold in the sky. The doctor's constitutional was of long standing; neighbours knew to within minutes when his tall figure would pass by, the elegant cane idly swinging, the tip of his cigar a reassuring beacon in the gathering dusk.

The doctor and his wife, regarded by all as exemplars of virtue, if not of rectitude, set the standard by which the neighbourhood measured its respectability. His profile of intimidatingly noble proportions aroused in the breasts of local wives a disturbing flutter, yet their husbands did not complain, and certainly were not jealous when their womenfolk visited the doctor's surgery for relief from all manner of minor complaints, usually to do with their female physicality. The husbands were bankers, successful merchants, men of commerce. They knew the doctor well, attended the same clubs and trusted him implicitly. He did not relish the telling of lewd stories and would walk away from anyone so doing. He was a man of learning and principle. No taint of scandal or breach of professional ethics had ever been associated with his name, nor were such expected. Dr. Cobden was a gentleman.

He paused in his stride to observe the rising moon, its fullness provoking a similar state in the doctor's chest. He was familiar with the sensation and its attendant emotion; unless checked it would degenerate into mild melancholia, for the doctor was not a happy man. Of late he had noted a tendency in himself to indulge in whimsical poesy; the darkness falling around him, for example, became a descending cloak of Cimmerian gloom, the full moon a lambent orb. Inspecting the ample bust of a patient this morning he had almost spoken aloud the word "Junoesque". He interpreted these literary indulgences as a mental flight from the reality of the present. While a student in Boston he had occasionally penned verses of a satirical nature for distribution among his friends; the more romantic or pastoral efforts he reserved for his own eyes. This re-emergence of poetical inclination, so long suppressed, obviously represented an unhealthy regression to the fecklessness of youth. Did this mean he was afraid of the advancing years? He was thirty-seven, firmly established in his practice, a much respected member of the community. Surely he was not dissatisfied with his lot.

The one identifiable thorn of discontent in his side was his wife's barrenness. Fourteen years of marriage had produced nothing but tears of apology from Emilia and constant reassurances of his love from the doctor. He had long since accepted the sterility of their union. Although a churchgoing Christian, he did not ascribe his wife's condition to God's will; a man of science, he knew that somewhere within Emilia a malformation, a twistedness, a lack of proper physical configuration prevented his relentlessly planted seed from taking root. This unfortunate circumstance bore on its reverse side an advantage the doctor admitted only to himself; he could engage in sexual intercourse with his wife whenever the urge came upon him without fear of ruining her slender figure. His passion for her remained strong and secret; Emilia believed his nightly mountings to be prompted by the desire for offspring, never by desire for its own priapic sake. Had she known, Emilia would have been profoundly shocked. She took no pleasure in the act herself, regarded it as her sacred duty, nothing more. Poetry and procreation, mused the doctor, and walked on.

His steps took him by the Episcopal church and he paused again to witness a flight of bats emerging from its steeple. Bats in the belfry, another phrase reminiscent of his youth, brought a smile to the doctor's lips. He decided he would succumb completely to morbid introspection this evening, opened the iron gate and strolled through to the cemetery. He selected a relatively new headstone free of grime and sat upon it. His occupation precluded superstitious fear of the dead; nevertheless, he extinguished his cigar out of respect. An elm whispered and rustled in the night air above his head. A twig fell on to his hat. Dr. Cobden removed his handsome stovepipe, whether to check if the twig had left an unsightly mark or as another sign of respect for the departed he could not decide.

The breeze brushed his scalp with gratifying coolness. He laid the hat on his knee and allowed random memories to crowd and coalesce in his mind, inwardly wincing at painful moments from yesteryear, recalling other, happier times with relish. Oddly, the least enjoyable of his recollections provoked a sharper reaction than the rest. He found he could summon sweat to his armpits and a knot to his stomach in exact replication of the agony he had suffered at the age of nineteen, when his father had made him stand before the entire family and confess to idleness and profligacy at college, resulting in abysmal examination grades. The ordeal had prompted him to mend his ways, yet the excruciating humiliation endured in memory, ready at the least provocation to reinvade his body, hot and palpitating. Compared to this, the resurrected wooing and winning of Emilia, a delightful experience at the time, prompted no more than a tepid warmth within him. Disconcerted, Dr. Cobden squirmed restlessly on the headstone and wondered, not for the first time, if he was possessed of a hopelessly melancholic disposition. One day, he assured himself, medical science would extend its knowledge beyond the merely physical and explore the teeming jungles of the brain.

The churchyard gate squealed. The doctor looked up apprehensively; if the church warden should find him seated on a gravesite his reputation would suffer. He stood hastily and attempted to identify the figure approaching the church door. The man, whoever he was, did not conduct himself with assurance; his clothing appeared rough, his manner furtive. The moonlight revealed a nondescript bundle in his arms. Intrigued, the doctor watched as the bundle was deposited carefully by the door. The man looked around briefly, failed to notice the doctor hidden in the darkness beneath the elm and hurried back to the gate. It squealed again, and his footsteps faded.

Dr. Cobden realised he had witnessed a scene worthy of the most mawkish theatrical melodrama. Before taking his first step toward the bundle he knew what it would contain. He knelt and examined the small sleeping face, plucked the expected note from a fold in the blanket and read the usual message: *This child is without a father and must now be without a mother. In the name of God I beg you to find for him a home of repute. May a sinning girl be forgiven.* This was an interesting variation on a hackneyed theme; the man was apparently so ashamed of his action he sought to disguise his sex in accordance with the dictates of convention. A sinning girl, indeed. The doctor found himself chuckling at the absurdity. He amused himself with the notion of chasing after the fellow, tapping him on the shoulder, saying "Pardon me, miss, I believe you dropped something".

Sobered by his own levity in the face of what was undeniably a tragedy despite its ridiculous trappings, he gently lifted the foundling and considered the options available to him. The church would no doubt send the infant to an orphanage where, unlike its stage counterpart, it would not grow up to discover it was the kidnapped offspring of wealthy parents, the victim of a dastardly plot to cheat it of its inheritance. Wrong would not be righted by final curtain; there would be no future reprieve for this abandoned scrap of humanity. The child's eyes opened and stared into his. Doctor and infant regarded each other in silence for some time. The doctor experienced a sensation of warmth and sadness. He identified it as pity. Without having made a conscious decision, he turned from the church and carried the bundle home.

Entering quietly by the back door, he placed the child on the kitchen table and unwrapped the grubby blanket. A boy, apparently sound. It kicked feebly at the air and ungraciously passed wind. The doctor noted its black hair and swarthy skin—a half-breed. Now he understood the man's charade.

A Negress of middle age entered the kitchen and stopped short at the sight of a baby among the crockery. "Where'd that come from?"

The doctor laughed. "Where all babies come from, Hattie. Get some hot water started and fetch clean linen. He needs a bath."

"You just deliver this'n?"

"Delivered him from a sorry fate."

"That child's got Indian blood in him, Doctor. You can see it right off."

"I know that, Hattie. Half the colour's probably dirt. You fix him up."

He passed through the house to the drawing room. Emilia was seated in her usual chair, crocheting. The doctor was eager to spring his surprise; from the moment Hattie entered the kitchen and consolidated the child's presence he had known the course he would take.

"Emilia, we have a visitor," he smiled.

"A visitor?"

"Before I introduce you, I have a question. If the opportunity for motherhood presented itself, would you take it?"

"William, please do not make a joke of our misfortune."

"The question is seriously put. Would you?"

"You know I would, if God so wills."

"Circumstance, rather than God, has been at work this evening, or perhaps fate." He placed an arm under hers. "Come with me."

"Is this a game, William? I find it in poor taste."

"Wait until you see what I have to show you."

He escorted her to the kitchen. The stove crackled; Hattie had departed for the linen closet upstairs. Emilia stared at the twitching, mewling bundle on the table, colour draining from her face. The doctor lifted his prize expertly and brought it to her. "A healthy-looking young fellow, don't you think?"

"William, please explain yourself."

"I found him by the church. Someone left him there, abandoned him." He produced the note. Emilia scanned it briefly, thrust it from her. "I do not understand." Her voice was cold.

"The child requires a home. We require a child. Was ever there a more obvious solution?"

A small gasp escaped Emilia's compressed lips. "Surely you've taken leave of your senses. The child is not white."

"Half-white. Around three weeks old, I'd say."

"William, please think before you say more. The charitable thing to do is place it with an institution."

"You have no understanding of such places or of the people who manage them. I would not willingly deliver a dog into their custody."

"I will not have an Indian child in my home. This is madness."

Her resolution irked him. "If his skin was white, would you reconsider?"

"Perhaps. If I knew the circumstances."

"Emilia, please allow a little kindness into your heart. This boy has no home, no family, no future. He has nothing but this one chance."

"The greatest kindness you can do for him is what I have suggested. We cannot raise an Indian. Consider the difficulties."

"I have."

He had not. Quite simply, he wished the child to be his. It felt as no other baby had in his arms. He could not have explained his dogged determination to possess, to cosset, to nourish the small life held against his waistcoat. Scores of babies had passed through his professional life, each one a personal challenge to his abilities. Some had lived, some had not; all received his utmost dedication, all were precious, yet none belonged to Dr. Cobden. Children of various hues were born and deserted every day in the poorer quarters of St. Louis, the unwanted result of casual liaisons, liquor and ignorance. He had never contemplated rescuing even one such from its fate among the slum dwellers. Perhaps it was the unique manner of this child's insinuation into his life that triggered so profound a reaction, perhaps years of frustrated parental yearning, or merely a masculine resolve to have his own way in his own home.

The doctor glared at his wife. She knew his mood had hardened, had become firm conviction; he would not be swayed. Reluctant to surrender, she lowered her eyes. "We will discuss this matter more fully, William."

"I think not. He *will* remain with us, Emilia."

"Will you not take into consideration my feelings?"

"Your feelings, my dear, are suspect. I am disappointed to find such lack of compassion in my own wife."

"William, that is unfair and you know it. I simply wish to point out the dangers of this . . . wild plan."

"There are no dangers."

Hattie returned, sensed the unhappy atmosphere and busied herself setting down towels, readying a large porcelain bowl. "I brung down an old shirt to put him in," she said, to fill the silence rather than to inform.

"That will be fine for now, Hattie. Suitable garments will be found in due course, I'm sure." He continued to glare at Emilia, his eyes now conveying a distinct message for her. Secreted in Emilia's wardrobe was a chest containing swaddling clothes. She had purchased them a decade ago in the belief that fine laces tailored for the newborn would summon life to her womb. The doctor had lectured her on her foolishness but allowed the clothing to remain. A year later he had entered her room to find Emilia pressing a silk christening robe to her abdomen, silently mouthing a prayer, unaware of his presence; he had left without disturbing her, shaken by the intensity of her mute supplication. His eyes, his tone of voice told Emilia what was expected of her. A wave of repugnance rose in her throat. The cherished satins were held in readiness for her own child; to soil them on this native brat would be an unspeakable crime.

"William. . . ."

"I do not wish to discuss this matter further."

Choking with anger, Emilia turned stiffly from him and left the room. Hattie lifted a large saucepan from the stove and poured warm water into the bowl. A lifetime of domestic servitude had honed her perceptions to an intuitive edge. She had divined the doctor's plan, knew of the swaddling clothes upstairs and was quietly appalled. An Indian in the house—the notion was downright uncivilised. She lifted the baby and deposited it in the water. A howl of outrage filled the kitchen.

"I don't believe this child's acquainted with soap and water."

"He'll get used to it. Man is infinitely adaptable."

He watched Hattie's large hands skilfully bathe and dry the squalling baby. Hattie noted the expression on the doctor's face, what she called a smile that don't know it's there. "This baby going to be here permanent?"

"He is."

There was no mistaking the certainty in his voice. Hattie towelled the dark hair already sprouting into a thatch. The howling had stopped. She sat the firm brown buttocks on a cambray shirt. Dark eyes stared into her own, direct and unblinking. "I expect you got a name picked out, Doctor."

"He'll be called . . . Joseph."

The name of his firstborn son had been chosen while the doctor was still courting Emilia. Joseph had been his grandfather's name. He rolled it silently on his tongue.

* * *

An unused room at the rear of the house was cleaned, aired, repapered in pale blue. The doctor bought a cradle lined with blue silk and a perambulator, and took his evening stroll in the company of the foundling.

Word of his unusual acquisition spread through the neighbourhood. That the Cobdens should adopt a child after so many years without issue was understandable, but an Indian? His fellow club members began to concern themselves with the doctor's state of health; no man in his right mind would behave in so foolish a manner. Knowing he could never have explained his obsession to them, the doctor enlisted the aid of science; the adoption was an experiment to determine the extent to which the influence of primitive heredity could be curbed by that of a civilised upbringing. Young Joseph would be raised among the affluent white class and would hopefully think and conduct himself accordingly. St. Louis society was sorely vexed. If the doctor's experiment proved successful, why, the philosophy behind it could logically be extended to the Negroes, and the South had built its prosperity on the concept of the African's intrinsic inferiority. Dr. Cobden's adoption of an Indian indicated his espousal of that most dangerous of heresies, racial equality. Their doubts began to multiply. Cobden was a Bostonian, no Southerner; his household's only servant was a free black woman hired for wages. Did this indicate the doctor's disapproval of slavery, the very cornerstone of life below the Mason-Dixon line? The question had not been raised when Cobden came to St. Louis to set up his practice, but was now of paramount importance. Was the city harbouring a viper in its bosom?

His club members convened secretly to delegate one of their number as spokesman and inquisitor. Dr. Cobden was invited to supper at the St. Giles and plied with food and drink. His companion, a cotton broker, lit cigars for them both, cleared his throat and began his painful duty. Politely, with a considerable degree of embarrassment, he expressed the doubts of his peers. The doctor's eyebrows lifted in astonishment. "I had no idea such a hornets' nest had been stirred. In all honesty, the wider implications had simply not occurred to me."

"And now that they have been brought to your attention?"

The doctor drew on his cheroot, allowed smoke to mingle with the sparkling chandeliers while he deliberated. The questions posed by his host had indeed occurred to him in the weeks following the introduction of Joseph into his home; he had hoped his neighbours and associates were not of similar analytical persuasion. The anxious face opposite him indicated this was not the case. He must tread carefully to avoid fracturing the rotten carapace of their prejudice. St. Louis was a fine city and he did not wish to leave.

He smiled disarmingly. "Surely one small baby could never topple a way of life that has endured for two centuries and more. Indians are not Negroes and, in any case, Joseph is half-white. It's highly likely that if he succeeds, as I hope he will, the credit must lie with the white portion of his blood."

This twisted rationale, so blatantly expounded, proved satisfactory. Dr. Cobden's reputation was buttressed once again, with perhaps a minor subsidence in the foundations, attributable to eccentricity. The stylish perambulator became a familiar and accepted sight along DeWitte Street, steered by Hattie in the daylight hours, by the doctor himself in the evenings.

At no time was Emilia seen with her adopted son, not in the street, nor on those occasions when ladies of the neighbourhood called in the afternoon to drink tea from delicate china cups and knit and discuss those inconsequential subjects deemed fit for the minds of women. Joseph was never displayed by Emilia for the benefit of her guests. When questioned on the child's progress she pronounced him fit and well, and changed the subject. When asked if she was in agreement with her husband's radical theory Emilia replied: "Dr. Cobden is a brilliant man, a graduate of the finest medical college in the country. It is not for me to question his judgement." From her behaviour grew the rumour that Emilia Cobden was not happy playing the role of mother to a half-breed bastard. The ladies of the area sympathised among themselves and visited the doctor's surgery less often with their trifling complaints, this being their only available form of protest.

The doctor took advantage of the decline in custom to lend his time and services to a charity ward lately established in a dilapidated cotton warehouse among the slums. This infirmary for the poor had been funded in part by the city, largely by private donation. Dr. Cobden had himself contributed a substantial sum toward the purchase of the building, and watched with satisfaction as walls were re-mortared, timbers replaced, paint applied to brick. He told himself his newfound concern for the indigent stemmed directly from Joseph; the child had awakened in him a social conscience that had for too long lain dormant. As his involvement with the ward grew he restricted his own practice to four days per week, then three. When the resultant reduction in income found its way to Emilia's household purse she demanded an explanation.

The doctor regarded his wife across the breadth of the drawing room, noted the tautness of lip which had become a permanent feature of her expression in recent months. "You are familiar, are you not, with the Hippocratic oath? I have sworn to dedicate myself to the alleviation of human suffering, Emilia. There is more of that commodity to be found at the infirmary in a single day than among the wealthy of St. Louis in the course of a year."

"That is no reason for reducing us to conditions of penury."

"Your description of our reduced circumstances is laughable. You have not, do not and will not experience *penury,*" he almost spat the word at her, "while living under this roof. I suggest you exercise a measure of economy in your domestic budget. Kindly do not raise this subject with me again."

He had never before addressed her with such scorn. Emilia was at first frightened, then angry and, after silence had fallen between them, resentful. William had become a changed man since the Indian came into their lives. The child had cast some kind of spell, transformed her loving and attentive husband into a remote, uncaring monster. It was not fair. She had striven with all her heart to conceive, and endured William's bodily attentions without complaint, had borne the disappointment of childlessness with fortitude, all for nothing, for a nameless brat with black hair and eyes and filthy brown skin. Rage welled within her again, sent a quiver to her jaw. Very well, if she must suffer then so must William. Emilia began to suspect the presence of lust in her husband's ruthless pelvic thrustings; the act was no longer performed in hope of procreation, but for sheer gratification of the flesh, she was sure. That would cease. Let him come to her room when next he felt the stirrings of the beast, let him approach her bed with scarcely concealed desire for her body; she would extract her own kind of satisfaction when his lust was met with uncompromising refusal.

She planned a speech, and when the doctor approached her two nights later delivered herself of it with the panache of an accomplished actress. "You are not welcome in this room any longer, William. Since you now have a son, and since I am fully reconciled to my childless state, no purpose is served by your presence here. Please leave without argument. My mind is very clear on this matter. Goodnight."

He turned, left without a word.

For several months the doctor did not go near his wife. They met only at mealtimes. Hattie served their food, flinching at the silence lying stagnant and molasses-thick between them. Pride held Dr. Cobden aloof; he waited for an apology from Emilia. Surely she could not tolerate the strain for very much longer. He at last realised his wife was under no strain, had adapted to the wordless conflict between them with far greater ease than he. The doctor became resentful of Emilia's composure, felt he was somehow being made to look a fool. He glared across the table at this woman who refused him her body. Food stuck in his throat, his stomach burned. She was laughing inwardly at him, mocking him with her daintily chewing mouth. He stood abruptly, threw down his napkin and strode from the room. Emilia did not look up. She congratulated herself on the success of her stratagem.

Later in the evening the doctor went to her room and entered without bothering to knock. Emilia was already in bed, the lamp turned out. "William . . . ?" She resisted with surprising strength until he hit her. With full knowledge of his actions, the doctor raped his wife.

When it was done he went to his room and dressed, picked up his silver-headed cane at the front door and walked through the streets of St. Louis until he came to the Mississippi. Watching the waters slide by, hearing the suck and lap of the shoreline, he allowed himself to think. His behaviour had been that of a madman. He failed to understand the monstrous change wrought in his personality; how could he have forced himself upon Emilia in so bestial a fashion? Worse, how was it possible he had raised his hand to her like some waterfront brute releasing his lust and rage upon a faceless whore? The thing was done, never to be forgotten.

"She will never look upon me with love again. . . ." The words sprang from him unbidden, slurred with anguish. The doctor felt himself drawn to the cold, unfeeling water. He could not swim; it would be quick, merciful. He took one halting step, faltered, fell to his knees. He cursed himself for a coward, spat on his finely tailored pants, knocked the stovepipe hat he wore so proudly from his head. Once, twice, he attempted to break the elegant cane across his knee, but the stout ash defied his strength. Defeated, he sat for some time, too weakened by the sense of his own impotence to rise.

The cold mud finally drove him to his feet, his passionate self-loathing reduced to leaden, formless misery. He walked away from the river, aimless steps leading him through streets alive with music and vice. Drunken laughter and foul language filled his ears, women beckoned him from alleyways. Cocooned in grief, he saw only the sidewalk.

"Been in some trouble, mister?"

He stopped, looked up. Two men stood before him, their eyes shadowed by battered hatbrims. "Been muddied up some, mister. Lost your wallet, maybe?"

He stared at them, aware of the danger in their slouching bodies, yet unable to muster the sense of fear required for defence or flight. Jangling pianos, raucous voices, the cacophony of human activity, all seemed far away. A lone street lamp burned fitfully some distance ahead, dribbling its light down grime-encrusted walls. He waited for the situation to develop as it pleased.

"Lost his tongue, that's for sure," said the second man. The first took a step forward. "Bet they wanted that fancy cane, mister. You bust their heads with it?" The smile beneath the hatbrim was brown with tobacco juice, its lifted corners vulpine. "You want to watch how you treat a handsome thing like that. Silver, ain't it?"

The doctor did not move. The man was puzzled; the well-bred features before him betrayed no fear, no anger, nothing. He interpreted the look as one of confidence, and eyed the cane with sudden apprehension; maybe it was a swordstick, the high-toner with the muddied knees just waiting for him to make a move before twisting the blade free of its sheath and running him through. The risk was more than he dared take.

"You take my advice, mister, and don't come around here. This ain't the right place for a gentleman." He stepped aside, ready to attack if the tall man hesitated, crabbed sideways to pass or quickened his step once past them; any sign of fear and he would know the cane was a stick of wood, nothing more. The doctor walked on, unhurried, leaving the incident behind, barely aware it had occurred.

For hours he wandered, criss-crossing unfamiliar streets until dawn. Tired, haggard, he found himself at last outside his home, and entered with the reluctance of a prisoner greeting his cell.

CHAPTER FOUR

Dr. Cobden began arriving home later in the evenings from his work at the infirmary. He ate alone in the kitchen, then went to the nursery to look at Joseph. Grave, dark eyes stared into his own. He held the child, spoke the meaningless words expected of a doting father, returned Joseph to his cradle and left. His visits lasted a matter of minutes. Once, leaving the nursery, he startled himself by asking "Have I made a mistake?" The voice was unquestionably his own. Shaken, he continued down the stairs. Lying awake in the hours past midnight he renewed his determination to make of Joseph a sterling citizen, a son to be proud of. There had been no mistake; everything depended upon that simple premise.

Cook, maid, and now nurse, Hattie went to the Negro quarter and purchased a conjure of buzzard bones and catfish skin to be worn under her dress. Protection from the black-eyed baby was necessary if she wished to keep herself free of the kind of trouble afflicting the doctor and his wife, trouble stemming directly from the foundling. It began the night he was brought into the kitchen and would continue, she knew, until blood was drawn and death ushered into the house. Hattie could feel those mighty black wings beating around the eaves whenever the wind blew, waiting for the right time to enter and enfold someone to that dreadful bosom. Hattie was determined it would not be her. She fed and cleaned Joseph with care, anxious to placate whatever spirit lived within him.

Emilia no longer received callers, never left her room. The doctor was not permitted entry at any time, and eventually ceased trying. His female clientele among St. Louis society no longer interested him; that is, he acknowledged his lack of interest for the first time. One wealthy woman came to him complaining of constant headaches, and was informed the pain came from her imagination in order to fill the void created by a largely useless and trivial way of life. Outraged, the woman spread her story and even fewer patients than before stepped through the surgery door. By 1861 the doctor's private practice had virtually ceased to exist. His club blackballed him without his even being aware of their decision; he had not attended for over a year. He was paid a meagre salary in recognition of his tireless service at the infirmary, a sum which amounted to almost one-tenth of what he had earned before Joseph turned his life upside down.

When Fort Sumter was fired upon the doctor volunteered his services as a field surgeon. His sympathies lay with the North, but he knew the soldiers of the Confederacy would require his skills as much as any Yankees. He moved across the country, digging out rifle balls, amputating arms and legs black with gangrene, filing the ends of sawed-through bones, trimming and stitching flaps of flesh. He worked without emotion in canvas field hospitals and commandeered buildings, apron spattered with gore, crimson hands seldom without an instrument in their grasp, his ears filled with screaming, groans, prayers, curses. His efforts were sometimes prompt enough to save life; more often they were not. He saw men by the hundreds buried in mass graves or burned for fear of pestilence; in time he would see them disposed of in their thousands. He breathed the nostril-clogging miasma of smoke and ruptured, rotting bodies that clung to the battlefields. He saw corpses feasted upon in the white heat of noon by swarms of brilliant butterflies, each twisted body trembling with the agitation of maggots within, bloodied uniforms hidden by living rainbow blankets. The doctor dreamed of blood and supurating wounds and shattered limbs, dreamed of a sculpted marble face, its beauty worthy of Michelangelo, and saw a hairline fracture split the brow, continue down through the nose and lip, divide the jaw; the divine face fell apart to reveal a slavering, crazed brute neither man nor animal, and the beast leered in recognition of Dr. Cobden and said, "I am your brother."

Despite her husband's absence Emilia continued to live in her room. Hattie brought food up to her, returned downstairs with empty trays and brimming chamberpots. The windows were kept permanently shut and the curtains drawn to prevent William climbing a ladder to invade her room, or, equally unsettling, spy upon her. She did not unlock the door to allow Hattie inside until a prearranged codeword had been whispered through the keyhole. She no longer bathed, fearing William may somehow have poisoned the water with his seed. No matter how often Hattie protested they were alone in the house, just the two women and the child, Emilia remained firm in her isolation; there would be no recurrence of the brutal act perpetrated upon her body, nor anything resembling it. Her room took on the appearance of some animal's lair, dark, filthy, malodorous. The worm of madness gnawed at her brain and grew fat.

Joseph knew someone lived upstairs. He could hear furtive sounds of movement if he stayed still for long enough, listening. The inhabited room was directly above the library. He spent a great deal of time there, climbing on to one of the comfortable armchairs, waiting for the soft footfall or muttered phrase which betrayed a living presence beyond the library ceiling. Whenever he heard these sounds a thrill ran through his body. It was not at all like the excitement he felt after waiting in the back garden for the squirrel who lived in the big tree to show his darting body; this was an altogether different feeling, tinged not with the warm flush of delight, but with the cool disquietude of fear.

He asked Hattie who it was that lived upstairs. "Your mamma, child. She ain't a well person, so you let her be."

This information puzzled Joseph; he had always assumed Hattie was his mamma. She took him with her to shops and markets and walked him through the public gardens in the same way he saw other ladies walking small boys and girls. He knew these ladies were mammas, had heard them addressed as such by their children, so Hattie must surely be his. How could he have another mamma hidden away upstairs? The staircase beckoned, its carpeting musty with dark allure. He had been forbidden to climb it by Hattie, had no memory of ever occupying a nursery on the upper floor. The mystery was intolerable.

He waited until Hattie left the house one afternoon to visit her sister on the far side of town, and tip-toed up the stairs. As his head drew level with the upper floor he felt a stab of guilt. He paused for several minutes then continued, heart pounding. The upper reaches of the house were hushed. A long corridor stretched before him, flanked by closed doors, the windows at its end shuttered against the summer heat. Joseph advanced step by cautious step. A picture hanging from the wall caught his eye, a near-naked horseman with flying hair and upraised lance in pursuit of an unbelievable animal, big and dark and humpbacked, with horns and bulging eyes. He stared at the scene, entranced by its patent absurdity; the men he had seen riding horses through the streets wore clothing, and he had never seen a cow that resembled this shaggy monster before him. He looked beyond the hunter and his prey, wondered at the flatness of the land, its horizon dividing the world into grass and sky. Where could this place be? Joseph had never been more than a mile from his home.

He grew bored with the picture, knew he had only stopped by it for so long because he was afraid to go on. Which of the doors was the right one? He concentrated, saw the upper storey in relation to the lower, knew the second nearest door led to the room above the library. He approached it quietly, a door like any other, the knob well within his reach. He grasped it, the brass slippery in his sweating palm, turned it slowly and pushed. The door did not open. Joseph understood that outside doors had to be kept locked because of people called thieves and robbers, but this could not apply to an inside door. He pondered over the possibilities and decided there were only two; his second mamma had locked herself in, or had been locked in by Hattie. The first was unlikely; the only place where a person needed to lock himself behind a door was the outhouse, where privacy was necessary while you made noise and stink. Obviously Hattie had been silly enough to lock the door without meaning to. He put his eye to the keyhole and saw only darkness. His other mamma was in there and couldn't get out, was probably starving hungry, too.

He knocked on the door and waited. Silence. He knocked again, a little louder this time. Maybe she was sleeping and couldn't hear. He knew Hattie kept a bunch of keys in her apron pocket, and hurried down to the kitchen, excited by the prospect of rescuing his other mamma and seeing her face. Hattie's apron hung on a peg behind the back door. He fetched a chair, stood on it, felt inside the pocket and found the hoop with its dozen keys. He raced up the stairs and began trying them one by one in the lock. There was movement in the room now, so she must have woken up. "I've got the keys, Mamma!" he called through the keyhole. "You can come out when I find the right one!"

He tried the fifth key, the sixth, turning each one firmly in both directions. He inserted the seventh. A thump from within the room made him pause; another thump, then the sound of something heavy being dragged across the floor. What could be happening in there, and why didn't she say something. "Mamma?" No answer. The dragging noise grew louder, the same kind of sound made when Hattie shifted the big kitchen table to clean under it. Why would his mamma be moving furniture around? The eighth key and the ninth did not turn the lock. Joseph became anxious. Would none of them fit? He could hear another sound now behind the dragging noise, a high pitched whimpering like a dog in distress, but that couldn't be; he would have heard a dog if Mamma kept one in her room. The door shook as something big was pushed against it, a wardrobe or bureau. "Mamma, what are you doing?" The whimpering continued. He tried the remaining keys, discouraged and confused. If there was a piece of furniture against the door how could he open it? The last key was inserted, turned, and proved as useless as the rest.

Joseph stared at the door. There was something here he did not understand. He put his lips to the keyhole. "Mamma, don't you want to come out?" No, she did not; he saw that now, for if none of Hattie's keys fitted the lock it meant Mamma had the only one. She had locked herself in and meant to stay locked in, had even barricaded the door to ensure it. He backed away, frightened by the whimpering. Somehow he had made his mamma afraid, made her give out those awful dog noises. She must have known Hattie had told him never to come upstairs. She would tell Hattie what he had done and he would be given a thrashing. He had done a bad thing and would get found out. His bowels quaked. Joseph ran downstairs, replaced the keys, then hid under his bed, eventually falling asleep.

The sound of Hattie's return woke him. Before she could learn of his crime he climbed through his window and hid in the big tree, wishing he could turn himself into a squirrel. It did no good. Hattie finally appeared on the back porch, calling his name. When he did not respond she came directly to the tree and peered among its branches.

"Child, you come down out of there."

"No!"

"You do what I say before you fall and bust your head! I got the responsibility and I ain't having no child bust his head in my care. You get down right this minute."

"I didn't mean it! I only wanted to let her out!"

"Let who out? What are you talking about, boy?"

"She got scared and wouldn't come out. I didn't mean any harm. . . ."

"Who did? Who got scared?"

"Mamma!" he bawled, and released a flood of tears.

Hattie looked down at her feet, easing the pain in her

neck, then up again. "Did you go up them stairs like I said you oughtn't?" Joseph howled even louder. "Well, did you?"

"I only wanted to let her out!"

His eyesight blurred, seeing only the tree-trunk inches away. He clung to it, determined never to come down. The back door slammed. Hattie had gone back inside. His tears stopped; snivelling, he waited. Hattie returned after a long while. "Child, you come inside now. There's cinnamon cake on the table, but it ain't going to wait for ever. Don't you be scared. Ain't nothing going to happen to you."

"Promise!"

"I promise. Now, come on down before you do yourself hurt."

He descended cautiously, ready to climb again if Hattie broke her word, little knowing she would no more raise her hand to him than she would to a mad dog or rearing horse. Hattie waited until his feet touched the ground, shook her head and went back into the house. Joseph waited until he remembered the cake, then followed. While he ate he told Hattie all that had happened. She wedged some snuff under her lip and drummed the table-top with her fingers. "I expect you done some figuring and you know your mamma ain't the normalest woman around."

"She made noises just like a dog. Why doesn't she want to come out?"

"That's just her way. She don't like to be outside of that room, and she's the missus so we got to do like she wants and not get her all vexatious. I been upstairs and she won't let me in on account of what you done, but I ain't blaming you. You oughtn't to of done it, but I reckon it had to happen sometime. Ain't nothing more curious than a boy. You won't go up there again, will you?"

"No. Is she really my mamma?"

Hattie hesitated, working on the snuff. The child was upset, she could see that. She tried seeing behind his eyes to the thing that lived inside him, but it was hiding; the tear-stained, cake-smeared face was that of an ordinary small boy. Should she tell him the truth, or wait for the doctor to do it? Cobden had been gone almost a year now, and didn't know how bad his wife had got, and what child would want the pitiful lunatic living in that stinking room upstairs for a mother? Hattie didn't know what it was that had driven Emilia to madness, but it started when the doctor brought Joseph home, that much she was sure of. Did her loyalties lie with the doctor, far away at the war and maybe even dead, with a madwoman living like a hog, or with this black-haired Indian looking at her with beseeching eyes? Hattie made up her mind; let the devil know where he came from and be done with it. "No, she ain't your mamma."

"Then, who is she?"

"Who's she? Child, you best be asking who's *you.* "

He watched her, struggling to understand the words falling from her lips, marching relentlessly across the table, entering him like a trail of busy ants, making his stomach tremble and lurch. "Your mamma ain't your mamma and your papa ain't your papa. He done found you like a kitten nobody wanted, found you and brung you here and adopted you. You know what that is?" A shake of the head. "He brung you into his home out of the goodness of his heart to look after you like a regular pa. He says most likely your real pa was a white man and your mamma an Indian. Them Indians got no shame, and some white men got none, too."

"What's an Indian?"

"That's folks that live out west of here, heathens and savages that ain't seen the way of the Lord, just living stark naked like animals."

He remembered the picture in the corridor upstairs. "Do they ride horses?"

"Ain't nothing else for them to do out there but ride horses and make mischief like you done today."

Joseph seized upon the idea of being the same as the long-haired man in the picture. "When are they coming to get me?"

"Coming to get you? Child, they don't even know you living in this world. Ain't no one coming to fetch you away

from here. You the doctor's boy now, for good or bad.''
This last slipped from her tongue before she could check it,
but Joseph appeared not to have noticed. He reluctantly
risked his last secure hold on a life that had somehow been
turned topsy-turvy in an afternoon. ''Aren't you my
mamma either?''

''How can I be your mamma? We ain't the same colour,
you and me.''

''Then, who is?'' His voice was faint now, losing heart.

''Ain't I just now got through telling you? Some Indian
woman was your mamma, and there ain't a way to find out
who, nor your pa neither, so quit asking. You's just you.''
Hattie fingered the conjure beneath her dress, wondering if
she had done the right thing after all. Surprisingly, the boy's
dark face had turned pale.

Joseph wanted more than anything to run up the stairs
and look again at the horseman, but he had given his promise. The kitchen air stifled him, made him want to vomit
the cake. He went out into the neglected garden and stared
at the tree, unsure what was expected of him. He teetered
on the edge of awareness, waiting for Hattie's revelation to
establish itself inside him. He was not who he had thought
he was, but had no clear idea who or what the true Joseph
might be. The tree before him, the house behind him, these
things were real, had substance which could be touched; as
they were yesterday, so they were today, and would be tomorrow and for all foreseeable tomorrows. The tree had
grown, the house been built, but he, Joseph, had simply
come into being, a child of faceless parents. His rootedness,
his attachment to the visible world had suddenly become as
insubstantial as a dandelion clock; all the remembered moments of his short life were whisked away by uncaring winds,
for each fragile moment had been built upon a lie, a great
untruth, an ignorance so profound as to leave him breathless. Joseph felt himself dissolving inside his clothes, melting
away like breath on a windowpane until nothing remained
but transparent emptiness. He knew if he remained still and
did not disturb the process he would float from his prison

of cloth and drift on warm breezes up and away from the yard, higher and higher over St. Louis. He would swoop and soar and ride the wind, and the wind would bear him westward.

He waited for deliverance, head bowed, eyes tightly shut. But the flesh of his body reassembled, sweating in the heat. Pain pierced his chest, sent him to his knees. Was this the arrow of God which Hattie had warned him about, the bolt from above sent to smite the unrighteous? He shook, doubled over in agony, too scared to cry out. The arrow was withdrawn through his back, leaving a cramped ache between his shoulderblades. Joseph panted for breath, praying silently for forgiveness, uncertain of his crime. He turned slowly to look upon the face of God, saw instead a high window, saw behind it a grey figure with tumbled hair staring down at him from a narrow split in the curtains; the woman who was not his mamma, the dog-whimperer transfixed him with her eyes. Between woman and child flowed a palpable wave of hatred shapeless and dark, spilling from the window, engulfing Joseph. Cinnamon cake rose in his throat, spewed on to the grass. He crawled on hands and knees to the porch, crawled under the stoop and continued on beneath the house where air and earth were cool. Spider webs tickled his face and festooned his clothing. He bumped blindly into the chimney foundations and stopped, feeling his heart gallop in his breast. He settled himself against the chimney bricks and remained there for hours, the spider-infested gloom less terrifying than the sunlit garden.

In his sixth year Joseph knew fear. He would not forget its bitter taste.

CHAPTER FIVE

In October of 1863 Dr. Cobden was granted leave. He returned home and prescribed for himself a regimen of good food, sleep and peace. Emilia received word of his arrival from Hattie and immediately barricaded the door, then hid in a wardrobe. The doctor did not go upstairs; a bed was made up for him in the library.

He summoned Joseph and was shocked at what he saw. The boy was solidly built, short for his years, but the chubbiness of childhood had deserted him completely. His neck and shoulders were already thick with muscle, his head of uncontrollable hair lowered with bull-like belligerence. "Joseph, look up. I am not at your feet." Black eyes glared at him from beneath a bulging forehead and thick brows. The boy's nose was short, wide, almost Negroid but for its powerful bridge; his mouth was broad, the lips well formed, his chin recessed but heavily boned. The doctor found his appearance disturbingly ugly. Joseph's hands lay at his sides, fists clenched. "You have grown, my boy." The eyes were lowered again. "Do you have nothing to say to your father after all this time?"

"You aren't my father."

The voice seemed absurdly high coming from the face of this small Neanderthal, yet the doctor was shaken by its intensity. Joseph continued staring at the carpet, working his toes inside his boots. The doctor realised his absence had resulted in loss of discipline; the boy needed to be taken firmly in hand. "I have told you once to look up. Your feet are not novelties to be regarded by the hour." Again the heavy head was raised, the face sullen, intractable. Man

57

and boy matched gazes for a long moment, and Dr. Cobden was surprised to find his own eyes lowered first. He ascribed his weakness to physical and nervous deterioration. "Do you have anything to tell me, Joseph?"

"No."

"You have had no adventures, made no friends?"

"No."

"Do you wish to hear of the war?"

"If you like."

The doctor controlled his rising temper, told himself the boy had grown unused to his presence, perhaps resented it. "I will not waste your time and mine with stories of shot and shell. There are no glories associated with warfare, Joseph. None. I thank God you are too young for service. I have seen more young lives thrown away on the field of battle than I thought possible. When you are a man I advise you to leave any country which threatens to go to war. There is no greater sin upon the face of the earth than to set armies marching against each other in the name of righteousness. The South will probably lose this war even though it appears momentarily to have the upper hand. I pray it does. It will almost certainly mean an end to slavery, and that is the only possible justification for carnage on this scale. Do you understand me, Joseph? I am talking treason. My hands serve the Confederacy but my brain is a traitor. You will kindly not repeat this conversation to a soul. Do I make myself clear?"

"All right."

"Weak though I am, Joseph, I will rise and strike you if you do not address me in a suitable manner."

"I won't tell anyone. Father."

Again they locked eyes. Joseph did not wish for confrontation with this man, knew he should drop his gaze first, but had he not been told to stop looking at his feet? He compromised by staring at the air above the doctor's head. Dr. Cobden wondered if he was being subtly mocked. The boy had become a stranger to him, a beetle-browed enigma. The ape-like stance annoyed him even more than the reluc ance to converse or show respect. "Pull your shoulders back, Joseph. Poor posture is not conducive to good health."

Joseph produced an almost imperceptible shrug and lumped into his previous attitude. The doctor grew angry. "Do you hear me? I said pull them back!"

"They're back!"

The doctor resisted an impulse to rise from his chair; he must not allow himself to be defeated by the boy's surliness. Joseph stared sideways at a bookcase, his mouth set. During the silence that followed, the doctor's professional instinct asserted itself; the boy was not deliberately slumped, he could see that now. "Joseph, remove your jacket and shirt."

"Why?"

"Because I tell you to!" He fought to soften his voice. "I wish to examine your back. Please do as I ask." Joseph flung the clothes on to a chair. "Now turn side-on to me."

He did so, and the doctor felt a familiar emotion steal into his chest; years of bracing himself for the announcement of bad news had never fully accustomed him to the task. He went to the boy, hoping his hands would disprove the evidence of his eyes. Joseph's skin trembled under his touch, a peculiarly animal reaction. "Do you ever experience pain in the spine?"

"What's a spine?"

"Your backbone. Does it ever ache?"

"Sometimes."

"You have developed a slight curvature of the spinal column."

"Why?"

"That I do not know. You showed no symptoms as a baby. This condition sometimes develops in later years, but it should not in a child your age. It must be rectified before it becomes worse. You must make an effort to hold yourself erect at all times."

"It hurts. It won't do any good anyway."

"Do not contradict me. I am a physician and you'll do as I say. Do you hear me?"

"Yes."

"You are either the most ill-mannered boy in St. Louis
or you are deliberately trying my patience."

"Yes, Father."

"Very well. You may leave. Tell Hattie I wish to ea
now."

During the next few days Joseph's resentment of the doc
tor turned to hatred. He was forced to stand in a doorwa
for an hour in the morning and an hour in the afternoon
hands clasping the frame on either side while he leaned fo
ward. He had also to wear a cloth headband attached by
cord to the back of his pants and pulled tight. His neck an
shoulders screamed, the crotch of his pants scraped agonis
ingly at his genitals. He removed the apparatus and refuse
to stand in the doorway. The doctor cut a branch an
thrashed him. Joseph disappeared for two nights and a da
and was returned by a mule driver, filthy and obdurate
Dr. Cobden took him to the library and sat him on a chai
with his muddied boots dangling above the carpet he pre
sented a pathetic sight.

"Joseph, do you wish to become a hunchback?"

"No." He had seen one of these people, a man of inde
terminate age who pushed a cart through the streets, beg
ging used clothes.

"Then I suggest—note the word—*suggest* you continu
with your exercises. Physical deformity is a great handica
in life. If pain is required to combat it, then pain must b
endured. I recommend this for the sake of your future hap
piness and well-being. Think upon the alternative."

Joseph resumed the torture, steadfastly refusing to cr
when the agony became almost unendurable. The docto
congratulated him on his perseverance, and Joseph was an
noyed to find himself grateful for the compliment. An un
easy truce developed between them. In the second week o
the doctor's leave Joseph was requested to join him in th
library.

"My boy, you have a great deal to cope with, but yo

must cope with more. I have noticed several books misplaced on the shelves. Have you perhaps taught yourself to read?''

"I only look at the ones with pictures."

"I thought so. You will begin school next week. In the meantime I will give you preliminary lessons in reading. Most boys your age already have a year of tuition behind them. If your mother was not bedridden she would have arranged matters in my absence. However, it is not too late. I believe you are an intelligent boy and will experience no difficulty. Fetch me a book—the one with the green binding.'' He pointed, Joseph took it from the shelf, handed it to the doctor. "This is a novel, Joseph, translated from the original French. It is the story of a hunchback. I am not mocking you. This book will make you fully aware of man's inhumanity toward those differing in shape from the accepted norm. When I return to my duties you may be tempted to discontinue with your exercises. This book will be an invisible rod with which to beat sense into yourself. It is an ugly story. Do you wish to read it?''

"Yes."

"Then, fetch pen and paper from the bureau."

Joseph's ability exceeded the doctor's expectations. Behind the boy's graceless manner lay a nimble intellect. He mastered the rudiments of spelling within days, was soon able to read and construct simple sentences with ease, even began haltingly, and with the aid of a Webster's dictionary, to begin M. Hugo's masterpiece. The doctor was well pleased; his son had the makings of a scholar. On the last day before his departure he took Joseph to a grade school of some repute, still operating despite the difficulties imposed by the war, enrolled him, advised him to heed the lessons of his teachers. He was to begin regular attendance the following morning.

Hattie and Joseph accompanied the doctor to the railroad depot and saw him depart. Joseph felt a pang of regret as the locomotive and cars steamed away, a novel sensation; for the first time he regarded this faraway thing called The

War as something in which he, Joseph, was involved. He wished it would end.

Hattie escorted him to school. Because of the train's late departure lessons had already begun when Joseph nervously took his seat. He felt the eyes of two dozen unknown boys boring into him from all sides. He heard nothing of the lesson. Surrounded by strangers, confined in a room which he could not leave whenever he chose to, Joseph panicked, and unconsciously let out a brief cry. The teacher stopped in mid-sentence. All heads turned to Joseph. He stared intently at his desk top, oblivious to the silence and the stares, passionately wishing himself away from here, wanting more than he would have thought possible to be back in the library with the doctor, hearing that patient voice explain, correct, encourage.

"The new boy will stand."

Joseph did not hear the command until it was repeated. He looked up, saw the grinning faces, knew his thoughts had somehow been divined; he was about to be punished for them. "The new boy will stand and come forward." He struggled to rise, caught his jacket on the desk lid, produced a loud bang. The class tittered. Joseph followed the aisle to the teacher's desk on its rostrum and stood before it, legs trembling, eyes fastened on miniature deltas of broken veins in the teacher's nose. "What was the purpose of that sound?" The question meant nothing to Joseph; he had heard no sound. Was it something to do with the lesson? The veins formed a surprisingly intricate network, a delicate tracery of red on white meandering through a landscape of pockmarks and yawning pores. "I will ask again, and for the last time, what was the purpose of that ridiculous sound?" A similar lacing of red infested the teacher's eyes, swimming on the surface, glistening, twitching.

"What sound?"

The class gave a combined gasp and guffaw; the newcomer was just asking for trouble, talking like that. The teacher silenced them with a glance. Joseph was unhappy

nd confused. Had he made a fool of himself by not giving
he right answer to a trick question?

"You made a sound, boy, a stupid sound, like a girl
aving her pigtails pulled."

He allowed the class to indulge in laughter this time; their
upport served to diminish the annoyance he felt at this new
oy's fascination for his nose, the feature which had long
go earned him the nickname "Old Plumnose." This boy
vould suffer for his lack of respect.

"Didn't you make such a sound, boy?"

"No."

"No, *what!*"

"No, I didn't."

The class howled. This was going too far; Old Plumnose
new sound carried quite a distance through the corridors—
vould, if not quelled, bring the principal from his office on
journey of enquiry. He glared about him to restore quiet.
The class waited, tingling with anticipation, grateful for Jo-
eph's unbelievable stupidity.

"You will address me as 'sir', boy. How will you address
ne?"

"Sir."

"That is correct. Now, why did you make that sound?"

"I didn't, sir."

"I maintain that you did." His teeth matched the yellow
f his eyes. Joseph had never seen so homely a man, was
uddenly embarrassed for him and lowered his eyes. Old
Plumnose scented victory and leaned forward from the ros-
rum, engulfing Joseph with fetid breath. "Didn't you!"

"I didn't hear anything, sir," mumbled Joseph.

"What! Speak up so we may all hear! You didn't hear a
eculiar sound?"

"No. No, sir."

"But the rest of us did, boy. Are you calling us liars?"

"No, sir, I just didn't hear anything."

"Are you deaf?"

"No, sir."

"Look at me when you address me, boy. And stand u
straight! Are you a hunchback?"

The word sank through Joseph like a stone. His ears fille
with roaring blood, his fingertips pulsed. From a great di:
tance he heard the braying of delighted boys. He lifted h
eyes.

"No!"

It was more scream than denial, so loud it produced
hush of surprise. Old Plumnose was aghast; the brat ha
dared shout into his face, stood not like a lamb ready fc
sacrifice but like some predator at bay, eyes flashing, mout
clamped into a straight line, body rigid with hate. Suc
behaviour was unprecedented in his entire career; it coul
not be allowed to pass unpunished. The class awaited h
reaction; if he did not crush this defiant insect now he woul
never again be able to control a roomful of rowdy boy:
would have to endure stares directed blatantly at his nos
It must not happen. He reached for the one weakness Jc
seph had revealed, fondled it, moulded it into a weapon c
humiliation.

Smiling, he said, "I think you are, boy. I believe you'r
a *hunchback.*"

The floor fell away beneath Joseph's feet, left him su:
pended in a void, laughter swooping around him like craze
birds. The veined nose and yellow teeth thrust themselve
at him. His eyes slid to one side, seeking escape. At th
edge of the teacher's desk sat an inkwell, a wooden pe
standing in its pool. He reached for it, grasped the sten
threw his arm back and plunged the pen with all his strengt
into the leering face, uncertain if the scream was his own c
his tormentor's. The pen dangled from a florid cheek, i
nib completely buried in flesh.

Joseph ran to the classroom door and flung it open, race
along a corridor, cannoned into a man as he turned a coi
ner, pushed himself away and ran on. Before him were th
double doors through which he had entered this castle c
torture. He clutched a handle, burst into sunlight and fre∈
dom and ran as he had never run before.

He returned home at dusk, weary and footsore from a day spent roaming the streets. Hattie confronted him in the hallway. "There was a man here looking for you that runs the school. He says you got to go and say you sorry for what you done or they going to fetch the law onto you. First thing tomorrow you got to go and do it."

"I won't!"

"He says they going to keep the money Dr. Cobden paid for schooling and not let you back there again, but you got to go and say you sorry or the law gets brung into it."

"No!"

"Child, you got to. Knifing a man, that's a crime. I can't hardly believe you went and done it, a boy your age."

"It wasn't a knife, it was a pen, and I'm glad I did it and I'm not going to say I'm sorry!"

"You quit raising your voice to me or I'll whomp you!"

Hattie and Joseph lifted their right hands simultaneously, Hattie with opened palm, Joseph with an extended forefinger pointed between her eyes. Hattie froze. The child was casting a spell! Neither moved for a timeless moment, then Hattie lowered her hand and hurried away to the kitchen. Joseph inspected his still outstretched arm with its accusatory finger, amazed at the effect it had worked upon Hattie; he had intended simply to shout some more at her, tell her to leave him alone, but when he had seen the expression on her face his voice had choked itself off. Hattie was scared of him! Hattie, so big and black and all-powerful was frightened of him! He did not ask himself why, assumed she was afraid of being knifed herself, ridiculous though the notion was. Joseph was content to have ended the argument without further loss of dignity. Confidence swirled through him, a new and heady wine, made him jubilant, heavy, substantial. He had defied Hattie and he would defy anyone else who came to make him atone for penning (he laughed at the word) that purple-nosed monster with the yellow teeth. A few seconds' recollection of the incident made him angry and frightened again; he thrust it to the back of his skull and calmed his racing heart, restored the equilibrium Hattie's strange reaction had created. He felt good again. He would defy them all, because defiance made him feel good.

Joseph waited in the house all the next day, preparing himself to be defiant. No one came. No one from the school and no one from the law. Hattie avoided him, fixed his meals but would not talk, tugged nervously all the while at the conjure hidden between her breasts. Joseph did not attempt to make peace with her; there would be no surrendering this mysterious power a pointed finger had given him. He did not use the gesture a second time, for there was no need; he knew it should be held in reserve for those occasions when it was imperative he get his way. Would it work on his father? The power would have come in handy to prevent the thrashing he had received for refusing to continue with his doorway exercises. Should he continue them now, with the doctor gone? The pain had been terrible. He had only done it because the doctor insisted, because he had been thrashed, because in some peculiar way he had wanted to impress the man. Looked at in retrospect his compliance and desire to please were pathetic. Why should he try to please someone who was not his father? He would not do so again. Defiance of an absent figure produced the same satisfied flush as had his defiance of Hattie. It was settled.

He went to the library, found the green book and began to read. He stopped only to consult the Webster's, to eat, sleep, defecate. His waking hours were bound in green leather, his emotions racked and strained by the injustices heaped upon the misshapen head and hump of Quasimodo. The outrageous unfairness of gypsy Esmerelda's trial filled him with hate, her rescue by the hunchback set him bouncing with glee on the armchair; the assault on the cathedral held his mouth agape, and discovery of the skeletons, hunchback and gypsy intertwined in death, crumbling when separated, produced a flow of unashamed tears.

He laid the book aside after five days of continuous reading, drained of sensation; he had lived another's life, then died. Joseph's world could never again be the same. He stood before the bookshelves, awed by the multitude of lives and worlds available to him. He chose another volume and immersed himself in the misery of Jean Valjean, followed that unfortunate's existence to its conclusion, opened Dumas' *The Count of Monte Cristo* and discovered yet more injustice. Could no man be a hero unless faced with overwhelming misfortune? Was this the only way in which a man could define himself, against great odds and the vicissitudes of fate? Joseph was convinced it must be so.

He read on, volume by volume, shelf by shelf, absorbing the lives of Greeks and Romans, Frenchmen, Russians, Englishmen from centuries past. Time and space funnelled through a room in St. Louis. Week by week Joseph became Ulysses, Gulliver, Robin Hood, D'Artagnan, Robinson Crusoe, a legion of heroes, a host of selves; his head swam with dangerous journeys, duels, dungeons, battles, the high seas, death, privation, revenge, thwarted passion, triumph. Sleet fell against the windows, then snow. He lived in the library, slept in the bed prepared for the doctor, was waited on by a sullen Hattie, his interior voyagings uninterrupted by occasional sounds of movement from the room above. He was no longer afraid of the invisible woman, had no interest in whatever calamity had driven her to madness; she was no damsel in a castle tower, merely the madwoman upstairs.

He exhausted the doctor's shelves of fiction and moved on to historical works, but found them unexciting, sampled Socrates and Plato and Thomas Aquinas only to find them dull. He opened medical texts, pored over the illustrations with horrified rapture, grew bored and closed them. He had learned to read in the fall, and already it was almost summer again. A restlessness invaded him; time, as measured by clocks, had resumed for Joseph after six months of magical suspension by the power of print. Outside lay Missouri, not Europe or Merrie England. Despair engulfed him. There were no more books.

* * *

He left the house for the first time since the doctor's departure, walked through town until he came to the river, stood there for hours watching the waters flow by. Ignoring the fact that most riverboats had been requisitioned for the war effort, he dreamed of riding down to New Orleans, finding a clipper and signing on as a cabin boy, sailing the world's oceans, beset by pirates and hurricanes. He retraced his steps homeward, planning how best to make his dream a reality.

"Hey, Hump!"

Two boys on the opposite side of the street were staring at him, grinning widely. One bent over and shuffled like an ape. Joseph wondered at their antics, then realised they were mocking him. He hurried away, paused by a store window to examine his reflection and stood aghast at what he saw. Behind his head rose what was undeniably a hump. He could no longer think of himself as round-shouldered or stooped. It was there, perched on him like a vengeful imp. He was a hunchback! Joseph was unable to drag his eyes from the apparition. His jacket hung at least eighteen inches higher at the back than at the front, had become too small altogether. Why had he not noticed the shortness of the sleeves, the uncomfortable tightness under the armpits? Uncut through the winter, his hair stood out in untamed clumps, almost wilfully unkempt. He looked like a clown. It was bending over so many books that had done this to him, he knew. He had allowed his fancy to be beguiled by daydreams of adventure while this grotesque mountain of flesh and bone and gristle had stealthily been growing on his back. He felt cheated, robbed; he had been lifted above the clouds only to be cast back to earth with malign force.

Passers-by were staring at him, had probably been staring at him all day while his own eyes were fastened on the ground, pushed there by his downthrust head. Joseph ran, boots thudding on the sidewalk, clamouring for attention. A woman in his path threw up her hands and screamed as he charged at her and fought his way past her skirts. A sound followed him along the street, a sobbing, panting, desperate sound he could not escape no matter how fast his legs churned; the sound became a word—hunchback, hunchback, hunchback—grew louder, rang in his ears, boomed in his heart like Quasimodo's cathedral bells— Hunchback! Hunchback! Hunchback! Jeering phantoms pursued him, screaming laughter through yellow teeth, flaying him with ridicule.

His lungs burned, forcing him to slow down and finally stop, sides heaving, face glistening with sweat. Joseph walked the last few blocks to his home with head bowed, eyes set firmly at his feet. He mounted the front steps, closed the door behind him, rested in the cool hallway. He would never leave the house again, never face those startled, amused glances, never sail the seas and know the delights of distant shores. Only one place afforded him the solace of privacy, a sanctum free from prying eyes. Joseph went to the library and locked himself in.

The house on DeWitte Street claimed its second exile from the world.

CHAPTER SIX

On the day Robert E. Lee surrendered at Appomattox and the tide of war ebbed at last, Emilia knew herself to be with child. She was uncertain how William had managed to impregnate her, but was without doubt as to her physical state. The thing inside her began clawing at her womb with hurtful fingers. It was large, and would not yield to her touch, a budding giant. This was obviously William's idea of a cruel jest, to swell her body, infusing her flesh with pain until she delivered the monstrous spawn of his lust.

To quell her torment she stole downstairs one night and removed the entire stock of laudanum from his surgery. Emilia sipped at the bottles constantly, drowned her discomfort in a languorous sea of dreams, lulled herself with narcotic sleep, serene, untroubled, sole passenger in a ship of dark design. When the last drop of nectar had been drained the pain returned, harsher, more insistent than before. A second midnight raid on the surgery yielded morphia, and Emilia took flight across endless skies of rainbow hue, a firmament of golden clouds and teeming suns, the radiant vault of heaven itself.

In time the last grains were absorbed into her body; drained of their essence, they lowered their host slowly, inexorably, on to a bed of thorns. Emilia's screams brought Hattie, candle in hand, to her door. Having long ago made a copy of the key for just such an emergency, Hattie let herself into the room. Emilia thrashed and writhed in a winding-sheet of linen and nightgown, filthy hair plastered to her face with sweat. Hattie struggled with her, surprised at the strength in Emilia's wasted body. Knowing she had no hope of subduing a madwoman by ordinary means, fearing the intrusion of neighbours if the screaming continued, Hattie bunched her fist and struck Emilia in the side of the head. Her body collapsed. Hattie held her palm over the open mouth, felt the hesitant pressure of breath. She stared at the gaunt features and thinning hair, wrinkled her nose at the odour of unwashed skin. "I wish you was dead, you crazy white bitch."

"Did you kill her?"

Joseph stood in the doorway, wrapped in a blanket. His voice betrayed no more than mild curiosity. Hattie felt a sudden chill; the boy had seen her hit a white woman. He entered the room, fanning the air beneath his nostrils. "Doesn't she ever wash?"

"She don't hold with it. I done my best to change the sheets and her nightdress. She don't allow it."

He came to the bedside. This shrunken, stinking creature bore no resemblance to the grey fiend that had glared down at him from the window four years before. "What was she screaming about?"

"Ain't no way to know what goes on inside of her head."

"Well, she's quiet now. You fetched her a good one."

"You ain't going to tell no one about that, are you, boy."

"Don't see why I'd want to. It's no one's business."

"Folks around here know she's peculiar, but if they hear such a ruckus they going to take her and lock her away someplace cruel."

"She wouldn't know the difference, I bet."

"Don't you talk that way. She done adopted you."

"The doctor did that, not her." He picked an empty bottle from among the twisted sheets, held it close to the candle flame. "She's been stealing from the surgery."

"She can't of done. I got the key. The doctor told me before he went away there's stuff in there that'll maybe wind up worth its weight in gold. He said to take care of it, and he give me the only key. This key right here." She selected a key from her hoop and flourished it under his nose for emphasis. "Ain't any way she could of took it."

"Then she's got another one hidden away."

Together they went downstairs to the surgery, found the door locked and the drugs cabinet empty. Joseph took a medical tome from the library and recited the symptoms of morphia addiction. "She's going to shout the house down. We'd better tie her up and gag her."

"Ain't there no other way?"

Joseph closed the book with a thud. "Not according to this."

She studied his warped form, the hair down to his shoulders now, spreading over the hump. With that and the blanket around him he looked more like an Indian than ever before, seemed almost to be deliberately cultivating an air of savagery. "You don't care what happen to her, do you?"

"No."

"Ain't you got no soul at all in you, boy?"

"Probably not. I'll get the clothes-line."

Hattie would not begin the work of tying Emilia to the bed until it became obvious Joseph's prognosis was correct; Emilia regained consciousness and began to howl and punch herself in the stomach. While Hattie held her down Joseph wadded a cloth and thrust it into her mouth, smothering the screams. He tied a bandage around her head to keep the gag in place and stood back, well pleased. He did not regard this woman as anything but an animal, and it was peculiarly comforting to know there was someone worse off than himself; he had no wish to see any improvement in her behaviour. He was gratifyingly disgusted when, after Emilia's limbs had been roped securely to the bedposts, she urinated, soaking the sheets and mattress. "Animal," he said.

"Ain't no animal, just a big baby is all, squalling and messing. You got to help me from now on, boy. She going to be some kind of trouble."

"I've got nothing else to do."

They watched over her for eight days, loosened the ropes whenever Emilia was calm, tightened them again when she

lung herself at the ceiling. The gag was removed whenever her breathing became laboured. She ceased to
cream; instead, there flowed from her lips a never-end-
ng froth of obscenity directed at William, Indians and
men in general. Emilia required water, cups, bowls,
buckets of water to drench the fire inside her. She drank
by the gallon, the water seeming to vanish into steam as
t hit the unquenchable heat of her belly. When at last
she was able to speak coherently Emilia looked at both
her attendants, turned to Hattie and said, "Make him
go." Joseph left. Emilia beckoned Hattie closer, whispered, "I'm having a baby."

"Is that so?"

"William came to me in the night and forced me to do
his will."

"What you going to call it?"

"Call it? No, it mustn't see the light. . . . It's a monster,
like that boy. It mustn't live. . . ."

"Don't you worry. Ain't no chance you going to have no
baby see the light."

"I don't want William's child, not any more. . . . It
hurts! Oh, oh, it hurts me. . . ."

Hattie bathed the pale and sweating brow. "You hush.
Ain't no baby going to get born in this house."

Fingers clutched at her wrist. "Don't let that Indian back
in here. He talks to it. They're brothers. I can hear them
whispering back and forth. . . ."

"He won't come in here no more. You rest easy."

Emilia drifted into an exhausted sleep. Believing the worst
to be over, Hattie quietly left the room, glad to be free of
its fetid confines. In dreams a man came to Emilia, a small
man, balding, with a kindly face; he resembled a clergyman
she had listened to on Sundays as a child. He warned her
of the pain to come, advised her to ensure the thing inside
her did not draw breath in a Christian world. How? Why,
it must be killed, forbidden exit from her abdomen, nipped
in the bud, as it were.

Emilia saw the wisdom of this plan and asked for specific

73

instructions. The small man with the kindly face whispered, "Downstairs, and hurry, you're beginning to feel the pain again. Do it before you wake up, that's my advice." She took a key from its hiding-place beneath the carpet and went down to the surgery, feeling her way in the dark, hearing Hattie snore in her room at the rear of the house. Emilia unlocked the surgery door. William's bag of surgical instruments was not there; perhaps he had been called away on some emergency, most likely a delivery. He would never deliver Emilia's monster, never never never. She went to the kitchen, found a knife with a handle of blackest night and a blade of moonlight. She kissed its edge, raised it in both hands and plunged it into her demon child, a cancer the size of a cannonball nested firmly in her womb. Emilia remained standing for a short while, surprised that her pain had not lessened, but grown stronger. She sank to her knees, nightgown sopping with blood. The kindly man was no longer with her, and Emilia began to suspect she had made a terrible mistake. The hall clock chimed softly three times. Hattie has been winding it faithfully all these years, thought Emilia, and died.

His wife had been buried for five weeks before the doctor returned home. Hattie explained the circumstances of Emilia's death. Dr. Cobden mourned the loss of his precious drugs; opiates were scarce.

He encountered Joseph in the library. Each found the other radically altered. The doctor's features were hollowed by fatigue and poor rations, his body reduced to skeletal proportions by recurrent fevers. He saw before him a parody of the hopes so long entertained for his son. The boy was a freak; worse, he appeared to take pride in his freakishness. The long hair had been clumsily braided, the blanket now a permanent fixture across hump and shoulders. The doctor ground his teeth weakly, kept his voice at a reasonable level. "What manner of creature do you take yourself for?"

"A hunchback Indian," said Joseph, equally determined not to provoke a disturbance between them.

"You did not continue with the exercises."

"No."

"Why not?"

"They didn't do any good."

"You should have persevered."

"A maple can't be an oak, no matter how hard it tries."

"Most poetic, Joseph, and utterly nonsensical. You are not a tree."

"No, I'm a hunchback Indian."

"Is your impertinence deliberate?"

"I'm not being impertinent, Father. Possibly facetious."

The doctor regarded Joseph with alarm; the child was not only deformed, but precocious. "I take it your education has proceeded along satisfactory lines."

"Yes. I stopped going to school."

"Explain yourself."

"I stabbed a teacher on the first day and didn't go back. They kept the fee."

A sudden weariness overcame the doctor. He waved Joseph away. Alone, he pondered the imponderable; if he had not brought the child home, would Emilia have retained her sanity, have lived? Perhaps not—he had assaulted her, raped his own wife like some invading Goth, and it was surely that act which had triggered her fall from the realm of reason. He could not blame anyone but himself. He tried to imagine Joseph at Harvard, found the thought laughable, yet the boy was without doubt highly intelligent. If the war had not removed the doctor from a position of influence would circumstances now be different? He must recover his strength before attempting any kind of confrontation with Joseph.

Hattie nursed the doctor for two months, gradually nourishing him back to a state of precarious well-being with whatever food could be had on the black market. Joseph had been ousted from the library, told to resume living in his own bedroom. He had complied. He was next ordered to strip clean Emilia's room, remove every object from it, scour the walls, floor and ceiling to remove the stench of years. He balked. "That's nigger work."

"That is an ugly word," said the doctor, "one I do not permit in this house."

"It's still nigger work."

"You refuse to do it?"

"Yes."

"Then, go to Hattie, call her a nigger to her face and tell *her* to do it."

Joseph cleaned the room with lye and borax. It took three days. He did not use the ugly word again. One day the doctor ordered him to remove his shirt and jacket. "Looking at it won't make it go away," said Joseph.

"I intend not only to look, but to measure."

"No."

"Yes. Are you ashamed to be seen without your shirt?"

"Leave me alone."

"I will, Joseph, just as soon as I have measured the contours of your back."

"I don't want to be measured."

"Kindly do as I ask before I become angry. I am a doctor. There is no need to feel self-conscious."

"I don't."

"Then do as I ask."

The doctor measured Joseph's hump from all conceivable directions and entered figures on a diagram. A few days later, his strength returning, he stepped from the house for the first time since his homecoming. He went first to see Emilia's grave, coincidentally located in the churchyard from which he had rescued the abandoned child. Dr. Cobden found the irony unsettling and did not linger there. His next call was to a harness maker, where he left a sheet of paper detailing exactly what he required. A week later the harness maker sent word of the special job's completion.

Hattie was dispatched to pick up the parcel. Joseph was sent for.

"I have something for you, my boy, something I'm sure you will hate."

Joseph eyed the parcel on the table. "Is that it?"

"It is. Open it."

He did so, and revealed a contraption rather like a back-to-front waistcoat of leather, with straps and buckles and rawhide laces.

"What is it?"

"I suppose it's a harness. Put it on."

"No."

"It will help straighten your back, at least while you wear it."

"I'm not going to."

"Indulge me, Joseph. Let me see if my calculations were correct. The spirit of invention is at work here."

"I said no."

"If you do not, I will order Hattie to give you no food from this day on."

"I don't care."

"You will, Joseph, you will."

Hattie locked the pantry. After a morning and afternoon without sustenance Joseph went to her, pointed a finger between her eyes. "Give me something to eat," he intoned. Hattie was unsure whether to laugh or shudder. "I can't give you nothing. I got my orders."

"Give me something to eat or you'll suffer."

"Boy, I suffered every day of my life. You get along and do what the doctor wants, then you can eat plenty."

Joseph thought long and hard. He did not wish to go out and steal food; he had not set foot in the street for over a year. Inside the house he was arrogant, truculent; outside, he would be timorous, insecure, a circus freak like Gwynplaine, the Laughing Man. He went to the doctor and was assisted into the harness. Straps were cinched tight, laces pulled and knotted. Joseph grew three inches in height, felt a bolt of pain run through him. "It hurts. . . ."

"That is to be expected at first. You'll adjust to it in time."

"I won't.'

"But you'll certainly try."

"I might."

"Hattie has managed to find us some meat for tonight. Would you care to partake of it?"

"It hurts like hell."

"Don't attempt to shock me with bad language, Joseph. Four years in the army have hardened my sensibilities. Is the pain really so bad?"

"Yes!"

"Then you must be brave and endure it. Indian youths are taught to remain in one position from sunup till sundown, no matter how their muscles complain."

"I don't give a damn what Indians do. This hurts and I don't want to wear it." He scrabbled at the buckles and knots, all located at the back, well beyond his reach. "Take it off me!"

"No. Be a man about this, Joseph."

"I don't want to be a man! I want to get this goddamn thing off me! Get it off!"

"If you do not behave yourself, you will not only forfeit supper, I will not remove the harness at bedtime. Do you wish to sleep in it, Joseph? I am the only one who can help you."

Joseph clenched his teeth, brought his anger under control. "You should have been an inquisitor."

"I'm delighted a child of your tender years is acquainted with the darker side of history. Have you read every book in this room?"

"Practically."

"Remarkable. You may be what is known as a prodigy. Do you know what that is?"

"It's some poor bastard that gets tortured by some other bastard that isn't his father."

The doctor permitted himself a bark of laughter. "My

boy, if you are not hanged in the meantime, you may some-day be a remarkable man."

He resumed his work at the infirmary. A small padlock was fitted to the harness; the doctor did not trust Joseph to wear it while he was absent from the house. He locked Joseph into the device before leaving in the morning, unlocked him before retiring to bed at night. Joseph asked Hattie to cut his hair back to a normal length, forced himself out the front door to the street and went in search of a locksmith.

"Get this off me without breaking the lock, then make me a key that fits."

"Can you pay for that kind of work, boy?"

"I've got five dollars." He had stolen it from a tin box in the doctor's bureau. "I'll give you more when I get the key."

"Turn around."

Knowing Hattie's loyalties lay with the doctor, Joseph kept his arrangement with the locksmith a secret. He went to the workshop minutes after the doctor's departure, was unlocked from the harness and spent the greater part of each day free of constraint. Towards evening he returned to the locksmith's and was trussed and locked as before. He was prepared to endure discomfort and humiliation until bed-time for the sake of food. The ruse worked for almost a week before the doctor noticed one evening that several buckles were incorrectly cinched, some of the rawhide laces knotted in an unfamiliar fashion.

"Joseph, have you bribed Hattie as your accomplice?"

"No, someone else. I'm not telling who."

"How does he unlock it?"

"Magic."

The doctor spent ten dollars on a specially strengthened burglar-proof lock and affixed it to the harness. "Your friend will find this no easy task, Joseph." The mood between them was almost one of competition, cool moves and coun-termoves made without emotion, a game played for its own sake.

Joseph presented his hump to the locksmith. "Can you get it off?"

The man tried hard, having conceived a liking for Joseph, but the lock manufacturer's boast was no idle one. "It won't come off, boy, not unless I cut through the hasp. It'll take all day and it'll be permanently broken. You won't fool anyone with it."

"Don't bother with the lock then, just cut the whole thing off me."

"You're sure about this?"

"Yes. Cut it off."

The locksmith sawed through leather with a sharp knife and the mutilated harness fell at Joseph's feet. He took it home, waited for the doctor to arrive, placed it before him. "I'm not wearing it any more. I had to cut it up to get it off. I could have had the lock broken, but it looks expensive."

"Go to the library, Joseph, and remove your pants."

Joseph survived the thrashing without complaint. Not a single tear escaped his eyes. As each blow fell he imagined it travelling from his raw buttocks up to a secret place deep inside his hump, where the pain was released without effect. Dr. Cobden wielded the freshly cut branch without restraint; something inside him had given way when Joseph showed him the ruined harness. He knew now he would never truly control the boy, never be able to guide him along paths not of his own choosing, never win Joseph's trust or love; Joseph would never acknowledge the doctor as his father, his mentor, his friend. The boy was ruthlessly independent, abnormally so, his strength a paradox in one so young and handicapped. The doctor assuaged his frustration and disappointment with every blow, loathing himself even as he drew blood. He collapsed into an armchair, breath whistling in his wasted lungs.

"Be a hunchback then. Get out of my sight."

Left alone, the doctor noticed flecks of blood on the ceiling; every upswing of the branch after Joseph's skin had been broken had left a delicate tracery of drops above his head; some had even arced over his shoulder and landed on the bookshelves. He shook uncontrollably, felt himself slide a little further down the descending spiral that had been characteristic of his life since the night Joseph entered his home.

CHAPTER SEVEN

In retrospect, Joseph realised the harness had been providential; it had obliged him to overcome his fear of ridicule and leave the house to seek help. True, his appearance still provoked stares and whispered comment, but with his hair barbered and, more recently, with a new suit of clothes tailored to fit he felt there was a place for him in the world. He dared to dream again of adventure in far off lands.

The doctor, his guilt mollified somewhat by the gift of clothing, attempted to reassert his authority. Joseph was informed he would attend school. Joseph informed the doctor he would not. The doctor called in the truant officer and Joseph was frogmarched away to school between two burly city employees. His escort and unique appearance made him an instant celebrity within the enclosed world of Throckmorton Academy. During the first recess, while Joseph debated whether to depart via the front gate or the brick wall by his side, a delegation of the curious approached him. Their spokesman demanded an explanation.

"I'm a reluctant student," said Joseph.

His audience puzzled over this reply and decided it meant no more than it appeared to mean. "What's your old man do?"

"I never met him. I'm a bastard. My foster-father's a doctor."

Such candour was unheard of. The crowd pressed closer, eager for more. "Are you a nigger?" ventured one of the less impressed.

"No, half-Indian."

"Jesus. What's that on your back?"

"My jacket."

"You're a hunchback."

"Yes, but don't say so. I don't like it."

"Gonna do something about it, Hump?"

Joseph promptly broke the boy's nose. "Be polite in future."

His success at the academy was guaranteed from that moment. An enclave of admirers formed about him whenever he set foot in the schoolyard. In class, teachers and pupils alike waited on his measured words; he always knew the answers required, but only gave them when asked directly. He volunteered nothing. The lessons, far below his own level of learning, bored him. He discovered that his penchant for sarcasm and disarming riposte, honed to an edge in his dealings with the doctor, had a natural home in the classroom.

"Joseph Cobden, give us the principal cause of the Trojan war."

"Lust, sir."

"Lust?"

"Yes, sir. Paris wanted to take Helen to bed."

"Silence in class! Do you have nothing further to add, Cobden?"

"Not really, sir. I don't know much about it. I'm a virgin."

And on another occasion: "Who can enlighten me with regard to the truncation of cones? Cobden?"

"Truncation of cones is a crime, sir. Cones are perfectly harmless."

"Remain after class, Cobden."

"May I ask why, sir?"

"Impertinence."

"That's what I thought, sir. Just checking."

The teacher attempted to cane him. Not wishing to create a martyr, he decided the punishment should take place in private. This was a mistake. When Joseph had received three strokes, a number he deemed appropriate for his transgression, he wrested the cane easily from the teacher's hand and broke it in two. He handed the pieces back. "The thing to do, sir, is not ask me any questions in class. That way I won't do any backtalking. I won't tell anyone about the cane, but don't try to do it again or I'll hurt you."

"You're a monster, Cobden. . . ."

"I know, but I'm doing my best to live with it."

Neither related the incident to a third party.

Joseph's body grew little in stature. At twelve years he measured five feet; at fourteen he had grown to five feet four inches, and grew no further. His neck, shoulders and chest were layered with solid muscle, his thighs and calves bulged to the point of making him appear bow-legged; his feet, however, were small, almost dainty. His ears were well formed, lying close to the sides of his head. He attempted to wear his cap at a fashionably rakish angle, but the massive dome of his forehead defeated his best efforts jauntily to shade one eye. Even the largest size in caps would not enable him to cover his head completely. He dispensed with a cap altogether, and the rest of the school followed suit. Joseph joked that as well as having a spare brain in his hump he possessed a larger than average specimen in his head. Brains or not, his scholastic record was no more than average. He took no interest in any lesson, did not study, regarded school not as an institute of learning, but as a place wherein he was a person of influence and renown. The doctor was disappointed, but not surprised at Joseph's dismal performance. "You realise, do you not, that you are throwing away whatever opportunities schooling may have opened up for you?"

"If I want to learn something I read a book about it. I don't need teachers."

"And what profession will you follow in the years to come?"

"I don't know yet. Something that'll take me away from here."

"The armed services?"

"That'd be just like school, and they wouldn't take me anyhow, not with my hump."

"Then it's the world of business and enterprise for you."

"I don't want to sell things."

"My boy, everybody sells something."

"Not me."

"So you wish to make your way through life without being subject to discipline or the necessity of earning a wage."

"That's it, more or less."

"I suggest you model yourself upon Jesse James."

"I've considered it, but I'm too easily recognisable to be an outlaw. The hump again."

DeWitte Street had declined in status during Reconstruction. Many of the householders' fortunes had been based upon the economic solvency of the South, upon slavery. The post-war world made paupers of them and their fine homes were sold, to be divided into apartments or reoccupied as boarding houses. The doctor once again had a three days per week practice among the clerks and drummers and carpetbaggers who inhabited the new DeWitte Street. His income improved slightly, but his mood did not. He was without a wife, had never truly been the father of a son. Joseph was not shaping as desired, was far too headstrong; this, coupled with a reluctance to face reality, would prove to be his undoing. Of that outcome Dr. Cobden was positive. He waited for the blow to fall, anticipated it with a measure of restrained eagerness. Like any man who knows he has failed, he hoped to redeem his impotence by having the last laugh. His final act of parental responsibilty took place on Joseph's fifteenth birthday, that is, the day on which the doctor had found and brought him home. Joseph had never been given gifts or a birthday party and so regarded this as a day like any other, resented, in fact, any mention of its significance. He was therefore primed for suspicion when the doctor broke the traditional silence of the breakfast-table.

"Joseph, I have a patient this afternoon, and I wish you to be present in the surgery when he arrives."

"What for?"

"An object lesson."

The patient had both syphilis and gonorrhoea. He did not object to Joseph's presence, assumed he was also a patient who had come to have his hump cured, if that was possible. He displayed his sexual organs with some pride; his mind had been deteriorating for years under the predations of disease. Joseph stared at the rotten penis. It hung like fruit savaged by birds, its length gashed and encrusted with sores, the surrounding tissue reddened, empurpled. His thighs and belly were clotted with buboes and lesser rashes.

"Hasn't gotten any worse, has it, Doc?"

"No, but only because it's as bad as it can get already. In fact there'll probably be a slight drying up between now and the time you die from it."

"Don't mince words, do you."

"What would be the point? You know what you have, how you got it and what it will eventually do to you. I can offer you a tincture to lessen the discomfort a little, but that's all."

"Better than nothing, I guess." He turned to Joseph. "I'm a victim of love," he announced, smiling. Joseph smiled in return, his stomach heaving.

The patient closed his pants and departed. Dr. Cobden steepled his fingers and looked across his desk at Joseph. "Many learned men in my profession advise boys your age not to practise self-abuse. They say it causes blindness and mental deficiency. It does not. I advise you to indulge as often as you please, rather than take yourself to a prostitute. Only a fool disregards the risks involved in that kind of transaction, and whatever else you may be, Joseph, you are not a fool. If you contract a sexual disease, I will have no sympathy for you. I will also have no cure."

Joseph took the doctor's advice, indulged in marathons of self-gratification. Drained, chafed, his bed linen twisted and gummed, Joseph one night realised this act of masculine expression was pathetic indeed. Was this how he would spend his life, spurting arcs of semen into nothing more substantial than air? He dreamed of women, a parade of smiling beauties, each one more than willing to gratify his least whim. They marched around his bed, discarding dresses and intimate frilly underthings until they stood naked, awaiting his command. Knowing nothing of sexual technique, Joseph mounted them all in the same uninspired fashion, his fist fairly humming. It was no good; his organ had given of its best, could no longer respond. He became depressed. Several of his acquaintances at school had boasted of amorous experience, usually of the kind paid for in advance. Joseph did not want this; the ghastly fruit of example hovered before his eyes, blotting out fleshy seas of bellies and breasts and thighs. No, not worth the risk, and even a whore probably wouldn't let a hunchback do it to her anyhow.

The doctor made no demands of him, did not berate him for poor grades, seemed instead to be waiting for something, a faintly superior smile on his lips. Smug, thought Joseph, he's acting smug. He asked Hattie if she had noticed the smile.

"This ain't a smiling house."

It was unsettling. He could not sleep at night, drowsed at his desk through the day, wondered where the sluggish flow of non-events was taking him. Like the doctor, he waited.

A new teacher joined the staff at Throckmorton Academy. Mr. Bascombe was a man of height and breadth, if not of learning, and had been selected for his unique ability to control even the most wilful of boys. The academy had suffered a steady breakdown of discipline in recent years, since the advent of Joseph Cobden in fact. Joseph's example was contagious and, though none could equal his performances, many tried, defying the various teachers with glib phrases and an insouciant manner. Mr. Bascombe was instructed to single out the hunchbacked ringleader and bring him to heel. The new man looked forward to his task.

Joseph's dormant perceptions were restored to wakefulness the moment Bascombe entered the classroom. The teacher stood on his rostrum and raked each row of desks with his eyes until they settled on Joseph, who knew immediately that the intensity of this stare was not due to his deformity, but because of who he was; the new man had searched him out and was laying down nothing less than a silent challenge. The directness of it worried Joseph for a moment, but he refused to be shaken. He had bested every teacher in the school, intimidated them to the point where they left him in peace, endured the occasional snide remark rather than risk confrontation. It would be the same with this newcomer, he was sure.

"My name is Mr. Bascombe, and I do not tolerate fools or timewasters. Above all I do not tolerate backtalkers. Any boy who backtalks me will suffer for it. I hope I make myself clear."

He did. The entire class noted the direction of his unwavering gaze throughout this introduction. A thrill of excitement ran along Joseph's wayward spine; a challenge had been flung down upon the classroom floor. Joseph did not hesitate. He raised his hand.

"Yes?"

Joseph stood. "On behalf of the class and the school in general I'd like to extend a warm welcome, Mr. Bascombe, sir. We hope your term here is a long and happy one. I'm sure I speak for all of us when I say how stimulating we find a new face, challenging almost. A new teacher brings out the beast—pardon me, sir, the *best* in us, and we look forward to making your acquaintance, intellectually and otherwise."

He sat down. A few titters were smothered. Bascombe

hesitated several seconds, taken aback by the suddenness of this polite broadside. The boy's gall was even worse than reported.

"Your name?"

"Cobden, sir."

"Thank you, Cobden. I look forward to the challenge, intellectual and otherwise. Open your texts."

Desk-tops were rattled, books shuffled, pages riffled, a muted fanfare preceding inevitable conflict. Every boy was tense with expectation. Bascombe's subject was mathematics, Joseph's lowest grade. Coincidence? Joseph asked himself, and felt a slight tremor of alarm; it would be all too easy for Bascombe to humiliate him in the name of learning. He knew he had only minutes, possibly seconds, in which to prepare a stratagem. Should he play for time with pretended self-reproach? Sir, I'm afraid I can't answer the question; I confess I'm the worst mathematician in the entire academy. Or should he bring his biggest guns to bear immediately, and let Bascombe know he was not afraid?

"Who can define *pi* for me?" No hands were raised. Joseph waited, not breathing. Yes, Bascombe's face was turning in his direction, the mouth opening like a cannon. "Cobden, can you define *pi?*"

He took a breath, knew he must try to bring down Goliath with one unerring shot. "It's a pastry consisting of a shortbread crust and top, filled with any number of savoury fruits. My own particular favourite is blueberry."

Joseph's cohorts howled their approval, delighted that he had not allowed himself to be intimidated. Bascombe's face did not change, but his hands clenched murderously.

"Stand, Cobden." Joseph obliged. "Come with me."

They left the room. Joseph assumed they would go to the principal's office. If they did, he would talk back until they expelled him, something both pupil and staff yearned for. To his surprise Bascombe led the way to the lavatories, empty of occupants during classtime. Before he could resist, Joseph was grabbed by the throat and pushed against the wall, the considerable weight of Bascombe's body pressed hard against him. "Sooner than expected, boy." The words were hissed into his face. Joseph raised his arms to push Bascombe away, and felt an agonizing pain explode between his legs; it blossomed through his groin and solar plexus until it consumed every part of his body, a pain so awful, so complete he could make no sound, draw no breath.

Bascombe withdrew his knee slowly, relishing the boy's open mouth and bulging eyes, then lifted it again, a short, fast jab as before. Joseph's testicles sought refuge inside his body, their hasty passage into his abdomen prompting a nauseous reaction; he vomited a solid jet of semi-digested matter. Familiar with the pattern of response, Bascombe had already released his hold on Joseph's throat and stepped clear. Joseph slid to the floor, back still against the wall, a second spasm flooding his shirtfront with vomit. Bascombe flicked a morsel of bacon from his shoe in disgust, kicked the shoe into Joseph's ribs to clean it, watched with satisfaction as Joseph toppled sideways, gulping for air. "Next time it'll be worse, boy. Learn to toe the line."

Joseph was left where he lay. Not wishing to be seen in this sad state by other boys, he waited until his body was capable of movement, then dragged himself from the lavatories and across to a secluded corner of the yard. Hidden from the school windows, he sat quietly and considered how best to fight this formidable adversary. Whichever way it happened, it would be the last thing he did at the academy. He would stay here no longer than it took to defeat Bascombe. In fact there was no point in continuing with the day's lessons; the mathematics class would soon be over, and he would not get the chance to confront Bascombe until tomorrow. Joseph picked himself up and left the schoolyard, nursing his empty stomach and bruised balls.

He limped through the streets, proud of the way he was nowadays able to ignore the stares he received, to feel nothing whatever. He went so far as to scorn people of normal proportion; they could never know the wretchedness of rejection or the peculiar strength it gave. Joseph liked to imagine himself a sword of Toledo steel, raised to white heat then plunged into bitter cold, tempered to an unbreakable keenness capable of slicing through any of the straight spines around him. Fire and ice, he repeated to himself, fire and ice.

He wandered aimlessly for most of the day, and in the late afternoon went home. He assembled a bundle of clothing and stole some bread, biscuits and a jar of preserves from the kitchen. The doctor had recently presented him with a razor and taught him how to negotiate with reasonable safety the eruptions on his cheeks. Alone in his room, he stropped the blade to an edge so fine it could sever a hair, then placed the razor in his pocket. At supper he could not eat. The doctor enquired after his loss of appetite.

"I'm just not hungry."

"Your face has a troubled look."

"Well it shouldn't have."

"Nothing has upset you?"

"No."

They sat in silence, the doctor eating slowly, methodically; he had lost his relish for food years ago, now ate only to sustain his body. Joseph forked the vegetables on his plate into a watery mountain. "What would you say if I told you I'm thinking of going away?"

"I would ask where you intend going, and why."

"West. I don't like it here any more."

"You're not yet sixteen, Joseph."

"I feel like about fifty."

"I am fifty-two, and I assure you our feelings have nothing in common. How do you intend paying your way?"

"I was hoping you'd give me some money."

"Why should I do that?"

"Because you've got some and I haven't."

"I will not encourage you to leave home. You're too young."

"But I'm strong."

"Nevertheless."

"So you're not going to give me any money."

"No."

"Then, I'll just have to find some elsewhere."

"If you can."

Joseph slept little, remembering passages from James Fenimore Cooper and Francis Parkman. Westward. The word sent a delightful shiver through him, raised bumps on his skin. A rolling sea of grass with shining mountains beyond, an inverted blue bowl of sky above, the land of his unknown mother. I'll be going home, he thought, and was seized with momentary dread. I'll be alone, won't know a soul. And I'm a hunchback. First comes tomorrow. He conjured Bascombe's face before him, made the nose larger and pink with broken veins, made the teeth more yellow, felt his rage quicken. His testicles ached with remembrance. He must be sure to stop short of actual killing, must control his temper; Joseph wanted retribution, not bloody vengeance.

At breakfast he attacked his food ravenously. "Your appetite seems much improved," said the doctor.

"I feel different today."

"Is it still your intention to leave this house?"

"I changed my mind," lied Joseph.

"I'm glad to hear it. You have a lifetime to explore the world. It should not take that long to discover that man is everywhere merely man."

"I'll train myself not to expect too much."

"You would do better to curb your sarcasm."

"I'll bear that in mind, too."

He fingered the razor in his pocket while walking to school, guts squirming with anticipation. His cronies in the schoolyard asked what had happened yesterday, why Joseph had not returned to class with Bascombe. "He got me, took me by surprise. But today I'm getting my own back.''

Word of the impending clash between teacher and pupil spread, and was common knowledge by the time classes began. The first lesson of the morning was geography. Joseph stared at a map of Europe and saw Bascombe's face leering at him from the continent, blotting out frontiers. I mustn't kill him, just hurt him.

The second lesson was mathematics. Joseph breathed steadily as Bascombe mounted the rostrum with an infuriatingly confident bounce in his step. He hectored the class for fifteen minutes on the subject of fractions, found them unresponsive and restless. The only boy in the room not fidgeting was Cobden; the brute sat calmly at his desk and did not once take his eyes from Bascombe's face. At last Bascombe understood; the boys were waiting. Cobden was not going to surrender his position without a fight. So be it. He would put a stop to the hunchback once and for all, reduce him to nothing. ''Cobden, what have I been talking about?''

''I don't know.''

''You don't know *what.*''

''I don't know what you've been talking about.''

An electrical charge seemed to fill the room during their exchange. Every boy ceased to move. Bascombe felt their hunger for sensation crowd around him, urging him silently to make his move, little Romans eager for gladiatorial combat, anxious to turn their thumbs down upon the loser. It would not be him.

''Come here, Cobden.''

Joseph stood and approached the rostrum. Bascombe produced a cane from his desk. ''You persist in trying to make a jester of yourself, Cobden, but you fail to amuse me. Go to the study room and wait.''

Joseph waited ten minutes in the empty room before Bascombe entered, carrying the cane. He swished it through the air a number of times, enjoying the sound it made. Joseph produced what he hoped was a sneer.

"Doing that isn't going to scare me."

"It should, Cobden. A flexible cane like this causes a lot of pain."

"Only if I let you hit me with it."

"There isn't a way you can stop me. I'm bigger than you, boy, and stronger and faster. The only way you can avoid what's coming to you is by running away. I won't be surprised if you try it; your kind are cowards at heart. I won't even stop you. There's the door, Cobden."

"I'm not going anywhere just now."

"Then hold out your hands."

"No."

"The longer you delay, the worse beating you'll get. Come here." Joseph walked towards him. "And take your hands out of your pockets."

Joseph pulled the razor free, flipped open the blade and slashed at Bascombe's hand, the one holding the cane. Bascombe's little finger was severed at the knuckle. He watched blood well and gush from the tiny stump, let the cane join his finger at his feet. Joseph walked past him, razor poised to strike again. Bascombe did not even hear the door close behind him, but stood looking at the finger by his boot, at the blood flowing down the seam of his pants.

Joseph considered returning to the classroom, flourishing the razor for all to see, bidding them a careless farewell. No, they were only boys after all, snotnoses, not worth impressing. Filled with the drug of triumph as he was, Joseph needed no approval from lesser beings.

He went quickly home. Today was a Wednesday; the doctor would be at the infirmary. Joseph went to the surgery, opened a cupboard and removed the cashbox he had known for years was kept in this place. Surprisingly, the key was in plain view on top of the metal box. Joseph inserted it and opened the lid. Resting on a neat stack of paper money was a note in the Doctor's elegant handwriting:

*Joseph, you are faced with a moral choice; either replace this
as you found it, in which case I will never know you attempted
to steal from me, or take it and never return to this house. If
you choose the latter option, bear in mind it will be the first
act of your adult life, and a life built upon theft can never be
worthwhile. I have done my best for you, fate has done its
worst. Only you can decide which has been stronger.*

"Fate, definitely," said Joseph, and counted the cash.
Ninety-three dollars, enough for his purpose. He replaced
the cashbox, then brought it out again, took a pen from
the doctor's desk and wrote on the note:

*A restless heart knows no conscience. I have great respect for
you. Goodbye. J.*

He shouldered his light bundle and went to the kitchen.
"I'm going away, Hattie. I just wanted to say goodbye."

"Where you going?"

"Out west."

"What you going to do way out there?"

"Whatever comes to hand. Thanks for feeding me all
these years."

"You got any money?"

"I just now stole some from the surgery cashbox. I left
a note."

"Ain't you ashamed? The doctor brung you up like his
own."

"I'm not his own, Hattie. I'm not anybody's." He held
out his hand. Hattie took it briefly in hers. Joseph hesitated, looking at her. "Tell me something. Why are you
scared of me? Is it the hump?"

"I ain't scared of you or no one."

"Sometimes you're scared of me, I can tell."

"No, I ain't. I'm ashamed of you is what I am. You
put that money back right now."

"I need it to get where I'm going. It's not his life savings or anything, and he won't have to leave me an inheritance seeing as we'll never meet again.''

"You put it back anyhow. You too young to be going out west."

"Goodbye, Hattie."

She watched him walk from the kitchen, heard the front door close, found she had been holding her breath. Gone, she thought, gone at last. The devil's cuckoo had finally weaned itself away from the nest and taken flight for the wilderness. Hattie surprised herself by detecting a faint pang of regret buried under a mountain of relief. Hold Satan to your tit for long enough and you'd feel sad when he quit sucking.

Joseph walked along DeWitte Street, his step light, an impromptu melody trickling from his lips. He headed for the railroad depot.

PART TWO
THE PILGRIM

CHAPTER EIGHT

Seated by a window on the train to Independence, tortured by the wooden seat, he watched Missouri roll by. His appearance and solitary state aroused whispered comment among the other passengers. He made no effort to befriend anyone, and the space beside him remained unoccupied until a drummer bound west sat next to Joseph and cleared his throat. "A fine morning."

"Fine enough," Joseph agreed.

The man was surprised at Joseph's voice, the cracked baritone of an adolescent; he had surmised, as many had before, that Joseph was in his thirties. The scowling face had none of childhood's contours; hatless, Joseph's forehead caught the sun across its considerable width, threw his eye sockets into deep shadow. The man imagined himself a great conversationalist, the kind who can talk to anyone from anywhere about anything, but Joseph's level gaze, incurious, unblinking, disturbed him. He beamed a hearty smile, his eyes resting on the hump over Joseph's shoulder. "Your first ride west, son?"

Joseph nodded and turned away. The man was offended; no one had ever refused his conversation before. He would not be rebuffed by a humpbacked child. There was nonwhite blood in there somewhere too, in fact the little brute was a mixture of everything the man held in contempt. "Business or pleasure?" he demanded, smiling still.

"Business," offered Joseph, after a long moment of speculation. The man's eyes had returned to the hump as Joseph had known they would.

"Kind of young to be a businessman, aren't you?"

"I'm fully equipped for this particular venture."

"What kind of venture might that be?"

"I intend charging people ten cents to rub my hump for luck."

The man's face reddened and he guiltily snatched his gaze from Joseph's back. Joseph smiled tolerantly, amazed and saddened that fools like this should consider themselves superior to him. "Goodbye," he said, and presented his hump to the man's face. Thereafter he was left alone.

At Independence, Joseph changed trains and rolled further westward, deep into Kansas. Telegraph poles drifted by with numbing regularity, sole representatives of the vertical in a land dominated by the horizontal. Every seat in the car was occupied, every overhead rack crammed with luggage. Joseph was ignored by the passengers around him. As day turned to night the prairie beyond the window darkened, became a frozen sea under reddened clouds, was gradually swallowed by blackness. The hours until dawn were long and uncomfortable. Joseph slept fitfully, his hump wedged into the angle between wall and seat, and awoke long before sunrise. The train appeared to have made no progress; the scene revealed by the first rays of light was identical with the landscape of yesterday, treeless, neverending.

Halfway through the morning the train slowed to a halt. The tracks ahead were buried under a living ocean of hair and horns. Passengers leaned from windows and gaped at the milling, heaving, snorting multitude that stretched, literally, to the horizon. The buffalo were moving at a steady pace, the nearer fringes of the herd kept at a safe distance from the train by blasts from the whistle, their hoofs raising dust enough to dim the sun. Joseph sat quietly, amazed at their ungraspable numbers. He thought of the picture in the doctor's home; brush strokes had been limned with reality, the creatures, humpbacked like himself, made concrete. The incident offered more to him than mere spectacle, yet he could not define its essence. He stared at the herd, oblivious to the excited chattering of his fellow passengers, lost in his own imaginings.

Five hours after it had been obliged to stop, the train edged forward among the dawdling tail-enders still crossing the Kansas Pacific tracks. Pistols and rifles were dragged from valises and luggage-racks, hundreds of rounds fired at the stragglers. Dozens fell, mostly cows slowed by calves. Another hour was lost while several of the carcasses were winched on to an empty flatcar at the end of the train. The rest were left to rot. The way ahead clear at last, the journey was resumed.

Stepping down at Hays City, Joseph experienced a fleeting moment of sheer panic; he knew no one, had nowhere to go. He swallowed his fear, scowled a little more to convince himself as much as others that his resolve was firm. He traipsed around the town, ostensibly seeking employment, in reality waiting for the agents of fate to channel his life into a new and excitingly different direction. He dared speak to no one. The agents of fate ignored him. As the day wore on and became afternoon, then evening, Joseph decided he must overcome his timidity and impose himself upon his surroundings by actively requesting lodgings for the night. He returned to a house he had noticed earlier, saw the handwritten sign still in the front window, knocked at the door. A woman of severe expression opened it and stared at Joseph in disbelief.

"I'd like a room, ma'am."

The woman recovered her composure. "The room is taken."

"The sign's still there in the window."

"That is a mistake. The room is taken."

She closed the door in his face. Joseph quelled the anger rising in him and walked on, found another boarding house, knocked on the door. A man opened it, a pipe jutting from his mouth.

"Looking for a room?" he asked.

"Do you rent them to hunchbacks?"

The man laughed. "I reckon you'd be the first. Come on

in.'' Joseph was led through to a small parlour, invited to sit on a chintz-covered sofa. The man looked at him with undisguised interest. ''Mind if I ask how old you are?''

''I'm twenty-three. You're probably wondering about my voice. It's part of being like I am. Dwarfs talk squeaky too, sometimes.''

The man nodded, knocked out his pipe over what appeared to be a small funeral urn at his side. Joseph wondered if the dottle was being mingled with human ash; he had heard that people in the west had peculiar customs. The man began tamping fresh tobacco. ''What's your name?''

''Joe Cobden.'' He had decided to employ the diminutive, hoping its blunt sound would make him appear older, tougher.

''Where are you from, Joe?''

''St. Louis. I'm looking to find work.''

''What kind?''

''Just about anything.''

The man applied a match to his pipe and peered through the smoke at his guest. ''Don't mind my asking, Joe, but you look like there's mixed blood in you, am I right?''

''I'm half-Indian.''

''That a fact? What tribe?''

''I don't know.''

''See, the problem is, Joe, my wife kind of runs the show here, and her folks weren't treated too kindly by Indians a number of years back, so she's not what you'd call partial to having them around, or half-breeds, neither. I'm in a peck of trouble if I let you take a room, see what I mean?''

Joe was already standing, picking up his bundle. ''The smart thing to do would be to put a lamp by the door, then you could see if your callers were acceptable before inviting them in.''

''No offence, Joe, it's just the way things are.''

''Am I going to find a lot of this out here?''

''A lot of what?''

''This 'Indians are shit' business.''

"Now there's no need for that kind of talk. I don't expect a man to come into my house and talk profanity."

"I'm leaving." He went to the front door, stepped outside into the gathering dusk. "If I bump into any whites looking for a room, I'll recommend this place."

"There's no need to get sore at me." The man's tone was aggrieved, defensive. "It's my wife that won't allow it. This is her house, see. If it was mine, you'd be welcome to stay."

Joe nodded tersely and walked away. Angry and footsore, he tramped the streets again as night settled over Hays City. Disenchanted, not daring to risk further humiliation, he returned to the railyard, found a secluded spot behind a shed and curled himself into a ball, too exhausted to be conscious of his discomfort. He dreamed of buffalo in teeming tens of thousands, felt the thundering of their hoofs throughout his body, awoke to find himself mere yards from the railroad track, shaken by an incoming train. The eastern horizon was already flushed with light. Surrounded by clouds of steam, Joe rose from his bed of earth and began looking for a job.

He entered every store, every livery stable, every business enterprise large or small which might conceivably require help. He was polite, called the women "ma'am" and the men "sir", smiled and said thank you when refused. It's because I'm a hunchback, he told himself, and so it was; Joe's startling appearance provoked instant rejection. Playing the role of humble indigent did not appeal to him. As the morning wore on Joe became frustrated, then angry, then aggressive. He stopped a man in the street by blocking his path. "I need a job. Got one?"

"No I haven't. Get out of my way."

"I'm strong. Forget the hump."

"Forget it yourself."

The man pushed Joe aside. Joe pushed back with all his strength. The man staggered and fell from the sidewalk, came up with an angry flush colouring his cheeks. Joe regretted his action immediately. "I'm sorry," he said. "I didn't mean it, I just got mad."

"If you weren't a humpback, I'd squash you like a bug."

A small crowd had gathered. The man hurried away, furious at having been bested by someone of Joe's stature and disability. Joe took advantage of the curiosity being directed at him. "I need a job! Who's going to give me one!"

Several onlookers laughed. "There ain't a circus in town!" shouted one, and more joined in the laughter.

Joe ground his teeth, forced his mouth into a grin. "I'm all through with circuses! They don't pay a man a living wage."

"Show me the man!" called the same heckler, and this time Joe saw who it was. He pointed, still smiling.

"Mister, I'll arm wrestle you to the ground for ten dollars."

The heckler was unwilling, either because he did not wish to match strength with a cripple, or because he had noticed the thickness of Joe's chest and arms. The crowd would not let him back down; he and Joe were jostled into the nearest saloon and seated at a hastily cleared table. Bets flew around the room, evenly divided. Joe and the man planted their elbows on green baize, grasped hands, waited for the countdown and brought all their strength to bear. Joe's opponent was not weak, yet he managed to resist for only eleven seconds before his forearm crashed to the table. A cheer for Joe rocked the bar and money changed hands. Joe climbed on to his chair. "Now who'll give me a job!"

"Can you swing an axe?" asked a voice at his chest.

Joe Cobden became a woodcutter in a land without trees. Eli Tilton was an easy man to work for; he asked no questions, demanded nothing but hard work, paid a fair wage. Tilton knew where wood could be found some forty miles away at Walnut Creek. He had a contract with the army at Fort Hays to provide fuel. The army wanted to build up its supply over summer and fall; in winter the route would become too hazardous and unreliable. Even now the trip to Walnut Creek and back was not without its dangers. Pawnee were known to frequent the area, which they rightly considered their own.

Tilton worked with a loaded Sharpe's rifle by his side, Joe with nothing save his axe. Each man cut two cords of wood per day and piled it into two mule-drawn wagons. When these were full they were driven to Fort Hays and unloaded. Tilton liked to imagine the grove at Walnut Creek was known only to himself, and swore Joe to secrecy. In fact the location was well known, but no one in Hays City wished to work so hard no matter what the profit, nor cared to risk scalping at the hands of hostiles. Tilton had cornered a demanding yet lucrative corner of a crucial market and knew it. He and Joe worked from sunup till sundown, seldom talked when not felling, sawing and splitting, ate together in silence. The arrangement suited Joe perfectly; he had no desire to discuss anything with anyone. His face and hands darkened to a chestnut brown, his torso swelled with new muscle, his hands blistered, the blisters eventually becoming calluses. Owning no hat, Joe let his hair grow into a black haystack for protection against the sun. The life had its own rhythm, toned the body, made no demands upon the mind. Joe was neither happy nor unhappy; he felt satisfaction at the completion of another day's work, the proof of his labour stacked around him, and had no trouble sleeping. He and Tilton did not agree or disagree about anything; two deaf mutes would have worked together in almost identical fashion. He was, for the moment, content. A woodcutter, he mused to himself, a profession found in fairy tales. The timber at Walnut Creek was sparse, afforded too little shade to be cool, was no more than a wooded declivity meandering for some miles before petering out in open prairie, the merest line of green on a plain of yellow brown. Joe imagined himself in Germanic forests of mystery and gloom, the haunt of witches and trolls, knew that he, dreamer of dreams, seeker after freedom and adventure would be cast in any fairy tale as a troll himself, certainly not as hero.

On a blazing day in late August, when the creek had become an exhausted trickle and the mule teams hung their heads and barely had the inclination to twitch flies from their skin, Joe climbed the slope to see if any breeze at all was passing across the land. As his eyes drew level with the prairie he saw a new mountain range of brown lumped along the horizon. A few steps more and the range resolved itself into a browsing herd of buffalo, perhaps half a mile distant. Their numbers were not so vast as on the occasion of Joe's first sighting, but his pulse quickened in response. He lowered himself from view and approached Tilton. "There's buffalo just a stone's throw away. How about I get us some red meat?"

"You know I don't like to make no noise. Noise brings Indians."

"Come on, Eli, there aren't any Indians around here except me. One buffalo, that's all. What we don't eat we could sell in Hays."

Tilton nodded at the big Sharpe's propped against a felled cottonwood. "Don't be all day about it."

Joe crawled on hands and knees in the manner he had heard was necessary, and took up position some hundred yards from the nearest animal. He took careful aim, squeezed the trigger. The rifle boomed and the buffalo of his choosing fell, its legs apparently pulled from beneath it. Joe waited for the herd to stampede but, apart from those nearest the target starting slightly as it went down, there were no signs of panic. Joe realised the wind was in his favour, surrounding him with the rank odour of buffalo; the herd had not smelled him, had not even heard the shot. He was tempted to take advantage of the circumstances by killing more, but restrained himself; one buffalo, he had told Eli, and one buffalo it would be. He stood and walked toward his kill. Shaggy heads lifted, tails were turned, and several thousand buffalo ran from Joe in alarm.

He stood by the fallen beast. Its eyes were open, already

filling with flies. The fifty calibre bullet had entered just behind the left foreleg and ploughed a path deep into the chest, burst the heart. Joe placed his boot against the matted hump and pushed; the buffalo's dead weight budged not one inch, seemed in death to have grown more bulky, to have become rooted in the very earth. The mucus-slimed nostrils were plugged with dust, the purple tongue lolled grotesquely, flecked with blood. Flies danced along the horns, the hump rose like a mountain. Joe almost regretted his act; the massive thing before him had moments before been alive, and now was dead because he, Joe, had so decreed. He had until now never killed anything larger than an insect.

Tilton came from the creek, stood beside Joe and looked at his kill without emotion. "Know what to do next?"

"No."

"Figured not."

He hacked at the hump with his knife, grunting with effort. "Best part of the whole animal," he explained, "the tongue too. Real delicacy, so they say. Never tried it myself. Puts me in mind of eating horse dick."

A fire was built. Joe tasted buffalo meat for the first time and found it good. He agreed with Eli about the tongue. They sold it and the remainder of the hump to an eating house in Hays City. The proprietor let them know he was willing to buy more of the same. Thereafter, toward the end of each stint at Walnut Creek, Joe put a saddle on one of the mules and set off to find buffalo in the near vicinity, a pack mule trailing behind. He rarely came back without at least one hundred pounds of flesh. Eli grumbled about being left without his Sharpe's while Joe hunted, but was persuaded to continue the practice for the sake of dollars. Joe demonstrated to him with pencil and paper that pound for pound, buffalo meat was a more lucrative commodity than firewood, and much easier to obtain; head in any direction and within an hour or so you came upon buffalo in abundance. They were everywhere, as plentiful as blades of grass, cash profit on the hoof.

They agreed to spend the winter months hunting buffalo. The army contract for fuel would expire in November, and they had no other work to turn to. Joe looked forward to the day when he would lay down his axe and invest his back pay in a brand new Sharpe's like Eli's. For the purposes of hunting, Joe would no longer be considered an employee, but a partner.

The teams were driven one last time to Walnut Creek, trees felled and split, the wagons loaded. While Eli attended to the final cords Joe headed into a bitter wind on muleback, an occasional snowflake touching his cheek, his skin crawling with cold. After the first hour he decided he would strip the hide from his kill and take it back to Hays to be made into a winter coat. After the second hour he was barely capable of thought. Teeth chattering, fingers locked around Eli's rifle, Joe had already turned back to the creek in despair when he saw buffalo in the distance. The mules were trained to stand unattended. Joe left them beyond the herd's feeble eyesight and crawled forward, found a spot on a rise two hundred yards from the nearest animals and felled one with a single shot. Removing the hide proved harder than anticipated, occupying more than an hour. The mules had to be fetched to pull the hide free, and by the time the hump, hams and tongue had been removed the afternoon light was fading. Joe loaded the pack mule, carefully balancing the meat and hide, then set off back to Eli and the wagons.

The last of the wood had been loaded. Eli smoked a pipe, stamped his feet, waited for Joe to return. The boy had infected him with enthusiasm for the new venture and he was anxious to begin. When this load had been delivered to the fort he would be free of his contract, an independent man with a reliable partner and a future. The day he walked into a saloon for a drink and saw a hunchback win an arm wrestling contest had been a lucky one. He knew as little about Joe's background as Joe knew of his. Eli did not wish to pry; a hunchback's story was bound to be a sorry one, and a half-breed hunchback's story was probably too dismal even to think about. The boy was a fine shot and would bring down plenty of meat, that was all Eli needed to know. Hunting in winter would be hard work, but the rewards would be great. Buffalo meat was becoming big business in Hays City now; he and Joe would not be alone on the prairie. He heard the sound of hoofs sliding down the incline and stepped out from behind the tree he had been using to shelter from the wind. The hoofs belonged to ponies, not mules, and Joe was not among the riders.

The weak shadows of November were lengthening when Joe returned. The wagons stood untouched, the mules, held in contempt by Indians, called "rabbit ponies", slaughtered in their traces. Eli's naked body had been left in the fork of a tree, his genitals crammed into a knothole in a parody of the sexual act. His cranium had been exposed by a scalping knife, blue-white bone with a few clinging strips of red tissue. Joe vomited while still in the saddle. He waited for an arrow or bullet to find him. When they did not he dismounted, dumped the load from his pack mule, took Eli's body from its obscene perch and arranged it over the mule's back, fingers and toes pointing at the ground. He covered it with the buffalo hide.

On the two-day journey to Fort Hays he indulged in fantasies of revenge. He would track down those responsible, would submit them one by one to fiendish torture, make them scream with pain until they admitted they had killed a man better than themselves, and were therefore unfit to live. Halfway to his destination Joe admitted it would never happen. Eli's murderers would remain forever faceless; the anonymous Indians were already beyond the reaches of justice. He removed the hide from Eli's frozen body, wrapped the stinking thing around himself to ward off the cold. The way ahead was already dusted with white.

A mile from the fort he replaced the hide over Eli's body for the sake of public decency. He told his story to the commander, was loaned two teams of army mules and a small armed escort, brought the wood from Walnut Creek and was paid for the job. Eli's spine had been broken with an axe in order to free him from the horseshoe shape his body had adopted on muleback. More or less straightened, he was placed in a coffin and buried in a cemetery outside the fort. The commander read the service. Joe was left with eighty dollars, a Sharpe's rifle and two wagons minus teams. He sold the wagons and his two remaining mules to the fort sutler, and was given a ride into Hays City on an army wagon headed there to pick up the garrison's pay.

Joe had never drunk liquor before, was not prepared for the consequences of his one-man wake. He stood in the bar where Eli had first seen him, demanded a whiskey and was sold one. The barman recognised Joe from his previous visit, was intrigued by his ugliness; Joe was a conversation-piece for the customers. Unless someone objected, he could stay as long as he wished, drink as much as could be paid for. A half-breed with a straight spine would have been thrown out immediately. Joe was unaware of his unique status. It would serve him all his life. The whiskey burned in a direct line to his stomach. When his breath was recovered Joe felt good, and so ordered another, and another. Talk and laughter boomed in his ears. His usual reserve was washed away on a tide of whiskey; he talked with strangers, told them of Eli's fate. His drinking companions, their faces swimming confusedly before his eyes, bought more drinks with Joe's money and expressed their regret. Joe thought he felt a hand touch his hump, but was unsure, too sluggish to turn and see; it was unlikely his new friends would have perpetrated such an insensitive act. He forgot about it, did not feel other hands surreptitiously touching him. Joe talked on, about his childhood in St. Louis, about the doctor and his mad wife, his schooldays, all of it lucid, incisively analytical, a brilliantly impartial summation of his life to date; those around him heard incoherent mumbling interspersed with cackling laughter. One of the drinkers said he worked for a circus in the east, had come to Kansas for live buffalo to display, had decided the easiest way to tame one was to capture it while still young. This had been duly done, the captive calf being held in a livery stable nearby. As a buffalo-hunter himself, would Joe be interested in seeing it? He accepted the invitation and prepared to leave, along with several more of his new friends. Joe was delighted that they should find his company so essential.

Out into the street, around corners, along more streets. Joe sang a ribald song he had learned at school; the men with him heard what they supposed was an Indian chant. They entered a livery stable. Joe drank from a bottle offered to him, drank again. Someone was touching his hump, this time he was positive. He turned to catch the offending hand, turned and turned and drilled himself into the earth like an auger, spinning, spinning, leaving the world behind, plunging deeper into darkness.

His groin grew warm and moist. He felt straw tickling and scratching at his back. Joe opened his eyes and saw the roof of the livery stable, realised he was naked. He heard low voices, laughter, and knew it was directed at him. Were they laughing at his hump? That warmth and wetness around his thighs, that peculiar tightness—had he pissed himself? Was that why they laughed? Joe raised his head with difficulty, brought his eyes into focus, but could not believe what he saw. A calf, no ordinary calf but a humpbacked buffalo calf, was sucking at his penis, which had risen to a hardened shaft. The calf sucked with a will, wondering why no milk flowed from this stiff teat. Joe absorbed the scene with a sense of unreality, unable in his drunkenness to fathom its meaning. More snickering came from the shadows, and Joe at last divined his predicament: I'm naked and a buffalo calf is sucking my dick and those men are all laughing at me. . . . Disgust and shame flooded through him in equal portions; his stomach rebelled, ejected alcoholic bile in a gush so powerful it temporarily blinded the calf, sent it bawling and blundering among the stalls. Joe rolled over, heaved the dregs of his stomach on to the floor and crawled towards the single oil-lamp illuminating the stable. Before he could demand his clothing a kick to the side of his head propelled Joe into oblivion.

A bucket of water was thrown into his face long after

dawn. Joe returned slowly to awareness, relishing the coolness trickling along his scalp. A man stood over him, an angry expression on his face. "Get on up." Joe staggered upright, in too much pain as the blood drained from his head to feel ashamed of his nakedness. "Get out," the man ordered. Joe wished only to comply. The man pointed to a corner where Joe's clothing lay scattered among the straw. Joe scraped himself clean of dried vomit and managed to dress himself, looked around with more alertness. "Where's my buffalo hide and gun?"

"I didn't see nothing like that, just the clothes. Now, get."

"They stole my Sharpe's and hide. . . ."

"I don't know nothing about it. If you got drunk and lost some stuff it ain't my fault. Indians oughtn't to drink. You get along now."

"Where's the calf? It was here last night, a buffalo calf for the circus. . . ."

"It ain't here now. Some feller took it to the depot hours ago. Be halfway across Kansas by now."

"Did he have my rifle?"

"I never saw no gun nor no buffalo hide. I ain't about to tell you again, Indian."

Joe shuffled from the stable. The morning light lanced into his eyes, made him fling up his hands for shade. He stood in the stableyard, swaying with concussion, hunger, dehydration. An alarming thought occurred to him; he slapped his pockets and found them distressingly flat. The proceeds from his sale of wood and wagons had been stolen. Joe Cobden owned nothing more than the clothes upon his crooked back.

CHAPTER NINE

During the winter of 1870–1 Joe did not hunt buffalo as planned. Instead he washed dishes and emptied spittoons and swept the floors of an establishment called the Anderson House, a restaurant for the undiscerning. The building was owned by Mrs. Adeline Attucks, a widow in her forties who seldom visited the premises. Joe slept in a store-room behind the kitchen, his back against the warm brick rear of the oven. The staff referred to him as "Hump" or "Humpy" behind his back, never to his face; something in Joe's expression warned them not to. One man, a waiter named Giddings, made an error of judgement while delivering a customer's order to the kitchen. Joe was scrubbing a skillet when Giddings entered and bumped against him.

"Can't you stand sideways to the sink, Hump? You're in my way like that."

Joe stared at him in surprise; he had assumed Giddings accepted his appearance with equanimity, had no idea the man looked on him with contempt.

"Well?" Giddings waited for him to move. There was room enough for him to pass if he wished; he simply wanted to make Joe look foolish, wanted him to acquiesce over a trifle, thereby proving the superiority of the norm over disfigurement. Understanding this, Joe felt his head swim with anger, his chest fill and overflow with a hatred which had festered since the incident in the livery stable. He removed his hands from the sink, dried them carefully, then placed himself squarely in Giddings' path. The skin along his spine quivered with tension. He could not bring himself to speak.

The rest of the kitchen staff were watching now, all activity suspended. Giddings, not an unintelligent man, realised he had provoked Joe with his insult, had somehow triggered within the hunchback a powerful resistance. The fact that Joe possessed self-respect despite his ugliness came as a shock to Giddings. He could neither understand nor condone it; a hunchback should know his place. Joe at last found a word to break the silent deadlock between them.

"Apologise."

Giddings could hardly believe Joe had the temerity to make demands.

"I'm losing patience, Hump. Are you going to move?"

"I want an apology."

"You won't get one, not from me."

"Then, I'll have to hurt you."

"I don't think so, Hump."

Without removing his eyes from Giddings' face, Joe reached for and grasped a metal colander. He held it before him, crushed it like a paper hat. Giddings felt the first twinge of misgiving; maybe he shouldn't have goaded the hump after all, but to back down now would be intolerable. He was not a weakling, believed he could match Joe in a fight. He attempted to pass. Joe grabbed the waiter by crotch and throat, raised him without effort and hurled him across the kitchen. Giddings struck a wall cupboard and sent its contents clattering to the floor about his tangled limbs.

He scrambled to his feet, furious at having been manhandled with such ease by a cripple. He picked a lengthy knife from the bench beside him and held himself in readiness. Joe felt wonderful; faceless Indians, nameless drunkards, a host of taunting voices from the past, all coalesced in the dishevelled form of Giddings. He tightened his grip on the crushed colander, a ridiculous weapon, and approached his opponent, blood humming in exultation. The knife was knocked aside. Giddings attempted to grasp Joe's throat— a hopeless tactic since Joe had very little neck. Joe delivered several blows to the side of his head in retaliation. Giddings' ear split and bled. He made a mewling sound every time the colander made contact and, hearing this, Joe stopped.

Mere seconds before he had wanted to kill; now, seeing Giddings cringe before him, inarticulate cries escaping his lips, Joe wished only to humiliate, to repay in kind. Giddings was nothing, a hollow man unworthy of his attention. He straightened the colander and jammed it on to the waiter's head, crowned him loser. No one had attempted to stop him; indeed, there were several smiling faces to be seen in the kitchen as Joe returned to the sink and plunged his hands once again into greasy hot water.

That night Joe lay behind the oven and could not find sleep. If he had been born without strength, life would long ago have squashed him like a snail. Without strength he would be helpless, a victim unable to retaliate, yet strength was his by chance, as was his twisted back—a good thing and a bad thing laid upon a newborn child like palm prints of white and black. If there is a god, Joe decided, he dispenses largesse without properly exercising divine wisdom, and since that is not a godlike act it suggests there is no god, certainly no god with anything remotely resembling human emotions and characteristics, neither a jealous nor a forgiving god, just a god of stone, a blind effigy unknowing of its acts. Joe had been granted great strength for no reason, had been cursed with a humped back for no reason, had been born, if the argument be logically extended to its fullest, for no reason. Existence without reason, existence for its own flawed sake, life without preordained purpose—these were the bleak tenets of Joe's first attempt to formulate for himself a philosophy. His conclusions did not fill him with despair, for his had not been a formal Christian upbringing; no crucifixes needed overturning since none had ever held sway over him. Joe felt very wise as he ruminated thus, perhaps even a little smug; let others kneel and pray to an empty sky, let them support their lives with nonexistent crutches; he, Joe Cobden, had found the truth, the awful, empty truth, and found it entirely acceptable.

* * *

Mrs. Adeline Attucks was told of the confrontation in her restaurant's kitchen. She paid a rare visit to the Anderson House to see for herself this hunchback with the spine like a question mark and the strength of two men. Mrs. Attucks had somehow convinced herself the object of her interest would be a giant; Joe's lack of stature proved disappointing when he entered the manager's office as requested. Joe saw a handsome woman, expensively dressed, her gaze frankly curious. He prepared himself for battle, convinced he was about to lose his job.

"I'm told you began a fight in my kitchen."

"No. I finished one."

"I do not like brawlers."

"Nor do I."

"Where are you from?"

"St. Louis."

"And you came to Kansas for what reason?"

"I had enough cash to get here. If I'd had more I would have gone to California."

"How does your job appeal to you?"

"It's the fulfilment of my every dream."

"You're educated."

"No, just smart."

"Smart people don't wash dishes and sweep floors for a living."

"I've had a measure of bad luck."

"Am I about to hear a familiar story?"

"I'm not about to tell you any kind of story."

Mrs. Attucks debated whether to admire his quickness or arrange to have him beaten for his impudence. He really was remarkably ugly. His refusal to ingratiate himself intrigued her. She decided to test him. "How does it feel to be a hunchback?"

"It feels almost normal once you get used to stupid questions like that one."

They regarded each other in silence for a short while.

"Your name is Joe?"

"Joseph."

"You may call me Mrs. Attucks."

"Are we going to be seeing each other socially?"

"I like the way you talk, Joseph, but don't overstep the mark. We have business to discuss."

"What kind?"

"The kind that involves making money. Is there any other?"

"I suppose not."

"The Anderson House isn't my only property. I also have a place just a few blocks from here. Have you ever heard of the Circus Maximus?"

"It's in Rome."

"It's now in Hays. It's a whorehouse. How would you like to work there?"

"I don't think I'd get too many customers."

Mrs. Attucks allowed herself a smile. "You won't be for sale. I need someone like you to bounce rowdy customers and anyone who gets rough with the girls."

"There are plenty of men in town who could do that kind of work."

"But they don't look like you. You're different. I like my place to be different. There are a dozen other places in town, but the Maximus prides itself on style, not just on the usual services. We'll put you in a decent suit of clothes, give you a room of your own and a fair wage. How does it sound?"

"I don't like to fight. I have to be angry to hurt anyone. They have to deserve it."

"The waiter the other night, did he deserve it?"

"He insulted me."

"So will some of the customers at the Maximus. They'll call you names when you ask them to leave, then you'll get mad and throw them out. You'll get a reputation in no time. Within a month you'll probably be sitting around getting fat. It's my business to know what people need, Joseph, and not just below the belt. I'd say you need to get out of that kitchen, and I'll bet mine's the only offer you've had."

Joe considered his options and found them wanting. By the end of the day he was ensconced in the best brothel in town. It stood two storeys high, and was among the first buildings in Hays to be constructed upon foundations of quarried stone; the large basement thus incorporated would prove useful during tornadoes and Indian uprisings, and was considered a perfect example of frontier forethought. Mrs. Attucks owned the place outright, had even participated in its design, which might best be termed Western Functional. There were no architectural frills and furbelows; indeed, the building resembled a clapboard warehouse rather than a whorehouse. Adeline Attucks wished her contribution to the town's grandeur to be solidly built and long-lived; she would have preferred that the Circus Maximus be made of brick, but her funds had been stretched as it was. At least it had been thoroughly whitewashed, unlike most wooden buildings; in fact the best brothel in town had been so coated with whiteness as to resemble some temple consecrated to arcane worship of all things immaculate. Like many a madam before her, Mrs. Attucks desired that her name be associated with civic pride in the years to come. Sadly, the Maximus (never formally entered into the municipal registry under that grandiloquent name) would become an anonymous hotel following Mrs. Attucks' death from cervical cancer in 1891.

Joe's first duty was to meet his fellow-employees. He had never been in such close proximity to women. Their perfume and the natural odour of their sex made his stomach lurch, his loins tighten. He felt like a fool as Mrs. Attucks escorted him through the building. The prostitutes looked at him with undisguised aversion; the sole exception was a Negress who proffered her hand like a man. "Pleased to meet you, Joseph."

He took the hand in his own, executed a mock bow. "Enchanted, Miss Serena."

The other women laughed at the ludicrous picture he presented. Joe compared their mirth to the sound of crowing poultry, and was grateful to Serena for not joining in. Mrs. Attucks led him away. "Don't be downhearted, Joseph. Most of my girls keep their brains in their ass. They'll get used to you in a week or two." She was well pleased with her purchase, for such was how she regarded Joe. As a child Mrs. Attucks had been fascinated by a painting which hung in her father's home. It depicted the court of some oriental potentate, and among the various subjects portrayed within that exotic tableau was one in particular which exercised a peculiarly repellent attraction for her, a hideous dwarf wearing a loincloth and jewelled turban; stationed by the throne, this diminutive monster stirred the air around its regal occupant with a huge feathered fan. That was a sight she yearned to see in her own establishment, something suggestive of lush decadence and the mysterious east. She knew it would never happen; that kind of thing was common enough in New Orleans, but in Kansas? She would be laughed out of business, and where would one find a dwarf in any case? The notion had been an idle fantasy, but one look at Joe and the image of grotesquerie and servitude had been instantly revived; Joe was the closest, most acceptable approximation of a dwarf she could have found hereabouts.

Next day Joe was dispatched to the only tailor in Hays City. This gentleman had wisely augmented his meagre business with an extensive haberdashery, and when informed of Joe's needs was immediately both jubilant and doubtful; at last had come an outlet for his sartorial creativity but, God in heaven, what a challenge! Joe was measured, a time-consuming process reminiscent of Dr. Cobden's preparations for the hated harness. Joe twitched and scowled as the tape was passed this way and that across his body. The assistant noting down particulars seemed intimidated by him, which served to make Joe even more uncomfortable. He returned to the Maximus, boots clumping on the wooden sidewalk. Did he really want to work there? Surrounded by sensuality, his mockery of a body would only seem more incongruous than ever. As a pauper, however, he had no realistic alternative. By the time he reached his own room any lingering doubts had been expunged by the cold prairie winds invading the streets. A brothel, whatever else it may be, is always a warm place.

Mrs. Attucks would not allow him to assume his duties

until such time as his new clothes were ready. Hammond, the man whose replacement he was, did not take kindly to Joe's presence. His was to be no voluntary leavetaking; Mrs. Attucks had noticed he was more often drunk than not, and made arrangements for his dismissal. A large man, strong, but beginning to thicken around the waist, he found Joe alone in a corridor and pushed him against the wall. "I don't think you're going to last too long in this job, Crip."

"No?" Joe was all politeness.

"No. I think you'll find you can't take it, all them troublemakers looking to cut your heart out. They'll do you plenty of harm, Crip."

"Thank you for the warning." He wondered if Hammond was going to knee him in the groin the way Bascombe had done while holding him against another wall in another life; he surreptitiously moved one leg across to overlap its fellow, found himself smiling at the absurdly mincing posture this gave him, one leg crooked daintily at the knee, toe touching the floor below Hammond's line of vision.

"What're you smiling at, Crip? Don't you believe me?"

"Of course I do. You've got an honest face."

"You're in for big trouble when they see who's doing my job, let me tell you. They won't have respect for no hump-back."

"The correct term is '*hunch*back', not 'hump'."

Hammond pushed him harder against the wall. "Hump-back, humpback, humpback," he sneered, blowing unclean breath into Joe's face. Joe felt no antagonism toward him, even felt sorry for the man; it must be humiliating to be replaced by a hunchback. He smiled in sympathy. Non-plussed, Hammond released him, shook his head in pity. "You won't last five minutes, not on a Saturday night. Why'd she pick you?"

"She thinks I look interesting."

"Jesus."

"I was wondering if you'd care to give me a few tips about the job—you know, how to handle a customer without anyone getting hurt, that kind of thing."

"I wouldn't give you no advice except one thing, don't count on not getting hurt."

"Thank you."

That night, his judgement affected by resentment and whiskey, Hammond deliberately provoked a customer into fighting him. Goaded beyond restraint, considerably battered, the customer drew a pistol and shot Hammond between the eyes. Mrs. Attucks was furious; incidents of this nature raised the premium she was obliged to pay the forces of law and order. She summoned Joe to her room.

"Do you drink?"

"No, I don't like the taste."

"Good. One drunk bouncer was enough. Tomorrow morning go to the tailor's. Tell him at least one suit has to be ready by tomorrow evening. I'll pay extra if I have to. I don't want to open for business without someone looking out for trouble."

"What's going to happen to the man that shot Hammond?"

"He knows a lot of people. He'll just leave Hays for a while. It pays to have important friends. I'm an important person in town, Joseph, don't forget that."

"I won't."

He was unsure if he liked Mrs. Attucks or not, and decided to postpone all moral judgements for the time being; he was, after all, engaged in the running of the Maximus himself, albeit on the periphery. Was a bouncer in a whorehouse any different from a bouncer in a saloon? He could find no satisfactory answer, and so ceased to ask.

Without any firm duties until the following evening, Joe wandered through the building, acquainting himself with the warren of rooms, allowing the women to become used to his presence. He held himself inwardly rigid whenever he passed women clad only in underthings, made himself ignore their casually flaunted femaleness, knew he must cultivate the habit of regarding them not as women, but as meat, receptacles of diverse male seed, spittoons of flesh harbouring a multitude of corrupting diseases in their wet and private places. He did this not to denigrate them, but to protect himself from hurt. A hunchback, he warned himself, had no right to expect anything of women; their love and their bodies were for ever denied him. He was reminded of this frequently, for the corridors of the Maximus were plentifully supplied with mirrors, an extravagance of which Adeline Attucks was justifiably proud.

In his wanderings Joe came at last to the basement. A small furnace, another luxury insisted upon by Mrs. Attucks, grumbled quietly in a corner, surrounded by substantial piles of wood; certain workers on the Kansas Pacific Railroad were instrumental in replenishing the supply, for which they received payment in the form of dalliance *gratis* in the rooms above. The furnace-room was not large, was separated from the remainder of the basement area by a brick wall, in the middle of which was a door. Joe studied this door with curiosity, enjoying the warmth and muttering of the furnace behind him. Prompted by nothing more than the mildest spirit of enquiry, Joe went to the door and turned the handle, pushed it open. Before him was a room containing a bed, a table and chair, many, many books arranged on shelving around the walls, and a neatly dressed Negro of some thirty years, all of this brilliantly lit by no less than five oil-lamps.

The Negro was in the act of selecting a volume from the shelves when he heard the door open. He turned, surveyed Joe calmly. He wore a pince-nez. Joe was surprised at that; he had never associated Negroes with the world of books and learning and eyestrain.

"How do you do," said the Negro in a pleasant tone.

"Excuse me, I didn't know anyone lived down here. I would have knocked."

"Please come in. You may sit in the chair if you wish, or on the bed. Both are comfortable."

Joe chose the chair. His host regarded him gravely. "I tend the furnace," he said.

"No one told me about you."

"They often forget I am here. I don't eat with the rest.

122

My name, since no one has told you, is Cyrus. Cyrus was a king of ancient Persia."

"I know. He conquered Babylon."

"You are a student of history?"

"No."

Cyrus indicated the shelves around them. Joe could see more books than bricks. "I have many hundreds of volumes. A great number are of an historical nature. May I know to whom I am speaking?"

Joe flushed at his own thoughtlessness. "I'm Joseph. I work here too." Cyrus raised an eyebrow. "I'm a bouncer," Joe added, and immediately felt uncouth; Cyrus, though his clothes were cheap, had about him an air of intellectuality, of refinement. Joe fumbled for conversation. "Are you from the South?"

"Were I from the South I would in all probability be unable to read or write. I am from Boston."

"So's my father—my foster-father I mean."

"But you, I would judge from your speech, are not."

"St. Louis."

"I have not been there, but I am told it is a city of pleasant aspect."

"I suppose so."

A silence established itself between them. Cyrus wore a polite smile, Joe restrained an urge to fidget. The only Negro he had ever had dealings with had been Hattie, and this man's character did not resemble hers at all. Joe felt intimidated, as he had in the presence of the doctor during his early years; perhaps it was the same precise Bostonian diction that begat his restlessness, perhaps the fact that the elegant phrases came from black lips. He told himself he was being foolish; it could not be that Cyrus' blackness provoked the disquiet in Joe's breast, for Joe was himself not Caucasian, had more in common with Negroes than with the whites among whom he had lived his life thus far. Watching the light reflect from Cyrus' pince-nez, Joe grasped the truth as it passed through his head, the last in a brief array of possible explanations: Cyrus made him nervous because Cyrus was, Joe's instincts informed him, a decent, sensitive, intelligent person. Joe was not prepared for association with such as he, had strengthened his inner self, plated his sensibilities with armour to ward off the crude batterings of inferior beings. Cyrus had, with a few softly spoken words, undermined Joe's painfully erected fortifications, threatened to invade the citadel of Joe's pride. It must not happen. Joe stood. "I expect we'll be seeing each other around."

"The chances of our meeting will be greatly increased if you seek me out, rather than vice versa. Most of my time is spent down here."

"I'll do that."

"You will be assured of a welcome."

"Thank you."

Joe left, determined never to descend the basement steps again. He had been granted strength, and strength was not a commodity to be squandered on friendship; to lay aside one's armour and allow contact with another, even a kindred spirit, would weaken the fabric of his identity, erode the persona he had adopted in order to survive.

Joe's new suit was delivered in the afternoon. He went to his room with the package, strangely excited, unwrapped the dark clothing and laid it on his bed. The pants were no different from any other pants, but the jacket was a travesty, the empty, sacklike back awaiting his hump an affront to the quality of the cloth and its meticulous stitching. He reluctantly undressed, put on the new clothing, compared himself to Quasimodo with his mock crown, the king of fools.

He sat on his bed and considered sneaking away from the Maximus through a back door, knew he would not; he had nowhere to go. As the afternoon became evening and snowflakes silently obscured the windowpanes, Joe continued to sit, staring at the floor, wondering if it would be better to be dead than alive. He ignored the dinner gong which sum-

moned the staff to their meal in the kitchen; Joe's appetite
for food had dwindled in accord with his appetite for life. A
chance meeting and a new suit had plunged him into deepest despair. On the washstand by his bed lay a small shaving
mirror. Joe picked it up and examined his face. I'm only
fifteen, he told himself. I've got years and years of life ahead
of me. He wondered how it was possible to endure life until
old age and death. What kept people sane for so long? How
did others manage it? The answer, of course, was simple:
other people were not hunchbacks.

When evening became night Joe was roused from his reverie by a knock at the door. He opened it. Serena beckoned
him out. "We've got customers." He followed her downstairs. She turned once to cast an eye over his suit. "You
look real elegant, Joseph."

"Thank you."

Adeline Attucks was in the parlour, surrounded by her
semi-naked wares. "Please be more prompt in future, Joseph. When there are customers in the house I want you to
be circulating among them. By all means get to know them.
We have our regulars here and they like to be acquainted
with the staff. It makes them feel welcome. But don't linger
in any one place for too long. Circulate, as I say."

"Yes, ma'am."

He went to do her bidding, aware of faces turning, conversations trailing off into silence. "By God," said a man,
"which lucky girl's going to service that?"

Joe turned, strode to the man's side. "Good evening,"
he said.

"Good evening yourself."

"I overheard your comment."

"No offence intended."

"Of course not. I just want you to get the facts right. I'm
not visiting, I work here."

The man smiled indulgently. "I guess you're the fetch-
and-carry man or something."

"I fetch people that aren't obeying the rules and carry
them out."

The man's eyebrows lifted with deliberate comicality. "You're a bouncer?"

"Correct."

"I don't believe it." He turned to his friends. "Does he look like a bouncer to you?" They agreed he did not. "You're Hammond's replacement?" asked one of them.

"I am. My name's Joe Cobden."

"Are you the fellow that half-murdered a waiter over at the Anderson House?"

"He said something rude about my appearance. I'm very sensitive about things like that."

"Maybe I could buy you a drink sometime, Joe," offered the first man in a markedly different tone.

"I don't indulge," said Joe, and walked on, willing the heat to leave his ears, commanding his heartbeat to decrease. He endured several more encounters of a similar nature in the course of his first night as Mrs. Attucks' new bouncer. Between conversations he observed the *modus operandi* of the Maximus, saw it was simplicity itself: men came in, dallied awhile in the parlour while making their choice from the women on offer, took same upstairs, were relieved of cash and semen, and returned to the parlour, whence they took themselves once again out into the wintry streets, poorer but presumably happier.

Joe carried an invisible sneer upon his face throughout the night; the customers he regarded as little more than brutes, no matter how well dressed. Adeline Attucks catered not only to hard-bitten trail hands and soldiers from Fort Hays, but also to the upper echelon of Hays City, such as it was: those who had made their fortune from the railroad when it came through, and the bankers and merchants that followed. There were no social barriers within the Maximus; a brothel run along these lines is a great leveller; once inside all men are equal, reduced to sameness by their mutual need for flesh.

* * *

At dawn the front doors were closed and locked. The whores came downstairs in ones and twos, heavy-limbed with fatigue, ravenously hungry. A solid meal was laid out ready for them in the kitchen. Joe waited until they had finished before relieving his own hunger. The cook set a plate before him. Joe ate with great appreciation and little finesse. "What kind of meat's this?"

"Kansas cow," said the cook, stacking pots and pans.

"Buffalo?"

"The same."

"I've eaten it before, but it didn't taste like this."

"That's on account of you never ate in my kitchen before. Buffalo meat's like any other, you have to know how to cook it to get the best out of it. Don't ask me for the recipe because you won't get it. You all finished now?"

"Yes."

Joe stared at his greasy plate. Somewhere out on the plains beyond Hays City men were hunting buffalo for meat, were making a living at doing what Joe yearned to do while he, Joe, worked in a brothel. Nothing could be more ridiculous. The plate was whisked from beneath his nose. Joe took himself up to bed and lay on his side for an hour, his hump preventing him as always from assuming a contemplative supine position, the kind favoured by daydreamers whose delight it is to conjure visions from blank ceilings. Joe projected his daydreams on to the wall beside his bed. His needs were simple: a horse and a gun, and command of his own life. The possibility of such seemed remote. He vowed to save his wages and buy his way to freedom. He fell asleep dreaming of silver dollars falling slowly from the sky like snowflakes, catching them in his hat, at which point he recognised the dream for what it was—Joe did not possess a hat. Thus cheated of even a facsimile of satisfaction, Joe drifted into deeper sleep and dreamed no more.

He awoke at noon with a feeling of mild euphoria, noted as he had noted many times before the restorative power of sleep. The doldrums of yesterday were gone. The new job was easy, well within his capabilities. He would perform his duties, earn his money, take it and leave when the time was right. The knot of tension in his stomach which had plagued him the night before had vanished. He felt confident enough to breakfast with the women. They, too, seemed more relaxed; none did more than glance at his hump. Several asked questions about his past. He told them of his woodcutting days with Eli Tilton, and of Eli's cruel demise. The whores expressed their sympathy, and Joe accepted their condolences as genuine, in fact he went so far as to regard the half naked creatures as perfectly normal human beings, their sole difference from the women leading respectable lives outside the Maximus being the nature of the work whereby they fed themselves. Provided he could control his yearning for female flesh, Joe anticipated cordial, even familiar relations with his fellow employees.

Thus braced, he went to the basement and knocked on Cyrus' door. As before, he was made welcome. Once seated on the only chair Joe's confidence deserted him. He was not adept at small talk, had never instigated a dialogue in his life, had always limited himself to defensive monosyllables generally designed to terminate discussion as quickly as possible; certainly he had never deliberately extended a conversation beyond the most basic of parameters. Now, facing an intelligent host obviously anticipating an exchange of views, Joe found himself tongue-tied. He cast his eye desperately around the room for inspiration, found none and so resorted to the banal.

"I guess you must be grateful to Lincoln," he said, squirming inwardly at his own fatuity.

Cyrus smiled. "I believe it is Mr. Lincoln who should be grateful to *us*. Without the issue of slavery to lend moral credence to his policies, the President would have been obliged to wage a war for purely political ends. You will recall he did not issue his proclamation freeing the slaves until several years after the war had begun. I personally believe he found it expedient to introduce a humane aspect into his political and military manoeuvrings at that time but, yes, I am grateful to him despite these shortcomings. I myself volunteered for service with one of the black regiments of the North but was refused. The arches of my feet are flatter than the proverbial pancake."

Joe felt chastised, humbled, foolish. "My father was in the war. He was a field surgeon."

"For the North?"

"Uh . . . no, the South. But he didn't do any fighting, just doctored the wounded. He wanted the North to win."

"He must be a man of staunch integrity. May I enquire how you came to be his foster-child?"

"He found me and took me home. I was just a few weeks old."

"Remarkable. Few white men would have adopted a child of your extraction. You must be grateful to him. I hope I do not intrude on your personal feelings."

Joe cast about for a suitably ambivalent answer, one that would convey his contrary emotions regarding the doctor. "I suppose I'm grateful to him the way you're grateful to Lincoln."

Cyrus seemed to find this satisfactory, nodded his head once or twice, continued to smile at Joe with unnerving insistence. Joe dredged his brain for a conversational gambit that was not asinine, but was unable to find one. Divining Joe's quandary, Cyrus asked if he had come to Kansas with a purpose in mind.

"Not a specific purpose," said Joe. "At least, not before I got here."

"But now you know what it is you want?"

Joe hesitated, uncertain of the reception someone as learned as Cyrus might give to his plans; they seemed childish of a sudden, the wishful thinkings of a boy. He debated the wisdom of revealing himself, decided it would do less harm than sitting like a stuffed cat, unable to speak. "I want to hunt buffalo."

"You surprise me. I had pictured you as a young man temporarily diverted from the path of learning by adverse

129

circumstance. You actually wish to hunt buffalo? That is your paramount aim?''

"Sure it is. Why not?'' Joe's voice was edged with annoyance. What right did this man have to sneer at his ambition?

Cyrus spread his palms in a placatory gesture. "I do not criticise you, Joseph. I merely express my puzzlement at your choice of occupation.''

"I want to be my own boss. Buffalo-hunting's the way to do it.''

"You may be right. Permit me to have my doubts.''

"I don't see you hatching any big plans.'' He sounded like a querulous child now, and knew it.

"I work perhaps three hours a day feeding the furnace. The rest of the time is my own to do with as I wish. As you can see, I use it to study.''

"For what?'' Joe could hardly believe his own rudeness; the words sprang from his mouth of their own volition. "What's the use in learning stuff if you're just a—'' he almost said "nigger'', "—a furnace-tender?''

Cyrus chose to ignore Joe's petulance, answered in an infuriatingly calm voice, the kind wisely employed against recalcitrant children. "I aspire to a life other than the one I lead, Joseph. I am a teacher by inclination. I assisted in tutoring Negro youths in Boston before the war, and afterwards attempted to bring the light of education to the South during Reconstruction. I was unsuccessful. In Mississippi I was attacked by white men and . . . ill-treated. I do not have the courage to return there. Instead, when I have saved sufficient funds I will establish a school for Negroes here in Kansas. The minds of the young are sacred vessels; they must be filled with knowledge before they are filled with ignorance.''

"That's very noble. If you save for around fifty years, I guess you'll have enough.'' I'll have to apologise, thought Joe, I'll have to apologise before I leave this room.

"I am not alone in this venture. There are interested

parties in Boston who will render assistance when the time is right, and my sister contributes every cent she can.''

''Your sister?''

''She works upstairs. Together we earn a healthy sum.''

Joe had seen a Negress at work in the kitchen, and there were at least two black maids in the building, but he did not enquire further, too angry with himself and with Cyrus. He felt he had been made to look foolish. Cyrus was storing up the wisdom of the ages, preparing to impart his knowledge to the uninitiated, while Joe simply wanted to slaughter dumb beasts for dollars.

''I hope you get what you want.'' His words were taut with resentment.

''I believe I will, with God's help.''

Joe decided Cyrus was not worth cultivating as a friend after all; any man who believed in God, no matter how articulate and erudite that man might be, was a fool. He stood abruptly, nodded at Cyrus by way of goodbye and left the basement. As on the occasion of his first departure, he promised himself he would not return. Joe Cobden was in need of cash, not confidants.

CHAPTER TEN

Joe quickly fell into the nocturnal routine of the Maximus. From early evening until dawn he prowled from floor to floor, not listening for, but hearing none the less the sounds of fornication. Profoundly ignorant of sexual matters, he mistakenly interpreted the cries escaping female lips as sincere, and was obliged to quell the jealousy he felt for those customers capable of arousing in their bedfellows such unrestrained ardour. At Throckmorton Academy an evergreen topic of conversation had been the possibility (rather than the probability) of a female enjoying the act of sexual congress as much as the male. Opinions had differed according to the personal experience of each theoretician, thus the known facts ranged the gamut from an inkling to a smattering.

His current work convinced Joe a woman was as capable as a man of enjoying copulation; the moanings told him so. Joe unknowingly extracted truth from these sounds of bogus rapture, but was rendered no happier for his newfound knowledge. Each carefully staged squeal and sigh cut into his self-esteem like a knife, each self-satisfied customer encountered in the corridors or on the staircase drove into him the spike of inferiority and resentment.

Whenever his emotions threatened to overflow, Joe employed a trick he had discovered to be most efficacious in allaying his torment; he simply imagined himself a buffalo, a lumbering, graceless, insensitive buffalo browsing unconcernedly for forage in the carpeted byways of the Maximus. The first time he utilised this protective device Joe had questioned his own sanity. Would a normal person envisage

132

himself as a beast in order to avoid pain? He did not have the answer, and thereafter became a buffalo, despite his doubts, on every occasion he deemed it necessary. It soon became second nature, and Joe's sense of inadequacy lessened. He accepted his imagination as a weapon to be ranked alongside his powerful body and determined character, and steadily regained the composure Cyrus had inadvertently crushed.

He descended once again to the basement, positive that this time he would not be bested, chiding himself at the same time for regarding each meeting with Cyrus as some kind of contest; Cyrus himself was obviously unintimidated by their encounters, probably had no idea Joe approached his door with such trepidation.

"Your life has been a busy one, Joseph."

"Busy? No."

"You have not come to see me for more than a week."

"I'll come down more often if you want."

"That would be pleasant. I thought you might have left Mrs. Attucks' employment, but my sister assured me you were still here."

"Which lady is she?"

"She works upstairs."

"I know, you told me. Does she work in the kitchen, or is she one of the maids?"

"Her name is Serena."

Joe thought for a moment and linked the name with a face. How could Cyrus sit there and calmly admit his sister was a prostitute? Joe was dumbfounded.

"Is something wrong?" asked Cyrus.

"Uh . . . no. I guess she's able to give you plenty of cash." Joe could have bitten off his tongue. "For the school, I mean. . . . More than if she was a maid," he concluded lamely.

"Serena earns far more than me, it's true. When our school is built it will have been largely her doing."

A long silence followed. To ask the questions Joe wanted to ask would have been the height of insensitivity, yet to leave the conversation dangling as it was made him feel ridiculous.

Cyrus smiled at Joe's consternation. "You find this strange?"

"No. Well . . . yes."

"I suppose it must appear unusual to someone who does not know Serena or myself. There is nothing to be wondered at. My sister shares my dream. Our people are in need of education now that they are free. Money must be raised to set this plan in motion. We cannot rely solely upon Negro organisations in Boston. Their funds are limited."

"I see."

Another silence blanketed the room.

"Perhaps you have more questions?"

"Not really."

"How remarkably incurious you are, Joseph."

"It's none of my business."

"I'm surprised the other women have not told you."

"I don't talk to them all that much. I don't talk to anyone."

Joe was unsure whether to regard Cyrus' revelation as the words of a brave man risking humiliation for the sake of unadorned truth, or as a fool for having bared a part of himself to the scrutiny of a stranger. Joe knew that hearts worn on sleeves generally become the target of crows. He no longer regarded Cyrus as his superior, knew it could only be because he had learned the man's sister was a whore; he knew also that this fact should not influence his opinion. Serena had been the first woman at the Maximus to talk with Joe as an equal, had never once stared at his hump, was personable and yes, even charming. Why then should he consider Cyrus a weakling and a fool for having revealed his relationship with her? Joe realised he had been applying to Cyrus the judgement expected from a normal man with normal prejudices—a ludicrous situation. As rapidly as he had decided Cyrus was not his superior, Joe reinstated him to that position and congratulated himself on his own moral sagacity and enlightenment. All this occupied perhaps three seconds; Joe's throat still held the reverberations of his last words. He held out his hand and smiled.

"My name's Joseph. Somehow I feel I've only just now met you."

Cyrus grasped his palm, not at all perturbed by Joe's whimsical display of fraternity. "Cyrus Paine. I'm pleased to make your acquaintance."

Thus a friendship of sorts was kindled, yet Joe's obstinate nature refused to relinquish that part of itself he considered strongest, the part which enabled him to survive among human beings without truly being one of them. A hunchback is ever and always a hunchback. He admired Cyrus and harboured a grudging wish to be admired in return, but could not bring himself to relax completely in the other man's company as a true friend would. For his part, Cyrus made no demands on his guest, did not pry into his background, filled the silences in their conversation with gracious ease. Joe appeared content to listen while Cyrus expounded on a wide variety of subjects, historical, political and, to Joe's chagrin, theological. He held his peace as Cyrus praised the wisdom of the New Testament and debated which of those stories in the Old were exaggerated and which were not. Fortunately Cyrus' scholarly rather than emotional approach to these despised themes lessened Joe's irritation, and he continued to visit the basement savant for these one-sided discussions.

Christmas is celebrated in a whorehouse as it is in any other house. For fifty dollars Mrs. Attucks purchased a small pine tree, part of a shipment which had been felled four hundred miles away in Minnesota and freighted west by some entrepreneur for those with yuletide spirit and stout wallets. The precious conifer, its needletips already browning, was set up in the parlour and festooned with the usual gay trappings. Presents exchanged among the women were opened with girlish enthusiasm and provoked many a squeal of delight and heartfelt kiss of appreciation. Joe went down to the basement with a gift, a slender ribbon of black sateen for Cyrus' pince-nez; no longer would he be obliged to return the lenses to his vest pocket when not required. The ribbon was affixed, the effect studied in a mirror; Cyrus pronounced it "eminently practical, without being ostentatious." Joe interpreted this as approval. He received in return a hat, no ordinary hat but a king of hats, a high crowned, wide brimmed thing of beauty in black felt with a dashing turkey feather in its band. It was quite unblemished, redolent of newness, and Joe suspected it had been purchased with Serena's rather than Cyrus' earnings.

"You'll be needing a hat when you get out among the buffalo, Joseph. This style is *de rigueur* for the plainsman."

"It's beautiful. Thank you."

"It is intended for wear, not just for admiration."

Joe placed it reverently on his head; the fit was perfect, but his hump interfered with the brim; he would have to alter it or wear the hat tilted forward—an impractical measure since it restricted his field of vision to the ground at his feet. Cyrus boiled a kettle on the furnace and together they reshaped the brim in a jet of steam, folding it up at the back to accommodate Joe's spine. The resultant rakish tilt from stern to bow gave the hat a personality all its own. Joe thanked Cyrus again and went to his room, there to place the hat on the top shelf of his wardrobe. It would not be worn again within the confines of the Maximus, but saved for the open prairie.

The gift reaffirmed in Joe the certainty that awaiting him was a future which would conform to the shape of his dreams; the hat was an investment in that future and was accorded almost totemistic significance in Joe's life. Every night before retiring he checked that the hat was in its appointed place and blew imaginary dust from its canted brim. This ritual act was usually followed by another. Joe's habit of transforming himself into a buffalo for the protection it afforded·him had become an addiction. He would strip all clothing from his body and get down on hands and knees before the full-length mirror inside the opened wardrobe oor. At puberty Joe's body had sprouted hair not only in he expected places but across his shoulders and down his rms. In two years it had thickened and spread to cover his ump entirely, even extended in tapering whorls down the mall of his back almost to the cleft of his buttocks. It lay n dark and curling swathes, a rippling mat that appalled nd fascinated Joe every time he saw it. If I fail as a buffalo unter, he told himself, I can always get a job with P. T. 3arnum: Joe the Buffalo Boy. He huffed and snorted at his idiculous, repulsive image, mocked it to lessen the gut-wrenching impact his reflection induced. I am a singular abomination, he thought, sometimes with an abiding horror hat such misfortune should be his, more often than not with stoic resignation. This is my lot; I can never be loved, I can only be free of love's responsibilities. Joe's night-time rum-nations ran along tracks as clearly defined and inflexible as hose of the Kansas Pacific.

On New Year's Eve he met his first challenge as a bouncer. The clientele, some of them familiar faces to Joe by now, were in a suitably festive mood. Hands were joined at midnight, the traditional ditty raucously invoked. Joe kept himself in the background, the only sober person present. When the final chorus had been sung many couples dashed upstairs, hoping to be the first to complete sexual union in Hays City in this new year of 1871. Others, too drunk for such activity, continued drinking in the parlour. Mrs. At-tucks did not sell liquor on the premises and usually did not permit bottles to be brought through the door; tonight she had made an exception to the rule, and was soon to regret her liberality. Shortly before one a.m. a cattle buyer by the name of Luther Finney, flushed with brandy and the prom-ise of fortunes to be made in his chosen field, was foolish enough to take exception to Joe's appearance.

"You!" he shouted, finger pointed. "Come here a mo-ment."

Joe crossed the room at a leisurely pace, felt his abdomen

clench in anticipation of trouble; he had been watching Finney for some time, noting the overloud hilarity and forced *bonhomie* that are often the hallmark of the bully and the fool. He stood before Finney, a neutral expression on his face. Finney took another pull from his bottle and beckoned Joe closer, leaned his head down to Joe's and said in a stage whisper: "Is it true that you're a rich man?"

"I'm afraid not."

"You're not? That's a shame, yes, it is. Someone as good-looking as you deserves to be rich, don't you think?"

"I agree."

"You agree? You really do?" He winked heavily at several of his friends, the effort jerking his head and unfocusing his eyes. "You think you're some kind of gay dog, h'm?" Joe smiled tightly, waiting for the point at which confrontation became inevitable. Finney smiled in return. "Know why I thought you must be rich? No? Because you're the only man I know that carries a cashbox on his back."

Overwhelmed by his own wit Finney staggered backwards, guffawing without restraint. Joe wondered if he should begin to assert himself now, or wait until this idiot said something even more insulting. He threw a quick glance around the room, saw that Adeline Attucks was watching from a far corner; if he wished to hold on to his job he would have to remove the offending article from her sight. He placed a hand on Finney's arm. "Pardon me, sir, but I think you've had a little too much to drink. I think it'd be a good idea if you left."

His hand was flung off. "You do, hey? I don't think that's a good idea at all, no I don't."

"House rules, sir. Unruly customers are requested to leave."

"Are they, now. Well I'm not going anywhere, not just because a humpback tells me to."

"I'm being polite, sir. I think everyone can see that."

"Your mother sells it, cashbox."

Joe kicked him hard in the testicles, as hard as he possibly could, not caring at that moment if he killed Finney with shock and pain. Finney sank to his knees, face bloodlessly white, mouth open in agony; his eyes rolled up into his head and he collapsed. Joe was truly angry now, quite prepared to do battle with anyone who took Finney's side. "Take him out or I'll drag him out by the neck."

Finney was removed from the Maximus without further incident; there was no mistaking the fury in Joe's eyes and clenched fists. Mrs. Attucks approached him. "Unorthodox," she said, "and definitely a dirty trick, but effective. I'm reassured by your performance, Joe, but one thing still troubles me. Will you be able to take care of business when someone deserves to be thrown out, but does nothing to insult you personally?"

"I don't know."

"I admire honesty, but it doesn't make me rest easier at night. You're here to uphold the rules of the house, not just to get your own back on morons who call you names."

"I know that."

"Good. Make sure you remember it."

The year had begun inauspiciously for Joe. He felt a measure of remorse at having kicked a drunk, no matter how deserving of punishment. Mrs. Attucks had raised an important point; could violence be triggered only if Joe's sensitivity was offended? Could he summon the impersonal callousness required to eject, possibly hurt someone against whom he bore no grudge? Ought he to injure anonymous persons simply because they transgressed rules laid down by his employer? If he found he could not, then he would quit. Mrs. Attucks would fire him anyway if he failed to execute his duties. He thought of the cold world outside, a friendless, moneyless place, and shivered. Joe decided he would deliberately make himself angry over whatever infringement of the rules required that someone be thrown out; he was not going to go cold and hungry for the sake of moral principle. The situation was only temporary anyhow; when he had saved enough to buy a horse and gun he would leave the Maximus, quit the job in his own sweet time. The place stank of perfume and female bodies, neither of which had any claim on the future of Joe Cobden, buffalo hunter.

Lying restlessly in his bed that night, Joe mulled over the implications of his strengthened resolve. Looming large among his misgivings was the fact that when he quit it would mean sundering the budding friendship with Cyrus, a thing he was of late beginning to value. A decision was required here, priorities in need of recognition. He reminded himself again of his need for self fulfilment, a longed for, somewhat vague condition dependent (of this he was sure) upon the possession of money, a bankroll, a grubstake. Cash was the true arbiter in this nebulous moral quandary. Finally achieving his goal would be compensation enough for leaving Cyrus behind. The man had intelligence and integrity, but no spirit of adventure whatever; he was an aspiring schoolteacher, and Joe had never had cause to admire the breed. He had never had a close friend and certainly did not need one now. By masking them with uncompromising certitude, Joe was fast learning the timeworn principles of expediency by which most men live their lives. He closed his eyes and allowed herds of phantom buffalo to trample his qualms under silent hoofs.

Having planned on leaving Cyrus behind in the indeterminate future, Joe did not wish to be reminded of his presence in the here and now. Better I should break off the friendship before it gets any deeper, he told himself, and was thereafter pursued by an annoying sense of guilt that increased with every day spent away from the basement. He would not allow his determination to weaken; if Cyrus wanted his company then Cyrus could damn well come upstairs and seek him out instead of living down there day and night like some kind of troglodyte.

One afternoon, while most of the whores were quietly sleeping, Joe was waylaid by Serena as he passed her door. "Joseph, could I talk with you for a moment?" He entered reluctantly and was invited to sit on a plush chair. Serena appeared agitated. "Joseph, you know I'm Cyrus' sister."

"Yes."

"Cyrus is a remarkable man."

"Yes."

She fiddled with a flounce on her blouse. "He deserves admiration and respect, don't you think?"

"I suppose he does."

"He looks forward to your visits, Joseph."

Joe stayed silent, felt his stomach tighten. Was this a reprimand? Serena clasped her hands nervously at her waist. Joe noticed for the first time how shapely they were, her knuckles pressed tautly against the skin. He wished he knew everything about these two people, wanted to hear them tell their story in detail. He would never have considered asking. Serena was waiting. Joe's fingers twitched with irritation. "Did he ask you to ask me why I haven't been down to see him?"

"No he didn't. That would not be a manly thing to do. Cyrus is a man." She emphasised the last word more than Joe thought necessary. Did she think he despised Cyrus for his bookishness?

"Sometimes I don't like company."

"Cyrus feels that way, too, but he has never turned you away from his door."

"Cyrus doesn't have to spend every night with a bunch of stupid arrogant bastards that think they're God's gift to the world."

"I know better than you what kind of men come here."

"Then, you'll understand why I like to be left alone."

"You can't want to be alone *all* the time, Joseph."

"Why not?" Did she mean that a hunchback ought to be grateful for having a friend? "Why shouldn't I like to be alone all the time?"

Serena went to the window and looked out at the steady drizzle of rain falling in the street, her back to Joe. "Cyrus doesn't like to be alone," she said.

Joe was infuriated. Was Cyrus' happiness *his* responsibility? What did these two want from him?

Serena turned from the window but Joe could not see her face, silhouetted as she was by the wintry light outside. "Cyrus is a highly intelligent man. There are probably few men in this part of the country with his learning."

"I don't doubt it."

"He needs someone to . . . discuss things with."

Joe had had enough. He stood. "All right, I'll give him the chance to wag his chin all he wants." He strode to the door, boots stamping the carpet.

Taken by surprise, Serena stretched out a hand to him, a melodramatic gesture since he was some five yards away. "Don't tell Cyrus I told you. . . ."

Joe shouldered his way through the empty corridors of the Maximus, thundered down the steps to the basement, hammered on Cyrus' door till it was opened. "Joseph, how pleasant to see you. . . ."

"I thought you might like to discuss the meaning of human existence or something." He entered and flung himself into the chair.

"Is something wrong, Joseph?"

"Yes there is, and that's my opening argument. Things are very, very wrong with the world, the world occupied by people, that is. Animals are probably happy. It's different for us, though, because we've got the brains to see how things *could* be and *should* be, but aren't. That's what makes us unhappy, the difference between imagination and . . . and actuality."

"That's an interesting theory, Joseph. . . ."

"Don't interrupt, please." His mind vibrating, Joe brought both barrels of his scattergun eloquence to bear on his impromptu diatribe; it was high time the world knew what Joe Cobden thought of it, by hokey! "The reason life's so awful is because it's so full of—" he groped for a word— "randomness! What I mean is, the haphazard collision of intentions and acts and incidents and . . . accidents and chance encounters and . . . uh . . . coincidences. None of them belong to a grand order of things, or an overall scheme, or a giant pattern or anything. There isn't one, there's just this godawful jumble of things happening with no guiding principle to hold it all together and make it *mean* something." He folded his arms with a confident air, well pleased with himself. "That's what I think. No need to ask what *you* think." There was a smile of superiority on his face now, almost a sneer; Joe had pondered long, passed judgement and found the world wanting.

"I think something has made you angry." Cyrus' voice was mild, his manner sympathetic, annoyingly so. Why was he not open-mouthed at Joe's revelation of life as it truly is? Joe was disappointed, but decided to press home with his argument, not so much to win a convert as to let Cyrus know what he thought of anyone foolish enough to have blind faith in forces unseen and unseeing. "You bet I'm angry. The stuff I've just been talking about makes me angry—not all the time, just when I can be bothered thinking about it. It's *there* whether you know it or not, whether you think about it or not, whether you feel bad about it or not. It's just *there.*"

"The randomness is there?"

"A big heap of it."

"Without purpose of any kind?"

"That's it, that's good. Without purpose of any kind."

"And where does God fit into this dismal vision?"

"He doesn't, for the very good reason that he doesn't exist. If God was around then the world would be as organised as the type on a newspaper."

"I have to disagree with you, Joseph."

"No you don't. You don't *have* to disagree with me, you feel *obliged* to disagree with me because you don't accept a world without God—am I right?"

"I cannot accept a world without goodness, without morality."

"Can't you? I can."

"Such a world would be intolerable."

"No, you get used to it, believe me."

"And the concept of right and wrong?"

"Abstractions; worse yet, they're subjective abstractions. What's right to person A is wrong to person B. Chances are they'll fight over it to convince the other he's in error."

"This hypothetical fight, is that itself not an example of wrong?"

"Not to A and B. It's different for person C, who's looking on though; he might think it's wrong. Then, again, he might just think it's funny or ridiculous. It'd probably depend on whether he's drunk or sober, or happy or miserable."

"This is both depressing and disturbing, Joseph. You live in a world without absolute values. How is such a thing possible? I could not live in such a place."

"Yes, you could. I do and I feel fine." Joe was feeling almost lighthearted now, partly because he was convinced his argument was inviolable, partly because it felt good to mock a Christian; there was nothing personal in the satisfaction he took from Cyrus' dour expression.

"You have convinced yourself of these things, Joseph. That does not make them so."

"True, I can't prove any of it, just as you can't prove the existence of God or any of your precious absolute values. It's kind of pointless to even discuss it. I just thought you might want to indulge in some stimulating conversation."

"You have come here to talk this way for my sake?"

"That's right, Cyrus, and I must say you aren't responding the way you should. When I engage in stimulating conversation I expect a little more liveliness from the stimulatee. Let's see a smile."

"I regret I cannot, not while I see you living in a world of nightmare."

"What nightmare? Prove it. I'm a happy man. I came down here to share it around. Look how happy I am." He bared his teeth in a rictus of ecstasy, waggled his head for added effect. Cyrus' face remained mournful, prompting genuine laughter from Joe. "Smile, why don't you? What could be funnier than you and me sitting under a brothel arguing about God?"

"It is my earnest hope to wean you someday from your philosophy of emptiness."

"You're welcome to try."

Cyrus did try, on that occasion and on many others. Now that Joe had openly declared himself an atheist it seemed his tongue, loosened by the disclosure, was inclined to compensate for its previous paralysis. His chief delight lay in trying to convince Cyrus, with many an example from Cyrus' own volumes on history, that God proved His nonexistence by His refusal to favour the righteous above the strong. "There's nothing above us but sky and stars," he would say, and Cyrus would shake his head with weary patience. Neither man managed to persuade the other of his folly, but the heat engendered by their exchanges fused their divergent personalities into that singular, two-headed thing, a friendship.

CHAPTER ELEVEN

As the weeks passed, Joe became more proficient at his work. Outright violence, he discovered, was unnecessary. He removed rowdies with politeness, gradually perfecting the technique not only of physically manhandling the miscreants, but of doing so with a charming smile and a humorous line in banter. The recipient of this treatment found himself escorted from a whore's room and jollied along to the parlour with one arm held behind his back while Joe chided him gently, as a mother would a restive child; at the front door Joe's captive would be expelled from the premises with a stout slap between the shoulderblades, a hearty benediction almost, a fond gesture of leavetaking from one man to another which did much to alleviate the humiliation involved. Most bouncers in similar establishments were in the habit of administering a boot to the seat of their victim's pants—not Joe.

Mrs. Attucks' girls no longer found him repugnant; familiarity bred acceptance, and for this Joe was grateful. For the first time since his woodcutting days with Eli Tilton a feeling of contentment came to Joe every afternoon when he awoke, the satisfaction of knowing that the night ahead would hold no challenges he was incapable of meeting. His dream of hunting buffalo was undiminished, but had been relegated to the indefinite future. Every week he banked his wage; he saw no sense in changing the direction of his life until his financial status allowed him to do so with impunity. Joe was fast becoming a fixture at the Maximus. The unchanging routine blunted the keenness of his desire for freedom on his own terms; what had once been a burning need quickly became no more than a dream postponed, a thing of no great urgency. A kind of lazy self-satisfaction enfolded Joe, lulling him with unfamiliar warmth. Thus, when Serena was murdered he found himself ill prepared for the consequences.

The first intimations that something was amiss came when Serena did not make an appearance in the kitchen at dawn to partake of the usual meal. No one remarked on her absence until the food had been consumed and coffee served. Jokes were made regarding the prowess of Serena's last customer; it was not often a girl was too exhausted to come downstairs and eat. Someone went to investigate. Joe was in his room, readying himself for sleep, when he heard the screams.

By the time he reached Serena's room it was packed with women staring ashen faced at the bed. Serena lay naked on her stomach, sodomised with a wine bottle, her neck broken. Adeline Attucks' lips were tight with rage. "Did anyone see who the customer was?" The girls looked at each other, faces twisted with horror and grief. No one spoke. Joe felt a peculiar sensation invade his head, a hollow rushing of blood, strong enough to make him lurch sideways; on his way to the kitchen some forty minutes earlier he had passed Serena's room and seen a man leave hurriedly. The man had looked around, seen Joe approaching and staggered backwards before recovering himself. Joe had assumed this was because the man was startled to see a hunchback. Long since inured to such reactions, he had thought no more of the incident until now.

"I saw him," he croaked, and every head turned.

"A regular?" asked Mrs. Attucks.

"No."

"Describe him."

"Just . . . normal looking. Average height, no beard or moustache. He wasn't a cattle hand. He had a suit on."

"His face?"

147

"I don't know. . . . There was nothing special about him."

"Go fetch the marshal. The rest of you, out of here."

Half an hour later Joe retold his story for the marshal's benefit while standing by Serena's bed. The marshal carried two pistols and was a person of some renown among law-breakers in Hays City. He reached across and twisted the bottle in order to see the label. Joe could scarcely believe the gross indelicacy of the act. "Take it out," he said. "If you want to see the label take the goddamn thing out."

The marshal turned and stared at Joe, his fingers still on the bottle end. "You tend your business and I'll tend mine." He turned to Mrs. Attucks, the only other person present. "This brand familiar to you at all?"

"We do not serve liquor here, Marshal, you know that."

"But I'll bet there's a bottle or two around for your own use, Addie. You a wine drinker? Can't be too many wine drinkers in town."

"I have never seen a bottle like that before. Please do as Joseph says. No purpose is served by leaving it *in situ.*"

"I wasn't planning on leaving it in sye-too, Addie. You wouldn't get the coffin lid on, for a start." He turned again to Joe. "Nothing more you can tell me about the feller?"

"No."

"You aren't the helpfullest witness."

"I'm sorry he wasn't seven feet tall with a scarred face and green whiskers. He just happened to be ordinary."

"Recognise him if you saw him again?"

"I think so. The first thing you should do is find out who in town sells wine."

"Like I said, you tend your business. Addie, this customer must have been a blow-in if your girls don't know him. That's going to make things a whole lot harder. He could already be outside of town. Likely as not he'll never get caught, you know that."

"Please do your best, Marshal. A crime such as this is . . . sickening."

He nodded his head several times in abstract commiseration, looking all the while at the dead woman's buttocks and the obscene bottle.

"I must arrange for the funeral," said Mrs. Attucks, and left. Joe watched the marshal. "Are you going to take the bottle out?"

"I'll get around to it when I'm good and ready, Hump. No use you stoking your boiler over it."

Joe leaned over and removed the bottle as gently as he could. The marshal made no move to stop him. "You shouldn't have done that till I said. That's evidence."

"It's still evidence. Left where it was it's a mockery." He handed the bottle over. The marshal declined to take it.

"Tell you what, Hump, you're so all fired up about clues and such, why don't you take a sniff at that bottle neck and see what kind of bookay that stuff had." He smiled widely. Joe resisted the temptation to throw the bottle at his face.

"You don't care who killed her, do you? She was a Negress, so you don't care."

"That's not strictly true, Hump. I don't give a damn what colour she was, just like I don't give a damn about you being a half-breed. She was a whore, that's why I don't care. You let the world into your bed and someday you'll fuck a murderer, that's the law of averages. Whores know the risk."

Joe set the bottle down on a table and left the room, fingers twitching with anger. A few steps along the corridor he halted. Had anyone told Cyrus? He hesitated, then descended to the basement and knocked on Cyrus' door. His knock went unanswered. He opened the door and entered. Cyrus was lying on his bed, arms by his sides, eyes staring at the ceiling. Only one of his many lamps was lit. Joe waited for his presence to be acknowledged. Cyrus neither moved nor spoke. Joe shuffled his feet nervously, unsure of his next move.

"Did someone tell you?" he asked. Cyrus did not respond. "I'm sorry, Cyrus. I liked Serena a lot. You must've been pretty close. I'm sorry," he said again, cringing at his own banality.

He fell silent. The silence deepened. Finally Cyrus spoke. "Was her neck broken as they said?" The words came from lips that barely moved, words in a dead monotone.

"Yes. It must've been quick that way."

"And the other thing?"

"Yes. I'm sorry."

"They say you saw the man."

"When they catch him I'll be able to identify him, Cyrus. His face was nothing special, but I won't forget it. When he's caught I'll be the one to put him under a rope, I promise."

Cyrus said nothing more. Joe lingered a few minutes, made insignificant in the face of another's tragedy, then moved towards the door. "Joseph." He stopped, turned to the bed. Cyrus lay as before, eyes fastened on the ceiling. "She was not my sister. Serena was my wife. No one knows. Goodbye, Joseph."

Joe could conceive of no appropriate reply. He left quietly and went to his room, there to consider Cyrus' revelation. The husband of a whore dwelling placidly beneath the place of his wife's couplings for cash—how was such a thing possible? Could a true man resign himself to such a bizarre situation without jealousy or rancour? Cyrus offered no evidence of such. Could it be that he had borne no love for Serena? Joe was uncertain how often the two had found moments of privacy, had assumed such occasions were limited, since he himself spent hours with Cyrus during that time of day when Serena, had she so wished, could have visited the basement. She had never done so to Joe's knowledge. That there had been communication between husband and wife was evident from the manner in which Serena had suggested to Joe that his company was missed by Cyrus, but from that time on, Joe was sure, he had been the only person to grace the chair in Cyrus' room, let alone the bed. An unsettling thought occurred to Joe; could it be that Cyrus was a man who did not desire women? Perhaps his marriage to Serena was the result of some mutually advantageous pact. Joe rejected the notion as hastily as he had concocted it; at no time had Cyrus touched him, or suggested in his conversation that such was his wish. Joe's instincts would have warned him of potential embarrassment had Cyrus been a lover of men, besides which Joe considered himself an unsuitable object of lust for either sex; to picture himself grappling with a male was only slightly more ridiculous than imagining himself in the intimate company of a woman. No, that was not the answer, and none presented itself during the hours in which Joe puzzled over the mystery.

Halfway through the night patrons of the Maximus, and some of the girls too, began complaining of lack of warmth. Joe was dispatched to the basement to investigate. He found Cyrus lying on his bed, one arm dangling to the floor. Under the severed wrist was a bowl, but Cyrus had underestimated the amount of blood that would be pumped from his body before his heart ceased, and the bowl had overflowed on to the floor. Joe walked across the already congealing tide of red and touched Cyrus at the temple. His skin was cold, cold as the untended furnace outside the door. Joe sat dazedly on the bed, boots paddling in sticky blood. A razor lay in Cyrus' right hand, its edge flecked with red. A single-syllabled refrain ran through Joe's head: no no no no no. . . . He could not stop it, even as he saw the envelope with his name on it propped against the pillow, even as he reached for it and tore the flap open—no no no no no no no. . . . The lone sheet of paper bore one line of neat calligraphy:

You are correct

Joe let the note fall to the floor. The paper began soaking up blood immediately. He stared at the lamp, avoiding Cyrus' blanched features; by the oil-filled glass base were the pince-nez. Joe picked them up and placed them carefully on the bridge of his nose; he had always wondered how the world would look through these dainty lenses. The basement became a smeared blur, a place of subterranean dread.

Joe snatched the pince-nez from his face and the walls swam
into focus again, a book-lined mausoleum under a whorehouse. He dropped them into his pocket, scarcely aware of
doing so. Joe felt weariness steal through his body; the night
was no more than half over, yet he knew he must sleep. He
removed the razor from Cyrus' hand and lay down beside
him, stared at the ceiling as Cyrus had done that last time
Joe had visited. He wondered what manner of despairing,
hopeless thoughts had invaded Cyrus' head as he lay there.
To kill oneself because a woman you loved was also dead—
the concept was alien to Joe's temperament and experience
of life. Would Joe kill himself because Cyrus was gone? No.
And yet he wished himself dead or, at the very least, oblivious. He knew his world would be a different place without
Cyrus; emptier, colder, harder. Joe gathered around himself the resolve that had been his before coming to the Maximus, the single-minded toughness of spirit which had taken
him from St. Louis to the heart of Kansas; it had enabled
him to survive adversity and disillusion before and would
do so now, he was determined. Warding off his wretchedness with a show of strength, Joe numbed his mind to the
full import of his discovery, drugged his fears with cloudy
resolution, and so fell asleep.

Joe's stillness beside Cyrus was interpreted by the girl
who entered the room shortly thereafter as death in tandem.
Too shocked to scream, she ran back upstairs to report a
double murder in the basement. Mrs. Attucks went to ascertain the truth behind the girl's hysterical gabbling.
"Mother of God!" she said, viewing the room, and her
voice roused Joe to wakefulness. He sat up. Hunchback and
madam looked at each other, astounded, uncomprehend-
ing. Mrs. Attucks, a veteran of strange sights and peculiar
situations, recovered her wits first. "What are you doing?"
she demanded, aware even as she spoke of the question's
absurdity.

"He's dead," explained Joe, still groggy from his brief
but surprisingly deep sleep. "Killed himself," he added,
sensing the inadequacy of his reply.

"Why are you on the bed, Joseph? I thought you were dead also."

"I just . . . felt tired." He swung his feet on to the floor, unknowingly crushed the bloody note. "Do you want me to get the marshal again?"

"No. There is no mystery here, no culprit to be found. Fetch down the kitchen help to get this mess cleaned up, then come back and get the furnace started again."

Joe's soles produced a sucking noise as he walked to the door. Mrs. Attucks stepped aside to let him by. "Say nothing of this to the customers," she advised. Joe nodded, eyes somewhat unfocused, and went to the staircase. Mrs. Attucks weighed his behaviour and found it unsatisfactory; no bouncer who worked for her should be so affected by the death of a nigger, and as for this peculiar business of Joe falling asleep right there on the bed next to the corpse—that was nothing less than perverse. If word of it reached the ears of her clientele, Joe would be a laughing stock; no one would respect him if they learned he had behaved in so abnormal a fashion. Physical deformity could be forgiven, aberrant conduct never.

Customers were not told, but the story circulated throughout the Maximus. Joe was once again the object of sidelong glances. The morning after the incident he overheard one of the maids tell another it was common knowledge that Joe and Cyrus had been lovers. Sickened, Joe locked himself in his room, sat on the edge of his bed and rocked back and forth for almost an hour, hugging himself, the only person who knew the truth, or at least a part of it. He could have told them of the secret marriage, but would not; he believed Cyrus had told him in confidence. No one would believe it anyway, since he could not offer a reasonable explanation for it. He wished he possessed one for his own peace of mind. Joe knew himself capable of surviving catastrophe of practically any kind, yet it annoyed him that he could not satisfy himself as to the causes of this serial tragedy, this mystery inside an enigma. If only he knew that much, the rest would be bearable. He could not blame Cyrus for the overheard rumour's ugliness, nor could he blame himself; the fault lay with humanity's unwavering predilection for the gutter. Joe's sense of outrage was blunted by sorrow, dimmed by bitter recollections of his life to date. This is where I belong, he told himself: nowhere. This is my country, the country of no people, though they swarm like flies. I am alone. Joe considered himself a scrap of rock surrounded by limitless ocean in which swam fish large and small, blowing their insignificant bubbles, mindlessly consuming each other. Only Joe, the wise rock, was capable of comprehending the raw emptiness of the universe.

A voice outside his door returned him from the further shores of wintry imaginings; his services were required in the basement, orders of Mrs. Attucks. Joe reluctantly descended the familiar stairs. Cyrus' door stood open and he forced himself to peer inside. The floor had been thoroughly scrubbed, the bed stripped, the bookshelves emptied; Cyrus' room had been rendered anonymous. Joe rammed wood into the furnace, stoked it to a dangerous heat, watched with satisfaction as the pressure gauge crawled higher; nothing would have given him greater satisfaction than to see the Circus Maximus blown to kingdom come. He would quit this very day, that much of his future was planned. He slammed the furnace door, went to his room and packed his few belongings.

A carpetbag in one hand, his hat in the other, he went to tender his resignation to Adeline Attucks. A knock at the door gained him entrance to her room. "Going somewhere, Joseph?"

"Away from here. I quit."

"Don't you think you owe me a few days' notice at least?"

"I can't wait. I have to leave."

"I understand. Maybe you aren't cut out for the job after all."

"I know I'm not."

"You'll have to forfeit your last week's wages for the inconvenience."

"That's all right, but I want to know where Cyrus is."

"That depends on whether he led a good life or a bad one." Mrs. Attucks did not often get the chance to display her wit, and was grateful to Joe for having given her the opportunity. But Joe did not respond.

"Templeton Morticians, three blocks east," said Mrs. Attucks. "Going to pay your last respects?"

"No one else will."

"Goodbye, Joseph."

He trudged to the undertaker's and asked to see the remains of one Cyrus Paine. A suitably cadaverous individual in a cutaway coat escorted him to the rear of the building. Two coffins lay side by side atop saw horses in a small windowless room. There was no stove in the room, therefore no discernible difference between the temperature here and that outside. Joe wondered if this was because Mrs. Attucks had not paid enough for the services of Templeton Morticians, or if the freezing weather was sensibly being utilised to preserve the deceased for display without offence to the olfactory nerves of those in attendance. Or maybe it was simply because the deceased were Negroes. Joe was the only mourner. He set his belongings down in a corner and approached the coffins. Serena lay in the nearest. To his shame, Joe had quite forgotten about her in his distress over Cyrus. Her head had been reset at the proper angle; she wore a high-necked dress which concealed bruises and swelling. Serena had been among the better-looking women at Mrs. Attucks' establishment, and made a fine corpse.

Joe moved on to Cyrus. His face appeared naked without the pince-nez. Joe remembered, took them from his pocket, and beneath the curious eye of the undertaker set them carefully in place. He would have preferred to keep them as a memento, but sending Cyrus to his grave without them was somehow unacceptable. I should have at least taken one of his books for a keepsake, thought Joe. I bet they're stacked somewhere in the Maximus. (Adeline Attucks had ordered

155

them fed into the furnace, the quickest means of disposal.) Joe knew he would not return there to find out. Joe's notion of human movement through time and space was simple, precise. He had no wish to revisit old haunts, the scenes of past incidents and encounters, be it DeWitte Street or the best brothel in Hays City; to Joe it would have seemed as unnatural as walking backwards. No, it was his self-appointed task to move ahead beyond this place into a future unfolding before him minute by minute, latent with the promise of newness and hope.

"Friends of yours, may I ask?"

Joe had forgotten the undertaker was there. "Yes," he said.

"Murder and suicide, like something from Shakespeare. Might I enquire as to the relationship between the deceased?"

"Brother and sister," said Joe after several seconds.

"Ah, of course. Marriage was, after all, impossible. I hope I am not indelicate."

"Why shouldn't they have been married?"

"As a friend, surely you knew. I would not have mentioned. . . ."

"Knew what?"

"I have overstepped the bounds of professional discretion. I apologise."

"I don't need an apology, just tell me what you're talking about."

"The gentleman had . . . met with misfortune, shall we say."

"No we won't, we'll speak English, please."

"He had been—there is no gentle word for his condition—castrated."

"He what?"

"Only a nigger, I know, but such a heinous crime."

"Castrated . . . ?"

"Without a doubt. I do not make mistakes of that magnitude."

Joe stared at Cyrus. The undertaker stared at Joe, wondering which style of coffin would best suit a hunchback; accommodating such a warped body for burial would be a challenge. Perhaps this friend of niggers was the lawbreaking type who would one day be brought to his door riddled with bullets, to be buried at the county's expense; one could always hope.

A tragedy of unbearable proportions was thus revealed to Joe by a chance remark. Expert opinion at Throckmorton Academy had maintained that a man divested of his testicles became grossly fat, talked in a high-pitched voice and was fit only for employment in a Turkish harem. Cyrus had appeared physically to be the most normal of men. Joe could only guess at the nature of the relationship between this couple, the sexual and emotional implications of Cyrus' horrendous loss. Townsmen in Mississippi had "ill-treated" him, that was what Cyrus had said. How could the man have uttered so mild an understatement without choking on hatred, without bunching his fists and thirsting for vengeance? Had the outrage been perpetrated before or after the marriage? Almost certainly after, for what woman would marry a man who had not the wherewithal to impregnate her? Then, again, what man, potent or not, would allow his wife to fornicate with strangers, even for so noble a cause as that espoused by Cyrus? The sheer impossibility of ever understanding reached out to Joe from the paired coffins, stole the air from his lungs.

He found his chest pressing against the rim of Cyrus' coffin, had allowed himself to lean forward beyond the point of equilibrium, sagged against the edge of this cheap wooden box containing the fleshly remnants of a wasted, tortured life, one lived in vain, a life of quiet application to a dream without substance, a dream to hide behind and forget the hideous injustice of a world in which so unspeakable an act could be accomplished with impunity. Was Cyrus a brave man or a fool? Was Joe a similar fool to persevere with his own kind of futile dream, lowly and accessible though that dream might be? Would Joe turn to Christ if his balls were cut off, or would he take the other, more obvious step and kill himself? Perhaps Cyrus had already been a staunch Christian before the incident took place, had used his existing faith to buttress himself against desperation and misery. Joe was sure of it; Cyrus had not killed himself because he had been castrated—that had happened years ago, too long for even the most delayed of reactions. No, he had killed himself because a woman who knew he was no longer a true man yet loved him anyway had been taken from him, left him alone with the chill knowledge that his life would hereafter be as empty as his scrotum. No amount of faith could possibly have compensated for that loneliness, that awareness of the void which waits until persons are stripped of hope before engulfing them. Joe felt the quintessence of Cyrus' life spill slowly from the coffin and settle around his boots, a turgid aggregate of courage and hopelessness, the dark and sluggish ebbtide of an existence endured with fortitude for as long as a beleaguered spirit would allow. *All for nothing* was the phrase that whispered itself in Joe's ear. He knew he would have to fight the insidious voice as Cyrus had done, resist it to the utmost. Joe would not concede that his own life might be as devoid of meaning as another's; his unsparing eye was quick to detect the emptiness of the lives around him, but would never acknowledge the similar state of his own—at least, not to the point where such self-knowing became unendurable.

Joe left Templeton Morticians, stumbled along the street, ignoring passers-by, his vision filled with a host of open coffins, each already with its brass nameplate screwed in place, rows of waiting coffins stretching to infinity. He walked until his legs tired of their burden, entered the nearest hotel and asked for a room. He was refused. "Because I'm a half-breed?" He was not surprised, not even offended; it was an inconvenience, not a tragedy, was even amusing if regarded from the broadest of perspectives. He tried elsewhere, was eventually admitted to a rundown establishment catering to the indigent.

He sent out for whiskey. When it arrived he lay on the putrid bed, the latest in a long line of transients, and began to drink, tentatively at first, remembering his last experience with liquor. This time, he told himself, there is no risk. This time I'm alone while I drink. It occurred to him that life itself would be less risky if lived in isolation; other people constituted a definite threat, a potential unbalancing of the interior harmony a man on his own might establish. Unfortunately, there was no profit to be had from the life of a hermit. Joe wanted cash. Dollars alone would prove to the world that a twisted spine is no obstacle to a man of grit and determination. Joe knew that so far as the world was concerned he was equipped for nothing more ambitious than the emptying of spittoons or the cleaning of stables; these were the occupations befitting life's unfortunates, but they did not suit Joe at all. The world must take notice, and the melodic jingling of silver dollars will call attention to any man.

Joe drank deeply. The whiskey burned his throat, fought its way down into his stomach with fiery speed and there blossomed into a beneficent amber cloud suffused with mellow rays of self-enlightenment. Joe relaxed completely under its influence. What a fool he'd been to avoid liquor for so long. He swallowed again, relished the heart-stopping gallop of alcohol down his gullet to swell the cloud of knowingness. Joe was unsure exactly what it was he was now positive about, but the feeling could not be denied; he was in possession of powerful secrets about . . . everything. His head nodded sagely in agreement, and the kind of enigmatic smile to be found on oriental statues spread across his face, a trifle lopsided to be sure, yet suggesting with its contours a knowledge so profound, so all-encompassing as to shame philosophers, kings and priests, all of whom, given the chance, would have surrendered their souls for the opportunity to sit for just a short while at the feet of Joe Cobden, savant extraordinaire. Yes, Joe knew all about life, and with every sip taken his knowledge expanded to embrace hitherto undreamed of attitudes and thoughts and perceptions, a marvellous pot-pourri of intellect and emotion galvanised, moulded, invested with breathtaking clarity by the startlingly original mind of Joe, the world's most renowned hunchback. He drank on, ingesting the catalyst whereby nonentities spin fabulous cocoons about themselves, instantaneous, reality-resistant fabrications born of self-doubt and the need for reassurance in a cold and uncaring world.

He emptied the bottle in five hours, sipping and sipping. When it fell to the floor and rolled with a hollow thud against the bureau he staggered to the washbasin and was violently ill; the basin was half-filled with sour bile before Joe's stomach ceased regurgitating what scant few scraps of food had been available for discharge. He crawled to the bed and lay on its creaking mattress, vowing never again to tempt fate by indulging in liquor. When he found himself praying for the cessation of pain in his spasm-ridden guts Joe stopped breathing, so great was his alarm; Joseph Cobden, self-professed atheist and truth seeker, praying to God! This was the worst crime he could have perpetrated against himself, and for so trivial a petition! Self-loathing drove him to the basin again, this time puking nothing more substantial than foul air. He clutched at the basin with trembling hands and croaked fitfully at its miasmic contents, fully aware of how pitiful a sight he would present to an onlooker. Never again. He found the bed with his knees (it being night, and Joe too drunk to be capable of lighting a lamp) and slumped across it, regret for his rash purchase evident in every moaning breath.

Just before he passed out Joe realised he had not thought once of Cyrus since opening the bottle. This time his dereliction of moral duty came as no surprise; a man capable of praying to a nonexistent god for relief was certainly capable of forgetting the tragic circumstances of a friend's death. That such a man was beneath contempt was Joe's final thought before succumbing to the force of gravity, which sucked him down into an endless hole.

CHAPTER TWELVE

By the end of March, Joe had whittled down to nothing the money he saved while working at the Maximus. He had barely set foot outside his room in five weeks. Food was sent up, and whiskey. He taught himself how to drink. Joe was headed away from the world of women, into the world of men; he must learn how to pass himself off as one of them. He rehearsed a joke for the time when tough buffalo-hunters would express amazement at Joe's capacity for alcohol; he would say, "Everything I drink goes into my hump, like a camel." A joke like that would show them he was not afraid to josh himself, would win him friends.

Thinner, weaker, looking older than ever before, Joe went in search of employment. An early thaw had turned the streets to mud. He loitered outside saloons, never venturing through the doors, avoided the possibility of ejection as a half-breed, reminded himself he could now scarcely afford even a beer. He waited, eyes searching the customers passing through to the cacophonous interiors, looking always for the marks of the buffalo-hunter: filthy clothing, unshaven cheeks, a Sharpe's big fifty and plenty of cash. Any such individuals were accosted. Sometimes they were associated with the buffalo trade, sometimes they were not; none wanted anything to do with Joe.

He was obliged to vacate his room, and spent a desperate night of forced wakefulness wandering the streets, seeking warmth. He had not eaten in two days. Towards dawn Joe found himself outside the livery stable wherein the buffalo calf had been set upon him. His reaction to the locale was without emotion; he could no longer afford the luxury of outraged dignity. He went inside, asked for a job, was told none was to be had.

Leaning against the stable walls, waiting for the sun to rise and warm his shivering body, Joe wondered if this was the lowest point in his life thus far. To be friendless and alone seemed a natural state of affairs, but to be without a nickel, that was a situation warranting anxiety, and plenty of it. Unless his luck changed before the day was out he would have to abandon the last shreds of pride and hire himself out as a cleaner of spittoons, a sweeper of dust. He could blame no one but himself, knew he had lingered too long in the anonymous safety of his room, soaking himself in liquor and dreaming fragile dreams. Now he paid the price for his foolish prevarication. I am a dog turd under the indifferent wheel of life, he told himself, and was surprised at his ability to manufacture so morbid a turn of phrase. Too bad I can't eat it, he thought. What would the doctor say if he could see me now? "Joseph, you have fallen no lower than I expected, that is to say, to a point beyond which there is no regressing. I am ashamed to find my worst fears confirmed. You are not a dog turd under the indifferent wheel of life, you are a wriggling worm within that turd, and as such totally undeserving of sympathy." Joe nodded his head. A wriggling worm; yes, indeed.

As the sun rose above the surrounding buildings half a dozen or so men began assembling by the corral, hard looking men on rangy mounts. Joe watched with growing interest as they were joined by a mule-drawn cook's wagon with its cargo of rattling pots and pans, and presently by three huge Conestogas of pioneer extraction, their hoops and canvas removed, each wagon requiring an eight-mule team. Joe straightened himself, scenting one last opportunity for deliverance. He approached the bearded man who appeared to be in charge, waited until the man's eye lowered to notice him.

"Are you running this outfit?" Joe made his voice as aggressive as possible, knew a whiner would get nowhere.

"What if I am?" The man looked at Joe's hump, not at his face.

"Buffalo-hunting?" Joe enquired, hands on hips.

"That's right. What's your interest?" His horse stamped nervous hoofs into the mud and was curbed impatiently. The rider wondered if his mare could distinguish between a normal man and a hunchback. Joe pointed at himself, ignoring the hoofs that threatened to crush his toes. "You need me along."

"Why?"

"I work hard but cheap, and if you don't hire me I'll fall down dead of starvation and you'll have to wait for years in purgatory before they'll let you into heaven."

The bearded man's lips may have smiled beneath the heavy moustache, it was difficult to tell. "Ever been around buffalo?"

"Hunted them last year until my partner got killed. Brought back plenty of meat."

"Are you the one who worked with Eli Tilton?"

"That's me."

"I heard about you. You worked in a cathouse, is that right?"

"Just for a while. Buffalo-hunting's what I do best."

The man scanned his waiting teams, looked back down at Joe. "Forty dollars a month and all the buffalo meat you can eat."

"Suits me. I don't have a rifle, though."

"Don't you worry about that. You just joined the Quincy Tubbs outfit. Get aboard a wagon."

Heart thumping with relief, Joe scrambled up the nearest wheel and on to the seat of the first Conestoga. The driver stared at him in disbelief, then shook the reins. Eleven men strong, the outfit passed through the outskirts of Hays City and headed south.

Joe introduced himself to his travelling companion. The driver merely nodded, his manner cold, unfriendly. Elated by the change in his fortunes, Joe refused to be intimidated, was confident he could win this surly fellow over. He jerked his thumb behind them at the empty bed of the Conestoga. "Must be counting on bringing back a whole lot of meat." The driver waited a moment before turning to Joe. His lip curled into a sneer. "Meat?" he said, investing the word with scorn rather than enquiry, then shook his head in pity. "Don't know nothin', do you?" he said, and spat between the traces. Puzzled, Joe made no further attempt at conversation. The man was obviously some kind of fool. What else were buffalo good for if not for meat?

A development of which Joe was unaware was about to alter the hunting habits of white men drastically, and change for ever a pattern of living established for numberless generations by the old Americans. J. N. DuBois, a Kansas City dealer in hides and furs, had in 1870 shipped several dozen buffalo hides to Germany; there, expert tanners developed a process whereby the hides could be hardened into serviceable leather, the equal, in fact, of cowhide. Scenting vast profits to be made from the herds of buffalo freely ranging the western territories, DuBois papered Kansas with circulars promising handsome prices for hides. Since no profit-making scheme can be kept secret for long, others learned of the new tanning process and advertised in a similar fashion. Thus was born an instant market for a hitherto ignored commodity. In the spring of 1871 began the autumn of the buffalo. It was to be a time of spectacular and unprecedented slaughter, of relentless extermination in the name of the white god Mammon, whose symbol is the writhing serpent transfixed by parallel lines. All unknowing, his heart filled with eagerness, Joe was about to take part.

Seated with his new associates around a campfire that night, Joe was careful to remain open and friendly, to take no offence at the questions put to him. Was his hump a source of pain? Always, he thought, a fountain of heartache. "No, it doesn't bother me." Was it true the dead nigger whore at the Maximus had a bottle shoved up her ass? "Yes." And Joe had a question of his own. "Did they find who did it?"

"Naw," said one of the men, "and never will do, I

reckon. Without a killing gets done in the street or a bar right there in front of folks there ain't a sure way to find who done the deed. Did you ever climb on any of them whores while you worked in that place?"

"No."

"Figured not." The comment was not malicious, simply matter-of-fact, yet Joe felt another sliver pared from his self-esteem. These men would never truly know him, would treat him like dirt if allowed. He would have to win their respect by excelling at their level. It would not be so very hard; Joe knew himself to be a crack shot.

"When do I get my rifle?" he asked.

The ring of faces around the fire fell silent, then erupted in laughter. Joe was panic-stricken. What had he said? Tubbs gave him a mock-serious look. "What rifle's that, son?"

"I told you I didn't have one, and you said not to worry. I thought you were going to lend me one. . . ."

The guffawing began anew. Tubbs shook his head sadly, chest quaking. "You're in the grip of a big misapprehension, son. You're here to skin buffalo, not shoot 'em. That's *my* job. Don't worry if you've got no knife. We supply that free of charge."

"But . . . why bother skinning if all you want is the meat?"

"Meat?" Quincy Tubbs raised his eyebrows and the men hooted their approval of his expression, that of a spinster aunt who has heard an indecent word. "We aren't interested in meat other than what we need to keep fed and healthy. What this outfit wants is hides. Three and a half dollars each is what they're willing to pay back east, and we intend supplying the goods."

His blushes hidden by the firelight, Joe gave a sickly grin, acknowledged the joke was on him. A buffalo-skinner. He recalled the effort required to skin the buffalo he shot on the day Eli was murdered. It had been a strenuous, bloody task. The delay it caused had probably contributed to Eli's death, since Eli had been left without his rifle, and had, in the end, proved unrewarding, the hide having been stolen along with the Sharpe's at the livery stable outside which Joe had been hired this morning. There appeared to be a kind of predetermined logic to the chain of events, one more example of the peculiar quirks of fate to be expected in a lifetime of random occurrences strung end to end until death. In any life coincidence and irony were bound to play a part; they were interesting nexes in an essentially erratic flow of happenstance, nothing more.

Talk around the fire grew desultory, ebbed with the flames. The outfit went to their beds in the various wagons, the ground still holding the soggy chill of departed winter. Joe rolled himself into blankets and prepared to cover his face with his hat when a boot kicked him in the shins. "Hump," said a voice beside him, "if I find you tryin' to pester me while I'm asleep I'll skin you alive." There were giggles from further along the wagon. Joe thought frantically. Had the stupid rumour about Cyrus and himself escaped the confines of the Maximus and become common knowledge throughout Hays? It was the only explanation for the warning. It had pursued him, tying him to the past at the very moment he wished to begin anew. His heart thumped painfully, his jaw clenched until he thought his teeth might break. "You hear what I'm sayin', Hump?" The question was accompanied by another kick. Joe could not identify the voice, but suspected it was the driver beside whom he had sat all day. He took a long and silent breath, made himself speak calmly, distinctly, aware that his reply would determine the nature of his future relations with the buffalo men.

"One," he said, "never call me 'Hump.' Two, if you kick me again I'll break your leg. Three, I don't know your face, so before I wake up tomorrow you'd better be up and about before I see who you are and mark you down for punishment."

Silence for the space of several heartbeats, a few titters from the other end of the wagon. "Big talker, ain't you," said the faceless man.

"Four, I don't like your voice, so don't say another word."

Another prolonged silence while the man decided whether to call Joe's bluff. He could not allow himself to be belittled by a hunchback; Joe might not know his voice, but the others did. He would have to reply. "Reckon I'll call you 'Breed' 'steada 'Hump'."

Joe ripped his blankets aside in calculated fury, leaped to his feet and reached for the man beside him as he attempted to rise. Joe grabbed his shirtfront and hauled him to his feet. Before the man could start swinging his fists Joe picked him up and threw him from the wagon. A Conestoga is a tall vehicle and the body made a satisfying thump as it hit the ground. Joe bundled the vacated blankets and flung them out alongside their owner, who picked them up and slunk away, cursing weakly. Joe arranged himself for sleep once more, the thrill of victory almost swamping his bitterness.

"Good move there, Cobden," said a voice.

"He asked for it," said another.

"Amen and good riddance," offered a third.

Joe said nothing; he would not forgive their giggling connivance so easily, nor their laughter around the fire. Let them wonder how he felt; his silence would earn him nothing but respect, perhaps even a little fear. He closed his eyes. I don't belong here, he thought. For all my daydreaming, I don't belong here.

Five days out from Hays City the Quincy Tubbs outfit established a semi-permanent campsite in the midst of rolling country scattered with herds of buffalo. The outfit rostered thus: one rifleman or hunter (Tubbs), one cook, nine skinners. One morning they set out to do what they had come to do, some mounted, others lurching and bouncing in one of the wagons. The cook was left behind to gather buffalo chips for his fire, prepare an adequate meal for their return and guard the camp. A nervous man, he spent a good deal of the day cowering in a wagon, waiting for Indians to appear and scalp him, wishing he had never left New York City.

Several miles from the camp Tubbs called a halt. He rode ahead to a rise, dismounted and peered over, lying on his stomach. A herd browsed below him, a wealth of easy targets. The wind was in Tubbs' favour. He singled out the cow which acted as watchdog for all the buffalo in that particular section of the herd. An army scout had told Tubbs of this peculiarity of the buffalo and instructed him in how best to take advantage of it: simply kill the cow and the beasts under her charge would be rendered defenceless, too stupid to decide for themselves if the popping sounds that reached their ears, followed by the slump of a nearby grazer to the ground, constituted signs of danger. Never had the killing of wild animals been so effortless.

Tubbs inserted a two and a half inch cartridge into the breech of his Sharpe's, took aim at the one cow which occasionally bothered to raise her head and sniff the wind. He squeezed the trigger and one hundred and ten grains of powder sent several ounces of lead smashing through the cow's lungs. She staggered but did not fall. Blood frothed from her mouth as the legs slowly buckled beneath her. The scent of blood made her neighbours restive, but caused no great alarm. They continued to feed as their guard bled to death mere yards away. Tubbs reloaded and fired again, bringing down a sturdy bull, reloaded and fired, reloaded and fired until the octagonal barrel of his gun grew hot. The plain below him was littered with dead and dying buffalo, and still the rest of the herd grazed on. He wetted a drawcloth and pulled it through the barrel several times until the metal cooled, then resumed killing. In the space of forty minutes he killed fifty buffalo, then stopped, not because there were no more within range to kill, but because he was unsure how many his skinners could handle in a day. Tubbs was a beginner at this trade, but was sensible enough to understand the parameters of indulgence; he was, after all, slaughtering for profit rather than for pleasure.

He waved the skinners forward. Their wagon topped the rise, its bulk and the sound of mule hoofs sending the nearest buffalo to a safer distance without provoking a stampede. Half a mile away they promptly forgot their panic and resumed grazing. Joe stared at the dead animals, impressed by Tubbs' speed and accuracy; only one animal had required more than a single shot to bring it down. He set to work with the other skinners. They worked in pairs. Joe, being the odd man out, moved from pair to pair as requested for some particularly difficult manoeuvre, usually the toppling of a buffalo on to its back. Once this had been achieved and the carcass held securely in place with pointed sticks, the actual skinning could begin. The first cut ran from the lower jaw down the belly to the tail. Lateral cuts were made from this along the insides of all four legs, terminating in a circular slash around the legs just above the hoofs. From the initial point of entry another cut ran around the neck to include the ears. The carcass was then allowed to flop on to its side. The hide was loosened a little at the cranium and peeled back to allow a rope noose sufficient purchase on a gathered knot of hide and hair. The rope was hauled upon until the hide began to peel off in jerks of several feet at a time. First to see the light of day was the hump, a small mountain covered in glistening fat of surprising whiteness; next came the forelegs, the back and ribs, the flanks and hind legs. The tail was peeled with one last tug, the hide severed just above the tuft of hair at its end.

The skinners quickly mastered the technique, and an air of friendly rivalry developed. Ten to fifteen minutes proved the average time elapsed from buffalo clothed to buffalo naked. Joe assisted, imitated, learned; his clothing quickly becoming plastered with grease, hair, fat and blood, plus numerous fleas, tics and other invisible parasites. He sweated and strained along with the rest while Tubbs sat in the saddle and passed among them offering advice, sometimes using the power of his horse to pull free a stubbornly adherent hide. The air buzzed with flies newly hatched in the warm spring sunshine; they feasted on exposed banquets of adipose tissue, spilled blood and the fresh excrement many of the buffalo had released as their final act before dying. Joe paused to sharpen his knife with the butcher's steel Tubbs had provided for each man, looked over the killing ground at the peeled mounds of flesh, scarcely recognisable now as having been buffalo. He felt a twinge of annoyance; all those tons of meat should not be going to waste. Still, there were buffalo by the million; it would surely take a century even to begin depleting their numbers. He thought no more about it. The hides were hauled to the wagon and loaded aboard.

The hunting party returned to camp at mid-afternoon. The cook, having reassured himself they were not Indians, rushed about in a frenzy of industry, performing those tasks he should have seen to hours ago. Work began immediately to scrape the undersides of the hides clean of any remaining flesh; both sides were then sprinkled with arsenic powder to kill the maggots and flies with which the living beast must contend, a task requiring gloves and the ability to hold one's breath. This accomplished, the hides were skewered at several points around their perimeters and pegged to the ground, hair side down, for drying. Darkness fell before the last hide had been attended to. The skinners, made ravenous by their labours, attacked their food with a gratifying fervour the cook could never have witnessed in New York City. Exhausted, replete, they took themselves to their blankets and were soon fast asleep. Tubbs, who had taken no part in the treatment of the hides beyond his role as supplier, remained by the fire to enjoy a last cup of coffee. Joe drank with him, fighting off weariness for the sake of establishing some kind of rapport with his employer. He did not seek favouritism, knew Tubbs was not the kind of man who required fawners, simply wanted him to know Joe was different from the rest, different in ways unrelated to his appearance.

"I could have killed them by the hundreds," said Tubbs. "They must be the most stupid animals in creation. This outfit's too small. I need another rifleman and a dozen more skinners."

"I could be that second gun," offered Joe.

"You don't have a rifle."

"You could buy one for me and take it out of my wages. I'm a good shot."

"Kansas is full of good shots, and with their own guns too."

Joe retired to his blanket, drifted into sleep wondering if he would ever be allowed to amount to anything. Reflections of so retrograde a nature rarely intruded upon his mind when fully awake.

The Quincy Tubbs outfit stayed in one place for three weeks. Every day for the first week Tubbs shot fifty buffalo. During the second week he shot sixty per day, his skinners now having honed their skills to a fine edge. In the third week the daily count sometimes rose as high as sixty-five. The immediate vicinity having been considerably thinned of beasts, the outfit shifted camp to the south and began anew, killing, skinning, piling hides higher and higher in the wagons. The mule teams sweated to haul their weight, the wagon wheels sank a little deeper into the prairie sod each day. For an hour every morning, Sundays included, Tubbs' rifle boomed like thunder. Tubbs was often to be seen smiling, and well he might, for the pickings were easy, child's play. God bless the Germans who invented the new tanning process, and God bless J. N. DuBois for alerting the west to the lumbering treasure trove in its midst. Puncture their mighty hearts, blast their lungs to pulp, watch them sink to their knees with dull bewilderment in their eyes; see them topple sideways, dying, while their fellows graze on unconcerned, pea-brained monsters too stupid to live, too boneheaded to inspire sympathy or regret; send a thunderbolt into the belly of this lowest and most plentiful of beasts.

Joe's whole body ached. Muscles that had grown slack in

Hays were stretched and tortured. He worked with an abattoir stench in his nostrils, a hateful, clinging stink of death and decaying flesh that penetrated his clothing and hair. The stench was a constant factor in the lives of the buffalo men, with them like the buzzing of flies from sunup to sundown, like the nightly snarling of wolves that fattened on their leavings. No predators needed to hunt; all they could feast upon and more was provided by man. Joe reminded himself before falling asleep each night that this onerous work was temporary, a steppingstone on the way to distant pastures of dollar green.

He was gradually accepted among the men. They included him in their conversation around the fire each night and, although their talk was of no interest whatever to him, Joe responded in kind, anxious not to appear aloof in any way. The truth was he considered himself superior to these hard and unsophisticated men; they would have been angry had they known his thoughts regarding their intellects, their humble aspirations (a piece of land), their physical crudity and their casual acceptance of what they assumed was their superiority over him. He let them believe what they wished, had no intention of antagonising them by correcting their appalling grammar or bridging the awesome gaps in their knowledge of the world. They were not evil men, were simply ordinary—a bad enough thing to be, in Joe's estimation. To Quincy Tubbs he gave grudging respect. The man was somewhat uncouth, and had flatly refused Joe's offer to shoot for him, but he possessed the natural qualities of leadership to which most men, no matter how divergent their personalities, histories and intelligence, will respond. And he had given Joe a job when no other would; that fact alone was sufficient grounds for Joe to work hard, seek to please. Tubbs noticed, and said nothing. He had no particular wish to be Joe Cobden's friend.

By the time the outfit returned to Hays City the Conestogas were groaning beneath their freight of stiffened hides.

Hays meant liquor, women, gambling, music, clean sheets, a bath, all the things hard-earned wages could buy. An entire floor of the Gable House Hotel was appropriated (its roof boasted not one gable) and, while the rest of the outfit formed a queue in the bath-house at the rear, Joe and another skinner accompanied Tubbs to the railroad depot, each driving a wagon.

For a quarter of a mile along both sides of the Kansas Pacific tracks the earth was hidden beneath stacked buffalo hides. The sight came as a revelation to Joe. Isolated on the prairie for two months it had been easy to foster the idea that the Tubbs outfit was plying a lonely trade; they had seen no other hunters, had not even seen any Indians, had seen nothing but each other and teeming herds of buffalo. Now it became apparent they were only one bunch among many; the stacked hides told the story. Tubbs quickly located a buyer, a price was agreed upon in five minutes, cash paid on the spot; Tubbs walked away richer by over six thousand dollars. Back at the Gable House wages were distributed to whoops and cheers.

Joe went to his room, locked the door and spread his cash across the bed. He saw nothing to promote whooping and cheering. This was what he had laboured so hard for; these crinkled pieces of paper were the measure of his stature as a man, and he did not stand tall. He counted the money again. Eighty dollars, out of which he would have to pay for his hotel room, food and drink. A new Sharpe's, a good horse and saddle would cost plenty. Working as a skinner he could not hope to afford the object of his dreams for a long while yet. Maybe he should ask around, see if some other hunter was offering more in the way of wages and inducements. But hadn't he done just that, and been turned down by everyone? Tubbs was probably the only one who would even consider hiring him. He was stuck with Tubbs, who, after handing out wages, had been left with a clear profit of five thousand dollars. Five thousand dollars! And all because he happened to own an expensive rifle. It was not fair. The man who already *had* money, in the form of a

Sharpe's (and the wagons and mule teams, don't forget them), was the man who ended up making the most money, and without even sweating for it. Every skinner did ten times the work Tubbs did—*twenty* times. Joe drew no political conclusions regarding the nature of capitalism from his pondering, simply wished it was he who owned the magical Sharpe's, instrument of his deliverance. Caught in a cleft stick, he thought. Very well, if he had to endure stench and filth and backbreaking work to get what he wanted, then endure it he must. But it still wasn't fair.

He brooded a while longer, then crammed the money into his pants and went for a walk. He went nowhere near the Circus Maximus. Hays was a big enough town to walk through without risking confrontation with faces from the recent past. Joe encountered the usual stares but did not allow them to upset him; his bad mood was fuelled by more practical considerations. Dollars and cents, his boots seemed to say as he clumped along the sidewalk, dollars and cents, dollars and cents. Suddenly Joe saw a face he knew, and almost stumbled with the shock of recognition. A man stood talking to another at a street corner. He cradled a Sharpe's in the crook of his arm. It had been the rifle which first caught Joe's eye rather than the man's face. This was one of the humorists who had got him drunk and subjected him to humiliation in the livery stable, Joe was sure of it. He turned away from the street, pretended to examine the goods on display in a store window. He peeked over his shoulder. The two men continued talking, did not notice him. The one with the rifle had been assisting the circus fellow, had helped him capture the buffalo calf that figured so prominently in their evening's entertainment. Had he had a rifle with him at the time? Joe thought hard, tried to penetrate the gauze time and distance and drunkenness had laid over the events of that night. No, he had not had a rifle. Some of the drinkers had worn pistols, but Joe had been the only one toting a Sharpe's, he was positive now. The rifle being cradled not five yards away was Eli Tilton's and, following his death, Joe's.

174

His heart thudded with rage, his lips pursed and puckered and finally settled into a trembling line. He sneaked another glance. They paid him no attention at all, but might do so at any time. Joe wished his hump would retract, render him anonymous, a store window gazer unworthy of closer inspection. He fretted for several minutes more while the two men laughed over something. Finally they separated. Joe followed his man to a saloon, waited outside for his reappearance. While he waited he mused over the vagaries of fate which had delivered one of his tormentors within striking distance, and holding in his arms the means of Joe's salvation. He forced himself to accept it as timely coincidence. How else could he conceive of it—as the manipulations of a guardian angel, a purposefully benign force hovering at his elbow, steering him through life? Ridiculous. It was chance, pure chance, and Joe concentrated on seizing the opportunity it offered to stand circumstance on its head and redirect his destiny along paths of his own choosing. He waited with impatience, sweating in the late-afternoon heat, a plan forming in his head.

His man smacked aside batwing doors and stamped off along the sidewalk, his meandering gait indicating the level of whiskey inside him. Joe followed, hat pulled low, trying to be inconspicuous, a difficult task for a hunchback. The man walked several blocks then turned into a narrow alleyway. Joe almost reversed his non-belief in guardian angels; an alley was perfect for his purpose. He left the sidewalk and followed. His man appeared to be the only other person in the narrow planked space between buildings. Guardian angels virtually fanned Joe with their wings when he saw the man stop, lean the Sharpe's against a wall and fumble at his crotch. He was going to piss! Joe almost swooned with gratitude. A pissing man will usually concentrate all his attention on the weighty business of finding relief; moreover, his hands, unless he is extraordinarily casual about the act, will be fully occupied directing the yellow stream away from his boots.

As he approached, Joe took the skinning knife from his

belt and nonchalantly reversed it in his grip; the handle terminated in a solid knob of metal, ideal for striking the unwary skulls of the unrighteous. Joe surprised himself with his eagerness. Was this the very first time he had truly wanted to do bodily harm? He debated the question for a fraction of a second, then planned the precise choreography of revenge. Yes, it would work. A quick glance behind to ensure the alley was still unpopulated, then he was alongside or, rather, behind his prey. The pisser had not looked up once, too fascinated by the sight of his abundant flow to bother confirming the presence of an audience, perhaps too drunk even to be aware of such. Joe brought the knife handle down on his neck with force almost sufficient to crush vertebrae, certainly strong enough to bring about instant insensibility. He slumped to the ground, still urinating vigorously. Joe scooped the leaning Sharpe's into his hand, sheathed his knife and walked on. The steps taken to change his life had scarcely caused him to break stride.

He went to a clothing store, purchased new pants, several shirts, some much needed socks and a jacket long enough to cloak his hump without baring his buttocks. Feeling like a king, Joe returned to his room at the Gable House. He literally hugged himself in congratulation, hoped the thief, whoever he was, was afflicted with a permanent neck-ache. He picked up the Sharpe's, kissed the oily lock and went along to Quincy Tubbs' room.

"I've skinned my last buffalo. From now on I'm hunting."

"Who with?"

"Preferably with you. If not, then with someone else."

"Ambitious, aren't you."

"Yes."

"Where'd you get the gun?"

Trusting him, Joe told all. Tubbs saw nothing to be ashamed of in Joe's tale, was more impressed by his gumption than he chose to reveal. He curbed an urge to ask for more details from Joe's past.

"Got any ammunition?" he asked.

"I can't afford any. Why don't you stake me for fifteen hundred rounds and take it out of our next trip's profits. I'll need a horse too."

"I might already have hired someone else."

"If you have, say so, and I'll stop wasting your time and mine."

Tubbs chuckled wheezily; he was three fourths drunk, but still very much in control of himself. "Tell you what, I'll stake you for the ammunition and the horse, but when the hides are sold and the skinners paid off you and me make a three way split of what's left over, two thirds to me, one third for you. That's to buy you a half share of the wagons and take care of what you owe me. The trip after that, assuming we get along all right together, we split straight down the middle. Still interested?" They shook hands. "You must be the youngest partner any buffalo man ever had."

"That just gives me more years to learn how to be the best."

"Like I said, ambitious."

That night Joe went drinking with the rest of the outfit. He did not tell them he would be hunting next time, not skinning. This might be the one and only occasion when he could drink with them as an equal; sitting high on a horse and carrying a gun makes a man different from his brother on the ground with a skinning knife. He drank as he had trained himself to, slowly and steadily. Because he was part of a crowd he was not called a half-breed and told to leave. The fact that he had plenty of money to spend also assured his tenure at the bar, one boot planted firmly on the rail, his head barely topping the beer-splashed surface.

"For a little feller you sure can drink," said someone.

"Everything I drink goes into my hump," said Joe, "like a camel."

They all laughed. Joe smiled crookedly. It was the high point in his life to date.

Well after midnight, totally drunk, Joe weaved his way back to his room. He lay on the bed for a while, decided it

made him feel ill to stare at the ceiling while it spun, and
so sat up. He took the Sharpe's in his hands and smiled,
examined it closely for the first time since recovering it that
afternoon. The smile slowly wilted. Joe was familiar with
every nick on the barrel of Eli Tilton's rifle, every scratch
on the stock. This gun was not Eli's! A dreadful chill ran
across his hump, dimpled his arms; his weakened fingers
almost dropped the Sharpe's. He brought it closer to his
face, turned up the wick in his bedside lamp, searched frantically for recognisable, exonerating features. There were
none. If the gun was not Eli's then it was possible he had
been mistaken about the owner's identity. Had the man
truly been among those who took him to the livery stable?
Joe was unsure of anything now. Panic set him restlessly
pacing the room, the rifle jerking at the end of his arm with
a life of its own. He flung it on to the bed, continued pacing,
convinced now he had robbed a total stranger of his rightful
property. Wait, he thought, maybe I'm so drunk I'm fool-
ing myself. He picked up the Sharpe's again, pored over it,
scrutinised it, nosed it like a blind monk deciphering a waterlogged manuscript. It was not Eli's.

"Oh, Jesus. . . . Shit!"

What to do now? Conscience dictated he should seek out
the wronged man, return the gun and apologise, perhaps
offer monetary compensation for whatever injury his neck
had sustained. Joe had brought that knife butt down hard.
What if the poor bastard had died? Joe moaned in consternation. He should never have come west. He should have
stayed in St. Louis, accepted his deformity and become an
articled clerk, a street sweeper, anything. He sat on the bed,
head cradled in his hands. If he returned the gun and was
not, by a miracle of forgiveness, prosecuted for its theft and
the accompanying physical assault, it would mean he was
back where he started, a humble, stinking skinner. He could
still smell the newness of his clothes. Soon they would reek
of blood and fat and buffalo shit. . . . No, they wouldn't,
because he was not going to return the gun. His mind was
made up in an instant. He would not deny himself this

opportunity for advancement, no matter how morally expedient the means. Joe knew exactly what he was doing, accepted his choice with full knowledge of its ethical shortcomings. Honest error now was compounded by deliberate wrongdoing. He would tell no one of his mistake, would play the part which, until a few minutes ago, had sat so naturally on his shoulders. He hoped the wronged man would not create too much fuss over his loss. In a town like Hays, where murder and mayhem were constant themes in newspaper editorialising, it was unlikely a simple battering and theft would excite much interest. But one could never be sure.

Joe set his jaw and awaited the outcome of his decision. He sequestered himself in the Gable House and did not set foot outside until Tubbs demanded that Joe accompany him on a buying expedition to resupply the outfit; partners were partners in town as well as on the prairie, and should share responsibility in all things. Joe grumbled that his share of the responsibility totalled only one-third, but went with Tubbs anyway, expecting at any moment to be waylaid by an indignant citizen with a heavily bandaged neck. The dreaded encounter did not occur. The necessary transactions completed, Joe hurried back to the safety of his room, where the stolen Sharpe's was kept hidden on top of the wardrobe.

While the rest of the men drank and whored Joe lay on his bed, anticipating the day they would leave Hays City.

CHAPTER THIRTEEN

Some legends do not pass into the public domain, but circulate only among those directly concerned with the milieu from which the legend has sprung. During the remainder of 1871 and the whole of the following year the buffalo-hunters of Kansas became familiar with the name Joe Cobden. Joe was not alone in his prowess with a rifle, and his weekly tally of buffalo was sometimes exceeded by those of his peers, but Joe had something the others did not; Joe had a hump, a buffalo-like hump, and when during his first winter as a hunter a heavy coat and cap were made for him from choice hide his appearance became so akin to that of the beasts he slaughtered his name was qualified accordingly. By the fall of 1872, when Joe was seventeen, the sobriquet Joe Buffalo was in common use among the brethren of hunters.

The Tubbs-Cobden outfit ranged from the Missouri to the Rockies, from Nebraska down through Oklahoma to the Texas Panhandle, shooting and skinning, but Kansas was where it had all begun and to Kansas the outfit always returned, six wagons and twenty-three men strong now, as efficient a killing machine as ever denuded the plains, and Joe Buffalo was its mainspring. His resolve to keep the stolen rifle no matter what, literally to blast his way to the top of a profession rapidly becoming overcrowded with experts, affected Joe's character in ways he found reassuring; moments of self-doubt came to him still, but with greatly reduced intensity. He was what he had wanted to be, a hunter of buffalo, a man (for remarkably few ever guessed his true age) with a reputation. That reputations west of the Missouri were generally purchased with the aid of gunpowder and lead and gaping flesh, either animal or human, was not a fact that Joe allowed to fill him with misgiving. The newly opened territories were a man's world, and contained within their westering boundaries a stage so vast, so impervious to normal emotion as to demand of its actors a minimum of dialogue and a preponderance of action, the most exalted (and opposing) forms of which are creation and destruction. Art requires an audience of adequate cultural receptivity, while death is democratic in its fascination, is instantly understandable to all. No amount of wordy mouthings is the equal of so decisive a final curtain as death, and it was thus the bringing down of manifold curtains which prompted appreciative applause in the west, rather than the dramas which preceded their fall.

Men of unremarkable character and intellect became the repositories of humankind's propensity for myth-making solely in consequence of their ability to destroy. Their names were writ large on the covers of dime novels and reward posters alike, heroes of the new western age, knights of the iron order; the living legends of their time. Few in the east questioned their right to the mantle of public renown, for the land of the demi-gods was far away toward the sunset, a place of unreal substance where events pursued their own course across a landscape unrelieved by moral precept, a wide open land laid bare for Mammon, whose spur is the free rein.

Like his fellows, Joe Cobden chose the narrow view that presented itself at the end of his rifle sights (hand-carved from bone nowadays to ward off the sun's reflection) and followed the herds with dogged determination, chasing dollars on the hoof through all four seasons. Like Tubbs, he never soiled his hands by touching the hides; all that was behind him now. He sat astride a splendid gelding and watched while others laboured to strip and clean and peg, a hundred hides a day, a hundred and twenty, folded along the spine and stacked in the wagons that squealed and groaned where no roads ran, wagons to be unloaded at the nearest railroad town—Wichita, Dodge, Hays—stacked again in endless rows alongside the tracks only for as long as it took the next freight to pull in, boxcar doors opened wide to receive the plunder of the plains and haul it back east. The machinery of capital demanded belts of leather to drive its lathes and drills and looms, endless belts on spinning wheels, humming and driving, whirring and clanking in sombre mills and factories.

The old Americans saw their herds, sacred gift of the Great Spirit who brought them into the world of men from a hole in the earth, dwindle in the space of twenty moons from abundance to paucity. A man could walk from sunrise to sundown on the naked, rotting bodies of buffalo without once setting foot on the ground. Prairie winds carried the scent of death to every plains tribe, a nostril-clogging stench of putrefaction signalling the end of their dominion. The land of their grandfathers' grandfathers was being stolen from them by white demons without souls, hordes of them, more than there are birds in the sky, a plague of white grasshoppers filling their eyes and mouths, blinding them, denying them food. Iron rods without beginning or end lay along the ground in pairs, supporting iron monsters whose breath was fire and smoke, and beside them on leafless trees were the singing wires that chattered and clicked in an unknown devil tongue. Everywhere the whites were digging into the earth, building wooden villages which sometimes were abandoned, sometimes grew and grew beyond all reasonable size and filled the air with noise and the odours of burning and metal and death. It could not be permitted to continue. Balance must be restored before the world turned upside down, casting all human beings into darkness. Protected from injury by magical incantations, secure in the rightness of their wrath, warriors rode out to destroy the advancing white tide. They killed the devils and their wives and offspring, the only sure way to root out the sickness. They ambushed the buffalo-hunters and took their scalps in retribution and sang fierce, exultant songs. But the whites were too many, the warriors too few, and the blue soldiers came to exact revenge, terrible, outrageous revenge, killing ten, fifty, a hundred, for the death of each white. And the buffalo continued to fall.

Now aspiring hunters paid a courtesy call at the nearest military outpost and were given cases of ammunition *gratis*, accompanied by a wink that said, "A troublesome Indian is bad. A docile Indian is good. A dead Indian is best. Hunger kills." And more buffalo fell, blessed by blue-coated representatives of white government. When all the buffalo had been killed, so they reasoned, why then the Indians would have to come willingly to reservation lands where they would be fed beef and taught how to farm crops like civilised folk. The distribution of free ammunition to hunters was unwritten, unofficial policy, and was executed with zeal.

Joe knew virtually nothing of Indians, was not particularly interested in learning. Indians were shadowy figures who rode their ponies below the skyline, furtive bands forever spying from a distance. He was prepared to tolerate their presence, had no objection when some fell into the habit of accompanying the hunters, eating those beasts brought down by the booming Sharpe's; it was a shame to waste all that meat. These were not *real* Indians of course, but whiskey Indians. Real Indians would never have abandoned their pride to feed on that which had been killed by whites, like the prairie scavengers. These Indians bartered their women for drink, and Joe did nothing to stop that practice either, it being none of his concern who took whom beyond the firelight to engage in transactions of the flesh. It relaxed the men after a day spent in hard labour, made them more cheerful. Fighting sometimes broke out over which squaw was whose for the night, but the injuries sustained were usually minor.

All this was regarded by Joe from the lofty heights of the experienced employer. He was not overly familiar with the men, seldom even had much to speak of with his partner.

Tubbs did not resent Joe's exclusiveness; he was a wealthy man now, they both were, and when the buffalo played out he and Joe would doubtless go their separate ways. Their relations were casual, based on mutual respect for each other's silence and independence, which are often equated with strength of character. Tubbs tended to admire Joe for not indulging in squaws as the skinners did, but by the same token he sometimes wondered if Joe was not perhaps a little too stand-offish; he was only a half-breed after all, and had been given his one and only chance for success by Tubbs and no one else. Not that Joe was surly or disrespectful; no, it was something else, a kind of smugness on the young-old face, a faintly supercilious air which could be detected on the odd occasion when Joe observed those around him without knowing he was himself observed. How a half-breed hunchback could possibly consider himself superior to anyone was something that puzzled Tubbs. He decided it must be on account of Joe's money; a heap of cash would turn the unlikeliest of heads. Once, considerably drunk, he had asked Joe why he was such a stuffed shirt. Unruffled, Joe said it was because he was going deaf as a result of several thousand small explosions having been detonated inches from his right ear, the human eardrum being no match for one hundred and ten grains of powder. Joe further explained that his expression, which Tubbs had mistakenly interpreted as superior, was in fact blankness, the natural result of being isolated, thanks to his hearing impairment, from his surroundings. Tubbs was almost convinced. He had ear problems himself, and like Joe had lately resorted to stuffing his canals with wads of cotton before opening fire on yet another herd. Almost convinced, but not quite. There was an equivocality about Joe which defied ready analysis, and a lesser man than Tubbs might have allowed himself to become irritated by the elusive something that lurked behind those dark Indian eyes.

His face may have been blank, but more often than not Joe's mind was active. The source of his cogitations was twofold. First, he dwelt at length upon the mystery of why it was that he felt no empathy with Indians. As a half-breed he should logically have experienced some inklings of kinship, perhaps not with the whiskey Indians, since they were beneath contempt, but surely with the free-ranging Sioux and Cheyenne who adhered to their traditional way of life. There was nothing about these people to promote contempt, yet he knew his feeling for Indians was basically that of any white man's—he wanted them to keep their distance and not interfere with white interests. He had heard of Indian complaints that the wanton slaughter of buffalo was producing starvation and hardship among the tribes, but could not fully credit the notion; there seemed to be so few Indians, so many buffalo. He concluded that his attitude was indicative of his upbringing; because he had been raised among whites he considered himself white. Others saw him as a half-breed, but Joe knew this was solely a matter of black hair and swarthy skin. To Joe's way of thinking the only thing which truly differentiated him from other whites was his hump. He had Indian blood in him, but blood meant nothing. He suspected that all men had identical blood. The thing that created individual identity was the manner of one's raising, plus those all-important random elements he had explained to Cyrus so long ago. In Joe's case these were represented by his deformity, a mad foster-mother, an absent foster-father, a wild imagination, a bad temper, high intelligence and, lastly, the social difficulties imposed by his mixed parentage. All these things added up to Joe Cobden of St. Louis, Joe Buffalo of Kansas.

He ruminated thus whenever there was nothing to distract him, but it seemed that the harder he tried to assimilate the lessons to be learned from his life and build a concrete picture of himself, a sense of exactly where he stood in relation to the world, the more evanescent became his awareness of self. He knew he was unique, yet felt at the same time he was . . . nothing. Left undisturbed, Joe lost all sense of time and place. He would stare at the sky or the horizon and feel all conscious thought and emotion drain away like a retreating tide, taking with it the flotsam of ambition, pride, frustration, rage, the tangled kelp of determinant factors accumulated over seventeen years of living. Memory itself seemed to escape through sieve-like holes in his consciousness, left him an intangible phantom inside a shell of flesh astride a horse, a mere wisp, two staring eyes relaying nothing to the dormant brain behind. He saw nothing, felt nothing, heard nothing but a faint susurration from his damaged right ear, a steady, barely intrusive whispering reminiscent of a seashell the doctor had once held to his head. "Hear that, Joseph? The sound of the sea." And Joseph had heard it, a faraway magical booming of surf, and smiled with sheer pleasure that such a thing was possible. The doctor continued, "It isn't the sea at all, of course, merely air moving in the shell's interior, and the pumping of your own blood." Joseph refused to believe it; the sound he heard was that of the sea, the shell remembering its birthplace, evoking within its spiral chambers the sun-dappled shallows. Joe returned from these excursions with reluctance, summoned back to Kansas by an impatient toss of his gelding's head, a shout from the skinners, or the passing of a chill wind across his face. As the phenomenon became more commonplace he learned to recognise the symptoms of its approach, and would deliberately isolate himself to invite the wayward sensations inside his skull.

Of a more mundane nature, but no less intriguing, was the secondary subject of Joe's ponderings: one Calvin Puckett. This individual had been hired by Tubbs six months before. Thin, weasel-faced, he was an expert skinner, the best in the outfit. Tubbs and Joe maintained a bonus incentive to spur the men on, and it was usually Puckett and whomever he had paired with who won the prize at the end of each week. Yet every time the outfit returned to a railroad town to sell the hides Puckett, unlike the rest, did not fritter away his earnings on liquor and women. It was rumoured he sent a portion of his wages home, employing the services of a letter writer to address the envelope, since he could neither read nor write. He retained only enough for food and lodging, always of the cheapest, but despite his parsimony he apparently had no conception of the profit motive, appeared content simply to do his work for the satisfaction it gave him. He always presented himself for rehire before the outfit pulled out for another foray among the buffalo.

Puckett and Joe had exchanged not one word in all that time, yet Joe knew Puckett hated him, suspected that someday Puckett would attempt to do him harm. He often caught the skinner staring at him for no reason, over his plate at supper, across a half-skinned carcass, knife in hand, standing by a wagon or wandering about the camp. There appeared to be no motive for this behaviour; Joe was sure he had never seen Puckett until the day he joined the outfit, knew he had in no way offended the man. Yet Puckett stared on. Joe's first tremor of genuine alarm was prompted by the sight of Puckett staring at him while using the pedal operated grindstone to hone his skinning knife. The look on Puckett's face was one of purest loathing. His gaze dropped from Joe's face to his knife held against the scraping wheel, then quickly back to Joe, an unmistakable message. Joe's patience snapped. He went to Puckett, kicked his foot from the pedal, stood with hands on hips, daring Puckett to push the knife into his chest. For just a few seconds Puckett's face twisted, then assumed its usual sullen expression.

"What'd you do that for," he said.

"You know why."

"I never done nothin' to you." His voice was querulous, aggrieved, the voice of a child whose sandcastle has been kicked over for no reason. Joe wondered if he had made a mistake, decided he had not.

"But you'd like to, wouldn't you."

"What're you talkin' about?"

Joe felt anger building inside him at Puckett's fake bewilderment. The skinner would not admit to anything, that much was clear; his aim appeared to be intimidation by staring, rather than direct physical confrontation. Joe realised then that Puckett was probably a coward, just a pathetic illiterate who disliked Joe because of his hump, in all probability resented having to work under a cripple, could only express his contempt with looks. Joe was disgusted with himself for having allowed the skinner's puerile tactics to have such an effect upon him. He felt a fool. Puckett would deny any accusations Joe cared to make; nothing could be proven. He tried to draw a semblance of satisfaction from glaring wordlessly into Puckett's eyes until they flickered and bobbed sideways. There remained nothing more to say, no final taunt to be flung, no parting shot that would not have fallen hopelessly short. Joe turned abruptly and walked away, rehearsing a demand to Tubbs that Puckett's employment be terminated when next they hit town. He did not want the skinner anywhere near him, staring, always staring, like some dog unjustly punished which can neither understand nor forgive its master. Joe changed his mind as quickly as he had formulated the demand; no purpose would be served by getting rid of Puckett. It would not be a victory, would be quite the opposite. He must not allow the skinner to upset him. Ignore the fool, that was the answer. Acknowledging his stares, reacting to his mystifying hatred would only give Puckett a sense of achievement. He pushed the entire incident to the back of his mind, turned a key, thought of other things.

For long hours after he had wrapped himself in blankets that night Calvin Puckett lay awake. Joe's challenge had upset him. For half a year he had been observing the hunchback, thinking his attentions unnoticed. The events of this afternoon had awakened him to the true state of things. He had been humiliated, but the experience was no novelty. Calvin Puckett was disliked by men, disliked by women, had never known a day's happiness in his life. His one accomplishment lay in being able to skin a buffalo faster than most. He had been born on a farm in Pennsylvania twenty-three years ago, had been beaten into submission as an unpaid worker by his father, had been unable to enlist the aid of his mother, who was herself mortally afraid of her husband. His various brothers and sisters bullied Calvin, took delight in tormenting him over his inferiority as youngest, therefore weakest, of the brood. The farm was not run successfully, and Abner Puckett fell into debt. He beat all the children at different times, but Calvin was his favourite target; he was small, ugly, whining, a natural recipient of casual violence. His father did not hate him during those early years, simply used him as a means of relieving his disappointment and anger as dreams of financial solvency receded. One of the cows broke its leg in a freak accident in the barn, and Calvin's nose was flattened; a crop failed to meet its expected yield, and Calvin's head was pounded against a wall; the oldest boy deserted the farm to fight in the war, and Calvin's entire body was beaten until blue, two of his ribs cracked. He hid in the woods until he had mended then crept home, starving, defeated, and was beaten again for his lack of gumption.

Calvin had never understood the notion of filial piety; he hated his father, had always hated him, and his father gradually came to hate him in return. Calvin waited. He had never been to church, had attended school for only three days before the oldest boy enlisted, necessitating the removal of Calvin from the schoolhouse to attend those chores so suddenly abandoned. He had no acquaintance with the Bible, but Calvin knew there was a god somewhere up above who would not tolerate such injustice as was heaped upon him at the farm. He waited for God to strike his father dead, prayed for deliverance, went about his tasks with stoic submission, avoiding his father's eye, avoiding, if possible, his fists and boots. One of his sisters ran off with a pedlar. Calvin considered hiding in the woods for a few days until the furore had died down, decided against it and took his ritual beating without flinching. When his father had exhausted himself Calvin pointed at him with a trembling finger. "God'll punish you," he said, and was knocked down again for his temerity. For several weeks thereafter Calvin's faith in God wavered; however, since he had nothing with which to substitute the unsteady edifice of belief he continued to hope and pray, albeit with less confidence than before.

On a sultry and overcast day in August 1867, God rewarded Calvin's fortitude by striking down Abner Puckett with a lightning bolt as he trudged across a field, an axe balanced on his shoulder. Calvin had not been privileged to witness the administering of divine retribution, but was the first to see his father's body in all its charred glory. The axe head was fused with the skull, creating the impression that Abner's brain had been of metal; the handle, still in the grasp of roasted fingers, was smouldering yet, as were the overalls covering the blackened body. A grass fire had flared briefly in the few yards surrounding the corpse, but had been thrown back from itself by fortuitous winds, probably a secondary benediction from God, who would turn the wind rather than see Calvin's inheritance reduced to ashes. Calvin sank to his knees and clasped his hands, offered thanks to his saviour (God, who had literally saved him from Abner, not Jesus, whose dubious self-sacrifice would not have been comprehended by Calvin had he heard of it) and was answered by the rolling, reverberating, mighty voice of God disguised as thunder, revealing itself only to Calvin.

Having had God's personal interest in his welfare revealed in so startling a fashion, Calvin began praying for the death of his mother and remaining brother (the oldest having failed to return from the war, although not officially listed among the dead) and awaited their imminent demise. Once these two were gone only his sisters would remain, and they, being female, would not inherit the Puckett farm; every acre he had watered with his sweat would be Calvin's and rightly so. He prayed and prayed and watched the skies, especially during stormy weather. But no punishment was meted out to those standing in his path. Three years passed. The brother who had gone to war returned by way of New York, Liverpool, Capetown, Sydney, Honolulu, Rio and Boston. He apologised for not having written, was accepted back into the bosom of the family without hesitation. To cap Calvin's frustration his mother remarried. His stepfather had two sons of his own, both older than Calvin. Could it be that God's attention was elsewhere? Calvin prayed for guidance. His future did not appear promising.

At last God revealed His design for Calvin's destiny. Wandering in the woods one day Calvin looked down and saw an arrow of stones pointing westward. He knew God had placed it there. Two small boys from a neighbouring farm were in fact responsible. They had been told this was an old Indian hunter's way of letting those following behind know which direction he had taken without their having to bother examining bent blades of grass and so forth. The boys had built the device for their own amusement. The arrow just so happened to point west. Ignorant of this, Calvin felt the reassuring hand of God in the breeze plucking at his already thinning hair, knew he must hasten to obey the Word or, more appropriately, the Sign.

He broke the news to his family. They breathed a collective sigh of relief; none of them liked him. His stepfather presented him with five dollars and a hearty handshake. "There's plenty of money to be made out west," Calvin was assured. The stepfather had no such knowledge, but did not want Calvin to change his mind. Calvin packed a bag. One of his sisters actually accompanied him to the nearest road. Calvin was touched; he had never suspected she had a sentimental attachment to him. For the first time in his life Calvin felt affection for another human being, an emotion formerly reserved exclusively for the Almighty. He bade her goodbye, blinking back an errant tear, and took the first step on his epic, God-ordained journey. His sister watched until he had disappeared around a bend, then returned to the farmhouse. Her mother looked up from the stove.

"Did you watch him like I said?"

"Yes. He went away."

"He didn't just go off into the woods the way he does?"

"He went down the road."

"You're sure, now?"

"I seen him walk till I can't see him no more."

191

"That's a good girl."

The way west was hard. Calvin suffered at the hands of men who considered him a fool. He knew he was not, but lacked the words to explain himself. Calvin retreated into ever-deeper silences. He reached Kansas and decided his journeying had continued long enough. He required surcease from torment. Too many had mocked him. The beatings delivered by his father were preferable; pain left the body after a while, but cruel remarks and cutting laughter seemed to be reborn with all their original intensity whenever Calvin remembered them, and he remembered every such incident. The lot of God's agent was not an easy one, but Calvin endured with fortitude, as he had been trained to do by the business of living.

One of a succession of jobs he had held on his journey westward had been that of butcher's apprentice in Cincinnati. Calvin had assisted at hog slaughtering on the farm, and applied himself to the butchering job with all the aptitude at his disposal. His employer had reluctantly been obliged to dismiss him after Calvin fell into argument with a customer over the weight of some meat. The customer accused Calvin of cheating, something Calvin would never have dreamed of. He denied the charge, deeply offended. The customer insisted, and Calvin became enraged that he, God's protégé, should be slandered so. He began to spit foam, fell to the floor twitching and thrashing in a thoroughly alarming manner. He was unsure of his actions during the next few days, but found himself bound for Kansas, and there, eventually, was given work by Quincy Tubbs on the basis of his butchering experience.

On the evening before the Tubbs-Cobden outfit was due to leave town for the open prairie, Calvin was awakened by a voice inside his head. "Beware the crooked man," the voice said. Calvin sat up and worried over the possible interpretations of this peculiar phrase. Was God warning him that his new employer was crooked, the kind who would cheat on wages? No, that could not be it; Calvin was not particularly concerned with accruing wealth, for pursuance of God's work was reward in itself. He fell asleep again, confident that all would be made clear when the time was right.

He did not have to wait for long. The very next day, as the outfit assembled in the street, a hunchback rode up to Mr. Tubbs and began speaking with him. Calvin knew this was the crooked man of whom he had been warned, there could be no doubt on that. He hoped Mr. Tubbs was aware of the danger he was in, talking to something like that. Calvin's concern quickly turned to bewilderment when it became obvious that the hunchback would be accompanying them. It was several days before Calvin understood that the monstrous little man was none other than his employer's partner! He could scarcely credit Mr. Tubbs' foolishness in allying himself with so wicked a creature. He flinched whenever the crooked man looked in his direction, with his devilish bulging brow and deep-sunk eyes and that ungodly hump on his back. Calvin felt himself in the presence of Satan or, at the very least one of his imps; God would not have warned him for anything less.

He watched, he waited, but the crooked man did nothing out of the ordinary. Calvin learned from the men that he was considered one of the best buffalo-hunters in the business. Calvin waited for God to reveal Joe's true identity. It did not happen. He waited, thinking himself unobtrusive in his surveillance until events proved this was not so. The crooked man had boldly challenged him, but Calvin had given nothing away. It was inevitable that evil would sooner or later scent the presence of good. From now on things would be very different between them. Calvin would have to be careful how he stepped now that the crooked man knew he had an adversary in the camp. Joe ignored Calvin, Calvin bided his time. And more buffalo fell.

CHAPTER FOURTEEN

The winter of 1872–3 promised to be the worst in living memory. By mid-December snowdrifts up to six feet deep had blanketed most of Kansas, transforming the plains into a white Sahara. Hunting would be too hazardous a pursuit until March. The shrinking herds stood as they had for centuries, shaggy heads into the wind, stolid, enduring, unmolested, blinking the frozen rime from their eyes, patiently awaiting the return of the sun. It was to be the last respite they would know.

Joe Cobden made a momentous decision; during this time of enforced idleness he would return to St. Louis and confront the doctor with evidence of his success in the outside world. The thought made Joe's heart race with a heady amalgam of anticipation and apprehension. He informed Tubbs of his plans, arranged to meet at winter's end here in Dodge. Conscious of his reputation, and of the unusual appearance which promoted and enhanced it, Joe had set aside a particularly luxuriant buffalo hide for preparation as a new coat. Instead, he would take the heavy robe home as a gift, a symbolic offering, a means of exculpation and conciliation. He paid for three tickets, purchasing the right to occupy the length of an entire seat; Joe had not forgotten his cramped discomfort on the journey out to Kansas.

The locomotive ploughed through a sea of snow, an iron prow attached to the cowcatcher. On several occasions progress was delayed by snowdrifts of forbidding depth. These were shovelled from the tracks by hand, a task to which Joe gave his strength along with other passengers so inclined. The hitches and halts, far from creating an atmosphere of impatience and exasperation aboard the train, were instrumental in welding diverse personalities whose only mutuality was their easterly journeying into a band of brothers. Bottles of whiskey were passed from hand to hand with boisterous camaraderie, the inefficient stove at the end of the carriage roundly cursed along with the blighted landscape of white beyond the frosted windows. Joe was recognised as Joe Buffalo by two men whom he had never laid eyes upon, and had to endure a drunken eulogy to his talent as a killer of beasts. The buffalo robe was passed around, admired and, naturally enough under the circumstances, coveted. His fellow passengers were prepared to overlook Joe's unfortunate ancestry in the light of his proven manhood, established despite a hump and Indian blood, substantiated by his reputation and, above all, by the gun standing at his side. This, too, was fondled appreciatively despite Joe's misgivings; even now he half-expected someone to scrutinise the Sharpe's and claim ownership. As a precaution against that possibility he had embedded his initials into the polished stock with tiny copper tacks, where they shone with the bogus gleam of mica in quartz.

Joe felt himself to be the most fraudulent of characters, a charlatan performing for a willing audience. Why this should be so, he could not understand, and to erase his doubts he played his role to the hilt. He told stories of his most successful hunts, enhancing the details considerably for dramatic effect, since there are few things less exciting than the slaughter of dumb animals who offer themselves so readily to the gun. Someone wrapped himself in the buffalo robe and galloped up and down the aisle with Joe in close pursuit, aiming his unloaded rifle, cursing elaborately whenever he missed. His prey uttered comical mooing sounds, never having come within hearing distance of a live buffalo, which does nothing but snort. This was what Joe had fought for: recognition, the approbation of men, tall men, hearty, open men with full moustaches and wrinkled eyes, with sturdy handclasps and ready laughter; men's men. And Joe was accepted among them. His self doubt was a foolish thing, a throwback to the past, a ghost to be banished with a confident wave of the hand. When Joe had at last fallen into a drunken sleep, one of the travellers described him as "a real interesting little critter."

Three days in transit, Joe arrived in St. Louis and hired a hackney to convey him to DeWitte Street. His footsteps slowed as he neared the doctor's home, the boundless optimism and confidence he had accrued on the train now leaking away. This was no conquering hero returning to accolades and wreaths of laurel; no Penelope awaited him behind the weathered façade. Joe felt the guilt and embarrassment of a schoolboy sent home with an unsatisfactory report card. He stopped by the gate, looked at the house for a long while, then went to the front door. His knock was timid, produced no result. He tried again, mustering strength enough to dislodge flakes of paint from the door. Had the place been so dilapidated when he left? He looked behind him, expecting to see every window across the street occupied by curiosity-seekers, but the panes were blank, backed for the most part by curtains drawn to keep out the cold. Joe stamped his feet, knocked again, pounded until he heard a bolt withdrawn.

The door was opened by a seemingly unchanged Hattie; no, there were deeper lines alongside her nose, and her mouth seemed thinner, more determined somehow. Joe held his breath, waited for some flicker of recognition. How could she stand there and say nothing? At first shy, then irritated, Joe nodded, smiled, hefted the bundled robe further up on to his shoulder in an effort to convey his wish to enter.

"Hello, Hattie."

When she did not respond he lost all patience and attempted to step past her. She blocked his way with her arm, slapped her hand hard against the door-jamb and held it there firmly.

"Where you think you're going?"

"Into the hall."

"No, you ain''t. You turn right around and go back where you come from."

"This *is* where I come from."

"Not no more. You get now, I'm telling you."

Joe set the robe down, rested the Sharpe's butt beside his boots. "I'm coming inside, Hattie. It's cold out here."

"First, you got to get past me. That ain't going to be easy."

"You're letting cold into the house."

Hattie removed her arm to close the door. Joe jammed his foot into place before it could be slammed shut. His heavy boots absorbed the blow, refused to be dislodged by several more attempts at slamming, then by repeated kicking from Hattie's boots, themselves no velvet slippers. He waited for her to tire, then pushed the door wide open, picked up the robe and went inside. Hattie walked away in disgust, leaving him to close the door for himself. He went to the living room, dumped his bundle on the sofa, propped the rifle against the wall. None of the furniture had been moved; all sat as before in the gloomy winter light seeping through the windows. Joe noted the panes were filthy on the outside, the grime overlaid by sparkling snow crystals. He went to the library.

The same books sat on the same shelves, the aroma of their leather bindings overcoming the mustiness of undisturbed air. Here it had all begun, the cultivation of a mind lying fallow, wanting only the sower's seed. Here Joe had cast himself as protagonist in paper worlds, places more real than actuality; here he now stood, having realised the only heroic role available to him, and recollected his juvenile questings from the comfortable hollows of the armchair. Full circle, he thought. He had journeyed from the imagined to the substantive, yet the transition afforded him less satisfaction than expected, left him with a puzzling sense of unfulfilment at having become the product of his own devising. It should have felt grander, much grander, to stand here at journey's start like some mariner having circumnavigated the globe; instead he felt more akin to a snake devouring its own tail. He had gone nowhere, accomplished nothing, become a creature of self-regard. He squashed the thought, pushed it away with such force his fingers flailed at the air. He was Joe Buffalo, had earned his name and reputation! No one could say it wasn't so.

He went to the doctor's room, knocked, entered. The room was empty, neat, redolent of mustiness and closed windows. Nothing had changed. Joe followed the sound of banging pots and pans to the kitchen.

"Where is he?"

"Where you think a doctor is this time of day?"

"He still works at the infirmary?"

"He does what a good man should."

Joe took this as some kind of rebuke. "Do you know what I've been doing all this time, Hattie?"

"Don't know and don't care."

She kept her back to him. Her truculence began to amuse him. He sat on a chair, rested his elbows on the table. "I've been hunting buffalo." No reply. She busied herself doing nothing in particular in the pantry. He drummed his fingers with impatience. "Did you ever hear the name Joe Buffalo? That's me. They gave me that name when I got to be top dog."

"Ain't impressed by no dog."

"Got anything for me to eat? I've come a long way."

"No longer'n it is to go right back there."

"Hattie, somehow I get the feeling you aren't glad to see me."

She let a pan fall with a clatter, turned on him suddenly. "You went and broke his heart. You went ahead and done it deliberate, even stole money to do just what you wanted and never mind nobody else, just up and stole and left and never give a damn. Well, don't expect no welcome home, not from me, and not from him. If I was you, I'd walk on out that door and never come back. I won't say nothing. He don't have to know you ever come by."

"I'm not going anywhere. I've come back to see how

things are and . . . make amends. I'm not leaving until I've done that."

"You don't have the littlest notion of what you done." She folded her arms and glared at him. There would be no food forthcoming.

Joe stood. "This is my home, too."

"No, it ain't. It never was and it ain't now."

He returned to the library, flung himself into the arm-chair and sulked, was soon fast asleep. He dreamed of climbing the stairs, the forbidden stairs to the upper floor, of opening the door to the dog-whimperer's room, seeing not a madwoman or even a dog, not even a room; he saw a broad plain, a piece of Kansas, and on the plain a million buffalo silently grazed, and far away, sprouting from the herd was a tree, a tall tree without leaves on its many, many branches, and at the top of the tree fluttered some kind of flag. He came closer, the buffalo parting to let him by, and when at last the tree was looming above him he still could not discern exactly what kind of flag it was that floated so lazily far above, even though there was no wind. And then the branches and boughs parted and he saw it was no flag at all, but a fish, a long and beautiful fish of reddish gold, its nose to the topmost branch, tail switching languidly from side to side in the breeze that was not there. The fish knew he was below, for it moved its fins and slowly rolled side-ways until one huge eye was looking down at Joe, a wise and round and unblinking eye.

"Wake up."

The doctor stood above him. A lamp had been lit. Joe got stiffly to his feet, unsure if he should offer his hand. The doctor was older, thinner. "Am I expected to kill the fatted calf?" His voice had become weaker, but had retained its corrosive edge.

"I came back to see how things are."

The doctor's eyebrow lifted. "Things are as you see them." A long silence. Joe swallowed the saliva accumulat-ing in his throat, an audible click. He rummaged in his pocket. "I owe you some money." He counted out a wad of bills, offered it to the doctor.

"What is this?"

"The money I owe you. Ninety-three dollars, plus interest. I've made it an even hundred."

"What money?"

"The money . . . I stole."

"Ah, yes. The money you *stole.*" The word was painstakingly enunciated to reinforce the barbed sarcasm in his voice. "Yes, I remember now. You *stole* some money from me, didn't you?"

"Here it is, every dollar. Plus interest."

The cash was still in his hand, the hand hovering halfway between the doctor and himself. No move was made to accept it; the doctor did not even look at it, instead stared into Joe's face. "I remember it quite clearly. I came home and found Hattie extremely upset. She said you'd gone, and taken some money with you. I'm not sure which she was more upset about, your leaving or the theft."

"The theft, I'd say."

"I would agree with you. And here you are back again."

"Do you want it or not?"

"Want it?" The eyebrow again, a look of deliberate bafflement.

"The money. Do you want the money or don't you?"

He thrust the cash at the doctor, who ignored it still. Both eyebrows were raised now. "Of course I want my money. I'm a poor man. I can't afford not to take back money that was *stolen* from me."

But still he made no move to accept what was offered. Joe slapped the bills angrily on to the table beside the lamp. Very well, he'd asked for this, deserved it, would suffer for it; let the old man enjoy his discomfort if it would do any good. Man and boy glared at each other as they had in the past. Nothing has changed, thought Joe, and smiled weakly, snorted through his nose to let the doctor know he would not allow himself to be intimidated indefinitely.

"These aren't the actual pieces of paper I *stole,* of course.

The *stolen* money was spent a long time ago, but this should do as a replacement. New cash is as good as *stolen* cash.''

"Are you attempting to make some kind of point?''

"I took it, I've brought it back. What do you want, blood?''

"That should not be necessary. Have you eaten?''

"Hattie wouldn't give me anything.''

"Hattie is a loyal woman. You offended her more than you did me. We'll have supper, and you'll tell me all.''

Hattie served them in icy silence. The doctor spoke of improved conditions at the infirmary and the latest medical developments in Europe. Joe volunteered no information about his travels, waited to be asked. To blurt it all out like a child was unthinkable under the circumstances. He should not have told Hattie he was a hunter; she had probably already told the doctor, hence his apparent lack of curiosity. I won't brag, he told himself, I'll wait for the right moment and let it fall casually, not try to impress him; he'd never admit to being impressed anyway.

"How is your back nowadays, if I may ask a personal question?''

"Sometimes it hurts. Not all the time.''

"That may stop soon. The male body ceases to grow past the age of eighteen or thereabouts. How old are you now?''

"Seventeen and a half.''

"Then you may find some relief in the near future. Of course the very nature of the deformity may give you pain for the rest of your life. I do not claim to be an expert on the condition.''

"If it keeps hurting, it keeps hurting.''

"An eminently practical philosophy, Joseph, and so poetically rendered. Do you find you have time to read while going about your business?''

"Not much.'' He waited for a response, received none. "I spend all day in the saddle.''

"Are you some kind of cattle herdsman?''

Joe ground his teeth. "I'm a buffalo-hunter. You may have noticed my gun in the living room.''

"I confess I did not. We'll retire there shortly and you'll show me. This stew is delicious, don't you think?"

The doctor allowed Joe to start a fire while he lit two lamps, then seated himself. When the kindling began to burn evenly Joe added more wood. The act made him think of Cyrus. He fetched his rifle and presented it to the doctor for examination. He pronounced it a "formidable looking weapon" and handed it back without hefting it for balance or raising it to his shoulder and sighting at an imaginary target—the things an enthusiast would have done. He had despised guns since the war. Joe was offended, thought the doctor had been deliberately offhand in his dismissal of the prized Sharpe's. He returned it to its place against the wall, dropped into a wingbacked chair and scowled at the fire. The doctor lit a cigar, offered the humidor to Joe.

"I don't smoke."

"Very wise. It tends to promote shortness of breath in later years. I still buy the finest, despite my penury. Every man must have one foible, and tobacco is mine. Do you have a foible, Joseph?"

"Yes, I'm an inveterate optimist."

The doctor brayed with laughter, his first uncontrolled display since waking Joe. He bent over and delivered himself of a hacking cough, his eyes watering. Joe momentarily considered leaving his seat to pound the doctor's back. He stayed where he was. The doctor brought his breathing under control, placed the cigar on a smoking-stand and gazed at the fire, for all the world as if he were alone in the room. Joe observed him surreptitiously. The man had aged. The firelight was kind, but the hollow cheeks and temples, the wattled folds of flesh beneath the jaw, these could not be gilded with the firmness of youth. Joe felt young and hard and strong. I'll still be young when this man dies, he thought. The doctor sighed, a long, wheezing sigh that set his pipes vibrating. Joe was alarmed, then disgusted (the sound conveyed a picture of clotted stalagtites of phlegm in the doctor's chest), then sympathetic. He rose, fetched the robe and draped it over the doctor's knees. The air was cold despite the fire.

"What is this?"

"A buffalo robe. One of the best."

"Did you kill this one yourself?"

"Yes. It'll keep you warm."

"Excessive warmth can prove debilitating."

Joe raised his eyes to the ceiling. "If you get too hot just take it off, or tell me and I'll take it off."

"I am not yet a cripple. I am capable of removing a robe from my own lap."

"Good. I'm glad to hear it."

He sat down again, fingers wrestling each other for supremacy. The fire crackled comfortingly, the coals glowed. Joe found himself thinking of fish without knowing why. The doctor seemed to be invested with vigour again, turning suddenly to Joe, his face, for the last fifteen minutes perfectly blank, now lively with enquiry. "And what will you do for a living, Joseph?"

Joe, startled from torpor, struggled for an answer. "A living?"

"Yes, yes, what will you do? Have you spent time considering the possibilities?"

Was the man senile? "I told you. I'm a buffalo-hunter."

"But when they have all been killed, what then?"

Joe chuckled knowingly, a trifle patronisingly. "They couldn't be killed in a thousand years. You haven't seen them. They're everywhere.

"An inexhaustible supply?"

"I believe so."

"And you will pursue this vocation until you fall from the saddle with old age?"

"Until I get tired of it. Or until I've saved enough to quit."

"Is this hunting a lucrative profession?"

"I've got over fifteen thousand dollars in the Western Kansas Pioneer Bank."

"Surely that is an exaggeration, Joseph."

"No."

The one word, delivered with a smug little smile, convinced the doctor he was not being lied to. He returned his gaze to the coals. The creature had done it; twisted, ugly, aggressively anti-social, the foundling waif had crushed the doctor's every hope and dream, crushed them to powder, then gone on to wrest a small fortune from a place no civilised man would care to visit, had bludgeoned his way to financial security as some kind of glorified abattoir slaughterman. Something was very much amiss here. The doctor was outraged by the implications of Joe's casual boast; it could not be that a wasted education coupled with a wilfully obstinate rejection of all normal mores should result so easily in success—worldly success to be sure, but yes, undeniably success as that word is interpreted throughout most of the world. The hunchback had become rich, would get richer. It was unbelievable. Bitterness washed over the doctor, flooded him with indignant sweat. He kicked off the robe. Joe rescued it from the predations of sparks. The doctor gripped the arms of his chair. He, a man of outstanding intellect and unimpeachable moral integrity, had through devotion to the poor and needy gradually become mired in the nether world of medicine for the masses. His reward had been a mad wife and wayward son, blighted expectations, a crumbling home, old age. It was not fair, and it had all begun with an impulsive stroll through a graveyard. He stared at Joe. As I have fallen, so this creature has risen. Now he mocks me, treats me like a decrepit fool, condescends to me; a hunchbacked Indian condescends to *me!* How, *how* was it possible? He watched as Joe's face shifted and swam in the flickering light, the bulging forehead an affront to the doctor's finely tuned sense of the aesthetic; a monster, a thing of muscle and sinew, a Caliban, probably vicious when aroused.

"It would have been the gutter," he said.

Joe looked up. "Pardon?"

"It would have been the gutter for you if I had not taken you in."

"Probably. I'm grateful."

"Are you, Joseph? Are you truly grateful? You have done nothing but defy me all your life."

"I'd prefer not to rake over cold ashes."

"Cold ashes, yes. . . ." That was the state to which his life had been reduced. Every day he assisted the sick toward recovery, if that were possible, made their last hours comfortable if it was not, every day came closer to the fact of his own death. He was only fifty-four years old, knew he looked a decade older. Suffering and sacrifice were the cause. He had much to be ashamed of, much to be proud of; the balance should have been equal, but was not. Perhaps, he thought, I resent him for his youth alone. Would I dare to be a hunchback for the sake of renewed vigour and a weighty balance of years left to enjoy? But enjoyment was surely not part of a hunchback's lot.

"Are you happy, Joseph?"

"No, but I'm halfway satisfied."

"Be so kind as to explain."

"I mean I feel I've accomplished something against the odds."

"Do you really? And what, precisely, is it that you have accomplished?"

Joe considered the doctor's question. How to answer truthfully without sounding like a braggart? How to convey the nature of the obstacles set in his path by prejudice and mischance without resorting to self-pity? He cleared his throat. "I made a place for myself in a world of straight backs. It wasn't easy."

The doctor considered Joe's answer. It was simple, honest, satisfactory. He felt resentment anyway. Together they watched the fire burn down without talking further.

For several days Joe attempted to mollify Hattie by chopping wood for the stove and chatting with her. She gradually relented, fascinated despite herself by his tales of Indians and treeless plains and thundering herds and cattle towns modelled on Sodom and Gomorrah.

"You must be right glad to be away from those parts."

"For a while, yes. It's nice to be home. But I'm going back."

"The doctor ain't going to like that. You left one time already. He don't have nobody but you. He's getting to be an old man now."

"I've got a business to attend to, Hattie. I can't just walk out on my partner."

"If you got the kind of cash you say you got, why don't you set up a business here in St. Louis? Then you and the doctor can be together."

"He doesn't need me that badly. We're not as close as you seem to think. Doesn't he have any friends?"

"just some other doctor like himself that works at the infirmary. Sometimes he goes to visit over at his house. But that ain't the same as having your own boy to talk to."

"I'm not his boy, Hattie. I never was."

"That's as may be, but he don't have nobody else."

Hattie wanted Joe back in St. Louis to be available when the doctor died (not long now, in her opinion) and so inherit and inhabit the house on DeWitte Street. With luck he would keep her employed there. She was well past middle age herself, and did not want to leave this place after almost thirty years. She felt she belonged here, the woman of the house. If Joe insisted on living in the west, he would sell the house and Hattie's life would be changed; at her time of life it was bound to be a change for the worse. She had thrown away the bone and skin conjure when Joe left, had not bothered to replace it now that he was back. Hattie was impressed with her own daring, and believed some good might come of it. She listened attentively while Joe talked, and gradually introduced into the conversation her theme of Obligation; Joe must stay, Joe must be a good son and look after his father, and when the father was gone Joe must look after his father's estate and all appurtenances thereof (herself included, was the implication). Hattie was practical; she had worked long and hard here and did not wish to be cast out to find a new way of life for herself, not while there was a chance to continue with the old.

For his part, Joe was determined not to be trapped by a sense of responsibility. He had come to visit, not to re-establish himself in the house. He would leave when good and ready. Nevertheless, he wondered if Hattie was right about the doctor needing his company. It was not apparent in his behaviour; since that first evening he had been civil to Joe, but scarcely brimming over with conviviality. Every night after supper he retired to his room to read, airily informing Joe he had lately rediscovered the benefits of literature as an anodyne for the physical weariness and emotional strain engendered by the nature of his work at the infirmary. He consented to use the buffalo robe for warmth, claiming it meant he could burn less coal, thereby saving money. Joe offered to meet the cost of fuel but was politely refused, was reminded that he had returned the money he *stole* and was therefore under no obligation.

Relations between the two quickly reached a frosty impasse. Joe grew bored. He toyed with the idea of visiting a theatre, but lacked the confidence as well as suitable clothing. He told himself he should not waste his time with frivolity anyway, without knowing if the playhouses of St. Louis were offering asinine melodramas or Shakespeare. He began to read again, but soon found it is not a distraction that can be pursued through the evening as well as the day without exhausting the eyes and imagination of the reader. He wondered if he should return to Kansas earlier than planned, then rejected the thought; it would be tantamount to defeat. He would not be driven from the house by the doctor's silence. At the same time he felt responsible for the old man's well-being, correctly interpreted this as the offspring of guilt; like many a person before him, Joe was learning that a crime committed within the family requires not only commensurate repayment but crippling interest before expiation can even be considered by either party. Maybe he should explore the possibilities of the doctor's friendship with his fellow physician; if it transpired that the doctor had a companion should he need one, then Joe could leave St. Louis with a clear, or at least a less muddied, conscience.

"Hattie tells me you have a friend at the infirmary."

"A friend?"

"Another doctor."

"That would be Dr. Hopkins."

"She says you sometimes visit him, have supper at his place."

"Yes." His voice was patient, bland, deliberately unco-operative.

Joe took a breath, told himself not to lose his temper, even managed a smile. "I just wondered when you were going to introduce us."

"Introduce you?"

"I suppose he knows I exist."

"There was a time when all of St. Louis, all those who counted, that is, knew of your existence. You were very nearly a *cause célèbre*, Joseph. Of course that was before the war, when such things were considered of importance."

"You mean my being half-Indian?"

"Precisely. Many people considered me mad."

"It must have taken courage. . . ."

"My own wife did not approve."

"I'm sorry."

"No need for sympathy. Every man bears full responsi-bility for his actions. I acted contrary to the social mores of the day and was crushed, at home and professionally, crushed like an insect. I bear no one ill will as a result of my failure. It is kismet. Do you know what that means, Joseph?"

"No."

"It means fate."

"Are you going to introduce me to this Dr. Hopkins or not?"

"Why are you so anxious to meet my colleague?"

208

"I'd like to look at someone else beside yourself and Hattie."

"An honest reply. Do you suppose Dr. Hopkins would wish to meet a buffalo-hunter?"

"I don't know. Why don't you ask him?"

"Very well. I see your insistence is not to be gainsaid."

"Is he married?"

"Dr. Hopkins is a widower, like myself."

"So I don't have to dress up or anything."

"Dress up?"

"I mean, is he the formal type?"

"No one expects a frontiersman to wear a Prince Albert, Joseph."

"Good, because I don't own one."

"I had assumed that was the case."

CHAPTER FIFTEEN

The meeting took place three nights later. Joseph accompanied the doctor to a grand street in Crève-Coeur. The house their hackney deposited them before was of the type usually referred to as "tasteful", that is, the home of a cultured and wealthy man. They approached the door, a massive slab of ebony with a brass lion's head knocker; elegant lanterns of wrought iron blazed welcomingly on either side. Joe had been informed of Dr. Hopkins' charitable work at the infirmary, of the private practice he still maintained four days per week. Joe had assumed this meant a string of rough men and broken, impoverished women entering via the back door, the same kind of sad parade that had graced Dr. Cobden's surgery years ago, before he had devoted himself fully to the infirmary. But this house, with its fluted columns, its neatly trimmed hedges and whitewashed windowsills, would never receive such woebegone clientele. Joe felt a pang of alarm, a suspicion that the doctor had somehow played him false. He was wearing the clothes he had come to St. Louis in, travel-worn, frontier clothing; if the interior of the house matched its façade he would look foolish indeed. The doctor rapped stoutly with the ring in the lion's snarling mouth, and the door was opened without delay by an elderly Negro.

"Good evening, Bartholomew. How is life treating you?"

"Tolerable well, Doctor."

They entered, handed over their coats and hats. The butler's face registered no surprise as Joe's heavy buffalo coat was laid across his arms. "Dr. Hopkins is expecting you, sir. Just go right on through."

The doctor strode confidently away, Joe at his heels, furious with himself for having set this farce in motion. The plush wallpaper and fine carpeting intimidated him, the obvious ease with which the doctor passed through the various rooms, each richly furnished, irritated him beyond measure, made him want to thrust his grimy boot between those long legs and bring him down. The doctor drew aside both wings of a pair of sliding doors and stepped into a handsomely appointed living room. A man of medium height, middle age and unprepossessing appearance rose from a settee, flung out his arms dramatically.

"William! Sit down, man, sit down. You must be chilled."

Joe squirmed for several seconds while pleasantries regarding the weather were exchanged. The doctor turned. "My foster-son, Joseph. Joseph, my good friend and colleague, Dr. Hopkins."

Joseph's hand shot out. "Pleased to meet you, sir." He waited for Hopkins' eye to roam across his hump and/or western attire, was surprised to have his gaze met with a strength and directness equal to the pumping handshake. "Welcome to my home, Joseph. William has told us a great deal about you. We're most anxious to hear of your adventures on the plains."

Joe grinned weakly. Us? We? There were others in the house? He would dearly have loved to floor the doctor with a blow for having failed to warn him. It would be of no use to complain, now or later—"But, Joseph, you simply asked if he was married, not if he had sired a family." He would have to make the best of an awkward situation. He prayed there would be no small children, creatures of guileless curiosity and thoughtless questions: "What's that thing on your back?" "That is a secret compartment into which I stuff annoying little snotbrains like you, sonny."

"Sit down, both of you. A little brandy to cut the cold from your bones?"

"Just what the doctor ordered."

It was a ritual question and reply, and their laughter had a well-honed familiarity to it. Joe joined in a nervous heartbeat too late. They settled themselves around a generous fire, delicate crystal winking in their hands. Hopkins beamed happily. "Charlotte will be down presently, I should think." Joe smothered a groan; oh Jesus, oh shit, it was going to be a woman who gaped unbelievingly at him, ten times, a hundred times worse than the prospect of a man's frank stare. He resisted the temptation to flee the room. Perhaps this Charlotte was Hopkins' sister, a shrivelled old maid, a spinster whose atrophied sexuality would not threaten him with rejection.

"Are the winters in Kansas as harsh as this, Joseph?"

"Uh . . . yes. Much worse." He plunged his lips into his glass to avoid elaboration. When was he going to see her? The doctors unknowingly eased his pain by talking of medical matters, to whit, the medieval practice of bloodletting by leeches and lancet, still recommended by a great many of their fellow physicians—a circumstance both men deplored. "Blood is the river of life, not sewage to be disposed of," declared Hopkins. "True, so true," murmured his companion. Joe's river was at full flood, rushing in crimson torrents beneath the skin of his face, a surging assisted by brandy. Perhaps she would be cross-eyed as well as ancient or, better yet, club-footed! No, that would only result in mutual embarrassment; mere plainness would suffice.

"Are frontier doctors qualified for their work, Joseph? Have you had occasion to avail yourself of their services?"

"No . . . uh . . . not me. Sometimes someone gets shot, or snakebit, or gets drunk and squats on his own spurs, and a doctor gets called if there's one around. I suppose most of them get by on luck rather than expertise. Maybe I'm doing them an injustice. I really don't know. . . ."

The door was opening, a woman entering the room. Joe's voice tapered off into fish-like mouthings. The most fearful of his expectations were confirmed; she was not more than twenty years old, and discouragingly, depressingly pretty. "Ah, Charlotte," beamed Hopkins, and rose from his chair, closely followed by Cobden and Joe, whose teeth already were grinding the pulp of his fear to bile that trickled in a burning stream down to his guts. Her dark hair was free of fashionable ringlets and ribbons, was parted centrally and arranged at her neck in a loose bundle (not pulled back tight and bunned, like a spinster aunt's) and from it had escaped—whether by artifice or by accident, Joe could not say—a provocatively stray tendril that fell to her shoulder. Her dress was simple, elegant, plum coloured, and revealed by its nipped waist the fact that her figure was slender and shapely. Joe stared at her face, searched desperately for flaws, but found not one in the regular features and warm, open smile.

"Good evening, Dr. Cobden. Do forgive my tardiness."

"Good evening, my dear. There is nothing to forgive, I assure you."

His hand, which had waved deprecatingly to dismiss her apology, now gestured to the hunchback attempting to hide behind transparent air, eyes glued to Charlotte, a sickly grin on his lips. "May I present to you my foster-son, Joseph. Joseph, Miss Charlotte Hopkins."

She bobbed her head briefly, smiled wider. "Most pleased to make your acquaintance."

Joe had already begun extending his hand before realising he was not expected to grasp her dainty palm, merely to nod in return, a modified courtly bow. He arrested the progress of his hand in mid flight, altered its course and crashed it against his thigh. "Pleased to meet you," he croaked, feeling his scrotum knot itself in agonising raptures of mortification. His face blossomed, a flare signaling the onset of acute self-consciousness. He wished he could remove his eyes from hers to seek refuge in remote corners of the room, but could not; they remained focused on Charlotte's (brown, he saw now, surrounded by whites of unsettling clarity, assisting the directness of her returned gaze) and would not be shifted despite dire warnings to himself of the consequences, namely her logical assumption that he was rude, ill mannered, graceless and boorish—all of it true, so true! He thanked her silently when Charlotte saw fit to end the unintended ocular battle by shifting her eyes to Hopkins. "Father, Daphne informs me supper is ready a little earlier than expected."

"Then we'll not keep her waiting. Hot food on a cold night is a sure remedy for what ails me." More laughter, fragile and evanescent. Joe wondered if more medical *bon mots* would be forthcoming during the meal, tried to prepare one himself; he must impress upon Charlotte the fact that he was intelligent, intellect being his only excuse for blighting the world with his ugly presence. Thank God (thank Dame Fortune, thank Lady Luck, anyone but nonexistent God!) the meal was already prepared; any delay before eating, delay that would have to be filled with conversation, and Joe would have burst with restrained effort, with curbed passion to impress. Yet to answer a question put to him from the pert mouth of this enchantress would have been an impossibility. Would one of Circe's swine have answered with anything but a coarse grunt? He had, at this point, been observing her for approximately thirty seconds, had known of her existence for mere minutes, was already hopelessly infatuated. He watched, twitching with jealousy, as the doctor offered Charlotte his arm and steered her from the room. Joe and Hopkins fell naturally into step behind.

"I hope our fare proves worthy of a returned adventurer, Joseph."

"I bet it will . . . uh . . . thank you."

They seated themselves around a table draped in pristine linen, set with elegant silverware. A maid, the first non-Negro in that role Joe had ever seen, entered the room bearing in her hands a silver soup tureen. Servings were ladled into bowls, the ante-bellum ancestry of the silver service discussed at length. Joe waited for the conversation to drift in his direction, waited to see which spoon was the correct utensil, waited for heaven to fall. With his very first effort he managed to slurp noisily, felt himself blush all the more furiously, hoped neither embarrassment had been noticed amid the discreet chinking of silver on china and soft candleglow. He sipped carefully at his next spoonful, waiting, waiting, eyes bent to the small lagoon of soup lapping at its silver shore, waiting, waiting. . . .

"Father tells me you have been hunting buffalo, Mr. Cobden."

His foster-father hunting buffalo? What was this? Joe raised his head, realised the question had been put to him, *Mr.* Cobden. Silence wrapped him in velvet wings, smothered his lungs, his brain, halted the spoon betwixt bowl and lip, froze him with sudden terror. Think, *think!* Answer! Don't let her mark you down as a fool. You are, after all, a seasoned veteran of the great plains, the possessor of a grizzled yet romantic allure, a breath of prairie wind bracing the politely stuffy confines of a St. Louis dining-room. Speak!!

"Yes I am . . . have been. . . ."

Good Christ, what a display of scintillating persiflage! He shrank toward his boots, ashamed of his own feebleness. She would know now what a hopeless, stumbling fool he was, would desist out of pity. But, no, the perfect lips were parted again in a sympathetic smile, no less, wide enough to dimple charmingly the smooth as marble cheeks.

"It must be a wonderfully exciting way of life."

Here was Joe's chance for redemption, to reinstate himself in her eyes, establish once and for all his towering knowledge and experience of life out there on the edge of civilisation. His lips trembled, his brain churned, his mouth opened. . . .

"I suppose so."

It was no use. Joe was defeated, the victim of creeping paralysis. But would his bewitching tormentor allow him surcease? She would not.

"I have seen drawings of the beasts, monstrous shaggy fellows. Are you not afraid to face them?"

"Not so long as I've got my big fifty." A nine year old lout, a feckless braggart with a slingshot, would have sounded the same. Joe cringed, but she appeared not to have noticed his juvenile display.

"A 'big fifty', Mr. Cobden?"

"Sharpe's fifty-calibre. We call it a big fifty."

"The Indians, are they not your foe? I have heard they regard the buffalo as their own."

Hopkins coughed elaborately, not wishing to have his young guest reminded of that unfortunate proportion of his river of life which ran redder than red. But Charlotte ignored his warning. "They must surely be a constant threat to your safety."

Inspiration presented Joe with an opportunity for absolution. "As a matter of fact," he said, his voice gaining power, "the Indians and I get along well together. I'm part Indian myself." He let it fall with the studied nonchalance of royalty revealing to peasants his proud lineage; perhaps she was a reader of Rousseau, would look upon him as a noble savage. "The Sioux gave me a name. They call me Pawahsetanteh. It means Buffalo Man." There; the lie had been blunt, forceful, had apparently convinced her. It was also, he realised, a test; if she was disgusted by his mixed blood, if she was not impressed by the candid manner in which he had alluded to his deformity, then she was nothing more than a pretty face. If, on the other hand, she respected him for his candour, it would indicate the presence of a woman of sensitivity behind the pleasing appearance, and if that were the case Joe would be faced with a considerable problem; if Charlotte Hopkins was a woman of intelligence and perception, it would be unbearable not to have her for himself. He searched her features for signs of distaste, suggestions of abhorrence. There were none. "How romantic!" she said, smiling still, her eyes reflecting the candlelight.

Joe was lost. The moment he had long dreaded had at last caught up with him, or he with it, the moment most men and women anticipate from an early age: the moment when they chance upon that person in whom they perceive the lineaments of mutual oneness, the promise of reciprocal yearning, the plain evidence of something unspoken, wordless assurance that the person before them is indeed The One. The instincts through which this message is received are notoriously inaccurate, often becoming entangled with commonplace lust, but such is the allure of unquestioning love that errors are seldom recognized until too late, at which time the players in this oldest of tragicomedies are released from the heights of bliss, real or imagined, and returned smartly to terra firma. Despite his cynicism, the like of which is usually found only among the middle-aged and hard done by, despite his contempt for the ordinary and predictable byways, Joe allowed his steps to be directed along the much trodden primrose path of romance, a dream-fuddled sleepwalker among millions similarly afflicted; like them, he believed his perceptions unique. Charlotte was no longer pretty, she was beautiful; no longer a politely attentive hostess, but a woman longing for reunion with that other, lost half of herself apprehended until now only in daydreams, that mystical figure, part brother, part lover, who is the quintessence of symbiotic fulfilment. Jettisoning his accumulated handicaps in an instant, Joe pictured himself as the long awaited object of Charlotte's desire. They would be one. It was written, preordained, fated, destined—dammit, the thing was kismeted!

All this had transpired in the time required to draw breath twice. Joe smiled at Charlotte. "Maybe not so much romantic as . . . gratifying. Indians are choosy about who they accept as a friend." He lied easily, fluently, steadily building a fiction based on dreary fact, elaborating, embroidering the plain rag of actuality. When he reached that point in his saga detailing the shooting match with William F. Cody (which Cody, to his chagrin, narrowly lost) Joe reminded himself of the Cobden-Tubbs outfit's cook, a liquor-ridden wretch who boasted pathetically of having created gastronomic masterpieces in New York City's finest restaurants. He wisely terminated his yarnspinning with an abruptness that had all the earmarks of modesty preventing the speaker from dazzling his audience further. The Hopkinses, father and daughter, had listened, Joe was convinced, with rapt attention. Dr. Cobden, unfortunately, had gazed at the ceiling throughout. Had he penetrated Joe's charade from the moment it began, and preferred to look elsewhere rather than accuse his fosterchild of outright lying? Perhaps he was simply annoyed that Joe had not seen fit to relay these grand adventures to him while they were alone, instead of waiting to impress a wider audience.

The second course had come and gone, and the third. During dessert Joe allowed the conversation to move away from himself, while still making pertinent contributions. He knew he had conducted himself with aplomb, knew he had made a more than favourable impression on Charlotte by the manner in which she continued to smile at him. Joe's confidence soared; he had found a woman prepared to accept him as a half-breed and, amazingly, as a hunchback. It was incredible, but her eyes said it was true. There was, after all his travels and travails, a Penelope for this misshapen Ulysses. He could at last divest himself of that hitherto necessary burden, his armour, and stand revealed as the vulnerable creature of spirit and flesh he truly was. It would be a new beginning. He positively glowed with euphoria, the condition being assisted greatly by brandy. How many glasses had he drunk? After the fifth Joe had stopped counting. It seemed to be acceptable in this household to help oneself to the decanter, and Joe availed himself, growing more mellifluous as the alcohol raced through his veins. Charlotte, he noted, did not partake, not that Joe would have objected to a female who imbibed; the act would have been in accord with her broadminded acceptance of so unlikely a suitor. Suitor? Joe discerned the drift of his own blurred thoughts, knew he was already considering how best to approach the ritual of asking for her hand. He gloated upon his overnight conquest of so perfect a bride while lecturing the two doctors on the merits of the Sharpe's over those of the Springfield. He had never fired a Springfield in his life; nevertheless, his damning speech (remembered almost verbatim from a conversation with Quincy Tubbs, who had once owned such a rifle) would have earned him a round of applause from the manufacturers of Sharpe's.

As all good things must, the evening came to an end. Joe had inadvertently smashed a wine glass, but had managed to pass the accident off with an easy laugh; to worry over trifles would have been ridiculous on a night such as this, with a new life in the offing. Yes, happiness and contentment were awaiting him, and Joe was determined to exit the stage with dash and flair. At the front door he bade Hopkins a hearty farewell and pumped his arm, then took Charlotte's hand in his to bestow a gallant kiss upon its creamy back. His nose reached the target before his lips, but the mishap was of no account; the deed itself had been accomplished, his seal of approval pasted on the hand that would soon be granted him by a proud and grateful parent. With a final wave from the gate, Joe and the doctor set off down the street, Joe's face creased with a smile. The doctor eyed his somewhat erratic gait with a flinty eye.

"Would you prefer to walk a short while before we attempt to find a carriage, Joseph?"

"I don't mind." Joe would not have minded anything.

"You appear to have enjoyed the evening."

"Yes I did. Didn't you?"

"It was most instructive. Correct me if I am wrong, but tonight was the first occasion on which you and I have appeared together in public since those balmy days when I pushed you in your perambulator."

"I don't remember that."

"It was especially enlightening to witness your behaviour."

"Did I do something wrong?"

"Not at all. You were a model of sobriety and rectitude."

Joe failed completely to discern the sarcasm. "I enjoyed myself."

"I have already made that observation. You seemed very much taken with Miss Hopkins."

"She's a wonderful woman, intelligent, sensitive. . . ."

"Yes indeed, a worthy prize for a worthy fellow. She seemed particularly radiant tonight."

"Do you think so?" Joe hoped the radiance was due to himself, and the doctor read his hopes as if they had been penned upon Joe's lightly sweating brow. He pursed his lips, savouring the last moments before Joe's downfall. "No doubt it has to do with her wedding a week from now. Anticipation and excitement will bring a flush to the most maidenly of cheeks."

"Wedding . . . ?" The sidewalk seemed to lurch under Joe's boots.

"Charlotte is betrothed to Mr. Langdon Birney. He is the owner of the Bluebird shipping line, a very wealthy young man indeed. Ah, I see a carriage."

The doctor hailed, the hackney halted beside them. He stepped aside to allow Joe entry first.

"I'm not going home."

"Not going home? The hour is late, Joseph."

"You go. I want to walk for a while."

"Are you feeling unwell? A little too much brandy, perhaps?"

"I'm all right. Go home. I'll be along later."

"Very well." He stepped inside the hackney.

"Why didn't anyone say anything?" Joe's voice was weak, plaintive.

"I fail to understand the question."

"About her getting married."

"Joseph, there are people in this world who demonstrate reserve in front of strangers, who do not blurt out their private business to chance acquaintances and dinner guests. It is one of the social graces. No doubt a second visit would have elicited the information from them. Under the circumstances, however, I feel an invitation will not be forthcoming. Do pardon my frankness."

"Because I broke a glass?"

"Destroying a part of Dr. Hopkins' prized crystal set was the least of your crimes. I believe you have tarried too long among savages. Goodnight."

He rapped with his cane on the roof, was borne swiftly away. Joe watched until the hackney rounded a corner and was gone. There was very little traffic at this hour. Light snow began to fall. Joe stood where he was for a long while, allowing snow to build up along the brim of his hat, his big, battered prairie hat with the turkey feather; wearing it to St. Louis instead of his buffalo hide cap with its festooning curls had been his one concession to sartorial decorum. I'll bet they laughed over the feather. The whole hat. And my coat. And boots. I'll bet once the door closed they had a good laugh over my hump. And everything I did and said. I'm a perfect fool. The depth of his stupidity left Joe numb inside, made him lightheaded with self-loathing, speechless at his own folly. Was it possible he had learned nothing, was still a child? More than likely, he concluded, aghast at the implications. How old must a body be before wisdom is acquired, how long before Joe could step forth to face each day without flinching at the memory of yesterday? His life to date seemed a complete waste of time, years of suffering and pain endured for nothing.

A carriage rattled by. The driver roared at Joe to get out of the way, and he saw he was still several yards out from the curb, had not moved since the doctor was driven away; moreover, he was freezing. He began to walk, head down, mind racing, fuelled with disgust and alcohol. He cursed the doctor, he cursed Charlotte Hopkins, the faceless Langdon Birney, anyone and everyone, but, above all, he cursed himself. When he finally tired of cursing he found he could no longer feel his face, so cold had the night air become. He hailed a hackney and clambered aboard.

"Take me somewhere I can get a drink."

* * *

He returned to DeWitte Street the following day, having spent the small hours in a police cell. He was bruised and bloodied, had vague recollections of a crowded riverfront bar, an insult, a fight. He could not recall winning or losing, or his arrest. Sufficient funds were found in his pockets to pay a fine. He had walked home, hoping the brisk morning air would clear his throbbing head. It did not, but his laggard pace, each footfall travelling the length of his body to reverberate inside his skull, meant the doctor had already breakfasted and left for the infirmary by the time Joe slowly mounted the steps to the front door. Joe was glad to avoid any confrontation. He slumped on to a wooden stool in the kitchen. Hattie looked askance at his puffed eye and crusted lip. "Been having yourself a high old time?" Joe attacked a loaf with his fingers, ignoring the breadknife at hand, devoured a chunk in record time. Hattie watched, repelled by the picture he presented. "You want butter to go with that?"

Joe wiped his mouth with the back of his hand. "Hattie, do you think it's possible for a person to be smart and stupid at the same time?"

"It ain't *im*possible. It depends."

"Depends on what?"

"On how big a fool you been, and how much of the foolishness you admit to. Any man that don't admit he's been a fool—now, *that* man's a true fool. How big a fool you been lately?"

"Pretty big."

"Well, so long as you know it, you can put it behind you."

"I've been doing that for years. I've practically built a small mountain behind me."

"You want something more to eat?"

"No, I want a drink."

"That part of your foolishness?"

"Part of it. Got anything in the house?"

"Never have been partial to drink, nor the doctor neither."

"You don't even have a bottle of something for cooking?"

"A man that's ready to drink cooking liquor, that man's a double fool."

Joe left the house, returned some time later, locked himself in his room and drank whiskey. His thoughts roamed the parched and rocky landscape of his past, attempted, with the aid of whiskey, to mantle his future in lush green. He fell asleep.

Joe awoke to darkness. He left his room, still clutching the bottle, found the doctor reading in the library. His head lifted as Joe entered. The sight provoked Joe to unreasonable anger; the doctor was too cosy, too smug, too satisfied with his miserable life. Couldn't he see how pathetic he was?

"I bet you're sorry you ever brought me in."

"What makes you think so, Joseph?"

"The way you look at me, that's what."

"I was not aware of looking at you in any particular way."

"You're not aware of plenty of things."

"You're drunk. Why don't we continue this conversation at a later date?"

"I want to talk now."

"Very well."

He closed the book on his lap, indicated a chair. Joe remained standing, struggling to articulate his rage. He wanted more than anything else to bring the bottle down on that fragile cranium with its thinning hair, make the complacent expression dissolve in pain. He set the bottle on the table. He had much to say, but could get none of it past his throat.

"I am waiting, Joseph. You said you wished to talk."

It had finally happened; the boy had been brought low by his own brash insistence on shaping events, changing the world to suit himself. The doctor had known full well that

223

any man, even a hunchback, was likely to fall under the spell of Charlotte Hopkins; he had held his tongue accordingly, hoping to lure unsuspecting Joe into her velvet web. The boy's insufferable cocksureness had been drained from him by the fangs of love, Joe their willing victim. It had been a pitiful thing to see, but the doctor felt no regret; Joe had had a lesson coming, a hard lesson. It had apparently been learned. A glow of satisfaction warmed the doctor's solar plexus. It was difficult to restrain a smile.

Joe took a step closer, but so woebegone was his expression the move lacked all intimidation. "I just want to hear you say you hate me as much as I hate you." His mouth was twisted, trembling.

"Do you hate me, Joseph?"

"I wish you could . . . I wish you could feel what I feel!"

"Under the circumstances, I doubt that I would enjoy the experience."

"I just. . . ."

He stopped himself. There were no words capable of expressing his wretchedness. The impossibility of ever resolving the emotions crowding his chest was evident in his own tortured silence, in the doctor's patiently raised eyebrows, in the very walls of the room. Joe was defeated. The doctor had won. Joe hated him more at that moment than any of those men who had openly mocked his deformity. Against the doctor's genteel innuendo there was no defence.

"When you found me I wasn't twisted, was I?"

"No, you appeared normal. The curvature came later."

"Would you have taken me home otherwise?"

"No, I think not."

"Thank you for being honest."

Joe swept the whiskey-bottle from the table. It flew straight across the room, still perpendicular, and smashed against the wall. The doctor did not move, did not take his eyes from Joe. He wondered, in all seriousness, if he was about to be murdered. Strangely, the prospect did not frighten him, had about it a certain awful inevitability, the last act in some squalid drama; the doctor was at stage centre, but felt himself watching calmly from the balcony, an interested spectator at his own imminent demise. A pain was growing steadily in his chest, and the doctor became aware that he was holding his breath, had been doing so for some time. He eased the pressure in his chest, hoping the strain would not provoke an attack of coughing; he did not wish to appear old and infirm before Joe.

"We are not brought into the world to be happy, Joseph."

"I know. I've always known."

"Then you will not be disappointed with your life."

The heat of Joe's fury cooled to a glacial flickering, a small and blue eternal flame. He extended his hand, his arm rigid as that of a wooden soldier. The doctor hesitated, took it. Joe felt the palm in his, dry, papery, cold, an old man's. He clasped it briefly, surrendered it.

"Goodbye. We probably won't meet again."

"There is no need for such dramatics."

"I'm stating a fact."

"I . . . I should very much like to know how you fare, Joseph. Write me letters, just one per year if nothing else."

"All right."

He had no intention of composing a single sentence. He left the library, collected his coat and gun, went to Hattie's room and knocked. She was seated by a small stove, knitting. Joe was shocked to learn she wore spectacles; Hattie had always seemed ageless.

"I'm going now," he said.

"This time of night? What you do, have another fight with the doctor?"

"I just think it's time I left."

"Won't be no train till morning."

"I'll wait at the depot. Chances are I won't ever be back, so goodbye."

"This place going to be yours someday. You got to come back then."

"I don't want any part of it."

225

Hattie saw her dreams of security snuffed out. The boy cared nothing for the house, had no conception of her fears. An uncertain future yawned at her feet. She had her pride, would not explain or plead, especially from someone half-white. Joe was not a devil-child, she knew that now; she had been younger and more foolish when she imagined the presence of evil behind those dark and staring baby eyes. No, he was just a man, and selfish like all men. All right, then, she would take care of herself, come what may, would anticipate nothing from anyone; that was the way a sensible woman conducted her life. If the doctor left her destitute (and she could scarcely imagine such a thing happening, despite her resolve to expect nothing), then she would go on living somehow. She believed the boy. He would not be back. She almost felt sorry for him, and took the hand he offered.

"Going back out there?" Her head jerked, denoting the west.

"That's where I belong." He did not believe this, but each of us requires a destination, a goal, and Kansas arbitrarily became Joe's; his money was there, after all, and cash can be both lodestar and anchor to a drifting vessel.

"Goodbye, Hattie."

"You be careful and don't let no redskins get your hair."

"They won''t."

He considered hugging her, decided not to; there had been a minimum of fleshly contact between them when he was very young, none whatsoever after he had learned to clean his own backside and bathe himself. Hattie knew Joe had been on the verge of holding her, saw his resolve weaken as he recalled their unspoken habit of physical exclusiveness. She was disappointed, supposed it was because Joe, unlikely candidate though he was, had been the closest she would ever come to raising a child of her own. Joe picked up his rifle, nodded at her, similarly afflicted with a sudden awkwardness; and went to the door. From behind, the absurd coat made him resemble a buffalo indeed. Then he was gone, his boots clumping down the hall. The front door opened, closed, and during the brief moment it stood ajar there came stealing into the house the freezing breath of old age and hopelessness and lost dreams and despair, which find their way into every home by and by. Hattie let the knitting fall from her fingers, stared at the stove with its warm and friendly potbelly. She should have married that free black, that Meade Hubbard, when he had proposed back in 1847. She had gone and turned him down for his arrogant manner. Young and foolish. A chill crept through her, dimpled her flesh. Hattie drew the shawl higher around her shoulders, pulled her chair a little closer to the stove, somehow felt she would never truly be warm again.

CHAPTER SIXTEEN

December had been an interesting month for Calvin Puckett. While the rest of the outfit disported themselves in the usual fleshpots Calvin communed with God. This remarkable dialogue took place over several weeks in a small hotel called the Eden. Someone somewhere had told Calvin that God created the very first man and woman in a place called Eden. Calvin could not read, and had taken up residence here simply because it looked cheap, not because of the sign outside. When the desk clerk had told him what the hotel was called Calvin sank to his knees and offered a silent prayer of thanks, overcome by the mysterious ways of God (someone had told him about these, too). The desk clerk, long since inured to such sights, common to any hotel on the cheaper side of town, assumed Calvin was drunk. There were quite a few drunks at the Eden Hotel.

Calvin spent a great deal of time in his small and evil-smelling room on the third floor, listening to the wind howl, watching the snowflakes dance and whirl. He had enjoyed the snowfall every winter back home, and watching it bury the rooftops of Dodge City sent shivers of ecstasy down his spine. He could watch for as long as he wanted, with no one to tell him there were chores to be done, no one to whip the backs of his legs with a length of old harness. There was just Calvin in Calvin's room, and God.

The manner of God's communication was as unspectacular as on that occasion when He had warned Calvin to beware the crooked man. His first message to the small room on the third floor of the Eden Hotel came while Calvin lay dozing on his bed, idly listening to the wind. These words were fed into his head by way of Calvin's left ear: "The road is long, the signpost true." He distinctly felt the message worming its way through, like a burrowing insect. It was in fact a louse, and it had made the foolish error of abandoning Calvin's hair for his ear, seeking greater warmth; what it found was wax, lots of wax, and the louse eventually perished among the gobbets of brownish residue which Calvin's mother always told him would one day be able to support a potato crop; she had not once suspected that Calvin's waxy ear would one day be the conduit of God's word.

The road is long, the signpost true. . . . Calvin pondered the possible meaning of this enigmatic phrase. Could it be a reference to the road Calvin had travelled to reach Kansas? It was the only road, or series of roads, he had ever had experience of, apart from the narrow country road that led to the schoolhouse back in Pennsylvania, and he had only used that a few times. What about the signpost? He had seen a lot of them on his way west; not one of them had seemed more true than the rest, all being reduced to sameness by Calvin's illiterate gaze. But wait. Could it not mean the arrow of stones in the woods near the farm, the very sign that had sent him on his wanderings? It had not been mounted on a post, but it certainly indicated a specific direction, just like the pointed planks at crossroads and turnpikes. Calvin hugged himself with glee. The road and the sign . . . of course! The components of the message had been identified. A little later he asked himself: what *about* the road and the sign? It still presented a puzzle. God surely was making him work hard for understanding. Well, it would come in its own sweet time, as his mother used habitually to say of death.

The divine messages began arriving at intervals of several days. "Seek not that which is not", "Sideways go, but never in between", "Evermore, yet often was", "Put not aside the cup", "Believe and not believe, always." In every case the voice was crystal-clear, deeply resonant, could be none other than the voice of God. And still Calvin understood nothing. ''Be with that which does not seek'', ''Above is the below of inside'', ''Each will be another, but not I'', ''Born is death to ending.'' Calvin began to fret, to berate himself for his lack of brains. All these words must mean something, but he could not even guess at possible explanations. ''Deep and wide, the boot is black'', ''Slowly and with careful step, climb not'', ''Be with the one waiting beside'', ''Delay not, yet also hasten.'' Then the messages ceased. He waited, but no more came into his head. God was done with whispering; God now waited for Calvin to act. He could not sleep, so great was the burden of his responsibility. God must by now be tapping His mighty fingers, clearing His throat with impatience. Calvin whimpered and whined and almost wished God had chosen someone else to be His representative. And then God came to visit.

It happened while Calvin was staring out his window, watching the snow as usual, marvelling at its whiteness, its purity. Nothing moved in the street below but gusting, drifting snowflakes. Calvin felt his mind gradually numbing with the cold that seeped through the walls and frosted panes, was unsure if his brain was shrinking or expanding, did not much care either way. He suspected he was waiting for something, not further messages—those had obviously stopped, at least for the time being. No, it was something else he waited for, and it would appear when good and ready. There was movement in an alleyway opposite Calvin's window, a sudden flurry of snowflakes, a surging and a swelling of whiteness, and into the street strode the wolf. Calvin knew immediately that this was no ordinary wolf, for it was white from snout to tail. The nose was black, the eyes yellow, and these three points were required to define the wolf from its background; with eyes closed and nose buried under a paw the wolf would have been invisible. It looked directly up at Calvin, sat on its haunches to let him know it would wait while he absorbed the fact of its presence. The white wolf was God made corporeal, His fur shifting, blending with the snow, the plume of tail melding with the curve of a snowdrift piled against a frozen rainbarrel. Calvin lost no time in descending to meet his maker.

Joe stepped down from the westbound train on Christmas Day with little yuletide cheer in his heart. On the frequently stalled trip from St. Louis he had brooded upon his failure to impress a soul in that city with his accomplishments. The buffalo coat on his back was sackcloth, the Sharpe's a weighty handful of ashes. Joe mourned for himself, for the blighted past and indeterminate future. His sole entertainment on the homeward journey (Is Kansas my home? he asked himself) was the pursuance of lengthy conversations with the doctor, one-sided harangues in which Joe accused, judged and condemned. The exercise brought him little comfort. No matter how well reasoned or passionate Joe's argument, the doctor always won, not by way of outmanoeuvring Joe intellectually, but by the simple raising of an eyebrow, the sceptical pursing of his lips. When the train finally steamed into Dodge well behind schedule Joe's mood was black.

He went to the Boston Hotel, where he knew he was acceptable, and took a room, considered sending out for liquor, decided he was too angry to drink. He lay on his bed and daydreamed instead of fabulous wealth, a mountain of dollars, towering testament to his ability for survival in a money-making world, riches the like of which had not been seen since the days of Midas, of Croesus. The doctor shook his head pityingly. Joe went for a walk, unable to take his ease after days of travelling; his back in particular was causing him discomfort. He tramped the streets, snow clinging to his boots, wind tugging at his hatbrim. Only those with urgent business were similarly engaged, heads bowed, coat-tails flying.

Company, convivial human company, that was what Joe needed to take his mind off things. He sought out Quincy Tubbs, found him at his second-favourite watering-hole half an hour later. Tubbs greeted him with a smile of astonishment. "What the hell are you doing back here so soon?"

Joe ordered himself a whiskey. "My plans for St. Louis didn't work out."

Tubbs' smile collapsed.

"It wasn't all that bad," said Joe, and Tubbs' mouth drooped even further.

"I guess you haven't heard."

"Heard what?"

"You've got your cash in the Pioneer Bank, am I right?"

"That's right."

"Not any more you haven't. No one has."

Joe's stomach plummeted. "Robbed . . . ?"

"Nothing so honest. The president sacked up everything in the safe and got on an eastbound train five days back. Word's gone out down the line, but the telegraph line's busted somewhere along the way. They most likely won't catch him. Did you have everything in the one place?"

"Everything."

"I'm sorry, Joe. There's plenty of men good and mad about it. Some even took off to find him and lynch him, but he had two days' start. Closed the bank on Saturday same as usual and no one saw him again, didn't even figure there was something wrong until the doors weren't open come Monday morning. You better have another drink on me."

Joe learned more. The Pioneer Bank of Western Kansas was independent, had no affiliated branches or companies, no responsible bodies which would make up the loss to customers. The money was gone, the bank defunct, and Joe's hopes likewise. He had several more drinks, enough to blunt the blow, but scarcely sufficient, in Tubbs' opinion, to provoke the hysterical laughter that soon followed. Joe could not help himself. Sweat and strain, he told himself, and what is your reward? Loss and pain. Sweat and strain gets loss and pain. That was when the laughter began, and once started it could not be stopped. Sweat and strain, loss and pain. Joe had to lean against the bar to remain upright while a distinctly unmasculine whinnying sprayed from his lips. The noise attracted attention, most of it sympathetic when the situation was explained. There were, regrettably, some present who secretly were glad at Joe's misfortune; they had watched his rise to fame, surprised at first, then resentful that a cripple should make of himself a success, when everyone knew that only a real man, a straight up and down man, deserved reward in this land of men. It was only right that the monstrous little breed should be brought down a peg, only right and proper and not before time, and they raised their glasses, recognising each other in their mutual delight, and winked and drained their whiskey to whatever was on the dark side of Lady Luck.

Joe declined his partner's offer of a loan, said he would make out somehow until hunting could be resumed in the spring. More than a little drunk, he left the saloon and battled his way against the wind for several blocks, determined to see the building around which his life had suddenly pivoted. The bank's doors were chained shut. Joe kicked at the icy steps in a rage, slipped and fell, became angrier still. He floundered in the snow, snarling at those people and inanimate objects which had conspired to rob him of pride and dignity and cash. He had a Sharpe's in his room, his gelding in a livery stable (fee paid in advance before he left for St. Louis, so the animal would not starve), warm clothing, and perhaps one hundred dollars in his pocket. Things could have been far worse, he reminded himself, and was so disgusted by the platitude he howled at his boots, a sight which would have drawn attention on a crowded street, but went unnoticed on this winter's day.

His rage was such it could only be walked off, and Joe stamped away down the street to divest himself of the hot serpents coiling through and squeezing at his guts. The biting wind became his enemy, cruel circumstance personified; he butted it and clawed at it and bored through it, gritting his teeth behind frozen lips, growling in his throat, every step taken against its brute power stoking rather than appeasing his fury. He tramped and stumbled and tramped on, burning the bank president in effigy, consigning him to the deepest of dungeons, torturing him with inquisitorial fervour, heaped all his bitterness upon the head of the thief, thereby granting the doctor a much needed rest.

He eventually came to the edge of town. That suited Joe. He ploughed on until he gained the summit of a ridge and there paused, sweating with effort, confronted by endless prairie, windswept and empty, a dreary expanse of chilled nothingness overhung with an iron-grey sky spilling yet more snow. The edge of the world could have presented no less hospitable a view. The north pole has its dramatic tumblings of shattered ice, its drifting crystalline mountains and glimmering aurora. Patagonia has the mysterious jagged skyline of the Andes, haunt of none but the soaring condor. Western Kansas is open, flat, a non-landscape, a featureless slate waiting to be chalked upon. The sight, rather than the wind, sent a shiver through Joe. His anger was spent. Who, confronted with such awesome emptiness, could maintain so emphatic an emotion as rage? Joe's dwindled away under the influence of the prairie to mere hopelessness. He had lost again. No sooner did his life take a turn for the better than the ground once again opened beneath him. Sisyphus at his eternal labours could not have felt less optimistic than Joe. He felt a sneaking need for comfort, for an encouraging slap on the shoulder from a friend, the reassurance that all would turn out well in the end, for the very things he could have received from Quincy Tubbs, had he offered the least encouragement. He knew he would never do so. Joe considered his position. He had been robbed, yes, but not run over by a train; he was young, in full strength, still possessed a horse and rifle, was under no obligation to surrender the captaincy of his future. He made up his mind; he would not only survive this calamity, he would thrive. Survive and thrive—he liked the sound of that. Joe squared his shoulders in a consciously manly gesture, defying the elements and fate together; in so doing he presented an enlarged surface for the wind to batter, and was promptly pushed on to his back. Determined not to interpret this in any symbolic fashion, Joe picked himself up, turned his hump to the gale and headed back to Dodge.

Calvin had been unable to find the wolf. He went first to the rainbarrel opposite his window, but falling snow, although light, had already obliterated any signs of its presence. He ran along the alleyway from which it had first appeared; the snowfall here was minimal, the plank walls rearing up three storeys on either side, yet even in this narrow, protected space there was no evidence of padmarks. Rather than conclude that there had been no wolf, Calvin deduced that God, in His wolf garb, had not touched the ground but held Himself above it by the merest fraction to preserve the immaculacy of His feet in this filthy human place. But where was He? Calvin ran up one street and down another, investigated every connecting alleyway without finding any trace of God. Had he failed some kind of test? Was God playing some incomprehensible joke? No, that was impossible; any God who would strike a man dead with lightning to aid one of His supplicants was not a jesting God. Calvin had been summoned from his room for a purpose, you could be sure of that.

Thus fortified with certainty he walked on, and would have missed Joe completely had not the wind removed his hat. Calvin pursued it to a street corner, retrieved it and had just completed jamming it firmly back on to his head when he chanced to see the crooked man trudging along, head down, oblivious to all but the area around his feet. Now Calvin saw why it was that he had been led halfway across town; he was to observe Joe Cobden, follow him and spy on whatever devil's business he was about. Warmed by excitement, God's henchman fell into step some twenty yards behind Joe and shadowed him to the edge of town and beyond. Joe did not once turn around—a fortunate thing for Calvin since the prairie around Dodge offered no cover whatsoever. He watched as Joe fought his way to a low ridge and stood there, apparently looking at something.

He stayed there a considerable time, not moving, and Calvin began to feel the cold seep into his bones. What was the hunchback doing, talking to some invisible demon, receiving instructions maybe? Calvin flapped his arms to keep warm and awaited the next development in this unexpected vigil.

It came sooner than anticipated. Lost in his armswinging, concentrating on the flow of blood beneath his skin, Calvin failed to notice that Joe had finished his devilish task and was now stamping back along his own footprints, these being fast erased by the wind. Calvin panicked, a condition which in him promoted stasis rather than action. He froze, became a statue, prayed Joe would walk by without seeing him, for although Calvin loathed Joe he also feared him. Where was the white wolf? Shouldn't some protection be afforded God's right hand man? But the godbeast was nowhere to be seen. Calvin closed his eyes, held his breath, became a tree, the last thing that would escape attention in Kansas.

Joe was almost upon him before he realised Calvin was there. He stopped abruptly, unable at first to comprehend what it was he was seeing. The person before him was Puckett, that much was obvious, but what was he doing out here with his eyes screwed shut, fists clenched into bulky knots inside his pants?

"Puckett?"

An eye cautiously revealed itself. Calvin wondered what to do now that he had been recognised. "Mornin'," he said. It was mid-afternoon.

"What are you doing, Puckett?"

"Me? Nothin' . . . I guess."

"Are you following me?"

"I just . . . just come out walkin'."

They stared at each other. Calvin allowed both eyes to open now, unable to hide behind his lids any longer. He shuffled his feet, glad of the opportunity to move his legs again and restore circulation. He would have given Joe a nervous grin had his frozen face allowed it. The wolf was still nowhere around.

"You're lying. You followed me out here."

"I never did!"

"Don't hand me that! You followed me!"

"I never! I come out for the walkin' . . . just walkin'!"

Joe wondered if he was armed. He had never seen Puckett with anything more lethal than a skinning knife, but in his expert hands that would be quite enough. "Turn out your pockets."

"Huh?"

"Empty them!"

Joe did not know how to cope with Puckett, could not be sure if he was a genuine simpleton or a clever actor hiding behind the mask of imbecility. He had heard that lunatics were often wonderful actors and could, if aroused, muster abnormal strength. The man could not be trusted. Calvin exposed his soiled pocket-linings, shamefacedly revealed a mucus-encrusted handkerchief wadded into a ball, several lengths of string and a smooth stone (from the apex of the stone arrow that had pointed Calvin west—he had kept it for a lucky charm)—the kind of things one would have expected from the pockets of a nine-year-old. Puzzled, Joe ordered the belongings replaced. Both men stood stamping their feet.

"Mighty cold out," offered Calvin.

"Enjoy the view," said Joe, and walked away, turning every now and then to make sure of the other's whereabouts. The incident had been disturbing. Joe liked to know the precise nature of whatever he was pitted against. He flattered himself he understood the doctor, and could usually form a reliable judgement of a man's character within minutes of meeting him, but Puckett was a creature of an altogether different species; confronted with such a peculiar individual, Joe felt almost normal by contrast. He would keep a careful watch on his heels from now on, would be constantly on his guard until Puckett revealed the true nature of his antagonism towards Joe.

Calvin stayed where he was until Joe had all but disappeared into the dark smudge that was Dodge. He knew he had failed at his appointed task, whatever that had been, and felt decidedly foolish. Thoroughly downcast, he turned for the town and found the white wolf in his path. "I'm sorry . . ." stammered Calvin, "I just . . . I never knew what to do. . . ." The yellow eyes appraised him, found him wanting; the tongue, a raw pinkness against the milky teeth and black lips, lolled derisively. Calvin hung his head, ashamed of himself, abashed before his lord and master.

"Next time just go ahead and kill him," said the wolf.

Time passed slowly: frozen days that chilled the marrow, invaded the very soul, starless nights of wind that moaned and whistled and sighed through walls built, unlike Rome's, in a day. Men shivered and looked at the sky and cursed through cupped and frosted fingers. The westerlies continued to howl, bringing to Kansas a wealth of snow from the roof of the Rockies. It was a long winter and a harsh one. Hunters and skinners by the hundreds were stranded in Dodge waiting for the thaw, and while they waited they drank and gambled and fought and contracted venereal diseases, and drank and fought again. On New Year's Eve they beggared their health with no more than the usual gusto, and so 1873 was ushered into being, its noisy inauguration differing not one whit in essential detail from the worn and wasted nub of the preceding year.

Having risen to prominence as a buffalo-hunter Joe did not readily countenance the idea of hiring himself out as another man's slave, but cash was required to sustain him until the thaw, when hunting could begin again. There was nothing else for it; he would have to take advantage of Quincy Tubbs' generosity and accept a loan. He concealed his loathing for the act with a display of casual *bonhomie* that rankled even as he performed, and which fooled no one. The arrangement was sealed with a drink—whiskey for Tubbs, gall for Joe. His pride demanded scapegoats and was offered three: the doctor, the absconding bank president, and Calvin Puckett. Two of these were far away, but Puckett shared the same square mile as Joe, and Joe did not like it. He stayed in his room and drank and brooded, and on those few occasions when boredom and frustration drove him into the streets he took care to glance over his shoulder at least twice in every block. Local wits said Joe Cobden was trying to catch his hump in the act of growing. He did not once catch sight of Calvin.

Joe longed for just one thing to comfort him during those days and nights of cold that froze the hands of clocks, a simple, everyday thing. Joe wanted a book to read. He thought of Cyrus' library, of the doctor's, and envied any man wealthy enough, stable enough, to own such a room, be it in basement or palace. One day, he promised himself, he would own a library and would stock it with such books as would reveal to him the secret truths men of wisdom have compiled over the centuries, books containing answers to questions that have baffled mankind since ancient times, questions such as. . . . Joe tried to think of a question, could formulate none more profound than whether the steak dinner served at Molly's Eating Emporium was more palatable than that served at the Boston Hotel.

On second thought a library was not what Joe yearned for. He had no need of ancient wisdom, for he had known the basic, the elemental truth since before his beard had sprouted, had always known, had seen the terrible, imperishable truth corroborated many times over in his short life, witnessed the confirmation of his instinctive grasp of reality's fundamental underpinnings, savoured the essence of existence which pervades all things, had rendered that essence into ringing phrases that echoed inside his skull, the distillation of all knowledge and experience passed down for a thousand generations, the most eternal of verities made concrete, carved in letters a mile high over the marbled lintel of Learning's temple, and the truth is this:

BOTH DISHES ARE INFERIOR—
AND ALWAYS WILL BE

CHAPTER SEVENTEEN

Spring came to Kansas, later than usual and therefore doubly welcome. With it came a satisfying rumour; the president of the Pioneer Bank of Western Kansas had been found, it was said, hanging from a staircase in a rat-ridden New York City hotel. Of the money he had stolen there was no trace; presumably this was the cause of his suicide, rather than guilt. Joe wondered what manner of lascivious delights his dollars had helped purchase, what lavish cuisine and suites of enchantment. The man had obviously gorged his belly and drained his balls until the cash was gone, or perhaps he had gambled it away. No one seemed to know for sure, and when he had heard four differing versions of the erring president's fate in as many days Joe began to wonder if there existed any corroborative facts. He suspected the stories were wishful thinking from those who had been duped, and ceased to speculate on which of the scenarios available most closely approximated the truth. He did not share his disbelief with others, likening their need for imaginary vengeance to the need of religious persons for God. If they wanted to chew on air, convinced it tasted like candy, let them.

Impatient after a winter of inactivity, the buffalo-hunters mustered themselves into outfits and headed for the horizon. Their coiled energies were released in a welter of killing, as if to make up for time lost. Prairie winds that had blown clean and pure all winter long now grew heavy again with the smell of death. Already the bones of previous kills littered the plains, bleached and scattered, skeletal garbage. Empty eyeholes saw the buffalo men pass by, blackened horns held a wisp of cloud between their crescents, jawbones lay among new green succulence; the ribs rising stark from segmented backbones clawed at the sky like the spars of some shattered armada. Across this open graveyard roamed the survivors, and into their midst came the hunters.

Even before the outfit left Dodge he had known this year would be different. Perhaps it was his debt to Tubbs, perhaps the closeness of Puckett (rehired as usual) or, not the least of possibilities, a change within Joe whose time had come regardless of circumstance. He was not the same person he had been in 1872, and as a consequence did not approach his work as buffalo killer with the same sense of dedication. His aim was sure, his weapon true, but of all the emotions available to him, satisfaction was the furthest from Joe's breast. He wondered at the change, attempted in idle moments to chart its shifting parameters. Gone were the quiet times when he could forget who and what he was; staring at the open sky no longer allowed him to drift away on the breeze. Joe Cobden was rooted inside himself, a prisoner within his body, trapped in this time, this place. The more he attempted to understand his condition, the more understanding eluded him. He slaughtered as never before, and if killing a buffalo required more than one shot Joe became furious, felt his reputation tottering. One particularly tough bull, a veteran whose hide was long past its prime, absorbed three bullets before consenting to kneel and die. For the rest of that day Joe trembled with anger. Conversation proved impossible; in answer to a question from Quincy Tubbs regarding the weeks ahead, Joe stared blankly at his partner, then turned and strode away. Tubbs sucked his teeth and wondered what the hell was scratching at Joe now.

Kansas in spring is mild. Kansas in summer is an ordeal. Those few clouds that stray above western skies are robbed of moisture, reduced to empty smudges of white yielding neither shade nor rain. Men roast slowly in the oven of their clothing, basted with sweat. Summer in Kansas is not a time conducive to interior monologue, to restive soul-searching and lengthy consideration of one's place in the *Weltanschauung*. At best, the sojourner in Kansas is able to remember his name at the end of each day, congratulate himself on his survival, and count his pay. That is enough.

Joe kept a stringent tally of the hides taken, pronounced himself out of debt in May; everything after that was profit, and Joe's barrel grew hot in pursuit of solvency. His right ear began to give him pain despite his earplugs (made of rubber now, cotton wads having proved ineffective) and a constant ringing, a sustained tone in the key of E accompanied him day and night, shortened his temper and curbed his speech. He felt he might explode, so great was the pressure mounting inside him, his ear a gauge on which a trembling needle inched inexorably into the red. He avoided Calvin Puckett if possible, knowing the sight of that thin face with its slack expression would provoke him as nothing else could. He had made no objections when Tubbs rehired the Pennsylvanian, determined to master his curiously ambivalent feelings for the skinner; he despised the man, was also afraid of him. This fear (once admitted, a difficult task for Joe) fostered anger, with himself for being afraid, with Puckett for being such a distraction. He reminded himself not to become intimidated by Puckett's dim-witted staring. He could not believe Puckett's fascination with him was solely the result of his deformity; the most ill-mannered and insensitive of men in the outfit had quickly accepted Joe's appearance, even the newcomers travelling with them for the first time. Confrontation was not the answer; Joe had twice attempted that tactic without meaningful result. He would just have to wait, and rely upon the passing of time to peel the layers of inscrutability from Calvin Puckett.

It was all too much. Joe took to drink, initially to aid him in finding sleep, but by August to assist him in facing each dawn. And still he could not define with exactitude the nature of his anguish. He enumerated his various problems; together they amounted to a handicap that might well have destroyed a character less strong than his own, but burdensome though these problems may have been, both separately and *en masse*, they did not explain Joe's overwhelming sense of desolation. He needed time to think, he needed a period of calm in which to resolve this insidious disquiet, he required the very things which were unavailable to him, and so the misery fermented, in time yielding a poisonous bile that gnawed with abrasive liquidity at his intestines.

Joe was unwell, and drank to cure himself. Whenever the outfit delivered its hides to a railroad town Joe stocked up on whiskey before they left. He took a canteen of whiskey along with him while in the saddle, and nursed a bottle by night. Tubbs refrained from criticism until Joe began requiring an average of two shots to bring down each buffalo.

"You're turning into a drunk."

"No I'm not."

They were mounted, a short distance from the latest killing ground, watching the skinners methodically peel hides from eighty-seven dead beasts. Tubbs spat tobacco juice for emphasis. "Sure you are. You're putting away plenty every day. Your shooting's gone all to hell. What's the matter with you?"

"I thought you were telling me."

"It's not funny, Joe. I don't want a drunk for a partner."

"I'm not a drunk, I'm a drinker."

"I mean what I say, Joe."

Tubbs rode off, the last person Joe wanted to disappoint, but ultimatums were one thing Joe could be guaranteed to resist; Tubbs wanted him to quit drinking, did he? Well, no one told Joe Cobden what to do, no one at all. He unscrewed the cap from his canteen, drank deeply. It tasted awful, but soothed the pain in his guts, hushed the eerie singing in his ear.

His intemperance did not go unnoticed among the men. Calvin in particular observed Joe's decline with interest. Was God's hand evident in the crooked man's inebriation? Calvin hated the taste of liquor himself, could not understand why anyone would wish to have even one drink, let alone sip the dreadful stuff all day long. Joe's fuddled aim was common knowledge now. Everyone counted the number of shots fired and matched this with the score of dead buffalo; his aim worsened daily, it seemed. He had never been a popular figure among the men as Quincy Tubbs was, and his company was now avoided altogether, not as a direct consequence of his drinking, which is a man's right after all, but because he allowed the whiskey seriously to affect the performance of his job. A man is what he does, or so ran the general thinking of the outfit, and when a man does his work badly, and is directly to blame for the deterioration, then he becomes less than manly and must be treated as such. Never having sought friendship among those on the payroll, Joe was at first unaware of the sidelong glances and sudden silences that greeted his appearance around the campfire of a night, or while breakfast was being dished out from the rear of the cook's wagon. His predilection for a separate existence blunted his perceptions, was assisted by alcohol in keeping from him the sorry picture he presented to the world at large. Calvin was aware of all this, but had filtered his understanding through the unique sieve of his mania. Joe was not undoing his life unaided, for the task had been undertaken by God Himself; invisible hands were thrusting the bottles into Joe's mouth, thirsty demons in his belly demanding more, the whiskey itself probably provided by angels as required.

As the summer wore on the heat became intolerable. Joe's unquenchable thirst for liquor had by now lowered his marksmanship to a ridiculous level. Strangely, this was not reflected in the weekly tally, for although by summer's height the buffalo count had been markedly reduced it was not due to Joe; there seemed to be fewer buffalo available for slaughter. Tubbs thought at first this was because the herds had changed their migratory pattern, but as the outfit roamed the prairie without encountering more than a fraction of the expected numbers it became obvious that a simpler explanation was called for. Other hunters, after initial success, were puzzling over the same lack of targets, mulling over the possibilities and eventually thinking the unthinkable: were the buffalo being killed faster than they could reproduce? Impossible; they were simply becoming more canny, hiding themselves from view, seeking pastures further afield in which to graze. Look harder, look longer, and a patient hunter would be rewarded. Some were, most were not. The bones littering the plains should have provided an obvious clue to the mystery, but were ignored as part of the scenery.

In the Tubbs-Cobden outfit a general feeling of unease had established itself; initiated by Joe's dissolution, added impetus was provided by the increasingly poor count of hides. The summer had begun well, but as the dog days advanced the rifles spoke less often, the skinning knives remained unwhetted, the wagons rode high and near-empty. It was discouraging, then irritating, then cause for debate and finally, alarm. Because men will always demand reasons for seemingly inexplicable occurrences, and because they do not always demand the most logical of explanations but that which will be emotionally rather than intellectually satisfying, the men of the outfit began to consider Joe the reason for their lack of success. He had sucked on a bottle and conducted himself with the kind of selfish unconcern which does not sit easily on the shoulders of he who aspires to leadership. For Tubbs they felt allegiance, for Joe Cobden nothing but resentment. He was a Jonah, had blighted their chances for profit, had somehow driven the buffalo away. They grumbled among themselves, elected a spokesman and approached Quincy Tubbs.

"The hunchback's got to go."

"He pays half your wages."

"There aren't going to be no wages without we start killing buffalo."

"He's not to blame for that."

"We think different. He goes, or we do."

"You can leave any time."

"We might just do that."

Tubbs went to Joe and relayed the mood of the outfit. "Things'd be a whole lot better around here if you'd cork the bottle, Joe."

"Cork my ass," said Joe, moderately drunk.

Tubbs saw his chances for a solution to the problem evaporate, and his tone hardened. "The boys are worried. . . ."

"Tell 'em to go chase themselves."

"This thing won't just go away."

"And you can join 'em."

Tubbs looked at Joe, saw him as he had on that first raw morning in Hays City, a stunted and misshapen creature with not one redeeming physical characteristic, the very essence of ugliness. The respect Tubbs had slowly assembled for Joe during their association had begun to wane from the moment Joe tilted his first bottle outside of a town; to Tubbs' way of thinking any indulgence which interfered with the hunting was unforgivable, especially now with the buffalo seeming to vanish into the emptiness around them. Observing Joe's bloated face, the heavy lidded eyes and weak sneer, Tubbs felt a part of himself detach and float away, and knew it for the closely guarded thing it had been. Quincy Tubbs was not a man to make friends easily, and until mere months before had regarded Joe as the friend closest to his heart. Joe did not know this, the emotion never having been expressed either openly or covertly; Tubbs considered such displays unmanly. Admitting his love for the hunchback to himself had been no easy task, and Tubbs was disappointed to find in Joe no trace of reciprocal warmth, no matter how low these hypothetical coals of affection be banked. Tubbs had not invested in true friendship since his childhood, and now felt his efforts had been wholly wasted. It was a bitter lesson for so professedly hard a man, and anger over his squandered love (a word he would never have applied, even grudgingly) quickly burned away any lingering wisps of fondness held in reserve. His affection, undeclared and unknown, had been thrown back at him with total disregard for the human niceties which existed even here on civilisation's furthest edge. Anger such as this, inexplicable to others, not comprehended in its entirety even by Tubbs, could not be ignored. Of a sudden he no longer wanted Joe Cobden for his friend.

"It's been my intention to dissolve the partnership next time we hit Dodge," he lied. "It may as well happen right here. There aren't enough buffalo to need two guns anyhow. I'm sorry, Joe, but you've had this coming."

The gist of Tubbs' words finally penetrated Joe's head. "You want to get rid of me?" It was a slap in the face, unjustifiable, an insult! He wanted to punch Tubbs square on the nose, trample him underfoot. A flush of rage rose from his chest, mottled his whiskered cheeks, expanded the veins lacing his eyes. "You want to get rid of me . . . ?"

"You know the reason. I warned you. If you don't leave, the outfit folds. I like this line of business." He produced a stub of pencil and scrap of paper, applied one to the other, handed Joe the result. "That's an IOU for your share of things. It's a fair figure. Take it, Joe." There was unmistakable strength of purpose behind his words, his voice, his very stance. Joe's anger was slowly but insistently nudged aside by shame. He had failed the one man who had given him a chance to make something of his life, and in so doing had failed himself. He could not speak, could barely look Tubbs in the eye, felt the hot core of his rage become a slough of guilt and mortification. He had done wrong. The IOU trembled in his hand. He could not define the numbers and letters, so shaken was he. In a matter of moments Joe had been reduced to a mere boy, a foolish youth caught aping the behaviour of adults. With something akin to shock he felt tears prickling at his eyes, felt his lips begin to quiver. No! He clamped his mouth into a line, squinted at the paper in his hand. He could not simply walk away, although that was what he wanted to do. He would have to say something, but what could possibly convey the flux of emotions inside him?

"I asked for it," he said finally, hoping Tubbs would be impressed by his candour, perhaps feel a little guilty himself for having hurt a friend, for having dismissed a partner in so blunt a fashion.

"You did that," said Tubbs.

Nothing remained to be said, only one thing to be done. Joe made up a sack of food, picked up his Sharpe's and mounted his horse with the usual monkey-like bound, watched by the entire camp. He kicked lightly with his heels, and horse and rider departed the Tubbs outfit for ever.

Watching Joe leave, Calvin experienced a rush of panic. He had heard rumours of discontent between the partners, but would not have believed Joe could simply pack up and ride off like this. What to do? He was here solely to keep an eye on the crooked man's activities, and don't forget what the white wolf said: Kill him. And there was Joe Cobden already topping the nearest rise, disappearing from view . . . gone! Calvin wrung his hands. It had all happened too quickly. Not a word had been said to verify it, but Calvin knew Joe would not return. Every minute lost took the object of his obsession further from him. Would God regard this as dereliction of duty? He must follow. Calvin was not a horseman, had always ridden in the wagons; he would have to pursue Joe on foot. The rest of the men were crowding around Tubbs; now was the perfect opportunity to slip away. Armed with teeth and fingernails, without so much as a handful of jerky or canteen of water, Calvin set off on a route that shielded him from view behind the wagons until he was over a ridge. Once out of sight he altered course until he could see Joe, quite some distance off by now. Calvin started running.

He ran and walked, ran and walked as best he could, but a man on horseback moving steadily across flat country cannot be followed indefinitely by a man afoot. For almost two hours Calvin was able to keep track of Joe by observing him as he passed across the tops of shallow rises, a little smaller each time. In addition to these sightings it appeared that Joe was deliberately leaving a trail to be followed, a paper trail, tiny shreddings of white barred with an occasional pencil mark; the IOU was offered to the god of pride in forlorn scatterings. Calvin picked up all those he could find, kept them clenched in the sweating palm of his hand until the paper had soaked up sufficient moisture to become whole again, a grimy wad carrying the impression of palm and fingers.

By mid afternoon pursuer and pursued were separated by many miles, and Calvin had reached the point of collapse. He did not know in which direction he had been heading, had only the vaguest of notions where the camp might be, not that he wished to return there; no, he must keep on until he found Joe, however long it took, however far he must travel, however brutally he must punish his aching legs, and roasted lungs. It was the will of God that he punish his body thus. By nightfall he was utterly lost, sole agent of motion on the darkening plain. His boots stumbled over buffalo bones until a skull brought him down. The air was warm, all the blanket Calvin needed, in his exhausted state, to fall quickly asleep. In the last moments of wakefulness he heard the cry of a wolf saluting the newly risen moon, and wondered if the wolf of wolves ever spoke in a voice other than human.

His first full day alone on the prairie taught Calvin many things: never set out on a journey of indefinite duration without adequate supplies; never follow a rider on foot; bring a map and compass. If his hat had not already been on his head when he left the camp he would doubtless have been sunstruck by noon. His body ached with the exertions of yesterday, his physical pain exceeded only by the knot of misery in his heart; once again he had failed to do his master's bidding. Would this be his punishment, this hopeless wandering among buffalo remains? Crows perched on roosts of bone tilted their heads in curiosity and flapped into the blue and empty sky, their desolate cawings the only sound. Heat sat firmly on Calvin's shoulders, a blistering weight absorbing the last of his strength. Hot winds moved sluggishly among the skeletons, parched his throat, dried the film of tears on his eyes until blinking became torture. Dying grass yielded to his boots and did not raise itself when he had passed by. He found himself falling often, usually without suffering great hurt. When this had happened a great many times he decided he would not get up again; better to rest where he was and gather what little strength remained. It was only yesterday that he had set out to follow Joe and here he was, dying. Just one day. Remarkable! Calvin had always known he was not a strong man, and here was the proof. A three-legged cat would have displayed greater stamina. He slept.

A crow alighting on his thigh woke him. Late afternoon, he reasoned. I should walk some more. The crow stood undisturbed for several minutes while Calvin sent messages to his limbs, orders waylaid *en route,* diverted and drained from his body into the yellow grass. Eventually, with a great deal of effort laced with self-pity, he contrived to raise himself. He stared about him, ignoring the cries of the disturbed crow. The wadded IOU dropped unnoticed from his fist. He walked on, one foot plodding before the other, clumsy and half-hearted. He did not even bother to choose a direction, so miserable was he at the unfortunate turn events had taken. He had done his best. It was not Calvin's fault if he was not smart enough to figure things beforehand and make adequate preparations. Now he would never get the chance to kill Joe Cobden and fulfil the destiny foisted upon him by the white wolf. It really was too bad. Calvin would have liked to repay the debt he owed God for striking down his father. When he dropped dead himself in the next day or so it would leave the scales unbalanced, the ledger blank, a source of shame.

Tearing up the IOU and throwing away the pieces had given Joe a satisfying glow, a squint-eyed, narrow lipped kind of feeling. Regret at having failed a friend had been replaced, now that he was alone, with a leaden emptiness, a sense of weightless plummeting. He had tried to lessen his gloom by inward rejection of Quincy Tubbs' last action, the fair and equitable purchase of Joe's share in the outfit. For many miles Joe tried to tell himself he had been swindled, taken advantage of, but within himself knew it was not so; he had reaped the reward of foolishness, had gotten off lightly in fact, the account all squared, the book closed. Then rage would come again to sweep away his equilibrium and tear down the hastily constructed citadel of understanding and acceptance. His mood alternated between despair and indignation, could find no comfortable perch anywhere. By day's end he had stilled these furious see-sawings to a maudlin pining for what had been, after all, two years and more of making real that which had been dreamed of. He had succeeded with a vengeance, that much was clear, had grown too confident in his ability to blast a way to personal achievement and what should have been its attendant happiness or, at the very least, contentment. The lesson learned was a simple one: disruptive phantoms of the mind are not dissuaded by ironmongery and gunpowder from pursuit of their own nebulous destinies, nor can they be drowned in liquor but, rather, thrive in that medium and are ultimately triumphant. Joe had been thrust from an ephemeral and vainglorious throne by his own cloaked and scheming courtiers, was now no more than a beggar in the kitchen. And all in the turning of a season.

CHAPTER EIGHTEEN

Ruminating on his wretchedness, Calvin was unaware of the railroad tracks until the toe of his boot struck the wooden ties. Marching parallel to the bands of steel, perhaps thirty feet away on the far side, were the multiple totems of progress, telegraph poles, a titanic fence with but a single wire. Calvin rushed across and put his ear to the nearest, eager for the chirrupings of civilisation. He heard nothing; no messages were being passed across Kansas. No matter, the rails were there. He ran back to the tracks and placed himself within their comforting boundaries. Now then, which way to go?

The tracks ran east to west, the setting sun told him that. After much debate with himself Calvin chose to walk eastward, since the sun's harsh glare at its current low altitude would have hurt his eyes; the sun in Kansas remains a force to be reckoned with until it is well and truly below the horizon. Hard, unyielding, ringing hollowly whenever he kicked at them, the rails cheered him immensely; they were the next best thing to a town. He could not eat or drink them, but they would lead him to a place where food and drink were to be had. That the distances between towns in Kansas could number a hundred miles and more did not deter Calvin from his optimistic bent; God had provided the rails, and the rails would lead him to safety. He strode into the encroaching gloom of evening with buoyant spirit and lightened step despite the dryness in his throat and the disgruntled rumblings of his belly. All would be well.

He continued walking long after his boots had been made invisible by darkness, heels thudding confidently against the ties and cinders of the railbed. Had Calvin known any tunes he would have been tempted to whistle or sing; as it was, even a nonmelodic humming proved too enthusiastic an exercise for his dehydrated throat and he wisely desisted. Calvin had always found it difficult to concentrate on more than one thing at a time; now that he had ceased to create music his mind was free to consider other things—the ever thickening darkness around him, for example. Where was the moon? Calvin searched, but could locate it nowhere—because the sky was hidden by black clouds! Why had he not noticed earlier? Clouds this dark meant rain, that magical substance which had last made an appearance in Kansas during May, and yes, the air was definitely cooler! Calvin felt a pleasant shiver of anticipation as the first distant flickerings of lightning lanced at the horizon, crazed scribblings in electric ink, instantly erased. Laggard thunder reverberated in its wake, the hollow booming pressuring a response from Calvin's wax-infested ears. He uttered discreet whimperings of excitement, as might a nervous dog. Rain was coming, wet and wonderful, cool and cleansing! He willed the wriggling snakes of light to advance and meet him, opened his arms to the muffled implosions of displaced air. Calvin ran toward the storm, eager for communion, had taken barely a dozen steps before the sound produced by his boots suddenly altered. He stopped immediately, knew he was standing on a bridge. Calvin did not like heights. He knelt and passed his fingers through empty air between the ties where seconds before there had been solid earth. He felt himself overcome by giddiness, and shuffled backwards on hands and knees to safer ground. Squinting, Calvin saw that the bridge, in his imagination an immensely long and unwieldy structure spanning a bottomless chasm, was in reality a modest trestle carrying the tracks some fifteen feet across a shallow wash, the merest line of erosion on the prairie, its bed just ten feet or so below the rails. Was that the trickling of water he heard down there, or the stormy tossings of dead grass? He clambered down the bank to investigate and found not a lifesaving stream (the water, little enough at the best of times, had ceased to flow in July) but a sad collection of clothing and bones which once had been a man.

These remnants were scattered for a short distance along the declivity, and had long since been robbed of meat by wolves. The clothing, before it had been torn apart by impatient fangs, had been of superior cloth. Calvin had never been told of the absconding president of the Pioneer Bank of Western Kansas, and was therefore unaware of the importance of his find. He was not afraid; once before he had examined the remains of a dead man during a time of thunder and lightning, and the occasion had heralded a new phase in his life. He could not know that the dead man had stepped down from a snowbound train one wintry night to stretch his legs; the platform from which he descended was directly over the bridge, and he stepped blithely into space, his eyes unused to the darkness outside the carriage. The wash had been filled with snow so lightly compacted as to impede his downward progress not at all. Beneath the snow were rocks, placed there not by nature, but by workmen of the Atchison, Topeka & Santa Fe railroad; their purpose was to hold intact the earthen banks under the trestle in case a flash flood should tear loose the soil and render the tracks unsafe. The president tumbled while in mid-air and landed upon his head. The blow was not sufficient in itself to kill, but the unconsciousness which followed was of a duration to enable cold, freezing, debilitating cold to invade the president's body. He had made no sound, and was not missed when the way ahead was finally cleared, the journey resumed. Not until the train was far down the line did passengers recall the small man with the worried frown; they assumed he had left to assist in the shovelling of snow and had returned to a different seat, another carriage. The money lay beside him in a leather bag. The president regained his senses for a short while, and pulled himself a little way up the banks of the wash before succumbing to his cracked skull and the cold. He was soon buried under fresh snowfall, one arm outstretched for the ties so impossibly near, and it was in this position the wolves found him during the March thaw. They were not particularly hungry, having recently killed a buffalo, and dismembered the president from habit rather than from need. The money bag was ignored; only a starving wolf will eat tanned leather.

Calvin nudged the bones this way and that with his boot, idly wondering who this unfortunate soul had been. The first drops of rain pattered on his hatbrim; a flash of lightning, very near now, illuminated the wash with brilliance, gave to every pebble a shadow. In the momentary dazzlement Calvin saw the bag, groped for it in the darkness that followed, found the handle and pulled it to him. As if awaiting the least encouragement its clasp sprang open; the interior of the bag offered itself. Cool wind passed across Calvin's brow; the raindrops accelerated their tattoo, striking the rocks, the trestle and rails, rebounding in a haze of shattered droplets. Lightning flickered between sky and earth, jagged bolts holding aloft a dark and tumbling temple of cloud. Thunder invaded Calvin's bones with its terrible vibration, set his fingers trembling. A whining noise rose in his throat as he reached inside, scrabbled through the bag with questing fingers. Paper money, nothing but paper money top to bottom and side to side, hundreds and thousands of pieces of money. Calvin could not count, but he knew dollars exist in various denominations; even if every one of these bills was just a single dollar it meant he held a fortune in his hands. How was it that the dead man had owned so very much? It was unthinkable that one person could possess this kind of wealth. A train robber! This was the only possible explanation; the scattered bones were those of a desperado who had met his fate, dying of gunshot wounds most likely, rich but doomed, expiring alone and without comfort. And leaving his riches behind. Finders keepers; the childhood ditty spoke to Calvin from the innermost recesses of his brain. Finders keepers, losers weepers. The loser was dead, beyond weeping, and Calvin was the finder who kept. So profoundly moving was the thrill of excitement that rippled through him, Calvin felt an urgent need to defecate. He lowered his pants, squatted beneath the trestle's meagre shelter and voided his bowels in a rush of excrement. The bag was still in his hand; he attended to his sanitary needs with several tens and a hundred. Had he been able to differentiate between the bills he would have used ones; Calvin was no wastrel.

Individual words caromed and collided within the pointed enclosure of Calvin's skull: Mine! was predominant among them, and Rich! was another, Soon! a more puzzling third. He was unsure what was meant by it; probably it implied great changes rushing from the future to meet him, staggering changes, the like of which had never before encroached upon his thinking. The nature of this imminent revolution was vague, so imprecise in detail while overwhelming in its inevitability that Calvin began to be afraid. Could he make so radical an adjustment? He huddled under the railroad trestle, rain drumming on his hat and shoulders, the smell of his own shit thick in his nostrils; tens of thousands of dollars lay at his side, a dead thief's bones at his feet. Calvin hugged his knees and rocked steadily for an hour or so, groaning with the weight of responsibility and the frightening abruptness with which his life had been rendered topsy-turvy. He did not once think of his empty belly, the white wolf, or the need to kill Joe Cobden. Calvin thought only of what he must do to keep the bag of money for himself. He did not want to be robbed by a compatriot of the dead man. Caution was called for. He closed the bag, untied his belt and passed it through the handle, joining the bag to his body. It was too bulky to rest on his lap; he ran it around behind himself and was able to sit on it. The fortune made a comfortable cushion.

Calvin closed his eyes to the white light flickering around him, to the endless drumrolls of thunder as the storm marched by. One need remained uppermost: to consolidate the certainty building within him that he had been granted the wherewithal to accomplish something grand, something truly astounding. Nothing else concerned him at this moment but the nurturing of his own budding self-esteem. For the first time in his life Calvin was able to conceive of himself as somebody of importance, a person of consequence. He would never have to skin a buffalo again, never be obliged to submit in tongue-tied agony while others ridiculed his silences and awkwardness. He would be a man to contend with. People would know the name Calvin Puckett and be awed by its utterance. Respect would be given him, respect long overdue. When he walked down the street eyes would watch, heads turn; hats would be raised in salute. He would take this bag of train robber's money and beat the world into the shape he desired, a shape essentially circular in design with himself at its centre. That was his rightful place, after all; the right hand of God deserved courtesy and deference, wanted and would receive no more than his due. Thus sat Calvin, contriving his future while the storm hissed and boomed around him, and perhaps it was possible his life would follow the plan laid out for it in this simplistic manner, for the cloudiest of pipe dreams may be given substance if the pipe be of gold.

Then he remembered God. Remembrance begat shame. Calvin had allowed thoughts of self-glorification to swamp his usual humble and unwavering devotion. Contrition made him wince and hang his head. God had provided the cash by having the crooked man leave the camp, by obliging Calvin to follow him and become lost, by directing his faltering steps to this place, this shallow crease in the prairie with its awesome secret. How many trains had rumbled overhead, oblivious to the trove? Dozens? Hundreds? God had kept them moving in order to preserve the bag of money for Calvin's arrival. He could not simply revel in his newfound riches without giving thought to the force behind it, the beneficent machinations of the Almighty. How best to pay tribute to His power and might? Calvin pondered, was pondering still when the storm dragged its tattered skirts away to the west. Out of concealment came the moon, and from its lucent influence came the answer: Calvin would build a church.

The wisdom of his choice was immediately apparent, for

no sooner had the decision been made for him by a small voice within than Calvin was overcome by utter calm, a tranquillity so vast a stone dropped into its heart would have been swallowed without a sound, without a ripple. A church! Calvin could not draw breath, so majestic was his vision, felt he would float from his body in ecstasy as the edifice reared itself before him, stone upon stone, assembled by unseen hands, walls rising to impossible heights until capped by the moon itself. The bag under his buttocks contained a house of worship comparable with no other. He would do it, would build a shrine to his god, and this determination to accomplish, to make his mark upon the world set Calvin's blood racing in rapturous tides from the maelstrom of his breast. His fingertips pulsed so painfully he would not have been surprised to witness them glowing redly in the dark; his entire body began to quake, a delightful shivering of such intensity it threatened to unseat him from his perch. It was then he realised the vibrations passing through him were being transmitted via the ground from an approaching locomotive.

Calvin's mood altered in an instant; gone were the grandiose imaginings of a moment before, and in their glimmering wake came the urge to be once again a part of the world of men. He scrambled from beneath the trestle and up the bank to the tracks. From the darkness in the west came a rumbling and a panting and an unblinking yellow eye crowned with showering sparks. Calvin was bathed in the beam of yellow light, felt an exultant pride in being illuminated thus when all around him was wrapped in gloom. The engineers could not fail to see him, but he raised his arms to make quite certain they understood his need.

Among the rules of the A, T & SF railroad was one which stated that at least one of the two men sharing the driver's cab be watching the track ahead at all times—an edict easily complied with in daylight, considerably harder to practise by night, when the headlamp's feeble glow revealed nothing but endless tracks receding into an infinite tunnel of blackness. Dulled by the monotony of such visual fare, the engineers often fell into a trance-like state despite the clash of iron couplings, the hissing of valves and the firebox's constant roar, all the usual cacophony of steam locomotion. So deep could this stupor become that the engineers, expecting nothing to appear in the funnel of light travelling ahead of them, would, when an object did appear, ignore it; the unexpected became the uncomprehended, ultimately the unseen. Locomotive 509 (*General Sterling Beamis*) clanked and chuffed and hissed past Calvin without either man in the cabin noticing God's right hand standing by the track, begging a ride.

He could not understand why the train did not slow down. Already a long string of cattle-cars was rattling by, their living freight engulfing him with the rank odour of dung and terror. Calvin was infuriated with the engineers for having deliberately ignored him, made up his mind never to let them into his church. Righteous wrath did not, however, furnish him with a means of leaving behind the scene of his transmutation; he would have to take action of his own accord. Calvin began running alongside the train, the bag bouncing and sliding across his hips. He matched speed with the cattle-car nearest to hand and grabbed at the ladder bolted to its side. With a heave requiring all his depleted strength Calvin swung his legs free of the ground and scrabbled with his boots for a foothold on the lowest rung. Secure after a fleeting moment of dread, heart drubbing his ribs, he inched up the ladder to the roof, slid across to the safety of the flat central catwalk and sprawled along it on his belly. Below him the cattle on their way to the stockyards of Chicago bellowed continually, jammed together in a ferment of bulging eyes, gouging horns, blood and shit, destined one and all for the sledgehammer and the cleaver. In this manner was the new apostle borne eastward.

In the last hour before dawn Calvin fell asleep despite his discomfort and awoke when halfway from the cattle-car roof to the ground. He had a fraction of a second in which to enjoy the sensation of weightlessness before his shoulder struck the stones and cinders of the railbed. He bounced away from the tracks, could just as easily have bounced in the opposite direction and been severed into portions by the wheels grinding past, and interpreted the lucky bounce as yet more evidence of God's guiding presence at his elbow. He was not badly hurt, not having had time to stiffen his body before it hit the ground; drunks often escape injury in this way without crediting God for it. He picked himself up, made sure the clasp on the money-bag was still secure as the last car click-clicked past him. As the train drew away, silence fell around Calvin, left him confused at the sudden absence of noise and physical vibration. He rubbed at his bruised shoulder, brushed dirt from his cheek, wondered what to do now.

He walked on. In time the horizon defined itself, a straight edge of greyness below a smear of palest blue. Calvin drew encouragement from the dawn, increased the length of his stride in its direction, watched it spread and wash across the sky. Now came the sun, a throbbing orange ball slowly ascending through bands of violet cloud. Calvin stopped to give the sight his fullest attention. He did not know that the sun is a flaming star, did not know that every star in the heavens is a sun, their fiery splendour reduced to benign silvery twinklings by sheer distance, did not even know that the earth is a sphere, had heard of no other country but America. Calvin knew nothing of science, knew only that men are cruel and God is good.

CHAPTER NINETEEN

An hour after sunrise he stopped again, this time to wonder at a long smudge on the horizon, a ridge topped with trees. The railroad approached from the south-west along a gently curving rise that gradually elevated the tracks some twenty feet above the prairie. A further half hour of walking told Calvin the rise eventually joined the spine of the tree-covered ridge, but before it did so the tracks veered off toward a town, and into that town strode Calvin, the bag in his hand now, in an approximation of normality. Calvin wanted no one to stare at him, to think him different from his fellows, for a plan was forming in his head, a plan contingent upon the degree to which this town proved itself worthy of his acceptance; he wanted it to be the right town, and so did not tempt fate by attracting attention with a bag hanging over his buttocks. The money swung at arm's length with every step. Calvin hoped he appeared casual.

There were few people around at this early hour to witness his arrival as he stepped from the tracks several hundred yards short of the railroad depot, and walked the rest of the way down what was obviously the main street. It was a small town, like many in Kansas, a cluster of some thirty commerical buildings and as many homes, bordered on the south side by the railroad tracks. A ten minute stroll took Calvin from one side of town to the other. There were farms roundabout, prosperous by all appearances, but farms did not interest him; Calvin's eye wandered to the wooded ridge, the only point of elevation for many a mile. He could discern no houses upon it, an unusual state of affairs; surely someone wanted his windows to encompass the views from the ridge, moderate though its height may be. But no one had. Very good. Calvin wanted the ridge for himself.

Another stroll back through the town proved somewhat unsettling; more people were about their business now, and several of them gave him scornful glances. Calvin paused before a store window and blanched at the pitiful figure reflected therein. Who could blame them for staring at such a scarecrow? His confidence began to seep away. New clothes, that was what he needed! He hid in an alleyway, extracted a handful of money from the bag and put it in his pockets, then ranged the street again until he found a window displaying male apparel. In went Calvin, trembling at his own daring. Out came Calvin some ten minutes later, a bulky parcel under his arm. The salesman had provided him with directions to the nearest bath house. This was located at the Calhoun Hotel, but the proprietor would not allow him to use it until he had first scrubbed himself in a horse trough at the rear of the building. Cleansed, dressed in new clothes that very nearly fitted his angular body, Calvin next visited a barber, easily found thanks to the red and white striped pole planted in the sidewalk. His narrow face freshly scraped, hair tonsured to the point where his ears stood out proud and white from his sunburned cheeks and neck, he re-entered the men's outfitters for what he had neglected to purchase on his first visit: a new hat. Perhaps his oversight was fortunate, for had he chosen a hat before gracing the barber's chair it would certainly have settled around his ears afterwards. Still clutching his bag, Calvin went to the window in which scarcely an hour before he had seen the dismal tramp; now was revealed a prince among men, a veritable dandy. Strutting a little, Calvin allowed his nose to guide him to an eating house, where he breakfasted on beef and potatoes and coffee, plus a quart of cool water. While paying his bill he asked directions to the biggest bank in town.

Calvin perched himself on the edge of a fine upholstered chair in the office of Nathan Bragg, president of the Farmers' Bank. Bragg was a busy man; only Calvin's new clothes

had got him this far. He had never before been in so sump-
tuously furnished a room, nor talked with so imposing a
figure as the muttonchop-whiskered president planted so
resolutely behind his walnut desk and thrusting belly.

"How exactly may I be of service to you, Mr. Puckett?"

"I. . . ." His tongue glued itself to the roof of his mouth.

"Yes?"

Calvin swallowed convulsively. "Who owns where the
trees are?" he blurted, almost tumbling from the chair in
his rush to rid himself of the question.

"Trees, Mr. Puckett?" Bragg wondered what kind of
strange bird had flapped into his office. He pulled an or-
nately fashioned watch from his waistcoat pocket, checked
the time and frowned mightily; this was a standard act of
intimidation used against those he considered his inferiors,
that is, virtually everyone in the county. "Trees?" he
prompted, growing impatient with the strangulated sounds
emanating from Calvin's lips.

"Just outside of town," babbled Calvin. "A line of trees
up off the ground. . . ."

"Are you perhaps referring to the ridge?"

Calvin nodded happily; this man was so clever and understanding.

"You wish to know who owns the ridge?"

Another nod, accompanied by an eager smile. Bragg began to doubt the wisdom of seeing this fellow; there was a
peculiar element in the facial construction, more than a hint
of degeneracy in the gangling limbs.

"Why, may I ask, do you wish to know?"

"I . . . I want to buy it . . . I *want* it!"

His mouth clamped shut, aware of its unseemly loudness.

Bragg pursed his lips and stared at Calvin, another ploy
to set lesser beings ill at ease. The ridge was owned by one
of his soundest clients, Lucius Croft, who owned a good
deal of land in and around the town. Purchasing the ridge
had been an investment, the lumber being considered at
that time a rare and precious thing. The south-west tip of
the ridge, the end closest to the town, had been denuded in

the early years of settlement, was now an eroding slope dotted with tree stumps. Then had come the railroad, and with it flatcar after flatcar of timber sawed and planed in the east, ready for immediate use. It was cheaper and easier to buy this than cut down the rest of the ridge, and the town had grown at an even faster rate. The ridge had been abandoned, its remaining trees allowed to grow unmolested, not worth the cost of felling. Lucius Croft had wanted to be rid of the land for years. It was too steep for farming, could never be of any practical use. And now came this awkward bumpkin with a desire for ownership, obviously a fool. Only one question need be asked.

"The ridge covers quite a stretch of ground, Mr. Puckett. Forgive my bluntness, but do you have the necessary funds for so large a purchase?"

"Funds . . . ?"

"Money," beamed Bragg, sighing inwardly.

"Yes," said Calvin. "A lot," he added. "A whole lot," he amended.

"Yes?" The president smiled wider in disbelief. He would tell his wife about this idiot with the sweat beading his upper lip. Normally a shrewd judge of character, able to detect a time-waster, Bragg should never have allowed into his office someone carrying such a disreputable looking leather bag: it appeared to have been out in the weather for some considerable time, as did its owner. Had the fellow somehow looked into his mind? The bag was being lifted for his unwilling perusal, set upon the polished surface of his treasured walnut desk, that filthy bag on the very symbol of his power! "Kindly remove that at once, Mr. Puckett!" Opening it. . . . He was opening it! What was in there, a gun? Was this a robbery? He drew in his breath, prepared to acquiesce at the sight of a pointed pistol. Instead there cascaded on to his desk a rustling avalanche of money, creased and crinkled, a slithering pyramid of dollars. Bragg's jaw dropped, his heart thudded with disturbing emphasis, and still more wealth spilled from the battered leather bag. Calvin stood with a beatific smile above the pile of bills. Several slid from the overcrowded desk and drifted to the carpet like autumn leaves.

"A whole lot," reiterated Calvin, and he did not exaggerate.

"My dear sir . . ." said Bragg, and the smile reasserting itself on his lips was for once sincere. This wonderful stranger had brought into his life the one thing guaranteed to set his blood racing, and no mean amount of it; the sum must be . . . enormous! "Mr. Puckett . . . sir, exactly how much do you have here?"

"I ain't counted it," said Calvin, suddenly afraid this resplendent fat man with the silk-edged lapels and perfumey kind of smell would discover he was unable to count beyond ten. His left leg began to tremble with nervous dread.

"You have not counted it? But, my good sir, that is . . . unwise, is it not? You must keep strict account of such capital. May I enquire as to its history?"

"History?" The name George Washington sprang into Calvin's mind; that was all he knew of history. His knowledge did not encompass what it was that George Washington had done an unknown number of years ago, just the name.

"I mean, Mr. Puckett, where did you get it?" Bragg smelled the fear drifting across his desk; something was wrong here, and he would get to the heart of it, ferret out the secret this simpleton was attempting to hide. His smile had not faded, had in fact widened to its broadest in an effort to reassure Calvin he was under no suspicion of wrongdoing.

"I . . . dug it up."

"Dug it up, Mr. Puckett? From where, a dollar mine?"

Calvin knotted his brow, wrestled with the question. "They don't get dollars from no mine," he said, puzzled, and the width of Bragg's smile decreased fractionally.

"Just my little joke, Mr. Puckett. You say you dug it up?" He spoke as to a backward child, saw this as the best means of making progress.

"I dug it up . . . in my uncle's yard."

"He was a wealthy man?"

"He had a whole lot of money. That money there. It's mine now. He said I can have it when he's dead. And he is. He died last week and I dug up the money. I want to buy all that land where the trees are. It's high up and that's what I want."

"Yes, indeed, Mr. Puckett, and I will be pleased to arrange the sale. It so happens the present owner of the property is a client of mine. Fear not, sir, the ridge will be yours. For an appropriate sum, of course."

"I got lots of money here. Is it enough?"

"I don't doubt it for a moment. But see here, Mr. Puckett, don't you think we should ascertain the exact amount you have before we proceed further?" Calvin eyed him with alarm. What was he talking about? Bragg divined his confusion. "Shall we count it between us?"

Calvin nodded. Bragg began assembling the bills into their denominations, stacking them in criss-crossed piles, ten notes this way, ten notes that. Calvin attempted imitation of the act, succeeded only in jumbling tens and ones and twenties and hundreds together. Bragg learned what he had needed to know; the fool could not count, could not read, in all likelihood could not write. He did not know where this phenomenal amount had come from and did not wish to know; a sum so vast in the hands of one so foolish could mean only one thing: it had been come by illegally. Best not to question its origin. The numbers were not sequential, were therefore untraceable. Calvin was still trying, a pitiful sight. Bragg warmed to his guest's quandary, encouraged him to slip free of pretence's barb. "Mr. Puckett, you're probably tired after your journey from . . . your home. Why not allow me to perform this tedious chore on your behalf. As a banker I am accustomed to counting large amounts accurately, and in a very short time. Will you permit me?"

"You go right ahead," said Calvin, relieved.

While Bragg counted and stacked, Calvin settled back in the upholstered chair and looked about him at the portraits and certificates hanging on the walls, at the wallpaper itself, consisting of a great many bunches of brown flowers, each one the same as the next; the motif had been chosen by the banker's wife. Calvin watched a fly crawl over the slowly diminishing pile of money, wondered if it knew how much was under its sticky feet. He looked forward to finding out himself. It was a whole lot, he already knew that, a whole lot of cash. He fell asleep in the chair, head sagging, his breathing punctuated with an occasional snuffle.

Bragg paused in his labours. How much more incentive did he need to make the most of this golden opportunity? The fool snored while a stranger counted his wealth! It would be criminal to allow a chance like this to pass him by. Bragg was a successful banker, but the town was small and he did not wish to be a big fish in a small pond for ever. A little deception here, where it would go unnoticed, and gigantic strides could be made in the direction of his dreams. He knew it was wrong, but there was something unnatural in allowing a cretin like Puckett access to so great a sum (twenty-three thousand so far, and rising) while he, a man of intelligence and drive, was stuck for the discernible future in a town limited in avenues for advancement. Look at the fool, head lolling like a sleepy hound's, mouth open, dead to the world while the very earth was eased from beneath his unsuspecting feet. He deserved it, had asked for it with his stupidity, and would get it. Bragg would be generous, though, would not rob him blind; there would be plenty left to play with. Why did he want to buy the ridge? It was worthless. What a wasted investment that would be. Still, if that was what the idiot wanted, that was what he would receive, and for a wildly inflated price. Lucius Croft would allow the bank to handle the transaction if Bragg promised a huge profit, would not begrudge him a larger than usual commission if all went well, and why should it not? It was painfully apparent that this dim-witted Midas could be twisted around the finger of anyone with a desire to do so. It was fortunate for him he had come to Nathan Bragg; there were plenty of unscrupulous characters in

Kansas who would have bilked him of the lion's share. Bragg was content with a jackal's share. He counted on while Calvin slept.

Forty-eight thousand, three hundred and fifty-one dollars. Bragg resisted the urge to throw his arms around the neat stacks and sweep the lot into his lap. He watched a thread of saliva link Calvin's lower lip with his vest. The sight hardened his resolve. He quickly and silently opened several drawers in his desk and transferred a good many bundles, counting as he did so; he took most of the hundreds, leaving the ones, fives, tens and twenties behind. Calvin snorted. Bragg froze, a sickly smile on his face as he lifted his head from the drawers. Thank God, the fool slept on, smacking his lips, air bubbling through nostrils sorely in need of a handkerchief. The banker was sweating as he locked the drawers and pocketed the key, could smell his own flesh, feel the dampness in his armpits. He breathed deeply to calm himself, closed his eyes, thought of what he had done, thought of the possible consequences if his act was ever discovered. Whatever qualms he had were deliberately thrust aside, silenced with a vision of his future, a comfortable and rosy coloured place, probably located in Chicago or New York City. The deed is done, he told himself, and now I must live with it. He did not anticipate any real difficulty in doing so. The smile reappeared on his face.

"Mr. Puckett?"

Calvin's eyes opened, darted around the room in alarm. He saw the money, located himself and smiled wanly. Bragg's expression was almost pitying. "You have a substantial sum here, Mr. Puckett." He Paused, took a breath. "Twenty-eight thousand, three hundred and fifty-one dollars. Does that tally with your estimate?" No answer. "Does that sound about right to you, Mr. Puckett?"

"I reckon."

"I suggest we deposit it in the safe. We don't want someone to come through the window and steal it while we're gone, do we?"

"We goin' someplace?"

"To see the ridge, and then to see the owner."

And that is what they did. Bragg hired a buggy from the livery stable and together fool and thief drove the two miles to the ridge. Calvin climbed to the top, looked across the town to the east, the prairie to the west, was exhilarated by the view, uninspiring though this was. Bragg stayed by the buggy, his mood fluctuating between fear and self-congratulation. Calvin descended from the ridge with eyes agleam. "I want it," he declared.

"And you shall have it," promised the banker.

They drove to the farm of Lucius Croft, a man in his sixties with an appetite for money undiminished by the years. Bragg took Croft into another room while Calvin was served coffee in the parlour by Croft's daughter. The two men plotted, Croft as yet unconvinced that someone would be fool enough to pay the price they intended asking. He was soon apprised of Calvin's stupidity.

"Ten thousand dollars for the property, Mr. Puckett," said Croft, drawing breath for the disclaimer he expected to make seconds later, a "Just testing your wits, Mr. Puckett," or a "You climb up a ways to me, and I'll climb down a ways to you and we'll meet where the price sounds best." He need not have bothered preparing himself.

"Have I got that much?" asked Calvin of Bragg, having already forgotten the bogus figure quoted to him in the banker's office.

"Yes . . . yes, indeed, Mr. Puckett. You have the amount and more much more."

"I want it to be all mine," said Calvin, meaning the ridge. The two men looked at each other over his head. Croft was almost disappointed that victory was his so easily; he had paid one hundred dollars for the ridge in 1855, had made a small profit from the lumber during that short-lived enterprise, had regarded the place as a millstone around his neck ever since. The price for a useless thing like the ridge should be haggled over. Croft was well known locally for his haggling; it was said of him that had he been in Judas Iscariot's shoes he would have bargained for more than thirty pieces of silver, and received them. He could not believe the thin and nervous individual perched on his settee, knees together, hat in lap, had actually agreed to the outrageous figure. It was like stealing from a baby, and the resultant unease this empty achievement created in his stomach made him pause. "You know you can't grow anything on that piece of land, don't you, Mr. Puckett? You know the boundary of the property lies where the flat land begins. You've got the ridge and nothing but. Every square foot has got gradient."

"Yes," said Calvin, smiling. The perfect location for his church had practically been flung at him, and all he had to do to make it his own was give this man some money. It was too simple; he almost felt that he was taking advantage of the old fellow.

"Then I guess the deal's all set." Croft was disgusted by Calvin's ready acquiescence, felt his lip begin to curl with contempt.

"Strike while the iron is hot," said Bragg. "I'll draw up the papers myself this evening, and tomorrow the exchange can be made. Does that suit you, Mr. Puckett?"

"Tomorrow?"

"Very early. The property will be yours by noon, I promise."

"I'd like that."

"And now we should be on our way." Bragg was anxious to be reunited with his desk.

"Where?" asked Calvin.

"Why, back to town. Do you have a room? There are several fine hotels."

"No."

"Then I will assist you in finding one."

"Papa," came a voice from behind them, "mayn't we offer Mr. Puckett the spare room for tonight? I'm sure you'll want to discuss many things with him."

Croft's daughter stood in the parlour entrance. She had listened to the conversation from the kitchen while pretending to rinse coffee cups. Her voice was as dull as her appearance; of her the locals said: "Some have got beauty, and some have got charm. Alma's got her old man's money." Croft was annoyed as she joined the men. He was obliged to keep her in the house (she was unmarried, despite her twenty-eight years) but did not wish to be reminded of her presence. His smile was stiff. "Mr. Puckett probably has other business to attend to." The smile was turned upon Calvin, who remained oblivious to its message.

"No," he said. He was contemplating sleeping among the trees on the ridge. That would be a fine place to spend the night, up there with the night breeze whispering among the leaves, the stars winking and blinking. And tomorrow it would all belong to him! He shivered in his clothes, could not stop, was scarcely aware of his palpitations. Only Alma noticed; the men were exchanging signals with fractional movements of the head and eyes. Neither wanted Calvin for company any longer than was necessary. Alma wondered if this pitiful-looking man had a chill, his hands were trembling so, his hatbrim bending beneath his knuckles.

Exasperated at the impasse, Croft glared at Calvin, who appeared to be staring at nothing in particular. Croft then transferred the glare to his daughter. Alma's face, he saw, was somehow different; she was staring at Puckett, totally absorbed in him. Was that a look of concern on her face? She generally maintained an expression possessing all the nuance of a brick. Into Croft's mind, an organ ever vigilant for opportunities at which to grasp, there came a sudden rush of understanding, and riding its coat-tails the lineaments of a wonderful plan. He beamed at Calvin. "Of course you'll stay and have supper with us, Mr. Puckett, and the spare room is yours for as long as you want. Alma, attend to it if you will."

"Yes, Papa."

Her face had assumed its usual neutrality, but as she turned away a keen observer may have detected a faint curving of the lips. All her adult life Alma had studied the folds of her father's brain with the intimacy of a laundress scrubbing grimy bedlinen, could define the shape of every thought as it twitched and squirmed beneath the folds like some restless sleeper warding off nightmare or shame. Alma had never encountered a man quite so despicable as Lucius Croft, had long suspected Bragg was cut from similar cloth; both men were conspiring to rob a man rich in dollars and poor in sense, and Alma was determined it would not happen—no indeed. She had made her mind up on it. As for her dear Papa's plans concerning herself—he was in for a shock. She had made her mind up on that, too.

Bragg departed. Croft excused himself, explaining that the farm's four hands were idle fellows all, and needed looking to around this time of day. Left alone in the parlour, Calvin's thoughts drifted away to the ridge. From the upstairs window of the spare room Alma saw her father enter the barn. While his wife had been alive that is where he had kept a supply of whiskey; he was not a drunkard, but relished the occasional tipple. The death of Alma's mother had not upset him greatly, his affection for her having exhausted itself within five years of the marriage, but out of respect for her memory he still kept his whiskey in the barn; a teetotal ghost would be a fearful thing to encounter in the house.

Alma descended the stairs, sat beside Calvin, who appeared not to notice her. She was accustomed to this response from men. There had been several suitors over the years, but Alma was intelligent enough to know they wanted only the large dowry and share of the farm it was generally assumed would go with her hand; any man as rich as Lucius Croft would pay plenty to rid himself of so ugly a daughter. Alma had pride, rejected them all. In Calvin Puckett she saw a person more pitiful than herself, and her generous nature, stifled for want of an outlet, enfolded him.

"Mr. Puckett?" He turned to her. "Mr. Puckett . . . I have something to say to you." His lack of response emboldened, rather than discouraged her. "You must not pay my father so much, Mr. Puckett. The ridge is of no value. You should offer far, far less. I say this because . . . I do not wish to see you cheated. Do not give him what he asks."

Calvin absorbed the gist of her plea, even took note of the passion behind it, but was unmoved. "I want to buy it," he said. He could not understand all this fuss about money. Money had turned his head when he found the bag, made him burn with a need for recognition, for personal aggrandisement, and that was wrong. A church, a tall and upstanding church in a high place would let the world know what kind of man Calvin Puckett was—the kind who knew God and was proud of it. He did not wish to haggle, to provoke any kind of uncertainty in his plans for the ridge. He had the money to pay the stated price, and plenty left over for a church. It was most peculiar that she should accost him in this fashion, demanding he jeopardise God's will. He would not do it.

"No," he said.

"You won't pay?" asked Alma, misunderstanding.

"I want it," said Calvin, and Alma's face, temporarily animated by hope, collapsed into its usual stoic blankness. The poor man was too stupid to understand. Stupidity usually angered her, but Calvin seemed so innocent of guile, so childishly stubborn in his determination she could not find him offensive. Alma noted the sunburned face and hands, the white neck and ears, the harsh creases in his clothing; the silly man had tried to make an impression on self-serving, heartless creatures like Bragg and her father. Could he not see what vipers they were? No, he could not; those pale blue eyes could no more detect the presence of evil than could the eyes of a newborn calf. Her frustration softened, gave way to puzzlement.

"Mr. Puckett, may I ask why it is you wish to own the ridge?" No one had asked, the men too eager for profit to be concerned with their prey's motives. Alma genuinely wanted to know; perhaps it would provide a clue to the intriguing combination of intransigence and naïveté seated beside her.

Should he tell her? Should a woman be the first to learn his secret? He was not uncomfortable in her presence—a

273

rarity in itself—and was cognisant of the effort it had required for her to malign her own father. He felt obligated.

"I'm gonna build a church," he confessed.

"A church, Mr. Puckett?"

"A big tall one, so everyone can see."

"Which particular church would that be, if I might ask?"

"Mine."

"Yes. . . . I mean, would it be Pentacostal, Baptist, Methodist . . . ?"

"Nothin' like that."

"Some other, perhaps?"

"Yes." He affirmed the reply with the artless smile of a child.

"And the name?"

"It don't have one. I'm thinkin' on it."

"Are you a very religious man, Mr. Puckett?"

He almost snorted with suppressed laughter. Was he a religious man? Only God's right hand, that's who. Still, she couldn't be expected to know that, nor could he bring himself to tell her, not yet anyway; maybe later when he was sure she could be trusted. It was nice to sit beside her and feel no fear, not like when he got near other women with their scornful looks and upturned noses, practically as bad as the men who didn't realise who he was, either. But this lady was nice, and partly from embarrassment at his own thoughts regarding her, partly to keep his awesome secret, Calvin lowered his head.

"Reckon I am," he admitted.

Alma had been religious during her girlhood—her mother's influence. Churchgoing had not kept Letitia Croft from an early grave. Thereafter Alma's piety had waned, especially when nightly prayers of impassioned intensity had not yielded a more graceful face and figure. She pitied this man his belief, pitied his homely appearance and guilelessness, laid a sympathetic hand upon his sleeve. "Mr. Puckett, I beg you not to do this. My father does not need ten thousand dollars. The ridge is worth only a fraction of that amount." She saw the narrow jaw flex with knots of muscle, knew further insistence would do no good. She removed her hand, stared at the floor, could not know that every atom of Calvin's being had thrilled at her gesture; his arm tingled at the location of her touch, seemed to throb with pressure that was no longer there. He cranked his head sideways and regarded her blunt profile. Calvin could not remember ever having been touched by a woman, could not recall his mother or sisters ever having touched him willingly or with the least affection. She was not pretty. Alma, was that what the old man had called her?

"Alma," he said aloud.

Her head rose, turned to him. "Yes?"

Calvin had not intended to speak. He blushed, an irrepressible, scorching blush that rose from his chest to his hair; a chameleon among beetroots could not have induced a more flagrant hue. Calvin swallowed the saliva gathering in his throat, set his Adam's apple dancing madly.

"Nothin'," he said.

One more snort and he would go back inside. Croft tilted the jug, savoured the fiery taste upon his tongue, gulped it down. He needed a man to share the jug with him, but the hands were in the north pasture. What he wanted was a son to trade liquor and stories with, but Letitia had never provided him with one. Their marriage had cowed him (she was a woman of strength) and he had never felt the urge to remarry. Every once in a while he paid a visit to a certain house in town to ease his physical needs. A son, that's what the place needed; all he had was a daughter ugly as sin and a nephew foisted upon him by the death of his brother in the war. The nephew was no farmer, nothing Croft would want to call a son, but he took care of the store on Decatur Street just fine, he'd give him that. Not much of a man, but a shrewd businessman, showing a pretty fair profit in the store ledgers. Taking over that place from the long-departed fool who had once owned it, the squaw-man, had been a clever move on Croft's part, one he had never regretted. A real man could plant his feet in two entirely different fields and flourish in both. He had hoped for romance between nephew Willard and Alma, but Willard was no fool, knew he could make a life for himself without hitching his body to such a sorry mare. Those not so picky had been shown the door by Alma. She was no fool either, knew they only wanted cash. And now had come a man with plenty of his own. Maybe now she would sit still and say nothing and flutter her eyes or whatever it took to snag a fish, a very rich and stupid fish. He hoped she was taking advantage of the privacy he had so thoughtfully provided, and was not hiding in the kitchen while the fish lay gasping for want of love. Could this Puckett be induced to see in her a desirable match? If he was fool enough to buy the ridge for so ridic- ulous a sum, the chances were fair he would see in Alma a reincarnation of Helen or Athena or one of those Greek sluts from yesteryear. He could only hope; some things were out of a man's hands entirely, in the lap of the gods. One more snort, and then he went inside.

Supper was not a success. The farmhands ate with Croft, Alma and their guest, and soon saw that Calvin was not a normal man. When they learned he was to purchase the ridge they nudged each other with their elbows and stop- pered their laughter with food. Conversation was mercifully sparse. When the hands at last removed themselves and Alma had carried the dirty plates to the kitchen, Croft in- vited Calvin into the parlour once more, offered him to- bacco, which Calvin refused, then set about filling his pipe. "Fine girl," he said, when clouds began erupting from its bowl. Since this comment was not a question, Calvin re- mained silent. "Yes," continued Croft, "a fine young woman. Wasted on a place like this, looking after an old man like me. Does a grand job of it, mind you. No com- plaints—no, siree—but it's just a shame, Mr. Puckett, a goddamn shame is what it is. Here's this young and able female, and what's the future hold for her? Nothing she'd care to think about, nor me. When I'm gone she'll have the farm, and a good one it is too, but I ask you, what's a woman alone going to do with a farm?"

He allowed the dilemma to hang in the air, supported by

innuendo, wreathed in pipe fumes. Calvin said nothing. Croft assumed he was cogitating, mulling over the implications of so tempting an offer. He'll come around, mused Croft. What other woman would have him, money or not? He puffed contentedly, allowing the fish fully to ingest the hook. Calvin stared at his knees and wondered what time he could go to bed. He was very tired, despite his nap in the banker's office. Croft watched with sinking confidence as Calvin's head began to nod, finally dropping on to his chest. Could it be that his words of invitation had been wasted? He glowered and puffed volcanic clouds in irritation. The fool, the stupid, blind fool! He'd be ten thousand dollars lighter come tomorrow, and he'd deserve it too, the goddamn jackass!

Calvin was revived an hour or so later, showed to his room by Alma. The house became quiet as lamps were extinguished and bodies lowered to creaking mattresses. The farmhands in their small bunkhouse behind the barn discussed the methods they would employ to bring a smile to the face of Alma, but allowed it would only work if the lady consented to wear a bag over her head so as not to frighten the stallion figuring so prominently in their plans. Croft lay awake cursing the insult implicit in Calvin's silence; he couldn't even lure an idiot into being his son-in-law. Damn! Alma contemplated her ceiling, asked herself this question: Will I, or won't I? In the town Nathan Bragg tossed and turned with nervous excitement beside his slumbering wife, planning a means of slipping the purloined twenty thousand dollars into the bank without alerting his clerks. There would be a way around the problem, he was sure; it just required the necessary folderol of paperwork and sleight of hand.

Calvin slept peacefully until a little after midnight, when he was shaken gently by the shoulder. Moonlight passing through the window bathed Alma in shades of greyish white, made of her nightgown a funeral shroud. Imagining her a ghost, Calvin's heart locked for one terrible moment, was clenched by a muscular fist. "Mr. Puckett?" He recognised the voice; her face seemed much altered by the hair cascading freely around it, hair falling almost to her waist. She knelt beside the bed, fearing her height gave her an intimidating aspect. "Mr. Puckett," she whispered again, and peeled the blanket from his chest. Calvin lay still, wondering at her behaviour, understanding nothing until she slid into the bed beside him, the bulk of her hips touching his lean flesh through the thinnest of cloths. He began to shiver. Now she was doing something he could not bear to turn his head and see, rustling and squirming and butting his jaw with her elbow as she raised her nightdress to form a collapsed ruff around her neck. The smell of her flesh made Calvin tremble in even greater agitation. When she took his bony wrist in her fingers and directed his hand to her breast his reaction was nothing less than galvanic; his spine stiffened, his legs straightened so quickly he feared his knees would break, and his fingers kneaded at the doughy mound in their grasp. "Shhhhh . . ." whispered Alma, although he had spoken not a word. She slid her free hand behind his bristling head, pulled it to her other breast, fed him her flesh. The moment Calvin's lips closed about her nipple his body ceased to vibrate, became instead a limp and pliant thing, its essence centred on his greedily sucking mouth. Calvin was a happy infant, and he mewled and whined in an ecstasy of oral bliss. There was no milk, but none was needed; the female softness offered so readily was all Calvin required to transport him to a distant time when his world had been severely limited, yet rich in promise, lush with gratification. That world had passed quickly, left him alone and vulnerable, sensations of safety and comfort a receding memory. The kernel of that memory germinated in the warmth of Alma's solid arms, flowered in an instant, attached itself to her breast like some rampant corsage. He was almost too eager, and Alma wondered if, while searching for the man within, she had not uncovered a suckling babe; he appeared uninterested in the rest of her anatomy. She reassured herself, stroking his short hair; there would be time enough to teach him the rudiments of procreation. For the present she was content to let him snuffle and suck and clutch all he wanted. When he paused for breath she had a suggestion to make.

Bragg returned to the farm by mid morning, laid a sheet of paper on the table before Croft, Calvin and Alma. "There we are. All we need are your signatures, gentlemen. Or your mark." He wondered why the daughter was present for this essentially masculine enterprise; perhaps she was to witness the proceedings. Croft looked particularly full of himself, and well he might. He would not have looked so pleased if he had known Bragg had already creamed twice ten thousand dollars from Puckett's wealth. He waited for someone to pick up the pen and sign.

Croft cleared his throat. "Mr. Bragg, let me acquaint you with a piece of news. This has happened sudden-like, but I'm pleased like any father would be. Alma here has consented to be Mrs. Puckett."

Bragg was stunned. What a pair, by God! What manner of children would be whelped from such a union? It did not bear thinking about. He shot his hand in Calvin's direction, a smile mobilising the flesh beneath his nose. "My most heartfelt congratulations, Mr. Puckett, and to you also, Miss Croft. What a surprise!"

"Almost as big a surprise to me as to you, Mr. Bragg," said Alma, and Bragg noted the smug expression masquerading as politeness. "Calvin and I have another announcement to make." The two men waited, both considering, then dismissing, the possibility of a lightning pregnancy. Alma looked first at one, then at the other, relishing the delay, wanting to remember this moment as a turning-point, a pivot upon which hung the balance of her years. "We have a request to make of you, Papa, something we wish to have as a wedding gift."

"Anything in my power, Alma," he beamed, still congratulating himself on the speed with which his scheme had flowered.

"The ridge."

Croft felt a monstrous clinging growth clutch at his throat, robbing him of air, stealing away his happiness. The bitch! The ungrateful, horse-faced bitch! Her own father . . . ! His mouth opened and shut, gaped in disbelief at her treachery. Bragg applauded briskly, delighted at the speechless fury mottling Croft's cheeks. "The perfect gift!" he crowed. "You wouldn't want an impoverished son-in-law, now, would you, Lucius? And this way the property is kept in the family for the best of motives." His commission from the sale would be lost, but he considered the loss worthwhile; he had never seen Croft so crestfallen, and the sight gave him more pleasure than he had thought possible. What a tragedy for the old skinflint. Wait till he told his wife. Wait till his wife told the town! Croft would never be allowed to forget the way his daughter, plump and unlovely, treated as an unpaid servant, had finally bested him. Croft shrank somewhat inside his clothing, appeared to lower himself by inches. He looked at Calvin, tried to discern a trace of laughter, of glee, of mockery in the foolish face. There was none. "Is this what you want?" he asked.

"I reckon," said Calvin, having been rehearsed for this small but vital role through the small hours of the morning by an unflagging Alma. He turned to her for a verdict on his performance, was rewarded with a smile. Croft sagged even lower, stared at the now useless bill of sale on the table before him. "Then, it's done," he said, and added silently to himself: And may you give birth to monsters and be as miserable together as a man and woman can be.

This admission of defeat filled Bragg's cup to overflowing. He pumped Calvin's hand again, said the only thing he could think of.

"Welcome to Valley Forge."

CHAPTER TWENTY

On the eight-day joruney to Dodge he saw only two herds of buffalo, and those in the far distance. Joe took a room at the Boston Hotel and asked himself what he could possibly do now. As part of the Tubbs-Cobden outfit his life had been made easier by his partner; it had been Tubbs who handled most of the business end of things, Tubbs who bargained for the best price and shook hands on every deal. Joe had really been no more than top gun. He could not bear the thought of setting up his own outfit and running it alone; the responsibility would have been too much, drawn him too deeply into the everyday physical world, obliged him to traffic with human beings every hour of the day. Impossible. He pummelled his pillow. No, he would not do it! There would be other work to engage in, he assured himself, but refused to consider what form this might take.

For a week he did nothing but wander the streets of Dodge and drink in those saloons where he was accepted, gradually becoming poorer, regretting having thrown away Tubbs' IOU. He could never ask for another to replace it; that would be too humiliating by far. He drank to rid his mouth of the taste conjured by wretchedness.

"Mr. Joseph Cobden?"

A man stood at his elbow, an easterner by the cut of his jacket and vest, all Joe's sidelong glance at first revealed. He leaned back a little to look him up and down. Great height was the first of his attributes, complemented by breadth of shoulder; a muscular neck supported the kind of head Joe had seen on statues in the public places of St. Louis; a brow of noble proportion sat upon a black ridge of

281

uninterrupted eyebrow, from which descended a nose of Grecian straightness; a broad and finely shaped mouth reposed above a chin so uncompromisingly thrusting in its contour as to stretch the skin into hollows under cheekbones wide as a Tartar's; of similar aspect was the moustache, thick and jet, drooping almost to the jawline. But it was to the eyes of this man that Joe felt drawn, eyes of so pale a grey as to appear empty, circles of cloudy sky within the leonine head. Joe had never before seen so imposingly handsome a man, found the tasteful suit of tweed ridiculous; so masculine a frame demanded chain mail and armour, a shield and broadsword rather than the cane of thickly knotted wood in his fist. The lips parted, teeth large and square as tombstones, yellow as old ivory revealed.

"Am I addressing Mr. Joseph Cobden?"

"You are."

"My name is Peter Winstanley. May I talk with you?"

"You may."

"Thank you."

The voice was not deep and rich and mellifluous, but high, almost feminine in pitch; this lion spoke with the magisterial authority of a swallowed mouse. Joe did not know whether to smile at the ludicrous sound or commiserate with its owner.

"Word has it you no longer hunt," squeaked the man.

"Whose word?"

"The general whisper."

"Are you English?"

"Yes. Do you dislike Englishmen?"

"I don't dislike one kind of man more than I dislike another."

The heroic features creased with a smile, delivered a piping ripple of laughter, absurdly infectious. Joe smiled, suddenly liking this giant.

"Would you consider guiding me on a buffalo-hunt, Mr. Cobden?"

"I might. How much?"

"I'm sure we'll arrive at a suitable figure." He raised his glass. "Your health."

"We should talk this over somewhere quiet."

"I have a room at the Mandan Hotel."

"All right."

They left. Joe found he had drunk his way through the afternoon and into the night. He lost his footing descending from the wooden sidewalk to the street, and was grasped by the collar before his knees could touch the ground. "Thank you," he said.

"Not at all," said Peter Winstanley, both men knowing he pretended Joe was not drunk. A cowhand in a similar state staggered against Winstanley before they reached the other side. "Pardon me," said the Englishman, although the fault had not been his, and the impossible voice captured the drunk's interest; he pursued the giant and the hunchback for several steps, unable to comprehend such contrast of form.

"Hey!" he called, and Winstanley turned. Joe turned a second or two later, his reactions hindered by the influence of whiskey. "What was that you said?" demanded the drunk. He wanted to hear that voice again, to be sure it really had been as high as he thought.

"I said 'Pardon me'."

The drunk was delighted. The voice was real, therefore the humpback must also be real, not the product of a bottle. What a sight to see! He returned his attention to Winstanley. "Talk some more."

"Goodnight to you."

He turned away, but the drunk was not satisfied. "Talk to me some more with that woman voice!"

Winstanley turned again. Faster than Joe's befuddled eye could follow, the gnarled and knotted end of Winstanley's stick swung from his boot to the drunk's left temple. Winstanley watched the cowhand collapse into a silent heap, rejoined Joe. "I dislike bad manners, don't you?" he piped.

"Yes, I do. What's that thing called?"

"This is a shillelagh, Mr. Cobden, Ireland's contribution to warfare. I never journey anywhere without it."

"I can see why."

They walked on.

Several days later this hunting party of just two men left Dodge. Winstanley had killed a great many living things during his thirty-eight years (Joe was told): pheasant and deer in his native land; wild boar in Bavaria; tigers in India; elk and moose and bear in Canada, lions, rhinoceros, elephants, cheetahs, crocodiles, anything that moved in Africa. He took the most impressive heads from his kills, had them mounted and sent to his ancestral home in Oxfordshire. Winstanley did not require a massive retinue of cooks and grooms and general hangers-on during these forays into the wilder regions of the earth; he prided himself on his ability to live off the land, despised the hordes of his aristocratic peers who had flocked to America, inspired with bloodlust by the world famous buffalo-hunt organised by William F. Cody and Lieutenant Colonel George Armstrong Custer in 1872 for the benefit of the Grand Duke Alexis, son of Alexander II, Tsar of Russia. Winstanley was himself a lord. He had come to Kansas not because such hunting expeditions had become fashionable among the wealthy, but to find and kill a beast of singular characteristic; not for Winstanley the common buffalo (he called them bison) which were the target of others. Brown buffalo heads already were decorating walls on both sides of the Atlantic, were no longer the conversation-pieces they had been just a few years before. The prize heads in Lord Winstanley's collection of trophies numbered three: a white elephant, a white tiger and a white rhinoceros. He had many other heads, over three hundred, but the whites, the rarities, the freaks of nature, these exerted a powerful influence upon the man. He had several polar bear heads but did not boast of them, rare though they were, for *all* polar bears are white. Winstanley had heard of another rare white creature, and desired it for his collection. He wanted a white buffalo. Joe assured him such things existed, mutants among their brown brethren. He had never seen one, but had once been privileged to examine a white buffalo robe in the office of an army colonel who had stolen it from the Sioux during a particularly virulent wave of army massacres. Joe had been convinced it was not a fake. The Indian tribes, he explained, revered the white buffalo for its rarity, and ascribed to it various supernatural qualities. Winstanley politely expressed his disinterest in what Indians might think. He wanted the head of a white buffalo on his wall, the hide on his parquet floor, would search until he found an albino beast and killed it.

There was much to admire in the man, notably his physical stamina and lack of formality. Joe called him Peter, and Lord Winstanley called his guide Joe, never patronised him, never bored him with stories of previous hunts or details of his private life, nor did he ever express interest in anything Joe might have to say about himself. This lack of curiosity was appreciated at first, then began to annoy Joe somewhat; he would have liked to talk with someone of intelligence about himself, someone capable of understanding his story's complexity; but Winstanley never asked. Together they roamed the plains in companionable silence, two long-haired and bearded men, one with the bearing of a knight, the other his trusty page. North to the Dakotas they went, meandering back and forth between the Missouri and the Rocky Mountains, in no particular hurry to no particular destination.

Summer heat gave way to the brisk winds of fall, then the first light snows of winter. They turned south to pass the season in Texas, killing only what was necessary to keep them alive, venturing into towns only when their supplies of flour and coffee and salt ran low. Whiskey was never a part of their equipage. Joe's vigour, depleted during the past year, was restored by the strict regimen of fresh meat and running water, by the cleansing properties of sun and wind and rain. They encountered few Indians and were never attacked, even when they once chanced upon a hunting party some twenty warriors strong. Neither man would have been pleased had he known of the names casually assigned them by this band of Cheyenne when they returned to their village and related the incident to their families: Woman Inside Him Calling, and Carries a Mountain on His Back. Joe assumed (correctly) that their bizarre appearance, one tall and godlike, the other squat and repulsive, was their permit to travel wherever they pleased. They avoided white hunters. Winstanley did not appear to need the company of men any more than did Joe, was in fact peculiarly insular for one born to the social obligations of high rank. Joe admired his penchant for aloneness, was also, as time passed, greatly puzzled by it. No explanation was ever forthcoming, and Joe assumed Winstanley's voice had blighted his life as Joe's hump had blighted his.

They did not find a white buffalo in Texas, nor in New Mexico. In Santa Fe a man asked Winstanley if he had a little woman stuck in his throat. "No," said Winstanley.

"Then you've got no balls," declared his interrogator. He wore a pistol.

"And you, sir, have no brain." Winstanley's voice never rose when annoyed, perhaps because it was already at conversational top register.

"Better take that back," warned the man. He had rehearsed the line many times, confident he would one day be faced with a situation like this if he tried hard enough. The confrontation took place on the porch of a general store, and was already attracting attention from bystanders.

"I never take back what I have given," said Winstanley with a smile. "Good day to you."

"Wait on there." The man with the pistol sensed he was faced with a coward. He was not a brave man himself, had purchased the pistol just a week ago to assure himself he was not afraid of anyone, had destroyed a great many bot-tles and tin cans while perfecting his aim. An avid reader of dime novels, he knew a man's gun should have notches carved along the butt, every notch representing a deceased human life, but bottles and cans did not count; this man's pistol butt was smooth and new and unadorned. He wanted to change its appearance very badly indeed; the cowardly giant with the falsetto voice would be his ticket to fame as a gunfighter, a man to be reckoned with. He could scent renown in the offing as his right hand hovered above the holster on his thigh. At this point his plans were disrupted by the realisation that his opponent did not wear a pistol, carried nothing but some kind of twisty-looking stick. He could not simply gun down an unarmed man; that was not the way to do it, not according to the dime novels.

While the seeker after fame deliberated his next move Winstanley broke his right hand with the shillelagh, and before he could recover from his astonishment his left hand was broken also, in case he should prove to be ambidex-trous. The man held his puffed and broken hands before him and howled. The onlookers thought it the funniest thing they had seen since Christmas, when a drunk tried to kiss his horse and had his lip bitten off.

"You're a very foolish fellow," chided Winstanley, wag-ging an admonitory forefinger.

"Good thing he's married," said one of the crowd. "Someone's gonna have to wipe his ass for awhile."

Riding away from Santa Fe, Winstanley had this to say: "Some people are absolute fools. Do you ever feel that with-out the likes of you and me the world would be a place of complete madness?"

Joe agreed wholeheartedly, added: "But there must be others the same as us."

Winstanley looked at himself, looked at Joe, and both burst out laughing. Where could two such as they possibly be found? The laughter and the thought that had produced it made Joe happy. Two of a kind, the *only* two. What a comforting notion. He tucked it into his breast and warmed it. Joe considered it possible—just possible, mind you—that his life had taken a turn for the better, all thanks to the titan beside him.

They journeyed north again. Joe noted the reduced numbers of buffalo, felt a slight pang of regret for his contribution to the slaughter that had so ruthlessly winnowed the great herds of yesterday, was glad he had been obliged to get out of that particular trade; there would not be too many hunters left in business at this rate. Hunting a white buffalo was an entirely different thing; it had a touch of the poetic about it, Joe thought. He had not felt so content in all his years. His falling-out with Quincy Tubbs was forgotten, useless baggage cast away that his progress might be speedier. He worshipped Winstanley, had been offended by proxy when it was suggested he had no balls. Joe knew for a fact that Winstanley had balls the size of chicken eggs and a penis that would not have shamed a pony; the two men bathed on occasion in the rivers and streams encountered in their wanderings, and were familiar with each other's nakedness. Joe was not ashamed of his humped back before Winstanley, knew the Englishman did not see in it a feature of any significance. Like Joe, he was celibate (he once revealed he had never married and had no wish to) and, although they led a Spartan existence together, no hint of homoerotic interest, either intended or accidental, ever passed between them. They were a nation of two, questing paladin and twisted shield-bearer, and the grail they sought was to be found among ungraspable distances and emptiness and solitude, a realm of earth and sky.

Sharing the beauties of landscape and nature was not enough for Joe; he wished to share of himself. One night while both men stared at the bubbling coffee pot with the enthralled expression of alchemists observing the transmutation of base metal to gold, Joe began to talk. The words flowed from him unhindered, every word a brick dislodged from the wall erected around himself at such great expense over so long a time, and when at last the rubble that was his life lay around him the entire story had been told. Joe sat, an emptied vessel, and awaited his companion's response.

Winstanley nodded slowly several times, as though savouring the last forlorn resonance of Joe's tale, poked at the buffalo chip fire with the tip of his shillelagh, said not a word. Joe felt the emptiness within him fill with dread. Had he told too much, given of himself until nothing worthwhile remained? Did Winstanley think him a fool and a weakling for having delivered so intimate and painful a narrative? He watched the handsome lips form a meditative moue, saw the luxuriant moustache twitch in contemplation of the moment. Was he deliberating at length, the better to reply, or was he simply too embarrassed to speak? Joe wished he had never opened his mouth, wished an eagle had plucked him from the fireside and carried him off, longed to reinstate himself as the strong and silent companion Winstanley expected him to be.

"You've had a hard time of it, Joe."

Nothing more was said. Winstanley revealed nothing of himself in return. Joe knew something had been lost, could blame only himself. During the weeks that followed he watched for signs that Winstanley now regarded him in a lesser light than before, but there was no change in the Englishman's demeanour, for which Joe was humbly grateful. He wished there was something he could do to atone for his immature *faux pas*—rescuing Winstanley from the clutches of a ravening grizzly bear, for example—but no such opportunity presented itself.

Days and weeks and months entwined, became a seamless ribbon one year long, and still no white buffalo appeared to bring their roving to an end. Winstanley cleaned and oiled his favourite elephant gun with care; it would not be fired until a white buffalo was the target. For lighter game he used his second rifle, a Martini-Henry. He called the elephant gun Wilhelmina. Joe considered giving his Sharpe's a name, but decided he must not imitate Winstanley out of sheer admiration; it would be far too easy to submerge himself totally in Winstanley's persona, which clearly was capable of ingesting him without a hiccup.

The man was a beautiful lake, deep and wide, yet curiously flat. No disturbing winds from the past ruffled the glassy surface, no creatures erupted from the depths to mar the tranquil reflection of its surroundings; it did not rise with rainfall or lower with drought. Winstanley was a body of water in stasis; there was about him a dream-like envelope capable of absorbing light without being obliged to reflect back a portion of the heat and brightness lavished upon it. The man seemingly was impervious, a world unto himself. He appeared to enjoy Joe's company—or did he merely tolerate it? Why had he divorced himself from the life of an English lord? Had he no friends, no family who might be anxious for news of the wanderer? Was this never-ending hunt all he required for happiness? He was obviously educated, yet never made reference to any work of literature or philosophy. Did he consider books unmanly? Did he suffer agonies of inferiority because of his piping voice? If so, how had he overcome them? And again, was there within him some inkling, some understanding of Joe as a fellow human being, or were his perceptions of the shallowest kind, ascribing to Joe the role of devoted follower, unquestioningly loyal, the equivalent of a faithful dog? Had Joe's confession of months ago fallen on ears not only deaf, but also uncaring?

It had taken a full year for these doubts to emerge, a year to overcome his awe for the splendid person of Winstanley. Joe had never been paid a wage, not a cent. Winstanley bought the few supplies they needed, but the agreed-upon two hundred dollars per month did not materialise. Until now it had not worried him. What need of cash when the sky was your ceiling, the earth your bed? Now the question rankled, was made even more complex by Joe's doubts that he had done anything to earn the wage. Winstanley was capable of surviving in rough country alone, obviously did not require Joe's expertise as a hunter, had apparently hired him for nothing more imperative than companionship. But of what kind? They spoke perhaps two dozen words in a day. These silences, for the past year interpreted by Joe as indicative of the deep and wordless empathy that existed between them as outsiders, riders beyond the pale, now appeared symptomatic of some ambiguous malaise, an encroaching paralysis of the camaraderie which, Joe now saw, may not have been present in the first place. Plagued by such questions, with all the time in the world in which to sift and ponder them, Joe was no longer happy.

Through the Dakota badlands they roamed, and now Joe simmered with resentment. He had invested a part of himself in the man riding ahead of him, and his investment had been sacrificial gold thrown into a bottomless lake. Winstanley was changeless, conducted himself today as on that first evening in the saloon and through all the intervening days, a man with one thought only, yet even this purported ambition to kill a white buffalo now appeared fraudulent. No inner fire consumed him; the grey eyes were narrowed not with bold intent, but because the sun demanded it. His approach to what had been presented as an obsession, an eccentricity at the very least, was altogether too casual, pursued at too idle a pace, was no more than a leisurely jaunt through the wilderness masquerading as destiny's call. The man was a fake. How was it possible that Joe could have been fooled for so long? He assembled reasons: Winstanley's very appearance inspired belief; his absurd voice had provoked scorn from others, circumstances Joe was acquainted with; it had been all too easy for him to see in Winstanley a story not dissimilar to his own, and from there had stemmed the admiration, the desire to accompany through fair weather and foul on a search for the unapproachable; in short, the infatuation. Joe had clung to Winstanley like a lovesick girl, expended emotion and faith and trust on a charlatan, a magnificent fraud; he had followed a dark and beguiling piper, and the discovery made him sick.

He reined in his horse. Winstanley was a short distance ahead. Joe could travel no further with this faker, this . . . pretender! Winstanley rode more than a mile before noticing Joe's absence. He turned and ambled back. "Is something the matter?" he asked. Joe heard no real concern in his voice, just an idle query; it was typical of the man. He could not bear to speak, afraid of what his mouth might say. Winstanley appraised him with pale eyes, in no hurry to receive an answer. Both horses lowered their heads and began to crop grass while their riders watched each other in silence. Above them wheeled a hawk, and above the hawk a blue infinity of sky. Neither man could decipher the other's expression.

"Is something wrong, Joe?"

"No!"

The word burst from him. Winstanley looked away to the northern horizon. Canada was no more than a day's ride off. He turned to Joe. "I don't understand."

"There is *no white buffalo!*"

He practically screeched. Winstanley looked away again. "Are you tired of all this, Joe?"

"Yes, I am. I've had enough. I quit."

"I don't have the money to pay you what I owe, not here."

"I don't care. I'm riding south."

"I'm sorry things have not worked out as they should."

"It doesn't matter."

Joe wanted to ride away now, this instant, before Winstanley did something to make Joe realise he was wrong about the man. Joe did not want to be wrong. He actually wanted to shoot Winstanley, pull the Sharpe's from its scabbard and put a bullet through him. He wanted to do this, he knew, because Winstanley was the only person in the world who knew Joe's story in its entirety. Joe regretted ever having told it, wanted its recipient dead. He was sensible enough to be horrified at his own desires, wondered if perhaps he was going mad. He must get away *now,* before he committed some unworthy bloodcrime to assuage the emotions stampeding through him, literally shaking him in the saddle. He did not want to harm Winstanley, simply wanted to be away, *away* from the sight of him.

"I believe I'll continue searching, Joe, perhaps into Canada."

"I hope you find one." He jerked his gelding's head up. "Goodbye."

"Goodbye, Joe. It's been my privilege to have known you."

He held out his hand. Joe made himself shake it, then kicked his heels. Winstanley watched him ride away. Joe knew before he had gone a mile that he had acted like a fool. It was to Winstanley's credit that he had never laid bare his soul as Joe had done. Joe had resented his strength, he saw that now. All his cankerous broodings, his malign imaginings and misjudgement of character had been the work of his own jealousy; from it had been manufactured a distorting lens through which Joe had seen what he wished to see, a creature inferior to himself. And now he knew it was not so. All it took was a mile. The truth was plain. He need only turn around, return to Winstanley and apologise. The Englishman would accept him back without reserve, and they would continue their search together. Joe kept riding south. I'll turn around and go back when I reach this next rise, he told himself, but kept on riding, over that rise and the rise beyond, and all the rises beyond that. His own cowardice and stupidity fascinated him. How can a man be such a fool? he asked himself, riding still. Is it pride? Is it stubbornness? He could no more turn his horse around then, or during the weeks that followed, than hold the sun at noon.

Sixteen years later, in a chapter of his memoir *Far Horizons, the Journeyings of a Hunter,* Winstanley wrote:

Of all the persons to have crossed my path in far flung reaches of the globe, Joseph Cobden was without doubt the individual least suited to his time and place. A product of miscegenation, a hunchback of withering ugliness, this unfortunate fellow possessed more intelligence than was good for him under such adverse circumstances, and clearly could not accept the lot which was his. It became apparent to me that Joseph, naturally taciturn by temperament, was bedevilled by memories of his unspeakable childhood, the details of which my reader will be spared, and was incapable of finding even a moment's peace, so great was the turmoil in his heart and mind.

Several pages later, after detailing his non-adventures on the plain, he wrote:

Nothing is so poignant as to witness the sudden decline of a man succumbing to his demons, and at so tender an age. It was with profound regret that I allowed Joseph to sunder our contract and return to Kansas which, for want of a better word, he termed his home.

The memoir was never published. There is no mention in it of the author ever finding a white buffalo.

CHAPTER TWENTY-ONE

There were no guests at the wedding. Croft was a grudging witness. Calvin moved into Alma's room at the farm. Plans were drawn up for a home of their own on the ridge. Alma wanted it to be located on the eastern slope, sheltered from the prevailing westerly winds, with a view of the town. Calvin was agreeable; he would cheerfully have lived in a tent while the church was built. The house of Puckett and the house of God were raised simultaneously, the church at the very crest of the ridge, the house a hundred yards away among the trees, further down the slope. Two local builders were contracted for the job, and they hastily assembled teams to assist them, teams of ten or so men each. Two teams would get things done twice as fast; Calvin wanted the jobs completed before the end of the year. Soon a trail was carved by brick and timber-laden wagons from the road nearest the ridge up the slope to the crest, and the sounds of hammer and saw disturbed the air.

Calvin would have liked to lend a hand, but was as clumsy with builders' tools as with the body of his wife. Alma endured his inept fumblings in silence, fearing to upset him with criticism, but when a week had gone by without consummation she devised a different stratagem. Calvin was ignorant of even the most basic physical aspects pertaining to intercourse between human beings but, Alma reasoned, as a farmboy he must surely have observed the couplings of cattle and horses. She presented herself to him one night as would a quadruped, and the sight of her buttocks, so round and full, triggered a response within Calvin equal to, if not exceeding, Alma's expectations; he lunged at her, organ at last stiff as a log, battering at her orifices Alma circumspectly guided it to its correct berth and clutched at the railings to avoid being butted from the bed under Calvin's onslaught. Thus was set the pattern for their matrimonial mountings. Alma put aside pride and dignity, prayed for an early pregnancy to save her from these nocturnal drubbings of the flesh. Croft was infuriated by the noise they made, prayed for early completion of the new house.

Rumour spread through Valley Forge, whispers that the church being constructed atop the ridge was to be a church unlike any other, a new kind of church with a new kind of name. The townspeople wondered if this meant Calvin was a Lutheran, or maybe an Episcopalian. They were assured by Croft that his son-in-law was *some* kind of Christian, else he wouldn't be spending a whole heap of money on a church, now, would he? Neighbourliness was sufficient excuse for locals to drive or ride out to the ridge and stand, hands on hips, watching the two buildings take shape. Calvin was always to be found near the frame of the church, sitting on a rock, watching, always watching, to the annoyance of the carpenters. Horny-handed farmers approached him, introduced themselves, commented on the weather and the swift progress of both buildings. Calvin answered them with polite monosyllables, proffering no information not directly asked for. His visitors eventually wanted to know the name of this particular church, and Calvin always answered: "I'm thinkin' on it."

"Mean to say you don't know?" was the typical reaction.

"Not yet. I'm thinkin', thinkin' hard."

"But it ain't like naming a cow. You got to know what kind of church it is beforehand, I reckon. What kind of religion you aiming to spout inside her?"

"I'm thinkin' on it."

"You a preacher yourself?"

"No."

"I guess you've got intentions to bring one in from somewheres else."

"Reckon I should?"

Calvin had considered nothing beyond the construction of his church.

"Are you saying, or asking, Mr. Puckett?"

"Huh?"

"I mean, are you telling me you aim to bring in a preacher, or asking me if that's what you ought to do?"

"I'm thinkin' on it; yessir."

And the seekers after knowledge would leave the ridge, shaking their heads, certain of only one thing: Calvin Puckett was a fool. They would tell their wives of Calvin's unhelpful answers and halfwitted manner. "What's the town need another church for, anyway?" they would say, angry at the thought of good money being wasted by an idiot. "We got two churches already, and they, by God, know what they're damn well called!" The wives, intrigued not so much by Calvin's imprecise religious leanings as by the fact of his marrying someone as spinsterish as Alma Croft, visited the ridge to satisfy themselves. They never approached Calvin, went instead to Alma, who spent a good deal of her time supervising construction of the house. It would be a fine home when completed, two storeys high, built around a central chimney of brick, with a steeply slanted roof to let those Kansas snows slide right off, and a broad, shady porch around three sides of the lower floor for relief from the summer sun.

"You'll be right proud of this place pretty soon," was the usual opening gambit of Alma's visitors.

"Yes."

"Be plenty of room for children when they come."

"I've planned for a large family."

"That's the only kind, generally," said the ladies who came to the ridge, and wondered if the lunacy their husbands insisted could be found inside Mr. Puckett's head was the kind that would be handed down to his offspring. Did poor Alma know the risk she was taking, being wed to a fool? Only someone as ugly as she would have been driven to take the chance. Well, all would be revealed in the Lord's good time, but it would just be a shame if the children had pointy heads and drooled.

Said one woman: "Seems to me this place used to be called Squaw Ridge back a good long time now."

"I have not heard it referred to by that name."

"Must be twenty years, maybe less. Squaw Ridge. The name never took hold. They say there's an Injun woman buried hereabouts. That's where the name come from. It weren't a burial ground, nothing heathen, just the one squaw, they say, but no one knows where exactly. She weren't a Christian, or there'd be a stone or cross. You might be a-building your kitchen smack on top of her."

"I hope not."

"Wouldn't be no smell, not after all this time. Just bones left by now, I expect. It's a mercy the name never took hold. I'd be mortified to live in a place called after some heathen Injun woman."

"If there *was* such a person."

"Oh, she's somewheres under us all right. You wouldn't call a place Squaw Ridge without you had a good reason for it, I reckon. What kind of a church is your husband building up there, Mrs. Puckett?"

"A special kind, Mrs. Lambert."

"What kind of special kind would that be now?"

"I have been sworn to secrecy."

Alma had ceased to ask Calvin for information; he did not interfere with her house, and she deemed it only polite not to interfere with his church. The wives went home to their husbands, their doubts confirmed; those two up there were as peculiar a pair as you'd find anywhere if you looked for a month of Sundays. The town had not experienced such common interest in a subject, nor such unanimity of opinion since Dr. Mudd had been sentenced to life imprisonment for allegedly conspiring to assassinate Abraham Lincoln.

Alma longed for the day when she could step outside her

father's house for the last time, surround herself with walls of her own. Calvin would be within those walls, of course, but the prospect was not too daunting—at least not during the daylight hours. She prodded her stomach. Was she filling out at all? No, no fatter than usual. Alma resigned herself to further indignities in the bedroom. Her plight would have been made bearable had Calvin evinced the slightest subtlety of emotion in the quiet moments following intercourse. Not once had he placed an affectionate arm around her or kissed her; when the act was completed he collapsed on to his half of the bed and began to snore. He also broke wind in his sleep. Alma was obliged to remind herself that nuptial bliss had not been an essential ingredient in her plan to be free of parental restraint. Things were better than they had been just a short while ago; were, to say the least, very different, which constituted an improvement in itself.

The church, being of simpler design and construction than the house, was near completion by November's end. It was not the towering edifice of Calvin's dreams, Kansas architecture being of the prosaic and practical school, but the steeple had been raised higher than was usual; its spire lanced uncompromisingly in the direction of heaven, pointing the way to salvation. A bell cast in Pittsburgh was shipped to Valley Forge on Calvin's instruction (by way of Alma's literate hand), was hauled into the steeple and affixed to an oak beam, to which was attached no ordinary rope, but a thick, white silken cord of sensual smoothness; Calvin did not want the coarseness of hemp in his church. He was the first to tug at the cord, the first to exult in the sound that reverberated across the town at twilight. The bell's tone was perfect, a harmonious pitch achieved, so Calvin and Alma were informed in a letter accompanying the shipment, by a careful fusion of nickel and silver to give the brass bulk of the thing a voice superior to bells of more common cast. Calvin considered the vast sum spent on it well worthwhile, yanked at the cord until exhausted. As the last tolling echoed away into the dusk he pronounced the sound just right; as he later said to Alma, it was a real bong, not a cheap clang.

The pews had likewise been ordered from the east, as was the pulpit, all of finest mahogany, polished to a sheen worthy of marble. The carpenters and the local architect who had designed the church considered it a big barn of a place, made even draughtier, now that the season was turning, because of a large hole in the south wall, a circle six feet in diameter. This was where the stained-glass window would be fitted once it was ready for installation. Calvin, with Alma's aid, had written to a man in Philadelphia famous for his expertise in this field, and included with the letter had been a drawing from Calvin's own hand, a secret design he had not cared to share even with his wife. A reply had been received, along with a staggering estimate of costs. Calvin did not hesitate, but despatched adequate funds to the master artisan. He had hoped it would be ready in time, but the master would not be rushed, and so the wind was kept from the church's interior by means of a tarpaulin temporarily installed for that purpose.

Calvin was approached one brisk morning by a salesman from Chicago. Together they craned their necks at the imposing spire. "Where's the cross?" asked the salesman. "I saw this place from the depot, just had to come up and see for myself if it's as grand as it looks from down there. You haven't got the cross fixed up on top, though."

"No," said Calvin, who had not even considered this Christian totem.

"Something else you've overlooked, my friend, something every bit as important as the holy cross, something I can assist you in obtaining at a special price set by my employers, God-fearing men all, for houses of the Lord."

"Huh?"

"A lightning rod, sir. You need a lightning rod from the reputable firm of McCluskie & Sons, purveyors of farm and building accessories since 1831, finest lightning rods inside or outside of Illinois. The McCluskie appliance will deflect all Jovian bolts from above, absorb their awesome electrical charge and send it straight down into God's earth. A church this tall, sir, requires a lightning rod of exceptional length. How high is the spire, exactly?''

''Pretty high,'' said Calvin.

''An understatement, sir, if I may say so. I would estimate not less than sixty feet. Would you concur?''

''I reckon.''

He did not have the faintest idea what ''concur'' meant, but he enjoyed watching spit fly from the salesman's lips.

''She'll come from the very tip of the spire, down the steeple to the roof, down the roof to the corner there, and straight down into the ground. Taking into account the angles and bends, I'd say eighty feet of rod are called for. I've an eye for measurement, and I'm seldom wrong by more than an inch or two. A McCluskie rod of that length, calculated at one dollar twenty-five per foot, would cost you one hundred dollars even. Does that sound like a bargain to you, sir, or does that sound like a bargain?''

''I reckon.''

The salesman pulled a small book from his pocket, began taking down details. Calvin pulled a wad of crushed bills from his pants, invited the man to select one hundred dollars' worth of paper. The deal was made. ''I'll telegraph head office in Chicago this very day, Mr. Puckett, and the appliance should reach you in not more than two weeks. Proud to do business with a man who knows how to make the right decision fast, and pays spot cash, too.'' They shook hands. ''What might the name of this church be, Mr. Puckett?''

Calvin told him. The salesman asked him to repeat it, then wrote down his words, an incredulous smile tugging at his lips. The salesman did not realise he was the first person to receive this information. Calvin had known for some time now, had been waiting for the right moment to speak. There was really just one name for this church; he should have seen that from the start, and saved himself all that effort. The salesman left the ridge, returned to town and sent a message from the telegraph office at the railroad depot. He then set out in a hired rig to visit the outlying farms and drum up more business for McCluskie & Sons. He expected it would be the usual ten dollars down and payment by the month with these farmers; their orders would be relayed via the slower, cheaper US Mail. The salesman had a good story to tell the other drummers encountered on his travels. Who would have thought a rich man could also be a madman?

The telegraph operator scratched his head, scanned the words he had transmitted, called the stationmaster in to confer. Together they brought in several others from the railyard to speculate, finally to laugh. This was too good to keep to themselves; word spread through town, was common knowledge by late afternoon, spread in a widening ripple of incredulity and mirth to the farmlands of Valley Forge in the days that followed. It had been obvious from the beginning that Calvin was a moron, but this! There was argument over the implications of the discovery. Did it constitute blasphemy, or should allowances be made for a half-wit? Should steps be taken to ensure Calvin's plan did not bear fruit, or was that kind of action unconstitutional?

Experts were consulted—Preacher Tub Davis of the Baptist Church on Arbour St. and the Reverend Dr. Lyman Wilkes of the Protestant Church on Decatur; the latter had joined Calvin and Alma in holy matrimony. These clerical umpires, seldom in agreement at the best of times, chose this forum to disagree once again. In a hastily convened meeting at the town hall they sparred before a delighted audience of councilmen, most of them merchants and the more prosperous farmers. Tub Davis recommended for Calvin a liberal application of tar and feathers, followed by swift ejection from the county. Wilkes rejected Davis' hot-eyed ranting in favour of a more moderate approach to the problem. It was undeniably true, he argued, that Mr. Puckett was not a man possessing the normal refinements and perceptions shared by this assembly, yet had he not spent a vast sum on erecting for the benefit of all citizens a magnificent church, indented the hitherto unbroken line of the ridge with God's thumbprint? The name chosen for his contribution to the community was unorthodox, to be sure, but perhaps it was not impossible he could be persuaded to change it, render it acceptable to the more conventional-minded.

"Conventional-minded!" howled Davis. "The man's gone and made an outright mockery of everything Christian folk hold dear! If you can't see that, if your eyes are so blinded by that man's gold, why, then, I'll just have to pray for you, brother Wilkes, and hope the light of the Lord'll let you see what the rest of us see clear as day."

There were murmurings from those gathered, and Davis interpreted this as encouragement; in fact most of the council men did not favour any kind of harassment. How many towns in Kansas had a rich lunatic for folks to talk about? Not too damn many, you could be sure of that, and there was no real harm in Puckett, just the kind of insensitivity to public opinion you'd expect from an idiot. He wasn't to blame for being that way, was to all intents and purposes an avid Christian, so why persecute him like those old Romans did? At the same time, things could not be allowed to continue as they were. All in all, ran the undercurrent of opinion, the Reverend Wilkes' plan stood above that of Tub Davis, who was the kind of fire-eater who'd pray for Satan to come down his chimney so they could arm-wrestle, brow to horns, for the souls of all mankind.

A vote was taken. Preacher Davis stamped out in disgust when the vote became clear. He knew why he had been defeated; the council was largely Protestant, a bunch of damn shopkeepers who wanted Puckett to spend money in their stores, and it was damn likely Wilkes was hoping for a handout, too. Tub Davis' own congregation tended to be poorer and less influential than the knot of vipers he'd just walked out on. Let them grovel before Puckett if they wanted, the Lord was observing their every self-interested move, and making note in the Book of Retribution. Damn! but he would have liked to see a good tarring and feathering.

Wilkes placed his hat squarely on his head and went to dissuade Calvin from his folly, with the blessing of the council. He was new to Valley Forge, that is, had taken over duties at the Decatur Street church a little over a year ago. He had a loyal wife, and a small daughter who was mute. Wilkes himself was an upright kind of man, with the bodily strength to follow a mule or chop a tree or shift a boulder, had that been the path he chose to take; he was the ideal custodian of God's word in a farming community, where manliness was the general rule, soft palms and bookish tendencies the badge of a parasite, representative of the effete east. Wilkes did not sit in idleness through the week, but drove a battered buggy around the farms, listening to the kind of problems that affect humanity everywhere, offering sensible advice, holding impromptu services if requested to do so, burying and baptising, sometimes even lending a hand with a farmyard chore. It was the women who needed him most. They could talk to each other of their woes, but that was like talking to their own reflection in a mirror; talking with the Reverend Wilkes was far more satisfying, him being a man. These women had been taught to doubt their own abilities, understanding and wisdom purely on account of their sex. It was somehow more meaningful to talk to a man, but their conversation had seldom been taken seriously by their husbands; not until Wilkes came along had the women been granted the privilege of a sympathetic and intelligent ear. He was manly, yet not a man as were their husbands, was as tactful and intuitive as a woman, but could never be accused of effeminacy. He would sit right down and help you split peas while you talked, and somehow it didn't make him one whit less of a man, made you trust him and confide in him. The farmers were not resentful of Wilkes' influence, trusted him themselves, admitted he was a real

hard worker, not just some head-in-the-clouds Sunday ser-
moniser spouting hearts and flowers talk that had nothing
to do with the other six days of the week. Wilkes was a
man among men. He covered a wide stretch of country
ministering to his flock, and was respected for the sincerity
of his efforts.

His wife Peg raised vegetables with some success in a
modest plot behind the rectory, the better to eke out the
inadequate stipend provided by the county, a quiet woman,
suffering some peculiar illness, it was rumoured. Daughter
Sadie had quickly become an object of adoration verging
on veneration when the family arrived at Valley Forge.
Five years old, very small, with the face of an angel, it was
not possible to look upon her without feeling a catch in the
back of one's throat; those eyes of deepest blue seemed to
bare the very soul of an observer, while simultaneously
inviting confession and offering absolution—an unnerving
experience at first, but one which mellowed to sympathy
and compassion when it was learned the child could not
utter a sound. Behind the soft white throat lay a malformation, a melding of fleshy tubes and valves and cords;
Sadie could breathe and swallow with ease, but no words
ever sprang from her mouth, not a cry or a cough, not so
much as a sigh. Her face, so young and yet so wise, possessed all the piquancy of a masterly portrait in oils, wide
of eye and pert of lip, staring, always staring with all-
encompassing intensity. Wilkes loved her more dearly than
he loved his wife, more dearly, were he to admit it, than
God's work. Prayer had done nothing to alter Sadie's condition, and Wilkes had slowly come to accept that this was
his punishment for taking enjoyment in the body of Peg,
from the time of their marriage to the present, when this
same body he had inserted himself into times without
number was losing its female contours, succumbing to a
wasting disease beyond diagnosis or medical aid. Wilkes
blamed himself for this also, and cursed the lustings that
plagued him, the weakness that had blasted his wife and
child.

Climbing the ridge to deliver his message, he put from him all thoughts of his own tribulations. This would be his first meeting with Calvin Puckett since the latter's wedding day; he had hoped a visit would be made to the rectory, but Puckett had visited no one, asked nobody's advice, had gone ahead with his church as if the building were an extension of his own home rather than a place designated for public worship. The McCluskie lightning rod was to be delivered to Mr. Calvin Puckett, care of the Church of the White Wolf, Valley Forge, Kansas. What on earth had caused him to choose such an outlandish name? Was he truly as peculiar as rumoured? Wilkes was looking forward to the confrontation. In truth, he found most of his congregation a trifle dull and predictable in their manner; he cared for them, but was all too aware of the lack of emotional or intellectual stimulation to be garnered from their company. Perhaps a madman would enliven Wilkes' tedious world.

He found Calvin where he had been told Calvin would be found, but not in the state he had anticipated; Calvin was fast asleep, stretched out on a pew. Wilkes cleared his throat several times. Calvin's eyes opened and he sat up, smiling with the sheepishness of a boy caught stealing cookies. Wilkes' hopes for an enlightened exchange of ideas faded away as he studied Calvin's face; there was nothing about it to indicate astuteness of mind or strength of character. He introduced himself.

"Set down, why don't you." Calvin clearly had forgotten his face.

Wilkes lowered himself on to one of the many cushions to be found on every pew, wondered which approach would best suit this fellow with the foolish grin and protruding wristbones.

"There are a number of people in town who are upset, Mr. Puckett."

"What about?" Calvin seemed genuinely concerned.

"About the name you intend bestowing upon this fine building."

Calvin squirmed with delight. "Bet they wished they

had of thought it up first," he said with pride. "It come to me just like *that.*" He attempted to snap his fingers, but Calvin's digits were not sufficiently co-ordinated to accomplish the act; they tangled in midair, flapped about ineffectively until called home to his lap.

"Many people feel it is an inappropriate name, Mr. Puckett."

Calvin stared at him blankly. Wilkes tried again. "They don't think it's the right name," he explained with a smile.

"It is, too! It's just exackly right!"

His expression was suddenly resentful, and Wilkes saw that kid gloves were called for; Puckett was obviously as sensitive to criticism as a normal person.

"May I ask why you chose that particular name?"

"That's my business, I reckon."

In times gone by Calvin would never have dared to be so aggressive in his own defence. He suspected he was being rude, but it just couldn't be helped. Who did this man think he was, telling Calvin he'd gone and picked the wrong name? There was no doubt whatever in Calvin's mind; he had chosen wisely. God had handed him the cash, the church and the name, and none of it could be denied or changed. He set his lips into a thin and determined line that did not go unobserved by Wilkes.

The minister wanted an answer, if only to satisfy his own curiosity. He studied the high walls, freshly painted with virginal white, as was the exterior, allowed his eye to roam across the flapping canvas covering the hole in the south wall, noted the richness of woodgrain in the pews and pulpit, the unblemished clarity of the window glass. A fine church, but for all its splendid newness Wilkes could not imagine a congregation to inhabit it of a Sunday. No one would dare set foot across the threshold until a suitable name had been found, until it was known for certain which arm of the Christian octopus it represented, until a legitimate clergyman arrived to assume the usual duties. None of this would transpire, of that he was certain. Calvin Puckett's resentful face told him so, and the mournful flapping of the canvas on this grey afternoon confirmed it. The church had been erected in vain, a naïve approximation of holy work, an idiot's dream. Wilkes' own chapel was in need of repair, had been for years. He would have mortgaged a small portion of his soul to be in possession of a building such as this, but of course that was not possible; its instigator, builder, owner and sole tenant would always be the child-man seated beside him, none other. What a waste, he thought, and hated Calvin's petulant nature and physical ugliness for a full half-minute before chiding himself for his lack of charity; the man was retarded in some fashion, and could not be held accountable for the foolishness of his acts, must have been born under the proverbial lucky star to have such riches, could never have acquired the kind of wealth represented here by engaging in the cut and thrust of commercial enterprise.

"It was not my intention to give offence, Mr. Puckett."

"I give it the right name."

"I'm sure you did. It's just that I, and others, do not understand this reference to a white wolf. It is not, so far as I am aware, a part of Christian theology. I was hoping you would share your special knowledge with me. It's clear you have been granted something which has not been given to others. Perhaps if it was explained, then we would understand."

Calvin was flattered by this appeal. Maybe he *would* tell. God wanted people to know the truth, else He wouldn't have revealed it to Calvin. Maybe it was his duty to share it around. He cast a look behind him to ensure they were not overheard, leaned close to Wilkes.

"It's God," he whispered.

"Where?" whispered Wilkes.

"No, the white wolf."

"The white wolf is God?"

Calvin nodded emphatically, smiling now, glad to have unburdened himself at last; truth was a commodity to be shared with those less fortunate than he.

"How did you learn this?"

"He showed me. Come right up to me and talked, close as you are right now."

"A white wolf."

"Yessir, white as snow. He told me I got to kill the crooked man."

"What crooked man might that be, Mr. Puckett?" They were whispering still, like two schoolgirls trading secrets. Calvin leaned even closer to Wilkes, brushed his ear with warm breath.

"Feller by name of Joe Cobden. He'll come along by and by. I got to kill him when he does. That's what God wants. I got to do it."

"Of course. Have you met this Cobden before?"

"Worked alongside of him a couple of years. A crookedy-back. He knows I know. He'll be along by and by, and when he does. . . ." Calvin made a dramatic chopping motion with his hand. "You tell everyone in town to watch out for him. It's best if I get a warning. That way I'll be ready."

"I understand. Has God told you anything else you feel you can share with me?"

Calvin frowned darkly, cogitated a short while.

"No," he said, the corrugations of effort leaving his brow. He was glad now that someone else knew what he knew. Alma had never asked. He was grateful to this man, whose name he had forgotten again, for obliging him to open his heart. Now there would be a whole town on the lookout for Joe Cobden, and he would be seen for sure. Calvin rubbed his hands together and smiled. Wilkes looked at those hands, overlarge, ugly hands, clumsy and chapped, the nails bitten down to ragged flanges of yellow horn. God would never have revealed himself to the owner of those hands.

He stood. "I'll pass your message on, Mr. Puckett."

"Good, good, that's the best way."

"Good day to you."

"You come again. You tell 'em anyone can come."

"I will, Mr. Puckett."

309

Wilkes went to the house. It was nearing completion, had already been painted a pale brown, with darker brown around the eaves and window frames, the doors and porch pillars; even the stable, some twenty yards away, conformed to this colour scheme. Wilkes thought it a handsome place, quelled comparison with the rectory's peeling walls and ever increasing lean to the west. A workman was placing the last of the roof shingles, and by the door stood a wagon laden with furniture, evidently not the first, for when Wilkes knocked and entered through the already opened door he found the hallway and those rooms adjacent to it almost completely furnished. Alma was directing the wagoneers in positioning an escritoire which, like the rest of the furniture, had been ordered by catalogue from Kansas City. She was annoyed at the interruption, took her uninvited guest to the front parlour, sat him down upon a sofa of immaculate newness.

"What may I do for you, Mr. Wilkes?"

She made a point of addressing him as "Mister", rather than "Reverend", did not dislike him as a man, but as a servant of the Church, an institution for which she had little respect. He chose to ignore the discourtesy.

"I have just been talking with your husband, Mrs. Puckett."

"That must have been fascinating."

He was shocked at her sarcasm. A woman who ridiculed her husband in front of others must be intolerable to live with. Could this be the reason Puckett spent so much time further up the ridge?

"You know, of course, his intended name for the new church."

"As a matter of fact I do not."

"He has not told you?" Wilkes was greatly surprised.

"Why should he? What he chooses to call it is none of my concern."

Alma avoided Wilkes' church, and was known not to frequent the meetings of Tub Davis; Wilkes therefore suspected her of being an atheist. He did not resent such people, but pitied them.

"He seems set upon naming it . . . the Church of the White Wolf."

Alma stared at him. A spotlessly new grandfather clock, wound for the first time just an hour before, punctiliously measured the silence from within its varnished cabinet. Alma felt something rise into her throat, an unfamiliar sensation, part bubble of air, part convulsion, unrecognisable until it spilled from her lips: laughter. She allowed it to flow, enjoying the novelty of merriment. What a perfect fool she'd married, what a joke of a man. And look at the minister, look at the dismay on his face; he probably wants me to have a word in Calvin's ear, thought Alma, and laughed even louder.

"If you would just talk with him. . . ."

She almost shrieked. Wilkes' face grew red; was the wife as mad as the husband? When Alma had calmed herself, Wilkes tried again.

"Do you have any idea why he chose such a name?"

"It's obvious."

"Yes?"

"He's simple."

"Come now, Mrs. Puckett."

"Everyone knows. You needn't deny it to spare my poor womanly feelings."

Wilkes looked at his boots in embarrassment; they were very muddy, had left gobs of earth on the new rug whose pattern, he noted, was vaguely Arabic, loop upon opulent loop, richly coloured, far grander than anything he had seen elsewhere in Valley Forge. The pattern was very nearly mesmerising; he wondered how long he had been staring at it, wondered also if Alma had noticed the mud he had tracked in. He looked up. She was waiting for him to say more, still amused by his stiffness. He decided he did not like her.

"Is there no chance he might be persuaded to change

the name, make arrangements to install an accredited minister of religion? It seems such a waste. . . ."

"I would say the chances of such a thing happening are very small indeed, Mr. Wilkes."

"That is not encouraging news."

"I'm sure you'll find an appropriate passage in the Bible to cheer you up."

Wilkes stood. "Good day to you, Mrs. Puckett. I shall find my own way out."

"Good day, Mr. Wilkes."

He left, hoping mud had been ground indelibly into the rug—a childish thought, he knew, but a satisfying one. "Good riddance," said Alma, as his boots clumped across the porch and down the steps.

And that, for the moment, was where matters were left.

CHAPTER TWENTY-TWO

The citizens of Valley Forge waited to see what Calvin would do when he finally realised he had raised a church that would never resound to sermon, hymn or prayer. It was almost Christmas. Imagine a church on Christmas Day, empty! It was a blasphemous notion, but, then, the white box on the ridge with its towering spire was not really a church, had not been built at the order of any orthodox ecclesiastical body, nor been consecrated by same. Whenever Alma ventured into town she was greeted with wolf-like bayings from small boys and saloon-porch loungers. To her credit, she acknowledged none of it openly, but once returned to the privacy of her home she would throw hand-embroidered cushions about the room, send them whizzing through the air with tassels flying; after one such public hazing she deliberately smashed a French vase costing more than fifty dollars.

Community spirit reached its finest flowering the night several loafers coated a stray mongrel with whitewash, hung a sign around its neck and stole up to the ridge. Alma was the first to see the unfortunate animal next morning, tied to the porch. The sign read: *Can I use my big white kennel now, please?* The mutt wagged a pitiful stump of tail and whined ingratiatingly. Alma freed it, removed the sign, waved her arms to scare it off, but it appeared to regard the porch as its new home and would not budge. She fed it, hoping a full stomach would render it more amenable. The whitewashed dog settled itself by the steps and grinned at her, tongue lolling. Calvin joined his wife on the porch, saw the dog and whistled at it. Surprisingly, the dog jumped to its feet. Calvin descended the steps with a lordly air. "Reckon I'll stroll on up to the church," he said, and did exactly that, the dog at his heels. Alma watched them disappear into the trees. Calvin had not remarked on the dog's woebegone appearance, or asked where it had come from, had failed completely to appreciate the ridicule inherent in the prank. He accepted the dog with the same benign incuriosity with which he accepted the existence of earth and sky.

Life was not working out for Alma as planned. Marriage had removed her at last from beneath her father's roof, had given her one of the finest houses in Valley Forge; it had also given her a simpleton to share her bed, a gauche adolescent of a man to whom she must offer her body whenever he pleased—and Calvin, now that he had mastered the intricacies of phallic penetration, pleased often. Alma's current role as social pariah had been years in rehearsal, first as the ugliest girl in school, then as the local old maid; now she was the wife of the village idiot. It was very nearly amusing. She wondered if certain lives are blighted from the beginning by some malign force drifting in the air, casually allocating misery here, discord there, heartache over yonder. Alma felt she had somehow received both her own share and someone else's. Unhappiness was the motive force behind her every thought and word and deed. Accordingly, none of these things had the capacity to alter her life one whit; she was trapped in a home smelling of fresh paint and varnish and wood and fabric, the newest yet oldest of cages. What made it unbearable was knowing she had walked in of her own accord, had even bribed the gaoler with her breasts for the privilege of incarcerating herself. Perhaps a child would make all the difference. She did not allow herself to contemplate the likelihood of giving birth to something of Calvin's type; no, it would be a bonny bouncing babe; and would make her happy. Contrary to custom, she hoped for a girl, believing this would preclude the possibility of any resemblance, physical or mental, between her husband and their offspring. An atheist by default, Alma found herself praying for impregnation every time Calvin clutched her shoulders or scrabbled for her bosom, his hips pumping with the energy born of excitement. Her torment seldom lasted more than ninety seconds on any given night.

During the day husband and wife had nothing whatever to say to each other. Over breakfast Calvin would predict the day's weather, and was never offended at Alma's lack of interest; he found it quite natural that a woman had no opinion to offer, for despite his thickheadedness Calvin had, over the years, absorbed some of the more basic tenets of the male attitude toward females. He was grateful to her for not obliging him to converse further. He spent a great deal of time asleep on one or other of the cushioned church pews, the dog asleep beside him, revealing a little more of its true drab brown colouring every day. Calvin was waiting for the stained glass window to arrive; beyond that event he made no plans. Cold winds blew across Kansas from the north and west, carrying no freight of rain or snow, empty winds passing across empty land. The sky remained blue and cloudless; the low winter sun crawled crab-like from horizon to horizon, dispensing light without heat, its arc sinking toward the solstice. Calvin lay on his back and stared at the ceiling of his church. Alma stared through the parlour window. Sometimes she read from a novel (ten yards of literature had been shipped from St. Louis, enough to fill the bookshelves in the study) but found it impossible to concentrate. Like Calvin, she waited.

On the morning of December 12th a long parcel wrapped in tarpaper and twine was offloaded from the caboose of the 10:23 westbound. The stationmaster inspected one end of the parcel where the tarpaper had torn, exposing the tips of four twenty foot lengths of metal piping. Calvin's lightning rod had arrived. The stationmaster now had to decide if he should send a message to the ridge, deliver the parcel himself, or wait until Calvin or Alma came to town and made enquiries. He was inclined to make them wait. Why should he put himself out for rich folks? Let them come and fetch it themselves. The stationmaster's son had asked for Alma's hand a year ago, and been refused.

That afternoon the day became overcast. Dark clouds moved in from the west, heralded by distant rumblings of thunder. People looked from their windows and stood in doorways to watch the approaching thunderheads as they spilled across the sky, swallowing the sun, absorbing all light, offering instead a leaden greenish hue that washed the world in undersea gloom. The earth shook, window-panes rattled in their frames as the aerial maelstrom passed overhead, its tumbling outer edges licking and curling. The black interior detonated continually, hatching electrical coruscations that flashed with the vividness of sparks struck from mighty wheels; this was an airborne engine of destruction, an amorphous beast consuming itself, stalking the plains on legs of lightning. Dogs howled, children were called in from streets and yards as the dark mass lowered itself over Valley Forge.

No rain or hail fell; the storm had come to rattle and quake, and to amaze with dazzling phenomena. The first of these appeared on Decatur Street, a glowing ball of bluish cast, perhaps twelve inches in diameter; it sped along the centre of the street some three feet above the ground, panicked horses tied to hitching rails, drove dogs to yelping madness and sent religious persons to their knees, convinced the Apocalypse had come at last. The ball hovered for several seconds at the edge of town, rose a little higher into the air and slowly tacked this way and that as it passed back along Decatur, for all the world like a balloon seeking out its owner. There were some who said it emitted a faint buzzing and crackling, others who insisted it went about its business in enigmatic silence. It bounced and bobbed, slid and hovered in close proximity to buildings without once touching brick or wood or plaster, for which many were grateful; they knew that had it done so the blue sphere would have burst, releasing a noxious cloud of pestilence and fever. Preacher Tub Davis was one who saw the thing, and swore it was a sign from the Lord, a warning to the townsfolk to mend their sinning ways and tread the path of righteousness. He fully expected the sky to disgorge a rain of blood, or maybe frogs, prepared himself to preach right there in the main street with his beard streaming red and a toad or two on his hat.

The miracle did not occur; instead there descended from the reverberating canopy of cloud a second ball, equal in size to the first, but having about it a yellowish hue. The interloper began its earthly investigations along Arbour Street, turned left to follow Chippewa and eventually rendezvoused with its glowing cousin halfway along Decatur. There were sober witnesses to what followed. Both balls rushed towards each other like tomcats, but rather than collide (which some aver would have resulted in a cataclysmic explosion, destroying the town and its populace), the blue ball and the yellow ball circled in tight formation, spinning about each other faster and faster outside Tom Clancy's Cloverleaf Saloon, blue and yellow, blue and yellow, until they blurred and blended, becoming a ring of green, now definitely humming at such a pitch it could be heard above the thunder crashing and rolling overhead. Tom Clancy himself declared that the thing's colour identified it positively as the spirit of St. Patrick. Why else would it have been so green, and performed outside the Cloverleaf? Then came the finale; with dozens looking on, the balls appeared to merge, to shrink their rushing perimeter and coalesce, becoming for one blinding moment a single sphere (still green, says Clancy, green as spring in Kilkenny) then nothing at all. It simply disappeared. There were some who maintained they heard the snap and crackle of electricity as the phenomenon took abrupt leave, and most were agreed it left in its wake the sharp smell of ozone. Scarcely had amazement died and explanations begun than a small boy came running down the street, larruping his thighs in excitement. "The church is on fire!" he screamed. "The church is on fire!" Men rushed in two parties, to the Baptist chapel on Arbour and the Protestant house of prayer along Decatur, but of course both parties were concerned for the wrong church entirely.

Calvin had seen the storm approaching from his church windows, saw the flickerings of lightning, felt the thunder draw a responsive trembling from his body. The dog (a piebald brown and white by now) whimpered with fear and fled to safety beneath a pew; it huddled there, blotched flanks shivering, ears limp with terror. "Ain't a thing to be scared of," assured Calvin. "It's just thunder and lightnin' is all. Won't do nobody no harm." The dog was not convinced and stayed where it was, a trickle of urine pooling between its hind legs. Calvin turned again to the window, admired the way the clouds resembled tumbling black water rushing along upside down, lightning dancing among the billows like crazed salmon. When the first bolt hit the spire Calvin thought someone had pounded upon the doors. Before he could reach them to find out who and why, a second bolt snaked from the boiling sky, struck the bell and set the belfry afire. As Calvin opened the doors chunks of wood were hitting the ground, dislodged from the steeple by the force of the blow, hissing with sap, their paint bubbling. From the bell itself came an endless peal, a humming vibration such as can be heard when the tongue has struck for the last time, the resonant sound seeming to linger for ever in the air.

Fire licked at the belfry supports, ate its way up the spire, made of it an elongated pyramid of flame. Calvin groaned deep in his chest, stood rooted to the earth, eyes fixed on the blaze above him. The entire steeple was burning now, and when the fire reached its base it found the beams supporting the roof, began to follow them beneath the shingles. Calvin's feet gave a little dance of vexation. Where was the rain, the cold and lashing rain to put out this ungodly fire? But the black clouds discharged only thunder and lightning. Smoke soon was pouring from beneath the roof as beams and rafters began to smoulder, increasing in volume and blackness as the fire discovered an entire ceiling to consume. Calvin ran around the building three times, sobbing with impotent despair. On his third circuit the dog burst from the open doors, stirred from its hiding-place by heat and noise; it joined Calvin in his hapless circling, short bow legs churning, piddling a little as it ran. Now the walls also were afire, the church a roaring box of flame. The bell, its beam reduced to charcoal, crashed to the floor and rolled forward into the vestibule. Calvin could see it as he ran by, its polished sides blackened and streaked with soot, his wonderful brass bell with the percentage of nickel and silver to give it just the right tone. Seeing it there, humbled, brought low, Calvin knew there was no chance now to save his church. Driven back at last by heat, he sank to his knees, watched his offering to God send rags of flame heavenward. Now the floor was alight, the boards aswirl with runnels of fire, the pews blazing in stately ranks. Windows burst from their frames, so great was the pressure of heat. Swooping winds rampaged between the walls and under the roof, sucking air through the doorway and empty windows; swirling funnels of flame leaped from floor and walls, touched and fell back again, were born anew seconds later in another gust of oxygen, rumbling and roaring, exulting in their power.

Alma was not aware of the blaze until she stepped outside, the better to view the storm grinding overhead. Once past the corner of the house, which blocked her view of the ridge's spine, she saw the fire not through the trees, these being too numerous to allow it, but reflected from the underbelly of the storm itself, a patch of rosy light in the midst of tumbling darkness. She knew its cause immediately, ran to the church, but could see Calvin nowhere. The rafters gave way with a crash, sending showers of sparks drifting high into the air; with the backbone of the church broken the steeple could not stand alone, collapsed backwards into the very heart of the fire, was joined by what little remained of the walls a moment later. The church no longer resembled a building, was more akin to some celebratory blaze, the kind usually accompanied by fireworks and crowds. A few main timbers remained standing at the conflagration's edge, charred and lonely as the stakes of martyrs. Had Calvin perished in the fire, too devoted to his folly to leave or, more likely, too stupid? For one guilt-ridden moment Alma allowed images of lawyers and wills and chests of money to crowd her mind. Had Calvin written a will? He could not write, did not have a lawyer! Did Kansas law automatically assign her husband's worldly goods to a grieving widow? And then she saw him, a pathetic figure among the trees, his clothing smudged and blackened. The ridiculous dog rested at the feet of Alma's ridiculous husband.

She skirted the smouldering patches of grass to reach him. Heat pulsed in waves from the fire, a furnace breath that scorched her skin even at a distance, crinkled her hair on the nearer side. Calvin did not seem to notice her, stood gaping at the sight before him. Alma touched his sleeve. "Calvin?" He turned slowly, eyes glazed, staring straight through her. "Calvin . . . how did it happen?"

He turned back to the fire, a shapeless heap of glowing coals laved with flame. "Joe Cobden done it," he said, as though realising it for the first time that very instant; his voice rasped in a throat parched by hot air. "Snuck right up and done it deliberate. . . ."

"Who did you say?"

"He done it all right. . . . I can smell him."

"Who *is* this person . . . ? *Where* is he?"

"Around," said Calvin, suddenly galvanised by the thought. "He's still around. . . . Got to be around here someplace. . . ."

He began searching among the trees. Alma was frightened. Was there truly an arsonist in the area, or had Calvin's mind regressed another notch towards outright insanity? At this time the people of Valley Forge arrived at the ridge, having driven buckboards and buggies and ridden horses from town as fast as they could, eager to witness the end of the white church. They swarmed up the slope, men and women and children by the dozen, by the score, and gathered around the blaze, eyes shining with reflected fire. Among them were Tub Davis and Lyman Wilkes, the former strutting with authority and satisfaction, the latter content to gaze at the crackling flames and wonder if this was a genuine example of God's will at work.

Davis was in no doubt on the matter. "Listen here, all of you!" he bellowed above the blaze and thunder. "Now you see what happens when a man sets himself up against the good Lord and makes of His name a mockery! God Almighty won't stand for it! He sent a sign! You saw it in town, the whirligig of light from heaven! And now this! The house of the Lord is a sacred place wherein His name must not be taken in vain! This,"—he gestured to the fire—"was an abomination in the eyes of the Lord, and He has destroyed it accordingly! There are no other paths than His path! Any that follow the serpent will be destroyed, and their goods and chattels alongside of them!"

There were ragged amens and hallelujahs from some of his followers, catcalls from the rowdy element, among whom a jug was circulating. People turned this way and that, toasting themselves on all sides with the fire's heat, but generally they stood facing it, for a fire is a thing to be admired on its own terms and for its own sake. The townsfolk stared at the glowing ruins of Calvin Puckett's church with the same rapt attention their ancestors had displayed before the lifegiving fires in their caves. This was a time they would be able to discuss for years to come, one of those stories that would grow from gossip to anecdote to tall tale to myth: The Day God Almighty Wreaked His Divine Vengeance upon the Mad Blasphemer.

Nobody approached Alma; their embarrassment at her shame kept them at a discreet distance. She noted the surreptitious glances in her direction, was not offended by the passing of the jug within sight of her, did not know how she should feel about what had transpired, therefore felt very little of anything. She experienced no sense of great loss but, rather, one of bemused indifference. It was a shame that so much money had been squandered on the church, but presumably Calvin had plenty more. It really was a very expensive bonfire. Let these people enjoy it, let them have their simple pleasure, their communal gloating. She despised them not because they laughed at her husband, for in all honesty she found Calvin a ludicrous specimen of humanity herself; no, she despised them because they were despicable, because they drew their strength and certainty from that hydra-headed institution, the crowd, the mob, the mass, in which many merge into one and are hidden by their fellows. Alma stood with arms folded, chin raised, the personification, she believed, of queenly disdain. The crowd saw nothing more impressive than a fat woman propping up her bosom.

Wilkes came to her side. "Is your husband uninjured, Mrs. Puckett?"

"He's looking for whoever did it."

"This was done deliberately?"

"So he believes. He has gone to look for a man called Joe Cobden."

"He mentioned the name to me. This Cobden is some kind of devil's henchman, according to Mr. Puckett."

"Then he probably does not exist."

"I am inclined to agree. Lightning was in all probability the cause. Several trees on the ridge have been struck in the past, I'm told."

The storm eventually rolled by, grumbling still, voiding its energies with vicious jabbings at the earth, and in its stead came the darkness of evening. The church settled into a heap of glowing embers, and the crowd began dispersing to their horses and vehicles at the foot of the ridge. Halfway there, however, they were treated to yet another episode in the Calvin Puckett versus God story. While passing the Puckett home its owner suddenly presented himself in their midst, a burning branch in his hand. Some say he sprang from the trees and scrub, others insist he had been waiting on the porch for sufficient numbers to pass by and make what followed an event that would not go unrecorded. With the clumsiness of a marionette under the control of an inebriate, Calvin passed the burning branch several times in front of his face, as if conjuring scenes of raging combustion to match those already demonstrated, then walked (if such a jerking of knees could be termed walking) to the front steps of his home and thrust the branch under them with the evident intention of setting the place alight. Perhaps he felt it only right that buildings raised concurrently and within shouting distance of each other should share a similar fate. Several onlookers laughed, were quite prepared to watch the flames take hold, but others among them took appropriate action and wrestled Calvin to the ground before the branch had time to do more than scorch the steps. When asked later why they did this, they said it was because of Alma, who was a normal woman despite her uppity ways and horse face, and didn't deserve to have her home burned out from under her by a lunatic. Two of the men who sat on Calvin's chest while he mouthed unintelligible phrases were carpenters who had contributed their talents to the raising of these walls, and did not wish to see the proof of their craftsmanship reduced to ashes.

Under Alma's instructions Calvin was taken inside and tied to a kitchen chair. A light froth had gathered at the corners of his mouth. Sympathetic offers were made to help Alma stand guard over her husband through the coming night, or until such time as he regained his senses (by which they meant until Calvin became once again a harmless idiot, rather than a danger to himself and others). It was commonly believed, following Calvin's attempt to incinerate his own home, that he had set fire to the church, possibly unable to live with the fact that it would never serve the purpose for which it had been erected, possibly for reasons incomprehensible to anyone but another lunatic. Alma chose to be alone. Her choice was attributed to pride by those whose services were refused, but they did not resent her for it; putting up with company after events like these would have put a strain on the most capable of hostesses. The crowd departed, leaving Calvin bound in the chair. Alma did not dare release him.

CHAPTER TWENTY-THREE

In the morning she went to the kitchen and was greeted by a repentant Calvin and a disgusting odour; God's right hand had shat himself. Alma untied the knots and freed her husband. He shuffled off to the outhouse to cleanse himself, contrition plucking at the corners of his mouth. Alma opened several windows. She kept a careful watch over Calvin throughout the day. He did not stray from the porch, had apparently forgotten the burnt offerings further up the slope, although the smell of cooling charcoal filled the air.

In the afternoon Alma received a visitor. Valley Forge was too small and law-abiding a town to require a sheriff, unlike the cattle towns to the west, but its citizens were reassured by the annual election of a constable as resident symbol of justice. Ned Bowdre was the eager incumbent in that year of 1873, a large and meaty man known and liked by the majority of townspeople. Along with his brother Milt he ran a successful farm on the north side of town, specialising in hogs. Sometimes Ned slept at the farm, sometimes in his small office on Decatur, depending on whether he smelled crime in the air. He had smelled plenty since yesterday's storm, and rode his straining mare up to the ridge, dismounted by the porch rail and came clumping up the steps. Calvin ignored him, and Ned Bowdre reciprocated; he had come to see the head of the house, and he knew which partner wore the pants in this particular home. Alma bade him be seated, knowing what was to follow. After a halting discussion on the storm and the fire Ned got down to business.

"It's not like this is personal, Mrs. Puckett, but folks are worried like you'd expect. Anyone's barn gets burned down and you know who's going to get the blame.''

"My husband's church was ignited by a lightning bolt, Mr. Bowdre.''

"That's not something you could prove, but there's plenty that seen him put the torch to this very house. That's evidence of intent. Anyone's barn gets burned down, I'll be obliged to put Mr. Puckett under lock and key for his own protection. You can understand the reason for it.''

Ned did not enjoy having to talk like this. Threats did not come easily to him, even when confronted by a brash drunkard just begging to be hit alongside the head with Ned's blackjack and hauled off to the jail to sleep off his liquor. Ned carried no gun, even had his badge modestly tucked away on the inside of his lapel. He had only been truly angry once in his adult life, when a man running in opposition to him for the office of constable had circulated the cruel rumour that Ned, accompanied by brother Milt, engaged in unnatural acts with their hogs. Ned had resented the insult to the animals as much as to himself and Milt, had stamped through election week with a face darkened by fury, unable to accuse the perpetrator for lack of proof. Fortunately, the voters knew a lie when they heard one, and had elected Ned for the third consecutive year. No one, not even the rumour-monger, knew that Milt did on occasion visit the hog-pen to alleviate the loneliness of bachelorhood. He would never have visited a brothel, fearing genital infection.

Ned picked his hat from its perch on his mighty knee, stood to leave. "It's my job obliges me to speak this way, ma'am.''

"I understand. You have nothing to fear from Calvin, you have my word.''

"I always accept a lady's word,'' was Ned's clumsy attempt at gallantry.

He took his leave. At the bottom of the ridge he passed a wagon heading up the trail to the house. The stationmaster had come with Calvin's lightning rod after all, not to expedite his duties but to drive home the Pucketts' misfortune with this gratuitous act of irony. He dumped the parcelled rod from the wagon in full view of Calvin, turned the team and drove away again. He would embroider the details of the delivery somewhat in order to be given free drinks at Clancy's and the Calhoun Hotel; Calvin and his ugly wife were favourite topics in the drinking establishments of Valley Forge, and anecdotes, no matter how feeble, were viable coin of the imbiber's realm.

Calvin ignored the long parcel as he had ignored the stationmaster, and before him the constable. He did not know who they were, was not interested in finding out. He wondered how Joe Cobden had found him so quickly. Maybe he had been sneaking around the area for weeks, staying hid till the church was finished and he could burn it down. Chances were he was around here still. Calvin owned no gun, had better get himself one quick. He rose and walked to town, a cold wind blowing about his ears. He examined every store window until he saw one fitted with bars, behind which were arranged a multitude of arms. Calvin entered and approached the counter, was recognised immediately by the proprietor.

"Something I can do for you, Mr. Puckett?"

"I want a gun."

"This is the place to get one. What kind are you wanting?"

"A rifle."

The proprietor lifted down a splendid weapon from the rack behind him. "Can't go no better than a Winchester, Mr. Puckett. Newest thing around, fifteen shot repeater. Just load her up and work the lever, your target won't know what hit it. What are you after, coyotes? Had a couple of fellers in here this week been bothered by coyotes killing their chickens."

"It's for a man," said Calvin, taking the rifle, savouring the smell of new wood and metal and gun oil.

"A present for someone, you mean?"

"To kill him with."

"Well now, you better not go around saying stuff like that, Mr. Puckett. Talk like that makes folks nervous. What feller is it you want to kill, if it ain't a personal question?"

"Joe Cobden."

Calvin sighted along the barrel. The Winchester felt good in his hands. He knew he would buy it.

"Joe Cobden. Is he a local man? I never heard the name."

"He's around here someplace. He burned down my church."

"Is that a fact? What's he look like, Mr. Puckett? I'll keep my eyes peeled for him around town."

"He's a humpback. Short and humpity-backed."

"Haven't seen anyone like that just recent. A humpback, that's the kind you'd remember if you seen him."

"I seen him. I see him again, I'll shoot him."

He pulled the trigger, slaughtering a tribe of Joe Cobdens. The hammer snapped home with a dull click. The proprietor, who had been questioning the advisability of providing a lunatic with a rifle, now saw that no harm would come to anyone; the poor fool was imagining things, making up humpbacks the way kids make up fairies.

"You'll be wanting ammunition, Mr. Puckett. Two boxes be enough?"

Calvin nodded, hefting the rifle, admiring its balance. The boxes were dumped before him on the counter. "You paying cash, Mr. Puckett, or do you want me to bill you?"

"I got no money on me."

"That's no problem. I'll just go ahead and bill you."

Calvin pocketed the boxes, shouldered the rifle and marched out. The proprietor wondered again if he had done the right thing, assured himself he had; there were no humpbacks hereabouts to get shot at by mistake for this Joe Cobden. He locked his premises and crossed the street to the dry goods store managed by Willard Croft.

"That crazy man your cousin married just bought himself a gun."

"You sold him a gun?"

"I sure did, a Winchester. Why not? He won't do no harm. He's after a feller called Joe Cobden, a humpback. He figures this humpback burned down the church, so now he's got to kill him. There ain't a single humpback around here, so no one's going to get hurt."

Willard, a slope-shouldered young man with a faint caterpillar of moustache, wondered if there was any advantage to be had from the situation. He knew his Uncle Lucius had wanted him to marry Alma, but at the time Willard considered himself too good for her. That had been three years back, and his various schemes to shake the dust of Valley Forge from his shoes and go westering in search of high adventure and cash profit had never materialised. His latest plan was to climb aboard a train to California and maybe get himself a good job with a shipping line in San Francisco. Christmas was eleven days away; he had promised himself he would decide by then. He did not relish the prospect of breaking the news to Uncle Lucius, who would call him an ungrateful young bastard and the like, and there was no real guarantee the right job would be waiting for him in California anyway; despite the largeness of his plans for advancement and wealth, Willard was a timid soul with an inflated impression of his own worth. If there was an easy way to get what he wanted, that was the path he would follow. If Calvin Puckett shot someone—and it was a distinct possibility, granted his state of mind—he would be arrested and hanged, and Alma would be a rich widow, the weight of her bank balance drawing a seductive veil over the depressing bluntness of her features. Willard would be willing to step into Calvin's shoes for that kind of money. California shrank to the size of a peanut.

"He'll probably just blaze away at a few trees," said Willard, hoping some unsuspecting person might wander in front of Calvin's sights. He wouldn't mind living in that fine new house; it was big enough not to have to look at Alma every minute of the day. She would no doubt appreciate a normal man after the idiot she'd married. And who, he wondered, is Joe Cobden?

Calvin arrived back at the ridge just as the first snow began to fall. He mastered the intricacies of loading the Winchester after many a fumbled attempt, levered a bullet into the chamber and went in search of his mortal enemy. The obvious place to begin was up by the church. The coals still had sufficient heat to produce a steady hissing as snowflakes settled on the blackened heap. Calvin looked for signs of the hunchback, who was at that moment entering Texas with Peter Winstanley. He searched the ridge until dark, then returned to the house. Alma asked where the rifle had come from. Calvin explained. When he fell asleep after supper, Alma unloaded the Winchester and returned it to the corner where Calvin had left it. Snow was falling heavily now. Alma turned out the lamp in order to see outside the window. The lights of town were hidden behind descending whiteness. Alma felt she was alone, a thousand miles from human warmth; a shiver passed through her. Behind her, still seated in his chair, Calvin saluted the coming of winter with a barrage of snoring. Alma leaned her forehead against the cold pane, closed her eyes and dreamed of another life.

Word of Calvin's purchase reached Ned Bowdre the following day. He visited the ridge. Calvin was prowling somewhere along its western slope, hunting Joe Cobden. Ned had with him a Winchester rifle, the identical model to Calvin's. He showed Alma how to remove the firing pin, watched her remove and replace it several times, then left, taking the rifle with him. When Calvin returned to the house for supper Alma fed him to repletion, waited until he fell asleep and removed the firing pin from his Winchester. Now he could play huntsman all he wanted, the rifle having been rendered doubly safe.

Alma visited Nathan Bragg at the Farmers' Bank.

"My husband is irresponsible with regard to financial matters, Mr. Bragg. I wish to make some arrangement whereby my signature alone will permit the withdrawal of funds and the payment of bills."

"I understand your concern, Mrs. Puckett, but in this state a woman may not interfere with her husband's business."

She resented his patronising tone, smiled a wintry smile. "Calvin has no business; he simply has a great deal of money in the bank, *your* bank, Mr. Bragg. Left to his own devices he will fritter it away or be robbed by some swindler with a clever tongue and plausible manner."

Bragg's cheeks flushed. "Yes indeed, Mrs. Puckett. These are unusual circumstances, for which provision must be made. I'm not a lawyer, of course, but I believe arrangements along the lines you've suggested might be accomplished were your husband to be, shall we say, 'interviewed' by a reputable doctor. If his conclusions are detrimental I'll gladly draw up a notarised document to the effect that, Mr. Puckett being of unsound mind, you, as his spouse, shall have power of attorney with regard to the money invested with the Farmers' Bank."

"Thank you, Mr. Bragg. Such a move will be in the best interests of all concerned."

He escorted her to the door of his office. "Good day to you, ma'am, and a merry Christmas. Please convey my regards to your husband."

"Good day, Mr. Bragg."

He closed the door after her, sent a silent curse winging in her wake. There were no feasible means of keeping her nose out of the accounts, but he had little to worry about; the theft had been perpetrated before Puckett's money had even been entered into the ledgers. Alma would find all the paperwork pertaining to her husband's capital in perfect order. Still, it was unnerving to be dictated to in so brusque a fashion, and by a woman of such irredeemable plainness!

Alma next visited the surgery of Dr. Elbert Whaley, two cramped rooms reached by rickety staircase from Shawnee Street; one room contained a desk, a stove and two chairs, the other a metal-topped table and folding screen, behind which was a hat-rack for shed clothing. The walls vibrated with the regular thumping of a printing press on the floor below, churning out copies of the *Valley Forge Courier*. Alma stated her need with succinctness. Dr. Whaley nodded as she spoke. He was fifty-three years of age, had practised medicine for twenty-six of them, the last eleven in Valley Forge. He was a widower, with intent to remain so. In his professional life Dr. Whaley had observed and prescribed for and operated upon many of the breakages and malfunctions that can afflict the human body, witnessed in passing more than a few of those psychological maladies which, if unchecked, can consume the soul. In his dealings with the former he was sometimes successful, sometimes not, his medical knowledge being only slightly more sophisticated than that of a veterinarian; regarding the latter he had formulated certain opinions without ever having achieved any true understanding. Such problems were beyond the scope of his certificates, were overgrown and febrile labyrinths, Stygian caverns populated by bat-winged horrors and the creeping worm of madness. He had no desire to tamper with those things which cannot be bandaged, trussed, dosed or stitched, and had long since convinced himself that persons suffering the torments imposed by invisible demons had been placed in that position by way of moral weakness and intellectual torpor, were stunted, unrealised human beings at the mercy of their own shortcomings of character. He had neither interest in, nor sympathy with, their plight.

Dr. Whaley knew of Calvin Puckett, his mysterious appearance in the town, his fabled wealth (only banker Bragg knew the full extent of this rapidly dwindling resource) and his Church of the White Wolf, now Church of the Cold Ash; he had already determined to his own satisfaction the nature of Puckett's incredible stupidity and wastefulness, and found the fellow wanting in practically every determinant factor which separates *Homo sapiens* from the lower vertebrates. He had no intention of examining such a dunce for curiosity's sake, but made up his mind, while listening to Alma talk, to avail his services for her sake. Several years ago, tiring of the almost anchoritic seclusion of his loveless existence, he had contemplated asking for her hand; she had intelligence and a steadiness of temperament he found estimable. Only her physical ugliness had deterred him from making the request; his wife, dead some thirteen years, had been a woman of considerable beauty and charm. Alma's sudden marriage to this clown from no one knew where had dented the doctor's esteem, but he was magnanimous, and ascribed her foolish action to a condition he privately referred to as "old-maid jitters", the realisation that wallflowers left unplucked will wither and die without ever having bloomed. It was a shame Alma had allowed herself to be snatched up by so inappropriate a gardener.

Alma fell silent. Dr. Whaley permitted an extended silence to preface his response; this had the advantage of imparting to his words a ponderous weightiness his patients found reassuringly profound.

"Very well. Do you wish me to visit your home, or will you bring your husband to me?"

"It would be easier if you would come to the ridge, Doctor."

"Will tomorrow morning be convenient?"

"It will. Thank you."

Calvin was prevented from hunting Joe Cobden the following day by hints that an important guest was coming to see him. He waited patiently in the parlour, the dog at his feet. He had not as yet given it a name. Dr. Whaley arrived by buggy at ten o'clock and ensconced himself in the parlour with Calvin. He emerged ten minutes later, found Alma in the kitchen, staring at the trees beyond the window.

"Why did you marry him?"

His forthright manner gave no offence. "I think you know why, Doctor. I'm sure everyone in town has discussed it at length. Is he mad?"

"I would classify him as a simpleton given to delusions, only dangerous when subjected to emotional strain. Who is this Joe Cobden?"

"I have no idea. It could be that he does not exist. Calvin may have . . . created him."

"Why would he give him a hunchback? Has he expressed a loathing of physical deformity?"

"Calvin expresses very little about anything. He appears to sleep on his feet a good deal of the time."

"Bragg can proceed with the document. Mr. Puckett is in no condition to be responsible for large sums of money. How on earth did he come by it, if I may ask?"

"He says he inherited it."

Dr. Whaley could accept this; he knew wealth was more often than not acquired or handed to those least deserving of it. That was the way of the world, the nature of things, a subject best suited for the diagnoses of doctors of philosophy rather than of medicine. He returned to town.

Several days before Christmas, Alma was officially made custodian of the Puckett fortune. To her dismay she learned that of the initial deposit of some twenty-eight thousand dollars (Bragg here was afflicted with a fit of coughing) there remained, after building and furnishing costs, a little less than half; nevertheless, she had promised herself a present, and a present she would have. The weather had deteriorated; snow twelve inches deep had to be contended with on Alma's two mile walk to town, soaking her skirts and chilling her feet. When the necessary documents had been signed she went to a horse-trader's corral at the edge of town and bought a sprightly mare and secondhand two wheeled trap; it was high time the stable was occupied. She had the trap loaded with oats and hay, straw and a horse blanket, plus food for herself and Calvin, then drove back to the ridge. It had hurt her to spend the money, but Alma was tired of walking hither and yon like some penniless tramp. It was a Christmas present; Calvin had his gun, and now Alma had her horse and trap. She called the mare Morgana.

There was no joy in the Puckett household on Christmas Day. Calvin was not aware of what day it was, and Alma saw no point in informing him. He went hunting for Joe Cobden as usual during the afternoon. Alma wondered what would happen should he shoot at a squirrel or tree for target practice and learn the Winchester would not fire. It had not happened yet; perhaps Calvin was determined not to squeeze the trigger until the imaginary hunchback was in front of him, in which case the rifle's defect would never be discovered. Alma spent the afternoon gathering dead wood and chopping it into lengths for the stove and fireplace. She did not trust the task to Calvin; the thought of an axe in his hands sent a shiver through her. In any case, she found she enjoyed the work, even took pleasure in greasing the pump in the front yard which drew water via pipeline from a creek at the base of the ridge, fortunately still unfrozen. The house required its own well, but Alma was unsure if such a luxury could be afforded.

Lucius Croft had not invited his daughter and son-in-law to his farm for Christmas Day. Alma had not seen him since moving to the ridge, doubted that their paths would cross intentionally again. The ridge was a castle beleaguered by a hostile, scornful enemy, moated with snow, domicile of a mad king and sorrowful queen. This state of affairs seemed only natural to Alma. She read her books and prepared meals. When she required company she went to the stable and talked to Morgana, lavished attention upon her dappled hide, curry-combed it to a fine gloss, raked out dung, replaced the straw beneath her hoofs, made sure the blanket was correctly cinched and hung, poured generous portions of fodder into the manger, stroked her neck and velvety nose for hours. The mare tolerated these lengthy intrusions with good grace, and on the twelfth day of 1874 was rewarded for her indulgence by being the first to learn that Alma's monthly blood had ceased to flow.

In February, when menstruation again failed to manifest itself, Alma went to see Dr. Whaley. He confirmed that she was indeed pregnant, told her to keep active and well fed, his advice for all women in this condition. Alma gave the news to Calvin, who eventually understood that he was to be the father of a child. His obvious joy was an embarrassment; Alma would willingly have recanted on all her atheistic notions and fallen into the arms of religion if only that would erase memories of the laborious and humiliating process of impregnation, make her the vessel of immaculate conception. She did not wish to share the months ahead with Calvin, made sure he knew he must no longer touch her at night. Calvin sulked when this stricture was imposed, but gradually made the adjustment back to celibacy.

The winter was mild by comparison with the previous year. On one of the bright and sunny days common to Kansas, when one's breath still forms a cloud despite the sky's brilliant blue, Alma backed Morgana between the shafts of the trap and prepared for a drive. When Calvin saw what transpired he begged to come along. Alma insisted on handling the reins herself. They drove for several hours, enjoying the chill bite of the air.

Arriving back at the ridge after this invigorating trip, they found a delivery awaiting them on the porch, a wooden box six feet square, six inches deep, stencilled here and there with the cautionary word FRAGILE. With the aid of a poker Alma prised one of the planks loose and found beneath it a circular something supported by an inner frame, the whole thing wrapped in layers of burlap, cushioned by pressed straw. More planks were removed, protective layers torn open, and there was the stained-glass window ordered so long ago. The box was pulled completely apart, the circular window rolled indoors. It was beautiful; no other word would suffice. Calvin's design had been sketchy, to say the least, and the master craftsman who implemented his wishes had taken a great many liberties with the overall concept. Calvin had specified a white wolf (had surrounded his crudely dog-like rendering with sections of coloured chalk, left the animal's silhouette blank to denote whiteness) and that much had apparently been understood by the artist, for the creature dominating the window was most certainly a wolf of milky whiteness; however, unlike Calvin's quadrupedal deity, this was a she-wolf with proudly swinging dugs,

beneath which squatted two chubby human babies in loincloths of ruby and turquoise, heads raised to give suck.
Around them in writhing abundance were the stems of some
outlandish vine equipped with thorns of daunting length
and leaves of vaguely oakish aspect. Surrounding all of this
were rays of golden light from some unseen source behind
the wolf, light even more benevolent than that of the sun.

Calvin was upset. He had not ordered two suckling in-
fants, nor a bramble bush. Alma pointed out to him the
subtlety of shading—how was this achieved in glass?—and
the brilliance of the colours, but Calvin was not to be mollified; he sat glowering at the fantastical disc with his lower
lip thrust petulantly forth. He would eat no supper. Alma
left him to sulk, and later rolled the window to a safe place
in the spare room behind the kitchen; she did not want
Calvin to put his foot through it in contempt. The door was
locked as a further safeguard.

As Alma pocketed the key she felt a stirring in her belly,
confused it for a few seconds with an urgent need to move
her bowels. The truth, when it occurred to her, sent Alma
quickly to the nearest chair, breath held in amazement. Life
had prodded at her from within, announced itself with fleshy
stirrings, but was it not too soon? Her heart raced. Was the
budding thing already drawing power from her blood,
adopting the shape of humanity? She felt faint, realised it
was for lack of air, resumed breathing. Perhaps she had not
felt movement after all; it really was much too soon, she
was positive. Alma waited. No further manifestation of internal life came; instead, there grew the certainty, attested
to by no discernible evidence, that not one life but two were
germinating inside her. Perhaps it was the influence of the
stained-glass window, the thirsty babes taking milk from the
belly of a wolf, but Alma *knew* beyond all doubt the precious
parasite in her womb was twofold. She held her abdomen
tenderly and smiled. Twins. She would be twice as happy.
Provided they were both girls, of course.

* * *

By mid-May, Dr. Whaley was able to confirm Alma's premonition. With stethoscope held against her swollen belly, he listened intently, and verified the existence of a double heartbeat, overshadowed by the mother-to-be's awesome thuddings, but undeniably there, faint patterings, sometimes in perfect unison, sometimes beating in fractional syncopation, one diminutive tympanist hastier than its twin.

"Strong and healthy," he pronounced, straightening himself. "And the same might be said of you, Mrs. Puckett. I don't think I've seen you looking so well in a long time."

He did not exaggerate. Pregnancy is generally supposed to enhance the appearance of expectant women, and like all popular falsehoods is more often proved untrue than not. The usual clichés—"blooming", "radiant", etc.—were in Alma's case no more than honest description. She carried herself with regal disposition, passing along the street, driving her beloved mare and trap, entering or leaving a store, and her new-found poise did not go unremarked among the women of Valley Forge. Alma began receiving visitors at the ridge, all of them female. They came to inspect the house for signs of dirt and neglect, and to ascertain the reason for her happiness, knowing it could not be anything so simple as her delicate condition. Had there been an improvement in her husband's mental state? they asked themselves, and went in ones and twos to find out. The house was spotless, but the source of Alma's constant smile remained a mystery. The younger women, virgins and those as yet unacquainted with pregnancy, declared nothing more than the prospect of such a blessed event was required to make a body satisfied. To them there was no mystery—Alma smiled because she was going to have a baby. The older women, those for whom pregnancy was forever associated with discomfort, ugliness and fear, were not convinced. Maybe, they whispered among themselves, she's going as batty as her old man. Alma was aware of their disgruntlement, could read the frustration in their eyes as they prattled about the hundred and one topics of local gossip in which she had no interest whatever, knew of their longing to find an answer, and drew an even greater measure of serenity from their baffled faces.

Her secret, if such it could be termed, was simple enough; every few days Alma would unlock the spare room and gaze at the stained-glass window. The babies delineated in lead were long-haired, asexual, their gender hidden by the brilliant loincloths, but Alma knew they were her twin girls, plump and jolly and a mother's delight. Had her reading extended beyond the historical romances of Sir Walter Scott and the copious outpourings of Dickens, had she ventured into classical works Alma might have learned that the two suckling babes were none other than Romulus, eventual founder of the city of Rome, and his sibling Remus, whom he was later to kill—both resolutely male. After long moments spent in silent observance of wolf and twins, Alma would redrape the window with an expensive linen tablecloth and leave, carefully locking the room after her; it contained, after all, a part of herself.

The summer heat became intolerable even to such an uncomplaining nature as Alma's, and by August she was more than prepared to be delivered of her womb's double burden. Calvin no longer sought the crooked man, but spent the greater part of each day asleep in a fringed hammock spanning the side porch, anticipating in his own lethargic fashion the birth of his daughters. Such had been Alma's assurance, and Calvin was sufficiently cowed by her confidence in this matter of sex to hold his tongue regarding hopes for at least one boy. One thing he knew—he would never, *never* strike his children the way his own father had struck Calvin, never make them work like slaves from sunup to sundown, never starve them of food or affection. These boys (or girls, or this boy and girl—the arithmetical permutations of twindom fascinated Calvin) would be happy, would have the childhood he had missed. He told Alma so,

and she patted his hand, irritated by his repetitious promises to her belly. "Of course they'll be happy. Now, run
along and leave me be." And he did. Alma was busy thinking, he could see that. Alma sure did a lot of thinking,
pretty near as much as Calvin did himself, and that impressed him a whole lot; yessir, he had himself a real smart
wife to figure things out. He reached down to scratch the
neck of his dog, and was content.

One girl would be named Letitia, after Alma's mother, and
the other would be called Coralee, because Alma liked the
sound of it. She ran the names over and over in her thoughts,
Letitia and Coralee, Coralee and Letitia, a litany not so much
of hope as of insistence. They had just better be girls, or there
would be trouble; Alma had knitted swaddling clothes of palest
pink in readiness, had the nursery wallpapered in pink and
cream. Even the crib was painted pink on her instruction.
Anyone could see she was tempting fate. She ate vast amounts
to feed her babies and sweated profusely in the summer heat,
no longer able to appear in public for fear of being unable to
walk any distance without suffering the humiliation of stopping to pant for breath like a dog.

Calvin was useless as a link with the town. Two or three
times a week one or other of the women concerned for Alma's welfare would visit the ridge, pick up a shopping list
from the stranded wife and fetch back from town those
things she needed, or thought she did; candy played a considerable role in Alma's diet. They did this from a sense of
social duty and a deeper female solidarity; a woman at the
mercy of an idiot, a *male* idiot, was sorely in need of assistance from her own sex. Alma was grateful for the help
offered, but still maintained a somewhat patronising attitude toward her visitors, unable to forget a lifetime of slights
and condescension from the people of Valley Forge, females
included. The women allowed her these airs and graces for
the privilege of being closely associated with such a peculiar
couple, the fountainhead of endless speculation.

* * *

In the Indian summer of September it seemed that the twins were at last eager to be free of Alma's womb. She went into labour early one afternoon, attended by Dr. Whaley, and now for the first time came pain, never-ending, backbreaking, unrelenting *pain*. Alma moaned, grunted, howled, struggled to turn herself inside out. Her bedsheets became drenched with sweat and her internal waters, eventually with blood. The babies would not be born. Dr. Whaley pushed at the mound of her stomach, trying to re-align the twins. The two women assisting him gripped Alma's slippery hands as she screamed. Calvin had run away to the far end of the ridge to escape the horrifying sounds emanating from the bedroom.

Dr. Whaley considered the plight of his patient; the twins had not turned their heads to the neck of the uterus as expected, were still more or less upright in the womb, and would have to be removed by caesarian section. He doused a handkerchief with ether, applied it to Alma's nose and mouth, granted her oblivion. "More hot water and fresh sheets," he told the women, and they ran to comply. Neither expected Alma to survive what was to come, offered hasty prayers none the less.

In the silence that followed Alma's anaesthetisation Dr. Whaley worked swiftly, opened her belly with the grim deftness of a cavalryman disembowelling an enemy of the nation, plunged his hands inside her body and brought forth two babies in a welter of blood. He held them to the light for a cursory examination; one child was living, the other dead, the umbilical cord of its twin wrapped around its neck. Dr. Whaley separated them, held the survivor upside down, smacked its buttocks, but could not make it inhale until he put his own mouth to that of the wizened blue monkey and inflated its lungs with his own breath. When its cries filled the room he cut and tied the cord, handed the squalling lump to the women for cleansing, turned to Alma and began to stitch, stitch, stitch, her insides with catgut, stitch, stitch, stitch, her outer flesh with horsehair, his hands, needle and threads slippery with blood. The raw gash was slowly reduced to a seeping line of red punctuated by horse-hair commas.

The women inspected both babies. The dead infant was female; her brother, bawling vigorously, tiny fists clutching the air, appeared to be physically normal. The boy's umbilical cord possessed all the dread fascination of a garrotte. "Strangled his own sister," said one of the women, and both shook their heads at such embryonic wickedness; here was a story to tell. Overhearing, Dr. Whaley informed them that strangulation is the cutting off of one's air supply by pressure to the throat; such could not have been the case with this uterine death since the girl had not been breathing, but absorbing oxygen from Alma's blood through her own cord, which was not entangled in any way. He could offer no explanation for the girl's death, and because of this it became self-evident, so far as the women were concerned, that their interpretation of events constituted the sacred and inviolable Truth; under that lofty guise the story circulated among the townspeople, inspiring many a gasp of horror that one so young could perpetrate so heinous an act upon his own sister.

Alma remained unconscious for two days, and awoke at around the time Joe Cobden took his leave of Peter Winstanley just below the Canadian border to begin his lonely ride south. She was feverish for a further ten days, kept alive only through the ministrations of Dr. Whaley. When the fever had passed and Alma was capable of raising herself to an upright position in the bed she demanded to see her twins. Mrs. Purdey, who had elected to stand watch by her bed on this day, presented her with a squalling pink thing layered in blankets despite the heat. Alma waited for a similar bundle, and when it was not forthcoming almost swooned with the shock of realisation. Mrs. Purdey related the tragic circumstances of the birth, was foolish enough to include details of the erroneous strangulation theory, offered her deepest condolences. Weakened by her ordeal, Alma felt a sorrow so great she imagined her heart would literally break. She had convinced herself two bouncing baby girls were arriving to brighten her life, and the tragedy's survivor was not even female. She thrust the baby from her, appalled at its ugliness and noise, and this act also spread through Valley Forge in the days that followed, along with whatever titbits Mrs. Purdey and her successors chose to reveal; for example, Alma would not choose a name for the child, nor would she breastfeed it (this task was undertaken by a wet-nurse) or allow it in the same room as herself. Her rejection was complete. Sympathetic to her disappointment in the beginning, Alma's nurses became less indulgent when her behaviour showed no signs of relenting. It was a disgrace, they said, the way she wouldn't even look at her baby, let alone touch it, and their sympathy was gradually transferred to the boy, who screamed and sucked and shat with regularity, oblivious to the drama set in motion by his entry into the world.

Everyone agreed it was useless trying to employ Calvin as a means of softening his wife's intransigence since she refused to see him also, and in the end it was Dr. Whaley, whose bedside manner could be stern when necessary, who demanded explanations and reform from the erring parent.

"The baby's yours," he said, "a fine, healthy boy any mother would be proud to have. Why won't you accept him?"

"I don't want it."

Her voice was sullen, filled with childish pique. Alma's appearance, so buxom and hale until her confinement, had suffered a startling change. From the moment she learned Letitia and Coralee were not to be, she had eaten only sufficient food to keep her alive, no more. Already wasted by fever, her flesh was fast collapsing around her, its former plump firmness sagging from jowls and armpits and hips in unsightly rolls and pouches. Her eyes were underscored with darkness, and her mouth, never quite level from the time of her own birth, now had an emphatic slant to the left, giving the impression of a permanent and deliberate sneer.

"These feelings of yours aren't unique. Other women have failed to love their children at first sight. The mood will pass. It must, if you're to fulfil your duties as a mother. You want to do your duty, don't you?"

"No."

"That's an ugly word, under the circumstances. Do you feel no shame? Do you intend ignoring your son for ever? You know that's not possible."

"I don't want it. Give it to someone else."

"A decent person does not shrug off responsibility. You wanted a child and your wish was granted. You cannot renege on a pact made with nature. Your obligation is automatic. The child is yours, you're his mother, therefore you'll care for him to the best of your abilities, whether you love him at this moment or not. That isn't the law of the state or the nation, it's the irrevocable law of God. Am I making myself quite clear to you, Mrs. Puckett?"

"Give it to God. Let Him look after it."

"Your attitude causes me a very personal kind of distress. I had considered you one of the more intelligent persons in the region, but of course intelligence is worthless unless allied to morality. Your behaviour is unforgivably selfish. You're not a child, you're a woman, but you apparently are not prepared to assume the responsibilities of that station. I see now that my estimate of your character was in error."

"I don't care."

"But you will, Mrs. Puckett. This immature behaviour cannot continue indefinitely. We're a small community. I know you don't consider yourself a part of Valley Forge, but that's another of your foolish misconceptions. Here you live, and here you'll stay, and while you're here you'll nurse your child as God has equipped you to. Every day you do not will make you more and more unacceptable to the locals. You cannot live among them without being a part of them. Do what you were meant to do, Mrs. Puckett, and you'll be forgiven. Everyone knows your marriage is . . . unusual, and they know the birth was both dangerous and tragic. For those reasons you'll be forgiven this rejection of the boy, but only if you cease *now*. There is no other path to choose." He picked up his hat. "Think carefully on what I've said. You'll see that I'm right. By doing as I say you won't be indulging me, you'll be investing in your own future. Good day."

He left. Alma could not deny the logic of his instruction. She thought hard, and was obliged by her circumstances to follow the path prepared for her by Dr. Whaley's argument: that of least resistance. When her nurse for the day entered the bedroom Alma asked to see her baby. Mrs. Lambert hastened to fetch the child from his crib in the nursery, handed him to Alma with a smile of such blatant victory Alma was tempted to hurl the bundle back at her, deny this surrender to the narrow and careworn corridors of motherhood. She did not. She took the baby in her arms, forced herself to look at it. It was ugly, as it had to be, granted its parentage. Mrs. Lambert beamed with contentment. Finally Alma could bear the woman's mawkish expression no longer.

"Thank you, Mrs. Lambert."

Dismissal was evident in her tone. She was left alone, took a breath, bared a pendulous breast and jammed the baby's mouth to her nipple. He began to suck, and Alma's lip twisted several more degrees from the horizontal; this hallowed moment, this timeless tableau gave her no more emotional gratification than had the slobbering attentions of Calvin. The act was wholly repugnant to her, and behind the stiff mask of her loathing a small despairing voice lamented that something intended to be wonderful was not.

A little later Calvin was ushered into the room by Mrs. Lambert. He approached the bed, nervously fingering his hat. Alma sat, propped up with pillows, the baby still at her breast. Her arms were as rigid as those of an idol, as rigid as her smile.

"Got ourselfs a baby," grinned Calvin. He had been allowed into the nursery once or twice under strict supervision, and even then had not been permitted to touch the child. The sight of his wife and son moved him very nearly to tears. He came closer, reassured by Alma's stillness and her smile. "A real fine boy," he said, bobbing his head up and down in agreement with himself. "Got to think up a name, I reckon."

I will play a role, thought Alma, and fool them all.

And for several years thereafter, she did.

CHAPTER TWENTY-FOUR

He could not return to hunting, had lost all heart for slaughter. The market for hides, flooded for three years, was now depressed in any case. But another market filled the void; it, too, was linked with the buffalo, not the living creatures but the dead. The prairie was littered with bones; wherever one looked, there they were, like white leaves tossed into windrows and left to settle, the bleached remains of once-mighty herds. The industrialised east wanted those bones, was prepared to pay seven to nine dollars per ton for them. The old bones were crushed for use as fertiliser, the newer bones prepared for use in the sugar refining process, in which their calcium phosphate neutralised the acid of the cane juice. Horns also were useful as raw material for buttons, combs and knife handles, and fetched as much as twelve dollars per ton. The hoofs made admirable glue. Joe Cobden worked in Dodge for several months as a stable-hand, and with his wages bought a second horse and rickety wagon, and set off into the open prairie to be a gatherer of bones.

He meandered across Kansas, piling his wagon high with skulls and backbones and ribs and leg bones, shoulder and pelvic bones. Whenever the load threatened to overflow, Joe took it to the nearest rail town and disposed of it. He was not the only gatherer. Apart from wandering souls like himself, farmers struggling to wrest a living from the land helped make financial ends meet by gathering bones. Outside every town along the Atchison, Topeka & Santa Fe and Kansas Pacific tracks were rows of bones twelve feet high, ten feet wide and hundreds of yards long, stacked walls of whiteness awaiting the next string of eastbound boxcars. It was not difficult to make a living. Joe could have made more cash by working with a partner, but preferred to be alone. He even found a measure of contentment in his solitary occupation. There was no one to distract him from the simple business of picking up bones, no one's gaze to remind him of his ugliness, no need to defend himself. The winters were not unbearably cold, and Joe continued picking the plains clean. His hair and beard grew long, and the smell of his clothing and body, unnoticed by Joe, grew foul.

Like the other gatherers, Joe had eventually to roam further from the railroads to find bones, but despite the extra time and effort involved the trade was still profitable. It would continue to be so until the end of the decade, by which time it was reliably estimated that in Kansas two and a half million dollars had been paid for buffalo bones, the price averaging at eight dollars per ton. It required approximately one hundred skeletons to make up one ton of bones. Thirty-one million buffalo had been slaughtered in Kansas alone. In Montana and the Dakotas and Nebraska, in Oklahoma and Texas, in New Mexico and Colorado the bone pickers were also hard at work, the fruit of their gatherings freighted east and rendered into useful products, rich reward for those men who had seen the means whereby worthless skeletons could be transformed into cash profit. It was entirely appropriate that the new five cent piece introduced in 1913 should bear on one face the head of an Indian, and on its reverse a buffalo, for the one could not survive without the other, and both were driven to near extinction in the heat of America's romance with Mammon; even this belated salute was typical of the nation's refusal to acknowledge guilt, for the nickel is among the humblest of coins. In the end, even Indians gathered buffalo bones.

Joe worked diligently, but without taxing himself or his team. The rhythm of his life was slow and easy. He was not greatly interested in profit, simply wanted to make a living.

For two years his wagon rolled across the prairie while he gathered, whistling and humming to himself. He reached the age of twenty-one years in the summer of the centennial, and was suddenly struck by the thought that he was at last a man. It was official. He felt no different. Across America towns and cities were preparing to celebrate the founding of the nation, their festive mood somewhat marred by the shocking news that General George Armstrong Custer and the Seventh Cavalry had been killed, one and all, by Sitting Bull's Sioux on June 25th at Little Big Horn. Somewhere in Kansas, lost on an endless plain, Joe Cobden pondered his future. Even the buffalo bones were thinning out now; he could probably continue for several years more, but was not sure he wished to. He was reminded of the hunchback he had seen in St. Louis as a child, the filthy, bedraggled creature who pushed a handcart through the streets, begging for cast-off clothing. Was Joe's current profession so very different? He mulled the question for days, disturbed by this new dissatisfaction with his life.

On the night of July 4th a million skyrockets filled the air across America, dazzling fountains of light, explosions of scintillating red, white and blue. The nation celebrated its pride and patriotic fervour; a great deal of whiskey and beer was poured down the national throat and a new generation of Americans was sired in the hectic flush of enthusiasm and drunkenness and general air of jubilation. Old Glory had never seemed a finer flag; it fluttered proud and free, and would never be furled.

Twenty miles north of Wichita, Joe saw nothing but the winking stars, heard no sound but the prairie wind and the chinking of bridle and bit as his horses munched the oats he had set down. He did not know what night this was. Perched on a buffalo skull by his campfire, Joe stared at the flames with sightless eyes, his body heavy with an unaccustomed weariness. The buffalo chip fire glowed softly, hissing a little in the night wind. Joe's eyelids trembled and closed, but despite his blindness he could see the figure seated in a chair on the fire's far side. It was a large and comfortable wingbacked chair, and its occupant was Dr. Cobden. He was smoking a pipe; this was unusual, for the doctor smoked only cigars. Joe supposed it would be up to him to speak first; he was heartily sick of this tiresome game of strength. "Are you warm enough?" he asked. The doctor was not draped in Joe's buffalo robe gift.

"It's a warm evening," replied the doctor, his manner equable.

Joe thought they might be able to have a pleasant conversation for once, instead of the usual bitter wrangle. "I never thought you'd come out here."

"This will be my only visit. I see you make your living with bones."

"They keep me alive." Did his voice sound defensive? He must rectify that. He was glad the doctor was with him. It had been almost four years since they last met.

"You look younger, somehow," said Joe.

"I'm a new man," said the doctor, and laughed; his chest sounded much improved, no longer had that hideous rattle.

"How's Hattie?"

"I regret to tell you, Hattie is dead, trampled by the team of a delivery wagon. She did not suffer long."

"You must miss her."

"I do, very much. Surprisingly enough, I also miss you, Joseph."

Both men stared at the flames. The doctor's pipe glowed with the eerie radiance of foxfire.

"Still in your favourite chair," said Joe.

"Of course. I find your own taste in furniture somewhat macabre."

Joe looked down at the buffalo skull beneath him. His buttocks fitted comfortably between the horns. "It's convenient," he smiled. "How long will you be here?"

A golden watch opened in the doctor's palm, seemed almost to be a part of his flesh. From it came a tune of such poignant familiarity Joe felt his heart lurch. He knew this tinkling melody, and yet did not know it. Listening to its delicate cadences he was seized with a curious sense of overwhelming loss, felt his body dissolve into magical paste, his skin burn with a pale fire. Joe could see right through the doctor's wristbones, right through the casing of the watch itself; its face bore three hands of equal length.

"Just for a short while," said the doctor. "I want very much to see you before leaving."

"Leaving?"

"An ocean voyage. I have promised myself a trip for many years now."

"Where to?"

"Uhmzarbidhar," said the doctor, or perhaps it was "Kahnbazdihar" or "Nahepthnitar". The name was layered with conflicting consonants and syllables, seemed to be many words in one. Joe had never heard of it before, had no idea where the place might be. He was saddened that the doctor was going away without him. The watch snapped shut; a mesmerising silence rippled from the doctor's palm. Already the chair was turning, pivoting, presenting the doctor's handsome profile. "Goodbye, Joseph." The flare of the wingback hid his face, left only the arm and knee, swept these from view in turn and began moving away. The chair shrank like some mysterious bloom gathered in upon itself, became smaller and smaller, vanished into darkness.

Joe pitched forward, awoke an instant later with his head dangerously close to the fire. The horses stamped nervously as he rolled over and leaped to his feet, slapping sparks from his hat.

"Time to sleep," he told the horses, and they calmed at the sound of his voice. Joe bundled himself in a blanket under the wagon, and before drifting into slumber tried to remember what it was he had been dreaming of before he fell from the buffalo skull. But it was gone, lost. He slept.

On the journey to Wichita a restlessness grew within Joe. Ambling along with only the rumps of his team and the sweeping horizon to look at did not produce the usual soporific balm of contentment. Something inside Joe had

changed, and Joe did not like it. The past two years of
solitude had treated him kindly; he did not wish to relinquish a way of life which suited him. Why had these doubts
arisen in his mind to plague him? Joe wanted only to be left
alone, to gather bones beyond the sight of men, to escape
the turmoil of knowing or caring for another human being.
Joe felt he had been hurt enough already. He had not, of
course, for any human who truly wishes to be alone, completely, utterly alone, has surrendered his humanity, made
of himself a hollow man. Joe's interior hummed and sang
with emotions aching for a chance to burst free and revel in
their own existence. Joe's capacity for self-deception was
infinite. He had learned the bitter lessons of cynicism and
self-pity, but had not yet acquired wisdom, which is the
ability to see both from within and from without. Joe's eyes
were nested firmly in his head but, although he faced forward, he gazed ever backward.

He disposed of his bones at the Wichita rail yard, hid
himself behind a shed and added the cash to a growing wad
he carried in a money-belt around his waist. Joe no longer
trusted banks and bankers. Two years of bone gathering
had netted him a profit of just under eight hundred dollars.
The money belt felt snug around his middle, almost like an
extra layer of muscle, but it did little to comfort Joe that
day. He stood by his emptied wagon, morosely watched a
train pull in from the east. A dozen or so passengers stepped
down into the morning sunlight. Joe noticed a family of
five, a man and woman and three young children, surrounded by bundles and suitcases held together with twine,
a sorry collection of belongings. What separated them from
others on the platform was their colour. Many Negroes had
moved to Kansas after the war, but were still vastly out-
numbered by whites.

Joe watched them, drifting closer out of curiosity. The
children clung to their mother's skirts as their father approached the stationmaster and asked a question Joe could
not hear. The stationmaster gave him the briefest of glances,
shook his head, The Negro thanked him. Joe was closer

now, and could hear the terse politeness in his voice. It was obvious the stationmaster had been deliberately unco-operative regarding the question asked. One of the children pointed in Joe's direction and squealed. Joe looked behind himself, expecting some remarkable sight, then realised *he* was the remarkable sight. He removed his hat, approached the family, smiling what he hoped was a friendly smile.

"Morning," he said, looking from one to another of their faces.

"Mornin' to you," said the man. His voice was neither friendly nor unfriendly, had in it the drawl of the South. The children were in terror of Joe despite his smile, or perhaps because of it. "Is there some way I can help?"

The man hesitated, looked at his wife, looked back at Joe. "Can you tell us how to get to Lucastown?"

Joe knew of this place, a settlement far removed from other towns, its inhabitants exclusively black. The Reconstruction era had not differed so very much from the antebellum years in Dixie; the removal of slavery's yoke had in most cases simply freed the Negroes to suffer abuse in places of their own choosing. Faced with rejection from the white communities, enterprising black settlers had established their own towns in much the same way that Swedes and Germans banded together in settlements from Minnesota down through the plains states. These five had come here to farm; Joe could tell from the man's calloused hands and the unnatural way his cheap new suit hung from his shoulders; somewhere in the bundles would be a pair of weatherbeaten overalls.

"It's around fifty miles from here." Joe pointed southwest.

"Is there a stage route goes that way?"

"No." And there never would be, thought Joe, unless the blacks set up their own.

"Is there a livery stable hereabouts we could hire a wagon?"

"There is, but they'd probably refuse you, or tell you they didn't have any wagons for hire even if there were wagons by the score right under your nose. Or else they'd charge you three times the regular rate.''

The man's face revealed nothing, no anger or resentment, remained a neutral mask, the art of hiding behind which he had learned at the age of nine. The children were losing their fear of Joe, having heard his voice, and had released their mother's skirts.

''Isn't there any kind of way to get there?'' she asked.

''Yes, ma'am, there is. If you'll just wait right here I'll be back in a minute or two.''

Joe fetched his wagon, drew up before the family. ''Climb aboard.''

''You're goin' to Lucastown?'' The man's voice was faintly suspicious.

''I am now.''

''How much?''

''No charge.''

They made no move to board the wagon. The woman looked at her husband, waiting to see if his features relaxed, to see if he believed this act of samaritanism.

''That's a right kindly offer,'' he said, his voice still not committed to acceptance.

''I'm a right kindly person,'' smiled Joe, and added, ''This isn't a trick. I'm not trying to fool you. I'll drive you to Lucastown. There's no other way you'll get there.''

The man traded looks with his wife, turned back to Joe and nodded. ''Thank you. We accept.''

The bundles and suitcases were lifted into the wagon bed. The children and the woman sat among them, the man sat beside Joe on the driver's seat. Joe offered his hand, gave his name. The man grasped his palm firmly. ''Cato Tyrell,'' he said, and turned to point out his family. ''My wife Niobe, and these three are Perry, Zerelda and Chadwick.'' The children giggled at the sound of their names, and the two boys punched each other lightly.

''Pleased to meet you,'' said Joe.

He stopped first at a general store for supplies, correctly divining that the Tyrells had only a few dollars between them, then followed a road south-west from Wichita. Cato Tyrell told Joe of his attempts to farm "back home" in Alabama after his freedom from plantation bondage, of the impossibility of ever doing so successfully under the share-cropper system, whereby white landlords (often newcomers from the North) held their tenants, black and white alike, in virtual thrall. Cato's brother-in-law, one of Lucastown's original settlers, had sent money for the family to come to Kansas by riverboat and train. They had nothing left, were in the brother-in-law's debt, but were glad to be out of Alabama and headed somewhere "with a future". Joe told them he was an ex-buffalo-hunter turned bone gatherer, nothing more. He liked the dignified friendliness of Cato and Niobe, the innocence and rambunctiousness of the children.

The two day trip passed quickly; on the second morning Lucastown hove into view, a scattering of dwellings on a rolling sea of grass. The brother-in-law was located, the Tyrells delivered to his door. While Joe helped unload their baggage he slipped four hundred dollars into a shabby valise. They pressed him to stay. He declined. Joe shook hands with everyone, including the children, who had accepted his deformity with the abruptness and totality of the very young. With a final wave he drove his empty wagon away from Lucastown. He felt good. It was as simple as that: he felt good.

Two hours later a horseman thundered up behind him, his mount lathered in foam. Cato drew up beside the wagon and handed Joe the money.

"We can't take it."

"It's a gift."

"We can't. Thank you anyway."

"But I want you to have it. You need it."

"I don't."

"You've got a family, I haven't."

"Please take it off me or I'll have to make you take it."

"I don't want it. It's for you and Niobe."

"We don't want it. It's a mighty kind offer and we're grateful, but we can't take it."

Joe's happiness was breaking up like a raft in white water. "But I want you to have it," he repeated, almost pleading now.

They searched each other's eyes for a tense moment.

Cato said: "No."

"It's to repay a debt," insisted Joe.

"What debt? You don't owe us nothin'."

But Joe could not explain. "Please keep it, Cato, not for yourself, for me. Keep it and let me feel good."

Another lengthy pause. "No," said Cato.

Joe pulled his buffalo gun from beneath the seat, aimed at Cato's heart. "Please keep the money and let me sleep at night." The gun was not loaded.

Cato said nothing. Joe said: "I'm not a white man. You don't have to be ashamed to take it. I'm a fucking half-breed, for Christ's sake!"

Cato tucked the wad of bills into his pocket. "You can put the gun down now."

"Do you promise to keep the money?"

"Seems you won't be happy till I do."

Joe lowered the Sharpe's.

"I thank you for the gift," said Cato.

"My pleasure."

"Anything I can give you in return?"

"If your cat has kittens, call one of them after me."

"We don't have no cat."

"Use some of the cash to get one."

Joe flicked the reins and the wagon moved off. When he dared to turn around he saw Cato walking the horse back to Lucastown. It had been a close thing, but Joe was beginning to feel good again. Being a benefactor was hard work.

On the route back to Wichita he strayed wherever patches of white indicated the presence of bones. Most of this area had already been picked over, and when he reached the town his wagon was barely half-full. He searched for the man who had given him such a fair price for his last delivery, but the buyer was not to be found. Joe was prepared to wait. He strolled around the depot's rail sidings, noted the amount of bones still being hauled in for sale. The long, bleached stacks alongside the lines seemed scarcely diminished since '74, when the bone market had well and truly boomed. It could not last, and this knowledge returned Joe's thoughts to those few strange days before he had met the Tyrells; then his dissatisfaction with bone gathering had been a kind of restlessness, a formless thing, but when the bones were gone he would be obliged to find alternative employment anyway. He preferred not to think about it on such a fine day.

A westbound train pulled in during the afternoon. Joe was seated on a stack of railroad ties some ten yards from the track. He stayed where he was, testing the reactions of those people seated by the windows. He knew they would stare at him, and it was interesting to note how unconcerned he felt about their shameless gawping. There were the faces, a whole row of them, staring at Joe as if he was some fabulous beast of antiquity, the Minotaur maybe, or the Gorgon; Joe would have liked to turn his audience to stone for their unthinking stares—temporarily, of course, just long enough to teach them a lesson in manners. They were leaving their seats now, as the conductor passed along the aisles, advising them of a twenty minute stopover while the fuel tender was replenished with wood and water. Joe listened to his voice passing down the train from carriage to carriage. The passengers disembarked for a hasty cup of coffee and an unspeakable lunch in the depot's restaurant. Joe sat on the ties and enjoyed the sunshine, proud of himself for not caring if he was the object of unprincipled scrutiny. They thought he was repulsive? Well, fuck 'em all. He smiled at his own good humour. It could only have come from his meeting with the Tyrells. It would be nice if he could somehow contrive to become a part of that kind of family, be accepted by people who knew what it was to suffer.

One passenger on Joe's side of the train had remained in his seat, possibly a veteran of railroad travel who knew the miserable fare on offer in the restaurant was not worth the effort of detraining. He was reading a newspaper. Joe waited for him to glance out the window and see the hunchback on the ties. Would he stare, or be too embarrassed? Some people were, but not many. The man turned the pages of his newspaper. Joe could not see which paper it was, and wondered if the headlines were still screaming for revenge against the Indians for their temerity in killing Custer and his men. While he watched the man reading, it occurred to Joe that he had seen this particular face before. It was an unremarkable assemblage of features, bland even, but Joe could not shake the feeling of recognition. It could not have been someone he had ever associated with for any length of time, or he would have been able to identify him immediately; no, it must have been someone he bumped into a long time ago, an acquaintance of minutes, rather than of hours or days. Who was he? Joe looked away, dredged his memory without success, looked back at the man, who read on, unconcerned, unaware of Joe's perusal. He had not looked even once from the window, concentrated all his attention on the newspaper. Joe felt the niggling resentment of frustration over trivia.

Now passengers were filing back aboard the train. Few of them looked at Joe this time; he had become part of the scenery, unworthy of their attention. The newspaper reader completed the last page, rolled his head to relieve a crick in the neck, glanced out the window and saw Joe. Their eyes met. The man stared for a long time. All the passengers were aboard now. The man was frowning as he stared, as if he, too, was trying to identify what he saw. A look of recognition suddenly altered his face; the change would have been imperceptible to anyone but Joe, who had been studying the man for fifteen minutes. He obviously knew Joe— not surprising when the ratio of hunchbacks to normal folk is considered—but he did not nod or wave or otherwise attempt communication. The locomotive's whistle blew, much to Joe's annoyance. The man knew him, but Joe still did not know the man. Who was he? He had turned away from the window following the sudden change in his expression, was now deliberately avoiding any further contact. Why would he do that? The whistle blew again. The driving wheels spun and grabbed, spun and grabbed, and a black cloud belched from the smokestack. The train slowly began rolling away from the depot. Joe was furious at his own thickheadedness. *Who was he?* The man could not be seen now, his carriage some twenty yards down the track. Joe slammed his fist against the wood beneath his thighs, swearing silently to himself. He had to know. *Think!* The last carriage clicked past him, and the caboose. Joe watched as the train became a small, dark square receding into the distance, topped by a thick black plume of smoke. It was no use. The face eluded him.

He sold his bones, set out once again for the open prairie. Three days later he still could not remember where and when he had seen the man before, and still it bothered him. He relived the events of that day by the Wichita depot many times, saw the train pull in, watched the mystery man read his newspaper, eventually look up, see Joe and react in a manner that could only be termed suspicious. Why? Maybe he looked guilty simply because he was told as a boy never to stare at cripples and freaks. But that was unlikely. Joe had formed a definite impression the man knew him not just as *any* hunchback, but as a particular hunchback. And following his guilty reaction the train had pulled out of Wichita, leaving Joe no wiser, puffed and clanked away, the caboose shrinking to a square, the smoke appearing to belch from its roof in a thick black plume. A black plume. Like those on the heads of black horses pulling a black hearse. Coffin in the hearse, body in the coffin. Body in the coffin is black also. Serena. Murder at the Maximus. The man on the train was the man whom Joe had seen leave Serena's room in haste, her last customer before dawn five years ago. The man on the train was the one whose face Joe had sworn to Cyrus he would never forget, the man he had promised to place under a noose.

The realisation left Joe lightheaded. Could he have been mistaken? He had made this error once before, had been convinced a man with a Sharpe's was the man who stole that Sharpe's from him. It had been the wrong man, a different Sharpe's. Maybe he was wrong again. But within that innermost chamber where instinct and intuition languish in modern man there lay the certainty that the newspaper-reader was indeed Serena's murderer. The knowledge sat inside Joe like an insolently squatting toad—Here I am, try to shift me if you can; you know you can't. The toad smiled a complacent smile, secure in Joe's helplessness. Too late, it croaked, you left it too late. Idiot. Now he's gone for ever. What a pathetic fool you are. Joe cringed before the toad, admitted his guilt to every accusation that bubbled from the creature's derisive lips. Yes, he was pathetic. Yes, he deserved to be banished from human society for his stupidity. It was true he had the brain of a snail and the heart of a flea, and, yes, he was the lowest of the low. He groaned aloud at his incompetence as fulfiller of promises, as agent of retribution. Joe was an avenging angel without wings or sword, helpless as a fledgling fallen from a nest. He cast himself into the deepest and fieriest of pits in an agony of self-loathing, could not stop trembling. A doorway to the past had opened, allowed caged memories to flap free and smother him with leathery wings. He had failed. If only he had recognised the man in time he could have grabbed his rifle, boarded the train and ordered him off at gunpoint. He had not done so, and now it was too late. He would have to live with the knowledge of his failure. Maybe it hadn't been the right man after all. Remember the Sharpe's! Yes, it *was*, it *was* the right man, and he knew Joe had seen him, and was only able to get away because of Joe's feebleness. He was obliged to force the truth down his own choking, resistant craw; Serena's murderer would go unpunished, Joe's promise to Cyrus would never be made good, and that was that. Joe ate shame and rage in equal portions, found them loathsome, indigestible; yet eat them he must, for the sought-after taste of requital would never be his to savour.

He continued to amble haphazardly, gathering bones, his thoughts numbed with guilt. He stared not at the sky, but at the wagon tongue and the Kansas sod passing slowly beneath it. The fine feelings of worth and pride nurtured by his brief acquaintance with the Tyrells had evaporated completely. When he at last came to Valley Forge, all unknowing of his origins in that place, Joe experienced nothing more significant than a resolve to do what he entered any town to do: sell his bones.

CHAPTER TWENTY-FIVE

There were no stacks of buffalo remains by the depot. Joe was not surprised. Driving into town he had noted the settled look of the surrounding country, guessed this town had been here twenty years at least, ·practically an ancient civilisation by Kansas standards; the bones would long ago have been cleared for the plough. He left his team in some shade, climbed on to the platform and went to the stationmaster's office. The door was open, but Joe knocked for propriety's sake. A man emerged from the gloom within, his cap identifying him as the stationmaster. Joe submitted to the usual openmouthed scrutiny with the imperturbability acquired through years of exposure to insensitive persons.

"Morning," he said with a smile. "Anyone around here in the market for buffalo bones?"

"Buffalo bones?" repeated the stationmaster, his eyes skittering over Joe, trying to take in as much of this carnival monstrosity as possible. "Bones?" he said again, in order to prolong his inspection. "No, I don't believe so. Used to be bones around here, but not for a good long while now.

"I've got a wagonload. How about if I unload them down the track a little way, and the next time a bone freight comes through from Dodge they could be slung aboard? You could collect the money for me if I'm not around, or you could give me, say, four dollars, and own them outright."

"I wouldn't want the responsibility, but you go right ahead and unload them. No one around here's going to steal four dollars' worth of bones."

Joe drove his wagon past the end of the platform and

362

began unloading. The task required little time or effort. Dry bones weigh less than new bones, in fact many unscrupulous bone gatherers would wet their bones before selling them in order to make them weigh more. Joe had never done this. The stationmaster strolled from his office and stood with hands on hips to watch Joe crown the pile with a skull.

"Been in this line of work long?" he enquired.

"A couple of years. I used to be a hunter."

"First you knock them down, now you pick them up, eh?"

Joe laughed politely.

"Didn't catch your name," said the stationmaster.

"Cobden. Joe Cobden."

The stationmaster was smiling for some reason. Joe assumed he smiled in an attempt to conceal the insult of his constant staring.

"Joe Cobden, eh?"

The stationmaster could feel a delicious tingling in his body, the like of which he had not felt since that distant day when he delivered the lightning rod, too late to save the white church. Everyone in Valley Forge had become familiar with the name Joe Cobden, wondering who this person was that Puckett chose to blame for his loss; a humpback, so the story ran, a humpback arsonist and invisible man. It had generally been agreed no such person existed, but as soon as the stationmaster saw this ugly creature standing all humped over in his doorway he had known, as if confirmation was whispered in his ear by spirits, that this was the very one Puckett had hunted for in vain. Here he stood, the humpback himself, Joe Cobden. The hand of fate seemed evident in the staging of this wonderful coincidence. What a story! He had to set the wheels of its next chapter in motion himself, before anyone else in town cottoned on to the fact that a legendary figure had suddenly been made corporeal among them.

"Mighty fine-looking skull on top there."

"He was a big one," agreed Joe.

"Matter of fact, it might be worth your while taking that skull along to a certain feller just outside of town. He's been hankering for a real good buffalo skull since I don't know when. He's got this thing he does, a hobby I guess you'd call it, collects bones and such, every kind of thing—cats, dogs, birds, makes no difference to this feller. Got a horse's skull right smack over the fireplace, so they say. One thing he don't have is a buffalo skull. I bet he'd give you five, maybe ten dollars for that thing."

"That's a lot of cash."

"That it is, but this feller's got plenty of dollars. Lives outside of town on the ridge. Just follow the road out and you'll see his place halfway up the slope. There's a trail goes right up to the front door. I can just about guarantee he'll want to see you, Mr. Cobden."

"Thanks for the information."

"Why don't you go right on up there? You wouldn't want somebody else getting a skull to him before you, now, would you."

The stationmaster bounced a little on his toes in anticipation as he watched Joe place the skull back in the wagon and drive off. He ran from the depot to Clancy's Cloverleaf Saloon, and from there to the Calhoun Hotel. Every drinker in both bars came out into the street to wait for the sound of rifle shots. Someone ran to alert Mr. Middleton the undertaker; Mr. Middleton's business had suffered a slump in recent months, and he would be glad for the extra income. The county would probably have to pay for the funeral, of course, since it was apparent the humpback did not have two thin dimes to rub together, but by God it would be worth it. The phrase bandied among the eager listeners was "pigeons coming home to roost". Mr. Andolini the barber used the word "vendetta", but no one knew what that meant; they didn't like the way Andolini was wringing his hands, either, as if he was actually upset at the prospect of a suitably bloody ending to the Puckett-Cobden feud.

Joe followed the road out of town, turned off toward the ridge, splashed across a shallow creek at its base and began to climb. The slopes of the ridge were heavily wooded for Kansas, and when the trees closed around the trail on either side Joe imagined himself in a different place entirely, one of the eastern States he had read about with their forested hills. The house, when he came to it, impressed him; not overly large, with a functional yet somehow appealing look to it. He was particularly taken by the sloping peaks of the attic gables, and by the shady porch extending around three sides of the building. That porch looked like the kind of place where a man could sit and relax and let the world go by. The neighing of a horse off among the trees suggested the presence of a hidden stable, its occupant scenting his own team. A mangy brown mongrel lay flopped on the upper porch step, one eye open to peruse the visitor. Joe set the brake and climbed down from his wagon.

He mounted the steps slowly, knowing dogs are generally excited by swift movement from strangers; the brown mutt closed its one wary eye in response to his caution. Joe knocked on the door. He could hear no sound from within. He knocked again, heard footsteps approaching. The door opened. The woman confronting him was thin, her face pinched, the cheeks drooping into dewlaps, her hair gathered with such harsh rectitude the shape of her skull was defined, the netted bun at her neck of cannonball solidity. There were strands of grey among the brown, although Joe reckoned her age to be around thirty. From her neck with its tight lace collar hung a slate-grey dress; its bodice emphasised the essential verticality of her torso, a stance almost unnaturally rigid; its hem brushed the floor, hiding her shoes. The woman's eyes were watchful, of a shiny blackness, like beads of onyx pressed into the sagging dough of her face. Her nose twitched as she caught Joe's prairie aroma. She resembled a small but angry and pugnacious dog.

"Yes?"

Joe removed his hat. Its wide brim tended to hide his hump when confronted by a person of his own meagre height. The woman's eyes did not appear to notice his deformity, did not stray from his own. Joe did not interpret this as good manners, but as a habit of the woman's; he judged her to be the kind who prides herself on her faculty for staring directly at people in a manner calculated to intimidate. Joe smiled broadly with yellowed teeth; he could never be intimidated by anything less than a man-eating tiger.

"Morning, ma'am. I've got something in the wagon that might interest the man of the house."

"And what might that be?" Her voice was as waspish as her appearance, brusque to the point of rudeness. Joe smiled even wider. He enjoyed meeting snappish types who thought he could be cowed by their superior mien.

"A buffalo skull. They told me down at the depot someone up here collects bones."

"I think you have been the victim of a practical joke."

"Pardon me?"

"You have had a joke played on you. No one here collects bones."

"What would be the point of the joke, ma'am? Jokes usually have a point."

"I'm sure I don't know. We are not interested in bones."

"Strictly speaking, it's a skull."

"Or in skulls."

They regarded each other a moment longer, then Joe tired of the confrontation. He believed her; it had been a joke at his expense.

"Sorry to bother you."

He turned away. Alma saw the hump, and something akin to a chime rang through her head. "Wait!"

Joe faced her again. She was staring at his back, and he wondered if this was the sole reason for her command; if so, it was the most blatant example of tactlessness he had ever encountered. He waited for her to return her eyes to his, smiling an ironic smile that would let her know he gave not two cents for her opinion. But her expression was not one of fascinated loathing. Had he chanced upon a bleeding heart, one of those folk who nurse the runt of the litter out

366

of misplaced sympathy? Joe girded himself to resist kindness; he had no need of it.

"What is your name?" The question was direct, but her tone had softened.

"Joe Cobden," he said, and was startled by the way in which blood drained instantly from her face, reinforcing the impression of flaccid doughiness. Her little pinched mouth had dropped open, as though he had said "Judas Iscariot" or "Napoleon Bonaparte."

"Joe Cobden. . . ." She repeated it in a whisper, had unconsciously leaned against the door jamb for support. She righted herself with a start, set her mouth in a grim little crease.

"They told you to say that, didn't they?"

"Ma'am?"

"You were told to give me that name."

"This conversation is drifting right by me. My name's Joe Cobden. No one told me to tell you. You asked me yourself."

"Is it truly your name?"

"Yes it is." He assumed she had heard of him during his transient fame as a buffalo-hunter.

She stepped aside. "Please come in."

Joe was taken to the parlour and invited to sit on a plush settee. The woman went off, returned minutes later with a tray bearing a coffee-urn, china cups and a plate of gingerbread cut into neat rectangles rather than frivolous little men. She set the tray down on a low table, sat at the other end of the settee to Joe. Coffee was poured, the plate proffered. This ritual intimidated Joe as no amount of staring could. He sipped self-consciously, chewed a morsel of gingerbread, aware, in these breezeless surroundings, of his own stench.

"My name is Mrs. Puckett," said the woman, leaving Joe nonplussed; the sentence had been presented as if it were some kind of revelation. Then the name's familiarity established itself. Puckett? Could this be the mad Pennsylvanian's sister? There had been stories about Puckett sending half his wages to a sister. "Mrs. Calvin Puckett," she amended, and the surprise of it almost caused Joe to choke; he had always considered Puckett about as likely a candidate for matrimony as himself and, what's more, the lunatic appeared to have married into money! This place had not been built on a buffalo-skinner's pay. He was thoroughly confused.

"We have been married some three years now. My husband has often mentioned your name."

"He has?"

"Forgive my bluntness, Mr. Cobden, but it is my belief he does not like you."

"He never did."

"May I enquire as to the reason for this bad feeling between you?"

"There isn't one. He started off by just staring at me, then he followed me around. Since we're speaking so bluntly, Mrs. Puckett, you . . . uh . . . you know he's not in his right mind, don't you?"

"I am aware of that. What else occurred between you?"

"Nothing. Peculiar looks and following me around, that's all. What kind of story did he tell you?"

Alma related the story of the church, of its destruction, of the blame laid at Joe's feet. Joe declared himself innocent. Alma believed him. Joe politely requested to know the source of Calvin's riches, since Alma's narrative had made it clear it was not her dowry which had raised these walls. He could not believe the story of an inheritance, but could offer no explanation more plausible. He consumed gingerbread absentmindedly while considering the incredible circumstance of his presence here, drinking coffee with Puckett the feeb's wife! He wanted something stronger than coffee, something to calm him, let him absorb these sudden revelations.

"Where is he right now?" said Joe. "Where's the gun?" Alma had told him of the Winchester. Joe did not trust it not to fire.

"The gun is hidden safely away, Mr. Cobden. My hus-

band has not touched it in two years. He is no doubt somewhere on the ridge. He roams back and forth, back and
forth, all day long.''

"Still looking for me?"

"I think not. Calvin is driven by some kind of engine
which feeds on delusion, but he is incapable of sustaining
any one delusion for very long. When he ceased to mention
your name he began hunting instead for an owl. He said its
hooting kept him awake at night. He searched for some
time, but did not shoot anything. Nowadays he spends his
time searching for a well. He insists there is water under
the ridge. He marches back and forth with a forked stick,
trying to find it. He may have forgotten you completely.''

Joe set his cup down. "Maybe it's best if we don't tempt
fate.''

"Mr. Cobden, please do not leave. Who knows, perhaps
confrontation with you will serve to jolt his brain, make him
stop this nonsense of searching for this and that. I assure
you, Calvin is perfectly harmless.''

"It might make him worse.''

"I will accept the responsibility.''

"I don't know that I can trust your judgement, ma'am,
if you'll pardon me.''

"Mr. Cobden, if I were not a sound judge of my husband's mental state, do you believe I would allow our son
to be alone with him for one minute?''

"Your son?''

"Noah is two, a fine boy.''

"Is he . . . uh. . . .''

"Noah is normal in every respect.''

It should be made clear at this point that Alma detested
Noah as much as she detested Calvin. The maternal instinct
had never asserted itself in her breast, yet no one, not even
Dr. Whaley, suspected the presence in Alma of a howling
outrage that she should be expected to toil for the benefit of
her unwanted son. Alma hid her true self behind the domestic mask of bustling activity, loathing the feel of her
child even as she tucked him into his crib. Her ability to

feel one thing and act another impressed her, and for two years she had drawn strength from the success of her deception. They don't suspect a thing, she told herself every night before closing her eyes, and the thought would be followed by a tight little smile. I'm just biding my time, thought Alma soothingly, just biding my time until the *right* time. Then watch out. Oh, but they would hate her, the citizens of Valley Forge, they would hate her and blacken her memory with their wagging tongues once she was gone. Good. She wanted them to hate her as much as she hated them. Alma did not know when the right time would come, or what elements would define its shape; she knew only that she would recognise the right time when it arrived. Joe Cobden had about him the aura of latent opportunity; he was a living, breathing prelude to, and catalyst of, the right time. He must not be allowed to slip away.

Alma ringed him with gossamer chains. She was determined to impress upon this gift from the gods the essentially tragic nature of her role as wife to a madman, martyr to a hopeless cause, but the task would have to be accomplished with stealth; he was far too intelligent to be swayed by either rhetoric or the swooning pose of a stage tragedienne. For Joe Cobden nothing less than what appeared to be denial of Calvin's condition would do the trick; he would almost certainly be impressed by that kind of forlorn bravery. As a hunchback, she reasoned, he will have suffered, will appreciate the suffering I have endured, will be sympathetic, and will co-operate. She was not as yet quite sure what she was doing, her head unable at this moment to plan with exactitude, but beneath her mental turmoil, which was itself kept well hidden from her guest, lay the icy core of Self, a nucleus hard and unyielding and impersonal as the mechanism of a clock. Its mainspring, uncoiling with the measured movement of an alert cobra, was determination, the yearning for a future away from this prison which had superseded the prison of her father's house, a yearning kept warm and alive with carefully banked reserves of ruthlessness, waiting, just waiting for the right time, the ideal moment, the conjunction of planets that would signify the hour of her escape.

"More coffee, Mr. Cobden?"

He nodded, mulling over the inadvisability of involving himself again with Calvin Puckett. He wanted to leave. Something here was not as it should be. He told himself his discomfort probably stemmed from the claustrophobic atmosphere one would expect to find in the house of a lunatic. And yet, for just a second or two, watching Alma pour coffee, he felt she, too, was mad; a spider, he thought, a little grey spider with perfect manners and a sad tale to lull her victim with, busily weaving her web around him while she sharpened her fangs and prepared to pounce. He blinked several times to rid himself of this obscene and unjustifiable vision. Mrs. Puckett was without doubt a fine person, concerned for her husband's welfare without bemoaning her own lot, trying, in her own polite and restrained manner, to enlist Joe's aid. The least he could do was co-operate.

"What do you want me to do?"

"Meet him."

"And?"

"Let happen what may. I repeat, the responsibility will be mine."

A child began squawling at the rear of the house. Alma excused herself, was gone for some time, returned to find Joe kneading his knuckles with tension.

"Have you made your decision, Mr. Cobden?"

"I'll do it. And you may as well call me Joe."

They waited another hour before footsteps clumped on to the porch. The front door opened and closed. Alma hurried out to the hallway. Her words reached Joe with ease. "Calvin, there is a visitor here to see you, someone you used to know."

"I seen the wagon. Who is it?"

The voice had not changed, was still a disquieting blend of boyish enthusiasm and suspicion. Calvin came barging into the parlour, saw Joe and stopped, as though encountering an unseen wall. He stared, his jaw slowly dropping. Joe stood, made himself smile.

"Afternoon . . . Calvin."

Nothing in the parlour moved. Alma wondered if Calvin would throw a conniption fit and foam at the mouth, or attack the hunchback. The intervals between tickings from the grandfather clock seemed somehow to be stretched beyond all normal bounds, frozen moments unnaturally extended, near to breaking point. Within the folds of Calvin's brain a variety of sensations fought for supremacy: confusion, shock, disbelief, rage, an emotional onslaught his mind was incapable of ingesting without serious danger of total collapse. He knew Joe, yet seconds later did not know him; so potent a symbol was the hunched shape before him, Calvin would not allow it to intrude upon and overcome his awareness, but deftly slid by it to fasten upon another familiar, but far less threatening focus for his eyes and brain. He raised a trembling hand, pointed a finger.

"Gingerbread!"

He hurried forward to clutch a handful. Joe he ignored completely. The remaining gingerbread was consumed in a convulsive rush of mastication and noisy gulpings. Joe was embarrassed for Alma's sake. Did the poor woman have to endure this kind of animal behaviour every day? Calvin turned to Alma with the empty plate. "Any more?" Alma silently took the plate, turned and left the room. Calvin gave Joe a sidelong look. "I like gingerbread," he announced.

"Me, too."

"I reckon I could eat it all the time."

"Mrs. Puckett makes a fine batch, all right."

Calvin's eyes wandered away from Joe's, looked around the room, observing the furnishings as though he were the visitor and Joe the host. Joe's misgivings had by now turned to pity. The poor bastard, he thought. No improvement. Can't even remember me. Probably just as well. "Nice house," he said.

"It's mine," Calvin admitted shyly, then his voice took on a swaggering tone. "I paid for all of it."

"You must be pretty rich."

"I am. I got a whole lot of money."

"Where'd you find it?"

Joe did not intend that his question be taken literally; he might just as easily have asked "How did you come by it?" or "What's the secret of your success?" A stealthiness of theatrical proportions clouded Calvin's features. He wasn't going to get caught by that kind of question; nossir. "I never found it. My uncle died and left it. It's a 'heritance." He pronounced it "hairtins".

"You're a lucky man," said Joe. He ascribed Calvin's facial contortions to idiocy, failed completely to note the clue thus offered.

Alma returned with more gingerbread. The situation's unreality almost brought a smile to Joe's lips; he sat and munched gingerbread with the man he had once been convinced was intent on killing him.

Alma was disappointed at Calvin's reaction; she still daydreamed of Calvin dropping dead while in a foaming convulsion, but it was obvious fate was not going to intercede on her behalf in so dramatic a fashion. She would have to instigate all change on the ridge herself, and that meant removing herself from it, taking herself a great distance from this house and its unclean memories. She sometimes wondered what had prevented her from departing before now. Was it a sliver of what society called "responsibility" remaining within her, a lingering remnant of the old Alma? She knew Calvin and Noah were babies both, and could not survive unaided, but did she really care? Alma was prepared to admit that, in all honesty, it was probably cowardice rather than any sense of moral indebtedness that had postponed her departure all this time. But now a replacement for her had arrived, someone to administer to her children's simple needs. Alma could depart, fulfil her dreams of freedom at last, and even do so with a clear conscience.

It was an arrangement made in heaven. The right time was very nearly within Alma's anxious grasp.

"Would you do us the honour of staying overnight, Mr. Cobden?"

During the wait for Calvin, Joe had described himself to her as an "independent entrepreneur". The irony had been intentional, but Alma did not detect it; she imagined Joe was ashamed to be a homeless drifter, and would leap at the chance of security. Alma was not ungenerous; she would give Joe what he secretly wanted. He simply had to be led to the waters of philanthropy and made to drink of them. She knew someone as ugly and friendless as Joe would be grateful for the opportunity being readied on his behalf.

"Thank you."

He did not really wish to stay there, but Alma's manner was heavy with unspoken obligation. Joe did the right thing and stabled his horses, promising himself he would leave tomorrow. Returning to the house, seeing the smile of gratitude bestowed on him by Alma, he thought he might extend his stay by one day more, just long enough to let her know that his presence was not going to effect any kind of change for the better in Calvin. He must be sure not to let Mrs. Puckett raise her hopes; her husband was a feeb, and a feeb he'd stay, Joe or no Joe.

He remained at the ridge for a week, had baby Noah thrust at him often, was soon dandling the child with careless ease, enjoying its delight at being thrown into the air and caught again. He carried Noah on rambling walks among the trees, sat with him on a tree stump at the ridge's blighted southern tip and talked nonsense for the pleasure it gave the child. They were sometimes accompanied by Calvin, but wherever they wandered Calvin insisted they pass by the low pile that had been his church. The clearing was now overgrown with blackberries, a profusion of thorny brambles hung with sour fruit.

Alma observed Joe's progress with satisfaction. She gave

silent thanks to the stationmaster who had tried to work a potentially deadly prank, and had instead provided her with a means of abdication; soon she would hand the crown of responsibility to Joe Cobden. Everything was working out to perfection, the machinery of deceit operating to plan. On a Tuesday Alma went to the Farmers' Bank and requested that half the remaining funds be made available to her on Wednesday. Bragg asked the reason for so large a withdrawal, and was told to mind his own business. On the morning of her departure Alma packed no trunks, took not so much as a valise. Joe watched her harness Morgana and drive into town as she had done the day before. When she returned he would tell her it was time for him to be moving on. The ridge and its occupants had provided him with an interesting, almost bizarre interlude, but he could not impose upon the Pucketts' hospitality for ever.

Alma drove to the bank, collected the money, headed back toward the ridge. She knew Bragg was watching from his window to see if she went to the railroad depot; she was not about to give him the satisfaction of seeing his suspicions confirmed. When she reached the turn-off to the ridge the trap sailed right past and kept going westward. By nightfall Alma was many miles from Valley Forge, but even darkness could not stop her flight. She drove through the night, guided by the telegraph poles and the A, T & SF tracks. By noon of the following day she had reached the next town. Morgana and the trap were sold at a small profit. The loss of her mare caused Alma considerable distress, but there was no other way. She purchased a ticket to San Francisco. By 1:35 she was rolling westward again behind an iron horse, with not a backward glance.

At that same time Joe went to town and began enquiring as to her whereabouts. Everyone knew his identity, and held him in conversation for as long as possible, providing him with fake assistance in order to glean more information from him. Joe knew his reputation as an alleged burner of churches had preceded him, and would have been amused by the crudely obvious subterfuges with which the townsfolk attempted to detain him in idle chatter had he not been so concerned for Alma. Where had she gone? He was directed to the office of the sheriff. Ned Bowdre had a year ago insisted that the title of constable, and the accompanying wage, were not commensurate with the time and effort he invested in the job; accordingly, he was made sheriff, and nowadays seldom ventured out to the hog-farm except to pay a social call on brother Milt. He was glad to meet at last the mysterious hunchback Joe Cobden, but could not enlighten him with regard to Alma's disappearance. He promised he would investigate. Joe was not reassured; he did not fully trust any holder of elected office, but there was no other course for him to pursue.

True to his word, Ned made enquiries, during which he talked with Nathan Bragg. The banker admitted Alma had withdrawn half the Puckett account; he had apparently been the last to talk with the vanished woman. Further investigation turned up a boy on the western side of town who said he had seen Alma drive by the day before, and he was positive she had not turned off the road to take the ridge trail, but kept right on past there until he could see her no longer.

Ned visited the ridge, told Joe what he knew. The conclusion to be drawn was obvious. Joe thanked him. Ned asked what Joe would do now. Joe did not know. Would Joe break the news to Calvin? Joe would. Ned departed. Joe laughed a bitter laugh; for a week he had accepted hospitality without realising he was being groomed for a role, that of surrogate parent. It was clear now that this had been Alma's intention from the beginning. She was a spider all right, and Joe had walked blithely into her parlour; her legacy was a comfortable web in which fluttered two helpless moths. Joe took stock of his situation; he could leave, in which case Calvin would presumably burn the house down by accident or design, possibly killing himself and the child, or he would run amok in some other lamentable fashion and be taken away to an asylum. Noah would probably be adopted; no, more than likely the locals would not want the son of a madman, and would send him to some distant orphanage, where the spirit would be crushed from him like juice from a grape. Joe could not let that happen.

First things first. He told Calvin of his wife's departure. Calvin ran off to hide among the trees. For two days Joe cared for the baby as best he could, even took some pride in the fact that it cried only three times, and never for very long. During those forty-eight hours of enforced obligation Joe discovered a part of himself he had never known to exist: the ability to forget himself completely while caring for another, totally dependent entity. So proud was he of his success, he even resented Calvin's reappearance on the evening of the second day, tired and dirty and hungry. Joe prepared him a meal. Calvin would not talk, ate in silence, then slunk off to fall asleep. The white wolf would have known what to do, but the white wolf had ceased to pad through Calvin's thoughts, had not visited for so long the tracks of his passing had been completely erased.

Joe lit an oil lamp, fed Noah, then himself. He had been inveigled into these peculiar straits, had been offered no choice, but his dominant feeling was not one of resentment, but of acceptance. He surprised himself with his lack of indignation at having been manipulated so skilfully by the grey spider. He watched Noah kick his feet in the air, a creature as vulnerable and trusting as a chick straight from the egg. I stand between this child and the pit, thought Joe. I can't leave. I won't. I don't even want to.

Noah shat. Joe cleaned him off.

It was a beginning.

PART THREE

THE WOODEN INDIAN

CHAPTER TWENTY-SIX

For the next four years Joe's sole worry was the state of Noah Puckett's intellect. At the age of six he still had not spoken a word. Joe took him to Dr. Whaley, who expressed doubts that the child would ever be normal. Joe returned to the ridge with Noah perched on his hump, Noah's favourite place, and watched him play in the yard. Was the doctor right, or could his opinion be disregarded as that of a quack? The boy appeared alert, fully cognisant of his surroundings, evinced a cat-like curiosity for everything that moved in the breeze or of its own accord. He had learned to walk with ease and was not misshapen in any way, although it was already apparent he would not be a handsome child. His limbs and their appurtenances were well coordinated, carrying him off on solitary explorations of the ridge, bringing objects close to his face for appraisal, and he scrambled with alacrity on to Joe's hump for rollicking rides around the yard. He was cheerful and good-natured. But he would not speak. Joe wondered if he had been afflicted with whatever it was that made Reverend Wilkes' daughter Sadie a mute. He watched in miserable silence while Noah played with a fallen branch, swishing it through the air, delighting in the flutter and hum of its leaves.

Calvin had remained sullen and torpid for eight months after Alma's departure. Slowly, he came to accept Joe in her stead; Joe performed most of the wifely duties of cooking and cleaning Calvin had come to expect from a woman. Joe did these things in order that the three males might eat and live together in something less than perpetual squalor. Calvin did not adopt this sensible attitude, secretly thought

Joe a servile and inferior being. He kept his thoughts to himself and Joe laboured on, mistakenly believing his efforts to be appreciated. He was apprised of Calvin's true feelings one night when Joe dished up beef for the third consecutive supper; he wanted the meat consumed quickly, before it spoiled. Calvin was not fond of beef, and threw his plate against the wall like a petulant child. Joe and Noah looked at the wall, looked at each other, looked at Calvin, who folded his arms stubbornly across his narrow chest, a mulish expression on his face. "I'm sick an' tired of it," he said, by way of explanation.

"Then why not say so? Now you'll have to clean the wall."

"I ain't cleanin' nothin'."

"You made a mess on the wall," said Joe, "and now you have to fix it."

"Ain't a-gonna."

Calvin raised his weak chin defiantly, confidently; he had never seen Joe display any mood but one of mild benevolence, was therefore totally unprepared for Joe's sudden leap from one side of the table to the other, sending his chair skittering across the floor. Joe's fingers closed around Calvin's throat, and he lifted the defiler of kitchen walls clear of his chair and shook him, like a dog with a snake. Joe did not enjoy his domestic duties, and resented any act which made his tasks more unendurable. It must also be taken into account that he had never conceived a liking for Calvin, whom he considered a sneaking, self-pitying, whining little weasel.

"Clean it up," said Joe, in what was a remarkably moderate tone, under the circumstances. "Clean it up, or I'll break your fucking neck."

He dropped Calvin to the floor. Noah's eyes were popping, waiting to see what happened next. He thought Joe was his father, Calvin some kind of poor relation or guest they allowed to stay around the place out of pity. Calvin scuttled away on hands and knees, badly frightened. He attempted to reach the door, but Joe blocked his way. "Clean it up right now." Calvin quaked before the monstrosity looming above him. Like a child, he knew he had done wrong, but thought it only natural that he should go unpunished, attended as he was by a servant. Joe's behaviour was like some nightmare come to life, dark and threatening, and Calvin squeezed his eyes shut in an attempt to relocate himself in the world of wakefulness. A hand grasped his collar and hauled him to his feet, and Calvin was faced with the dreadful notion that this awful thing happening to him was real.

"You're a lazy, useless, dopey shit-for-brains. I'm sick and tired myself, sick and tired of the way you slink around here like a whipped dog half the time and a fucking king the other half. Are you going to clean up that mess?"

Calvin nodded with atypical vigour. Joe released him gently, allowed his feet to touch the floor before releasing his collar. "Then, go and do it. Now."

Calvin did it. He wanted to cry at the injustice of his humiliation. A few sniffs and tears escaped him. "Quit blubbering or I'll make you do the whole damn house!" roared Joe, and Calvin's intimidation was complete. Joe felt much better for having disciplined his host; he had allowed Calvin far too much leeway solely on account of his feeble-mindedness, let him laze around the place without lifting a finger for himself or his son. Resentment had been building in Joe for four years. Now it had been released, and he knew conditions in the house would never again be oriented around Calvin's likes and dislikes. It might even help the idiot to grow up and take charge of his life, assume the responsibilities of fatherhood, although this was unlikely. Definitely a step in the right direction, thought Joe.

Noah apparently agreed. "Serves him right," he said.

Joe swivelled his head to regard Noah. "Pardon?"

"He made a mess, so he can clean it up," said Noah. There was nothing whatever wrong with his voice.

Joe was both relieved and exasperated. "How is it we never heard you express an opinion before?"

No answer. Noah resumed eating. Joe looked at Calvin, who had noticed nothing out of the ordinary in hearing a boy, supposedly mute, open his mouth and offer comment. Joe's annoyance was again directed at Noah. "Why didn't you talk before? All this time we thought you couldn't talk. . . ."

"I *did* talk. You never heard me."

Joe wanted to shake him as he had Calvin, but restrained himself. Was it a joke? he wondered. Is a six-year-old capable of playing such an extended prank, holding his tongue for years? It seemed impossible, but the boy insouciantly forking up his supper constituted proof that it was not. What kind of kid *is* this? Joe asked himself. He decided to say nothing, and—such is the mind of a six-year-old—Noah himself soon forgot whether his muteness had been the product of arrested development, or a self-imposed silence perpetrated for the amusement it afforded him to see a look of concern on Joe's face. As had Calvin until the night of flying beef, Noah regarded Joe as someone whose sole reason for existence lay in being available to serve him, as cook, as cleaner, as means of locomotion and source of entertainment, but in this he differed in no way from other children. He liked Joe, but any child will use the object of its affection without compunction or remorse.

After Noah's revelation Joe was wary, felt he had somehow been duped, made a fool of. He made himself forgive the boy, who was only six, after all. Joe was tempted to take Noah into Dr. Whaley's office and stun the old fraud with a display of verbosity and intellect unequalled since young Jesus lectured the elders; he wanted that pompous quack to know himself for what he was, nothing more than a bonesetter. Joe did not pause to equate his dislike for Dr. Whaley with residual feelings of resentment against another doctor, the one who had dominated his own childhood. He saw in Noah the child he once had been, a creature disadvantaged, looked down upon, yet possessing a mind of preternatural sharpness, a thing to be honed until razor-edged, a tool with which to carve a place for himself in an adverse world. Joe did not knowingly compare himself to Dr. Cobden in his skyrocketing hopes for what he was sure would become a prodigy of some kind; nor, like the doctor, did he countenance for one moment the possibility of disappointment or personal betrayal with regard to these gilded intentions, these best laid plans.

He set about educating the boy, beginning with the alphabet. Every day, for at least three hours, Joe poured knowledge into Noah's ear, a gratifyingly receptive organ, and watched proudly as letters, words, sentences and eventually coherent phrases began to flow from the boy's pen. Joe instilled in Noah a sense of the world's vastness, wishing him to take a cosmic view of things. "Valley Forge is just a tiny place in Kansas, which is just a portion of America, and America is just one country among dozens. There's so much of the world that one person could never see all of it, not if he lived to be ten thousand years old."

"Why can't I be ten thousand years old?" Noah had not yet learned arithmetic, since Joe disliked the subject, and therefore had no true conception of the figure's size.

"Because people don't live that long."

"But I want to see everything!"

"Well, you can't! You'll see as much as you can in seventy years and drop dead like the rest of us."

"It isn't fair," sulked Noah.

"No it isn't, and that's the big lesson to be learned from life. Nothing is fair. Understand that and you can call yourself a wise man."

"I want to see all of it."

"Too bad, small-fry. Write down all the reasons why you think you should be allowed to live ten thousand years."

Joe sent away for books on geography and history, learned a great many things from them himself before passing the knowledge on to Noah. He read to the boy from Alma's shelves of adventure and romance, held him spellbound with tales of excitement and love and chivalry and death in distant lands, tales of times long gone, realms of enchantment bound in leather. Some of his own favourites were among them. He ordered more fiction from a St. Louis bookstore's catalogue, delved into what was to become Noah's own favourite kind of unreality, the works of Edgar Allan Poe and Nathaniel Hawthorne. Joe was made to read the tales of terror many times over to an openmouthed Noah. He had become an accomplished actor by way of these narrations, adopting different voices for the various characters, investing his delivery with all the mystery and ghastliness required, enjoyed these stories every bit as much as the boy.

The bond between them was indisputable, their waking hours spent together for the most part, in lessons, in reading, in easy silence on long summer days, in vigorous discussion on every conceivable subject during the chill flurries of winter, when men and boy were housebound, slaves to the roaring fireplace. In time, when he had overcome his fear of Joe, Calvin also partook of these fantastical journeyings, listening with an intensity equal to that of his son. All three shared domestic chores. They were a family, and Joe was undeniably its head. Joe's money had long since been spent. Calvin's account at the Farmers' Bank had been returned to his charge following the flight of Alma. Joe was not told how much cash remained, and assumed (incorrectly) that there was plenty. Their needs were few, once the library had been fully stocked, and the money seemed capable of supporting them well into some indefinable future. Joe enjoyed the lazy way of life established on the ridge, felt no compunction to work for a living, felt he was entitled to be fed and lodged at Calvin's expense in return for his services as parent, teacher and companion to the Pucketts.

In the fall of 1882, when Noah was eight years old, a representative of the Valley Forge school board came to the house. The board deemed it time for the boy to attend lessons, instead of running wild through the trees like some kind of Indian. Joe thanked him for the board's thoughtfulness, promised to make arrangements, showed him the door. He did nothing, of course, and in time the school board's representative called again. Had Mr. Cobden forgotten their little talk of several weeks ago? Joe adopted a contrite expression. Oh, how remiss of him, he'd gone and let things slide completely. Maybe next year. But the representative insisted. Joe assured him he would send Noah along to the schoolhouse the very next day. He did no such thing. Noah thought this a wonderful game. He knew no one but Calvin and Joe, had formed no friendships away from the ridge, felt in no need of extraneous distraction in the form of organised schooling, loved the way Joe mimicked the rectitude of the board's envoy after that person had departed. "The child must receive an education," pontificated Joe, hands on lapels. "The nation demands it, Mr. Cobden. The youth of today is the citizen of tomorrow. Strength through knowledge is our passport to the future." He leaned close to Noah's gleeful face, narrowed his eyes accusingly. "Do you not agree, h'm?" Noah applauded Joe's wicked impersonation, and together they awaited further developments.

On his next visit the representative was accompanied by Ned Bowdre (still in office) who took Joe to one side and politely requested an explanation. Joe told him the boy was already receiving adequate teaching here at home. Ned allowed the boy seemed bright enough, considering the way he hadn't talked all those years, but the law was the law, and Noah would have to spend at least four years in school to comply. Joe did not like being dictated to by an anonymous body of persons who were doubtless less smart than himself, probably nowhere near as smart as the boy. When the forces of law and education had departed, Joe and Noah held a council of war. Their hands appeared to be tied. Joe could only suggest that if Noah misbehaved himself badly enough the teacher might lose patience and send him home again; it seemed his sole hope for reprieve from the smothering horrors of school.

With a heavy heart, Noah dragged his feet to the schoolhouse on the corner of Shawnee and Decatur, entered the yard and stood for a moment, sullenly regarding the writh-ing commotion of skylarking boys, the more demure knots of girls, who scrupulously avoided any acknowledgement of the rowdier sex. All eyes turned to witness his uncomfortable arrival. Noah was terrified. They were all short people like himself, with a few hulking exceptions, but he felt no kinship whatever with them; they might just as well have been a flock of staring flamingoes. He squirmed inside his boots, considered turning tail to run back home. One of the hulking exceptions, a lout of fourteen named Tyler, already aping the narrow stupidity of his father, approached Noah with a confident swagger.

"Who're you?" he demanded.

"Noah Puckett."

"Your pa's an idiot."

Noah knew the boy was referring to Calvin, for whom he had no great affection. Despite having been told several times by Joe that the child-man was his natural father, Noah still associated the hunchback, rather than the fool, with feelings of reciprocal warmth and admiration, the emotions supposedly inspired by parenthood. Unable and unwilling to explain all this to his interrogator, Noah said nothing.

"He's an idiot, ain't he?" insisted Tyler.

"I suppose so."

It seemed pointless to deny what was obvious; still, being forced to make that kind of admission out loud was surely a prime example of bad manners if ever Noah had heard one. "But it's none of your business," he said, and immediately felt better. He was not intimidated by Tyler's size; Joe was big, and Joe had never hurt him. He was unprepared for the sudden shove that set him on his back in the yard, the focus now of every child's attention. Tyler revelled in his power; Noah looked very small and weak at his feet. Noah did nothing, still mystified at this unwarranted aggression; he had only said what needed saying. This was entirely without precedent in his life. Then he remembered a host of exciting books peopled with braggarts and bullies—this boy was one such as they! Noah understood at last why every eye was watchful for the retaliation he was obliged to muster in compliance with tradition. Life really was very much like a book, he saw it clearly now. But he did not get up. Heroes wore rapiers, and Noah had not so much as a pocket knife. He had to make the effort, though, or he would be perceived as that other literary figure, the coward, which was even worse than being a braggart or bully. Halfway to his feet, Noah was pushed down again by Tyler's boot.

"That's not fair!"

This complaint introduced mirth to the yard. Even the girls laughed. They all knew who Noah Puckett was, had sometimes glimpsed him on the streets with that awful humpback Indian, the one that burned down the church Noah's idiot father built up on the ridge. It seemed natural somehow that the son of an idiot should be held to the ground by Tyler Grier's boot. He looked very silly, and they showered him with all the laughter he deserved.

One child abstained: Sadie Wilkes, who never took part in anything the others did. At thirteen, she was among the oldest of the girls, and this was to be her last day at school; with her mother so poorly, bedridden now for many months, Sadie was needed at the rectory to look after her while Reverend Wilkes administered to his flock. She watched Noah's humiliation without sympathy for the newcomer; he was no more than another small boy to Sadie, and all such were no better than pesky, yapping dogs, to be avoided whenever possible. She turned away, went around to the far side of the schoolhouse to be free of the girls' shrill laughter, the raucous hooting of the boys, children all.

Sadie's body bled once a month, had done so for two months now. The stigma of womankind was hers, and she was both terrified and proud to have been singled out thus by Jesus, who only allowed exceptionally good girls to shed their blood as he had done; this was the information her ailing mother had given her, the last effort of a dying woman—dying, so she thought, of a surfeit of physical attention from her husband—to instil in the mind of her daughter an unbreakable link between God's everlasting curse on all daughters of Eve and the need, the crucial, never-to-be-forgotten need for chastity. Once let a man touch you, and the bleeding would stop, and Sadie would no longer be blessed in the eyes of Jesus. God had doubly blessed her, said her mother, in that he had also frozen her tongue, that she might never spread vicious gossip and idle chatter, which are the bane of wives the world over.

A stout woman of grim countenance and advancing years opened the schoolhouse door from within and shook a brass handbell at the gathered children, silencing their clamour, scattering the ring that had formed around Noah and Tyler Grier. They filed into the wooden box of learning under her watchful eye. Noah stood and brushed himself off. "You! Boy!" said the woman, Miss Woodcock by name. "Shift yourself this instant!" Noah shuffled into the schoolhouse, receiving a smart blow to the side of his head as he passed within reach of her free hand. "Fighting is not permitted in the yard," she explained, and pointed to an empty desk at the rear of the room. Noah sat. He wanted to cry, could feel the tears prickling his eyes, his mouth beginning to tremble; first the bully, now this horrible-looking lady with the iron-grey hair and fat behind—it just wasn't fair! He saw the bully leering at him, waiting for him to blubber. Joe wouldn't want him to blubber, so he did not. He gazed at his splintered desktop and radiated hatred for every living thing inside the schoolhouse. He wouldn't come back here willingly, not if it was going to be like this every day.

Lessons began. The ages of the pupils ranged from seven years to fourteen; accordingly, they were arranged in groups, given different tasks. Since Noah had joined the class a year later than most, Miss Woodcock had to determine his intelligence and place him either with his own age group, or with those younger. She asked if he understood the principles of the alphabet. "I know all that," he assured her. "Oh, do you now?" said Miss Woodcock with a glacial smile. "We'll just see how much you *do* know." She handed him a reader and sat back with a look of gloating expectation; she knew Noah's history, knew it was impossible, living as he did with a crazed father and deformed hanger-on, shiftless idlers both, that this boy should be anything but ignorant. Miss Woodcock did not like small boys, nor large boys, nor men. She also disliked most women; only for very young girls did Miss Woodcock feel anything resembling kinship and sympathy. The blight of Miss Woodcock's life had been her name. When only eleven years old she had been told what a cock was, and it was not a male chicken. A cousin had added to her embarrassment by showing her something his father, a retired fur trapper, had brought home from the Rocky Mountains years before: a wooden phallus, used in symbolic fashion for ceremonial purposes by one or other of the heathen tribes beyond the pale of decency and civilisation. A wood cock. "This is you," said the cousin, wagging the obscene thing under her nose. Miss Woodcock conceived her hatred of small boys and her own name at once, and for ever. No cock, wood or flesh, had ever been allowed near her from that day on.

"Well, what are you waiting for?"

Noah commenced reading. The sentences were so childishly simple he deliberately gave his voice a sing-song lilt to express his contempt for such paltry stuff. The reader was snatched from his hands, another thrust at him. "Now this one." His performance improved, stimulated by a slightly more complex challenge, yet even this meatier fare did not strain his capabilities. The entire class listened, amazed at such erudition from someone who minutes before had been flat on his back in the dirt. A third book, the school's most advanced reader, was offered to Noah. He opened it at random and read with careless aplomb, showing off, putting all these fools in their place. Knock him to the ground and laugh at him, would they? Hit him over the head, eh? Well just let them see how smart he was and they'd change their ways pretty quick. Miss Woodcock was appalled by his assurance; this had to be squashed immediately, before the wretched child made her a laughing stock. She took the reader from him in mid-sentence, cast about desperately for a club, was granted inspiration.

"What are five and eleven?" she demanded.

"They're numbers," said Noah, and the class brayed.

"Don't act the fool with me. Add five and eleven."

Noah consulted his fingers, only to have them slapped with a wooden ruler. "In your head, and silently," said Miss Woodcock, hoping she had found his Achilles heel. It seemed she had; after an extended silence Noah offered his answer. "Fifteen?" More laughter, and Miss Woodcock did nothing to stop it. Noah blushed, furious with himself, angry at Joe for not having bothered to teach him numbers with the same diligence he had brought to reading. Miss Woodcock at last raised her hand for silence. "Twenty-three and eighteen," she barked, and Noah hung his head.

Sadie watched his humiliation from her desk, her face the only one among the pupils which did not register delight at the public humbling of Noah Puckett. She cared nothing for him, just as she cared nothing for any of these children from whom her dumbness kept her for ever apart. Noah Puckett was a thin and ugly boy with a thin and ugly face, the eyes set much too close together, giving him the wily look of a fox. His only interest for Sadie lay in the coincidence of Noah beginning his schooling on the very day hers ended. She would be glad to be free of Miss Woodcock and her unrelenting bad humour, glad to put behind her the strident discord of the schoolyard, the arguments over trifles, the ridiculous and self-important allegiances between girl-friends, their whisperings and gigglings. She knew they hated her for her tranquillity, her intelligence and her beauty. Sadie's father had once pointed out to her the resemblance between herself and a very fine picture of an angel, painted by an artist of long ago; Sadie might well have modelled for the radiant being, and was secretly pleased that her person was thus associated with holiness. She was not a vain girl; her beauty was for Jesus, none other, and it was her deliberate abstraction from everyday emotions and perceptions, she knew, that aroused the ire of girls and women, the confused adoration of boys and men. Noah Puckett would have fallen under her spell, given the opportunity, but Sadie did not regret that he would never have that chance; she took no pleasure from her influence on those around her, simply acknowledged its results, as she acknowledged the rain that fell unbidden from clouds.

At the end of the school day Noah returned to the ridge and stamped into the house with his brow lowered, lips set in a line.

"How'd it go?" asked Joe.

Noah stared at the floor. Joe suspected the worst had happened.

"Why didn't you teach me how to do numbers!"

"Did they ask you to do arithmetic?"

"I didn't know *anything!* They laughed at me! Why didn't you show me how! You should've!"

Joe shrank from the accusation. He knew he had avoided the subject because of a personal loathing for the formal and intricate dance of digits that is mathematics, had left the boy unprepared for that particular branch of learning.

"I don't know much about it myself," he admitted.

"I know *that,*" said Noah, and left the room, almost knocking Calvin over as father entered and son exited.

"Somethin' happen?" asked Calvin, watching Noah leap from the porch and disappear among the trees.

"He didn't know how to do sums. They laughed at him."

"Oh."

Calvin thought it perfectly natural to be laughed at, since he had always been laughed at. There were worse things in life. He tried to think of some worse things, instead found himself wondering what was for supper.

The rectory was a place of musty odours and hushed silence. Her father was out. Sadie went to her mother's room, quietly opened the door and looked in. Mother was awake, staring at the mottled ceiling, arms resting at her sides. Sadie tiptoed to the bed, bowed low to plant a dutiful kiss upon her cool brow. Her mother's head, flesh wasted to cords and planes, lay nested among plump white pillows like an offering of withered fruit, the hair wispy and sparse as webs of grey mould. "Bless you," she breathed, and the stench of what Dr. Whaley had diagnosed as "advanced inner putrefaction" was wafted to Sadie's exquisite nostrils. She betrayed no trace of disgust, smiled warmly, arranged the quilt that did not need arranging, smoothing it across her mother's hollow chest.

It was clear Peg Wilkes was dying, but Sadie was not dismayed at the prospect; soon her mother would be raised from her bed of pain and gathered to the arms of Jesus, her rightful place after so much suffering. Sadie believed wholeheartedly in an afterlife, a kingdom of heaven, splendid and serene, a garden in the clouds wherein the virtuous are rewarded for their faith, their sorrows washed away, their earthly torment laid aside with magical ease. There would be a great many tall trees there—unlike Kansas—and the ground would be covered with brightly coloured flowers exuding a fragrance that bordered on the sensual, the perfumes of paradise floating like mist in forest glades, and among the treetops would flit and sing a multitude of small and friendly birds. There would be rabbits, too, and other soft and furry animals, but nothing too large to hold in one's arms and stroke; there would be no cats or dogs or flesh eaters, only those gentle creatures content to graze on herbage. Sadie would sip nectar from the petals of golden blooms, thick, sunwarmed nectar of ambrosial sweetness, and would wander freely among the hills and dales, her silken robe touched by the benign fingers of a scented breeze. With a start she realised she had pictured herself among these sylvan surroundings, rather than her mother. There was something vaguely sinful about her blissful meanderings, a dereliction of duty almost. Mother would join the exalted throng of garden dwellers long before Sadie, that was the thing to concentrate upon. She would soon be there, free of pain, her body made whole, and Sadie would join her after an appropriate passage of years. Strangely, she could not imagine her father in heaven. Perhaps there was another section for men.

The dying woman breathed evenly. Whenever she was not balanced on the sharp edge of pain her body slid into the vale of uneasy dreams, assisted by Dr. Whaley's bottles of laudanum; gathered to the arms of Morpheus, rather than of Jesus, Peg Wilkes sought the scattered isles of relief in her sea of torment. Sadie crept from the room.

No more school; from now on the rectory would be her domain. She went quietly from room to musty room. The furnishings were poor, but Sadie was satisfied; riches and comfort on earth were the surest way to prevent entry to heaven. This family was truly blessed by poverty. She knew there were some folk in town who were poorer, but that was because they were shiftless, not devout. Sadie heard a horse and buggy clopping along the alley beside the house, and went out to assist her father in stabling the mare.

She prepared supper. Wilkes told her of his day. A hired hand on the Tisdale farm had vowed he would become a regular churchgoer if God gave him a winning hand in a tense game of poker last Saturday night. He had won over two hundred dollars and, rather than let him forget his vow, the other hands made him swear in front of the Reverend that he'd be along to church come next Sunday, or the devil'd burn his tail good. As Wilkes put it: "Some join the flock of their own accord, others are directed by false signposts, but arrive safely just the same." Sadie smiled. She knew her father appreciated a response whenever he produced a witticism. He asked if she was glad to have done with school, and Sadie nodded with enthusiasm. He prepared a sermon while she washed and put away the dishes.

Later in the evening Wilkes visited his wife, taking her some rewarmed soup. She was awake, gripped by frightful abdominal spasms, her lips clenched. He quickly set the soup down, poured a large dose of laudanum, prised open her jaws and spooned it into her mouth with one dextrous movement. Within minutes her thrumming pain eased. He bathed her sweating brow. She declined the soup, took his hand in hers; her clutching fingers had the strength of a baby's.

"I want to go soon, Lyman, *soon*. . . . "

"Now, now, you know you mustn't talk that way."

"Why does God let me suffer so . . . ?"

He could think of no reason that truly made sense. God's mysterious ways were unfathomable to man; one had to have faith, or one became bogged in an atheistic mire of unanswerable conundrums and hideous contradictions. All would be revealed at the foot of the throne. Wilkes thought it impolite, to say the least, that his wife should ask such a pointless question; he forgave her, since it was obviously the pain which had prompted her doubt, rather than impiety. But she would not desist. "Why . . . ?" she asked again, and this time he grew annoyed. The smell in the room was awful, invading his nostrils, probing his throat with feathery ticklings, and for one dreadful moment he thought he might vomit. A basin stood handily by the bed; his wife had, in recent weeks, taken to bringing up portions of her interior self. This could not go on. A thought of mercurial swiftness passed through his head, left its message indelibly stamped before he had time to capture and crush it: I wish she was dead and gone. . . . Wilkes was horrified at his own lack of charity; this woman, this scrap of mortifying flesh was his wife! He sank to his knees by the bed, pressed his lips to her limp hand, kissed the sharply indented knuckles, fought off another urge to regurgitate his supper.

"My darling, I pray daily . . . hourly. . . ."

Already she was drifting, drifting, thistledown on the languorous swell of narcosis, borne away on the irresistible tides that surged within a small green bottle.

Wilkes went to the cramped parlour and sat for an hour, brooding. For almost six months he had slept on the uncomfortable settee, unable to endure the nearness of his wife in their bed. He undressed slowly, dazedly, drew a nightshirt over his head, turned and went to Sadie's door. He knocked lightly, turned the handle and entered. His daughter was in bed, reading by lamplight. He noted the title: *The Pilgrim's Progress*. She lowered the book as he approached her bed and sat on its edge, watched as he lowered his head to his hands. "She is much, much worse. The end must surely be near. . . ." Sadie did not move. Wilkes looked up, gazed at her lovely face. Yes, he thought, an angel. He took her hand in his own, infused his heartbroken expression with the nuance of request, a silent beseeching. Still she did not move. Wilkes raised her hand to his mouth, breathed the unique aroma of her skin, felt the pliant softness of her fingers.

Suddenly he fell upon her, his action half lunge, half swoon, and held her to him as a drowning man might clutch a drifting spar. Sadie stiffened. Three times this had happened since her father had taken to sleeping in the parlour, three invasions of her bed and her person, times of crushing weight and relentless physical assault that left her body sore and wet, her face reddened by the scraping of his whiskers. He had told her on each occasion that he must join himself to her or die. Sadie had believed him; she did not want her father to be wasted away by illness as was her mother. She permitted the baffling act to be perpetrated upon her, regarded it as some kind of sacrifice, her body an altar on which a ritual must be performed to stave off Wilkes' death—although this pagan image disturbed her—and had become slightly less confused each time he made known his need for physical conjunction.

But this time was different. In the interval since his last nocturnal visit she had begun to shed the blood of the Lamb from her belly, the very symbol of her oneness with Jesus; her mother had told her many times over that a man would stop that flow, dam her red offerings to Christ, plug the fountain of her sacred outpourings with a bung of mortal flesh and render her imperfect in the eyes of the Lord. Sadie attempted to push her father away, but already he was in the bed beside her, had slid beneath the covers with the urgency of an animal seeking its lair, had raised the hem of her nightdress, was moaning in her ear, pushing at her with his hips, with the rod of his manhood, ignoring her fragile resistance, entering her with a groan. Sadie knew this was very wrong, a flagrant abuse of her soul's temple, but against her father's strength there could be no resistance powerful enough to halt his hoarse grunting into the pillow beside her face, the brutal insistence of his loins. She ceased to struggle, lay as though dead, allowed his chest and belly to thud against her, forcing exhalations from her, interpreted by Wilkes as reciprocal passion, urging him on, spurring him to a paroxysm of spurting seed and strangulated breath.

Wilkes collapsed across his daughter's breast, inhaled the scent of her unbound hair as his body knew the blissful passivity that follows release. He loved his daughter very much; it was she who enabled him to survive, to endure the strain of his wife's decline, to go about his daily tasks with a face betraying nothing of the demons gnawing at him from within. He was aware the community admired him, knew they came to his church out of respect for his worth as a man as much as for their habitual need of reassurance that their lot on earth was temporary, a prelude to the glories beyond. It was Sadie who held the key to his continued deception, Sadie who enabled him to prevail against the suffering that misfortune heaped upon him, and yet Sadie was herself a part of his dilemma. Wilkes believed he had caused the decay of his wife's body with his unrelenting lust, and now that she was no longer available for the easement of his desire, Wilkes had set about polluting the sacred vessel of his own daughter, whose eternal silence was also, he was sure, the result of his concupiscence—had forced upon his own flesh and blood the poisoned kiss of incest. But what else could he do? Sexual longing encroached upon his every conscious thought and restless dream. There were half a dozen wives among his flock who would willingly have succumbed to his masculinity had he been fool enough to make his wants known, but a devious liaison such as that was unthinkable, could never be kept a secret in this place of wagging tongues and watchful eyes. It must be Sadie or no one, and his lust for her, he reminded himself, was tempered with genuine love, which surely exonerated him somewhat. He knew it did not, and his momentary rapture was gone, driven away by guilt. Why did he allow a thirst so quickly slaked to dominate his life? It would be better to have himself made a eunuch, and be able to live in peace with his conscience.

A wetness along his cheek brought itself to his attention. Had his anguish driven him to tears? He raised his head, saw that it was Sadie who cried. He erased the line of her tears with his thumb, fearful that it might be he who had caused this display of sadness. Made gentle by remorse, he withdrew his flaccid penis from Sadie and kissed her damp cheeks with a tenderness that went unnoticed. Sadie felt a great weight of sorrow pressing against her breast, a weight that continued even after her father had clumsily eased his bulk from her and lay like a dead man at her side. He had destroyed the thing that made Jesus love her, crushed it beneath him, oblivious to her mute protest. Now there would be no more blood, and Mother would be furious at the way in which Sadie had thrown away her dowry, allowed herself to be rendered unsuitable as a bride of Christ. She must never know. Sadie would say nothing, was sure her father would also be silent. If only she had a voice, perhaps she could have stopped him, but Mother said her silence was another of God's gifts. It was all horribly confusing.

She stared at the picture of Jesus hanging on the wall beside her bed, lost herself in the limpid eyes, the abundance of soft and waving hair, the demure beard and raised hand, in the palm of which a small scar leaked neat droplets of blood. He was the most beautiful human being the world had ever seen. Sadie engaged in silent conversation with the picture of Jesus every night before turning out her lamp. His eyes gazed directly into her own, and his smile, so faint as to be almost invisible, told her he understood her every problem, and loved her as he loved no other. She stared anxiously at the picture; had the tiny smile disappeared? Was Jesus disappointed at her weakness, her lack of resistance? It wasn't my fault, she implored, but the corners of the smile had definitely turned down. Jesus appeared sad, aggrieved, and it was Sadie's fault. She lacked the temerity or insight to blame Wilkes, and her soul wilted under the stern reprimand of Jesus' eyes.

Wilkes roused himself from the slumber into which he had nearly drifted, kissed Sadie perfunctorily and went to his makeshift bed in the parlour. Sadie examined the picture one last time before surrendering the room to darkness. His face was sorrowful still. She wept freely before falling into an exhausted sleep, her thighs uncomfortably gummed.

CHAPTER TWENTY-SEVEN

Noah had found a retreat for himself, being of an age when a private hideaway becomes paramount among a boy's needs. He discovered it by accident, while engaged in the juvenile pastime of destroying living growth with a stick wielded like a cutlass. He had attacked the edge of the blackberry patch on the ridge's crest, hacking at the tough and thorny stems like some prince cutting a swathe through magical briars to find an enchanted castle and sleeping maid. Tiring of the effort required to inflict even a modicum of damage to the hardy bush, Noah contented himself with wandering along its periphery, prodding at the dreary foliage in frustration. At the southern end he saw a rabbit dash from the thicket and go scampering off into the trees with white scut bobbing. Noah examined the area from which it had emerged, and saw an opening among the general tangle and overhang of vines. With his stick he lifted aside the nearer stems and saw that the opening extended back into the heart of the blackberry bush, a miniature tunnel terminating in darkness.

He could not resist. On hands and knees he crawled inside. Its width barely accommodated his narrow shoulders, and several times he was obliged to fend off stray tendrils threatening to rake his face and hands. The tunnel had been made by something larger than rabbits, but he could detect no animal odour, was therefore not afraid of encountering fang and claw at its end. What Noah found was without doubt a lair of some kind, a natural open space deep within the thicket, perhaps six feet across and four high. Blackberry vines grow in arcs, and the walls of this bower were gracefully curved, laden with thorny deterrents to rearrangement. It was an igloo of brambles, and Noah was delighted to have found it. The earth floor was studded, he saw by the green light filtering through from the outside world, with what appeared to be black nuggets; these crumbled when extracted and subjected to pressure, and he identified them as chunks of charcoal. This was, he reminded himself, the site of the famous burning, the one his schoolfriends assured him had been ignited by Joe Cobden. Noah had remonstrated with them, tried to explain Joe's non-vindictive nature, but had changed nothing by his efforts. The Church of the White Wolf had passed into legend, and the story of its rise and fall could no longer be tampered with, especially by someone who had not even been born at the time. Pellets of dung scattered at random testified to casual occupancy by rabbits. Noah was having none of that; this was his place now, and any rabbit venturing into his domain would be in for a big surprise. Joe had taught him how to set up a rabbit-snare, and Noah decided he would plant one just inside the entrance. This place would be his secret. He would not even tell Joe.

On his way out Noah saw something his eyes, moving from brightness to darkness, had not seen on the way in. At arm's reach from the tunnel wall, entwined with bramble stems, was a dully shining object. He knew immediately what it must be—the church's brass bell—and poked at it with his stick. He found it could be reached at the cost of a few scratches, but remained firmly in the barbed embrace of its resting-place. He would cut it free with a knife on his next visit.

The Reverend Dr. Lyman Wilkes buried his wife late in October. He had chosen a coffin at Mr. Middleton's undertaking establishment, the cheapest model of all, a raw pine box speckled with knotholes, had then been struck by guilt, changed his mind and spent money he could ill afford on Mr. Middleton's most expensive casket, a polished behemoth of fine cedar, with nickel-plated handles. The graveyard at the south-eastern corner of Valley Forge was thronged with mourners. They came not because Peg Wilkes had been much beloved—she had never truly become a part of the community—but because her husband was universally respected; his flock came to offer their condolences, and the area outside the cemetery's picket fence was thick with wagons and buggies and teams. Everyone agreed Sadie looked like something out of a picture book with her perfect face, white as chalk, framed in a bonnet of black. Her father read the eulogy, praising his wife's virtues, notable among them being her forbearance under constant pain. His fine speaking voice cracked halfway through with emotion. There were tears in his eyes as he closed his Bible and uttered a hoarse Amen. Sadie threw a posy of asters into the open grave. Heavy clods of Kansas earth thudded against the coffin lid, spattering the asters with soil. Sadie thought the sound reminiscent of someone knocking drunkenly at a door, an irregular thumping, solid and insistent, yet somehow not hopeful of gaining entry. Gaps between the coffin and the grave walls were quickly filled, the flowers swallowed, the lid sinking beneath a rising tide of earth.

The mourners began making their goodbyes to the grieving widower, delivered brief messages of hope and perseverance, all sincere. Sadie watched until the grave had been transformed into an oblong mound, patted into shape with shovels, a neat job. She continued to stare at it until the last of the mourners had driven away. Wilkes approached her, laid a consoling hand on her shoulder. She pushed it away impatiently, as she would an over-friendly cat, stared at the burial mound, at the wooden marker with its two lines of biography and plaintive epitaph: *She Shall Be Newly Risen.* Sadie knew her mother was already among the forests of heaven, tiny birds circling her head, alighting on her shoulders and arms.

"We must go home now."

She followed him back to the rectory, stepping in his bootmarks across muddy ground, two figures in black beneath a grey and lowering sky.

He came to her nightly now, to hold her and drain himself into her belly. Her bed was narrow, and when he was done he would return to his own room, occupy the bed so recently vacated by his wife. Sadie's eyes, her most startling feature, dimmed slowly but steadily, lost the light of intelligence and awareness, became somehow flat and opaque. Her movements were sluggish, her response to questions a blank stare. The town, Wilkes included, supposed she was still in mourning for her mother, had no idea Sadie mourned the loss of her blood-ties with Jesus. She had known it would happen if her father persisted in lying on her; her mother had told her so, and had been proven right. No more blood came from Sadie, and in her sorrow she became ill. Over Christmas and the New Year the lustre of her eyes grew ever more dim, like guttering candles. She spent much of her time lying on her bed, gazing at Jesus, begging him for guidance. The noble face offered neither encouragement nor forgiveness. His brow had darkened with the subtlest of frowns, indicating his disapproval of Sadie's weakness. Jesus' favour had been withdrawn, as it would be from any sinner who had cast away the badge of blessedness. He gave no second chances. His raised hand no longer offered the proof of his sacrifice, but was lifted to bar Sadie's entry to paradise. Her misery was profound, a cloak wrapped thrice around herself, cocooning her from all hope, its folds stiffening by the hour. Wilkes was himself in despair over her haggard appearance and listlessness. He spent more time with her after intercourse, holding her in his arms, covering her unresponsive lips with kisses. Her silence, a lifelong thing, was now absolute; even her eyes had ceased to speak. He considered taking her to Dr. Whaley, but that man was associated in Wilkes' mind with pain and suffering, with lingering death; he could not expose his beloved Sadie to such malign influence. In his anguish Wilkes truly believed the doctor would transform whatever ailed Sadie into a concrete disease; left alone, there was always the possibility she would recover. He did nothing but pray for her, and his daughter drifted further from reality's shore.

On a morning in January, a morning of bitter cold, Sadie awoke to the sound of her name. The voice was her mother's, and came from the yard. Sadie rushed to the window. Snow had fallen in the night, had been coated with glittering transparency by freezing rain in the hours before dawn. Her mother was calling to her from beyond the stable. Sadie hurried into her warmest clothing, laced up her boots and tied her bonnet, all with movements so fleet anyone who had observed her in recent weeks would have been greatly surprised. She crept from the house, anxious not to awaken her father; Mother would not want him around when they met. She floundered through snow at least one foot deep, its crust frozen and slippery, crunching underfoot, rounded the corner of the house and arrived behind the stable. Her mother was not there, but her voice came to Sadie with the crispness of winter air from further down the alley, and Sadie followed it from alley to street, from that street to another, and so to the edge of town. Few saw her at this early hour, and Sadie noticed no one, had eyes only for what eyes could not see, followed the bidding of her numbed ears and began walking along the road west, away from Valley Forge. There was little cover for her mother to hide behind, but still she did not appear, and Sadie grew afraid, felt she might be the victim of trickery. But the voice was her mother's, of that she was sure, and Sadie maintained her dogged and graceless stumbling through the snow in pursuit of it.

Understanding came when the ceiling of grey cloud was lanced briefly by a cluster of sunbeams; for one moment these slanting blades of light stabbed at the earth, and their target was the ridge. Sadie watched them strike diamond sparks from ice-laden boughs, saw the ridge transformed instantly from featureless snowy hump to splendid jewel embedded in the broad belly of the land. Sadie knew unquestioningly that this place was her destination. She did not need the voice now, hurried as best she could along the road, turned on to the ridge trail and floundered upward through an avenue of trees. The voice returned, drew her away from the trail, deep into the silent stands of blackjack and cottonwood, their every branch and twig hung with snow, sheathed in ice, a crystalline forest, the voice echoing faintly, alluringly among its thousand frozen sentinels.

She wandered among them as the clouds folded back upon themselves and released a flood of sunlight over the ridge, dazzling Sadie with reflected shimmerings and whiteness. Ice on the trees began melting within minutes, punctuating the silence with watery patterings. Slender rods of ice dropped from twigs, so fragile they shattered on impact with snow; the boughs and trunks began releasing pipes and curves of ice, a host of weary knights shedding brittle greaves and breastplates.

Sadie fell at last, her vaporous breath exhausted. Her mittened hands sank beneath the snow, and welcome coolness numbed her cheek. The voice had departed, leaving a tinkling silence in its wake. Sadie felt herself slipping away, merging with a dream, was beckoned to by her father, a distant figure in black, his words lost in the vast white plain between them, and still further off was another figure, her mother, silently lifting her arm, not to beckon but to point heavenward, and when Sadie looked up she saw the face of Jesus spread across the sky, and knew the snowy plain on which she stood was the open palm of Jesus Christ. In its centre there now opened a canyon of red, a yawning stigmata stretching to the very feet of her father, drawing him irresistibly to its edge, threatening to swallow him, suck him down into its crimson depths; but now the plain was tilting, tilting until almost perpendicular, and Sadie toppled from unimaginable heights, down, down through layers of churning cloud, down to a landscape brushed with white, down to a ridge of frozen trees and into the familiar envelope of her body.

She jerked with galvanic suddenness, found herself staring at the dark root of an elm. Where was she? Shivering, she raised herself and looked about her. She had come to the place of trees, the ridge. Why? Frightened, bitten to the bone by cold, Sadie stood and began to walk. She did not retrace her steps, wandered aimlessly, looking not at the ground but at the network of stripped boughs above, at the intricate tracery of their meshing, tree with tree. The sun had gone. Now the crest of the ridge was a gloomy place, and Sadie quickened her step. Although her fingers and toes were numbed beyond feeling she could sense heat radiating from her face, and the scalp beneath her bonnet crawled with sweat. In the pit of her stomach small animals squirmed and fought for scraps of food—no, they were squabbling over something else, something they hid when once they realised she was watching, small and naked mole-like creatures with blind eyes, repulsive, hiding their secret, coated in slime. Sadie fell to her knees and vomited, her stomach heaving, the convulsions so strong she was jerked forward several inches. The sight and odour of her discharge set her heaving again, and Sadie crawled away to find cleaner air. She felt very ill indeed, and wondered if perhaps she was dying.

Something pricked her palm right through the mitten; she had almost crawled into a snow-covered blackberry thicket. Sadie had heard of this place, knew thorn bushes now grew where a church had burned down. Noah Puckett's house would not be far from here. She regained her feet, wondered in which direction the house lay. She could not choose, felt her resolve dwindling, leaving her body while she stood there undecided. Which way? A sound reached her burning ears—a gunshot? It came again, sharp and clear, a faint echo trailing after. And again. An axe! The echo deceived her for a short while, but soon the axe strokes became more distinct as she neared their source. Now Sadie could smell woodsmoke, and a moment later stepped into the clearing in which sat the Puckett home. Joe Cobden was chopping wood in the yard. She watched him set a thick chunk upon the block, raise his axe and split it with one blow. He resembled a picture she had seen once in a book of fairy-tales, a monstrous thing, an ogre. The ogre split both halves of wood into quarters. The ground around the block was littered with wood chips, and nearby was a stack of kindling. The ogre halted in his labours, turned his head a little. Had he scented her? He had, and was turning fully around, a quizzical expression on his bestial features. Sadie was not afraid, although she knew ogres ate children for breakfast. The ogre smiled grotesquely, revealing yellow fangs in its whiskered face; the long hair falling across its forehead was dark and tangled, strands covering the eyes set deep into its skull. It sank the axehead lightly into the block and came toward her, smiling still. Sadie felt no fear. I must be very sick, she thought, not to be scared. She looked beyond the ogre to the house, wondering where Noah Puckett was, then found her eyes drawn to the roof, and the sky beyond. Before Joe could reach her, Sadie Wilkes collapsed in the snow.

Noah was dispatched on foot to town, his mission to alert Reverend Wilkes and bring him back. He was thrilled to be chosen as messenger of possible doom, and flung himself into the task with gusto. Joe brought Sadie inside and set her down on the floor before the fireplace, hoped its crackling heat would help restore blood to her dangerously chilled extremities. Calvin chafed her hands while Joe attended to her feet. Sadie's breath was shallow, her parted lips pale. Joe noted the flecks of frozen vomit on her sleeves.

"She goin' to die?" Calvin quavered, made nervous by the look of concentration on Joe's face.

"Maybe not. Keep working."

Blood was encouraged back to her fingers and toes after half an hour of vigorous effort. Both men rested once it became clear she would not suffer frostbite. It had been a close thing, and Joe barely had time to wonder what Sadie was doing up here on the ridge before her body began to convulse and buck, despite her apparent unconsciousness.

"What's she doin' now . . . ?"

Joe attempted to hold her midriff down, but her spine would not stay on the floor; her body flexed and arched, and Joe, attempting to hold her down, feeling the plumpness of her belly beneath his fingers, suddenly knew what was about to transpire. "She's going to have a baby. . . . Get some water on the stove and boil it up! And bring the spare sheets from upstairs! Quick!"

Calvin hastened from the room. Now what? thought Joe, unsure whether to hold her down or let her body dictate its own requirements. He could hear Calvin in the kitchen clanging a full kettle on to the stove, then racing into the hall, clumping up the stairs two at a time. And still Sadie's eyes were closed. Could she feel no pain? Joe understood childbirth to be a hurtful business. What was he supposed to do? Nature took the problem from his hands; before Calvin had time to descend the stairs with a cascading armful of sheets the muscles of Sadie's belly pushed from her a slithering foetus. Joe heard the faint sound of its emergence, felt her muscles slacken. He lifted the skirt away from her flooded thighs, hesitated, pulled down the thick woollen undergarments, saw the half-formed thing nestled there among wrinkled cordage: an embryonic human, head, torso and limbs all present, eyes, nose and mouth etched on the swollen head. Joe lifted it carefully. "Get a knife," he said, and Calvin scampered away. Joe looked at Sadie Wilkes' premature child, barely a handful, quite dead. It would have been a girl.

Soon after, Wilkes' buggy drew up outside; with him were Noah and Dr. Whaley. Noah led both men indoors, still excited at the importance of his role. To his annoyance, Joe sent him straight out again.

"But I want to see what happens . . ." he whined, and was turned and given a push by Joe.

"Well, you can't. Make a snowman or something."

Sadie lay in Joe's bed, eyes closed, her face pale. Wilkes was aghast. "Where are her clothes?"

"By the fire. They're wet."

"You did not have the right to remove my daughter's clothing!" His voice was building to a stentorian timbre worthy of the pulpit, his face, reddened by cold, infused now with anger. "What in heaven's name made you think you had the right to do such a thing!"

"Wilkes," said Joe evenly, "your daughter just had a baby. There was a mess you wouldn't want to see a dog in. We cleaned her off. She won't even remember it. The baby's dead," he added.

Wilkes' gusty outrage died somewhere between diaphragm and teeth. "A baby. . . ."

"Almost a baby." He turned to Dr. Whaley. "It's in the kitchen if you want to see it."

"Presently," said the doctor, and bent to roll back Sadie's eyelids. "Has she been frostbitten?"

"We got to it just in time."

"She was all froze up," said Calvin.

The doctor pulled back the quilt, lifted the nightshirt Joe had slipped over Sadie's limp body, examined her genitals. "You attended to the cord?"

"Yes."

Sadie was covered again. Wilkes was furious with the doctor for having exposed his daughter's naked thighs in front of the hunchback and Calvin Puckett. Dr. Whaley went to the kitchen. Wilkes did not accompany him. "I should like to be alone with my daughter," he said. Joe and Calvin went to stand with their backs to the fire in the living room. Dr. Whaley joined them there.

"Mr. Puckett," he said, "would you do me a kindness and dispose of the foetus?"

Calvin looked at Joe.

"Bury the baby," Joe translated. "Use the back door so Noah doesn't see you. Take it a long way from the house."

Calvin went to the kitchen. The thing was wrapped in

burlap, for which he was grateful. He had seen no resemblance to a person; it looked more like some kind of frog. He took it away to do as Joe said.

"About six months along, I'd say," said Dr. Whaley.

"I could see it wasn't ready."

"You did a fine job, under the circumstances."

"Think she'll come out of it?"

"Probably. She's very young, basically healthy."

The doctor knew Joe Cobden did not like him, knew it was because he had considered Noah subnormal during the boy's years of silence. He had obviously been wrong, but did not care to raise the subject. Neither man broached the issue of the foetus' paternity. Conversation languished until Wilkes marched stiffly into the room.

"She must be taken home," he announced.

"That is not advisable," said Dr. Whaley. "Moving her without good cause will only aggravate her weakness. A day or two spent where she is will do more good than harm."

"I insist that she return home with me."

"The buggy is yours, Reverend, and so is your daughter. If you wish to put the two together and risk her health, I have no legal means of stopping you. If, however, she pays any kind of price for your foolishness, I'm sure it will be no secret around town whose fault it was."

Wilkes glared at him. Joe was impressed by the easy manner with which the doctor had his way. Wilkes turned to the fire, furious; he had expected to find in Whaley his ally, not his adversary. He did not enjoy being contradicted in front of hunchbacked Joe Cobden. At least the moron was not present. He was shocked to find himself regarding his daughter's saviours in these terms, far removed from the concept of everyday gratitude, let alone Christian charity.

"Very well," he conceded, "but I shall stay here with her."

"That is between yourself and Mr. Cobden."

"No objections," said Joe, who had plenty. He knew

Wilkes was regarded with extreme favour by the community at large, especially since the death of his wife, but Joe
could not warm to him. Wilkes had done nothing wrong
that Joe knew of, and his bad grace at the moment could
logically be attributed to concern for Sadie, but somehow
Joe did not like the man, wondered if perhaps he was jealous of Wilkes' broad shoulders and imposing height, the
manly thrust of his jaw, as he had secretly been jealous of
Peter Winstanley's physical beauty. But, no, that kind of
muddled thinking was long behind him. He disliked Wilkes
for no apparent reason, rejected him as a dog will sometimes reject by instinct a stranger with whose history and
habits it is unacquainted.

The doctor was driven back to town. Wilkes returned to
the ridge with clothing taken from Sadie's closet. The afternoon was well advanced by that time. "If I may be
allowed, I'll set up a chair in the room with my daughter,
and sleep on that."

"You're welcome to the settee."

"Thank you, no. A chair will suffice." Wilkes hoped
never again to sleep on a settee, his own or anyone else's.

Noah was allowed back into the house once the dead
infant had been disposed of. He was told Sadie was suffering from nothing more debilitating than exposure. He was
annoyed at Joe for having shut him out over something so
trifling, and eager to impress Wilkes, a new audience for
his cleverness. Throughout a rather strained supper Noah
performed diligently, encountered hostility and indifference. At first grateful to him for relieving the general awkwardness with his disgraceful showing off, Joe finally had
to cap his enthusiasm with a terse order to be quiet and
eat. Noah hated him for that. Noah had in recent weeks
found several reasons for resenting Joe's authority, trivial
incidents in the grand scheme of things, but to an eight-
year-old the very essence of tyranny—and Joe wasn't even
his father! He favoured Joe with a scowl to express his
grievance. Joe ignored him. Calvin wished Joe hadn't shut
Noah up; the boy was a treat to watch sometimes, mim-

icking his schoolteacher—"No, no, no! We do not say *ain't*,
Tyler Grier, we say *is not*. Do you wish to be an ignoramus
all your life?" Another voice: "I *ain't* ignorant." And he
told some pretty good jokes, too: "What did the farmer
say when he saw three holes in the ground? Give up? Well,
well, well." He was a clever boy all right, maybe even
smarter than his old man. Calvin was proud of him. The
supper was concluded in silence.

When Noah and his father had retired to bed, Wilkes
and Joe sat by the fire in a parody of conviviality, Calvin's
decrepit old dog slumbering between them. The subject of
Sadie's baby squatted behind them in the darkness like
some uninvited and unsavoury guest whose presence would
eventually have to be acknowledged. Wilkes, undoubtedly
in Joe's debt, felt it incumbent upon himself to speak first.

"This has come as a great shock to me," he said, and
he did not lie.

"I suppose it would to any father," said Joe politely.

"I cannot imagine who is responsible. Since the passing
of my wife, even before that time, my daughter has been
solely occupied with tending to her domestic duties. Or so
I thought. Someone has taken advantage of her during the
hours I spend on my rounds. But who would do such a
thing to a defenceless girl, a mute? God in heaven, there
are beasts in human form among us, Mr. Cobden. Who
could it have been? Surely no one in Valley Forge would
be so heartless. Do you think it possible some tramp or
drifter came to the door asking for food and . . . seized the
opportunity? Itinerants are known for their low character."

"As a long-time tramp and drifter myself, I can't agree.
A home and a job don't confer sainthood on anyone."

"I meant no offence, of course. I simply wish to understand the facts of the incident. It must not be allowed to
rest here."

"Here's exactly where it should rest, unless you want
the whole town to know your daughter was pregnant to
some unknown man, if he *was* unknown."

"Are you suggesting she *allowed* this to occur?"

"I'm suggesting it didn't happen in your front yard. You say she's never away from home, so that's where it happened, inside, and she probably let him in because she knew him. Once the door was closed he probably went ahead and . . . seduced her. She wouldn't have let a stranger indoors, not if you've taught her your opinion of tramps and drifters."

Wilkes swallowed the insult as part of his penance. He knew he was the father of the nameless thing now buried somewhere among the trees, yet a part of him, a growing part, clung to the scenario offered by Joe; he *wanted* to believe the perpetrator was another, flayed his mind to discover who, *who* among the men of Valley Forge could possibly have been responsible for this hideous crime against a girl of tender years. Wilkes clenched his fists as though to strike the anonymous rapist, smite him in righteous wrath. He seemed close to tears as he considered his helplessness in the face of such insidious evil, while the other part of himself, knowingly guilty and frightened, watched his display of parental outrage with the impartiality of a drama critic. He knew he had convinced Joe Cobden with his performance, despite the hunchback's personal antagonism toward him; it was a role he felt he could sustain for the few days he was obliged to spend in this house. Neither of the dual selves jostling inside him questioned for one moment the need to avoid detection and punishment, nor doubted the rightness of Wilkes' hypocrisy. The twin gods of self-interest and self-deception, thus propitiated, achieved equilibrium. Wilkes was to be their slave for ever, need give no public obeisance, but must always be in their thrall—and in return they would grant him immunity from disgrace. The twin gods persuaded Wilkes it was a bargain. It did not once occur to him that Sadie might betray the identity of her seducer. Why would she? He was her father, when all was said and done.

Minister and hunchback watched as faces and forms

were kindled and destroyed among the pulsing redness of the coals, Wilkes directing his steps around a sinister corner, to tread hereafter the dark side of his particular street, Joe deriving ironic satisfaction from the presence in his bed, at long last, of a female; the situation was not without humour.

Wilkes slept in a comfortable armchair with a footstool to support his legs and a blanket around him, six feet from Sadie. He spent all the next day at her side, feeding her, reading to her (he was surprised at the Puckett library's extent) and simply holding her hand. Joe told Calvin and Noah to leave them alone. At the first opportunity (while Joe was out in the yard) Noah knocked at the door of the sickroom and entered. Wilkes looked up with annoyance; he did not like this weasel-faced boy with his deplorable manners and insistence on attention.

"Is she all right?" asked Noah, approaching the bed.

"She is much better."

"She must have come to see me."

"I beg your pardon?"

"That must be why she was up here in the first place."

"And how did you make her acquaintance?"

"At school."

"My daughter has not attended school since May."

Noah knew Sadie Wilkes had left school the very day he had begun, but this did not deter him from believing she had come to visit him. Noah thought himself highly regarded from one side of town to the other. If Wilkes couldn't see the logic of it, that was Wilkes' fault. Noah thought grown-ups the most stupid and obtuse things in all creation. Even Joe, whom he admitted was pretty smart, often let Noah down by making him do things he didn't want to do, by excluding him from places he wanted to be. Take yesterday—Joe had picked him to run for help, which showed he trusted Noah to get the job done, and what happened when he got back? He was shown the door, that's what. No, he couldn't come in and see what the grown-ups saw, know what they knew. Build a snowman,

Joe had said, and don't bother us. It was infuriating. When Noah was a grown-up himself he would make anyone who had ever insulted his intelligence cringe and grovel before him and beg forgiveness, which, after glorying in their humiliation for a while, he would grant. Noah looked forward to that; it was one of the main incentives to hurry up and grow old. When he was well and truly old—say around twenty—there would be nothing he would not have done or seen, and everyone would like and respect him. He would probably let Sadie Wilkes marry him if she was still pretty enough. It was a shame she couldn't talk, though. How was she going to tell him she thought him the bravest and most worthy of men? He supposed she would write it down on paper.

"Is she going back to school?"

"Sadie will be performing the duties of a woman at home. She has recently lost her mother."

"I know. Joe said Mrs. Wilkes was better off dead, being sick like that."

"Did he, indeed?"

"I haven't got a mother, either."

"I am aware of that," said Wilkes, checking his impatience.

"She ran off. No one knows where she is."

When confronted with this uncomfortable fact at school, Noah had wisely adopted an affirmative rather than a defensive stance, had even gone so far as to suggest that his mother had fled the ridge because everyone on it was peculiar-looking, himself included. The other boys had been astounded at his candour, knew it was pointless taunting someone who agreed with them, and so accepted him among their disreputable ranks. The girls, of course, thought him loathsome, but this was their usual opinion of any male their own age. In his heart Noah knew his mother had done a terrible thing, running off that way, and he secretly believed it must have been something he himself had done that caused her abrupt departure. He had known for years now. He sometimes wondered if that was why he had not learned to speak until late, and even then had held his tongue until the night Calvin had thrown his supper at the wall and been yelled at by Joe until he cleaned it up. Maybe he had somehow thought that if he stayed quiet his mother would come back. But was a little kid like he'd been at the time capable of that kind of reasoning? Noah could not remember what it felt like to be himself just a few years ago; his former self was a stranger to him. It was as though awareness extended only a little way into the past, and a long way into the future. He had been a different boy back then, would be another boy entirely a few years from now. Noah understood and accepted the concept of transition without ever having heard the word.

He leaned closer to Sadie, who was awake. "I went for help," he told her. "You would have had your fingers and toes drop off if I hadn't done it."

She knew the boy before her was Noah Puckett. Father had told her she was in the Puckett home, and had been ill. Beyond these few facts she knew nothing, and was not concerned with learning more. She wished Noah would go away; his voice was loud, his staring intrusive. She closed her eyes.

"Perhaps we should leave Sadie alone," suggested Wilkes. "She's very tired."

"All right."

Noah went to the door, waited for Wilkes to follow, saw that the "we" had been formal, rather than accurate. He left Wilkes sitting by the bed, was insulted by the feeble trickery employed to get rid of him. Wilkes would have to grovel more than most before Noah would forgive him.

He went outside, helped Joe stack wood for a while (Joe's idea, not Noah's) then wandered off among the trees. That was where he saw the tracks, two deep sets of bootprints in the snow. He followed them, scenting a mystery. Why would Joe and Calvin have come out here? The tracks halted by a tree. Either the two men had sprouted wings and flown away, or just one man had come this far,

stopped, and turned back. The snow was disturbed—
something had been buried here. Noah scraped away the
snow and soil with mittened hands, found the burlap bundle, unwrapped it and saw its pathetic contents. He was
both fascinated and repulsed. Look at the tiny fingers and
toes, the creased eyelids, the tiny nubbin of nose and little
fish-like mouth. Noah knew a baby when he saw one, although this was the first he had ever touched, certainly the
first dead one. It was cold, the flesh frozen. The story was
plain. Sadie Wilkes had had a baby, and it had died, and
everyone thought it was so sad they didn't want Noah,
who wasn't a grown-up, to know about it. Did they think
he'd bawl his eyes out or something? They really were a
stupid bunch. Well, he'd found out their secret, simple as
ABC, and to consolidate his new-found power over the
stupid grown-ups Noah did not rebury the baby where
Calvin had left it, but took it instead to the blackberry
patch, pushed the bundle ahead of him through the thorny
tunnel to the briar igloo within. In the centre of this natural dome sat the brass bell, rescued and placed here by
Noah, its sides smeared by the heat of long ago. He moved
it aside, set to work with his case knife and soon had a
hole of respectable depth gouged in the cold earth. He laid
the bundle to rest there, shoved soil back over it. The resultant mound was covered by the bell, restored to its central place of honour. There! He did not know exactly why
he had done this, but was glad he had. Somehow it made
him smarter than anyone else. Then he went and did as
he had been told to do yesterday—he built a snowman.

Sadie was taken home the following afternoon. Noah
was sorry to see her go, in a way, but consoled himself
with the knowledge that she had left a part of herself at the
ridge. He liked to imagine that she knew he knew; it was
an unspoken secret between them, one more thing to be
kept hidden from the adult world. For several weeks after
Sadie's departure Noah held conversations with her inside
his head. As in real life, she did not speak, simply smiled
warmly and nodded every now and then. She understood

him perfectly. He did not visit her at the rectory, fearing this might bring his fantasy crashing down. Eventually he ceased to converse with her remembered image, which had begun to blur and fade. He felt himself poorer for its loss, and for some time thereafter conducted himself in a manner described by Joe as being "like a bear with a pine cone up its ass". Noah did not find this funny. He was finding very little to laugh about these days.

A year after the death of his wife, the Reverend Dr. Lyman Wilkes married eighteen-year-old Mary Raffin, daughter of a local farmer, and swiftly impregnated her.

CHAPTER TWENTY-EIGHT

In 1884, Nathan Bragg informed Calvin he now had a grand total of forty-one dollars and nineteen cents remaining in his account. A week later Calvin guiltily told Joe, who went to the Farmers' Bank for corroboration. It was given. Bragg took pleasure in delivering the news; the twenty thousand dollars he had stolen from Calvin Puckett had not become the basis for a larger fortune as planned. He had invested the money in the east, and his investments had foundered disastrously. He was no worse off financially than on the day Calvin had entered his office, had in fact prospered on the legitimate side; but the stolen money had been earmarked for glorious expansion, a means to a more prestigious end, and events had drained the cash from Bragg's pockets with a suddenness that left him trembling with bewilderment and fury. Now, many years after his own loss, it was gratifying to witness the final trickling away of the wealth he had allowed Puckett to retain. Bragg knew it was foolish to blame Calvin for his deplorable judgement regarding the secret investments, but blame him he did. Now they were even.

Joe returned to the ridge. For eight years he had not worked for a living. During the first six of those years he had Noah to build a life around, but since the boy had begun his regular schooling it left Joe with the greater part of each day in which to do precisely nothing. His belly was creased with fat, and he was not yet thirty years old. Consultation with Calvin was pointless; Calvin's solution to the problem would be to wring his hands and shake his foolish head and look to Joe for guidance. Joe would have to get a job in Valley Forge, and it made him angry. The residents of the ridge were unique in the county, hopeless misfits all—well, perhaps not the boy, who had yet to prove himself worthy of this epithet—and were granted that special treatment accorded only to the truly unacceptable. Joe was perversely proud of his role as social leper, and did not relish the idea of humbling himself by asking for employment. He thought hard, seeking alternatives to the looming shadow of wage work. What could he do, what talents did he possess that could be made profitable? He could bounce rowdies out of a brothel, and he could shoot buffalo; neither ability was in demand hereabouts, the local brothel being a discreetly run business which operated strictly for the benefit of a regular clientele (one required recommendation from a known customer to gain access) and the buffalo long gone, the last of the herds eking out a huddled existence on the open plains of Canada.

Was there a commodity here on the ridge which could be commercially exploited? There were only the trees. Everyone in town bought their lumber and firewood at McGruder's woodyard down by the A, T & SF tracks. McGruder shipped his timber in from Minnesota by the flatcar load, and was a wealthy man, having secured a virtual monopoly on the wood trade after buying out a rival woodyard several years ago. McGruder was also a councilman, and prevented any other merchant establishing a similar business by the simple expedient of withholding his approval of a trading licence. He charged what he liked for his timber, but was not foolish enough to overstep the boundaries of prudence; people bought from him because they must, but he took care not to beggar them in the process. Joe had never had recourse to McGruder's yard for firewood; the ridge was littered with dead trees and boughs split from trunks by ice storms and wind. The house had never suffered for want of fuel for fireplace or stove, and there was plenty left over. Joe took a brisk walk along the ridge, took note of the abundance of suitable wood, confirmed what he already knew—the solution to insolvency lay under their noses!

He began work immediately, used his team—venerable beasts now, grown unused to work—to drag a fallen tree from its resting-place to the yard in front of the house, where he proceeded to chop a quarter of it before dusk. Over supper he told Noah and Calvin of his plan. Calvin allowed it was real smart thinkin', but Noah expressed no interest in the project whatever. Undismayed, Joe had a wagonload of split wood ready by noon the next day, and drove it to town. He stopped half a block down the street from McGruder's yard and hung a hand lettered sign from the seat: *Firewood—entire wagonload $10!* This was half McGruder's price for a like amount. He waited only a short while before making a sale to Andolini the barber, whose robust wife was in the process of opening a restaurant on Decatur—the Vesuvius, it was to be called—and the kitchen fires would require vast amounts of kindling. Joe made a verbal contract there and then with Andolini for at least two wagonloads per month. He stacked the load behind the restaurant-to-be and drove home in triumph.

Thereafter, he poured his energies into woodcutting, and never failed to find a customer for each load, usually within the hour. It was impossible for Joe's curbside dealings seriously to affect the profits of the timber yard, but McGruder did not take kindly to competition in his chosen field, no matter how small. He enlisted the reluctant aid of Ned Bowdre to press home his complaint, and together these two confronted Joe seconds after another successful sale.

"There, you see?" trumpeted McGruder, pointing to the cash in Joe's hand. "Do your duty, Sheriff!" A small man, he pranced about under Ned's nose like a frenzied and very foolish dog attempting to elicit reaction from a bull.

Ned nodded at Joe, whom he quietly admired for his intelligence and his indifference to the general need for public approbation. "Got yourself a nice little business here," he said.

"Nice enough," said Joe, who had conceived a grudging regard for the sheriff over the years.

"Mr. McGruder says you're breaking the law."

"What law's that?"

"The retail marketing law," interjected McGruder. "Have you got a licence to trade within the city limits? No, you haven't, so you better quit right now or get taken into custody for violation of the law."

Joe regarded McGruder's reddened face with equanimity, even gave him a smile, turned to Ned Bowdre. "Where's the city limit, Sheriff?"

"Oh, I'd say around two hundred yards past Henneker's livery stable."

"Thank you."

He drove off. Next day he stopped the wagon two hundred and five yards from the edge of town. Word of the conflict between Joe and McGruder had already circulated through excitement-starved Valley Forge, and quite a crowd went out to buy wood and place orders and see what would transpire. Disappointingly, McGruder's hands were tied; Joe was operating outside the law's jurisdiction, and so long as money was exchanged for wood at least two hundred yards from town there was no legal recourse with which to thwart him. Once Joe had pocketed the cash he was free to enter the town for the humble and non-profitmaking chore of delivery. McGruder fumed, pored over state lawbooks pertaining to trade practices, but could not fault Joe's business method. There were many citizens who enjoyed witnessing McGruder's impotence, and deliberately turned from him to infuriate the man even more. Riding the crest of a popular wave, Joe was given more orders than he could handle, and the jagged star of commercial transaction rose brightly above the ridge.

Calvin was recruited to help stack wood in the wagon, and to offload it at the buyers' back doors. There was a slump in business during the summer, when fuel was required only for cooking, and the pause gave Joe time to consider a problem facing him as a direct outcome of his success; almost all the fallen timber had been cleared from the ridge now, and he was faced with the necessity of felling live trees if the business was to continue. He did not wish to strip the ridge as Lucius Croft had set out to do a quarter-century before. He counted the number of trees within a measured square, twenty yards to a side, calculated how many wagonloads could be had from each tree, and found that a margin for selective felling existed which could maintain the business without unduly affecting the ridge's dense growth, at least for the forseeable future. He simply had to choose trees at widely spaced intervals, and thus avoid the gradual creation of an eyesore. Joe felt good. He rose early, worked hard felling, dragging, sectioning with a crosscut saw—Calvin at one end, himself at the other—splitting, loading, selling and delivering. He fell into his bed at night exhausted, and slept the sleep of the just.

There was an unsought-after consequence of all this: Joe became casually acquainted with many in the town who previously had known him only by sight and by repute. To their astonishment they found him courteous, well spoken and reliable, not the grunting brute his appearance suggested. He had lived on the ridge for eight years, and only now was he beginning to be accepted as a legitimate resident. The consensus of opinion whittled the proportion of Joe's Indian blood from one half to one quarter—he couldn't be a true half-breed, not with that pleasant manner—it must be the hunched back and long hair that created an impression of savagery, the ridged brow and heavy, underslung jaw that made one think of a surly ape. He was three-quarters white, by God, and deserving of sympathy on account of his ugliness. Why, that Calvin Puckett would have been carted away years ago if not for the way Joe Cobden ran things up on the ridge, and the boy would have run wild too, instead of being the smartest pupil in school. According to Miss Woodcock, who had experienced a change of heart and now saw in Noah the reward for her long and thankless years as a schoolteacher, the boy would go far, possibly even to one of the east's finer colleges (if a generous sponsor could be found) and was the kind of young man who would bring credit to his hometown, take the names of Valley Forge and Miss Woodcock out into the vastness of the world. Yes, indeed, there were folks beholden to Joe Cobden, and not just because he kept stoves and fireplaces filled at a reasonable price.

During the time Joe's business began truly to thrive, Mr. Middleton the undertaker fell prey to pneumonia, and was laid to rest in one of his own coffins. He left no family to inherit the funeral parlour; he left no outstanding debts, either, and was therefore deemed a good and worthy man whose professional services would be missed, it must be admitted, more than his dauntingly silent and withdrawn personality. His property became forfeit to the county, and it was decided by the councilmen of Valley Forge that they should sell the business to another undertaker. For a while people were afraid to die, fearing they might be buried in a packing crate, or simply wrapped in a blanket, stitched up in a sailor's shroud and laid to rest in disturbing proximity to the earth and all its worms.

The council members agreed such a state of affairs could not be allowed to persist, and so placed advertisements in several midwestern newspapers. They received two replies, one from a Mr. Hutchins of Illinois, the other from a Mr. Pike of Iowa; both were qualified as morticians, but it was generally thought that Hutchins' letter and *curriculum vitae* were more impressive, the careful penmanship gracing stationery of a distinctly superior type. The council urged him to proceed with all haste to Valley Forge, where the populace held themselves in readiness for death, awaiting his timely arrival to breathe their last, utter death-rattles of relief and topple obligingly into one of Mr. Hutchins' wooden chambers of eternal repose. He did not arrive, and several elderly persons hovering at the portals of infinity were cautioned to keep the flame of life flickering on. The council wrote again, cursing the US Mail for its tardiness, and still

Mr. Hutchins of Illinois did not arrive. Some members detected the odour of mendacity, suggested Mr. Hutchins had found a position in some town he considered more congenial. There was nothing else for it—they would have to accept Mr. Pike of Iowa, despite that gentleman's blunt style in correspondence:

> *Sirs, I am available for the services your community requires. Enclosed are references and a list of my credentials. Your asking price is acceptable. I await confirmation. Respectfully yours, Joshua Pike.*

The new undertaker arrived by train in April of 1884, bringing with him his wife, daughter and aged mother, "a regular hayreem" as some of the loungers on Tom Clancy's porch expressed it. The family Pike and their trunks and baggage were transported by wagon the short distance from the depot to their new home on the corner of Decatur and Wyandotte, a two-storey dwelling. The ground-floor was the business area (the funeral parlour itself, with stands to display the various models of coffin available for peace everlasting) with a basement workshop where jaws were wired, rectums plugged, embalming fluid pumped and stage make-up applied to render the dead fit for the eyes of the living. At the rear was a stable occupied by the hearse and its team, both horses somewhat spavined with age, but willing pullers both, certainly capable of hauling the dead from this world to the next; above were the living quarters, an amplitude of rooms, most of them never used by Mr. Middleton, but necessary for a family of this size.

And what of this family? How did they, as strangers, impress the few who had immediate contact with them following the departure of the 2.18 westbound? Their wagoneer summarised them thus: Mr. Pike —tall but fat, with a face like an uncured ham with a moustache stuck on it; Mrs. Pike—little and skinny and all scrunched up like a dog waiting to get kicked; Mother Pike—a crone, shrivelled and mean-looking as a hungry old turkey buzzard, and last of all the daughter—thin, with a worried look and no chest, maybe twenty-seven or twenty-eight years of age (she was twenty-three) and definitely an old maid in the making.

The stationmaster corroborated these pithy portraits, and Clancy's porch clientele agreed; the Pikes looked about as miserable a bunch of people as you could expect to find at a funeral, or in this case at a funeral parlour. It was not anticipated that they would in any way liven up the resolute dullness of Valley Forge, but in this their detractors were mistaken. No sooner had the Pikes entered their new abode than Mother Pike (seventy-six years old) began mounting the stairs, complaining bitterly at their existence, a veritable goat-path to one of her advanced years, and having reached the midway point appeared to tire of this unwanted effort and promptly descended, utilising all parts of her anatomy bar her legs. Miraculously, the only bones broken were in her left forearm and wrist, and these were diagnosed by Dr. Whaley, who was fetched immediately by the wagoneer, as merely hairline fractures, since he could neither feel nor hear the grating ends that would have accompanied a compound fracture. He applied splints and plaster, and several men assisted in carrying Mother Pike upstairs to her room. She decided which was to be her room by being carried from one to the other, and settled on the biggest, located on the corner and illuminated by no fewer than four windows. A bed (Mr. Middleton's) was trundled from a room further down the corridor, quickly made up with sheets and counterpane, the men dismissed, and the old woman left to the care of little scrunched up Jessica and worried old maid Phoebe.

Grandmamma, as she was called within the family, was not happy to have been ousted from the Pike home in Iowa, had not wished to come west, thought Kansas as visually exciting as a table-top, and was determined to make the family do penance for having uprooted her in so heartless a fashion. She could not vent her bile upon Joshua Pike, for he was her own son, her darling boy, incapable of wrongdoing; she was therefore obliged to make life a misery for her son's wife, whom she despised for a weakling and a fool, and the offspring of their union, equally despised, but for vastly differing reasons. Phoebe gave as good as she got, and left Grandmamma in no doubt as to the mutuality of their hatred. Between these two, grandmother and granddaughter, there flowed a passionate loathing, undeclared, yet as palpable as breath. But Phoebe, as well as Jessica, was at Grandmamma's mercy, for as surely as Joshua Pike ignored them both he doted upon the welfare of his mother, and expected of his wife and daughter that they should attend to her needs, great or small, with the willingness and alacrity due a woman of such venerable and sensitive character. They obeyed—he was a man, they mere women. All money trickling into the Pike household came from his professional toiling over the dead, and he did not allow them to forget his position as custodian of purse strings; by handling the bodies of the dead he kept alive four human beings, and this god-like role granted him absolute authority over the conduct of all under his roof. He worshipped his mother with a fierce loyalty—both had been deserted by a wastrel whose sole contribution to the world had been the casual siring of a son—and would countenance no opposition to her installation on the domestic throne. Pike was her grand vizier, Jessica and Phoebe her slaves. Grandmamma so loved her son she had convinced herself the decision to leave Iowa had been forced upon him by the two women, rather than the reverse.

Lying now in unwelcome surroundings, her arm and wrist throbbing painfully, she planned how best to consolidate the power granted her by old age, a doting son and personal viciousness. And the answer came to her, an answer inspired by the vindictive pettiness to which this woman's character, made strong in her youth by marital abuse and social hardship, had now been reduced; she would stay right where she was, in this room, in this bed, would rule her minions from this couch of infirmity, a toppled idol still demanding its full share of sacrifice and offerings. What a wonderful scheme! She almost forgot her discomfort at the thought of Jessica and Phoebe waiting on her, serving her with the deference and fear accorded a queen. The idea would probably not have occurred to her had she not tumbled down the stairs and been put to bed. Her legs were quite uninjured, as was her back, apart from bruises, but no one knew this except Grandmamma, and Grandmamma well knew the position of strength to be had from withheld information. She had arbitrarily decided to be a cripple for as long as it pleased her. Her slaves would find out soon enough.

Jessica and Phoebe unpacked everything but Pike's equipment—these grim instruments were handled by him alone; everything else was women's work, and he left them to it. Mr. Middleton had left behind the basic tools of his trade, but Pike found most of these hopelessly antiquated, more like instruments of medieval torture. His own collection of scalpels and clamps, tubes and bowls and pump was gleamingly new; a fresh start in a distant town demanded newness in all things, especially newness of outlook, a forward-looking approach to life, a rejection of the past and its association with failure. Well might Pike attempt to erase recent memories, for he had been dismissed from his office as instructor at the Des Moines School of Embalming after having been caught swindling the administration by spiriting away substantial portions of chemical stocks for private sale. The discovery of his crime had not been made public, prosecution waived, the trustees fearing for the school's reputation, but Pike's dismissal was inevitable. He told his family he was tired of teaching, and wished to return to practice. He refused to discuss the sudden decision, even with his mother, and so the Pikes had come west to Kansas.

Pike considered seeking out the town hall in order to introduce himself to the council members, if they were there, but decided against it; let them come to him, as come they must to collect payment for the building. The sale would cost Pike the greater part of his savings, and he hoped for a substantial number of deaths in the next few months to feed his family. Exposure as a swindler had left him with a bitterness ripened to bursting, a constant gnawing at his self-esteem; it was not knowledge of his paltry crime that kept him awake at night, grinding his teeth and vowing vengeance, but the fact that he had been incautious enough to allow detection of his misdeeds. Remembrance of his humiliation before the board of trustees made him twitch his shoulders, squeeze both hands in murderous impotence. He laid out his instruments in the cabinets along the basement wall, examined the stone-topped table, identical to the table he had used in his Iowa practice, touched the cold surface upon which he would soon be preparing the dead of Valley Forge for burial. Middleton had apparently been a conscientious practitioner of the embalmer's art, for all was spick and span, the only indication of the nine weeks that had elapsed since his death a light coating of dust; Pike would have Jessica attend to it. His only complaint regarding the house was the unfortunate location of the rooms in which they would live; his mother could not traipse up and down stairs all day, and would to a certain extent be marooned on the upper floor. Still, she had no great love of the outdoors and would, if made comfortable, probably be happy enough.

While she and Phoebe unpacked the Pikes' belongings, Jessica fretted over the lack of beds. Their household furnishings from Des Moines had been loaded aboard a boxcar on the day they had departed that city, but had fallen behind the family *en route* to Kansas, it being easier and swifter to transfer people from one train to another than boxes and crates and disassembled bed frames. Joshua had been told the greater part of their belongings would reach Valley Forge within twenty-four to thirty-six hours after the family's arrival, which meant that for the time being there was only one bed—the one left behind by the deceased mortician—in which to sleep four people, and that one bed was already occupied by Grandmamma, who would not share or relinquish her hold upon it any more than a lioness would surrender her cubs. There was a battered sofa which might afford slumber to one other person, but this left two still without a place to lay their heads. Jessica knew which two it would be—herself and Phoebe, naturally. Grandmamma would keep the bed, Joshua would recline on the sofa, and mother and daughter would have to content themselves with Mr. Middleton's armchairs, which were not to be compared with the much nicer armchairs on a train somewhere between Iowa and Kansas. Still, they would have to do.

Jessica fussed with the business of sweeping and dusting, attempting to lessen her anxiety over the unexplained, or partly explained, move to a new town, when everything had been so comfortable in Des Moines. She could not understand Joshua's need for what he termed "expanding horizons", had been reduced to tears after politely requesting a more detailed explanation; the request had been met with angry shouting. Joshua was in a terrible rage about something, she knew, but he would reveal its cause to no one. That was Joshua's way, and nothing would ever change him. Jessica was terrified of her husband. He was a large man, impressively so, it had seemed to her as a virginal twenty-year-old, and she had gladly consented to marry him. A mortician had almost as respectable an occupation as a doctor, or so she had thought, but time revealed to Jessica what had been revealed to the wives of other morticians— people do not wish to be closely associated with the family of a man whose clothes reek of formaldehyde and other, more sinister odours. The Pikes had remained a family apart, the newlyweds and the mother-in-law, soon joined by baby Phoebe, after which event Joshua explained to Jessica that their occasional conjugal associations must cease. Jessica was not upset by the proposed abstinence; she did not enjoy the physical couplings of marriage, and was content with one child. She was in fact grateful for having been spared any further discomfort in the marital bed.

When Phoebe was eight her parents began sleeping in separate rooms, and never again shared the intimacy of casual bodily contact within the same bed, let alone sexual union. When Phoebe heard from other girls at school that their parents slept in the same bed she was greatly puzzled. Why on earth would they do such a thing? When procreation (or a garbled and highly romanticised version of it) was explained to her she knew something was very much amiss in the Pike household. Jessica was greatly embarrassed at her questions, fobbed her off with hastily concocted excuses involving her husband's "restless sleeping", which rendered a comfortable night's rest beside him impossible.

An intelligent girl, Phoebe had sensed the insubstantiality of this answer, and thereafter held her tongue while she observed the distance set between each member of the family. Nobody touched anybody else, that was what it boiled down to, and Phoebe was saddened by the implications of this discovery, for it meant that in her home there was no love. Papa doted on Grandmamma, but between Papa and Mamma there was a void, a nothingness composed of condescension on her father's part and fearful timidity on her mother's. Further observation revealed a terrible secret—Mamma was deathly afraid of Grandmamma, more afraid even than she was of Papa. The old lady's weapons were identical to her son's; her eyes and tongue derided Jessica at every opportunity, let her know she was a fool, a *clumsy* fool, what's more—look at the way she served the family at table, dithering and spilling in a fluster of abortive efforts to please her judges, her tormentors. Phoebe was at first embarrassed for her mother, then learned to hate her for her lack of grace and poise; she saw Jessica through the reptilian eyes of Papa and Grandmamma. Not until many years later did Phoebe realise she had wronged a good and kindly woman by despising her lack of social accomplishment; all such talents would have been wasted anyway, since no one ever called at the Pike house to shake hands and rub elbows with the members of a family that dealt with death on such intimate terms—what other house in the neighbourhood had a parade of dead people passing through its basement? Even Phoebe's closest friends at school let her know she "smelled funny".

The first lesson in Phoebe's moral rehabilitation occurred when she was fourteen. On a bright summer day one year before Pike became an instructor at the embalming school, Phoebe had stolen downstairs to his workroom to escape the heat. She knew a dead lady was down there, had seen the body brought to the house that very morning. She was not afraid, for no one in the family had ever bothered to tell her the kind of stories that send a shiver down juvenile spines and cause cadavers ever after to be associated with terror. Phoebe wanted to be surrounded by cool air, and knew the brick basement was the place to go. She was strictly forbidden entry to Papa's workshop, but did not allow this to stop her. The door to the basement steps was not locked; Papa obviously thought a stern warning was sufficient to keep her away. But it was hot, so down she went. The lady lay on a big stone table, and was covered completely by a sheet. Knowing she had already broken a cardinal rule by being here, Phoebe decided she may as well look at the lady while this opportunity presented itself; it would be the first dead person she had ever seen from right up close, never mind the silly stories they told about her at school—things like washing her hands in an upended skull filled with water before supper, and playing knucklebones with real human bones.

She lifted one end of the sheet and a mass of russet hair was revealed, but before Phoebe could touch it or inspect the face below the hair she heard footsteps descending from above. She quickly hid herself beneath a bench over by the wall. Two oblong windows were set in this wall at ground level, up by the basement ceiling, their glass stippled to prevent spying from the backyard; the light filtering through cast a deep shadow under the bench, and Phoebe's dark smock and hair blended perfectly with the gloom.

Her father removed his jacket, rolled up his shirtsleeves, whisked the sheet from the dead lady with one deft flick of his hand. The lady had no clothes on at all, which gave Phoebe a shock; she had never even seen her own body naked in a mirror, let alone someone else's right before her eyes, and the sheer expanse of white flesh thus disclosed seemed most unreal. Papa went to the woman's head and stroked her hair. Phoebe thought he must feel sad for her, and was trying to comfort her even in death. Then his hands strayed to the lady's bosom, another anatomical feature with which Phoebe was unacquainted, and began doing something very strange, stroking and kneading the mounds of white flesh, just like Mamma when she made bread, pushing and kneading and . . . flipping them about, making them flop first to one side, then to the other. Phoebe did not understand this at all; even more confusing was the moment when her father leaned down and actually put his mouth to the tips of those bosoms. Papa was kissing the dead lady's bosoms! Phoebe had to stifle a fit of giggling. This was just the silliest thing she had ever seen, for heaven's sake, and what was Papa doing now? He went to the other end of the table, stood there for several minutes, hands deep in the pockets of his pants, moving there, as though fingering the spare change he kept, but there was no clinking of coins, just the faint sound of friction as his knuckles brushed against cloth. Then he did something that sent Phoebe's hand to her mouth—he opened the buttons of his pants and brought forth an object Phoebe had seen on dogs and horses, but never on a man. Was Papa going to wee? But he did not point it at the floor, he allowed it to point at the ceiling. How was that possible? And then he began tugging furiously at it, as though it had done something wrong and must be punished, and while he tugged at it he made strange moaning sounds and pushed his open pants against the cold and unshod foot of the dead lady, pushed his fist-enclosed thing right up against the creased sole, made the toes jump as he attacked it. And then there was a flash of something that caught the light and vanished, a little leaping arc of dull whiteness that cascaded over Papa's hand and the dead lady's foot and lay there, glistening like the imprint of a snail.

Her father seemed almost to sag over the stone table, leaned against it with his belly, huffing and puffing, and his eyes looked at nothing. Now Phoebe no longer found the sight funny. Something here was very wrong. She did not fully understand what it was, but knew with every uncorrupted atom of her being that what she had witnessed was a bad thing, a wrong and shameful thing that would never be raised in conversation at suppertime, or at any other time. Papa had done something private and secret; Phoebe knew he would be very angry were he to find out she had seen him do this thing. He took a large handkerchief from his pocket and wiped his hand, his other part, and the lady's foot, then folded the handkerchief carefully into a square and replaced it in his pocket. He buttoned his pants, then set about the normal business of a mortician, readying the cadaver, inside and outside, for public display in one of his finest caskets. Phoebe stayed crouched under the bench for more than two hours, until his task was completed and he left.

She was silent for days afterward, and looked at Joshua Pike as though seeing him for the first time, as though he was not a man at all, but some lumbering beast in human guise. She could not identify his crime with words, but knew it for what it was, and thanked God her father had never cultivated the habit of kissing or touching her.

The second incident transpired almost a year later. Grandmamma was seated beneath the oak in the backyard, perched on a comfortable chair beside a small table, on which lay a turkey-wing fan and a small silver bell. Phoebe was watching Grandmamma from a window at the back of the house, hiding behind the curtains. She did not know why she was spying, but enjoyed the activity immensely; to look at someone while that person was unaware of your scrutiny was a delightful feeling. Through the open window came the steady droning of insects, a restful, lulling sound. Phoebe watched as Grandmamma picked up the silver bell and sent a brisk tinkling across the yard to the kitchen, where Mamma was preparing supper. Mamma did not delay for a moment, but came out to the yard, followed the short brick pathway to the oak and stood before Grandmamma, hands fiddling nervously with her apron strings.

"I want a glass of cool water," said Grandmamma, her words passing through the window to Phoebe's ear. Phoebe knew Grandmamma's real name was Beatrice, but Phoebe's secret name for her was Snapdragon, because of the habitual bad temper suggested by her voice; her furrowed lips squirmed as she spoke, as though every word left the taste of lemons in her mouth.

Jessica went to the kitchen, drew water into a glass, returned to the oak and set the glass down beside Snapdragon's turkey-wing fan and silver bell. She stood waiting, perhaps expecting thanks, or another command, or more likely a curt word of dismissal.

"What is this?" Grandmamma eyed the glass along the bridge of her nose.

"You asked for some water."

"Is that what you've brought me, water?" Grandmamma was smiling, Phoebe noted, a disturbing sight.

"Yes," said Jessica, beginning to worry that she had once again done something wrong.

"Just plain, ordinary water?" The smile was broader, like that of a crocodile opening its jaws.

"Yes. . . ."

Snapdragon sent the glass flying from the table-top with one sweep of her hand, sent it spinning through the air, water dispersing in a brief silvery spray. The glass shattered against the brick pathway, a shockingly loud noise; the silence that followed was made more profound by the abrupt cessation of all insect scrapings and raspings, an awful, engulfing silence Phoebe did not dare profane with even one exhaled breath.

Snapdragon's eyes narrowed. "I wanted *barley* water," she said. "Fetch it."

And Jessica did, returning with a new and brimming glass. While Grandmamma sipped, Jessica knelt and began picking up the pieces of broken glass. "That's sensible," said Grandmamma. "We don't want you cutting your feet. You wouldn't be able to run your little errands. Make sure you get all of it."

Another sound came to Phoebe through the window, the sniffling of her mother as she attempted to restrain her tears. It was a horrible sound, and Phoebe wished she would be quiet. She was not sorry for Jessica so much as embarrassed on her behalf. When Jessica returned to the kitchen Phoebe could hear her still, despite the several rooms between them; she was sobbing openly now. Grandmamma could hear it, too; there was a little smile on her wrinkled mouth. Phoebe thought her repulsive; it was the smile, that look of righteous satisfaction wrenching at her lips. Jessica sobbed on, the sound drifting through open doorways from the kitchen to Phoebe. How awful it must be to feel that way, she thought. Only after several minutes of deliberation did it become clear to her that, although her mother was weak and silly and embarrassing to be near, she would not be that way if only Papa and Snapdragon would be kind to her. Phoebe herself had never been kind to Jessica, a shameful thing to admit. That would change. And Snapdragon had *not* asked for barley water the first time, Phoebe was positive, and it proved what should have been obvious to her for years now—that Grandmamma took deliberate pleasure in tormenting Jessica; it had not been the usual case of a crotchety old lady not getting along with her daughter-in-law, but a brazen instance of outright provocation, an act designed solely to humiliate poor Jessica. Now that she had seen the truth, Phoebe was outraged. Did other families behave like this towards each other? Surely not. It was a conspiracy within the Pike home, a plot to make Mamma feel stupid and inadequate, and even though Phoebe had to admit Jessica was undeniably a little clumsy, and often said foolish things, there was no need for Papa and Snapdragon to mock her with their looks and silences and barbed tongues. They didn't like Mamma, that's what it was; they didn't like her, and wanted to remind her of their distaste on every possible occasion. They even enjoyed doing so! It was unthinkable, but it was true.

From that moment Phoebe allied herself with Jessica against the two monsters in human form who tormented her so. It was not an easy task. She did not enjoy putting her arms around Jessica to comfort her, since Jessica's body gave off a slightly musty odour, an unfortunate glandular secretion which had been instrumental in curtailing the sexual liaison between man and wife; it seemed also to be growing stronger as Jessica aged. But Phoebe did rally to her mother's cause when circumstances demanded solidarity against superior forces, and no rebellion could have been launched with a more devastating broadside than Phoebe's first open move in support of Jessica, some weeks after the barley water incident. Supper had proceeded along its usual lines, a stolid cutting and forking of food, the scraping of knives on plates reminding Phoebe of unbearable fingernail scratchings on school blackboards. The food would not descend her throat. She knew the silence could not last, waited for a comment from the enemy, felt relief when at last it came.

"This meat is tough," said her father.

"Like leather," agreed her grandmother.

Jessica hung her head in tacit submission to their judgement.

The time had come. "The reason the meat is tough," said Phoebe, "is because Mother is not given enough money to buy meat of better quality."

Forks paused *en route* to mouths hanging open in astonishment. A look of consternation passed between her father and Snapdragon, and during those few speechless seconds Phoebe saw that it was high time Papa also had a secret name, and it would be . . . Mr. Meat! He was big and fat and worked with human flesh, as a butcher does with cattle and sheep, and it was of meat that he complained. Mr. Meat. She smiled at her plate, the only diner still eating.

"What did you say?" asked Mr. Meat.

"My mouth was not full," said Phoebe, the thrill of challenge setting her nerves a-tingle. "You must have heard." She was tense, eager, fearful, an inspiring *mélange* of emotion; she knew she could not be bested, knew the confidence creeping into her body would not go away, had been waiting until now to be revealed in a way Mr. Meat and Snapdragon could not misinterpret. Phoebe had done nothing less than overturn the precepts of behaviour expected of young girls before their elders and betters. She knew it, and was proud of it. Let them try to fight me! she thought. Just let them try!

"Go to your room immediately," said her father.

"Why?"

The question elicited a gasp of horror from Snapdragon.

"Go to your room!" thundered Mr. Meat, and Phoebe lost all control. She had not intended it, but of a sudden felt herself possessed by a demon with unanticipated and total charge of her tongue. "I haven't finished eating!" she screamed, and stood, flinging her plate against the ceiling, where it shattered and descended in clattering pieces.

Even Jessica was aghast. All three adults stared at Phoebe as she stood with thighs pressed against the table-edge, body leaning forward, readying itself for aggression. No one present had ever seen a more startling sight.

"She's mad . . ." said Grandmamma.

"No, I'm *not!*" screamed Phoebe, and reached over to tip Grandmamma's plate into her lap.

"Noooo . . ." moaned Beatrice Pike, as though receiving a lapful of scorpions.

"What are you doing!" Mr. Meat was also standing now, thoroughly confused; he could do nothing to stop Phoebe upsetting his own plate, which dribbled gravy down the legs of his pants.

"Shut up!" screamed Phoebe. "Shut up! Shut up! Shut up!"

She barely recognised the voice as her own; the demon had taken over completely. "I am now going to my room!" she howled, and marched off, mounted the staircase to her bedroom, closed the door behind her. She wished she had a key. Papa would be up to visit her soon. Phoebe sat on the bed, then stood again; she must not allow him to bully her as he had bullied Mother, nor must he be allowed to think her mad, or the battle against the darkness surrounding Jessica would fizzle out like a damp firecracker. That must not happen. Phoebe knew she was being very brave and grown-up for a fifteen-year-old, and was proud of it. She breathed slowly and steadily, waiting for the footsteps on the stairs, heart hammering still in the aftermath of excitement. Had she really thrown her supper at the ceiling and tipped plates over Mr. Meat and Snapdragon? Oh, what a wild and outrageous thing to have done! Had the neighbours overheard? Her fists were clenched resolutely, her mouth set in a firm line. I will be strong and brave, she promised herself, strong and brave enough for two.

Now the stairs creaked beneath the weight of Mr. Meat. Phoebe became as rigid as a ship's figurehead, arms held stiffly at her sides. The door opened; her father had never seemed so huge, so much a presence of threatening flesh. Mr. Meat, she repeated to herself, Mr. Meat, Mr. Meat. . . . He had a belt in his hand, a wicked length of leather. The door was closed behind him. Phoebe noted the flushed cheeks, the fury in his hooded eyes. He had not noticed or removed a shred of potato skin from his moustache, so foul was his temper when he left the supper table. "Before you are punished," he said, his voice flat with controlled anger, "I should like to have an explanation."

Phoebe's stomach fluttered, her bowels loosening. He really was a huge man; bloated, that was the word, a big bloated whale—no, a walrus, with that moustache. She clenched her buttocks as hard as her fists. "You mustn't treat Mother like a slave," she said, and was disappointed at the whisper in which this all-important message was delivered. She swallowed and tried again. "You mustn't bully her." Better, that time; firmer, with the timbre of defiance, if not of authority. His face registered nothing at all. Had he heard? "You and Grandmamma talk to Mother as if she was a silly child. You mustn't do it any more. It isn't right."

He advanced one step towards her. "Hold out your hands," he commanded, still in a deadly monotone. "Place them together, palm up."

Phoebe felt her arms beginning to rise, held them down with a stiffening of resolve, a determination to make of this moment a turning-point in the blighted history of the Pikes.

"If you touch me I'll tell Mr. Storbeck what you did to Mrs. Storbeck."

There. It was said. He was blinking—once, twice, thrice—was that a sign of alarm? "What are you saying?" No change in the voice; he really did not seem to remember. Did this mean Mrs. Storbeck had been only one among many? It stood to reason that half her father's cadavers would be female. Phoebe had not even considered the possibility that the strange and disquieting ritual between living man and dead woman was anything but an isolated act of madness. "Mrs. Storbeck," she reminded him, impatient with his blankness. "She died last year. She was here, in the basement. I saw what you did."

His eyelids were flickering rapidly now. "I do not understand you. Hold out your hands."

"I saw what you did! I was under the bench! I saw all the things you did, all the horrible dirty things, and if you touch me I'll tell Mr. Storbeck! I'll tell everyone!"

Pike made no further move toward Phoebe, allowed his eyes to leave hers and dart to the corners of the room, searching out eavesdroppers. How could she possibly have seen? "I have told you never to go down there. . . ."

"But I did, and I saw, and if you touch me I'll tell!"

She knew he was afraid; his eyes betrayed him. He looked very foolish indeed, a big fat walrus all puffed up with his own importance, floundering helplessly in his guilt. Oh, what power in a string of little words! He seemed to be sagging before her, shrivelling to obscurity, a silly walrus with potato stuck on his moustache. Phoebe felt the exultant hum of victory invade her bones, felt inches taller, an imperious queen passing judgement upon an erring page—no, a humble potlicker from the stables. Should she be magnanimous? "You must be nicer to Mother, and Grandmamma must be too."

"You will not speak of this to anyone."

She was uncertain if this was a threat or a request, and was annoyed at his lack of inflection; he should show some gumption—he was her father, after all. "I won't say anything if you do what I said."

Pike established a pact with his daughter by turning, leaving the room, closing the door behind him. She listened to his footsteps descending the staircase, took a deep breath and released it. Had she truly done the impossible and defied her own father, bearded the lion in its own unsavoury den? It seemed she had, and Phoebe did a little dance, back and forth across the room, up on to the bed, over to the window overlooking the backyard. The table and chair were still there beneath the oak, but Mother would never again wait on Snapdragon, fetching and carrying. It would be the start of a new life!

It was not. Pike and his mother treated Jessica with elaborate politeness for six months, to her confusion, and began steadily to regress thereafter, until life proceeded as before. Somehow the threat of disclosure to Mr. Storbeck, once having been voiced, never again had about it the urgency and desperate willingness to act which had so frightened Pike on that first occasion, and Phoebe knew he would not allow a similar outburst to shield her or her mother from punishment. Instead, she lectured Jessica on the need for strength and pride, on the right of every person to stride through life unencumbered by shackles and chains, all to little or no avail.

"But I don't *have* chains," Jessica would protest. "That's just silly, dear."

"I don't mean literal *chains*, Mother, I mean . . . an attitude, a way of treating you as though you *did* have chains."

"But I don't, dear."

"Can't you see the way they treat you? Doesn't it make you angry that they expect the kind of service from you they wouldn't get from a slave?"

"Who, dear? Honestly, I don't know what you're referring to, Phoebe, all this talk about slaves and chains. Mr. Lincoln set the darkies free years ago, when you were just a little girl."

"Mother, I'm trying to make you aware that Father and Grandmamma do not treat you with respect. Can't you see the look on their faces when they criticise you for every little thing?"

"But I deserve it, sometimes."

"No, you don't, you *don't!*"

"You mustn't upset yourself like this. You worry so much about me and really, I'm perfectly happy, dear. When you're older you'll understand."

Poor Jessica could not admit to her many humiliations, for acknowledgement of her ill-treatment would have obliged her to seek a remedy, a change in her way of life, and that was something she knew she could never accomplish, not even with Phoebe's willing assistance. Phoebe despaired of ever bringing about the least degree of self-awareness in her mother, of awakening her dormant strengths and making whole her flayed pride. Jessica would not co-operate, refused to see her husband and mother-in-law for the self-righteous, overbearing, hateful creatures they were.

For eight years, throughout Pike's tenure at the Des Moines School of Embalming, Phoebe remained under a roof that stifled her freedom as surely as a coffin lid excludes the light of day, her sole reason for staying a sense of responsibility toward Jessica, who thwarted her efforts at every turn by evasion rather than confrontation. Phoebe wept for her mother's weakness and stupidity and vowed to leave, to find a life for herself far from the stink of formaldehyde, a world away from the poisonous exudations of the two people she hated most. Her education was terminated at the age of sixteen; she was expected to make herself available to gentleman callers, but of course none arrived. Phoebe was not overly attractive, and her father was not a wealthy man. What was there to entice a suitor?

And so Phoebe undertook to help her mother do the hundred and one things that must be done to keep a house clean, to feed its occupants and attend to the many needs of an elderly woman. It was work of wretched monotony, wholly unrewarding, and Phoebe endured only by way of the satisfaction she felt at having halved Jessica's burden. It was probably the most she would ever be able to achieve, and the prospect of performing domestic tasks at least until her mother died made Phoebe quail; dullness and irretrievable waste spread their insidious stain throughout the flux of her thoughts, and set about swallowing her youth.

Thus freighted with bitterness and woe, with loathing and spite, the family came to Kansas. On the journey west from Iowa, Phoebe composed a poem, matching its rhythms to the clicking of iron wheels:

> *Unhappy band of travellers*
> *That seek a distant land,*
> *Your yearnings are as temples built*
> *Upon the shifting sand.*

It was very bad, she knew, but it was hers alone, a kind of secret.

CHAPTER TWENTY-NINE

It quickly became apparent to the citizens of Valley Forge that the Pikes were an unusual family. The grandmother was never seen, was reportedly bedridden with some kind of back ailment, although she would not permit Dr. Whaley to examine her. Pike's wife appeared in public rarely, usually on a Sunday in Reverend Wilkes' church, where she said not a word. There was talk of feeblemindedness from some, of chronic shyness from others. Curiosity-seekers wishing for a glimpse of her had to time their casual strollings-by to coincide with Jessica's once-weekly washday foray into the yard beside the stable, where a clothes-line whipped about in the winds that are seldom still in Kansas. There she stood, a little woman with a big basket, the wickerwork overflowing with linen, and beside her was the daughter, not much bigger herself. Phoebe had ceased to be a novelty early on; with her daily round of the stores for food and household essentials she became a familiar face along Decatur. The storekeepers found her pleasant enough, but she did not linger to trade gossip with anyone, a peculiarity regarded by some of the local women as standoffishness. They thought Phoebe considered herself their superior, and marked her down for a fall, the kind Pride goeth before. Pike himself was necessarily a public figure; his profession brought him into contact with the recently bereaved, some of whom described him as a model of solemnity and solicitude, others as "slick", by which they meant he had about him a distasteful unctuousness. But no one said he didn't provide a decent funeral.

Whenever Phoebe thought of the house she did not see it

as a whole, from the outside, nor did she separately picture the various rooms inside; she saw the staircase. Twenty-three steps in all, the number of years in her life, the staircase rose to another world, a claustrophobic place papered in flowered patterns of mauve and brown, a place with but one highway, the narrow corridor leading to the throne room of this world's undisputed ruler, the wicked, the fiendish, the evil queen of darkness—Snapdragon! She perched herself like a spider in the middle of her bed, and her invisible webs ran to every corner of her domain, upstairs and down, their tremblings and twitchings conveying to her the placement and doings of her subjects, who were summoned before her many times each day with melodic tinklings of her silver bell. Many times they toiled up the twenty-three steps to do her bidding, and many times down. Every morning Grandmamma insisted on being bathed, then fully dressed, although she would not move from the bed all day; she also demanded daily brushings of her long white hair, of which she was justly proud, then had its length pinned up in a heavy knot at the nape of her neck. Together Jessica and Phoebe attended to her needs. Phoebe had a frequent daydream in which she wound Grandmamma's long tresses around her wattled neck and pulled them tight, choking her until her face became as black as her dress. A variant on this theme involved taking hold of Grandmamma's brow and jaw from behind and twisting her head sharply to one side, snapping her neck as easily as one snapped slivers of wood to start a fire in the kitchen stove. These daydreams were no compensation for the drudgery. Phoebe hated her grandmother, hated, hated, *hated* her, and whenever her foot was placed on the first of the twenty-three steps in response to the delicate but insistent tinkling from above she took into her body a deep breath before proceeding to step number two and all the rest, as if preserving a lungful of the less adulterated air to be found on the ground floor, retaining its essence to enable her survival in the poisonous upper reaches of Snapdragon's realm; then up the dreaded staircase she went and into the *sanctum sanctorum,* to receive from the lips of the queen herself—the Word.

"Open the curtains. It's like a tomb in here."

Would that it were, thought Phoebe, with you as the corpse.

"Fetch my knitting."

May the needles slip and stab your black heart.

"Close that window. Do you want me to catch my death of cold?"

Actually, yes.

"I want vegetable soup, good *thick* soup. Lots of bits and pieces."

A little hemlock, a pinch of belladonna, a few tasty morsels of deadly mushroom?

"I want something to brighten up the room. I want a plant in a pot."

Some poison ivy, perhaps, or an arrangement of stinging nettles.

"I want a stand for my potted plant, so I can see it without breaking my neck."

A service I would willingly perform.

"Rub my back. The pain is terrible today. Did you get the linament I like?"

It has pure alcohol among its ingredients—highly flammable—perhaps if I rub hard enough. . . .

"Be sure and get all the dust out of the corners. It's choking me."

May there be dust storms of Saharan proportions.

And the most odious task of all.

"Empty the pot. And rinse it out properly."

Phoebe would dearly have loved to empty the sloshing chamberpot over Grandmamma's head, drench her with piss, drape her with stools; what a cheering sight that would be! These vindictive imaginings were often so intense Phoebe questioned her own sanity. Did she truly wish Grandmamma dead? Yes, yes, she did, dead and buried and rotting beneath the ground. Only then would Mother be free; but, no, not even then, for there was the equally insidious domination exerted over Jessica by her husband, still only in early middle age, and blessed with his mother's iron constitution. His method, unlike Grandmamma's constant mistress-servant style of nudging Jessica toward nervous collapse, was to ignore her completely, whatever the hour of day or night, across the dining table, during chance encounters in the corridor; he did not see her, never addressed a question or comment in her direction, and when questioned himself—oh, brave Jessica, actually to *speak* to him—he would direct a blank look at a point somewhere beyond Jessica's shoulder and answer with a terse yes or no, usually the latter. As a tactic it was every bit as effective as Grandmamma's. The old lady's death would solve only half the problem. Really, it would be so much simpler if Mother herself were to die. And the self-recrimination returned: how can I even *think* such a thing?

But think such thoughts she did. Household tension increased during the winter of 1884-5, when Grandmamma insisted on having a stove installed in her room. This was duly done, and yet another task, that of keeping the thing fed with wood, fell to Phoebe. Upstairs she went with laden arms, a trail of bark chips in her wake, upstairs and down again. The door to Grandmamma's room was kept closed to shut in the stifling heat, and her silver bell, exquisite instrument of torture, could no longer be heard down in the kitchen, was scarcely audible even at the foot of the staircase. But Grandmamma was not to be thwarted, and remedied the problem by insisting that her darling boy provide her with a stout walking cane; she specified that it be tipped with metal, and the reason soon became clear—instead of ringing her ineffective silver bell to summon Jessica and Phoebe she now thumped on the floor beside her bed. The sound travelled with depressing clarity to all parts of the lower storey. There was no escape.

Grandmamma's stove consumed prodigious amounts of wood, seeming to swallow entire trees as the winter progressed, its iron potbelly glowing redly. Pike cast about for cheap fuel to keep the monster sated, and was told by one of his customers (a farmer whose wife had died in childbirth, one of Dr. Whaley's failures) of Joe Cobden, the hunch-backed part-Indian that lived up on the ridge and sold the cheapest wood in town. Pike was given the story of Mc-Gruder's attempts to stop Joe's harmless commerce, and of Joe's retreat to the city limits. The hunchback could be found there on any Monday, Wednesday or Friday morning to take orders and receive cash. Pike presented himself on a brisk but clear day and stated his needs. Joe Cobden wrote down the particulars in his notebook, promised delivery the following day. No, he told Pike, he didn't split the wood before delivery any more, didn't have time to do more than fell and saw the wood into manageable sections; nowadays the customers had to split their own. Pike was not worried; the price was more than satisfactory, and the women would get plenty of good healthy exercise splitting the wood into stove-sized chunks. He went home well pleased with himself.

Joe delivered as promised next day, drew his wagon up behind the stable and began throwing wood on to the ground. It was easy work, Joe having recovered all the strength he had lost during his years of idleness. Halfway through unloading, he paused to admire the fat rumps of his new team. One of the original pair that had hauled him across the prairie in his bone-gathering days had died of old age, and the other, the gelding on whose back he had ranged far and wide in pursuit of buffalo, was too old now for work, spent the time remaining to it in the stable or the nearby pasture Joe had cleared and fenced. The new team was a solid investment in his small but thriving business. Joe stooped to pick up another section of wood, and heard a sound that caused him to stand upright again. It was music, very faint, coming from somewhere inside the Pike house— from the upstairs, he guessed. He could not identify the melody, his musical knowledge being confined to the home-spun tunes sung across America, usually accompanied by squeezebox and harmonica. This was something quite different; it did not compel one to tap a foot in unison with its rhythm, was sometimes quick, sometimes . . . *hesitant,* was the word Joe chose after listening to it further, almost like water purling and trickling along a narrow stream, dropping now and then over shelves of rock, pooling for a moment then rushing on, its tempo revived.

Then it stopped and, in the silence that followed, Joe understood that part of the music's fascination for him had been his certainty that he had heard it before. But where? A lovely sound like that, how could he have forgotten? The crystal clarity of its notes suggested a music box, but for some reason Joe was positive the melody had sprung from an opened watch, one of those elegant pocket pieces that plays a tune when its face is consulted. But had not the melody lasted much too long? A watch had a spiked metal disc too small to do anything but repeat a few bars *ad infinitum.* One of the Tubbs-Cobden outfit's men had owned such a watch, his prized possession; it gave out a sprightly rendering of "Dixie", and was much admired until a skinner, a survivor of the first battle of Bull Run (Union forces) had deliberately stepped on it and ground the "stinkin' Reb toon" underfoot, provoking its owner first to fisticuffs, then to tears; the watch had been given to him by a sweetheart, he sniffed, who had then passed away. This was a blatant lie; the watch had been stolen from a drunk in a Dodge City saloon. Joe was sure that what he had heard was a musical watch, a very big watch maybe, that could play for minutes on end. He wished he could hear it again. Magically, the music obliged. Joe dropped from the wagon with simian ease and followed the enchanting sound to its source.

Long before her world had been overturned by things seen in gloomy basement and sunlit yard, Phoebe had been a contented little girl, never more so than on the occasion of her eighth birthday, when Papa, in an atypical act of munificence, had bought for her a truly wonderful gift. Its sides and lid were carved from teak, delicately chiselled in bas-relief with a multitude of gambolling forest creatures; around and around in a neverending chase they leaped and bounded and padded—deer and badger and fox, hare and wolf and shambling bear—an untamed menagerie nose to tail. On the lid were carved swallow and swift and falcon, stork and eagle, their every feather rendered in impossible detail. Phoebe had stared at the box, struck dumb by its beauty. "Open it," Papa had said, and when she did so out had spilled a heavenly sound. On the inside of the lid was a mirror which reflected Phoebe's bedazzlement. Papa showed her how to lift out the shallow wooden tray—"for keepsakes", he explained—and expose the musical machinery within; not one, but four different metal rollers studded with tiny spikes produced the melody, each taking up the refrain as the preceding roller completed its allotted quota of bars. "It's lovely . . ." breathed Phoebe. "All the way from Bavaria," said Papa, but so far as Phoebe was concerned it came from fairyland, from the ethereal landscape of the moon. It was not until much later that she detected what may have been the artisan's cryptic signature; one of the frolicking animals, a deer, had an arrow in its neck, partially concealed by the network of antlers belonging to its parallel mate, but definitely there, a sly intruder in a scene of sylvan innocence. Phoebe prided herself on being the only person ever to have noticed the arrow, and never mentioned it to a soul.

Throughout her childhood the box had been a good friend, its music never failing to transport Phoebe elsewhere; it was not a melody to cheer one up, being far too subtle a piece for that, but it did assist, with its spillway of sound, in providing the hint of magic every young life requires. She did not listen to the box daily, kept it for those times when her patience and fortitude finally gave way, when black despair enfolded her. Then she would bring out the music-box to remind herself there is beauty in the world. On this particular day, having been reprimanded by Grandmamma for not coming to her quickly enough after being summoned by the thumping cane, Phoebe needed reminding. Of late her resistance had fallen to such a low ebb she had not the strength or will to fight back, to engage in the usual sneering match, using what Grandmamma called her "wicked sassmouth", and that fact depressed her even more than the loss of her physical stamina; Phoebe did not know if it was tired legs or a heavy heart that made each trip upstairs a little more difficult than the last. Seated by the window in her room overlooking the backyard, she waited for the music to bathe her in waves of relief. It did not happen. She felt nothing. Had she listened too many times over the years, and worn out its magic? The sound was as clear as ever, the tiny spikes on each roller plucking at the tips of metal fringes, extracting notes of crystal sharpness. As a child Phoebe had called the sound "spinkly", meaning spiky and twinkly. Today it was nothing more than noise, almost irritating in its brightness and clarity. She closed the lid, shut it off, sat staring at her hand resting on the carved birds. It was the hand of an old woman, dry and wrinkled, its back already flecked with the pale freckles that would one day become liver spots. I'm only twenty-three, she thought; there must be something in store for me, something good. She opened the lid again, listened to the music. Of *course* she still found it moving. The day on which she did not was the day they could bury her.

Something hit the windowpane beside her—an extra heavy snowflake? But it was not snowing. She looked outside just as another woodchip hit the glass. Below her stood the most grotesque individual she had ever seen, the town hunchback, the wood man they called Joe. He mimed opening the window. Puzzled, she did so, and waited for him to speak. Was there a problem regarding the wood? She saw he had offloaded about half the delivery already, recalled having been partially aware, throughout her cogitations, of a thudding and thumping in the background of her thoughts.

"Yes?" she said. The air outside was much too chill for her to be standing at an open window.

"What's it called?" said Joe.

"I beg your pardon?"

452

"The music. I've heard it somewhere before, but I don't know what it's called."

The box was still open. Phoebe closed it. " 'Für Elise'," she said.

" 'Furry leaves'?"

" 'Für Elise'. It's German. Für means 'for'. 'For Elise'. Beethoven wrote it for a woman called Elise."

"Beethoven?"

"Yes, Beethoven. Have you heard of him?"

"I've heard of him. I don't know where I heard the music, though."

"Wait one moment, please."

Phoebe closed the window, draped a heavy shawl around her head and shoulders, picked up the music-box and went down to the yard. The hunchback stood waiting. It was curiosity, she supposed, that had brought her down here, the urge within us all to see for ourselves the freaks of the womb. She would not have done it had she thought him self-conscious about his deformity, but it was he who had thrown woodchips at her window and begun the conversation; in fact he seemed almost cockily assured. She was nearly intimidated by his ugliness, but there was something approximating a smile on his lips. She handed him the box. He turned it around and around, marvelling at its craftsmanship. "Never seen anything like it before," he said. "It's a work of art."

"Yes, it's very beautiful. It's from Bavaria. I've had it a long time."

His hands were big and rough, the backs thick with hair, ridged and corded with pulsing veins. She wondered if he ever wore gloves during winter. "Look at this," he said. "There's a deer with an arrow in its neck. Did you notice that?"

"Yes. There's only the one."

"Peculiar."

He opened the box. Phoebe removed the keepsake-tray (empty—it always had been) and showed him the intricate clockwork mechanism solemnly turning, the spikes glinting in the weak sunlight. "Für Elise" played through to its plangent conclusion. Joe closed the lid, admired the box again, handed it back to her.

"Thank you," he said.

"You don't remember where you heard it before?"

"No. It'll probably come to me in the middle of the night."

She had expected him to grunt, not talk, to employ the pidgin tongue of dime novel Indians—"Heap nice box makum good music", or some such; she was surprised at his obvious intelligence.

Neither had anything more to say. "Back to work," smiled Joe, and returned to his wagon. Phoebe went inside. "Peculiar" is definitely the word, she thought, and wished he had not discovered the arrow so quickly; it was as if he had stolen a tiny, hidden portion of herself. By day's end she had ceased to think of the incident at all.

In the early days of spring Phoebe experienced one of the most hurtful moments of her young life. She fell in love with a stranger. It happened thus: Pike ordered his coffins from a carpenter in Kansas City who specialised in this line of work, and each month received a shipment of half a dozen or so in the styles ordered. The coffins were wrapped in thick cardboard and tarpaper, glued and bound with twine to prevent their varnish being chipped or scratched in transit. Pike himself usually supervised their unloading from caboose or freight car, anxious for the preservation of his costly wares. In the last week of March he fell into a fury because the arrival of his latest shipment coincided with a funeral. Pike drove the hearse himself, and considered himself irreplaceable (any child over the age of nine could safely have performed that part of the job), so Phoebe was dispatched to the depot in his stead to supervise the unloading of the precious caskets. It was a raw and blustery day, the heat of summer still far away, and Phoebe awaited the train's arrival inside the depot, rather than on the windy platform, happy enough to perform any task which got her away from the house.

The train arrived on time, and Phoebe went along to the caboose to watch as five tarpaper-wrapped coffins were slid out and lifted carefully down to the platform. Mr. Henneker who ran the livery stable was supposed to pick them up and transport them down the street to the funeral parlour, but he had not yet arrived. Phoebe was not worried; there was no sign of rain, and no one would steal the heavy boxes. The locomotive huffed and hissed as water from the tower sluiced into its tender. Several passengers had disembarked to stretch their legs during the five-minute stopover, and it was among these strollers that Phoebe saw the man with whom she fell in love. He was young, upright, well dressed, handsome. Her own idle perambulations around the coffins was halted. She stared at the young man. He was less than five yards away, having descended from the last carriage. He looked at the depot, at that portion of the town to be seen from where he stood, and finally at Phoebe. His glance slid by her, fastened on the coffins, interpreting their shape; and then, noticing that she stared at him, he reached for the brim of his hat, gave it a polite tug, smiled as he did so. It was not so much the fact that he had a set of very white teeth that caused her intestines to knot, nor the fascinating creases that formed around his lips and eyes; it was his voice. "Afternoon," he said, and the sound of it was rich and warm and full, the voice of moist daydreams made real, simulacrum of all things passionate and virile. Phoebe could find no voice of her own with which to answer this siren call of maleness. Invisible arms were wrapped around her, squeezing the breath from her lungs, forcing blood to her head in a foolhardy rush that almost caused her to reel against the coffins. I must be ill, she thought, and had to shift her leaden feet to remain standing—how humiliating it would be to fall down in front of this Adonis, to see him immediately classify her as a silly, swooning female; and yet, he would be obliged, would he not, to rush to her aid, to lift her in his arms like the hero of some cheap fiction . . . ? No! Phoebe inhaled cold prairie air, doused this unworthy fantasy with a chill dose of reality. The man was probably married. She looked at his hand—no rings. What difference does it make if he's unmarried? she remonstrated with herself; the man has simply stepped down from a train to relieve the monotony of his journey. He is not staying here. He is going away and I will never lay eyes on him again. Some woman west of here will have him all to herself. She hated him for having revealed his existence to her, wished she had not come to the depot. Phoebe turned away, faced the end of the wooden platform, concentrated on the shining rails stretching to the horizon.

Behind her the conductor called for boarding. She would not turn around for one last glimpse of him, she would *not!* The whistle blew, once, twice, and the locomotive began to move, taking up the slack between cars, the clash of iron couplings progressing from front to rear. Phoebe did not dare turn until the train was gone, its snorting borne away on the wind. And then, into the desolation which filled her came a strange notion: the young man had not boarded the train, still stood mere yards away, waiting for her to turn again, a knowing smile on his lips—yes, he had recognised her, as she had him, and could no more have climbed back aboard the train and continued westward than plucked the sun from the sky. He stood behind her at this very moment, and when she turned he would find her charming look of incredulity irresistible, and the two would rush to each other's arms, drawn by the magnetism of love.

She turned. The platform was empty, of course, and now Phoebe really did feel ill. The narrow deck of planks yawned with emptiness, with total absence of *him*. She then did the unthinkable—she sat on a coffin. Phoebe stared at the toecaps of her button boots and wished she were dead. Thoughts of marriage, dreams of being *loved* had been ruthlessly put aside for so long she had assumed they would never surface, and now, like a scaled monster rising from the deep, had come this pitiful fantasy, concocted in an instant, coloured with all the vividness imagination can provide, a gaudy and insubstantial bauble suspended on a spider's thread. It fell with a crash that left her robbed of feeling, arms crossed, hands clutching at her ribs. I am a fool, she told herself. Like any fool, I deserve punishment, and this is it. The pattern of her life became brutally clear; she had allowed herself to drown while busily keeping her mother's head above water, had subordinated all personal wants and needs in a concerted effort to keep Jessica from being devoured by those closest to her. This was her reward, this resounding hollowness in the pit of her stomach, this awful dislocation of the soul. She continued to sit on the coffin, sightless, far removed from the depot. I must get away from here. . . .

"Miz Pike?"

She lifted her head. Henneker stood before her, accompanied by one of his sons. "Wagon's waiting," he said.

Phoebe made no move to rise. Henneker's boy looked to his father for an explanation; Phoebe's face was so blank, her body so still.

"May as well get the job done, Miz Pike," said Henneker.

Phoebe nodded once. "Yes," she said, and after several heartbeats rose from the tarpapered coffin to let them proceed.

For several weeks thereafter, Phoebe was afflicted with what she termed "lunacy". Despite her unending and bitter self-castigation she thought constantly of the young man; his casual "Afternoon" became the preamble to imaginary conversations in which Phoebe told him everything, absolutely everything. She did not complain or bemoan her lot, for that would not have endeared her to him, simply stated the facts of her existence, the loathsome, degrading, incontrovertible facts. When she had told her tale in a straightforward and admirably restrained fashion he held her tightly in his arms, overcome with the sadness generated by her wasted years. "I had no idea such a life was possible," he murmured into her hair. "From now on things will be different. Everything will change. We are going away from here, and will never return. Your mother will accompany us. My home is large, has been empty for too long. We will all be happy together." And they boarded a westbound train, herself, Jessica and Horton Winfield (the name she had chosen for him), and rode the shining rails toward a bright new day, absurdly happy, content at last.

She indulged in this daydream while washing dishes, preparing meals, cleaning the house, enduring the silent mealtimes, while walking down the street, even while sitting in the Reverend Dr. Lyman Wilkes' church, ostensibly listening to a sermon on the theme of brotherhood among all men. Wilkes' voice drifted across his congregation, lulled her with its partially comprehended phrases. She believed nothing he said, but was not offended or annoyed by his sincere prating. Phoebe knew that God, if He existed, would never have allowed a dead woman's foot to be sprinkled with her father's onanistic seed. The sight was too grotesque to have any place in a world governed by forces of good *or* evil; it was simply pathetic. Phoebe attended church because it was expected of her on this seventh day of every week. She did not object. It was something to do.

Wilkes' voice droned on, assuring his flock that Jesus is the brother of us all, the protector, the good shepherd. Phoebe did not wish to be a sheep, would rather have been a ravening wolf dashing among the flock, slashing woolly throats with her fangs, letting free this much-vaunted blood of the Lamb that Wilkes spoke of. Words, she thought, mere words, shallow approximations, stunted guideposts to *feelings*, which can never truly be understood by another. Even ideas, such as the one being propounded by Wilkes, were only structures of words, each succeeding layer raising the edifice further from its intuitive base, the flimsy scaffolding of words supporting with their effrontery and arrogance a tower of Babel, aspiring to the heights of understanding, the summit of knowing, yet by their very nature incapable ever of reaching that distant place. Waste, thought Phoebe in her despair, sheer waste, a noble experiment at best, foredoomed to failure. Reality lay in the surging of one's blood, the quickening of the heartbeat, the fierce desire to plunge over the waterfall's lip and hurtle down to froth and foam, to be tumbled and buffeted by the maelstrom of passion, to be carried away on the dark and febrile current of yearning—that was what Wilkes should have been preaching about. Phoebe had no actual experience of love beyond her impossible longing for the man on the train, had no criterion by which to judge the validity of her belief, but would willingly have staked her life on its truth. She imagined a mighty finger crashing through the roof, pointing to the top of her bonnet— *"Unbeliever!"*—and thought of being blasted by a heavenly bolt of lightning. It would not happen, she knew; Ben Franklin with his kite and key had stood a far greater chance of incineration. Phoebe would have traded endless pristine draughts of Christian love for one bubbling goblet of lust. The word (another of those straw scaffolds) repeated itself, swamping Wilkes' syrupy mouthings. Lust. Lust! She wanted the touch of a man, but not just any man; she wanted the touch of the one she could not have, the one who had come and gone, and left her reeling.

Beside her, Pike allowed his mind to wander. It did not wander far; he thought of Wilkes' daughter, the beautiful mute who every Sunday received the collection plate from the last pew, the pew where the Pikes usually sat. Today she had taken the plate with its modest freight of loose change from Pike's own hand, and their fingers had accidentally touched. He had felt the plate jerk slightly as she attempted to move her fingers away without losing her grip on it. She was the loveliest creature he had ever seen, and it grieved him to know she thought him repugnant, a fat middle-aged man who tinkered with the bodies of the dead, probing with his embalmer's hose and nozzle at their intimate orifices before her father said his piece at the graveside and buried the results of Pike's efforts. No wonder she did not wish her hand to touch his; it was understandable, especially in one so young. It hurt anyway. He wished his own daughter was half as lovely as Sadie Wilkes, but what could you expect from the womb of a woman like Jessica? He had married her not for her looks, which were negligible by anyone's standards, but because he erroneously believed her to be the heiress to a small but healthy fortune. Jessica had inherited nothing from her parents but debts, and was obliged to sell her home (which Pike had anticipated living in) to repay her many creditors. What a waste Pike's married life had been, what a desert! His mother had toiled like a slave to send her only child to medical school, had scrimped and saved (her own words, oft repeated) without assistance from husband or family, was chagrined at his failure to pass exams, at his pragmatic opting for embalming as a second, more realistic choice of profession; she had relented when he showed promise in this less decorous trade, only to plunge once again into acrimony over his choice of bride.

And she had been right; he never should have married Jessica. It had been the act of a naïve young fool. But he had paid the price for his folly like a man, had accepted his lot, and not sought solace in the arms of other women, apart from . . . and Phoebe had seen him. Damn her! Despite the passage of time he still cringed at the memory of his confrontation with a witness to his crime. It was clear Phoebe had seen only the one incident, and it had never again been mentioned following that incredible display of tantrum at the supper table and in her room all those years ago. Had she forgotten? She was civil to him, but that meant nothing. The sword of Damocles she held over his head had been considerably blunted by attrition, especially since the death of Mr. Storbeck some six years after that of his wife. The wife! Now, there was the kind of woman he should have married, full breasted, with a narrow waist and generous hips, wonderfully rounded buttocks, abundant hair and a throat of marble, not a bundle of sticks like Jessica. Yes, yes, he could picture those large and flaccid breasts still, their weight carrying them to her armpits as she lay on the stone slab. He had wanted to have her. Have a dead woman.

Usually he contented himself with self-abuse, but the body of Mrs. Storbeck had called forth a beast from within, a dark and hideous thing with a mind of its own. There she lay, and he had wanted her as he had never wanted any living woman. His desire had shocked him deeply, frightened him, forced him to quell the stirrings of the beast and perform no more than the usual rite of sexual release. God in heaven, what if he had succumbed to his desire and actually mounted her? Would Phoebe have stayed quietly beneath the bench, or rushed screaming into the street to bring disgrace down upon his head? Doubtless that is what would have occurred. His own strength of character had saved him from that dreadful fate; a weaker man would have gone ahead, and probably been gaoled for life. It had been a narrow escape. If only Jessica had resembled Mrs. Storbeck, what a marvellous marriage it might have been. Perhaps even Mother would have warmed to a type like Mrs. Storbeck, and not hounded her as she had hounded Jessica. But, no, it was doubtful that Mother would have approved of *any* woman sharing the life of her boy; even the Virgin Mary would not have been good enough. His beloved wife seated on one side of him, his dutiful daughter on the other, Pike tried to concentrate on the sermon and ignore his stiffened penis.

On the short walk home along Decatur, Jessica wondered if the man-that-wasn't-there, as she called him, would bother her today. The man had made his presence known for the first time just a few weeks ago; he had not knocked on the door or accosted her in the yard, nothing like that, had simply let her know he was there behind her. He used no words, but she knew he was there, even though when she turned around to see him he had vanished. One day she would turn quicker than he expected, and would be able to see just what he looked like. Jessica did not know if the man-that-wasn't-there was cruel or kind. He was simply *there*. Sometimes he did not visit for days at a time, but then would come the familiar sensation along her spine, and the wordless message—something like: "I'm back again"—

would be relayed to her. It was all very puzzling, but she dared not discuss it with Joshua, oh, dear me, no! He would tell her (if he told her anything at all, didn't just lower his eyes to his plate and continue eating) not to be stupid. That was his favourite word when dealing with Jessica—stupid. "You're stupid," he would say, as casually as he would observe that the sky is blue. "You're quite remarkably stupid, Jessica. I have never encountered another woman as overwhelmingly stupid as yourself." He had never hit her—well, not for many years now, not since Phoebe was tiny—and he did not drink, like so many other men did. She had much to be grateful for, really. She just wished he wouldn't keep insisting she was stupid. Jessica knew she was not the most intelligent person in the world; she was smart enough to know that much, but being told again and again of her shortcomings seemed unfair. One day he would hit her again, she knew that also; he would tire of telling her, and would hit her to make her understand once and for all that she was stupid, stupid, *stupid!* She had never told Phoebe of this fear, this looming dread; Phoebe would only worry all the more about her and give one of her funny little lectures about being strong. Really, Jessica couldn't see what being strong had to do with anything. When your husband wants to hit you no amount of strength will stop it happening. So she told Phoebe nothing, nor did she tell her of the man-that-wasn't-there. One day Phoebe would meet a present-able young man and marry, and on that day Jessica would be thrown to the lions. Without Phoebe she would be cast down to the deepest pit of hell. Imagine—just her and Joshua and Beatrice. . . . It was unthinkable. They would kill her. She had seen the look in their eyes. They hated her. Only Phoebe kept her alive. Phoebe would *not* meet a presentable young man and marry. No. Jessica reassured herself on that point, wondered why she had considered the prospect, even for just a second or two. Phoebe was not the type to go gadding about, flirting with men, attending church socials and the like where eligible bachelors congregated; in fact it looked as though Phoebe would end up on the proverbial shelf—a comforting thought. It was a shame, Jessica supposed, but she could not help feeling relieved; what terror in store if Phoebe was ever to leave! No, it was better this way. She knew it was selfishness that caused her to think like this, but every life deserves one good thing in it, and Phoebe was the one good thing in Jessica's. They were almost home now. She wondered if the man-that-wasn't-there would surprise her with a visit. Jessica had not felt his presence behind her since Thursday.

Phoebe had time to untie her bonnet and hang it on a peg behind the door before the pounding began. The ceiling shook beneath Grandmamma's flailing cane. Jessica looked up with the abject appearance of a rabbit watching a hawk plummet from the skies, growing larger and larger. "I'll do it," said Phoebe, and was rewarded with a look of naked gratitude from her mother.

With the reluctance of an aristocrat on her way to the guillotine, Phoebe mounted the staircase. Grandmamma did not stop her pounding until Phoebe had entered her room, closed the door, crossed the room and stood at last by the bed, strongly resisting the urge to take the cane from that gnarled hand and bludgeon Grandmamma to death.

"Yes?" Her voice was icy with contempt.

Grandmamma pointed with her cane to the chamberpot on the bedside table. "Get rid of it."

"I believe I've asked you several times to cover it with a cloth."

"What for?" snarled Grandmamma. "You know what's in it."

Fifty years ago she would have blushed to mention the contents of a chamberpot, even five years ago; it seemed that old age was loosening some of the more prudish screws that had held together that phenomenon known as a "respectable woman". She had recently accustomed herself to these blunt utterances, found they gave her a certain pleasure. The foulest word she had ever spoken aloud in her life was "bugger", and she had not known what it meant anyway. For that matter, she still did not, but bodily waste was another thing altogether; she understood *that* clearly enough, and liked to think that Phoebe and Jessica were shocked by her new-found impropriety.

"Cover it anyway. It smells less."

Phoebe draped a large napkin over the pot's rim. Grand-mamma exposed her gums in a grin. By God, but she hated this girl! It was almost a joy to hate this way; reducing Jessica to trembling servitude had been far too easy. Phoebe was the one who kept Grandmamma's fires smouldering, with her narrowed eyes and tight lips, those looks of una-dulterated loathing, equal to Grandmamma's own. It was good to have someone to hate when there was nothing else to do but grow old and die. "Take it away!" she screeched.

Halfway down the stairs Phoebe had to stop and lean against the wall to control her trembling. Then she contin-ued downstairs to the outhouse.

CHAPTER THIRTY

Lucius Croft was seventy-seven years old now, and he, too, nursed a bitter flame that kept him alive; he hated Calvin Puckett. Calvin had stolen his daughter away from him (as Croft saw it) and had robbed him of the ridge. Not only that, but he had driven darling Alma from his door after tiring of her, sent Croft's only child off into the darkness for ever! The bastard! Croft wanted very much to hurt Calvin Puckett, was not prepared to accept Calvin's simplemindedness as a mitigating factor, had, for his own purposes, chosen to ignore the thing that made Calvin victim, not perpetrator in the affair of Alma. Above all, Croft wanted Noah. He had never had a son, but a grandson would do just as well. For the first six years of Noah's life Croft had no interest in the boy, having heard that he was hopelessly backward, incapable even of speech. Then had come the news that he could talk after all, was not only normal but smart as a whip. By the time Noah was thirteen it was generally acknowledged that the boy was some kind of prodigy, what the editor of the *Valley Forge Courier* called "our fair town's whitest hope, an example to youth everywhere". Lucius Croft wanted that boy more than he had ever wanted anything in his life. He was one of the community's wealthiest men; not only was his farm a model of industry and profit, but the store on Decatur, still managed with admirable flair by nephew Willard, was an unparalleled moneymaker. Lucius Croft was rich and clever, and he wanted Calvin Puckett, who was poor and stupid, to be ground into the dirt.

On a day when he knew Joe Cobden was in town delivering wood, and Noah at school, Croft paid his first visit to the ridge since he had surrendered it as a wedding gift in 1873. Calvin did not at first recognise him, and was too surprised to be embarrassed by his gaffe when Croft introduced himself. He invited the old man to come inside and take a seat, this being the full extent of his ability to play the role of host. Croft lost no time, knowing he would probably have to repeat himself several times in order to drive home his message. First, he asked if Calvin was aware of his son's superior intellect. Calvin was, and beamed proudly. Was he also aware that Noah would require further teaching at big schools away from Valley Forge, colleges in the east? Yes, Calvin had heard that. Was Calvin worried about where he would find the cash to pay for college when the time came? Now that it was mentioned, Calvin was. Had he heard of the practice of sponsoring, whereby a well-to-do man paid for the advanced schooling of a bright boy who otherwise would not receive the benefit of higher education? No, he hadn't, and Croft leaped into the breach.

"There's a man who'll pay Noah's college fees gladly."

"Who?"

"Me."

"You gonna pay for Noah to go to college?"

"Let's be frank. You've got no money of your own. You live on what Joe Cobden earns woodcutting, don't you?"

Calvin nodded. "Joe looks after us real good."

"But he doesn't have enough to send Noah to college, does he?"

"He don't?"

"He'd have to cut down every tree on the ridge twice a week to earn enough for college fees."

Calvin wondered how it was possible to cut down the same trees twice, figured that it wasn't, and understood at last that Noah's future was in jeopardy. "There ain't gonna be enough," he said, and there was a note of panic in his voice.

"Not unless you accept the money from me."

"I'll do it, and thank you kindly."

"First there's got to be a contract between us."

He produced two sheets of paper, handed them to Calvin, upside down. Calvin did not know the difference. "This is a loan paper, one copy for you and one for me." Croft did not wish to use the word "mortgage" for fear Calvin knew it and would realise what was afoot.

"Loan paper?"

"It says that I'll loan you fifteen hundred dollars, using the house and ridge as collateral."

"Collateral?"

"A wise man never loans money to anyone who's flat broke, Calvin. You've got a fine home and property here. These things are called collateral. Thanks to them you can accept a loan."

"You said you was gonna give me money." Calvin was becoming confused.

"A loan amounts to the same thing. You wouldn't expect me to hand you the cash out of the goodness of my heart, now would you? Life just isn't like that. Fifteen hundred dollars is a lot of money, Calvin."

"More'n a thousand?" This was the largest sum Calvin could imagine. He did not know it was ten times one hundred, just knew it was a whole lot.

"A thousand, plus another half-thousand."

"Is it enough to pay for college?" asked Calvin, impressed.

"Oh, plenty, yessiree." Croft had no true idea of college fees. "Just sign on the bottom line," he said, righting the papers.

Calvin went to fetch pen and ink, returned and carefully wrote his name, the only two words he had ever been able to master, after much instruction from Joe. He signed both copies, and in this way mortgaged everything he owned.

"Thank you, Calvin. And here's your money."

Calvin stared at the thick wad of bills. It sure did look like a lot. He took it gratefully and squashed it into his jacket.

"I surely do thank you."

"What good's family if they don't look after each other? We're related by marriage, Calvin, don't forget that. Just sign the receipt and that'll take care of business."

Calvin signed. Croft folded it inside his own copy of the mortgage agreement and tucked the precious sheets away. He had Calvin Puckett right where he wanted him, safely in his pocket.

"There's another matter I want to talk to you about."

Calvin adopted his alert expression, the one that meant he had to frown a lot with concentration; he was ready now for this other matter.

Croft cleared his throat. "I know you think Joe Cobden's a good man. So do some other folks around here, but there's a certain letter come into my hands and I figure you should know what's in it."

"Letter?"

Croft fetched another sheet from inside his jacket and handed it to Calvin, who stared with blank incomprehension. "A letter for me?" No one had ever written Calvin a letter before.

"Not for you, for me. From Alma."

"Alma . . . ?" Calvin knew who Alma was; he had been married to her! "Alma . . . ?" he repeated.

"Want me to read it to you?"

"I reckon . . ."

Croft took back the sheet of paper. The letter had been written by a prostitute he visited once a month, to ensure the handwriting had a feminine look to it. The prostitute, who worked in the discreet brothel on Chippewa, had been well paid, sworn to secrecy. She thought it was some kind of joke.

" 'Dear Father,' " read Croft, " 'it is with a heavy heart I put pen to paper and inform you at last of the reason for my departure from Valley Forge so many years ago. I am at present living in Boston. I am nursemaid to the children of a wonderful family whose name I cannot tell as I do not wish to involve them in my past. I will never return to

Kansas, not while I know the misshapen fiend Joe Cobden is living still in what was once my home. For it was he who caused my flight, he who drove me from my home and the side of my husband. It is only with great difficulty that a woman may talk of certain things, and my fingers tremble at this telling of my tale. Father, it was my misfortune to be much admired by the hunchback, who began forcing his unwholesome attentions upon me whenever Calvin was not there. I resisted with all my strength, but said nothing to my husband, whose guest Joe Cobden was. I feared he would not believe me if I spoke of the hunchback's unseemly advances. And then the dreaded thing happened—Joe Cobden ravished me on the settee in the parlour' ''—this detail was a spur-of-the-moment addition by Croft, who thought it would give the letter greater credibility; he was gratified to see Calvin, who was perched on the settee, give a slight jump—'' 'while Calvin was occupied elsewhere. He clawed at me like a brute, and had his way. I could make no sound, as his hand was across my mouth all the while. When he was done he told me never to tell of it to anyone, or he would kill us all, the baby too. Terrified, I fled for my life . . .' ''

The letter continued with a description of her new life in Boston, but Calvin heard none of it. Joe . . . and Alma! On the very settee he was sitting on! He stood up, began pacing around the room. Croft, having concluded, did his best to look sympathetic. "It must have been a cruel ordeal for such a gentle woman, maybe even made her a little crazy. Only a crazy woman'd leave her home and child and run off the way she did." He did not bother to remind Calvin that Alma had, in her distraught state of mind, coolly withdrawn half Calvin's money from the bank before departing. The success of this scheme depended upon Calvin's penchant for suggestibility. Tell him something in a convincing manner and the chances were he would believe it, and if he believed it he would either drive Joe Cobden from his home or kill him. If the latter, Calvin would be hanged or incarcerated in an institution; if the former, Calvin would spend the fifteen hundred dollars, since Joe Cobden would no longer be around to chop trees and earn money, and when the fifteen hundred dollars were gone, why, then, in would step Croft, waving his mortgage in one hand and adoption papers in the other. No one would deny his claim to either the ridge or the boy. Machiavelli could not have devised a simpler, more propitious stratagem. He folded the letter and replaced it in his pocket.

Calvin's world had come unhinged, the past and the present separating, flying apart. All this time he had thought Joe was his friend, and he had gone and done that awful thing to Alma, made her leave the house and never come back. He had not thought of her for years now, but Croft's visit had rekindled memories of a poignant and highly selective nature, memories of what Calvin considered the good things to be had from marriage, revolving for the most part around the kitchen table and the marital bed. And Joe Cobden had gone and taken it all away from him. You couldn't trust nobody, *nobody!*

Croft knew the thrill of seeing a job well done. The poor fool looked like he'd been kicked by a mule. He stood, placed his hat on his head. "I'll take my leave now, Calvin. You'll likely want to be alone. It's the worst kind of news one man can give another, but I told myself you deserved to know the truth, letting the hunchback live here like you do. I won't be giving you advice; no man needs that in a case like this. I'll just say that when I find a snake in the grass I don't just let it lie there. Nossir, I go ahead and reach for a gun." He went to the door, paused. "At least our other business will have brought you a ray of sunshine. Good day to you."

Calvin said nothing, had failed to understand; the loan was already forgotten in the light of the awful disclosure about Joe and Alma. He watched Croft depart in his smart buggy, then went to Joe's room, where the Sharpe's big fifty and the Winchester were kept. The firing pin had been replaced three years ago when Noah, as most boys do, had wanted to learn how to shoot. Joe taught him with the Winchester, the Sharpe's having too powerful a kick for a small boy, and after having destroyed a number of harmless birds and squirrels Noah had tired of the rifle and returned it to Joe's permanent care. Calvin found it in a wardrobe along with a box of ammunition, loaded it and went back to the parlour. He took a seat by the window, the rifle across his knees, and waited for Joe to return home.

He kept turning to look at the settee, pictured them there, could not help himself, and finally began to wail, tears flooding his face. How could Joe have done such a bad thing? Joe was good to him and Noah, had been right from the start. Calvin tried to remember how Joe had come to the ridge in the first place, but was unable to recollect the scene. Had he known Joe before that time? He was unsure. It didn't matter anyway. What mattered was Joe Cobden had gone and done it with Alma, with Calvin's *wife*, in Calvin's *home* even! Right *there* on the settee that Alma got from a catalogue and never wanted him to sit on unless his pants were clean. He saw her there now, with her rear end in the air, skirts raised out of the way and that . . . *hunchback* clutching at her, pushing at her, riding her like a horse, *making* her do it, *hurting* her, hurting his *wife!*

Galvanised by rage, Calvin sprang from the chair and emptied all fifteen bullets from the Winchester into the settee, peppered the striped sateen with holes, splintered the upholstered framework, blew one leg clean off. It was not enough. He ran out to the yard, fetched back the axe, began chopping the settee in half; this accomplished, he dragged the halves outside, ran back inside for kerosene, sprinkled the wrecked furniture with lavish oily rain, ran inside again and returned with a burning stick from the stove. The settee ignited with a *whoosh!* Calvin had been too liberal with the kerosene, and woodchips scattered nearby from Joe's chopping block also caught fire. Enraged though he was, Calvin did not want to set the yard on fire. He removed his jacket, swiped at the burning ground and succeeded in thrashing these minor flames into submission. His jacket began to smoulder, having itself received a dangerous splash or two of kerosene. He attempted to save it, but was forced in the end to throw it on to the fire, where it was quickly consumed. He had no memory of the fifteen hundred dollars in one of its pockets.

The settee was still burning when Joe's wagon entered the yard. Calvin was jumping around the flames, screeching incomprehensibly. When he saw Joe climb down, Calvin ran inside yet again and burst from the front door with the axe in his hands, leaped from the porch to the ground without touching the intervening steps and ran full tilt at Joe, the axe raised. Shocked by Calvin's apparent madness, Joe froze. Why was the settee on fire? Why was Calvin running at him with the axe? That Calvin was intent on killing him became more obvious with every thudding footfall, was emphasised by the thin scream trailing from Calvin's distorted mouth. Joe turned and ran. Calvin pursued him around and around the yard, his speed hampered by the weight of the raised axe and his own natural clumsiness. Joe had no trouble keeping well out of reach and, once realising there was no immediate danger to his person, began finding the situation funny. He began to titter as he ran, casting glances over his shoulder to ensure Calvin was still stumblefooting along at a safe distance, the whole thing just too ridiculous for words. "What's wrong?" he kept asking between bouts of laughter. "What the hell are you doing? Put the axe down! What's the matter with you anyway?" But it made no difference. Calvin ran in pursuit until exhaustion caused the axe to fall from his hands. When he saw this happen, Joe stopped, beginning to tire himself. "Why don't you tell me what's wrong? And why's the settee on fire, for Christ's sake?"

Calvin ran at him again, arms outstretched, fingers clawing for Joe's throat. Joe grabbed his wrists and held him off. "Stop it, Calvin! What've *I* done? Just tell me what it's all about!" Calvin kicked at his shins. Joe lost patience, threw him to the ground and went to the house, hoping to find some kind of answer within. He picked up the axe in passing and took it with him into the hallway, then the parlour. The floor was littered with woodchips, the wall spattered with bullet holes, Calvin's Winchester lying on the floor. Joe picked it up, checked that it was unloaded. It had been, of course—at the settee.

The front door slammed. Calvin stood bristling in the parlour doorway. "Get out," he said, his voice caught somewhere between a hiss and a moan. His entire body shook.

"Why?"

"You know why, you . . . you dirty *dog!*"

"No I don't. Supposing you tell me."

"You know, you know, you *know!*"

"I don't! Why'd you burn the goddamn settee!"

"That's where you *done* it! You done it *there!*"

"Done *what? Did* what?"

"Alma!" screeched Calvin. "You done it to *Alma!*"

Calvin's knees buckled, depositing him on the floor, where he sat with his back against the parlour door and bawled with the utter abandonment of a child. Joe felt helpless, confused beyond all understanding. What had happened here in his absence? What was this nonsense about himself and Alma? Done it to her? Done *what?* He cast his thoughts back eleven years, sought answers in memory. No, he hadn't done anything to her. He went to Calvin, stood over him, too angry still over the axe attack to kneel and comfort him. "Look, you're going to have to explain a few things. I want to know what you think I did to Alma. I only knew her for a week before she left, remember?"

"That never stopped you!" howled Calvin. "You *done* it to her!"

At last Joe understood the accusation's meaning, if not its source. "Don't you know me better than to think I'd . . . do something bad to Alma?"

Calvin's breath came in sniffles, gasps and, finally, hiccups. His tears ceased, and he scowled at the floor, mouth turned down with exaggerated truculence. He plucked spitefully at the carpet between his thighs. He suspected maybe Joe had a point there, but he did not want to admit it. Deep within Calvin was a kernel of resentment, and Joe was its unlikely cause. Calvin knew Joe had done good things for him, but at the same time it had always bothered Calvin that his own boy should have more respect for Joe than for his father. He had seen it from the time Joe came to stay at the ridge, and especially since the time Noah had started talking and reading all those books Joe showed him how to use. Joe got all the things Calvin, as the boy's father, should have been getting. It wasn't fair, and he resented it. He felt guilty about his resentment, knew it was unworthy, but would not release his hold on it. Like a petulant child scolded for doing what it knows is wrong, Calvin wanted to hit back, to blot out his sense of foolishness and shame. Knowing Joe was right, knowing Joe was *always* right, infuriated him. He tugged more and more threads from the carpet, creating a small hole. It was *his* carpet, wasn't it? He could put all the holes in it he wanted, could put all the holes he wanted in the settee, and he'd darn well done it, too! In fact the whole darn place was his, Calvin's, to do with as he pleased, to have whoever he wanted inside of it, and to ask whoever he didn't want inside it to leave. No one could stop him from doing that, not even Joe. The knowledge of this power, the power of possession, of dominion, gave strength to his disgruntlement. It was high time the king took charge of the palace.

"Go 'way," he said.

"I can't hear you when you mumble."

"Go away!"

It came from the pit of his stomach, and from the tiny cupboard at the back of his mind wherein was kept the injured remnants of his pride. On this day Calvin Puckett, unloved by all since the day of his birth, abandoned by wife and son, made use of by a scheming hunchback—on this day Calvin Puckett would darn well have his own way!

"Go away! Go away! Go awaaaaaaaaaaaayyyyyy!!!"

Walking home from school, swinging his lunch pail at arm's length, Noah resented his own tramping feet. Many of the boys at school had ponies, and Noah did not. Shanks's mare was all very well for dumbass farmers' sons, but Noah Puckett was destined for great things, for a shining future. Miss Woodcock told him so, fluttered around him like a broody hen, offering encouragement he did not need, anoying the hell out of him in fact. He indulged her, kept to himself his dislike for the teacher who had once deliberately humiliated him in front of the entire class, the teacher who nowadays doted on him. Noah thought she was a stupid old cow. She got herself all flustered just because he could tell her about Sennacherib and Alexander and Charlemagne. All she could think of was sending him off to college when he was fifteen; all she worried about was getting him a sponsor who would stake him to a chance at that shining future. Noah wanted what Miss Woodcock wanted, but he wished he didn't have to put up with her fussing as part of what was required to get it. College. Topeka, she said, or maybe Kansas City, and if he excelled in one or other of those places, why, he'd have the wherewithal to go even further east, to Yale or Harvard. Those were magical places, capable of transforming a Kansas nobody into a man of renown, a mover of mountains and shaper of destinies.

Noah was unsure what exactly it was that he wanted to be, once manhood had been achieved, just so long as he was both rich and famous. Miss Woodcock kept telling him there was "no limit" to personal achievement in the United States if a boy was smart enough and willing enough to get where he wanted to go. She had presented him with a biography of Abraham Lincoln, had written on the flyleaf *Mighty oaks from tiny acorns grow,* just to reinforce the intended message. He had read the book, since reading remained his passion, and was impressed by Honest Abe's rise from rail splitter to President. Something like that would suit Noah; you couldn't get much more famous than being president of the whole country, and he assumed the job was well paid. Mind you, he might just decide to become one of those captains of industry he read about in the papers. He might be a railroad baron. Or another Thomas Edison. There was an annoying abundance of choices. Still, he was under no obligation to pick one this early. The big problem right now was the lack of a pony. Joe had once offered him the use of his decrepit old gelding that could barely get from one side of the pasture to the other, but Noah wasn't going to make a laughing-stock of himself by shuffling up to the schoolhouse on that old gluepot; no future president/tycoon/inventor was going to let people point and giggle and think him a fool, not if he could help it. Better to stick with walking. Abe Lincoln had to walk to school. Joe's old nag had dropped dead a few weeks later anyway.

When he reached the house Noah was surprised to see Joe packing his few belongings into the wagon. The remains of a fire smouldered in the yard. Calvin stood on the porch, his Winchester (bullets spent, but he had forgotten) held ready in his arms. The scene was so laden with inexplicability Noah stood where he was for a moment, wholly confused, then went to the wagon.

"What's going on?"

"Ask your father," said Joe tersely, and continued loading.

Noah mounted the steps to the porch. "What happened?"

"Ask *him*," said Calvin. "He knows."

Noah had always known adults were fools. He went back to Joe. "He won't say."

"He thinks I raped your mother."

"Raped?"

"You're old enough to know what that is."

"Why's he think that?"

"I don't know, but if you ever find out be sure and write me a letter about it. I'd kind of like to know myself."

"You're going away?"

"Have to. Worn out my welcome, looks like."

"But you can't just *go*. . . ." Life without Joe? Unthinkable. Little knots of panic were beginning to form along his spine, making him squirm.

Joe climbed aboard the wagon, wanting to get this over with quickly, be gone before the boy fully realised what was happening and did something that would only complicate a situation already bordering on lunacy.

"I want to come too!"

Something like that.

"Well you can't."

And Joe drove away.

Noah turned an accusing eye on Calvin. "Why'd you make him go?"

"He knows."

"I don't!"

"It ain't fitten for ears young as yours."

"You stupid shit! You're an *idiot!*"

"Don't you go talkin' at me that way!"

"Idiot!" Noah screeched, fists bunched.

"Don't you call me that! I'm your pa!"

"No you're not! *Joe* is!"

This was the worst thing Noah could have said; Calvin, in his lack of sophistication, tended to interpret in a literal fashion anything said to him, and Noah's announcement blared at him like the trump of doom—Joe was Noah's father! Not only had he raped Alma, he was the father of her child! That the alleged rape occurred two years after the birth of Noah was ignored in the harsh light of revelation. All three of them—hunchback, wife and boy—were together in a plot to make Calvin look a fool! He had been wickedly deceived all along the line, and everyone had known but him! All the laughter Calvin had ever heard directed at him in his life now returned, redoubled, a hollow cacophony of belly laughs, guffaws, titterings, hootings and howlings, a great flapping blanket of sound, billowing and snapping in winds of outrage, and at every snap the laughter increased, became the baying from a million throats that merged into one, a giant screaming throat that yawned above and around him, swallowed Calvin, sucked him from the porch and drew him up into a whirlwind of sound, spinning, spinning, his ears seeming to explode. . . .

Noah watched the Winchester fall clattering at Calvin's feet, saw his father clutch at his head, spin around once, trip and fall down the steps to lie thrashing in the yard, limbs jerking, fingers clawing up earthen clods. Threads of foam spilled from lips champing at air, producing a sound Noah thought the most dreadful he had ever heard: "Nungh, nungh, nungh," said Calvin, over and over, one heel drumming a spastic tattoo on the bottom step, the other gouging furrows in the ground. Noah ran down the trail away from the house, ran until he caught up with Joe, screamed his name. The wagon halted.

"He's dying! He fell down and spit everywhere!"

Joe dropped from the driver's seat, hoisted Noah up to take his place. "Get Whaley."

They sped in opposite directions. When Joe reached him, Calvin had become rigid as a board. Joe carried him indoors like an unwieldy length of firewood, laid him on his bed and waited for the doctor to arrive.

"Lucky he didn't swallow his tongue," said Whaley. It was early evening. "Epilepsy," he explained. "Nothing to be done about it. You've never seen him this way before?"

"No."

"It won't kill him, not unless he swallows his tongue, as I say, and chokes. If it happens again, get a spoon down his throat to keep his tongue from rolling up and blocking the oesophagus. Don't use your fingers; he may bite them off."

"That's all?"

"There's no cure. He won't be incapacitated by it until he has another attack. That may happen next week, next year, there's no predicting."

Dr. Whaley left. Joe and Noah stared at Calvin, who appeared to be deeply asleep. Joe wondered if the same thing had happened when Alma left. On that occasion Calvin had disappeared for two days. Who knows what might have happened to him during that time? He had never spoken of such an attack, probably would not have remembered it anyway. Whaley had said he might have no recollection of this afternoon's fit.

Noah wished with all his heart that Calvin had died. He felt no remorse or guilt for feeling this way. With Calvin dead, Joe would have no reason for leaving, and life at the ridge would be both simpler and happier. What boy wanted a fool like Calvin for a father? Come to think of it, what boy wanted a hunchback for a father? Noah reminded himself he was not like other boys, and could therefore want what he liked. Tiring of what seemed to him a pointless vigil, he went early to bed, and lay thinking of his life to date. It had all been most peculiar, by any standards. Had Abe Lincoln ever dug up a dead baby and buried it again? Noah had not been back to the blackberry patch since that day. He told himself it was because he was now too old to be scrambling through the undergrowth, but at the back of his mind there lurked the notion that the place was haunted, that a tiny ghost rose from the ground every night, only to find itself imprisoned within the brass bell, trapped like a genie in a bottle. He had no intention of crawling into the heart of the thicket ever again. I'm too old, he said to himself, really much too old.

Joe could not sleep. He had unloaded his belongings from the wagon, stabled his horses. He did not know where he could possibly have gone, had he continued on his way down the ridge trail to Valley Forge and the world beyond. Calvin's feeble mentality had driven him away, and Calvin's eccentric body had brought him back again before he had gone two hundred yards. Fickle fate at work? Joe had not attempted analysis of life's perverseness since his early days in Kansas. He lived from one day to the next, appreciating those things which gave him pleasure—watching Noah grow up, for example—never allowing himself to be surprised or dismayed over the bad things that sometimes intruded upon what was basically a congenial and unhurried existence. I must be getting old and complacent, he thought, but the prospect did not worry him; complacency was easier to deal with than anguish. He conjured up incidents, relived emo-

tions from his childhood and youth, could barely recognise
the rages, the tempestuous miseries endured, the naïveté
compounded by ignorance and downright stupidity, the
hopeless longings and crushing disappointments, his pride
and his shame. It had all happened to someone else. Joe felt
something very near to contentment as he considered the
twistings and turnings his life had taken to bring him here
to this house, to this chair beside the bed of its mad owner.
He suspected life had very few surprises left for him now,
certainly none he was incapable of handling. He was thirty-
two years old.

CHAPTER THIRTY-ONE

Calvin remembered nothing of that day's events. Joe and Noah did not enlighten him. Life on the ridge proceeded as before, until Lucius Croft came to the door. "I want my grandson," he declared. He was puzzled at Joe's continued presence in the Puckett home, and it was impatience, following the apparent failure of that part of his plan, that drove Croft to the house on the ridge, demanding what he considered to be his own. Calvin did not know how to cope with the intruder, so Joe took charge.

"You can't have him."

"I want my grandson!"

"You already said that. I'll repeat myself too. You can't have him."

"This is not a suitable home for a child."

"What's wrong with it?"

"The boy has no proper parents."

"Neither did I, and look what a wonderful character I grew up to be."

"Let me have him, at least to visit."

Croft's voice had a catch in it that Joe thought genuine. The poor old bastard, he thought; he's all alone. "Wait here," he said. Croft had thus far not got beyond the front door.

Joe talked with Calvin and Noah. Calvin had no opinion. Noah thought it might be interesting to see his grandfather's place, and Joe could see no real harm in it. The boy went off with the old man, was returned late in the afternoon filled with cake and candy, slightly ashamed at having indulged himself like someone years his junior; he excused his gluttony with a reminder that cake and candy were never in supply at home. He liked Croft well enough, but it was kind of disgusting the way the old fart kept talking about his wonderful daughter that had been led astray. Noah could not tell if he truly believed this nonsense or not, decided not to contradict this human horn of plenty, and so opened his mouth only to stuff it with more confectionery.

With this first visit a pattern was established. It was a pity Joe remained unaware of Croft's role in promoting the allegation that he had raped Alma, for had he known the truth he might perhaps have been on guard against the subtle campaign for Noah's heart Croft now began to wage. For all that he had convinced himself Alma was the perfect daughter who had been driven away by an unsuitable husband, the greater part of Croft's brain and nature still functioned as of old—with an unswerving determination to get hold of that which he considered his by right of his age, his wealth and his cunning. Croft had rewritten the past to suit himself, and was entirely capable of composing the present with a view to the future.

Joe suspected nothing until the day Noah returned from the Croft farm not in Croft's buggy, but on a fat-bellied pinto pony with a gleaming new saddle. Noah rode him around the yard several times, calling out to Joe and Calvin to come see what he'd got. Joe was angry. He would have liked to buy the boy a pony himself, but could not afford to do so. The firewood trade was bringing in a healthy sum, enough to feed the three of them and still leave a good few dollars over each week. Joe was saving those dollars for Noah; if anyone was going to be his college sponsor, it would be Joe Cobden. Had Noah been dropping lead-lined hints to Croft that he considered walking to school the burden of a bumpkin? Joe was willing to bet he had.

"Isn't he a beauty!" Noah proudly stroked his pony's neck.

"He sure is," said Calvin.

Joe had to agree; the pony was a handsome beast, splashed broadly in black and white, with a shaggy mane and tail. The saddle was the best money could buy. Noah also sported new boots, riding boots, high-heeled like a Texas cowboy's; his walking days were obviously over. Joe swallowed his anger, stroked the pony's velvet nose, narrowly avoided having his fingers nipped. "What's his name?"

"Wicked. He's got a wicked gleam in his eye."

Just like some people I know, thought Joe.

From that day on Noah rode to school, to Croft's place, to all points of the compass. The pony was a new and living toy, but it made him feel like a man. He wanted a rifle scabbard to tie on to the saddle, so he could carry the Winchester and look like a real rough rider. Joe said no. A week later Noah had the scabbard, in stout leather, and a rifle of his own to place inside it, a brand new Remington.

Joe went to see Croft.

"You've got to stop buying him everything he wants."

"Why?" Croft had a confident smirk on his weathered face that Joe found infuriating.

"Because you're spoiling him. He doesn't need a damn rifle."

"The rifle is what tamed this great country, Mr. Cobden. Every boy should have one and be trained in its use as part of his American heritage. Without the rifle Kansas and every other state would still belong to the Indians."

"What are you trying to do, Croft, buy him?"

"I don't need to buy Noah. The boy's related to me. There are blood ties between us." And not between him and *you,* Indian, was the implication.

All Joe could do was forbid Noah to carry the rifle to school.

The following week Croft bought him an expensive dove-grey stetson, wide brimmed, with a deep dent in the crown. It increased Noah's height by twelve inches, puffed up his vanity beyond measure. Joe hated the sound of Noah's boot-heels clumping through the house, was sure the boy did it to annoy him. He hated also the careless way Noah treated his new possessions; the pony was often ill-groomed, the rifle unoiled. Joe informed Noah he would not be fed until he had attended to these chores. Noah promptly rode over to "Grandpa" Croft's farm and stayed two days, eating all he wanted, under no obligation to lift a finger for horse or gun. He returned home only because he found Croft a bore, and because the farmhands laughed openly at his cowboy outfit. Before Joe allowed him into the house, Noah had to present one burnished pinto and one gleaming gun for inspection; Joe also made him clean the mud from his boots for good measure, hating himself for standing over the boy like some kind of tyrant, yet seeing no other way. Noah must not be allowed to sink into the velvet-lined pit being prepared for him by Croft. He decided to approach the problem head-on.

"The old man's trying to bribe you. He wants you to belong to him, like a son."

"What's wrong with that?"

"I'll tell you what's wrong with it—he's an old shit, that's what. He knows very well you belong here with Calvin and me. It's us that brought you up, not him. He didn't even care if you existed until now. Can't you see that, or are you too taken up with the stuff he keeps buying you?"

"There's no reason he shouldn't buy me stuff."

"I'm not saying there is. It's his motive I don't like."

"What's wrong with it?"

"I already told you; he's trying to buy your goddamn soul."

"That's stupid. You told me people don't have souls, just bodies and minds. You said souls are made up by the church to keep dumb people happy."

"I mean . . . symbolically. You know damn well what I mean, so don't try to sidetrack the conversation. You're beginning to suffer a bad case of smartmouth, and I don't like it."

"What are you gonna do about it?" Noah jeered, half afraid of what might follow. Joe's reaction surprised and disappointed him; he had expected a slap in the face, received instead a look of sorrow, the first he had ever seen on Joe's ugly puss.

"It's too bad," said Joe softly. "You're turning into somebody I don't want to know."

Noah felt awful. The best part of him was still bound to Joe and the ridge by years of closeness, of affection, of respect. He did not want to drive any kind of wedge between them, but he did not want to be told what he must and must not do. All he needed, literally, was a firm hand. Joe should have slapped him. They both knew it. Noah went to his room. Joe remained by the fire for a long time, wondering if his grip upon those things he had come to hold dear was slipping.

Phoebe walked several steps past the sign before understanding its significance for her. She went back. In the window of Croft's store was a sheet of whitewashed cardboard, carefully lettered in black: *Help Wanted. Apply Within*. The sign might just as well have applied to Phoebe herself, as to the store; she needed help the way a drowning man requires it, and in recent weeks had concluded that assistance would arrive in only one form—cold cash. With money, Phoebe could take herself and Jessica away from Valley Forge. She did not know where they could go, or what they would do when they got there; it was the act of leaving which occupied her thoughts, and here before her was the means whereby she could purchase tickets to freedom. *Apply Within*. She did, and fifteen minutes later walked out with hope humming its seductive harmonies in her breast.

Pike was outraged. His daughter *working? Serving* people? Letting the community think he could not afford to *feed* her? He forbade Phoebe ever to take up the position Willard Croft had said was hers, even forbade her another visit to the store to tell Croft she must rescind her services. Phoebe allowed him to make his points several times before assuring him she would do exactly as she pleased; she was twenty-five years old, and quite capable of deciding for herself what to do with her life. Pike tried a different approach. "And what of your mother? Is she to perform all domestic duties on her own? Are you prepared to double her burden? Are you really so selfish?"

"Mother's burden would be halved if only Grandmamma had the decency to stop wanting something fetched up to her every five minutes. It's *her* that makes hard work for us both in this house."

Pike was shocked. "Are you saying your grandmother is to blame for her condition? You would blame a helpless, crippled woman of advanced years for the work you are unwilling to do?"

"She isn't crippled. She's quite capable of getting out of bed and looking after herself. There's nothing wrong with her that strong words from you wouldn't cure."

"Have you forgotten your grandmother had the misfortune to fall down the stairs on our very first day here?"

"She broke her arm, Father, not her legs or back. There is nothing wrong with her."

"Oh, yes? And why, pray tell, is the poor woman bedridden?"

"Spite, I should think."

"Spite? Explain yourself."

"Very well. She doesn't like Mother or myself, so she does her very best to make us work on her behalf. She's mean and petty and spiteful."

Pike came very near to hitting his daughter, and both knew any further provocation would carry him across the borders of prudence and restraint. "You will apologise for that remark," he said, the jugular vein pulsing hotly above his collar.

"You wish me to say I'm sorry?"

"I insist upon it."

"I'm sorry Grandmamma is mean and petty and spiteful."

His hand met her cheek in a surprisingly loud slap. The blow had not been overly hard, knocking Phoebe's head sideways without upsetting the balance of her body. Her cheek flushed redly with the imprint of his palm. She was glad to have been hit; it made the undercurrent of loathing she felt for Pike easier to support. Phoebe sometimes liked to think of herself as a beleaguered castle; now the drawbridge was well and truly up. Pike's blow had made of her an unassailable fortress, battlemented with pride, armed with the hot lead of scorn.

"Thank you, Father," she said evenly.

Pike was trembling with fury. He did not know if Phoebe was sincerely thanking him for having corrected her lamentable attitude with a well-deserved blow, or mocking him. "Go to your room!" was the only possible response to so nebulous a phrase.

"To my room . . . of course!" said Phoebe with a smile, as though this was the most original and welcome suggestion ever to have reached her ears. "To my room!" she said again, and swept by Pike with the nonchalance and hauteur of a duchess. Pike wondered if perhaps his daughter was demonstrating the symptoms of incipient mental aberration; he had come to accept that Jessica was evincing all the signs generally associated with feeblemindedness—forgetfulness, blank stares, an annoying habit of suddenly turning to look behind her—and would not have been surprised if the seeds of madness had been inherited by and were beginning to manifest their growth in Phoebe. Was any man more cursed with ill-fortune than Pike? He thought not, and in the blackness of his mood forgot that he had not managed to extract from Phoebe an apology for her remarks about Grandmamma, or a promise to surrender her job at Croft's store.

Willard had long ago abandoned plans to leave Kansas in pursuit of adventure and excitement elsewhere. Every passing year had rooted him more firmly in the familiar soil of Valley Forge, and these roots became longer, deeper and even more tangled when he married. His wife had disappointed him in some respects, but he could not fault her domestic industry or her willingness to prepare his favourite foods; the bedroom was another matter, one that Willard's mind lurched sharply away from whenever his thoughts strayed in that unpromising direction. Children had resulted from their joyless couplings, making Willard a man in the estimate of himself and his few cronies, and because of this he regarded his wife not with love, it was true, but with a genuine, if moderate, affection. He was neither happy nor unhappy, and his moustache still resembled a sparsely furred caterpillar. Satisfaction came in the form of success at the store, in knowledge of his skill as a manager and salesman, and the promise of a sizeable inheritance when Uncle Lucius finally went to his reward in heaven. Until recently the old skinflint had had no one else in the world to leave his farm and store to, no one at all; Willard had dismissed Noah Puckett as a possible contender for these post-mortem prizes-to-be years ago, but now word of Croft's sudden and unstinting generosity toward the boy had come to his attention, and Willard was afraid. He lost several nights of sleep over these stories, and only managed to revive his spirits by telling himself Uncle Lucius would never let his labours go unrewarded; the old man was simply being open-handed, was indulging the boy because Noah was his grandson, not because Croft was grooming him for the role of heir.

So well was the store doing, Willard had decided to take on one other person as a sales assistant, and the very first applicant was ideal for the position. Willard had known Phoebe as a customer for over two years, ever since the Pikes had come to town, and admired her no-nonsense approach to life, her brisk intelligence and her unwillingness to engage in idle gossip—a vice his wife was prone to. He made his satisfaction known by asking Phoebe to remove the *Help Wanted* sign from the window personally. He was sure they would get along well together as employer and employee.

During her first few days Phoebe familiarised herself with

the range of stock. The store had expanded greatly since the time of its founding, and would not have been recognised by its former owner, the squaw-man, who had set up shop with little more than a barrel of crackers, a barrel of molasses, a bolt of cloth and a keg of nails. Now one could buy a brocaded scarf or damask towel, a lace collar, bead panels and braid trim, buttons, pens and nibs, boxes of stationery, needles and yarn, thread, thimbles and pincushions, suspenders or a hairbrush, a keepsake box or some gloves and hosiery, a tobacco pouch, soap (shaving and toilet), candy, bracelets, lockets and stickpins, drapery hooks and chains, caps and bonnets and dozens more frills, fripperies and furbelows. That was one third of the store; the second section was reserved for boots and shoes of every type from satin slippers to thudding, steel-toed brogans, and in the third section were to be found lamps and oil, butter churns and moulds, cutlery and enamelware, buckets, tubs and ladles, crockery and diverse household utensils. The store, as Willard was wont to say, thrived like a weed, a weed that had over the years become a flowering vine, from the various branches of which he harvested a steady crop of dollars.

Phoebe quickly mastered the skills of salesmanship, even took pleasure in assisting a customer in making up his or her mind regarding a purchase. Willard congratulated himself on having found the perfect assistant. Phoebe found the atmosphere congenial, the work itself no more demanding than her wage made worthwhile, and did not once regret having made her choice. She never discussed the store at home, and Pike chose to ignore her disobedience by never mentioning her place of employment or alluding to her lowly status as one who served others—except to demand rent from her, of course. Phoebe complied; it was only fair.

One day Joe Cobden walked in and caused trouble. Willard had sold him a pair of stout boots, and Joe had already paid for them and picked up his parcel from the counter when he indicated a cardboard placard behind Willard's back. "Did you know your sign's misspelled?" he asked. Willard turned. The sign had been hand lettered by himself, as were all the signs inside the store. It read: *Button's—20 cents per doz Sock's—$1.00 pr.* He could see nothing wrong with it. "The apostrophes are redundant," explained Joe. "Plurals don't require apostrophes. One button, two buttons; one pair of socks, two pairs of socks. No apostrophes."

Willard was not pleased at Joe's observation. Like many literate people, he had somehow failed to absorb some of punctuation's basic rules; he did not, for example, know the difference between "your" and "you're". "It looks fine to me," he said stiffly.

"Didn't I explain it properly?" asked Joe. "The punctuation's definitely wrong."

Willard gave him a stony look. The nearby presence of Phoebe, overhearing all this, made it twice as bad. There were two or three customers listening as well, pretending to browse among the shelves. "It's perfectly all right," he insisted.

"You don't believe me?" Joe sounded amused, rather than offended.

"What would an Indian know, anyway?" said a middle-aged customer, the tip of her nose reddening with outraged racial pride.

"Ma'am," said Joe, "rest assured, I know whereof I speak." And he took off his hat (Phoebe would later tell Jessica he had "doffed" it) and made a bow to the woman, a smile on his face.

The customer was not inclined to take this exaggerated civility lying down. "What would an Indian know, anyhow?" she repeated, this phrase representing the full intellectual thrust of her argument. Her nose had now passed from pink to puce.

"More than some whites," said Joe, and walked out.

The woman gasped. Willard fumed. Phoebe watched Joe through the window as he slung his parcel into the wagon and drove off. When he had asked her for the name of her music box's melody she had thought him surprisingly forward, but had ascribed this to frontier manners; now she thought him almost rude. She had known many of the signs in the store made incorrect use of apostrophes, but was too polite to embarrass Willard Croft by pointing this out to him. Joe had done so in much too blunt a fashion. She almost felt sorry for Croft, felt nothing but contempt, however, for the woman who had tried to make Joe Cobden ashamed of that half of him which was Indian. He had handled her rather well, really, thought Phoebe with a smile.

"Back to work, Miss Pike," said Willard, and when she saw his fussily pursed lips under that silly little moustache and the angry flush on his cheeks she no longer felt sorry for him, reminded herself she hadn't the time or the emotion left over to feel sorry for anyone but Jessica and herself. Back to work she went, checking off stock against a list; wondered, before putting the incident behind her, just how smart a person Joe Cobden really was.

Willard went to the storeroom at the rear to calm himself, despite the presence of customers; Phoebe could take charge of them. Phoebe, Phoebe. . . . He should not have let the hunchback upset him. Now Phoebe would think him a fool, rising to the bait like that. And what if the signs *were* wrong? Phoebe was an intelligent young woman, would know if they were or not (and he accepted, of a sudden, that they were) and would think him another kind of fool for not having used the correct spelling, or punctuation, or whatever it was, in the first place. He did not care what the customers thought, did not appreciate the woman having taken sides with him, cared only about the light in which Phoebe Pike saw him. Willard Croft realised at this point that he was falling in love with her—he, a married man! Had he been a religious fellow he might well have prayed for deliverance from the grip of this madness. As it was, he wished he kept a bottle of whiskey on the premises; he needed a stiff drink and some time to himself in which to quell this rising foolishness before it endangered everything he had worked for.

On her way home from the store, Phoebe found herself dawdling, reluctant to enter the Pike abode above the funeral parlour. Jessica had made no complaints over her extra work, but Phoebe had on occasion intercepted looks of muted reproach, a kind of "Can't you see what you've done to me?" expression. It infuriated Phoebe that her mother could not appreciate her efforts, could not take the long view; Phoebe had told her of the plan to save money, to take Jessica with her and leave Valley Forge for ever. Jessica had been frightened at the prospect. "Oh, no, dear, that's not right. I can't do that. Your father would never forgive me. I'm his wife, for richer, for poorer, in sickness and in health. . . . You don't understand. I couldn't just *leave*, dear. It wouldn't be right. . . ." Phoebe understood all too well; Jessica was the blind one, refusing to acknowledge the jaws grinding her to pulp, inhaling deeply the rotten breath of matrimony gone bad, making believe it was perfume. Jessica had mired herself in the slough of unquestioning duty up to her scrawny neck, and would probably extol the virtues of her lot as the filth invaded her nostrils. Very well, if Jessica was unwilling to flee, Phoebe would save money for her own sake, would leave when she had saved enough, and the devil take her mother—enough was enough! She felt unreasonably guilty over her new-found independent stance; for too many years she had pictured herself and Jessica as being chained to the same rock, allied in their torment, and now it was clear that an ever widening strait separated them. Phoebe felt on the one hand that the time spent championing her mother's cause had been wholly wasted, and on the other that she was selfishly planning to abandon the one person in all the world who depended completely upon her for support. The two emotions were irreconcilable. Phoebe sometimes wondered if she would have the courage to leave when the time came; irrationally, she found comfort in knowing the day of her departure was still (according to her purse) far distant.

When Phoebe entered the kitchen she found Jessica nursing a badly bruised hand, which she attempted to hide. Phoebe insisted on examining it. "How did this happen?"

"I don't know, dear. I forget. . . ."

"Mother, you wouldn't forget something as painful as this. How did it happen?"

"I must have caught my hand in the door—yes, in the door! It hurt so much I had to sit down. . . ."

Jessica's face told Phoebe this story was untrue. Only one thing would place her mother in fear of telling the truth, and Phoebe marched upstairs to confront that thing. She flung open Grandmamma's door without bothering to knock, the shock of her action eliciting a startled shriek from Grandmamma, ensconced as usual on her bed. Phoebe did not bother closing the door behind her, but walked swiftly across the room to the bed and hissed into Grandmamma's face these indecorous words: "You old hag. You shitting, pissing, evil bag of bones. If you hit her again, I'll kill you." She picked up Grandmamma's cane, the weapon employed, she was sure, against Jessica's hand, and threw it into the corner of the room. Another little squawk of surprise came from Grandmamma's gums as the cane rebounded from the wall to the floor, rolled and lay still. Phoebe leaned even closer to her enemy, her voice still soft, hissing between her teeth. "Soon the maggots will have you all to themselves, the big, fat, filthy maggots crawling all over you and through you in a box under the ground, gobbling up your eyes and your guts and your brain, and I'll be so happy thinking of you down there I'll dance a jig. I'll jump over your grave and click my heels. . . ."

Grandmamma inhaled a lungful of air preparatory to a bout of screaming, but Phoebe clamped a hand over her mouth. "No," she said, "we're not going to call for help, and we're not going to struggle, are we? I might keep my hand here a little longer than is wise. . . . Do you understand me? Touch her again and I swear I'll poison you so you die in agony. I'm not going to say any more, and you aren't going to say anything at all, not one word, or I'll pick up that cane and break it over your head."

Phoebe removed her hand, straightened herself, glared at the chalk-white face below her. Grandmamma was shocked by Phoebe's passion; she knew the girl hated her, but

493

this . . . ? She would not be cowed so easily, no she would not; no slip of a girl was going to make her shrink from battle. "I want my cane," she croaked, defying Phoebe's stricture. Phoebe stared at her, as though deciding what punishment this infringement of her orders merited, then went to the cane, picked it up, took it to the bed. She raised it high above her head and brought it crashing down alongside Grandmamma's thigh; another inch and her leg would have been broken. They traded looks of loathing before Phoebe turned and left the room, slamming the door so hard it could be heard by Pike in the basement.

Grandmamma picked up the cane and thrashed her bed in frustration. She had only given Jessica a good whack because the clumsy fool had spilled coffee on her bed quilt; she had not even hit her very hard! And then Phoebe! What an ordeal for a woman in the twilight of her years! A death threat, no less; the promise of murder! She flailed at the quilt, pounding a long groove beside her legs, pounded until her chest began to pain her. She sometimes experienced uncomfortable twinges there, and attributed them to wind. Grandmamma was too proud to countenance the possibility of expiration by heart failure. The Angel of Death himself would have to come flying down through the ceiling to cut off her head with his sword; anything else would be anticlimactic, an unsuitable ending to the struggle that had been her life.

And what of Sadie Wilkes? It had been four years since the abortive delivery of her child; she was seventeen now, had lost none of the luminous beauty of her childhood, was still the loveliest female in Valley Forge. Her stepmother, Mary, was only twenty-one, already the mother of a boy and girl. Mary was a gregarious and lazy individual who objected not at all when Sadie continued performing the greater share of household chores, was so used to the situation by the time her children arrived she took it for granted that Sadie would do everything for them but offer her milkless breasts. Mary did not like Sadie very much, despite her willingness to lighten Mary's load. The reason for her antipathy was so obvious even Mary, who was not particularly intelligent, had to admit it; Sadie was beautiful, and Mary was not. That was reason enough to dislike her stepdaughter, but she thought her feelings well disguised by the constant prattling she subjected Sadie to throughout the day. In the evening and at night, of course, she reserved her conversation exclusively for Lyman Wilkes, who would have preferred that she remain silent. He had married her solely for the release to be found between her plump thighs. Mary, from a farming background too intellectually restricted to have received anything resembling instructions or warnings against the social consequences of acquainting herself with the demon Lust, accepted the incessant mountings of her husband without guilt or shame, was in fact one of the few women in the county who actually enjoyed intercourse; she even looked forward to the time each night when her husband joined her in bed. She knew he took pleasure in her body, and it was only this which prevented Mary from being consumed by jealousy, for it was obvious to her that Wilkes loved his daughter more than he did his wife. All Mary had to offset this imbalance of affection was the allure she held for Wilkes during the hours of night; at all other times he ignored her, endured her meaningless chattering with an expression of fortitude that would not have gone amiss on the face of job.

Sadie still worshipped Jesus, addressed all her silent yearnings to the picture on her bedroom wall. She had never learned to hate her father for the thing he had done to her, had no clear memory of her pregnancy at all; she knew only that her blood had returned, and had continued until now with monthly offerings to Jesus. She communicated this to no one, not even Wilkes, who was an officially accredited authority on all things pertaining to God and His only begotten son. The blood-pact between Jesus and Sadie was a secret, and would remain one. She knew Mary was jealous of Wilkes' love, but did not allow this to sadden her; Jesus had said it was merely one more rock in the road to salvation through his as-yet-undisclosed plan to make of Sadie's life a triumph. Sadie wondered what shape her existence would one day take, and waited patiently to have the meaning of Jesus' promise revealed in all its splendour. Until that hallowed moment she would content herself with caring for Mary's babies and seeing to the usual domestic tasks, would conduct herself with quiet grace, attracting the attention of no one.

CHAPTER THIRTY-TWO

There was a delayed repercussion from Calvin's fit, aggravated by the long-overdue demise of his decrepit but beloved dog (still without a name at the time of death) and as a consequence of these disturbances to his system Calvin once again took up his old habit of searching for something on the ridge, searching, in fact, for the thing Alma had told Joe he was out looking for on the very day Joe arrived; Calvin was seeking water. With a forked hazel stick grasped in both hands, arms held before him like a sleepwalker, Calvin prowled among the trees, waiting for the tip of the stick to tremble and point eagerly downward at some underground spring. He did this for weeks, covering every square foot of his property, but the hazel stick only pointed at the earth when Calvin's skinny arms grew tired. Water continued to be pumped up through a pipeline from the creek below the slope.

Disappointed at the failure of his mission, Calvin spent several more weeks brooding, and eventually was roused from his brown study by yet another notion, one that sparkled with promise, sent him racing to town for equipment—Calvin was going to dig for gold. He was convinced, for no good reason, that beneath the ridge there was a seam of precious yellow metal, a rivulet of frozen sunlight trapped beneath the earth, awaiting the impatient tip of his pick, the frantic scrape of his shovel. There was no talking him out of his folly, no restraining his determination, and word of Calvin's new obsession soon spread through the homes and watering holes of Valley Forge. Not since Alma's departure had Calvin provided the town with such a convenient butt for their laughter.

Calvin was immune to scorn by way of the very foolishness which provoked it, and by the two miles which separated the ridge from the town. Joe merited laughter by association, but was very nearly armour-plated in this regard and responded not at all. But Noah suffered. His fancy hat and boots and his pony had distanced him from every other boy in school. He had never truly been accepted among them as an equal at the start of his schooldays, and thereafter had so easily and so often proved his intellectual superiority to the rank and file he stood no chance of ever being invited to partake in the activities of that substratum of social congregation, the gang of kids. This had not bothered Noah overmuch at the time; he was not bullied, was tolerated as some kind of freak, an encyclopaedia in high heeled boots, a thing which served a need in the schoolyard—the necessity for one individual to be set apart as different, in order to reinforce the sameness of the rest. Calvin and Joe had long served a similar need among the community at large. But the one-man gold rush on the ridge brought a renewal of personal abuse. Now the glamour of Noah's possessions seemed unbearably pretentious to others; the midget cowboy with the twelve-letter words and snooty ways was only crazy old Calvin Puckett's kid after all. Off with his hat, and into the mud with it!

To the adults of Valley Forge he was no longer the town's whitest hope. That title had been draped around his neck for too long to remain convincing; fame in the offing does not have the same cachet as fame achieved. He was just a boy with big ideas about himself and his future. "Prove it," seemed to be the unspoken command on the public's lips. Only Miss Woodcock kept faith, determined that Noah should vindicate her existence by stunning the world with his brilliance and erudition. She made enquiries of a certain learned body in Topeka with regard to the possibility of a scholarship, since it was apparent no one intended sponsoring the boy to college, not even old man Croft, who would have been better advised to spend his cash on that worth-while venture rather than on ponies and rifles and saddles. Unbeknown to her, Lucius Croft did in fact intend sponsoring Noah to the moon and back, if that was necessary, but was not inclined to make his intention known; it would have interfered with his scheme to snatch back the ridge.

Whenever he was not assisting Joe with the sawing of logs into sections, Calvin dug holes. He dug them here, he dug them there, always six feet deep—the commonly accepted depth of a grave. If he discovered no gleaming nest of nuggets before reaching that depth, he promptly refilled the hole and began digging elsewhere. After the first six months a pattern to his labours began emerging. It was Noah who noticed it first. "He always digs on the east side of trees. Why does he do that?" Joe asked Calvin, and received the news that Calvin was no longer searching for a gold seam created by nature, but a crock of gold buried by man. The existence of such a crock had been revealed to him in a dream; Alma had revealed it while floating several inches above the ground, pointing at the earth with her naked toes, assuring Calvin that if he dug on the east side of a certain tree the treasure would be his. Calvin had remembered the directive to dig on the east side, but had forgotten which tree; he was therefore obliged to dig a hole beside every tree on the ridge. He was confident he could accomplish this Herculean task before old age overtook him, maybe even in time to pay for Noah's college fees, by hokey!

Noah and Joe despaired of convincing him his efforts were wasted, and their mutual display at least served to unite them, although not to their former closeness. They had, alas, steadily drifted apart since Lucius Croft insinuated himself between them. They were not enemies, were reasonably relaxed in each other's company, but had lost that preternatural affinity which had long been the essence of their friendship. Joe saw in Noah the emergence of a personality not dissimilar to his own at the age of fourteen; a studied arrogance sat upon his shoulders, a bristling wall of porcupine defensiveness surrounded him—Don't touch me, not unless I say so; which I won't—and beneath it all lay a terrible fear, formless, omnipresent, the very mainspring of Noah's wild gyrations of mood. No longer a boy, not yet a man, convinced of his simultaneous superiority and baseness, he was an evanescent diagram of potential disaster or glory, a being in tortuous flux. He was also, and in equal measure, an awkward and pimply little lout with permanently soiled underclothing and a ferocious and constant need to spurt his semen, a cornucopia of jism, a creature utterly indifferent to anything having no direct bearing upon his own interests and needs, the embodiment of self-absorption.

Calvin dug holes well into the summer of 1888, and finally struck something other than dirt and rocks; he found a skeleton beneath a cottonwood tree. Frightened by what his shovel had revealed, Calvin ran to the house and fetched back Joe. Together they dug carefully around the bones and exposed the thing from top to toe. There was no coffin surrounding it, no evidence of a shroud, not even of clothing, this having been rotted away completely by thirty-three years of rainfall seeping down through the earth. Joe could not tell if it had been a man or woman, assumed it was the remains of a pioneer. There was no grave marker, no cairn of rocks, nothing to indicate the body had been buried by someone who felt a sense of loss. Perhaps the unfortunate being had died of cholera and been rushed under the sod with fearful haste.

"Reckon we oughter tell someone?" asked Calvin.

"No need," said Joe. "It can't have been a relative of anyone around here."

They reburied Millie's bones. Calvin began digging another hole some distance away.

A short while after this incident, Lucius Croft was faced with a decision; it was now one year since he had gulled

Calvin into mortgaging the ridge, and the details of the contract stipulated that the fifteen hundred dollar loan be repayed at the end of twelve months, along with the one hundred and fifty dollars interest which had accrued over that time. Croft wondered if the money had been spent. Joe Cobden was still making a fair profit, enough to support himself and both Pucketts, so chances were the loan had been squirrelled away for the purpose Croft had purportedly offered it—college. He wanted to know exactly how matters stood. Of late the boy had been visiting him less often, and when at the Croft farm exhibited a truculence that bordered on the insolent. It was time to haul on the reins, lay to with the whip and bring the boy to heel, make him acknowledge just who was in control of his future.

He went one night to the ridge, intent on confrontation and victory. The mortgage and cash receipt were produced. Joe and Calvin stared at them in bafflement. The signatures were undeniably Calvin's, but he could not recall how they came to be on this mortgage agreement and receipt. Croft made a point of letting Joe know that the existence of these papers had been corroborated by Nathan Bragg of the Farmers' Bank, and by Croft's lawyer in town, Purvis, so if Joe was thinking of ripping them up and setting fire to them he could just think again. Joe, who had been contemplating exactly that, handed the papers back to Croft. Calvin was close to tears. "I don't remember nothin' . . ." he said, over and over. Croft could hardly believe his luck; the fool had obviously lost the cash somehow, and played right into his hands.

"The debt's due by the end of the week," he crowed.

"Why don't you let him off," said Noah, speaking for the first time. "You can afford it."

"That isn't sound business practice, boy. Your father signed a mortgage and accepted money from me. The debt's due. It's as simple as that."

Noah left the room, apparently in disgust. Joe was glad to see him do it, thought such an act would let Croft know the boy was not completely in his pocket, still had a sense

501

of moral allegiance. Joe was quite mistaken; Noah was merely worried he might be called upon to sell his rifle and pony to help repay the debt stupid Calvin had got them into. He flung himself on his bed and cursed his father for a fool, eventually relieved his anger by way of masturbation.

Croft had interpreted Noah's exit as had Joe, but was not worried by it; in time the boy would learn to recognise the true face of human affairs, which is the Janus mask of owners and owned. Noah had to accept that he would someday handle with coarsened fingers the squalid coin of human endeavour, stamped on one side with the rich, on the other, larger side with the luckless poor. By whatever means possible, it is better to join and remain among the former; that would be his lesson to the boy, the only lesson truly worth chalk and slate.

"You'll have the money by the end of the week," said Joe.

Croft was surprised; hard worker though he was, Joe could not possibly have saved that much. "Going to rob a bank, Mr. Cobden?"

"That's my business. You'll get your money. You can leave now."

Smiling, Croft stood. "You fellers should learn how to hoe a straight row, then you wouldn't get into trouble like this."

Joe had saved fourteen hundred and eight dollars in the four years he had been in the firewood business. He borrowed the rest from Andolini the barber, who liked him and whose business was profitable, whose wife's Vesuvius restaurant was even more so. He would work off the debt with firewood. The money was handed to Croft, who could not understand how the ridge had slipped from his grasp. On his monthly visit to the Chippewa Street brothel he was made impotent as a result of his fury, failed even to succumb to his favourite prostitute's oral blandishments. The old man considered revoking his most recent will, in which the bulk of his wealth and property were left to Noah, but stopped himself; it was not the boy's fault, it was that god-damn hunchback who'd gone and spiked his guns, goddam-mit!

At around this time Valley Forge lost one of the town's best men. Ned Bowdre had been enforcing the law as con-stable and sheriff for over fifteen years. He had never mar-ried, for despite his imposing size and strength Ned was depressingly, stubbornly shy. The one person who under-stood this was Ned's brother Milt, also a bachelor. Ned one night paid a surprise visit to the hog-farm he owned in part-nership with Milt and, having found the house empty, went to the pens, where he found hogs aplenty, but no Milt. Ned proceeded to the barn, through the slats of which lamplight could be seen, and upon opening the door was confronted by the incredible sight of Milt engaged in coitus with his prize sow Cleopatra, bent low over her back, crooning into her ear with the ardour of a pauper wooing a silk purse. Ned backed out of the barn without being detected and rode quietly away, shocked by what he had seen—his own brother a hog-humper! The rumours that had circulated during his first election campaign had been true after all!

For days he brooded on his discovery, did not dare go anywhere near Milt for fear of throttling him, the damn animal! He walked around town with a tortured brow, ig-nored all greetings, did not see familiar faces, was a man adrift on streets that no longer seemed the same, peopled with citizens who would one day find out (if they had not already) that their sheriff was brother to a goddamn. . . It was too much for a decent man to bear. Ned Bowdre's spir-its sank down into his size sixteen boots and stayed there, blunting the alertness which might have saved him.

Valley Forge had never known a bank hold-up, but on this day was about to experience its first. Two young men filled with self-justification and adrenalin walked into the local branch of the Kansas National Bank (from which Joe had withdrawn fourteen hundred and eight dollars the previous week) and demanded that two sets of saddlebags be loaded with money. The horrified tellers obliged, and the robbers, resisting the urge to run, left the bank and crossed the street to their tethered horses. Ned Bowdre, by one of the quirks of fate which make philosophers shake their heads and mystics smile knowingly, was crossing the street toward the bank at that very moment, for no reason other than that the bank stood on the shady side of the street, and it was a hot day. He took no notice of the two young men with saddlebags slung over their shoulders as they came towards him; Ned's thoughts were elsewhere, flickering darkly upon the possibility of the truth leaking out before the next election. He frowned at the prospect, felt despair dragging at his mighty frame. The robbers knew who Ned was the moment they saw the badge winking on his shirt and the mean-looking frown creasing his brow—a sheriff, and he was coming right at them! Panic-stricken, the nearest young man pulled a pistol from his belt and shot Ned in the chest at point blank range. Ned understood, in the last conscious seconds of his life, that he had been shot, but did not know by whom, or why. I'm having a run of real bad luck, he thought, and died.

The robbers mounted their horses and rode out along Decatur. No one stopped them, for virtually no one in town carried a weapon more lethal than a pocket knife. The murderer and his accomplice made their way south and west to San Antonio, where they perpetrated a similar hold-up. Texas Rangers tracked them for three days and put five bullets in one young man, four in the other.

Joshua Pike had to use his largest and most expensive coffin to accommodate Ned Bowdre, and Reverend Wilkes praised the sheriff's dedication to duty; the word had gone around that brave, foolhardy Ned had attempted to arrest the robbers by using the power of his voice alone, had left his gun holstered and had died because of it. That was how the *Valley Forge Courier* wrote up his obituary, and that is the way his death was recalled ever after. Milt, unbeknown to himself the peripheral cause of all this, was heartbroken, and did not pay attention to Cleopatra for several weeks.

Mounting guilt over her plans to leave town, and in so doing abandon her mother, drove Phoebe to the surgery of Dr. Whaley. She thought, in her innocence, he might be able to help. Without relinquishing her hold on Pike's dreadful basement secret, she made it clear to the doctor that her father was a cold and heartless bully who dominated her mother to the extent that Jessica was fast sinking into a state of what Phoebe kindly referred to as simplemindedness. "She used to turn around quickly, as if she expected to see someone standing behind her. She even did it once or twice in front of Father. He can't stand to see her do anything . . . peculiar. He shouted at her. I asked her why she does it, and she said, 'Do what?' and . . . smiled. But she doesn't do that any more. Now she keeps looking at the corners of the room, any room, and when I ask her why, she says she can see insects running about, see them from the corner of her eye, but when she looks directly at them they're gone. I'm afraid she might . . . lose her mind."

Phoebe stared at the hands clenched whitely in her lap. Dr. Whaley leaned back in his chair, steepled his fingers. "And you think your father is to blame for this condition."

"Yes. That is, he makes it worse, much worse. And so does my grandmother. She . . . bullies her. She always has done."

Dr. Whaley's medical training and his considerable experience of life enabled him to classify most people. He knew all humans are as distinct, one from the other, as snowflakes, but the differences are often minuscule; certainly there exist categories of convenience into which most people can be fitted without discomfort. Phoebe, in Dr. Whaley's estimation, slotted without too much effort into the *virginal female, sexually ignorant, intelligent but prone to views of a hysterical nature—needs husband* category. Alma Puckett, née Croft, had been of similar persuasion, but in her case, of course, a husband had compounded the nature of her misery. Dr. Whaley did not doubt, having met her once or twice, that Jessica Pike was a woman of deteriorating mentality. He likened this condition to a kind of biological dam, its existence as yet unconfirmed by science, located in the brain; before the dam are spread the pleasant pastures of normality, cosily nestled between the timeless hills of Family and Nation (or perhaps Family and God, or God and Nation—the doctor's own religious convictions often wavered, during which times he removed God from the picture—it was difficult to place a dam between three hills, anyway) and behind the dam lay a dark and forbidding body of water, shoreless, depthless, seething with all manner of crawling, darting, slithering *things,* mindless but alive, ever ready to spill over the dam and invade in their swarming multitudes that way of life decreed by the Constitution (and God) as the finest in all the world. Jessica Pike's dam was fast eroding, no doubt of that, and the first of the gibbering, gulping *things* were already among her quiet pastures, blinking in the unaccustomed light, preparing to burrow deep, like moles, like worms, to lay and incubate and hatch their poisonous eggs. It was probably only a matter of time before she succumbed completely to madness, but that was no reason, *no reason* for this pernickety little miss to blame her father. That was an act of almost unforgivable ingratitude, but he would treat her kindly; she was considerably distraught, unable to see reason, seeking to plant the blame for what was inevitable on the nearest doorstep. Blaming the grandmother as well was an indication of just how far she was prepared to stoop in order to satisfy herself she had found the answer to the unanswerable. She was only a woman, and would have to be guided gently but firmly to the truth.

"I think you may be doing your father an injustice, Miss Pike."

She raised her head. "I'm *not,* really I'm not. I'm afraid if she doesn't improve, Father will have her . . . taken away.'' Her hands flew apart, hovered aimlessly and collapsed again to her lap. ''What has Mother ever done that she should be this way? Why do these things happen to people who don't deserve such suffering?''

''Those are questions for Reverend Wilkes. As a doctor I can only tell you that people with mental illnesses either get better or, more commonly, worse. It's all in the lap of the gods in cases like this. All you can do is what you appear already to be doing—care for her, give her love and kindness.''

Phoebe leaned forward eagerly. ''Would it be possible for you to ask my father to do the same? He . . . he has no patience with her. He only makes her worse. When he speaks, Mother cringes like a dog. Won't you speak with him . . . please?''

Dr. Whaley was becoming annoyed; calming a patient (he classified Phoebe as such, despite the fact she had come to him on behalf of another) was one thing, pandering to her immaturity and foolishness quite another. ''Miss Pike, you must understand I cannot impose myself on your family circle. Your father is the head of the house. I've known Mr. Pike in my professional capacity for several years now, and he has always struck me as being a reasonable man, doing a difficult job well. There's a social stigma attached to undertaking, you know. It isolates a man, his family, too, I don't doubt. I'm sure you must be exaggerating his adverse influence upon your mother. Perhaps he is every bit as unhappy with the situation as you, but that's not for me to know. Unless he approaches me in person regarding this matter I'm merely an associate, the man who signs the death certificates before your father prepares the deceased.''

She stared at him for some moments. At first he thought it was because she had seen the logic of his argument, and was assimilating this new-found understanding. Then he saw that it was something quite different; she was glaring at him, her lips tight.

''You won't speak with him?''

He resented the terseness in her voice. Just who did she

think she was, coming in here blithely to diagnose and prescribe? She was virtually dictating to him, or attempting to. "I will not. I'm sorry."

Phoebe stood with an abruptness that startled him. "Thank you for your time, Dr. Whaley. I realise now I must fight alone."

"Don't you think you're overdramatising just a little? How's your own health?"

"I'm well, thank you," said Phoebe, icily polite.

"Are you sure? You look quite flushed."

"I'm flushed because I'm angry. Good day, Doctor."

And out she went with a swishing of skirts, her neck rigidly perpendicular. She even had the brazen nerve to slam the door! Dr. Whaley shook his head, drummed his fingertips on the desk to ease his annoyance; Phoebe Pike was definitely a native of the Hysterical Female tribe whose number, he estimated, was legion.

The summer passed, and chill winds blew across Kansas. On the ridge the trees began shedding their leaves in flurries of yellow and brown that were blown against the stumps of Joe's fellings and the low mounds of Calvin's refilled holes. The ridge no longer resembled a place given over to unmolested nature, was scarred and pocked with the signs of steady commerce and foolish enterprise, the woods gradually being depleted. Joe knew he was spoiling the beauty of the place, but had no choice; to eat he must fell trees. But, no matter how many he laid low, they would never yield profit enough to replace the savings he had handed to Croft. If Noah went to college, it would be by courtesy of the old man. Joe resented his accelerating influence, saw the wrinkled and cunning face every time he swung his axe.

Like the buffalo before them, the trees continued to fall.

Phoebe had become a fixture at the store. Willard continued to worship her in his own stilted and guilt-ridden fashion, his longing for her evident only in the more than fair wage she received each week. At night, lying beside his sleeping wife, he conjured Phoebe's unremarkable face before him and covered it with lascivious kisses, even went so far as to undress her and touch her most private places. He also held sparkling conversations with her, explaining every aspect of himself, recounting his youthful aspirations to seek out adventure, sadly thwarted by involvement with his uncle's business. He had sacrificed his dreams to repay the kindness old Croft had demonstrated by taking him in after the death of Willard's father in the war. If not for that obligation—who knows—Willard may have gone far 'and achieved much. But he did not regret the humdrum nature of his calling, for without it he would not have met Phoebe, who nodded and smiled and assured him she understood, and would, had circumstances permitted it, have reciprocated his love. As it was, she, too, concealed her longing beneath the polite, everyday conversation that passed between employer and employee. Willard usually found it difficult to sleep following these interminable fabrications, so great was the distance between imagination and reality. He was a very unhappy man.

One afternoon in October a woman entered the store, a farmer's wife. "Good afternoon, Mrs. Pacey," said Phoebe. The woman was a regular customer, but today her slab-sided face, usually cheerful, reflected unrelieved misery. A purse was clutched tightly in her hands. "I want a veil," she said, in an alarmingly dead monotone. "A black one," she added. Phoebe had not supposed, after seeing her face, it was a wedding veil she required. She went to the appropriate shelf and fetched two black veils of slightly differing quality. Mrs. Pacey stood at the counter, eyes fastened on nothing. Willard, having disposed of the only other customer, came to her side. "Not someone in the family I hope, Mrs. Pacey," he said, with a frown of concern. He wished Phoebe had brought only the more expensive model from the shelf for perusal; the Paceys were one of the county's better-off farming families.

"Our little girl died last night. . . ." Her voice tailed off, was without inflection. Her mouth remained open after the last hushed syllable had drifted away.

"Oh, surely not! Little. . . ." He had no idea of the name.

"Carrie," droned Mrs. Pacey. "Diphtheria. . . ."

Tears welled in the corners of her eyes and rolled unheeded down her cheeks. Phoebe was embarrassed in the face of such naked grief; she would never have cried in public herself, but was sympathetic to any woman whose pain was this great.

"My Frank's down at your father's now," said Mrs. Pacey to Phoebe, "getting things fixed. . . ."

She then made a horrible sound, a kind of strangulated gulping. Phoebe knew she must do something for this unfortunate woman, but could not think what it might be. Willard saved her further anxiety by dragging a chair from the shoe section and placing it behind Mrs. Pacey, who sank gratefully on to it. Phoebe was impressed by Willard's solicitude. Willard picked up both veils and held them inches from the woman's face. "Which would you prefer, Mrs. Pacey, the ninety cent model or the two dollar?" Phoebe was suddenly appalled at his insensitivity; he had not seated Mrs. Pacey out of concern at all, had simply wanted a captive target for his sales talk. She felt a vaguely nauseous sensation crawl up into her throat from the pit of her stomach. She had known from the beginning that Willard Croft was a fussy and officious man, a salesman first, last and always, but until this moment she had found his company tolerable. Looking at him now, detecting the false commiseration of his pudgy features, she was revolted. "It's a real tragedy," he was saying. "I can't tell you how sorry I am, ma'am. This kind of thing seems to happen to the most decent, hardworking members of the community."

"I'll have the ninety cents," sniffed Mrs. Pacey; tragedy was no excuse for extravagance.

Willard handed both veils back across the counter to Phoebe, who surreptitiously wrapped the two dollar model in brown paper, then returned the cheaper veil to the shelf. She watched with ironic detachment as Willard collected payment.

Returning home in the early evening, Phoebe paused at the top of the basement steps. Pike's voice could be heard upstairs. She quickly descended to the permanent cool of his workshop. Mounted on saw horses was a coffin no more than two feet long. Phoebe approached it, peered inside. The corpse of Carrie Pacey had been dressed in white swaddling clothes; she had been just eight months old. Tiny hands were folded in repose across her chest. She appeared to be sleeping. Phoebe stared, appalled yet fascinated. What kind of world was it wherein something as vulnerable and innocent as a child could have its life snuffed out before it had truly begun to live? God's mysterious ways were not sufficient to stem the flood of anger and helplessness gathering in her breast. Phoebe was, as a rule, too concerned for her own particular torment to consider the sufferings of the world at large. She was not one to fuss and coo over chubby babies, had no room inside her for the warm emotions commonly attendant upon the newborn and the very young, but the sight of Carrie Pacey's tiny puckered mouth and closed eyelids, too new even to be creased, made her tremble. A dead baby has no meaning—none at all. It is the antithesis of all that purports to explain life in terms of beneficence and light, the doctrine of the caring god. Sparrows fall, stars explode; none is missed, for the void is soon filled by another, and tears wept over the dead vanish into earth and air. Phoebe was compelled to touch its cheek, withdrew her finger as though burned; such coldness belonged to marble, not to yielding flesh. She fled the basement, felt the abyss yawning beneath her, that emptiness everlasting through which all plunge from dawn till dark.

Throughout supper Jessica's eyes kept skittering away from her plate to the conjunction of walls and ceiling, three intersecting planes aswarm with insects. She had never been able to ascertain just what kind of insect they were, no matter how hard she stared—in fact the more she stared, the quicker they vanished. She supposed they had a hole up there somewhere, a tiny crack one couldn't see without standing on a chair. She pictured herself standing on a chair, and tittered. "Jessica. . . ." came the solemn warning from Pike. She guiltily forked up another mouthful of fried potato, chewed busily for a while, then allowed her gaze to wander back to the ceiling corner; yes, they had returned, dozens of little black things, possibly hundreds. "Jessica!" snapped Pike. His voice was so sharp she whimpered with fright, dropped her fork with a clatter on her plate. "Pick it up again," said Pike evenly, "and eat. Do not look at the ceiling, do not look at the floor. This is a clean house. There are no insects of any description inside; no ants or beetles, no centipedes or cockroaches. Do I make myself clear?" Jessica hid her face. "Do I make myself clear, woman?" She looked up, timid, terrified. "Yes, dear." Phoebe felt she would choke. The silence until the dishes were gathered was thunderous.

The Pikes retired early. Phoebe undressed to her chemise, sat before her dresser mirror and unbound her hair. When it lay along her spine she began brushing half-heartedly at it, pulled at knots, separating strands, ruing its disappointing thinness. Tiring of the effort, she let her arm fall to her side. The brush slipped from her fingers to the floor with a soft thud. She did not bother to pick it up. Her limbs seemed made of lead. Phoebe stared at her unflattering reflection. What a beauty, she thought; what a beauty indeed. The planes of her face were irregular, her features unemphatic and slightly lopsided, her expression one of utter blankness; even her lips had sagged apart a little under the influence of her mood. I feel absolutely nothing; not a thing—no hate, no love, no fear, no joy. Nothing.

She blew out the lamp, climbed into bed, lay staring at the ceiling, a broad plain indented by hidden rafters. A dog barked on the far side of town; another answered, closer, baying hysterically for several minutes, setting Phoebe's nerves on edge. When quiet was restored she began to weep. Tears rolled unimpeded down her face, chilled her ears and neck, soaked into the pillow. I'm so sad, so sad, so sad I wish I were dead, dead and gone and away from here. Take me away, take me away, take me away at break of day. Lay me down, lay me down, in the graveyard of the town. Let me lie, let me lie, beneath the all-encircling sky. She was unsure about the all-encircling sky; it sounded like a line from someone else's poem. Try again; something a bit more ambitious. After much lip chewing she thought she had it.

> *Sea of grass on which I lie,*
> *Bear me up with hope anew—*
> *Let me drown in depths of sky,*
> *In hemispheres of boundless blue.*

She admitted it was clankingly, thuddingly bad, as always. Still, she had composed only half a dozen or so poems in her life, was a rank beginner. What must it be like to be a poet, to compose verse while sitting dreamily by some summer window, a gentle breeze stirring the lace curtains, with perhaps the sound of waves in the distance? What perfect bliss would flow from such a life. There would be a voice below in the garden, a hearty male voice encouraging an infant to take those first few trepidatious steps. His jacket would be removed, his sleeves rolled up to reveal tanned forearms; Horton Winfield, train traveller and stealer of hearts, lifted their baby to the sunlit sky, and father and child laughed delightedly together, while upstairs in the bay window Phoebe penned another stanza of what would later be hailed as *a masterly début; the fairer sex have found their doyenne*, etc.

Phoebe slapped herself sharply across the face. Fool! Stupid idiot of a weakling! *That* is a dream. *This* is life, this lying in bed as though in your coffin. A night freight rumbled through the depot, clanked and clanged across the points and sidings. The engineer, a reckless soul who delighted in disturbing honest slumber, hauled hard on the whistle cord. The sound cut through Phoebe like a blade, for there is no more mournful cry than that of an American steam locomotive's whistle; in no way resembling the reedy piping of its European counterpart, the lowering wail of a freight echoing across the open prairie is the last sound that will be heard before Armageddon, a fiery bellow that soars momentarily, then falls away to an agonised moan from the belly of the wheeled beast, rising and falling, rising and falling, declaring to the emptiness: I am here . . . but I am already going. . . . Here . . . and going . . . Here . . . and gone. The tears returned. I'm alone, alone, all, all alone. . . . (That was Coleridge, wasn't it?) Even in her grief she plagiarised, made a mockery of her torment, could not stop her tears with levity, found this pitiful and wept all the more, even pulled the pillow from beneath her head and howled into its downy plumpness. Could anything be worse than this life of hers? Eventually she calmed her quaking chest, slowed her breathing, held herself tightly for consolation. And what was the outcome of this sorry parade of emotion? Phoebe had to relieve her bladder.

She refused to keep a chamberpot beneath her bed, so down the stairs barefoot she went, through the hall and the darkened kitchen, across the yard and into the outhouse, where she sat shivering while a meagre trickle of urine passed from her body, then back inside. Passing the door to the basement, she paused for the second time that day in that spot. There was a noise from the bottom of the steps, and a thin line of candlelight could be seen below the door. Was Father working late? No, for she had heard his snores on her way downstairs a moment before. Had he perhaps left a light burning inadvertently? She opened the door and knew, even before she heard the softly cooing voice, that someone was in the basement. Phoebe tiptoed down the steps, her legs and arms dimpling with the cold, and saw Jessica standing in her nightgown by the tiny coffin, her back to the steps. What was she doing, and saying? The words were meaningless bubbles of sound, and they caused the hair to rise on Phoebe's neck.

"Mother . . . ?"

Jessica turned. Carrie Pacey's corpse was cradled in her

arms, encouraged by Jessica's dreamily plaintive voice to suck at her exposed breast, hanging like a dried fig in its face. Phoebe felt the icy coldness of the brick floor travel up her legs and spine to clutch at the base of her brain, felt herself rock slightly on her heels. The thing had finally happened, the scales had tipped; her mother was, by any definition of the word, mad. Phoebe stepped closer, moving slowly for fear of startling Jessica into realisation of her behaviour, arousing awareness that might provoke some kind of violent reaction, a dropping of the corpse, perhaps, or loud screaming.

"I tried to make her feed," said Jessica, "but she just keeps on sleeping." She was smiling contentedly, indulging the little one's capricious refusal to suck; Phoebe had been that way sometimes as a baby, but she had hoped things would be easier with this second daughter.

Shaken, Phoebe found her voice. "She probably doesn't want any. Why not put her back in the cradle, if she wants to sleep . . . ?"

Still cooing softly, Jessica replaced the corpse in its coffin. "There," she said, "now you stay quiet."

Phoebe closed Jessica's nightgown. "Time to go back to bed, Mother."

She picked up the candlestick, took Jessica by the elbow and began escorting her toward the steps. Jessica allowed herself to be guided, as though blind. "I'm so tired . . ." she said, "so very tired. . . ."

After bedding her mother down safely, Phoebe returned to her room. She was still awake and staring at the ceiling when the sun rose.

CHAPTER THIRTY-THREE

In Mid-October Noah paid a visit to the Croft farm. Croft had Noah saddle a horse for him and they rode out beyond the boundaries of his land, a long ride. "What are your plans, boy?" he demanded when they stopped to let their horses graze.

"Plans?"

"College and such."

"Been considering it."

Noah usually adopted the clipped frontier manner favoured by Croft whenever he was in the old man's presence. Croft knew he did it subtly to mock him, and Noah knew he knew. Croft was unsure if this constituted sass or spunk.

"Your daddy ever find that money I loaned him?"

"No."

"Got any idea where it went?" Croft thought it was suspicious the way Calvin kept digging those damn holes all over the ridge; he'd probably buried the cash, then forgotten where.

"He's dumb enough to have wiped his ass with it," said Noah, and Croft leaned over to lash his forearm with the plaited leather quirt he liked to carry for show—only a Mexican would actually use a quirt on a horse. Noah yelped and pulled on Wicked's reins to keep him from dancing away.

"What was that for!"

"He's a fool, but he's your father. You want to call him names, call 'em in your head, quiet-like."

Old hypocrite, thought Noah. It was becoming more and more difficult to talk with him, and Noah only did so for the sake of the money he counted on getting from him. Croft knew that too.

"Plans, boy," he reminded Noah.

"College," Noah snarled, "I'm going to college."

"And just how the hell are you going to do that without money?"

"My teacher's rustling up some cash from somewhere, a state scholarship or something."

"Scholarship! That's fancy talk for charity. You want to be a charity case, boy?"

"It's all I can get." Unless *you* crack your wallet, he added silently. The whole subject of his schooling bored Noah. He had stopped dreaming of Yale and Harvard, found himself dreaming instead of warm latitudes, island-studded seas. Wanderlust, the very thing which had brought Joe Cobden to Kansas, threatened to take Noah Puckett away. But he was not yet ready for such a step, and knew it. He revealed these secret yearnings that brewed and stirred in the back of his mind to no one, least of all to old Lucius, who still had not disclosed whether or not he intended paying Noah's college fees. Noah knew this was to keep him on his toes, keep him polite and docile. He was quite prepared to play along. Who knows, maybe the old man would even leave him an inheritance, not that Noah was the least bit interested in running a farm or store—that was for dumb-asses—but he could sell them for plenty and use the proceeds to go adventuring. Still rubbing the quirt mark on his arm, he understood that even an anticipated windfall must sometimes be waited upon to the point where it causes a distinct pain in the neck. He wanted to get out of Kansas, away from all this endlessly flat nothing; he wanted to see the Rockies, tall and glistening with snow, wanted to see an ocean stretching away to the horizon, a different kind of flatness—blue nothing! The Rockies, of course, would be populated by dusky Indian maidens eager to rob a wayward lad of his virtue for a few strings of beads; even the ocean had long-haired mermaids basking on foamy crests, sport-

ing with naked breasts among the blue and rolling troughs.
For Noah, Kansas was a prison without walls or ceiling.

"All you can get, eh? But not all you reckon you deserve,
am I right?"

"Anyone with brains deserves a chance."

"That what you think you've got under that ten gallon
headwarmer, brains?"

Noah did not grace this taunt with a reply. Croft was in
a more cantankerous mood than usual today. Noah thought
him a little more senile each time they met.

They rode on a mile or so, came to a buffalo wallow forty
feet across, a saucer-shaped depression so worn and trampled by generations of buffalo bathing in dust it would not
support grass. There had been no buffalo in the vicinity of
Valley Forge for twenty years; even when the hunters had
been doing a brisk trade elsewhere, this stretch along the A.
T & SF tracks had already been cleaned out. Croft thought
it a shame, in a way; they were damned impressive animals,
but Indians and buffalo had to go if civilisation was ever to
take permanent hold out here.

"How's your Indian friend doing?"

"Same as usual."

"Know where he got that money from?"

"No." Joe and Noah never discussed personal matters
nowadays.

"From an Eye-talian barber, that's where. Has to chop
wood for that fat Eye-talian wife of his the rest of his life to
repay the debt. He's put himself well and truly in the red.
Know what that means, boy?"

"Yes."

"Come to think of it, Indians are always in the red."

Croft barked at his own wit. Noah consented to sneer;
the old skinflint really was becoming obnoxious, but not
unbearably so, not yet anyway.

"And supposing you get this government charity, then
what?"

"Then college," said Noah. Was the old fool going to

518

cover everything twice? "College!" he said again, making no secret of his impatience.

"Afterwards! Afterwards! And don't use that tone with me or you'll get this across your insolent face!" He brandished the quirt again, his cheeks mottling.

"I don't know!"

"Well, think, boy, think!"

Noah wondered what Croft would like to see him become; that would be the safest thing to throw back at him. "Maybe a farmer," he said.

"Farmer? Don't hand me those horse-apples, boy! You don't want to be a farmer any more than I want to be a fencepost! I know when I'm lied to, and I don't have to take it from a piddledick like you!"

"All right then! A lawyer!"

"Lawyer? Liars and thieves and swindlers, the lot of 'em!"

"You've got a lawyer!"

"The biggest liar and swindler and thief I ever met! If I trusted him to shine my shoes I'd be barefoot!"

"Well, *what,* then?"

"Make up your own mind, boy! Don't be dictated to like some kind of woman! Use the brain you claim to have!"

"The Army!" Noah yelled in desperation.

"That's more like it. Grant was in the Army! Grant got to be President!"

"Good! I'm glad you approve! I'll join the Army and be President!"

"Quit that hollering! Damn, but I sometimes think you're half crazy!"

"We know where I get it from, don't we!" Noah was beginning to enjoy this shouting match, but made sure he was not too close to his grandfather's quirt.

"We do that, by God! I'm warning you now, boy! Keep that tongue good and civil or there'll be blood on the moon! I'm no fool! I know what you want! Well, you won't get it, not from me, not if I don't feel like it, let me tell you! You're out for what you can get, young as you are! Well, not from *me,* boy, not from Lucius Croft! You see if you can get it somewheres else! Just you try getting it and see if I'm wrong! I'm your only chance, the only chance that'll ever come your way! You better toe that line and toe it good, I'm warning you!''

Noah was alarmed at such a display of temper, could not see how he had caused it, decided Croft had turned well and truly senile today, would maybe even choke on his own spit if he kept it up. Noah waited for him to clutch at his throat and topple from the saddle, but it did not happen. Croft glared at him, breath whistling in and out of his lungs.

"You don't want to make such a fuss, not at your age,'' said Noah, to show he was not afraid of any loud old man.

"They wouldn't take you in the Army,'' wheezed Croft, "not even if they were paid. You've got no discipline. None.''

Noah was pleased that Croft thought so; why would anyone want to be disciplined? "I wouldn't go in the Army if *I* was paid,'' he said. "Or to college,'' he dared to add.

"You're a contrary young fool,'' said Croft. "I can see that now. You'll come to nothing, boy. There's no way to stop you.''

Noah suddenly became aware of what was happening; he was talking himself out of that which, minutes before, he had been desirous of having. He needed Croft's cash, got by one means or another, if he was ever to go adventuring. Lying about wanting to go to college was perfectly sensible, but telling the truth was not. "I'm sorry,'' he said, the words sounding feeble and insincere even to his own ears. "I *do* want to go to college. . . .''

"Well, your teacher better get you that government money, boy, because that's your only hope now.''

"I didn't mean all that stuff,'' whined Noah, unnerved by the tremulous anger in Croft's voice. "I apologise.''

"Don't even have the craw to stand by what you say,'' snorted Croft. "You're no good. You've got bad blood.''

The words bludgeoned their way through Noah's head. Bad blood. I've got *bad blood.* . . . He wanted to do many things at once—kick his pony's flanks and ride away, lean over and punch the old man, fall on his knees and beg forgiveness—all of a sudden everything had gone wrong! Just because Croft had raised his voice and tried to bully him like a little kid, he'd gone and shouted away a fortune, yelled his future into flight, and it wasn't even his fault! Bad blood, that's what had done it. He would have kept his mouth shut when the old man started ranting if it hadn't been for the bad blood making him answer back, making him lose what he had worked (for acting the part of dutiful grandson was work of a wearisome kind) so hard for. It wasn't fair! Joe had told him a long time ago that nothing is fair. Expect nothing and you won't be disappointed, he'd said, and Noah had thought it just what you'd expect a hunchback to say, because hunchbacks had no right to expect anything good to happen to them anyway. But *he* could, Noah Puckett could, because he was *special,* he was *smart.* Now had come the realisation that what made him special was not his brains, but his bad blood! It explained a great many things about himself—his moods, his wild dreamings built upon juvenile whimsy, dime novel adventure. It was bad blood, Calvin's blood, the blood of a madman. The time had come to face up to it—he, Noah, was half mad. Everything made sense once that unwholesome premise was accepted. He almost felt grateful to Croft for having revealed the truth to him this way. *I'm half mad with bad blood!* Noah was a man now, a *mad*man. He would have fitted into college the way a hyena fits into a sitting room. How could he ever have thought *that* was the life for him?

"What are you laughing at, you young fool?"

"I'm a hyena!"

"You're Puckett's boy all right," said Croft, his voice made calm by what had been revealed to him on this wintry afternoon. He felt cheated. For almost two years he had paid attention to Noah, bought him gifts, let him know there was a steady man in the family, someone who would help him achieve what would otherwise be denied the son of a feeb, had squandered time and money attempting to groom

the boy, preparing him for the world beyond the horizon—
and now just look at him, look at him! A hyena. Was he
truly half mad? Croft had not meant it, but Noah had
seemed to seize upon the insult, was behaving as though it
were not only true, but something to be proud of. It was a
big disappointment, almost as big as losing the ridge, and
it had taken only a minute, this overturning of expectations.
Croft felt sick at heart.

"You watch out, boy," he said. "You don't have the
Lord on your side." He did not know why he said that. He
had wanted to deliver a ringing reprimand, something to
leave the boy shaking in his socks, but invoking the Lord
like some idiot preacher was not the way to do it; suggesting
to Noah that his attitude had about it the odour of sulphur
and brimstone was ridiculous—even Croft did not believe
it (he had not set foot inside a church since Alma's wedding)
and he felt foolish as soon as the words had left his mouth.
The boy did not seem impressed, either, just sat there on the
horse Croft had given him and sneered. Croft formed the
disturbing notion that Noah would, at any moment, pull his
rifle free of its scabbard and send a bullet into him. It was
the eyes, and that twisted, smirking mouth that convinced
him it would happen. I'm afraid of a boy, a boy! He banished his fear with another warning, a more sensible, be-
lievable warning—again, hardly original:

"You'll come to a bad end."

"I know."

"You're on my land. Get off." They were miles from
Croft's land, were on open prairie belonging to no one. It
was the boy again, making him say foolish things. He realised he wanted Noah to ride off first, did not want to present
his back as a target.

"All right."

Noah rode away from his grandfather, and Croft felt
weights descending on to and lifting from his shoulders; he
had lost his grandson, but was free of a ton of trouble. That
boy was riding for a rope as sure as Kansas is flat. Noah
had not once broken the law, nor showed signs of so doing,

yet Croft's conviction was firm; Noah was as good as hanged already. Bad blood.

"Good riddance," he said, and rode slowly home. He supposed he would have to change his will. No, he would wait awhile; Noah might see sense and come to heel, the bad blood be washed away. Then again, the moon might be made of cheese.

One day late in the fall, Phoebe decided to visit the ridge before all the leaves had been stripped from the trees. She could have asked for permission to visit from either Joe Cobden or Noah Puckett, both of whom entered the store from time to time, but was disinclined to do so, whether from shyness or pride she could not say. Joe made her feel . . . jittery, not because of his deformity, which she had become used to, but as a result of the mock-courtesy with which he greeted her whenever they met. They had never spoken of anything bar the business of exchanging coin for goods, and yet he never failed to sweep his hat off in her presence like some stunted cavalier, would incline his bony head a few degrees and say, "Good morning to you, Miss Pike. I trust you're well on this fine day?" or "Cruel necessity has brought me once again to your emporium of delights—we're out of matches." Or (and this, stupidly enough, had inspired her to make the trip to the ridge) "Fall is upon us again, Miss Pike. The furry leaves are falling by the million in my part of the world." She had smiled, as usual, at his deliberate silliness, but the reference to "Für Elise" she somehow resented, suggesting as it did a secret shared by just the two of them. Yet even as she dismissed his behaviour as foolish at best, mildly insulting at worst, she chided herself for her lack of charity; the poor man was a hunchback, and probably felt he had to conduct himself this way, or be obliged to scuttle through life with never an upraised glance, ashamed to be seen among the normal. She decided she would respond in kind the very next time she saw him, but he had not revisited the store by the time Phoebe knew she wanted very much to see those falling leaves. Asking Noah Puckett if she might visit the ridge was quite out of the question. Just yesterday he had come in and slapped money wordlessly on to the counter, extracted two sticks of licorice from a jar and walked out again, definitely not in a mood to grant polite requests. She found him a perplexing, almost unpleasant youth, and often imagined him with a candy cane in one hand and a Bowie knife in the other, a vision not so very far removed from reality.

And so, unasked, she set out one Sunday afternoon while Pike and Jessica were in church (Phoebe pleaded a monstrous headache) to walk to the ridge. The walk itself did much to uplift her deflated spirits, and by the time she reached the avenue of trees sheltering the trail up to the Puckett place she found herself, like Sadie Wilkes before her, called away from the wagon ruts, lured off among the trees not by some disembodied voice but by the desire for privacy; she did not wish to encounter a wagon or rider on the trail, wished to have this cold and windy day all to herself, for privacy was a luxury usually to be found only within the familiar walls of her room. Phoebe took a childlike delight in kicking her way through the rustling carpet of leaves, crunching them underfoot, swishing them aside with the hem of her skirt, her cheeks invigoratingly cold, the edge of her bonnet flapping.

She had not felt so alive in a long, long time, even made little humming noises in her throat as she sent her boots through a particularly dense windrow of crinkled foliage, sent showers of darkened leaves into the air like frightened bats, to be whisked away on the wind. She even broke into a run! How long had it been since she had done such a girlish thing? She ran for the sheer gratification of physical movement, unconcerned with however she might look or sound, exultant in her aloneness, imagining herself a wood sprite flitting through her tangled domain. Why had she never come here before? Trees, trees, glorious trees! Why was the ridge not inundated with pleasure-seekers like herself, pining (a pun! a pun!) for the sight and touch and smell of these wonderful creations, tall and stately, broad and shady (well, in summer they would be shady)? She could only presume their spirits were so withered by apathy and indifference they did not feel the lack, were not aware of deprivation; that they might simply have respected the law of private property did not occur to her. She actually flung herself against an ash tree, hugged its trunk, pressed her face against the bark until her skin hurt. What a performance! If anyone had seen her they would assuredly have thought her mad. Phoebe looked around, chastened by this possibility. There was no one.

She slid to the ground, sat with her back propped against the bole of the ash, did something she could not recall having ever done before—she released an identifiable sigh of contentment. Oh, novel sensation! She did it again, but self-consciousness robbed it of the glorious satisfaction she had felt the first time. Stilled at last after her dash along the ridge's spine, Phoebe's body seemed to take root where she sat. If at that moment she could somehow have turned herself into a tree, she would have; she could not bear the thought of trudging home again. Joe Cobden and the Pucketts were lucky to live here, free to wander through the woods at any time they pleased. Phoebe had noticed quite a few stumps, and was reminded that the ridge was where Joe Cobden cut down these tall and shady trees for a living, so perhaps he was not in the habit of tripping gaily through the undergrowth as she had done. What a pity; all forests should be declared sanctuaries, she thought, for the trees themselves, and for those whose peace of mind depended upon them. She idled away her time with such thoughts, only gradually becoming aware of the cold seeping under her dress and into her bones. Time for another run! Last one to the school gate gets her pigtails pulled!

Phoebe ran and ran, crossing and recrossing her path, ploughing through leaves, leaping fallen branches and swooping between the trees with arms outstretched like some black owl in search of sustenance. She eventually collapsed with her back to another comfortable trunk, her boots inches from a mound of earth, another feature of the ridge she had noticed; presumably these were the refilled holes resulting from Calvin Puckett's search for treasure, the story of which, once it had circulated through town, had caused the usual smiles and shaking heads—"That Puckett," they said, "he sure is a fool." Phoebe closed her eyes and thought of a pirate chest brimming with golden doubloons, precious jewels, ropes of pearls, the answer to all her prayers—freedom could surely be bought by the year, by the decade, if one had sufficient diamonds. Into this fantasy crept a disquieting sensation, that of being silently observed. Phoebe opened her eyes.

The wolf was no more than five yards distant, facing her, an old, old wolf with a white snout and dirty grey hide, its left back leg trembling, lip lifted in what Phoebe at first thought was a snarl, but apparently was a scar, for although the rotting grey fangs were exposed no sound came from the wolf's throat. Phoebe sat as still as the tree behind her, not daring even to breathe. The wolf continued to stare, seemingly unafraid. She saw now that the scar which lifted its lip in a permanent sneer continued up the side of its white snout to the left eye-socket, which was empty, the unsupported lid drooping sadly. Phoebe almost felt sorry for the animal; the trembling hind leg robbed this old plains hunter of any threatening appearance it might imagine it still possessed, made her think of a palsied Civil War veteran who wants to believe he could still defeat the enemy singlehanded. But she took care not to provoke it.

The wolf looked away from Phoebe, a brief reconnoitring of the area; there was just this one human, and unafraid. The wolf was seeking a place in which to die. It was tired and old and weak and alone, and in pain; it did not seek to prolong this condition, had exhausted itself climbing the west side of the ridge to this place of clashing trees, hoping there would be a hideaway here it could make its own, a place to die. Its nose told the wolf what its rheumy eye could not—

this human was not going to move—and so the wolf turned painfully and limped away, and was soon lost to sight.

Phoebe stood and hurried in the opposite direction, disturbed by what she had seen. She passed a blackberry thicket in what appeared to be the ridge's only treeless space, and came at last, through no deliberate plan, to the Puckett home. She stopped at the edge of the clearing, just a few feet away from the spot where Sadie Wilkes had stood to watch Joe chopping wood. Phoebe could either turn around and go back among the trees (and risk encountering the wolf again) or she could follow the ridge trail down to the road that would lead her back to Valley Forge. Or she could knock on the door. It would be impolite, to say the least, simply to walk up to a home one had never visited before and expect to be welcomed. But that is what she did.

Noah answered the door, stood gawping at her for several seconds before responding, "Hello, Miss Pike." He could not have been more surprised if it had been Abe Lincoln on the doorstep.

"Good afternoon, Noah." She gave him a nervous smile, still not quite believing she had had the temerity to impose this way. Noah recovered himself somewhat. "Uh . . . come in."

He led her to the living room. Joe and Calvin were sprawled in huge armchairs before a blazing fire, Joe whittling at a piece of wood, Calvin watching him. Their faces grew blank when Phoebe entered and stood before them. "Good afternoon, Mr. Cobden, Mr. Puckett. I hope I'm not disturbing you."

"No," said Joe, and was unable to say more. What was Phoebe Pike doing up here?

"I have just seen a wolf," she said. "I don't think it would have attacked me, but I thought it wise to take myself out of its path, so to speak. I hope you don't mind."

"A wolf?" Joe suspected some kind of trick concerning the Church of the White Wolf. But that was not only before Joe's time, it was well before Phoebe Pike's time, and anyway, she was too sensible a person to have any part in tricks. It was a coincidence.

"Yes, not far from here. He seemed very old and lame."

"You're sure it was a wolf, not a dog?"

"It was too large to be a dog."

"I've never seen one around here." He turned to Calvin. "Have you?"

"Never did," said Calvin brightly, his thoughts apparently uncluttered by memories of his church. "Nothin' around here to keep a wolf alive, not 'less he eats chickens like a coyote."

Joe remembered something called manners and vacated his chair. "Please," he said, indicating its much-hollowed interior.

"Thank you." Phoebe sat.

"Did you fall over?"

"Pardon me?"

"You're covered in leaves."

"I sat down."

"Oh."

A silence. Joe turned to Noah, lurking by the door. "Get some coffee, would you?"

Noah was about to tell him to get it himself, but went and did as he was told, banging a kettle savagely on to the stove. He was upset by Phoebe's presence here, upset and excited. He could not remember when there had been a woman in the house. Sadie Wilkes did not count, having been a girl. Phoebe seemed to make the room, the very air around her, different. He wanted her to go away, yet at the same time wanted to show her his room; why, he did not know, since it was a pig-sty, quite unfit for the eyes of a guest. He went back to the living room, not wanting to miss anything by watching water boil. Phoebe was examining the piece of wood Joe had been whittling. "But it's really very good," she was saying, "especially considering you only have the one knife to work with. I believe woodcarvers have a great many tools." The wood had been hacked and pared into the shape of a squirrel; the tail was too weighty, it being almost impossible to suggest feathery lightness in so dense a medium as wood, but the proportions were correct, the sideways tilt of the head suggesting alertness. Noah was instantly jealous. He returned to the kitchen and made coffee, his face grim.

Despite Noah's glowering silence, the gathering became a surprisingly jolly affair. Joe and Calvin also were aware of the difference a woman makes to a room grown used to males alone, and both did their utmost to be amusing hosts, resulting in much cackling and whinnying from Calvin whenever Joe made a witticism simple enough for him to understand, and some genuine laughter from Phoebe herself.

"The thing you have to watch out for when you're skinning a buffalo is, the animal's got to be rolled on to his back and kept there by propsticks, or else he'll flop over on his side. I remember a time when I was working away, cutting down the belly with my knife, and this big bull all of a sudden topples over, breaks the sticks that're holding his legs up in the air and practically squashes the life out of me, and I said to him, 'Get off! What do you think you're doing?' And the big bull says, 'Don't blame me. You keep tickling my belly, and I can't stand it.' "

Noah thought it was a pathetic joke, but the others all roared as though it was the funniest thing they'd ever heard. Calvin was braying like a jackass. Noah thought furiously, trying to invent something funny, but nothing would come to mind; trying to create humour when one's mood is black is like attempting to swim while wearing armour. He sat and glared at them, reserving the greater part of his anger for Joe, who was holding forth like some kind of court jester, which he probably would have been if he'd lived a few hundred years ago with a hump like that, just like the crippled dwarf-jester in Poe's "Hop-Frog". Joe and Calvin were behaving like a couple of schoolboys showing off for some stupid girl, a thing you wouldn't catch Noah doing, not if you waited for ever, nossir, not him. . . . "What's the difference between stealing a cat and watching one sleep?'' he said.

All three adults turned to him. Noah wished he hadn't spoken; it was a feeble joke, it really was.

''Well?'' said Joe. ''What's the difference?''

''No difference—they're both catnapping.''

They laughed! Were they idiots, or what? No one should laugh at such a dumb joke. It must have been because they were already in a good mood from Joe's even dumber jokes. Laughter seemed out of place in this living room, like a fart in the schoolroom. Now, *that* was funny, almost as funny as the dirty duck joke he just now remembered. Noah wished he could have told that one, but of course he couldn't, not with Miss Pike there. He moved closer to the fire, dumped another chunk of wood on to the grate as an excuse to be beside Phoebe's chair. He could smell her, smell the strange and beguiling odour of her; it was not a perfume, was the ineffable femaleness of her body coming right out through her dress, swamping the smell of the fire and the upholstery that had not been cleaned for years and the feral odour of three bachelor males. Around Phoebe Pike there drifted an invisible cloud redolent of warm flesh and skin, of long tresses frustratingly bound and bonneted, of small bones and delicately shaped hands and feet, of the fact that she sat to pee, sat as she was right now in the chair by the fire, her little button boots side by side, not sprawled apart the way Joe and Calvin always sat. She was mere inches away, close enough to touch and, although Noah was wedged between Phoebe's chair and the fireplace, he felt greater heat from the chair as he squatted there, watching the way her little teeth and gums shone wetly in the firelight, at the crease in her cheek when she laughed, and the way her eyes seemed actually to sparkle. He had always considered her a very ordinary-looking person, and could not understand this sudden metamorphosis; it would be interesting to see if she still looked this way when next he went into the store. He knew he would be going there more often in future.

They drank coffee and talked about small things and

laughed a good deal, none of them fully comprehending why it was that this unexpected visit had proved to be the most enjoyable two hours any of them could remember. Phoebe could not but wonder at the ease with which she conversed; these three strange persons were as vastly different, one from another, as they were collectively from the average citizen of Valley Forge. They plied her with more coffee and a lazy daisy cake. "Who made this? It's delicious!" and Joe hung his head, somewhat abashed to admit the fingers that had sifted and beaten and stirred had been none other than his own. Phoebe had a second slice, to Noah's annoyance. Joe had once offered to teach him a little cookery, and he had scornfully refused; if he had gone ahead and learned how, maybe she would've praised Noah's cake. It was not too late to learn, though; he would ask Joe for instruction tomorrow.

Only when the grandfather clock struck five did Phoebe extricate herself from the armchair. "I must be going home. Thank you so much for your hospitality. I . . . I've enjoyed myself very much." They escorted her to the door, all three, and clustered about her like Goldilocks' ursine trio.

"Be sure and come again," said Joe.

"Anytime at all," Calvin nodded enthusiastically, face happily sore from all the grinning he'd done today.

"We don't get too many visitors out here," said Joe, "so we appreciate when there's a knock on the door." He hoped the hints he was dropping were not overly heavy; that would have embarrassed everyone.

"I *will* come again—next Sunday?"

"What about the wolf?" They turned surprised faces to Noah. "There's a wolf out there, remember?"

"He's right! There's a wolf! Darn wolf right out there!" gabbled Calvin, imagining a monster the size of a barn rending Phoebe limb from limb.

"I was going to hitch up the team anyway," said Joe. "It's getting too dark to walk all the way to town. It'd be night before you got there."

"I don't want you to go to all that trouble, really. . . ."

"No trouble."

Noah saw his chance. "She can use Wicked. It's easier."

"I suppose so," Joe admitted. "I could pick him up next time I'm in town. . . ."

"No! I'll go, too. There's the wolf, and I've got my rifle. . . ."

"And what do you intend riding? Wicked isn't hefty enough for two."

"I'll walk in and ride back. It's easier than harnessing the team."

Joe saw the determination in his face. "All right. Go saddle up."

Phoebe was assisted into the saddle, where she insisted on sitting like a man for fear of falling off, and was led away by Noah, the reins in his hand. She waved goodbye. Joe and Calvin waved in return until horse and humans were swallowed by the darkening tunnel of the trail.

"That's a nice lady," said Calvin.

"Yes, she is. Wonder why she came up here?"

"Company?" suggested Calvin and, as every idiot is once in a while, he was right.

Phoebe felt like a queen being escorted by a pageboy, riding on this, her very first horse, one hand clutching the saddle horn, the other perched regally on her hip for balance as Wicked lurched and swayed beneath her. How on earth did riders stay aboard when a horse galloped? She could barely see Noah's hat by the time they reached the base of the ridge and were ambling along the trail towards the town road. Neither had spoken a word.

"Oh, dear," said Phoebe, "I think an angel is passing."

"Huh?" The hat shifted as he turned to look up at her.

"When an angel passes, nobody can talk," she explained, prompting him gently.

"I was thinking," he responded. Did he sound resentful?

"Well, I won't ask what your thoughts are. I'm sure they'd be very private at this time of evening."

"That's all right. I was just about finished thinking anyway. See that star, the red one?"

"Where?"

"Right there where I'm pointing."

"Oh, yes." She could not see his arm, let alone a star.

"That's Mars. Mars is the god of war in Roman mythology. Some people think it's Greek, but it isn't, it's Roman. The Greek god of war was Ares, but most people don't know that. The Romans stole a lot of gods from the Greeks and just changed the names."

"How fascinating."

"They stole Zeus and called him Jupiter, and later on the English called him Jove, but it's all the same god."

"Is that what you were taught in school?"

"They don't teach anything in school except 'the cat sat on the mat' and 'two and two are four'. I already knew before I went to school. We've got a lot of books at home."

"I can see why everybody says you'll soon be on your way to college."

"Well, maybe. . . ."

"Don't you want to go to college?"

"I used to. Now I don't know anymore."

"Is there something else you want to do?"

"I haven't made up my mind yet."

"Was it Joe who taught you things before you went to school?"

"I suppose," he admitted grudgingly. He did not want to talk about Joe. "It wasn't Calvin, that's for sure." He had never called his father "Pa" or "Dad" or any of the other paternal diminutives; calling him "Calvin" lessened the bond between them, made the link more casual.

"I'm sure Mr. Puckett had other things to do," said Phoebe, slightly embarrassed at his tone.

"Oh, sure, like watching the grass grow, and digging holes in the ground all over the place."

"Is he digging a well?" asked Phoebe, knowing he was not.

Noah snorted. "He's got this stupid idea there's a pot of gold buried under a tree, only he doesn't know which tree. Everybody knows about it."

Including me, you mean, thought Phoebe. He thinks I'm patronising him, and aren't I? But she could not stop herself. He was a boy, and she could not talk to him as she would a man. "Did he find a treasure map that started him off?" Oh God, now he'll think I'm such a stupid *grown-up*. . . .

"Nothing like that," said Noah evenly. "He just woke up one day and started digging, said it all came to him in a dream. He's a lunatic."

"You really shouldn't say that, Noah. He's your father. There have been lots of famous people who were struck by a vision. Joan of Arc . . . and . . . lots of people in the Bible." She cringed at her own words. What a fool I must seem. It's because I'm unused to children. . . . He'd hate to be called a child. Youth. Young man. . . .

"Yes, but they saw angels and stuff, not pots of gold. Know what he's found so far? An old skeleton, and he buried it again."

"You mustn't be too harsh on him, Noah." Be charitable, young man.

"That's easy enough for you to say, Miss Pike. He's not your father."

"No. . . ."

A host of angels trooped past until the lights of town were closer.

"Soon be there, Miss Pike."

"You must call me Phoebe now that we know each other better."

"All right."

And more angels, fingers to perfect lips, accompanied them to Phoebe's door. She dismounted with some clumsy assistance. "Thank you, Noah. Bringing me all this way was the act of a gentleman."

"Any time," he said, with a reasonable attempt at braggadocio, and crowned his efforts by springing into the saddle with the litheness of an acrobat. He had been practising that trick for some time, hoping it would one day (or night) come in handy. He even tipped his hat, and Phoebe hoped he did not see her smile in the feeble glow from the upper storey windows.

" 'Night, Miss Pike."

"Goodnight, Noah, and thank you again."

He wheeled his horse and galloped off down the street. At the edge of town, where darkness encroached once more, he slowed Wicked to a walk. The saddle beneath him was warm from her body. He was pretty sure he had impressed her with his horsemanship, but then, recalling their conversation, saw that he had conducted himself like a schoolboy. Just a week ago he had congratulated himself on discovering he was a madman, unpredictable, a unique and dangerous being, yet tonight he stood revealed under his true colours, not the midnight shade of a brigand's flag, but milksop white. Pathetic! Just . . . pathetic! Every word he had uttered on the walk to town came rampaging back through his head; foolish words, inadequate, shallow, the words of a *boy*. And he had gone and jumped on to his horse like some circus trick rider to impress her. She was at least ten years older than he, for God's sake! What did he think he was doing? She was probably laughing at him right this minute, and he did not blame her one little bit. (Phoebe was in fact undergoing interrogation as to her whereabouts until this late hour.) Noah rode slowly against the night wind back to the ridge, wrapped in gloom. Winter's coming, he thought. Winter's coming, winter's coming. . . .

CHAPTER THIRTY-FOUR

But before it came Noah was informed by a jubilant Miss Woodcock that she had obtained permission for him to take an examination which, if passed (and pass he assuredly would) automatically guaranteed him a place in one of Topeka's leading schools until his eighteenth year, when he would be given a further helping hand towards the university in Lawrence. To qualify for this largesse, Noah must present himself in Topeka to sit for the examination on December 3rd. The news made him feel sick. He did not want to go to one of Topeka's leading schools, nor to college. He did not know what he wanted. Too craven to state clearly his opposition to this development, Noah said nothing, acquiesced by silence. Miss Woodcock was ecstatic; once Noah had been launched upon the waters of the world her job would be completed, her long years as a schoolmistress rewarded beyond expectation. Noah was to be the culmination of her hopes, the crowning glory of her career.

But who would accompany him on the trip to Topeka? Calvin would be useless, and Miss Woodcock had classes to teach, December 3rd being a Monday. The only suitable chaperon was Joe Cobden, whose schedule was such it could be rearranged to accommodate a day's travel by train to Topeka, a day spent there for the examination, and a day's return travel. Joe was agreeable. He and Noah set off early on Sunday morning, endured the nine hour journey to the state capital on the A, T & SF, found a hotel which would accept them (both were newly barbered and dressed in their sprucest clothing, anticipating trouble in this regard) and spent a restless night, Joe because his mattress was lumpy,

Noah because his thoughts were engulfed by dread of examination day, lurking just the other side of dawn.

The exam would not be held until eleven, in the civic hall. They breakfasted and went for a stroll, admired the colonnaded stone splendour of the Statehouse, idled their way along the main streets, ears nipped by cold. Noah pressed his face to a store window filled with secondhand bric-à-brac. "Can I have those?" He pointed to a pair of unusual spectacles reposing between a battered cornet and (strange to find this in Kansas) a Scotsman's sporran. "What for?" asked Joe. The spectacles were tinted a deep shade of green, looked like something a blind man might wear. "I want them," said Noah. "Can't I have them? Please?" Joe was not in the habit of buying Noah gifts, not since the business with Lucius Croft and the pony, but there was a note of desperation in the boy's voice which Joe attributed to nerves over the impending examination. He did not want to aggravate that condition and be held responsible if Noah failed. "You can have them if they're less than a dollar." He handed Noah a bill, waited for him to come out again. He hoped the green spectacles cost more than a dollar, but Noah emerged from the store wearing them. "All you need now is a tin cup and a cane," said Joe, but Noah seemed mighty pleased with the peculiar lenses. "It's like being under water," he said. Topeka had become some Atlantean civilisation submerged for millennia, the sky a shallow sea of cloudy green. Now almost as outstanding in appearance as Joe, Noah wandered along, looking this way and that in amazement, staring at the people swimming upright through these watery streets.

Joe asked directions and they arrived at the civic hall with a half hour to spare, both of them stiff with cold by now. A great many boys, at least fifty, stood around in knots, accompanied by adults. "There's more here than I thought there'd be," said Noah. "They're from all across the state," Joe reminded him. "If this was the east, there'd likely be thousands. Think you can lick 'em?" Noah pulled his stetson down until the brim touched his green spectacles.

"Easy," he said, his voice quavering. "Good," said Joe. The boy's nervousness was transmitting itself to him; he wanted this whole thing to be over and done with.

At fifteen minutes to eleven, boys and adults were herded inside, the boys divested of hats and coats, then ushered deeper into the building. Joe sat in an ante-room festooned with hanging hats and coats, littered with anxious parents. The examination was scheduled to last three hours. He settled himself to wait.

Noah visited the lavatories before entering the examination room; all the boys had been warned they would not be allowed back into the room once they had left it for any reason whatever. He used a flush toilet for the very first time, saw the brown muck that had exploded from him carried away by a miniature whirlpool. Someone was vomiting in another booth. His stomach gripped by nervous spasms, Noah used the toilet again immediately, was almost sickened by the stench of his own excreta. He then joined the rest in the high-ceilinged chamber of torture. Fifty or so desks had been set out as in a schoolroom, and a scholarly-looking gentleman on a rostrum gave the candidates last-minute instructions—no talking, no cheating, no leaving the room until at least one hour had elapsed. Examination papers and writing-paper were distributed by tight-lipped assistants, laid face down on each desk. Inkwells had been provided. Every candidate had his own pen. The scholarly gentleman consulted his pocket-watch.

"You may turn over your papers and commence."

The room filled with a rustling that echoed among the rafters. *Place name in upper right hand corner of all submitted sheets. Number pages.* Noah did this with a trembling hand, then looked closely at the first question, something about the Louisiana Purchase. The words swam before his eyes; he had removed the green spectacles, but it was as though he wore them still, imposing a translucent screen between himself and what he perceived; the question paper was not real, nor were his pen and hand, the desk on which they rested, the floor beneath him and the building roundabout. He looked at several more questions, trying to make sense of them—Wolfe and Montcalme at Quebec, something about the Crusades, and then, oh, horror, the mathematical sheet! *If X numbers divided per hour π calculate tons required multiplied by equilateral square root of decimal point hypotenuse equation degrees. . . .*

Noah began to tremble all over. *I can't do any of this. . . . I can't, and I don't want to anyway. . . .* He gaped at still more questions. *Imagine you are the mayor of your town. State clearly and succinctly what changes you would make in order to maintain a thriving economy and ensure political harmony for the future, utilising the precepts established by American democracy.* Noah wrote his first word—*Dynamite!* His spirit soared when he realised what he had done; not only had he begun with a question halfway down the question sheet, he had given it a ridiculous answer. But it felt wonderful to have written that word. Change Valley Forge in order to maintain and ensure, etc.? Why, certainly—just light this fuse and take cover! With one word he had relinquished all obligations the examination paper, the civic hall, Miss Woodcock and the editorials of the *Valley Forge Courier* held over him. Fuck 'em all! He wasn't going to do this goddamn dumb-ass exam! Fuck it! He proceeded to fill the page with curlicues radiating in eloquent sweeps and curves from an elaborate scroll around *Dynamite!* When that page was filled he began another, this time drawing ships, trees, horses, none of them exhibiting any great eye for composition or perspective. Finally, to establish once and for all that he had absented himself from these hushed proceedings, he set down on paper the dirty duck joke:

Q. How do you fuck a duck?
A. Put your dick in its quack.

Nothing more remained to be done. Noah set aside his pen with a sense of great accomplishment. Looking around, he saw bowed heads, frantically scratching pens, lolling tongues and furrowed brows. Noah was beyond all that; he was free, had renounced the familiar and accepted mode of conduct, sidestepped all popular expectation, had circumvented the presupposed route to his future with an act as simple, as irrevocable as Alexander's hacking apart of the Gordian knot. He was vastly satisfied, immensely proud of himself. A sweep of the sword, a stroke of the pen, it was all the same; Noah had cast himself off from whatever comfortable berth might have been prepared for him, set adrift his tiny boat on tides responsive to moons others could not see, would ride currents of unimaginable strength and speed to unguessable destinations. A long voyage or a short one, under an entirely different hemisphere of stars, it was he who had taken that first step by severing the cord that bound him to his past and that other, now vanished, future.

On the rostrum stood a blackboard, and on the blackboard was chalked a list of times: 11:00, 11:15, 11:30, 11:45, 12:00 and so on until 2:00, when the exam was to end. The candidates had been told no one must leave during the first hour. This presumably was to prevent those who panicked at first sight of the questions from marching straight out and blighting their chances for ever; a boy obliged to sit for an hour might well calm down, steady his nerves and get to work, a little behind the others, perhaps, but still with plenty of time left. That was how Noah interpreted the rule, and he was right. The scholarly gentleman looked at his watch and drew a line through 11:15. Fifteen minutes! He'd only been here fifteen minutes! It had felt like an hour at least. He had changed his life in that time, accepted that he was indeed the madman from Valley Forge, the bold adventurer unafraid to grasp at whatever opportunities precocious destiny might see fit to fling down in his path. And here he sat, forced to simmer in the ferment of his own bold juices for another forty-five minutes! The world awaited him, the spinning planet hummed in anticipation of his setting foot outside the examination room and on to unconquered soil; earth and sky attended his next decisive move. . . .

He stayed where he was. If he left now, Joe would only ask questions, but if he waited until noon he could bluff his way, say the exam was so simple it had taken him only one-third of the allotted time to complete. That was the way to do it. He couldn't simply walk out now and tell Joe he had decided to seize the future by the scruff of its nebulous **neck;** Joe wouldn't understand. No one would. He had to bluff, give himself time to absorb the changes fully, prepare himself for whatever was to follow. It was an ignominious beginning, but prudence dictated that he stay where he was for the time being. His caution was buttressed by fear, for heroes are seldom created overnight, not outside the pages of a book.

Joe had almost fallen asleep in the ante-room despite the murmurings of parents, guardians, whoever they were. He had closed his eyes to shut out the stares directed at him where he sat on a bench. A nearby stove lulled him with warmth, and Phoebe Pike drifted across the forefront of his mind, unbidden, but not unwelcome. A nice person, Joe told himself, amended that to a nice *woman;* no sense in denying she was female. Since his days at the Circus Maximus, Joe had adhered rigidly to the practice he developed there of perceiving women in exactly the same neutral light as men; it was the only way in which to subdue the writhing beast within, the monster of sex. Seventeen years later, his body approaching the detumescence of early middle age, the monster was easily calmed, spent most of its time in hibernation, its heartbeat slowed almost to the point of cessation. Phoebe Pike would not disturb the monster's slumber were Joe to dwell upon her remembered image.

As a person, though, her worth was easily determined; she was . . . nice. A music box had led him to her four winters ago, and in all that time he had never thought about her with anything more than the usual benevolent indifference he applied to persons anywhere. He suspected she was more intelligent than most, but that was all. It had been no music box that had drawn her to the ridge, so what had it been? He guessed, with considerable shrewdness, that Phoebe Pike herself did not know—at least, not on any conscious level. She was lonely, he decided; probably her life at home was not all that might be desired (Joe had an unusually jaundiced view of family life) and she had no friends her own age that he was aware of. She was lonely, definitely, had come to the ridge to find conversation and company (Joe flattered himself she had recognised in him a similarly intelligent being), had been struck by doubt or nerves at the last minute and concocted the story of the wolf to get her through the front door. It was a white lie Joe found easy to forgive, under the circumstances, and he was glad of that afternoon's pleasant frivolity, just a week ago yesterday. The proposed second visit had been cancelled, since Joe and Noah had to travel to Topeka, but when they got back he would be sure to ask her out to the ridge the following Sunday. She was only the third woman he had ever seen there; the first had been Alma, the second Sadie Wilkes. Had her father ever found out who made Sadie pregnant? If so, he had not shared the news, and rightly so. Joe despised gossip, having on diverse occasions been its target.

"Joe?"

Noah was tugging at his lapel, a curiously child-like and intimate act, it seemed to Joe, one he would not nowadays have associated with Noah the Sullen. Joe's eyelids were still grainy from his discomfort of the night before, and his interrupted dozing by the stove had been no help at all; even his throat felt thick and clogged. "All through?" he asked, the words rasping.

"Yes. Can we go now?"

"No reason why not."

He lifted Noah's hat and coat from a peg on the wall, handed them to him. The other adults were watching them closely, some whispering. Joe stared back at them while Noah readied himself for the cold wind outside.

"All set?"

A nod. They left, and the wind lifted their coat-tails. Noah donned the green spectacles.

"How'd it go?"

"All right."

"You were the first out. Must've been easy."

"Can we go home now?"

"Our tickets are for tomorrow. Don't you want to rest up a little after all that brain-squeezing? They've got a theatre here. We could see a play tonight."

"I want to go home. We can change the tickets."

Joe laughed. "Homesick for the ridge already?"

"I just wanna go home!"

"Keep your teeth in. All right, we'll go home."

Joe glimpsed the face of a clock overhanging the street. 12:09? He had thought it must be at least 1:30. Joe did not own a watch.

"How long were you in there?"

"In where?"

"In the garden of the seven sacred virgins, where the hell do you think. How come you're out so early?"

"I told you, it was easy. I did it and came out."

"The whole thing?"

"Yes!"

"Don't you think it would've been smarter to take it slow and make sure the answers were right? Leaving after an hour strikes me as being reckless." No response. "Doesn't it strike you as being reckless?"

"No."

They returned to the hotel and packed their single valise. Joe paid the bill. "Come again," said the clerk, who had not once taken his eyes from Joe's hump.

"I'd love to," said Joe, "but I don't think you'd let me. I shat in the bed."

They walked to the depot, where Joe changed their tickets. The next westbound would come through in sixty-eight minutes. Noah's face was pinched and white, made paler by the ridiculous lenses.

"Can you see where you're going with those things?"

"Yes."

Something was chewing on the kid's ass, that was obvious.

"Hungry?"

"I guess so."

They both ate beef sandwiches in the depot restaurant, finished up with mugs of scalding coffee. Noah said not a word, his face hidden by the spectacles and his hatbrim. Observing his skinny wrists and long white fingers, his silent profile dipping into the coffee mug, Joe understood that Noah had failed. He had been unable to complete the exam, had not breezed through it like the genius he fancied himself to be, had probably sat, terrified, for much of that single hour. He's scared shitless, thought Joe; everyone back home's waiting to deck him with laurels or crucify him, and the poor little bastard knows it. Should Joe show that he knew, or should he leave the boy alone? Noah's hands were shaking now, sending ripples back and forth across the surface of his coffee. I'm finished, he thought; finished, finished, finished. . . . All the dash and pride he had felt were now gone, whisked away by cold winds on the walk to the depot. No one would ever see what Noah had done in the same light Noah saw it; they would think he had failed, pure and simple. And hadn't he? He was not sure himself any more, and his doubts gnawed at him, turned the coffee to acid, to broth of shame.

They had not exchanged a dozen words during the wait, and once aboard the train sat on opposite seats beside a window, both staring out at the level bleakness of Kansas in December. For hour after hour they did not move or speak. Joe could read nothing in Noah's hidden face. Finally he had had enough of this polite tiptoeing around what was on both their minds.

"Want to tell me what happened?"

"No." Noah's voice was cracked with tension.

"How long till the results come out?"

"Dunno."

"Miss Woodcock must have told you."

"I dunno. Early New Year."

"Think you'll have a story ready by then?"

"What story?"

"You know what story. You'd better get ready for a lot of screaming."

Noah turned away, looked out the window, strained his neck to keep from facing Joe. Joe let the matter rest. He wondered how Lucius Croft would react to all this, was slightly ashamed of himself for hoping it would create a nice wide rift between the old man and Noah; something good might come out of it after all.

The train arrived at Valley Forge several minutes past midnight. They tramped the two miles to the ridge. Calvin woke up when they entered the house, but Noah would not respond to his questions, went straight to bed.

"Reckon he's tuckered out," said Calvin, eager to excuse his genius of a son.

"That train ride takes it out of you."

"Did he win?"

"We won't know for a while, but listen—don't expect too much."

"Huh?"

"Don't go counting on him getting the scholarship or anything."

"Why not?"

"Just don't, that's all. You'll only be more disappointed if you count on him winning."

"Why?" Calvin's mouth was hanging open with concern.

"Because he didn't win, that's why."

"But you just now was sayin' you won't know for a while. . . ."

"Calvin, you're just going to have to take my word. He didn't win."

"Why . . . ?" Noah not win? That was impossible.

"I don't know why. Nerves, maybe. He won't say, and don't go bothering him about it. He doesn't feel too good right now. The best thing is to forget about it."

"Forget about it . . . ?"

"That's what I said."

And Joe made himself a meal to silence any further questions. Calvin watched him eat, his face woebegone. Something bad had happened and, as usual, he did not know what it was.

* * *

It was a bleak Christmas. Phoebe Pike visited once before Christmas Day, and was puzzled by the air of despondency inside the Puckett home. Joe did not invite her back, knew he should have tried harder to entertain her, but could not do it alone; Noah had fled when she knocked at the door, and all Calvin did throughout the visit was stare at the fire. A disaster.

On January 5th, Joe asked at the post office for any mail addressed to the ridge, but there was none. He went in every day until a letter for Noah arrived. Joe took it home, handed it over. Noah opened it when alone. Out of a possible one hundred he had scored one per cent. He was curious. Had they given him that one lonely mark for having spelled *Dynamite!* and his own name and the dirty duck joke correctly? Enclosed with the official notification of grading was a letter from Mr. Ward Peck of the State Board of Education:

Young man—your disgraceful paper has been brought to my attention, and it is without regret that I inform you it has been decided by myself and other members of the Board that you will never again be considered for one of this body's scholarships. Some boys have to sit for the examination twice before becoming eligible, but this second chance will not be extended to you. You are seriously at odds with all things respectable and worthwhile, and a major disappointment to your teacher, who has been informed of what transpired. You must answer to her for your obscenity and timewasting. It is beyond my understanding how an American youth could have penned such filth. Several members of the Board voted to have you brought before a magistrate, but I do not believe your kind is worth such effort. I trust we will not be hearing from or of you again.

Noah tore the letter to shreds.

When school resumed he did not dare to face Miss Woodcock. Noah's schooldays were over. Joe did not try to make him go, simply pointed out that refusing to apologise to Miss Woodcock was the act of a coward. Noah said being a coward was just fine with him. Joe thrust an axe into his hands. "From now on you can earn your keep." Noah submitted to Joe's silent disapproval for weeks thereafter, and was spared no sympathy over the painful blisters that formed and burst and formed again on his unpractised palms.

The news of Noah's failure became public property, presumably by way of Miss Woodcock, who resigned her post as schoolteacher on only twenty-four hours' notice, packed her few belongings and departed from Valley Forge on a night train, when there was less chance of her being seen at the depot. A new teacher was not found for several weeks, and the pupils were grateful to Noah for this unexpected holiday, despite having him held before them by their parents as an example of what they must not become. The ridge was once again a focus for general gossip and speculation; some maintained Noah's examination results had been so spectacularly brilliant the State Board of Education had dared not admit it, not wanting their fellow Topekans to know a boy from a small town like Valley Forge had bested the brains of the capital. But to most this theory made no sense at all; it was clear Noah's paper had been disgustingly filthy, for why else would a good woman like Miss Woodcock have slunk out of town like that if not from a sense of guilt at having tutored such a foulmouthed (or penned) brat? Some said the offending paper had had to be burned, for fear it would fall into innocent hands, deprave and corrupt by association and example.

Noah himself did not escape public disdain, since Joe insisted that he accompany him when delivering wood. They had only to drive down Decatur to attract the attention of everyone on the sidewalks; even people inside stores and houses who saw them pass by would come out to stare. Noah sat as though carved from basalt, ignoring the stares and impudent remarks—"Hey, genius! Know any good jokes?" How much did they actually know? Surely Mr. Ward Peck had not informed Miss Woodcock of the exact nature of his crime, word for word. Noah never did find out that the details had reached Valley Forge by way of a brakeman on the A, T & SF whose cousin Sally in Topeka was married to the best friend of one of the examination graders; the dirty duck joke had been passed from man to man without soiling cousin Sally's ears, and been passed from the depot to Clancy's Cloverleaf Saloon and the Calhoun Hotel in the space of an evening. "Quack! Quack!" cried small boys whose older brothers frequented these drinking establishments. "Quack! Quack!" A local bard composed a limerick to celebrate Noah's humiliation:

> There was a young man name of Puckett
> Who straddled a duck for to fuck it,
> Said the duck— "Off my back!
> You're too big for my quack—
> If you give me a dollar I'll suck it."

When this ditty reached Noah, courtesy of one of his former schoolfellows (Tyler Grier, who had pushed him into the dirt on his first day, now himself an ex-student and farmhand) Noah was mortified, yet grateful that the poet had granted him a dick too big for the duck's quack; cruelty modified by a compliment.

"Like the attention you're getting?" asked Joe one day. They had felled an elm and were sawing it into lengths, hot work even in January.

"Water off a duck's back," said Noah, and grinned wryly.

Joe had to admit that was a pretty sharp riposte; maybe the boy wasn't going to sulk away the rest of his life after all. They worked on.

Lucius Croft could not believe it. He wrote to the State Board of Education for confirmation of this ridiculous story, and received it. Now that he knew the facts, he wondered why he had doubted the rumours. Hadn't the boy proved on that last ride together that he was not normal? Puckett blood had triumphed over Croft blood. It was a bitter blow. He had hoped against hope there might be some kind of compromise or reconciliation between himself and Noah, but fate had decreed otherwise, he saw that now. First thing in the morning he would go into town and have Purvis revise that last will, reinstate Willard as the recipient of Croft's not inconsiderable legacy. But tonight he would get drunk.

Alone in the farmhouse, legs covered by a blanket (his shanks seemed to get colder than the rest of his body) in front of a comforting fire, a bottle of whiskey and a lamp on the table beside him, Lucius Croft proceeded to invoke, then drown, the various persons (living, dead and departed) who haunted him. He poured and drank, poured and drank for several hours, stopped long enough to replenish the fire clumsily, then poured and drank again until past, present and future swam around him in provocative circles, just beyond understanding's reach, mocking him. He brooded darkly upon Noah's misdeeds, tried to comfort himself with the decision to change his will, failed to do anything but make himself more miserable. Why had the boy done it? Croft would have been prepared to go ahead and pay for Noah's college fees, the Topeka disgrace and his apparent madness notwithstanding, anything to perpetuate his own blood, but, coupled with the fact that it had become clear Noah had no intention of ever again visiting him at the farm, pride dictated that the will be changed. Lucius Croft was not going to pander to some precocious child just because he happened to be Croft's grandson, nossiree, not him. He fell asleep, failed to hear the snapping and popping of the fire's newest log.

The smell of burning woke him. Croft's blanket was smouldering in several places. Not fully awake, he panicked and flung out his arm, and on its sweep back towards the blanket to beat out the smoking patches his hand connected with the lamp beside the wiskey bottle, flinging it against the brickwork around the fireplace. The lamp's glass base shattered, splashing oil across the hearth and the blanket, which flared instantly. Too drunk to move quickly, Croft was awash with flame before he could prevent it. The blanket had tangled around his lower legs and, despite his best efforts to stand, Croft could do no more than topple to the floor and thrash wildly, attempting to smother his burning hair with a small scatter rug. His screaming woke the farmhands, who dashed into the house and put out the burning hearth and blanket before the house itself was threatened.

Croft was unconscious but still living, his legs and head horribly burned. One of the men rode to town to fetch Dr. Whaley, but when he at last arrived there was little the doctor could do except inject Croft with morphine. He recovered his senses for several minutes, but could say nothing. He died shortly before dawn.

Dr. Whaley took the body to Joshua Pike, and did not exaggerate when he described as "challenging" the task of making Croft presentable for public display. Pike, when he saw the charred head, glumly concurred, but cheered up when he took Whaley at his word and approached the problem as a general would a campaign. He first snipped away the worst sections of scalp and replaced them with a special putty; this substance also served to patch up the less obvious burns around the temples. All in all it was a fair job, but the complete loss of hair was vexing. He telegraphed a salon in Topeka and ordered a wig, then proceeded with the standard embalming process. It was not yet midday.

By noon the following day the body of Lucius Croft was ready for perusal by members of the public. One of the ground floor rooms (in which frugal Mr. Middleton had himself assembled his cheaper coffins) had been transformed by Pike into a nondenominational chapel of rest for the benefit of those corpses not directly linked with the Protestant or Baptist churches. The windows were hung in funereal black, one wall was dominated by a plain wooden cross (there were no popish crucifixes in Valley Forge) and the open coffin reposed on a table draped in black velvet. Several vases of freshly cut flowers (hardy winter varieties, virtually odourless) did unfair battle with the exudations from Croft's burnt flesh, and those mourners who filed in to pay their respects (a surprising number, considering the deceased's skinflint reputation) held handkerchiefs to their noses rather than to their eyes, which in any case were dry. They came out of curiosity, for word had spread regarding Croft's hairless state; one of the farmhands who had assisted Dr. Whaley described to anyone who would buy him a drink how the dead man's scalp had resembled "a rasher of bacon, all crisped and cooked and crinkled up". That was the sort of thing one didn't often see, and so they came, singly and in groups, to see what undertaker Pike had managed to accomplish for the unfortunate departed. The wig had arrived just this morning, had been given a hasty but artistic pruning by Pike (it was a woman's wig—blonde) then lightened to a venerable whiteness with careful dustings of finely sieved baking powder until an approximation of Croft's former colouring was achieved. A few artfully combed strands also helped hide the puckering of puttied temples. If one did not look too closely, one could not readily detect the fraud.

A murmur of disbelief rippled the tranquil filing-by when none other than Noah Puckett arrived! Townsfolk marvelled at his nerve in thinking himself worthy of attendance, but Noah appeared to notice nothing, not their silence, nor their stares. A sudden buzz of whispering followed his exit from the chapel of rest after a brief but intense inspection of Croft's remains. Everyone in town knew by late afternoon, and on the following day a large crowd flocked to the cemetery to see Croft put under—also to see if the boy would have the gall to show up; he had taken onlookers by surprise yesterday, but today they were primed to call out "Shame!" and "Hypocrite!" and "Quack! Quack!"

Preacher Tub Davis had insisted on handling the burial service despite the fact that Croft's daughter had been married by Wilkes. Lucius Croft, he insisted, had himself been married in a Baptist chapel back in Missouri, and was therefore closer to Tub's church than to Wilkes'. No one knew how Tub had discovered this information, since he was not a Missourian himself, and had never met Croft before coming to Kansas, but no one was willing to challenge him on this point, not even Willard, whose mind was occupied with other matters. Tub Davis had seldom seen such a gathering at any graveside, and only wished it was attributable to a general respect for the recently deceased; he knew it was not, of course, having heard of the errant grandson's outrageous visit to the funeral parlour (wearing some kind of blind man's dark spectacles, it was said—as a calculated insult to the dead man and all those present, Tub didn't doubt) and, like all the rest, he anticipated some kind of confrontation when the boy attended the burial. He hoped the mourners would have the decorum to wait until after his own contribution to the issue before tarring and feathering the young blasphemer, and preferably outside the cemetery's picket fence; retribution for the living was one thing, respect for the dead a different animal entirely. Tub thought there should be special areas for the meting out of punishment against the ungodly, and sometimes wished public stonings were not confined to the Holy Land and centuries past.

But Noah confounded all their expectations by staying away. A keen resentment was felt by the crowd; they had come hoping for something exciting, something about which they all agreed, and the little bastard had gone and dashed their hopes! They shuffled restlessly, seven or eight deep around the gravesite, and Tub Davis, divining their mood of frustration, quickly whipped through the usual praise for the deceased (whom he had met only once or twice and disliked intensely on both occasions—Croft, in turn, had thought Tub a psalm-spouting lunatic) and abandoned his prepared lesson from the Bible in favour of the kind of speech closest to the heart—the inspired harangue. "My friends," he began, although a great many of those gathered here were from Wilkes' flock, not his own, "before us lie the mortal remains of a man who died with hope and expectations unfulfilled! Our great reward lies in the Hereafter, but while we dwell in this vale of tears, it's only human to expect satisfaction from one or two things on this here mortal plane!" This was a radical departure from his usual message, to whit: Nothing you do or say on earth is of any significance unless directed to the greater glory of God and the accruing of heavenly favour. Nevertheless, the crowd listened, hopeful of some controversial statement.

"You all know, like I know," Tub continued, "of the grievous disappointment this good man suffered just recent. My friends, we are all of us a part of the good Lord's flock, and we have got obligations, one to another. But if those obligations are spurned and tossed aside on to stony ground, why, we all of us suffer for it! And the one who did the spurning is accursed in the eyes of the Lord, let me tell you!" He glared about him as though awaiting contradiction; none was forthcoming. "You know who I'm talking about, friends and neighbours, and I just want that person to know his pernicious and flagrant act of defiance has not gone unrecorded! There's a dark corner of hell reserved special for them that careth not for their fellow man and trample on the expectations of their elders! The young have a bounden duty to perform, and that is to heed the words of them that knows best! Them that follow not the path of duty will be blasted by the wrath that knows no let-up, in this world *and* the next!"

He continued in this vein for a good ten minutes more, but barely kindled a spark of response from the gathering. The Protestants had always thought Tub a ranting fool, and saw nothing here today to change their minds, although he was right about the duty of the young. The Baptists present suspected Lucius Croft had not truly been one of them, and they thought it unwise of their preacher to appropriate an unsaved soul in this way. Tub looked and sounded just fine thundering away from up in the pulpit, or dunking new members of the flock while standing up to his waist in the nearest creek, but with an old reprobate like Lucius Croft lying in the coffin instead of a regular churchgoer like themselves, the effect of his speechifying was considerably reduced, and there was only one apologetic "Hallelujah" throughout. None of them needed reminding of Noah Puckett's sins; what they needed was Noah Puckett in the flesh, not to tar and feather him, but to furnish their lives with a little spice, an *event*. They wanted something to *happen*. Harsh words and Sunday rhetoric were not enough. Their resentment against Noah had worsened, not because of his crimes, but because he had tantalised them by appearing at the chapel of rest, then left them disappointed at the graveside. It was a bitterly cold day, and they would have preferred to stay at home.

The coffin was lowered without further delay, the waiting pile of earth returned to the hole. Those who felt they should speak the traditional phrases of sympathy went ahead and spoke them to Willard Croft, who stood with his wife and bored children by the cemetery gates, ready to receive such offerings. He had closed the store for the day out of respect, and had therefore expected Phoebe to be present at the burial. She had not come, and he was upset at her absence. Still, perhaps it was just as well since his wife was here. Neither woman suspected Willard of harbouring toward Phoebe anything but an employer's regard for a good worker, but he sometimes liked to imagine that his wife was desperately trying to ascertain just who her husband's mistress was, praying for a clue to the identity of whichever perfumed hussy was stealing his love. His wife would have been amazed, had she known his thoughts. Why on earth would anyone want to steal Willard away from her? There was in fact one very good reason, one which Willard himself had learned only yesterday. He stood by the cemetery gates, telling himself it was best that Phoebe was not here to fan the flames of his wife's suspicions, and accepted with sorrowful visage the condolences made every fifteen seconds as the mourners filed past on their way home.

Willard was not feeling in the least sorrowful, for lawyer Purvis, custodian of the old man's affairs, had let slip the information that Croft had made out two wills, the first leaving everything to Willard, the second, which left everything to Noah, automatically nullifying the first. Purvis had by roundabout conversation insinuated he was prepared to forget the existence of the second will (witnessed by his own clerk, who would keep his mouth shut) if Willard would see fit to reward him with, shall we say, fifteen per cent of the inherited property's current worth, payable over a period of three years to avoid suspicion? Willard thought fifteen per cent a reasonable figure, and had seen the paper which would have made Noah the wealthiest young man in the county incinerated before his eyes early that very morning. He was possibly the only person content with the day's proceedings, and found it difficult to maintain his dolorous expression.

On the ridge Joe and Noah chopped wood while Calvin began a new hole. It was a day like any other.

CHAPTER THIRTY-FIVE

The man-that-wasn't-there had come and gone. So, too, had the swarming insects, and Jessica knew why—the little green lizard had gobbled them all up; only a tiny little fellow he was, but such an appetite! They hadn't a chance, all those scurrying, scuttling whatever-they-weres; he pounced on them and ate them in the twinkling of an eye, and his merry little eyes *did* twinkle, just like black beads they were, and sometimes he blinked just one clever little eyelid—*winked* at her, the little dear, just to show how much he cared, and the corners of his mouth turned up ever so slightly in a half-smile.

He was such a handsome little fellow, emerald green from nose to tail except for his belly and pulsing throat, a lovely shade of palest yellow. Pounce, pounce, pounce! Whenever the insects began crawling into the corners of her vision, there he was, a flash of green, and didn't they just scatter! But not before he'd caught a few more and gobbled them down. He was weeding them out, harrying their flanks, routing their plans for conquest. With the little green lizard for her ally Jessica felt she stood a chance against the swarming soul-eaters (for such was the role of the insects— to consume her soul until none was left). The insects were under the command of Joshua and Beatrice, the lizard under the command of Phoebe, and their battleground was the nebulous landscape, sometimes fantastic, sometimes drear, of Jessica's mind. Back and forth went the battle, back and forth, first one side gaining ascendancy, then the other, but of late it was the valiant lizard which had triumphed more often than the foe; no matter from which direction they came, those swarming soul-eaters, there he was! Gobble, gobble, gobble, and entire regiments were decimated, mown down by his scything jaws, pursued by those nimble legs that sent him scurrying hither and thither among their broken ranks as they scattered before him. Crunch! Crunch! went their horrible little bodies as he bit into them, chopping them in half while their nasty barbed legs kept on wiggling. Oh, wonderful green lizard, triumphant again! He was her only friend through the day, now that Phoebe worked at the store, the only one in whom she could confide; in fact she told him more than she had ever told Phoebe, that was how much she trusted him, and his twinkling beady eyes blinked back tears as she told him just how awful things were in this place called her Life, and even nodded his sweet little head now and then to show he understood. Don't worry, he told her, I'll eat them all up, every single one. And tears of gratitude would leak from Jessica's eyes at his bold announcement. Bless you, little lizard!

She took Grandmamma's lunch to her room on the special tray with legs that could be set up across Grandmamma's knees. When all was arranged, she turned to leave. "Don't go yet," said Grandmamma. "I want some company while I eat. Sit." Jessica did not wish to talk to her, wanted to leave the room as quickly as possible, but there was no disobeying that imperious tone of voice. She sat on a chair and immediately began to fidget restlessly. Grandmamma forked up the stew Jessica had prepared. Jessica watched the wrinkled and bloodless lips move, saw the hollowed cheeks writhe as each mouthful was thoroughly chewed, the lean jaw champing like some steam-driven machine; then another forkful of stew would be tipped into the gaping orifice and those lips meshed again as the jaw machine resumed its implacable champing. Where cheekbone met jawbone a ghastly knob beneath the skin moved back and forth like an indecisive mole, and its burrowings tugged on Grandmamma's large and pendulous ears, moving them fractionally, like the wings of a moth when it is deciding whether or not to fly.

"What are you staring at?"

"Nothing. . . ."

Grandmamma chewed on, her jaw that of a cow, her eyes those of a hawk. Jessica made a brave attempt at removing her eyes from Grandmamma's, but failed; her gaze was drawn irresistibly to that of her tormentor, and she was rendered immobile by what she saw, as a small creature is said to be held spellbound by the unblinking eye of the snake which is about to devour it.

"How long do you think it'll be?" asked Grandmamma.

"Be . . . ?"

"Before they take you away."

"Take me away . . . ?" She felt she must somehow have missed the opening sentences of this conversation; whatever was Beatrice talking about?

"To the madhouse," said Grandmamma, wiping stew from her chin.

"Why . . . why would they do that?" Jessica did not fully comprehend who "they" might be, imagined an army of insects dragging her "away", her body supported on a million tiny carapaces, their hateful, scurrying legs creating a kind of whispery scratching sound. The thought made her feel quite ill, and she clutched at her skirts to make sure no insects were climbing her legs. Where was her little green lizard?

"Why?" said Grandmamma. "Because you're mad."

Jessica stood, convinced she could feel the horrible tickling of their feet as they swarmed up over her boot-tops and on to her legs. She thrashed feebly at her skirts in an attempt to drive them away.

"Sit down!" commanded Grandmamma, and Jessica obeyed, her skin crawling. "Just you stay sat till I'm all through talking to you," warned Grandmamma, "and don't fidget like that! Sit still!"

By a concerted effort of will Jessica managed to locate the lizard. He was over by the wardrobe, and he knew she was being attacked. Yes, here he came, racing across the floor with his darling little tail whipping back and forth. He disappeared beneath her skirts.

"Mean to say you didn't know you're mad?"

"I am not mad," said Jessica, thinking not of the insult but of the green lizard, even now creating chaos among the invaders in that gloomy world beneath her trembling skirts. Kill them! she silently pleaded. Kill them all!

"Yes you are. Crazy as a loon." The stew was excellent for once. She wished there was more, but it would have been a mistake to compliment Jessica. There would be none of that. Grandmamma's taunting served her as both appetiser and dessert; no meal was complete without a garnishing of spite. Watching Jessica's foolish face twitch was a delight.

"You have no right to talk to me this way. . . ."

What was this? Resistance? There would be no revolt of the slaves in the Pike home; no, indeed. "Be quiet while I'm talking!" shrieked Grandmamma, and Jessica's quivering mouth shut, although her lips continued to tremble.

"Know what they do to you in the madhouse?" Jessica did not know. Was the sensation on her legs the insects or the lizard, or both? "I'll tell you what they do," said Grandmamma. "They chain you to the wall stark naked and whip you till you mend your ways. Sit *down!*" Jessica had attempted to rise, but now sank again on to her seat of torture. The lizard apparently could not see in the darkness of her skirts, for her legs were aswarm from ankle to hip. "And if that doesn't work," continued Grandmamma, "they put you in a hole in the ground like John the Baptist and piss all over you!" She loved the sound of that word, so like the sound created by the substance itself. "Pisssss . . ." she hissed at Jessica, "piss all *over* you!"

Jessica sprang to her feet this time, her lower half alive with scrabbling, nipping insects. They must not be allowed above her waist! She moaned like a dying thing and ran from the room, beating at her flying skirts.

"It won't be long now!" howled Grandmamma. "It

won't be long now!'' And for once she knew her words were not mere tauntings, but prophecy. The way Jessica had fled the room was proof! Imagine a normal person hitting herself across the thighs like that. The creature was mad all right, mad as a June bug.

When Phoebe arrived home she found Pike standing over Jessica in the kitchen. Jessica was weeping and whimpering, Pike ordering her to "Stop it! Stop it this instant!" Phoebe placed herself between her parents. "Leave her alone!" Pike surprised himself by obeying; let her look after the fool if that's what she wanted. It was not a man's business to pat the hand of a hysterical wife every time she broke into tears. It was the noise, rather than the foolish explanation she had given him, which caused him such annoyance, the horrible mewling sound Jessica made, like a kitten being smothered by a pillow. He returned to the basement. The dead were sometimes better company than the living, it seemed. The dead, at least, did not babble of lizards.

"Mother, take a deep breath."

Jessica inhaled jerkily, released a sigh that became a moan, a sound both anguished and pathetic. Phoebe took her gently by the hands. "Tell me what happened." She expected to hear of some petty cruelty perpetrated by her father.

"It's the lizard . . ." sniffed Jessica. "My little lizard can't keep up with them any more. . . ."

"What lizard?"

"My little green lizard. He eats them all up, but there are too many. They were . . . everywhere!" She ended with a little shriek and beat again at her skirts.

Phoebe held her mother tightly, offered the soothing panacea of meaningless sounds to which babies and animals often respond when upset, and Jessica's flailing hands eventually were still. "Why not have a lie-down?" suggested Phoebe, and Jessica, swayed completely by her gentleness, nodded weakly. Phoebe led her to her bedroom, closed the shades against the remaining sunlight, removed Jessica's boots and covered her with a blanket. Lying there, her thin face atop the blanket still agitated, flanked by clutching fingers, Jessica appeared the most helpless thing Phoebe had ever beheld; her vulnerability begged for surcease, invited the grinding heel that would crush her once and for all. Phoebe imagined her mother giving one final yelp of alarm as the heel descended, and then the silence, the blessed silence that would follow—no weeping, no foolish talk of lizards, no need of a weary champion to defend her, no anchor and chain of obligation to keep Phoebe in Valley Forge any longer. She had saved almost two hundred and ten dollars, enough to buy a train ticket and lodgings in some distant city, would have left already if not for Jessica. But the burden around her neck would permit no flight, and Phoebe submitted to its intolerable weight with resignation.

Jessica's eyelids closed, fluttered like dusty moths for a moment, then were still. Phoebe tip-toed from the room, closed the door behind her without a sound. She continued down the corridor, still on tip-toe, but stopped when a sound was heard from Grandmamma's room, a soft thud followed by the creaking of her mattress. Phoebe went to Grandmamma's door, knelt and peered through the keyhole. She had never spied in this fashion before, but did not stop now to consider her action, for there before her was a sight that set her heart racing—Grandmamma was out of bed! She was halfway across the room, walking! Now she stooped to retrieve the cane that had fallen from the bed and rolled across the floor. Phoebe could scarcely believe her luck.

The door crashed open while Grandmamma was still stooped to pick up the cane, and in her surprise she could not decide whether to stand upright or sink to her knees, and her mouth hung agape in the frozen leer of a gargoyle. Phoebe surveyed with satisfaction the picture Grandmamma presented, bent in half, swathed in black, like an old peasant woman bowed beneath a bundle of invisible sticks. "Why, Grandmamma," said Phoebe, smiling the smile of an enraptured saint, "you're up and about! And we all thought you were crippled!" She brought her hands together like an ecstatic postulant, declared, "It's a miracle!" with all the sarcastic verve she could muster.

Grandmamma's state of shock was broken by Phoebe's voice. She snatched up the cane with a purposeful grip, as if to punish it for having revealed her sham, scuttled back to the bed while still bent over and scrambled on to her throne, the middle of the mattress. Now she gripped the cane with the defiant authority of a queen about to ward off bloodthirsty revolutionaries with her sceptre, and her eyes blazed with the light of outraged indignation.

"Think how happy the news will make Father," Phoebe continued, "and Mother, too, *especially* Mother. She won't have to fetch and carry for you any more. And just think, Grandmamma, you can relieve yourself in the outhouse instead of using the pot! It's the start of a new life," she enthused. "Aren't you happy?"

"I can't walk," stated Grandmamma, her voice hollow.

"Can't walk, Grandmamma?" Phoebe adopted an expression of puzzlement and consternation that could have been seen from the back row of any large theatre. "But I saw you, dear Grandmamma."

"You didn't see anything!" snapped Grandmamma, doubly annoyed by Phoebe's mockery; being found out was bad enough, but this stupid play-acting was too much for her pride. "You didn't see a *thing!*" Her chin was up, her neck stiff, the wattles on her throat flushed and trembling.

Phoebe's hands had been clasped in mock-delight beneath her chin; now she placed them firmly on her hips and let her face harden.

"I saw you."

"You didn't!"

"I *saw* you."

"No!"

"Yes!"

"Get out!"

"You miserable old hag!"

"Witch! Witch! You're trying to kill me!"

"I'd love to! I'd love to see you dead!"

"Get out!"

"Not until you admit you can walk!"

"I *can't* walk!"

"I *saw* you!"

"You didn't, didn't, *didn't!*"

"You old faker! Horrible, *horrible* old . . . *bitch!*"

Grandmamma swung her cane like a cutlass, but Phoebe was beyond her reach. "Get out! Get out! Get out!" she screeched.

"Get out yourself, you liar! Liar! Liar! Fake!"

"I'm a *cripple!*" howled Grandmamma, and so fervent was her acting she actually believed it, and began weeping tears of pity for herself. But Phoebe would not be swayed.

"You're a disgusting, horrible old *fake!*"

Phoebe had left the door open behind her, with the consequence that Jessica was cowering beneath her blanket in the next room, and Pike, having heard the fracas from down in the basement, was at this moment thundering up the stairs to investigate. He entered Grandmamma's room, red of face from his exertions and from anger; only *he* was allowed to raise his voice in this house.

"What is going on here!"

"I caught her walking, Father. She's not crippled at all. I always knew she wasn't, and now I've *seen* her out of bed."

"Liar!" wailed Grandmamma.

"She's a selfish old woman, making Mother wait on her like a queen when she's perfectly capable of looking after herself."

"Liar! Liar!" Grandmamma waved her cane feebly, turned an imploring face to her son. "She's telling *lies* about me. . . ."

Pike was furious with Phoebe. "How dare you make such an accusation! Your grandmother is crippled. You will apologise!"

"I'll do no such thing! I saw her! She's deliberately made herself a millstone around Mother's neck, made her slave away day and night for nothing! You mustn't let her get away with it any longer!''

"Do not raise your voice to *me!*"

Grandmamma's head wagged tragically on the stalk of her neck. "Oh, oh . . . lies and spite . . ." she babbled. "Why does she hate me so . . . ?"

"You will apologise to your grandmother!"

"I will not!"

"Apologise!" His jowls were an apoplectic purple.

"No!"

They glared at each other, both made speechless by such intransigent opposition. Like a seasoned veteran of the boards, Grandmamma sought to resolve this impasse with a dramatic foil to their hysterical shouting; with a horrifying gurgle, she clutched at her throat and fell backwards on to the pillows. Pike immediately rushed to her side and took her in his arms. "Smelling salts! Quickly!" he barked over his shoulder.

Phoebe folded her arms. "No."

"Do as I say!"

Grandmamma faked a convulsion, throwing herself about in Pike's arms, then suddenly lay very still. Pike dashed from the room, leaving Grandmamma's head open-mouthed on the pillow, gargling unpleasantly on air. One arm flopped dramatically from the bed and hung like a dead branch. Phoebe admired the conviction behind the performance, and applauded lightly. Grandmamma's eyes opened and swivelled to focus on her.

"Disgusting old hypocrite," said Phoebe.

Grandmamma's eyelids snapped shut again as Pike rushed back into the room, a phial clutched in his paw. He unstoppered it and waved the thing about beneath Grandmamma's nostrils until she gasped and pushed the phial away. The sharp reek of spirits of ammonia filled the air.

Phoebe went to the door. "Don't bother asking me to fetch Dr. Whaley, Father. I'm sure you'll find she's recovered by morning. Except for her legs, of course."

She went downstairs, tied on her bonnet, wrapped herself

in a heavy shawl and left the house. The sun was sinking somewhere behind the clouds, and the ceaseless Kansas wind flayed her cheeks and brow. Where to go? There was nowhere but the ridge. It would be dark before she got there, and she had not been invited in any case. Perhaps they no longer liked her. The last visit had not gone well, and since then the ridgefolk (that is how Phoebe thought of Calvin, Noah and Joe) had suffered once again at the hands of gossip-mongers over Noah's débâcle in Topeka. Joe in particular seemed more surly whenever he came into the store. She did not like to think that her friendship with these three peculiar men was at an end, for without them she had nothing. But she would not intrude uninvited.

Phoebe spent the next hour walking up and down every street in Valley Forge, dreamily reliving the discovery of Grandmamma stooping for her cane, and the screaming match resulting from it. In the end she returned home, knowing Jessica would be in no condition to prepare supper on her own, and the Pikes spent the remainder of that evening in a frosty silence born of mutual antipathy and indigestion.

Noah's spindliness had given way to strength; his body seemed almost to swell overnight with layers of lean muscle. His beard sprouted at last and Calvin presented him with a razor on his fifteenth birthday (having been reminded of this event by Joe). The boy had, to all appearances, become a man, but remained as sullen as ever, now with a powerful body and razor-slashed face befitting his saturnine mood. He worked alongside Joe with the truculent intensity of a mute slave, one no owner would dare to lash for fear of provoking murder. He grew stronger and more silent by the day, and knew his job so well Joe had only to indicate which tree was to be felled for all subsequent conversation to be made redundant, unless prompted by Joe for its own sake. Once, by way of experiment, Joe said not one word from dawn till dusk, waiting to see if Noah would respond by opening his mouth to stave off the silence that grew between them like a wall. Noah said nothing. How had he found such appalling strength of purpose, and why did he exercise it in this childish game of weakling-speaks-first? Was this brooding, speechless creature the same entity Joe had once carried joyously upon his hump? They sat on the same fallen trees, ate the same food at the same time, but faced in different directions, sweat drying on their brows, bodies thrumming with the idling energies of blood and sinew, re-fuelling for their next task in this endless cycle which brought the trees of the ridge to the stoves and hearths of Valley Forge.

The house was no longer a home, had been stripped of all warmth and confraternity, was now no more than a roof under which the residents sheltered from sun and rain. The culprit was Noah. He knew it, and so did Joe. Calvin suffered the most from this atmosphere of strain and gloom; like a dog, he knew something was wrong, but could not identify the exact nature of the problem, knew only that the house had become a mighty quiet place lately. And like a dog he dug holes; not to bury bones, but to unearth answers to questions he was incapable of formulating. Mealtime conversation had been reduced to a "Pass the butter" formality. Calvin had several times attempted to broach a topic of mutual interest, but his efforts were lame and resulted in even stonier silences. He gave up, as had Joe, and an iron-clad hush descended between all three with the weight and finality of a portcullis; they could see each other, could even touch, had they so chosen, but lived in separate spaces, each one inviolate.

One evening when not a single word had been spoken for over an hour, Joe decided he had had enough. He laid aside the buffalo he was carving and flung his knife at the ceiling, where the tip of the blade lodged in a rafter.

"I've got an announcement to make," he began, and Noah rose from his chair. "Stay where you are!" commanded Joe, and Noah hesitated, torn between obedience to and rejection of such unaccustomed peremptoriness.

"This concerns you," said Joe. "It concerns all of us. This place is like a graveyard. Nobody talks. Day and night it's the same thing—nothing. Not a word."

"That's right," agreed Calvin. "Nobody says nothin'. I seen it for weeks now. . . ."

Joe continued. "When people stop talking it's because they've got something on their mind, something they should say out loud and be done with it. Calvin, do you have something on your mind?"

"No," admitted Calvin.

"You're not feeling bad about something?"

"I reckon not."

Joe turned to Noah. "How about you? Got anything on your mind?"

"No," denied Noah in a voice that trumpeted *Yes!*

"I don't believe you. I think you've got so many god-damn grievances in your head you don't know which way to turn."

"What makes you think you know what's inside my head?" Noah employed his most scornful manner in an attempt to alter the direction this fireside chat seemed to be taking.

"I can read your face, that's how, and you've got misery written all over it. Why don't you spit it out, kid, and we can all start being friends again?"

"You don't even know what you're talking about," Noah sneered.

"Sure I do, and you know I know. You're the most miserable thing on two legs since Jesus got a hernia. You sit there every night with a face like a knothole and don't say a word. I've had enough. Say what you need to say, whatever it is, and let's act like civilised people again."

"I've got nothing to say," said Noah, and added: "Not to *you.*" He said it without thinking; he knew Joe was not to blame for any of the tidal sludge of sorrow that rocked back and forth within him, could not have said who *was* to blame, apart from himself, and that was too sweeping an admission to make.

"Oh, it's *me*, is it? You've got some kind of beef against me, have you? Let's hear it."

"I told you, I'm not saying anything to you." Noah wanted this to stop right now, before it led to a point which, unlike the silences, proved to be beyond his control. Noah found it easy to generate a feeling of unease throughout the house, but was too cowardly, in his misery and selfishness, to instigate any kind of confrontation that might resolve or alleviate his unhappiness. He gave no thought to anyone else's happiness.

Joe would not be denied. "Why won't you say anything to me? You haven't been saying anything to Calvin, either. Well?"

"I told you. . . ."

"Tell me something else! What's the matter, can't you find the words? Don't you know how to say what you mean, college boy? Spit it out, *genius.*"

Joe knew he was exceeding the limits of familiarity, but if there was ever to be a rapprochement within these clapboard walls it would require considerable bloodletting beforehand.

Noah's face blanched. The turmoil within him, until this moment simmering in its own stale juices, now bubbled hotly, too volatile for the cool parryings of wordplay. He launched himself across the few yards separating him from Joe and aimed a clenched fist at his face, the first time in his life Noah had deliberately attempted to harm anyone. Joe dodged too late and felt knuckles rake his jawbone. The stubble was so harsh Noah's hand was skinned, and this made him even more furious. They grappled in front of the fireplace, stumbled over the armchairs and crashed into Calvin, standing dithering by the kindling box. Down went all three in a thrashing knot of limbs. Calvin's head cracked against the brickwork and he let out a screech so piercing Joe and Noah immediately disengaged, fearing they might somehow have killed him.

Calvin blubbered woefully, felt the blood leaking from his scalp. "Get a wet cloth," said Joe, and Noah did so. Calvin was crowned with a sopping rag, yelped as his wound stung and cold water ran down his neck. Joe and Noah made a great fuss over him, helping Calvin to a chair, assuring him he was not badly hurt, brewing a fresh batch of coffee to placate him. Calvin enjoyed all the attention, did not see that they were using him as a convenient distraction from the dreadful thing that had happened—Noah had attacked Joe or, if words can be considered weapons, Joe had attacked Noah. Violence had never been a casual guest at the house on the ridge, and the protagonists felt like foolish children. Calvin was placed between them like some neutral zone between warring nations, and when he could be fussed over no more they avoided each other's eyes. Now was the time for their enmity to be resolved, yet neither seized the moment, and so the thirty second fracas became nothing more than a temporary blast of steam released from an overheated boiler.

In the days and weeks that followed, Noah took pains to be on speaking terms with Joe and his father, but their conversations were stilted and self-conscious, confined to the commonplace topics on patient standby for those who wish to be polite without truly communicating anything of their interior selves—weather and work were the subjects discussed, and the nameless canker inside Noah began to grow again, and a reciprocal boil grew on Joe. Several times he was on the point of throwing down his axe and begging Noah to explain how he felt about . . . everything. But he did not, worked on, telling himself whatever was in Noah's head and heart was strictly the boy's own business. At Noah's age, earlier even, Joe had cut off his teacher's little finger with a razor and boarded a train for the west; no one had known the least thing about his needs, his pain, his plans. Noah might even resent the intrusion, as Joe would have. No, best leave him alone to do private battle with his demons; they might destroy him, or Noah might use them as stepping stones to a clearer view of things. Either way, Joe convinced himself, it was none of his business; Noah was too old now to be pampered with well-intentioned advice. In his own way, Joe was as merciless and unyielding with Noah as Dr. Cobden had been with Joe, but of course he did not see the situation in that light.

Worse was to come, and the unwitting catalyst was Phoebe Pike. Joe knew there existed a social debt which he must repay; Phoebe's second and last visit to the ridge had been an embarrassment for all concerned, and the fact that he had not extended another invitation since that time (because conditions there had not improved) might be construed by Phoebe as condemnation of her; simply put, she might think they (Joe in particular) didn't like her, when the very reverse was true. But what to do? Joe could not subject her to another tense afternoon at the house, with its doggedly unoriginal conversation and tamped-down emotions. Nor could he see her on his own, for that would appear as though he were paying court to her, and nothing could possibly embarrass her more; imagine a presentable young woman being courted by a hunchback—unthinkable! And yet he was determined the tenuous link between them should not be allowed to rust away. How was this social deadlock to be resolved?

Late in April, Phoebe approached Joe. He had delivered the latest consignment of wood to the yard behind the Vesuvius restaurant, and was preparing to drive his wagon on down the alley to Wyandotte Street and thence homeward, when Phoebe appeared. She had planned this apparently accidental meeting with great care, having noted the regular deliveries to the Vesuvius, and was making use of her lunch hour (in actuality thirty minutes) to effect this chance encounter.

"Hello, Joe."

He looked down, startled yet pleased by her sudden appearance. He felt shyness and guilt welling inside him, but had the good sense not to show it. "I haven't seen you in a while," he said.

"That's because you haven't been in the store." Her

manner seemed cheery enough, a smile on her face, no accusing or hurt look in her eyes; maybe she didn't resent his social neglect after all. "You must have all the thimbles and thread and shoes you need," she said.

Phoebe Pike had no one to talk to. In all of Valley Forge, Joe Cobden was the only person she knew with whom a conversation might be not only possible but enjoyable. For the sake of a few minutes' exchange of words she had plotted this moment of reacquaintance. Both wore awkward smiles. Joe, already seated on the wagon, could think of nothing else to say but: "Can I give you a ride anywhere?" That was not what Phoebe wanted to hear; she had engineered this meeting for the very reason that the alley was almost always free of traffic and passers-by. This was to be a private conversation, yet here was Joe already suggesting they go elsewhere. But if she said no he might very well simply drive away; she did not doubt he was quite unaware of her need. Compromise was called for.

"Yes, you may take me to the depot."

"The depot?" Was she buying a ticket, going away somewhere? He wanted very much to know, but thought it would probably be impolite to ask; he did not want her to think he was another nosy Valley Forger.

"I want to look at the train schedules," she explained.

"Climb aboard."

It was not until the wagon had turned from the alley on to Wyandotte that Joe realised how peculiar this would look to anyone who saw them. What business did Phoebe Pike have, riding on his wagon? Phoebe too seemed aware of the incongruity, and on the short drive to the depot sat bolt upright, looked straight ahead. Neither spoke, both feeling themselves closely scrutinised for those few hundred yards. If anything, this served to unite them, distanced though they were, for both despised the prying, Argus-eyed thing called Community, and when the depot was reached Joe not only assisted Phoebe down from the seat, he accompanied her on to the platform. Let them stare! And stare they did.

Phoebe went to the schedule pinned on the outside of the stationmaster's office. Made confident by their newly bonded, as yet unspoken solidarity, Joe now felt he could ask: "Where are you going?"

"I don't know where I'm going, or when." Her eyes roamed the list of arrival and departure times, eastbound and westbound, absorbing nothing.

"Planning ahead?" He was relieved to learn she did not intend leaving immediately.

"I suppose so, yes. Daydreaming." This last word was uttered in so unmistakably plaintive a tone Joe could not fail to understand at least a portion of Phoebe's need.

"You don't like it here, do you?" It was a flat statement, and he did not expect contradiction; Phoebe's wistful expression as she stared at the schedule told all.

"I dream about leaving. Every day I imagine how it would feel to get on board a train and be taken away . . . anywhere."

She turned from the wall and wandered slowly to the far end of the platform, followed after a moment by Joe. The stationmaster had been straining to overhear their conversation through his open window, and was disappointed when they strolled out of earshot. He had heard enough, though, to furnish him with a grievance that would later be shared by other citizens. Not happy here, was she? Just who the hell did Phoebe Pike think she was, not to be happy in a fine little town like this one?

Joe had never seen anyone look so distracted, empty almost. Phoebe stared at the horizon as though waiting for a tidal wave or range of mountains to rear up before her. "What keeps you here, Joe?"

"Calvin. He needs looking after."

"Don't you ever feel the need to leave this place?"

"Sometimes."

"I stay here for the same reason you do. Mother would shrivel like a leaf and die."

"Obligation can be a heavy burden," said Joe, aware that his words sounded like some kind of platitude. He felt he owed this woman more than platitudes, but could think of nothing more to say. So he gazed at the horizon also. They were looking east. It was not so many miles to St. Louis. For a young adventurer he had not journeyed very far, had seen only the eastern slopes of the Rockies during his wanderings with Peter Winstanley; everything beyond, what might be termed the *real* west, was as unknown to him as Arabia. Kansas sat fair and square in the heart of the country, a long way from the shining seas on either side, a long way from mountain and forest and desert, was the empty bottom of the shallow saucer that is America. He felt like a failure. Facts were facts, and the fact was Joe Cobden was a humble woodcutter. For all his alleged brains, he made his living by chopping down trees and selling them. His way of life suddenly struck Joe as being vastly unsatisfactory. What's more, he was leading Noah down the same narrow path, apprenticing him as he had done. But the boy would soon tire of the dull repetition, would lay down his axe for the last time and declare himself free, would saddle his horse and depart. Joe could not hold himself accountable for Noah's life, only for his own, and what a pathetic life it was—a woodcutter, the lowest of the low.

"Sometimes I wish she was dead," said Phoebe, "so I needn't worry any more. Does that shock you?"

In his current frame of mind Joe could not have been shocked by anything, no matter how morbid, especially so understandable a wish. "No," he said. Funnily enough, he had never wished Calvin dead. It was only now, today, that he had become dissatisfied. Phoebe Pike was, with her own confession of misery, obliging Joe in some indefinable fashion to look askance at his life, to judge it with a cold and unflinching eye, and it could not but be found wanting. There was nothing of which to be proud, no great achievements, not even his transient fame as Joe Buffalo. He had survived, had helped a feeb survive and had nurse-maided the feeb's ungrateful son; that was all. Nossir, not a life to be trumpeted abroad, not one to be entered into the history books. He wondered what domestic horrors had produced so bleak an outlook as Phoebe's, but naturally he did not ask.

Their conversation thus far did not seem unnatural to Joe, for these two misfits now had a marginal understanding of each other's woes, enough to recognise and salute a kindred stoic without making undue fuss over the discovery. The very brevity of their words proved, one to the other, that little more needed to be said—for the moment, at least. Joe offered a ride back to the store. Phoebe said she would walk. On impulse, Joe said he intended taking a ride on Sunday. Did Phoebe enjoy riding? She who had been on horseback only once, and then at a walk, said she did. Joe would be at the junction of the westbound road and the ridge trail at noon, if Phoebe cared to join him. It was not necessary to explain why he would not bring a horse to her house.

They parted. As she watched Joe drive his wagon away, it occurred to Phoebe that they had been standing on the very spot where she had seen the handsome young man step down from the train such a long time ago. On this occasion there had been no train, no coffins, no handsome young man, just a shabby hunchback. What a queer coincidence.

CHAPTER THIRTY-SIX

"Why do you need it? You've got one of your own."

Joe had asked to borrow Noah's saddle.

"Because I'm taking both horses out. They've done nothing but haul the wagon for as long as I've had them. A ride'll do them good."

"You're taking both of them at once?"

"Right, but I don't want to have to swap a saddle from one to the other when I switch, so I need yours."

"I'll ride the second horse for you."

"No thanks, I want to work them both myself."

"Why?"

"That's just the way us Indians do things," said Joe, and faked a laugh. He wanted the ride with Phoebe Pike to be a secret not only from the people of Valley Forge, but from Noah. Maybe he was being ridiculous, but the thought of anyone knowing that he, the ugliest thing in creation, was taking a woman riding sent a cold chill down Joe's question mark of a spine.

"I was going to take Wicked out for a ride on Sunday," Noah lied.

Joe saw he was deliberately being difficult. "How about if I hire the saddle for a dollar."

"I'm not that mercenary. You can have it."

Noah walked off, left Joe feeling like a fool. But he had the use of the saddle.

On Sunday, Noah watched Joe leave, riding one horse, leading the other. He watched until horses and rider had disappeared at a walk along the trail, then bounded from the porch and ran as fast as he could along the top of the ridge to a point where the junction of the trail and the road leading to town could be seen through a gap left by felled trees. He waited several minutes before Joe appeared. For no discernible reason, Noah wanted to know which way he went; he just wanted to know. Joe was hiding something from him, and hiding it badly. Joe stopped at the junction, let the horses crop grass. What the hell kind of ride was this, halted before it went a quarter of a mile? Then he saw a figure in black approaching along the road from town. He suspected it was Phoebe Pike, but distance prevented certainty. Joe dismounted, assisted her on to the second horse, remounted, and together they rode west along the road. Noah raced further along the ridge to the southern end denuded of trees by Lucius Croft. He could see clearly across the stumps and eroded gullies to the road. It was Phoebe Pike, he was sure of it now. He watched until they turned off the road a mile distant and began riding at a leisurely pace across open prairie.

"You cunt," breathed Noah. "You fucking cunt of an asshole bastard. . . ." He meant Joe, not Phoebe. He sat on a stump, his limbs shaking.

They rode slowly, Phoebe being an unpractised horse-woman.

"You'll have to get yourself a split skirt if you're going to ride like that," said Joe. Phoebe had again refused to sit sidesaddle.

"I'm quite comfortable."

The horses ambled on. The day was mild and sunny, prefiguring spring. Phoebe had removed her bonnet.

"Does your family know where you are?"

"They think I'm walking. I don't go to church any more. Father was scandalised when I stopped."

"Does he think you'll burn in hell?"

"No, I don't think he believes in hell. He just thinks it looks bad for his daughter not to attend church like everyone else."

"How about you, you don't believe in God?"

"No. There are only people. And animals and mountains

and seas. . . ." She threw back her head, let the sun shine full in her face. "And sky."

"I don't believe in God, either." He considered explaining how his hump had led him to atheism, decided it would be in bad taste; worse, it would make her think he felt sorry for himself, which he did not. "You're right, there are just people. And things."

"Are you acquainted with Mr. Darwin's theory of evolution?"

"I read his book. It took five weeks."

"And do you believe we are descended from monkeys?"

"I do, and my belief is reinforced every time I drive along Decatur Street. If man was created in the image of God, then heaven must look like Valley Forge. I'd rather be related to any kind of ape."

Phoebe laughed. Joe was proving to be as amusing as on that first visit to the ridge. "Did you ever see the wolf?"

"Wolf?"

"The one I saw last fall, the lame wolf with one eye."

"No, I think you were privileged to witness its one and only appearance."

After an hour they stopped and dismounted. The ridge was a low hump on the horizon, which elsewhere stretched without interruption. With the flair of a conjuror producing a rabbit from a hat, Joe extracted from his saddlebags an oilpaper package of sandwiches and a canteen of water. "Not exactly pheasant and wine," he admitted, "but, then, this *is* Kansas."

They ate, talked and were silent, talked again, asked casually probing questions, gave lightly veiled answers. Both revealed only an iceberg's tip of themselves, yet both were aware of the vast hidden bulk of endurance and disappointment the other thought it polite to hide, and both respectfully ignored the other's oversight. Eventually, they talked of other things.

"Did Noah really write an obscene joke on his examination paper?"

"Yes, not a bad one either. He says he made it up himself."

"Might I know it?"

"Pardon?"

"Would you tell me the joke? I'm sure every man in town knows it by now, but the women have by and large been kept in the dark. We have a sense of humour also."

"You want to hear a dirty joke?"

"Not just any dirty joke—Noah's joke."

"But it's . . . well, it's not really suitable for a lady's ears."

"Mr. Cobden . . . Joe, you surprise me. I had thought you were aware I'm not a churchgoing Christian woman. I'm not a prude, nor am I a red-lipped harlot, and I don't think hearing something amusing will turn me into one."

Joe delayed as long as possible. Telling Noah's joke to someone like Phoebe Pike was very difficult for him. His procrastinating came to an end when she began tut-tutting and shaking her head, as though he were some foolish schoolboy who had forgotten his lesson. With halting reluctance, minus the confidence and panache with which all dirty jokes must be told, Joe revealed Noah's brainchild.

"That's really rather witty," said Phoebe, and laughed.

Joe gave a sickly grin, wished, now that it was over, he had given the joke the delivery it deserved.

"What does he plan on doing with his life now that college has been removed from his options?"

"I don't know. Neither does he. I doubt that he'll stay around here."

"What about Mr. Puckett? Does Noah feel no responsibility towards him?"

"Noah knows I'll look after him. I wouldn't blame him if he left."

"No, I suppose the young shouldn't be restricted by unnecessary . . . obligations."

Phoebe did not wish to be reminded of her own trouble, and their talk meandered lazily among more innocuous pastures, browsing without haste, ingesting further personal revelations of a minor character until the warm sun made conversation too arduous a task. Phoebe had not expected the afternoon to pass so pleasantly. What an interesting man Joe Cobden was. She was sure no one else knew this side of him, not even the Pucketts. What a pity Joe was deformed; if not for that, he would be—she hunted for the correct word—presentable? acceptable? Acceptable to whom? With a start she knew—to herself. A flush crept into her cheeks as she hastily suppressed a picture that had formed unbidden on the periphery of her thoughts, a picture of herself and Joe Cobden engaged in coitus. Phoebe was twenty-eight years old and a virgin still. She did not wish to remain so, but had studiously avoided the various annual occasions of festivity that included dancing among their attractions. It had become customary, every July 4th, for certain young men to place bets on whether this would be the year when Phoebe Pike climbed down off her high horse and took a stroll into the dark with some local Lothario while the fiddles sawed to drown whatever sighs must come from the direction of their departure. Phoebe's virginity was a state of mind and body made almost palpable by her desire to be rid of it. For five years Phoebe had been sure of one thing—the man to whom she gave herself would not be found in Valley Forge. Joe Cobden had escaped inclusion with the male populace of noncontenders for her hymen simply because it had not occurred to Phoebe that a man of his configuration would even consider himself a suitable object for the bestowal of her sexual favours. She could never give herself to a hunchback, no matter how clever, how kind, how understanding.

She felt guilt for her out of hand rejection of this man. His unfortunate appearance was not Joe's fault. Could it be that he entertained thoughts of a sexual nature toward her? Surely not; a hunchback would never countenance the possibility, would know such a thing was . . . impossible. Wouldn't he? Joe was leaning on one elbow, eyes half-closed, watching the horses graze. A moment ago Phoebe had thought she knew him very well; not the complete man, of course—there were obvious gaps in the personal history he had related (no mention of the part his hump had played during his formative years) just as there were gaps in her own potted autobiography (no basement discoveries)—but now she wondered if she knew him at all. Were dark flickerings of a sexual tendency stirring in his mind at this moment? But surely cripples and the very ugly purged themselves of such expectations, if they had them at all. Perhaps they were compensated by Nature (who will improve a blind man's sense of touch and hearing) by being denied the urges that would in any case go unsatisfied. Of what use would the need for love be to a hunchback? It could only be a burden, and Phoebe thought Nature sufficiently benign to have withheld this, rather than add it to the obvious stigma of physical deformity. Then she reminded herself of Jessica, a woman burdened with encroaching madness—was she not in need of love? Nature, she was forced to admit, is without sympathy, is wholly indifferent to suffering, be it simple or complex. Joe Cobden probably wanted love every bit as much as Phoebe. How very sad. Had he invited her on this ride for the purpose of expressing his desire? Nothing of a coarse nature would pass his lips, that was clear after his embarrassment over the joke, but equally disturbing was the possibility of him declaring his fondness, his regard, affection, respect—any of the euphemisms whose meaning would be immediately apparent to the recipient. She prayed he would say nothing. How could she respond to any such declaration without hurting the poor man's pride? Then, again, he might simply have invited her for a ride because, like her, he wanted someone to talk to. Had he guessed their meeting in the alley behind the Vesuvius had been deliberate? Perhaps she had made a terrible mistake in arranging it. He might have misinterpreted. I must be calm, she thought. I must not alarm myself.

Watching her from the corner of his eye, Joe thought Phoebe Pike more attractive than usual, especially with her bonnet off, but of course that was the kind of thing he should not be thinking of, not if he intended seeing her in private like this. She'd run a mile if she thought he wanted anything more than conversation from her, and he didn't, not when he'd issued the invitation anyway. He ordered his thoughts to about-face and march in a different direction, but a thought in Kansas, like a traveller, has nowhere to go that does not resemble its point of origin, and in a very few minutes Joe was again observing Phoebe with an appreciative eye. Aware of what he was doing, he felt guilty, then sad; linking himself romantically with this woman was just about the worst folly he could possibly commit. He had to stop it *now*. But he could not, not until he made himself imagine the look on Phoebe's face were he to reveal himself to her in a state of undress; her expression could be likened to that of someone who has bitten into an apple and discovered therein one half of a wriggling worm. He felt easier following this interior revelation and reaction, convinced himself his idle daydreams had been well and truly drenched in cold water.

One of the horses lifted its tail and released a deluge of dungballs that accumulated in a pungent and lumpy cone. Joe noticed that Phoebe did not turn her head to avoid seeing this potentially embarrassing sight, and was reminded once again of her unique character; not a blush, not a simper had he ever seen, none of the things he had come to expect from a young woman—but then, what did he know of women? The only females he had ever become acquainted with were the whores at the Maximus. They had not been the coarse harridans of his expectations; nor were they particularly modest with regard to their persons, all in all had been convivial company. But the Maximus had not prepared him for Phoebe Pike, who was at this moment wondering why it is that some animals—goats, rabbits, horses, etc.—release shit in the form of individual balls, rather than lengthy turds. She presumed it had something to do with eating grass.

They rode back to the Valley Forge road, as together, yet apart, as on the ride out. Phoebe dismounted at the junction with the ridge trail, thanked Joe sincerely and began walking back to town. Joe had not extended an invitation for next Sunday, and Phoebe was unsure if she was offended or grateful. Joe felt he needed a full week in which to mull over the implications of what he was doing before committing himself to another secret assignation with her. It might be best to finish things before he allowed himself to become obsessed with what he could never have. He was not a happy man as he led the horses into the stable, unsaddled and brushed them, and was still ruefully cogitating when he set foot on the porch. Noah was seated on a tilted chair, boots up on the porch rail, his eyes hidden by the green spectacles. "Enjoy your ride?" Joe nodded abstractedly and went inside without even bothering to lie about his afternoon.

Noah hated him for that, and made a vow to get even somehow for the deception. Noah's life was a blank. He was bereft of all aspiration, had nothing to look forward to, seemed incapable of planning any kind of future for himself, was mired in the present like a fly in molasses. His strongest emotions were reserved for a general resentment against the townspeople, a more concrete bitterness directed toward Calvin, solely on account of his father's addle-pated helplessness, and also toward Joe, because Joe was strong and smart and seemed to have more than a hunchbacked halfbreed deserved; certainly he appeared happier than Noah, and Noah did not like that at all. Ever since the winter he had withdrawn into himself, unprepared for a life that did not involve public acknowledgement of his brilliance. All that had been thrown away in the examination room, could never be revived, not that he wanted a return to that way of life; no, he wanted something else, but could not imagine what. Escape from Kansas was still the dominant theme in the undercurrent of his thoughts, but even this aim was muted, nebulous, had been indefinitely postponed while Noah recovered from the double blow of public humiliation and the fact that old Croft had left him nothing, not so much as a nickel. That also was to have been expected after the way he had behaved, but the outright rejection still hurt.

All Noah's exultant devil-may-care attitude on examination day had been carried away on the wind, left him not a bold decision-maker but a bungler, a blindly thrashing fool caught in the repercussive net of his own foolish and ill-considered acts. No one admired him; even Noah found his former posturings ridiculous in the light of what had happened, but this did not prevent him from experiencing a maudlin self-pity whenever he considered his plight, for Noah had not yet made the great leap into adulthood which recognises that responsibility for events arising solely from one's own choices must be shouldered by the one who chose, whether those events prove advantageous or disastrous. Noah shrugged off his responsibility, with the result that blame for his misery must needs be affixed elsewhere. Joe's deception made him the obvious candidate.

Noah was disgusted by the thought of Joe romancing Phoebe Pike (romance was the only possible reason for a secret rendezvous) and resentful of the fact that Phoebe had apparently co-operated, walking out from town that way so no one would see them meet. Why did she want an ugly creature like Joe, when Noah was ready and willing to give her everything of himself? It was not merely puzzling, it was infuriating, and Noah was determined matters would not be allowed to continue as they were without interference from himself. Having made up his mind on this he felt somewhat better, and set himself the task of bringing about vengeance against these two people who had slighted him so shamelessly.

Nor was Noah the only person planning trouble for Joe. The death of Ned Bowdre left vacant the public office he had occupied, and the town council quickly appointed a successor to wear Ned's badge until such time as an election could be arranged. Although Valley Forge had suffered only that one day's lawlessness in all its thirty-five years, the council now felt itself to be surrounded by other potential bank robbers and murderers, and so appointed a man known to be uncompromisingly tough in his attitude to saddle-tramps and ne'er-do-wells; any stranger entering town from now on would have to account for himself to the satisfaction of Perce Lafferty. Perce had itched to be sheriff for several years now, but was never a popular figure like Ned; Perce liked to lord it over folks, and from the moment a star was pinned on his lapel he changed for the worse. He carried a long-barrelled Colt's revolver on his hip and more or less abandoned his half-share in the hardware store to his partner, the better to devote himself to the task at hand: ridding Valley Forge of undesirables, troublemakers, misfits of any kind who might send a nervous tremor through the stout hearts of this town's worthy citizens.

Perce hailed originally from Missouri and was a fervent Baptist, much to the gratification of Preacher Davis. Perce was a regular churchgoer and was not known for womanising or drunkenness, was not unduly harsh with his wife and had never shortchanged anyone at the hardware store. The council was convinced it had found a man of iron to wear their badge of tin. Perce didn't like Joe Cobden. Joe was half-Indian as well as being just plain damn ugly, and Perce's cousin Brock had been killed by Indians up in Dakota in '74. That was reason enough for Perce to wish Joe Cobden would put a foot wrong sometime while Perce was there to see it and come down on the hunchback like the wrath of God.

He did not buy his firewood from Joe on principle, preferred to pay those extra dollars and get his fuel at McGruder's woodyard. McGruder admired a man of principle, especially one placing money in his pocket, and again used his influence within the council to try to bring about a change in the law with regard to trade practices and the city limits; Joe Cobden had flaunted his wares under McGruder's nose for too many years, and now that Valley Forge had a hard man propping his boots on the sheriff's desk instead of that wishy-washy Ned Bowdre the time was ripe for a statute that would be backed up with direct and uncompromising enforcement if necessary. He proposed that the city limits be extended to a distance of three miles beyond the present boundary "to prepare for expansion in the fast-approaching twentieth century". As before, anyone selling any kind of goods within the city limits had to have a licence, and those applying for said licence must henceforth go through a rigorous process of investigation, culminating in three favourable votes from council members, before being granted legal inclusion among the trading fraternity. Willard Croft, another powerful councilman nowadays (he still ran the store, had placed the farm under a manager) seconded the proposal, and a vote was called for. McGruder lost by seven votes to five, but over the next few weeks, in conjunction with Willard, he managed to convince two of the opposing members to see things differently. This change of heart was accomplished by liberal gifts of wood from the yard, and shoes and other goods from Willard's store. Again the new amendment was proposed, and this time was passed, entered in the statute books and made operative within a week.

And now Joe's persecution began. Perce Lafferty explained to Joe just why he better get his red ass the hell away from what *used* to be the city limits before he goddamn well got his hump throwed in gaol for flagrant violation of the new statute, and he also better pray he was *real* good friends with three council members or he could just forget about doing business after today in *this* town.

"Thanks for the information," said Joe.

"No charge. Now, git."

"Is your wrist tired, Sheriff?"

"What the hell's that supposed to mean?"

"Your hand's been resting on your gun butt these last few minutes."

"It's right convenient for hauling iron, Indian."

Joe would dearly have loved to suggest to Perce that his wrist was tired from having played with himself overmuch while dreaming of his favourite catamite, but he wisely refrained; instead turned his wagon away from its customary spot two hundred and five yards from Henneker's livery stable and returned home.

He was licked. The ridge was well within the new three-mile city limit (and since when was a pipsqueak of a place like this called a city anyway?) so he could not ask his customers to pick up their own wood and hand over cash at the house, not without "conducting business or trade within the precincts of Valley Forge" *sans* the all-important licence, which he would never get in any case; he knew they would have thoroughly enjoyed watching him beg for one, only to be turned down. He would not give the council that satisfaction. He had for several years now been delivering wood to a councilman's home; the cancellation of that order a week ago should have alerted him, but it had not, and he was left defenceless. Disenchanted as he was with his profession, he did not resent the loss of his business as much as he hated the active malice behind the legal manoeuvrings which had brought it about, but retaliation was out of the question; Perce Lafferty was a dangerously belligerent man, one to avoid confrontation with unless one's ancestors were white as far back as Adam.

Had Joe overcome his rage and applied for a licence the chances were good he would have received one, for there remained five members of the council who resented the way McGruder had steamrollered the statute into actuality. These five men suspected bribery behind the turning of two coats, and would willingly have endorsed Joe if only to grease that self-satisfied little crocodile McGruder's rails. But Joe did not apply, and none of the five men thought to apprise him of his chances, for council members do not approach half-breed woodcutters, not even when a reciprocal need is served. And so Joe Cobden stewed in a speechless rage for two days, then accepted the inevitable and informed his erstwhile customers he had been driven from business. Some of them were genuinely sorry, and said it was a shameful way for folks to behave, but no one led a revolt against the council's edict; in truth, they were divided on the issue, for while they would henceforth pay more for their firewood (McGruder now having a monopoly) they were at the same time proud of the fact that Valley Forge now extended three miles more in all directions, enough to make a citizen lift his chin a little higher, by God!

Joe's sole champion was Phoebe. Once she learned of the new trading law she demanded an explanation from Willard Croft, who was somewhat taken aback by her seemingly causeless anger. She insisted Joe had been victimised because of his Indian blood, and Willard was obliged to exercise his sternest demeanour in restoring the impertinent creature to her place. He loved her as a schoolboy loves the buxom Spanish lady on the inside of a cigar-box, but she could not be allowed to place herself above him on a moral issue, or any other issue. He was not only a councilman, therefore wholly supportive of its decisions and deserving of respect for his loyalty; not just her employer, therefore the natural recipient of even greater esteem—he was first and foremost a man, and as such could not be argued against.

But Phoebe insisted upon the last word. "I find your attitude disappointingly petty, Mr. Croft, I must say. I am now going to lunch." And out she swept, without pausing to affix her bonnet.

Croft's annoyance was dissipated by puzzlement over the exact meaning of her words. Disappointed? That suggested she held him in high regard; one had to be admired before someone could be disappointed in one. He forgave Phoebe her foolish and ill-informed tantrum instantly, for this was his first inkling of possible secret yearnings for him on her part. Yes, he had definitely hit upon something here; it was just a question of interpretation, seeking out the hidden meaning behind what apparently was harsh criticism. But he had seen the dove among the snow—oh yes—and his heart fluttered at the discovery. Phoebe was undeniably a contrary miss, but he rather admired her spirit. Of course, a few months of marriage would put her nonsense to flight— but that could never happen, not while his wife lived. In rare moments Willard lingered over the likelihood of an early death for Matilda. It was probably too much to hope for. Still, at least he knew Phoebe admired him, and despite their little scene of a moment ago he felt very pleased—with her, and with himself.

Joe told Andolini the barber he would have to hire a wagon and go to the ridge to pick up the remainder of the wood owing him; Joe did not dare drive a wood-laden wagon through town for fear of prosecution. Andolini understood; only a few more loads were required to repay the debt in any case. Joe wondered what to do with his life now that he was no longer a woodcutter. Noah, too, was out of a job, but appeared undismayed. "It was boring," he said. "It put food in your mouth," said Joe, and Noah sneered at such a plebeian attitude.

He was glad the new sheriff and the council had brought Joe down in the world, but did not draw from it the kind of personal satisfaction that would have followed had he, Noah, been solely responsible for Joe's downfall; that private reckoning was yet to come. He waited for several Sundays, anticipating another request for the use of his saddle, a request he would take delight in refusing. But Joe asked for nothing, rode nowhere, and Noah began to suspect things had not worked out with Phoebe Pike as Joe had planned. And why should they have done? What normal woman would want a hunchback, for God's sake? His jealousy slackened, and he looked at Joe now with a condescending, almost pitying eye for the jilted lover. It meant, of course, that Noah once again stood a chance. Phoebe would not turn him down because of his youth, would probably see his lack of years as a bonus when compared to an old man like Joe. Noah's face was still narrow and foxy and occasionally infested with pimples, but his body was lean and strong and his spine straight as an arrow. He would rub in the irony of his conquest by borrowing Joe's saddle to go riding with his lady love.

But first he had to issue an invitation, and over this necessary step he faltered, postponing the moment from day to day while he thought out the best approach, casual yet forceful, with which to convey his desire. By early June he could wait no longer, and rode into town as though at the head of an invading army. Wicked was tied to the hitching-rail outside the store, and Noah clumped across the sidewalk and went inside. There were several customers awaiting service, and he browsed among the boots and shoes until they were gone. Then Willard Croft, not Phoebe, asked what he wanted. Willard did not like Noah for the sense of insecurity the boy's relations with Lucius Croft had engendered in the past, and for the fact that Noah would have inherited the farm and the store had not lawyer Purvis done the gentlemanly thing and provided Willard with the opportunity to keep everything in the family, the *real* family. He found it particularly annoying to have to look at Noah while his eyes were hidden behind those sinister blind man's spectacles. Noah did not reply to his question, and Willard took this for insolence. "If you do not wish to purchase anything I must ask you to leave," he said.

"I'm still looking," said Noah. "When I find what I want I'll let you know."

He could not abide Willard's fussy mannerisms and the silly little excuse for a moustache that twitched on his sweaty upper lip, a moustache even less substantial than Noah's own, and was gratified to see Willard exit to the back room in a huff that was intended to let Noah know Willard was not going to stand around waiting for the likes of *him* to make up his mind.

"Hello, Noah."

"Afternoon, Miss Pike."

Damn! He'd intended calling her Phoebe right from the start; she'd told him to that time when he took her home from the ridge. He could not think what to say next. All his carefully prepared introductions to the subject of a Sunday ride had suddenly fled his brain.

"How is Joe these days?"

"He's all right." Damn Joe, it's *me* you should be asking about. . . . "Sitting around doing nothing," he added, in an attempt to convey a picture of indolence and sloth.

"Isn't it dreadful what they've done?" said Phoebe.

"Please let him know I support him. The council ought to be ashamed. What will you do now?"

The question was inclusive, but Noah chose to interpret it as personal. "I'll find something else, something with more life to it. There's a big world out there waiting. This could be a blessing in disguise." Jesus, was it really *him* talking this horseshit? He began to blush, knowing he sounded a fool. But Phoebe was apparently not concerned with what Noah might be feeling, asked: "What will Joe do?"

"Him? I don't know. Nothing, I guess."

"That doesn't sound like Joe. I'm sure he'll think of something."

Noah felt his Sunday suggestion yammering for release from the back of his throat, but could say nothing; Joe seemed to stand between himself and Phoebe like a pane of cloudy glass, allowing them to see each other, yet somehow distorting not only their appearance, but their very words. He had to speak, had to ask her before his chest exploded. But before he could utter a syllable two women entered the store and came straight to the counter, ignoring Noah for the godless young scarecrow he was. Phoebe excused herself to attend them. Noah stood where he was for half a minute, seething, then walked out and rode back to the ridge, hating Phoebe Pike as much as on the day he had seen her with Joe. Or had it been Joe he hated that day . . . ? No matter, he hated them both now. Any woman that rode out on a Sunday with a hunchback was not worth caring about anyhow.

And as Noah thrust her from him there came springing into his chest the resolution he had until this moment lacked; the wish to be gone from Valley Forge was now compounded by the will, and these two inducements straining in tandem caused Noah to leave his horse waiting by the porch while he went upstairs and began assembling a bundle of clothing that could be tied on to his saddle. He would not take a bag or suitcase; such things were for milksops who travelled by train or stagecoach. All a real man needed were a few basic totables and a rifle.

Joe rounded a corner of the house in time to see Noah swing into the saddle. Something looked different. He saw the bundle tied behind the cantle with leather laces, and understood.

"Going somewhere?"

"What's it look like?"

"Any particular place?"

"No."

"Told Calvin?"

"He's off somewhere, digging."

"Wouldn't take long to find him."

"I don't have time."

"Yes, you do. What you don't have is the guts to face him and say you're leaving."

"Look, just leave me alone."

"You can be alone all you want after you've said goodbye to Calvin."

"No!"

"Your mother left like this."

"I don't care."

"You're a coward."

"That's what *you* think! A coward wouldn't pack up and leave!"

"Sure he would. You think you're going to find something wonderful out there, don't you? You won't. It's just a different kind of shit."

"You sound like you're about ninety years old."

Joe felt he had heard this conversation before, a conversation in which he, Joe, had spoken Noah's lines.

"Got any money?" Joe asked, his throat dry.

"I don't want anything from you."

Joe's mind churned to find suitable parting words. The kid was actually leaving, he didn't doubt it now, and for all Noah's obnoxiousness, for all his weakness of character and personal, inexplicable enmity towards Joe, he did not want to see him go. He supposed the doctor must have felt something like this when he read Joe's farewell note. At least Noah hadn't stolen anything. Presumably.

"Don't kill anyone, and don't get killed."

Noah did not answer, trotted his horse across the yard to the ridge trail and was swallowed by the trees without once looking back. Gone. Joe sat on the porch steps. You little shit. You fucking little shit. Thanks for letting me break the news. He sat there for almost an hour before setting out to find Calvin.

The latest hole was on the thinly treed western slope of the ridge, and Calvin was sure this would be the one to yield that elusive crock of gold, just as he had been sure of the other one hundred and thirty-eight. This one would be different; he could smell the difference already, and laid on with pick and shovel, humming a tuneless melody to himself. He was not aware of Joe until the boots standing by his head caught his eye. Calvin figured he must be getting pretty deep down now, because Joe looked mighty tall above him, and he knew for a fact Joe was just a little feller.

"Ain't found it yet," said Calvin, happy for the company.

"Noah's gone."

"Gone?"

"Took some clothes and rode off."

"To town?"

"Further than that. He wasn't exactly sure himself."

"When'll he be back?"

"Hard to say. He's just a boy, Calvin. He's got to move around, find himself."

"But . . . where'd he go?"

"Just wandering. Don't go and get upset about it."

"But he never said nothin'. . . ."

Calvin's voice rose an octave every time he spoke.

"He didn't want to upset you by saying goodbye. He thought it'd be better this way. And he's right; you would've got upset, and that's what you don't want to do."

"He never said nothin'. . . . I'm his old man!"

"He knows that. He said to me, 'Get Calvin drunk and

he'll feel better about it,' and that's what we're going to do, you and me. We're going to crack a bottle and get howling drunk.''

No prospect could have held less appeal for Joe; he wanted to think, to collect himself into a resilient bundle, lace it up tight and label it: *Joe Cobden—Do Not Disturb*. It would never be marked *Fragile*.

''How come he never said nothin' before he went?''

''Because he thought it'd be better this way. You've dug that hole deep enough. Go any deeper and you'll be up to your knees in Chinamen. Come on and we'll crack that bottle.''

He helped Calvin from the hole, led him back to the house. With luck liquor would relax him, hopefully stave off any kind of fit that might already be building behind his confusion and dismay. Calvin walked like a man in a daze, clutching Joe's arm for support. He missed his footing while mounting the porch steps, was half carried by Joe into the living room and placed on the sofa. His breathing was shallow and rapid. Joe fetched glasses and a bottle of whiskey that had been bought almost a year ago; liquor had never been a staple in this house. He poured a shot, helped Calvin to gulp it down, wiped the excess from his stubbled chin. Calvin lay back, his head on an embroidered cushion.

''She ain't gonna come back. . . .''

''That was a long time ago. It's the boy that's gone this time. But he'll be back after he's stretched his wings. Here, have another shot.''

More whiskey was poured down Calvin's throat. Joe took a swallow himself, then sat by the sofa to wait for whatever was going to happen, hoping the kind of outrageous hope that borders on prayer, willing Calvin to be calm, assisting his will with more whiskey. Calvin continued to babble of Alma, held conversations with her about nothing. Joe wondered what had become of the little grey spider who had snared him so very cleverly with her silken thread. Would she laugh to learn he was here still, tending to her husband

and child? Child? She'd whelped a selfish little bastard that took after his mother.

In time Calvin's lips ceased to move. Bubbles formed in the corners of his mouth, but did not excite themselves to froth; these shining spheres were not the harbingers of epilepsy, were simply the product of whiskey and Calvin's tendency to breathe through his mouth. He slept, was snoring gently by sunset. Joe lit a lamp, seated himself in an armchair where he could keep one eye on Calvin, and proceeded to get drunk himself. He found he was not as bitter as he ought perhaps to have felt, considering the events of recent weeks, and assumed this meant he was getting tougher as well as older; he was a beat-up old boot, and old boots are seldom surprised by the stones they encounter. He congratulated himself on his toughness, drank a toast to his ability for survival, drank several more and began to wonder if the doctor was still alive after all this time. Joe had never once written, had told himself after the first few years that the old man was gone by now. He would no doubt have laughed to see Noah riding off like that, would have turned to Joe and said: "Here is exemplified the cyclical nature of human affairs, Joseph. Observe well and learn something of your fellow man." Joe drank a toast to Dr. Cobden, and another to Hattie, whom he presumed also to be dead. He wondered, too, whether Noah would have proved less truculent if old Croft had kept his feet on his own land and not invaded the ridge with gifts and interference. Maybe, maybe not. Joe had been an opinionated and unbending little shit himself at Noah's age, had got that way without outside influence. But, then, he had always blamed the hump for that. If not for his hump he might have become someone quite different, might even have become a doctor himself under old Cobden's tutelage, would certainly never have become a buffalo-hunter. The hump had changed his life as surely as a mountain changes the course of a river. The hump, the hump, the hump. . . . If not for his hump he would not be sitting here, drinking himself stupid and attempting to unravel the myriad stitches comprising the rough and ragged tapestry of his life, a futile task if ever there was one.

Drunkenness crept through his veins, numbed his toes, his legs, crept inside his head, smothered the crispness of those observations engendered by alcohol, swathed them in grey cotton until thought itself became a skewed pattern of random associations; scenes from the past, remembered emotions, distilled reminiscence, a blanket of fuddled and bemused observation seemingly free to flap and settle where it pleased, eliciting from Joe nothing more than a soft grimace or grunt. His eyelids began to sink, his lips to pout and droop. His glass hit the rug with a discreet thud, spilled the last few drops of liquor unheeded. Joe roused himself, felt the need to void his bladder, clumsily guided himself to the porch rail and pissed a magnificent stream on to what should have been a flower bed but was not, since no one on the ridge could be bothered planting seeds.

While he pissed, Joe saw dancing points of light before his eyes, not the fabrications of insobriety but actual points of green and yellow light, pulsing vividly, hundreds of them, *thousands,* bobbing about in a formless dance delightful to behold. When he at last recognised them for fireflies about their nightly business, Joe laughed, and could not understand, as he stood there with his penis cooling in the breeze, why his laughter was becoming something else, an irregular spasm of sound painful to deliver, difficult to control. He was crying, blubbing like an infant, and so ashamed and confused was he by this discovery he cried longer and louder, until his face was as wet as the earth below the porch.

Drained of tears and urine, his head barely attached to his neck, Joe returned to the living room. Calvin snored on. "You're missing all the fun," said Joe, and covered him with a rug dragged from the floor, removed the fringes from Calvin's face and trudged upstairs to his bed. Too drunk to find or light a lamp, he stumbled over various wooden obstacles in his meandering path to the mattress. Over the course of time Joe had whittled a bestiary which would have pleased that other, ark building Noah with its inclusiveness, culling from memory and imagination and book illustrations every kind of creature, spanning creation from frogs to elephants. They occupied shelves and cabinets and the floor of his room, a room presided over by a buffalo skull mounted on the wall above his bed. Hung on a peg thoughtfully provided by the builders for a holy cross, vacant eye sockets stared from this cranium of bone and horn at a host of kindred animals silent and still as itself. This was the skull Joe had brought to the house on the ridge thirteen years before, the skull the stationmaster had assured him would find a buyer there. Thirteen years. Joe was not superstitious, expected bad luck at any time or place, irrespective of numbers. He flung himself on to the bed and passed out.

CHAPTER THIRTY-SEVEN

Joe did something strange after Noah left: he went to the spare room, a seldom-visited repository for junk of all kinds, and rescued from its shroud the stained-glass window. Joe pushed the several hundred pounds of glass and lead uphill like a cannoneer manhandling the wheel of an artillery-piece, set the window upright between two trees at the northern end of the blackberry patch and wedged it firmly in place. Sunlight invested the glass with life; the chubby twins and white wolf glowed, seemed almost to burst from their single plane and come tumbling from the window into this corporeal world of solidity and dimension.

Joe was pleased, but not yet content. From a Montgomery Ward catalogue he ordered three sets of guitar strings, then began carpentering in the yard. He sawed and planed, hammered and glued, and his efforts resulted in three boxes, each four feet long, eight inches wide and two inches deep, bearing on one broad surface two widely separated holes, each four inches across. The guitar strings were mounted on pegs and stretched above the holes, and there they were— three Aeolian harps. Joe hung them in the trees around the blackberry patch, and the wind tirelessly plucked and thrummed at them from the moment he stepped away to admire his handiwork. The sound of the harps was imperceptible from any great distance, but as the patch was approached became apparent to the ear in gentle gustings and murmurings, a wind-borne sighing of so plangent a tone the listener may well have thought it the exhalations of melancholy dryads in some ancient glade, the distant reverberations of strings idly strummed by immortal fingers.

His satisfaction was great, but his pocket near-empty; having obeyed some inner aesthetic dictate, Joe now was faced with the problem of feeding himself and Calvin. Cash must be found, but from what quarter? If only Calvin could remember what he had done with the money Croft had loaned him; but naturally Calvin could not. Practicality, that was the keynote, a sober mustering of the facts, from which would be drawn a solution. Joe pondered, Calvin silently fretted, alarmed by the intensity of Joe's concentration; things must be pretty bad all right for Joe to frown so.

"Animals," said Joe at last. Calvin stared blankly at him, waiting for more. "All the stuff I whittled. I can sell it."

"Sell it?"

"Not around here—in Topeka, or maybe Kansas City. People like carvings of animals to put around the place, shadow cabinets, mantelpieces, shelves. . . ."

"Tables!" trumpeted Calvin, inspired.

"There, too."

Joe selected his half dozen best and boarded a train for Topeka, wandered around until he found the kind of store that dealt in furnishings and knick-knacks, requested an interview with the manager, was granted one, made his pitch and was successful, but received only one dollar for each carving. The manager contracted for the fifty or so still littering Joe's room, then proceeded to explain certain facts. "Bulk, Mr. Cobden, that's the answer, production in quantity." He picked up a rhinoceros. "Something as small as this is manufactured much quicker by the casting process; one hand-made mould produces thousands of reproductions, dozens, maybe hundreds every day. Wood-carving on a small scale is hardly a sound financial enterprise."

"But I don't know how to cast things. All I can do is carve." Joe was crestfallen; each animal had taken a week to produce.

The manager led him to the window, pointed across the street to a splendid green awning emblazoned in gold with the legend TOBACCONIST. Beneath the awning, by the doorway, stood an imposing figure—a war bonneted wooden

Indian clutching a handful of cigars, his free hand raised in stiff salute. "There's your answer, Mr. Cobden. If bulk is not for you, then tackle *size*. A cigar store Indian is traditionally wooden, never cast. Every tobacconist in the country wants a Hiawatha outside his store, and they can only be produced by hand. I happen to know that particular specimen cost two hundred dollars, paint and varnish included. Have I struck a spark, Mr. Cobden? I believe I have. Hardwood only now, none of that trashy pine, not for something intended to stand exposed to the elements year in and year out."

Joe thanked him, shopped around for a set of wood-carving chisels, rode the A, T & SF back to Valley Forge, dispatched the remainder of his menagerie to the helpful manager, then set out to find a tree containing an Indian. He located an elm of such height and girth it surely contained three, and cut it down. Now, wherever he looked he saw Indians, lurking in their barky boles, silent, grim-faced, awaiting release. Why, the ridge had a veritable tribe hidden away. Joe thought they should be given a name. He had always thought it ironic that the north-south streets of the town were named after long-vanquished eastern tribes— Chippewa, Wyandotte, Shawnee—never after the still troublesome tribes of the south-western States; he doubted that there was an Apache Street in the entire country. The people Joe intended liberating from their arboreal prisons deserved a name all their own; they would be called the Buffalo tribe, and every one of them would be a chief.

With Calvin's help Joe sawed the trunk into three eight-foot lengths, then put pen to paper in an effort to establish exactly what kind of Indian to create. Semi-naked? Fully clothed? Since his knowledge of anatomy was limited, Joe decided his first attempt would be draped in shirt and leggings for artistic convenience, and drew a sketch representative of his conception. War bonneted or not? Yes, if he was to look like a chief. He stood the first of the eight foot columns on its end in the yard and began work under the fierce July sun. If it required a week to carve a life-sized squirrel using only the leisure hours of the evening, he should be able to hack out an Indian in the same time by working all day.

He soon saw it would take longer than that; it took three days for the suggestion of a human figure to emerge from its cylinder of elm, eight days more of careful chipping with mallet and chisels (fearful all the while of making the kind of error that would reduce the thing to handcarved kindling) before a recognisable cigar-store Indian took shape. The war bonnet was the hardest part, the wall of feathers flaring up and back, obliging Joe to hollow out the space between feather-tips and the top of the head; the figure must be convincing from all angles, could not be left with a solid wood head-dress like a hussar's shako. The fringes dangling from the extended arm also gave trouble, being of a daunting thinness, but the hazard was safely negotiated, and four days more of painstaking work led to the emergence of the completed figure, still chisel-marked, unpainted and unvarnished, but identifiable. Its bodily proportions were subtly misaligned, the placement of the limbs somewhat awkward, and the bulky moccasins suggested severely clubbed feet; the hand clutching the cigars was as uncompromising as a bear's paw, the other (holding a tomahawk against the chest) of altogether more convincing design; the face was of an appropriately hawk-like cast, yet somehow conveyed the impression of idiocy. Praxiteles would have turned his head sorrowfully away; Michelangelo would have attacked it in a rage for its offensive quasi-humanness. Joe was forced to admit his first attempt at a life-sized figure was not a success.

But never mind, there stood ready to hand two more of its woodbound cousins, and Joe began again, labouring from first light until it became dangerous to wield a cutting tool in the lambent afterglow of day. Covered from hat to boots in woodparings, reeking of sweat, Joe would walk down to the creek and fall in, wait until his pants and shirt were thoroughly soaked, then squelch back up to the house, where Calvin was doing his best to prepare supper. Joe would rescue him from this chore for the sake of his own stomach, and after eating would wearily climb the stairs and sleep as though drugged. The second Indian was a great improvement on the first, but still not up to Joe's self-imposed standard, was not yet a $200 Indian. Funds were still leaking steadily from the ridge. Joe spent an evening cleaning, oiling and polishing Calvin's Winchester, went to town the next day and sold it for cash to buy food, then came home and took up his chisel and mallet for a third assault upon the high citadel of Art.

On August 16, 1889, Joe Cobden completed a $200 Indian. The first credible chief of the Buffalo tribe stood in the yard and glowered across the intervening distance at Valley Forge. Joe spent precious money on pots of paint, brought the chief to colourful life, then lined up all three efforts for comparison; seen together, they appeared to illustrate the rise of Man from his bestial ancestry, the chief standing resplendent beside his misbegotten cousins. "Looks mighty fine," opined Calvin, and Joe was in modest agreement. He chopped the cousins to kindling, offended by their inferiority. "What you gonna do now?" asked Calvin, who still had not fathomed the reason behind Joe's creation of this splendid wooden being.

"Sell it, what else?"

Joe rode the train to Topeka in the caboose with his chief, not trusting the railroad to deliver the goods unchipped. For a dollar he hired a hand-trolley from a porter at the Topeka depot and trundled the chief through the streets until he found a tobacconist's without benefit of a wooden Indian. He asked the proprietor to step outside for just one minute, showed him the chief. The tobacconist was interested. Joe demanded the full price. The tobacconist offered fifty dollars. After three minutes of wrangling the chief changed hands for one hundred dollars. On his way back to the depot Joe detoured to pass by the store to which his animals had been sold. Several were in the window, their price tags indicating three dollars, a healthy profit for the store. Joe had been wise in deciding to market the chief, and all future chiefs, himself. He crossed the street to examine the Indian that had altered the course of his life. It really was a far more accomplished piece of work than his own, and Joe studied it closely, ingesting every curve and plane, storing away details for his next attempt. Then he went home.

While Joe was gone, Calvin made a strange discovery. While on his way to the latest hole he decided to look once again at the stained-glass window and listen to the wind-harps. The sight of the white wolf did not revive unpleasant memories from the past, for Calvin had very nearly forgotten that phase of his life; it was just a picture in coloured glass, and it impressed him greatly. He liked the sighing and moaning of the harps also, liked the way the sound made him feel happy and sad at the same time; Joe sure was clever to make them sound that way. But on this day Calvin found he was not the only admirer of Joe's handiwork; while still some distance off, he saw a figure standing before the window, gazing at it with the stillness of total absorption. The figure wore a skirt and bonnet, and Calvin assumed it must be Phoebe Pike come to visit again after so long. Calvin liked Phoebe, and hurried up behind her. The harps were humming mournfully in a light breeze, and she did not notice Calvin's approach until he spoke.

"Mornin', Miss Pike."

She turned, but the lovely face was not Phoebe's. He recognised her, though, even if six years had passed since she gave birth on his living room floor; a face as lovely as that was not easily forgotten. She was a young woman now, and Calvin was suddenly shy in her presence. He remembered she could not talk, and cast about desperately for words. If he'd known it wasn't Phoebe he would not have disturbed her, felt guilty for having intruded on her admiration of the window. "Pretty, ain't it?" he said, and Sadie turned again to the stained glass, then nodded at Calvin. "And them boxes Joe fixed, they put out a regular moan, I reckon, kind of like . . . ghosts." He almost frightened himself with the notion of spirits wandering along the ridge, shuffled his feet in embarrassment, wished the onus of communication did not rest so heavily on his sloping shoulders; apart from that one nod Sadie Wilkes had done nothing to help lighten his burden. Still, what else could she, a mute, have done? Calvin tugged at his hatbrim. "If you'll excuse me, I got work to be doin'." And he walked off backwards, nodding and smiling.

When Joe returned the following day, Calvin told him about the encounter. "I figure she must've come up here a few other times and we never seen her till now."

"Maybe she likes the privacy. You didn't frighten her, did you?"

"No I never." Calvin was offended. "I treated her polite. She can lookit the winder any time she wants."

Another tree was felled, another chief begun. Sometimes Joe stopped work and wandered up to the blackberry patch; he hoped each time to see a woman there, but the window cast its coloured shadow on the ground unseen, the harps thrummed for his ears alone. He stood for some time, as though attempting to summon a female form from brightness and wind-song, then returned to his work.

A woman entered Croft's store; this was Amy Scruggs, prostitute, and it was her particular conceit to be called (in her professional capacity) Varina Cleburne. Amy worked in the brothel on Chippewa. She was a regular customer at the store, having an insatiable need for worthless gewgaws, most of them worn once or twice then discarded. Amy Scruggs was biding her time in Valley Forge, knew she would one day move on to greater things; she had lived and worked in the town for several years now, was in reality too lazy to shift herself to a larger, more profitable venue elsewhere. It was Amy who had written the bogus letter from Alma at Lucius Croft's request, was the unwitting instigator of Calvin's horrific fit. It would not have made her unhappy, had she been made aware of her role in that small tragedy, for Amy liked to see things "stirred up". Things did not often get stirred up in Valley Forge, and she was obliged to en-

gage her thoughts in the making of trivial choices in Croft's
store, to pass the time and use her cash. Everyone knew
who she was and what she did, as they knew the two other
women similarly engaged in the same house, but the three
women conducted themselves with decorum while in public,
and wore nothing but severest black. They did not call attention to themselves, were therefore tolerated by the womenfolk of the county (for the brothel served an area extending
beyond the city limits) who had no power to change this
state of affairs in any case; so long as men wanted prostitutes available they would be there, inviolable (but not inviolate). Even Tub Davis had given up preaching against
them, and Sheriff Perce Lafferty considered the Chippewa
brothel a fixture, rather than a blot on the landscape, a
necessary evil, as he was forced to remind his wife whenever
she lectured him about its existence.

There were some women who could not accustom themselves to the idea of prostitutes walking freely about the
streets (not soliciting, just walking), treading the same sidewalks as respectable folk, breathing the very air inhaled by
clean-living citizens. Such a woman was in the store when
Amy/Varina entered and began browsing among the goods
on display, the same woman who had doubted Joe Cobden's ability to spell better than a white man. She stared
openly at Amy, who enjoyed the look of outrage on her face;
things could very easily get stirred up in such a situation,
and Amy was in a reckless mood. Waited on by Phoebe,
she tried on every bauble within reach, eked out her parading in front of the mirror with sighings and posturings calculated to infuriate her audience. She was particularly vain
with regard to her hands, which were very fine hands indeed, being of a naturally pleasing conformation, their softness enhanced by lack of acquaintance with the rigours of
farmwork or domestic chores. A great many trays of rings
were placed within her reach, and she poked and picked
among them fastidiously, as though fearing to touch brass
when silver and gold alone were worthy of her.

"I don't know," she said. "Nothing seems right somehow."

"How about this?" Phoebe held up a locket and chain. Amy Scruggs fascinated her; she had the character and personality of an overindulged and intellectually indifferent child, but her body, the thing beneath that blackest of black dresses, had known the touch of men, had been penetrated by them, pressed and held beneath them times without number. Amy Scruggs *knew what it was like,* and Phoebe, although she admired nothing about this vapid creature, was envious. Unlike most local women she did not resent Amy's presence, welcomed the nearness of that body which had known the lustful embraces of men, drew from its aura of sensuality a measure of excitement; carnality by proxy, as it were. "You can put a picture inside it."

"Oh, I've got so many already."

And a different man's picture in every one, thought the indignant customer behind Amy, but said nothing. Phoebe took from the display cabinet a tasteful cameo brooch. "This is nice. We got some in just last week." Amy eyed it without interest. "Oh, I don't know. It's only a brooch. Don't you have anything different, I mean something really *new?*"

"I'm afraid not." Phoebe knew exactly what Amy was doing, wanted her to continue until the woman eyeing her said something or burst a blood vessel with suppressed anger. Phoebe, too, was in a reckless mood that day. She attributed her wickedness to the heat, wished she were a dog lying on the cool earth beneath a water-tank, not serving behind a counter in an airless store.

"I just can't make up my mind." Amy examined the cameo again. "I suppose it *is* kind of nice."

"Your dress will set it off perfectly." Phoebe was not lying, had never told a lie in order to sell something.

"Maybe I'll take it. I just don't know."

When the game eventually grew tiresome for Amy she purchased the brooch and swept out, nodding casually to the woman in passing. It had been a bravura performance, but Amy was wise enough to depart the stage without waiting for encores. Willard had witnessed all, was not surprised when the woman turned to him, eyes lit with the fires of outrage.

"Mr. Croft, it's disgraceful that a creature like that should get service in a respectable store!"

Willard slid into his standard placatory manner. "I'm just a businessman, Mrs. Allen. I can't accept one person's money and not another's."

"That woman's money is *tainted*."

His ploy having failed, Willard turned to Phoebe, his brow lowered. "Miss Pike, there is no need to serve that young woman with such enthusiasm."

"Pardon me, Mr. Croft?"

"Just don't be so helpful. Let her find what she wants, pay for it and get out. Smiling and pointing things out only encourages her."

Phoebe arranged her features into their blandest contours; the little worm wasn't going to make *her* his scapegoat. "But, Mr. Croft, you've always told me to give her every respect. She spends more money in here than anyone else in town, you said."

"I'm sure I did *not* say that, Miss Pike."

"I could have sworn you did, Mr. Croft."

Willard swivelled his body as if mounted on castors. "Mrs. Allen, you must see our latest footwear, just in from Kansas City. . . ."

But Mrs. Allen was already halfway through the door. Willard was furious with everyone concerned, excluding himself, and went into the back room to sulk. Sometimes he wondered if loving Phoebe was a sensible course to pursue. If she ever again embarrassed him like that he would . . . yes, he would *fire* her! It had been going on for too long; he could no longer sleep at night, lay beside his wife, resenting her carefree slumbers, his mind filled with Phoebe Pike. No more! Just let her put her foot across the line one more time. . . .

* * *

The evenings had become unendurable, as they did every summer. Heat was hungrily absorbed by the house through the day, would not disperse at night no matter how many windows were opened. Pike sat in the living room, entering figures into a ledger. Some yards away sat Jessica, ostensibly knitting, looking furtively about her for her guardian in green; he had not visited her for several days now. Phoebe sat in her room upstairs, trying to read, wishing herself in some cool and distant place. In the next room Grandmamma rubbed peevishly at her chest, trying to ease the pains of wind; she needed wind *out*side her, not inside, needed a good stiff breeze to make her feel better.

Jessica lowered her knitting and searched openly for the least sign of her little friend. Where was he?

"What are you doing?" Pike did not even look up from his work to ask the question.

"I'm not doing anything. I'm knitting. . . ."

"One cannot do two things at once," he told the ledger, "even when one of those things is nothing."

"Yes, dear," said Jessica, eyes roaming the floor.

"Stop that! There are no small green lizards in this room. There are no lizards of any description, nor are there any giant sea-snakes, dragons or unicorns. Kindly attend to your knitting."

"Yes, dear."

The ceiling thudded beneath Grandmamma's cane and Jessica jumped.

"See to it," said Pike, his head still lowered.

Jessica hurried upstairs. "I want cooling," said Grandmamma, thrusting at her a broad fan of woven raffia. Jessica wordlessly applied herself to the task. "Faster!" ordered Grandmamma, and Jessica swatted the syrupy air with increased vigour. "Sweep it, *sweep* it! Don't just flutter it back and forth. *Sweep* the air across me. Put your arm behind it." Jessica swept, and Grandmamma's thin lips parted with bliss.

Jessica's arm tired quickly; she resorted to her left hand,

but this too could not sustain the effort required of it. "I have to stop for a little while . . ."

"Nonsense. You've only been doing it for five minutes. I want to see that fan pass three feet each way. I don't want disturbed air, I want a *breeze*."

Jessica fanned for as long as she could, then let her arms collapse at her sides. She waited for the scorn, for the sneering that was sure to follow. But Grandmamma (again suffering discomfort in her chest) said simply: "Fetch me some water." Jessica went to the tray set on the dresser by the open window; a night wind (nonexistent) was supposed to keep the carafe there cool. As Jessica's cramped fingers closed about its neck to lift it from the tray, she chanced to peek into the mirror; no sound behind her prompted that glance into the reflected room, but look she did, and what she saw caused her heart literally to skip a beat. From the neck of Grandmamma's dress rose not the head of an old woman but a lizard. It was not Jessica's cheery champion, it was cold and grey and terrible to behold; from the scaly reptilian snout darted a black tongue of alarming mobility, its flickerings accompanied by a faint hissing. The hooded eyes observed her, the creature believing itself unseen; the tongue curled and snaked and probed at the air, retreated to the barely open maw with its rows of ferocious teeth, darted again, stretching to an impossible length, this time returning to the trap-like jaws bearing in the grasp of its flexile tip something small and green. The floor opened beneath Jessica, sent her reeling through corridors of darkness.

Phoebe heard the pounding of Grandmamma's cane and wondered at its message; she had heard Jessica's voice in the next room just a moment before, could not imagine why Grandmamma would want two slaves at once. She tried to ignore it, but the thumping continued until Phoebe's patience exploded in a flurry of dark thoughts, each one a picture of Beatrice Pike undergoing torture ingenious and prolonged. Her arrival at Grandmamma's door coincided with that of her father, and together they entered. Grandmamma's cane pointed at Jessica, sprawled inelegantly on the rug, her dress soaked with water.

"She fell down. No reason for it." She thought Jessica must have strained herself with all that fanning, hoped she would recover soon to fan on. Phoebe went for the smelling salts, found the phial improperly capped, the contents evaporated. Jessica was taken to her room and placed on the bed. "Probably the heat," said Pike, not terribly concerned if it was not, and returned downstairs.

Phoebe stayed until her mother recovered herself and sat up. The wet cloth sliding from her forehead startled her; Jessica had no recollection of her collapse or its cause. Phoebe helped her undress, fetched her knitting from the living room (Pike made no comment on this evidence of recovery) and sat with her until Jessica finally fell asleep. Phoebe retired to her room and followed suit, sinking, sinking through welcome layers of nothingness.

When all under this roof were at last asleep there came the long-awaited breeze, no cooler than the air it displaced but alive with movement, pushing aside the torpid exhalations of the town, passing along the empty streets, through open windows, brushing aside curtains with light-fingered stirrings, flowing silently from room to room, enveloping sleepers in movement, making them dream of sluggish waters that ran with the warmth of blood.

Jessica rose from her bed. She was nine years old and had wandered out into the meadow to pick flowers. She plucked a knitting needle from its sheath of loops, held it before her like a posy; she wanted to show it to Mamma.

Grandmamma dreamed of warm molasses being poured along her thighs; then, in a fusion of dream and wakefulness, realised she had urinated. She had never been incontinent in her old age and was very much ashamed, felt as she had when this mishap occurred during her girlhood; she had gone and wet the bed again, and *punishment* would follow. Her eyes opened fully and saw a figure beside the sodden bed; she must be dreaming still, for the figure resembled a ghost, with trailing grey hair and a flowing white robe, and in its hand . . . a knitting needle. Beyond it the curtains billowed in languorous undulation like wings, and Grandmamma knew this was no dream, knew the Angel of Death had come for her at last, could feel his icy hand clutch at her heart and squeeze, squeeze so hard, a vice without pity, crushing her chest slowly, irresistibly, while the deathly visitor stood unmoving, moonlight gleaming dully on the needle held before him like some instrument of judgement, a silver dagger drawn between the hemispheres of her brain.

Her mouth formed a hollow cavern (her teeth grinned gleefully in their bedside tumbler) and from the cavern came the sound of a soul's departure, a strangulated croaking made awful not so much by the inhuman scrapings and scratchings in her larynx as by the lengthy silences between them. I'm dying, thought Grandmamma, and from the cavern, frozen now in a rictus of dread, there drifted an endless sigh, a steady hiss as of escaping steam. The eldritch sibilance uncoiled, spiralled upward into darkness.

And Jessica, having showed Mamma her flowers, departed as she had come, to sleep the untroubled sleep of the very young.

One particularly repugnant medieval torture was the stacking of rocks upon a board laid along the body of a heretic, the weight being steadily increased until the sought-after confession was gasped out. Phoebe felt just such an intolerable board had been lifted from her when Grandmamma was discovered next morning, jaws agape, eyes wide and staring. Dr. Whaley wrote "vascular arrest" on the death certificate and Phoebe's heart sang. Pike was shocked by Grandmamma's demise, then withdrawn, downcast. For the first time in her life Phoebe saw her father grief-stricken, yet she had no sympathy for his sense of loss, rejoiced that one half of the army marching for possession of Jessica's mind had fallen headlong into a bottomless chasm; she felt she could successfully cope with the remainder. She gloated over the death, was aware of it and was not ashamed. Jessica seemed not to understand her liberation at all, wanted to know if Grandmamma would require special attention while in her sickbed. Phoebe assured her Grandmamma would require nothing more of Jessica. "Nothing, *ever*, " she emphasised. But Jessica could still not accept the suddenness with which her burden had been removed, and fussed about the house in search of reassurance, small and green.

Pike began the task of preparing his mother for burial, his hands shaking. He could barely bring himself to observe her nakedness, went about the usual preparations in a daze, trying to convince himself this was not Beatrice Pike stretched out before him but some anonymous farmer's wife. Contact between his fingers and the corpse caused fits of trembling augmented by a peculiarly insistent sensation of guilt. Had he done his best for her, rewarded her for those early years when, abandoned by her husband, she had poured her every resource into Joshua's future greatness? She had wanted him to be a doctor—he had failed. She had not approved of Jessica—Pike had married her none the less (for the best of motives, he reminded himself—financial gain with which to support Beatrice—an incentive rendered hollow by the subsequent revelation of Jessica's penurious circumstances). Beatrice had wanted grandsons, but Pike had provided her with nothing more than Phoebe, inheritor of Jessica's mental instability, a perpetual thorn in the flesh of this body before him, his mother. He had not devoted sufficient time to her since the move to Kansas, had never wholly accepted her protestations of incapacity despite his shouting matches with Phoebe, yet had deemed it his mother's right to conduct her life from the narrow confines of her bed if she so decided. All in all he had much to be ashamed of, was grateful for just one thing—word of his dismissal from the Des Moines School of Embalming had never reached her ears.

He laboured on in the basement, forcing the hosepipe down her throat and deep into her chest, pumping in embalming fluid. He extracted the hose and steeled himself for the most onerous task of all; he must now force a nozzle up his mother's anus and fill her bowels with a soapy solution to flush out her excrements, then thrust another hose up her to inject the preservative. He could not do it. Better that she should be left semi-embalmed than that he subject her to this final indignity. He dressed her in a dress of black taffeta and the shoes she had not worn since arriving in Valley Forge. To compensate for having left her bowels professionally unmolested he decided to bury her in his most singular coffin. This was made of cast metal, was not the usual box, but consciously styled according to the contours of the human body in much the same fashion as an Egyptian sarcophagus; it even had a small but stout glass window set into it, permitting a view of the deceased's face, but most people found this bizarre feature unsettling. The Fisk Metallic Burial Case came in two halves which met with the precision and finality of an iron maiden's embrace, and was marketed by a Cincinnati company which had begun by manufacturing stoves; it was casually referred to by the foundry workers as "Ironsides". Vice President John C. Calhoun (the proprietor of the Calhoun Hotel claimed kinship) had some years before been buried in an airtight Fisk, but the price was prohibitive, and Pike had never been able to convince potential customers the thing was not somehow "heathen", suggesting as it did the shape of the body within; they much preferred the utilitarian wedge or, better yet, the ubiquitous oblong, the design for which, greatly reduced, could well have represented a child's pencil box. Very well, what was unacceptable to Kansans was to be lauded (Pike considered his customers bumpkins for the most part), and the Fisk Metallic Burial Case would make of the funeral an affair to be discussed for ever, granting Beatrice the kind of immortality that would long outlast the efficacy of embalming fluid.

She was placed in the chapel of rest, and proved to be the most popular exhibit since Lucius Croft. Many observers thought the cast-iron casket an inappropriate chariot to the afterlife and did not hesitate to say so, once out in the sunlight again. The old lady was crammed in there like canned preserves, a downright undignified way for a man to treat his own mother, putting her in a giant candle-mould that everyone else in town had the good taste not to buy for their loved ones; and why was the lid already closed, obliging all to squint through that itty-bitty window? And the weight, by God! It would probably sink below the six foot level at the first rain, probably keep right on sinking through the ground till it got to hell's back door. It just wasn't right, nossir.

The funeral was well attended. Six husky men struggled beneath the casket to the graveside and laid it across the wooden supports, which immediately sank several inches into the crumbling earth around the grave's perimeter. A subtle but distinct surging by those nearest the hole was later remarked upon; everyone knew it was because they had expected the monstrosity to go crashing down to its appointed place without further ado. The groaning supports continued to sink; earth trickled downward throughout Wilkes' service, irregular patterings of pebble and soil raising four bifurcated cones along the neatly spaded rectangle at the bottom of the grave.

Wilkes spoke the final words, closed his Bible with a portentous thud. The same six men lifted the casket with ropes while the wooden supports were removed. All six took an involuntary step forward as the awesome weight of the thing extracted its due; torsos thrown back, strongest legs extended, the six-man team fought a losing tug of war against gravity and iron. Eventually the brute lay where it should, Grandmamma's face staring blindly from the tiny window like some deep-sea diver succumbed at last to oxygen starvation. The ropes were released (some say thrown) into the grave, their hempen coils evoking not the usual rattle and thump of rope on wood but the sound of brief abrasion, as when a poorly thrown hawser strikes a capstan before sliding off.

It was at this moment that Jessica pointed to the casket and fainted. Consternation! The mourners surged with abandon now, and a man and woman pressed to the brink of the grave by those behind toppled headlong, the man spraining his ankle upon impact, the woman's fall made gentler by coils of rope. When she recovered from the surprise of her fall she found her face inches from that of Beatrice Pike, and in her confused state of mind imagined those ancient eyes staring into her own. Her scream aroused even greater alarm among the roiling bystanders, and the two in the grave (excluding Grandmamma) were joined by another, this person's fall being cushioned by his predecessors. Hoverers on the brink demanded to know what had caused one woman to faint, a second to scream, but were given no comprehensible answer until the screamer was hauled to safety, whereupon she announced to the world, "She's alive! She's alive!" prompting further hysteria; more women fainted (or pretended to—the pretenders were for the most part young females who seized the chance to throw themselves into the arms of their baffled beaux) and several daring fellows deliberately jumped down on to the Fisk Metallic Burial Case to investigate this unbelievable claim. Grandmamma's lowered lids indicated eternal slumber, and the men said so. Perhaps the matter would have rested there had not Jessica chosen this moment to revive, and the first words from her lips were: "She looked at me. . . ."

The burial could not proceed until the casket had been opened, death confirmed once and for all. Pike was outraged. "I will not permit it! My mother is dead. No one could survive the injection of embalming fluid. The lungs are filled. . . . I absolutely refuse permission!" But he was ignored. He turned to Reverend Wilkes for help, but the man of God could only say that "under the circumstances" it was unthinkable to continue without first ascertaining the exact state of the—he almost said "the deceased"—of Mrs. Pike. Furious, Pike sought the assistance of Sheriff Lafferty in preventing this sacrilegious disturbance of his mother's final rest, but Perce had already grabbed a rope and begun organising a team to haul the iron casket back into the light, a task requiring twelve men. Pike fumed and fretted, pow-

erless to stop them. Phoebe led Jessica to the shade of the
hearse, away from the crowd. "Mother, did you really see
it?"

Jessica looked across at the mêlée, nodded slowly. "She
opened her eyes and looked at me. . . . She isn't dead, I
know it. . . ." Her voice was rising in panic.

Phoebe held her, spoke soothingly. "They'll find out.
They're going to look and make sure."

"She isn't dead. . . ."

"Yes, yes, but they have to be sure."

A Fisk Metallic Burial Case, once sealed, is a difficult
beast to open again, its screws being plentiful, tight-fitting
and deeply countersunk. A boy was dispatched to town for
a screwdriver, rode off on muleback. The mourners clustered around the casket as they had done while it reposed
in the chapel of rest, but now they scrutinised the pale features within more closely; some swore they saw Grandmamma's nostrils quiver, others were positive her eyelids had
stirred as they gazed, and a few insisted her cheeks had
begun to bloom. Pike literally turned his back on them,
went and stood in the cemetery's furthest corner until the
boy returned, jumped from his lathered mule and handed
Perce Lafferty a screwdriver. Thirty minutes later the last
screw had been removed. The lid was raised and set aside.
Grandmamma awaited the touch of enquiring hands, but
no one appeared willing to initiate the necessary contact
between living and dead, if dead she was. Someone suggested Dr. Whaley should be present to conduct an examination and there was general approval of this plan, but
before a rider could be sent to fetch him Phoebe pushed
through the crowd and knelt by the casket. She peered
closely at the bloodless face, asked for a mirror, was given
one by Amy Scruggs (one of the very few women in Valley
Forge who carried such an item of vanity on her person)
and held it above the nose and mouth. No mist formed.
Phoebe stood, handed back the mirror.

"My grandmother is dead."

She returned to the hearse, waited beside Jessica while

the test was repeated. There could be no doubting the verdict—if eyes could not discern the presence of death, noses could; one of Pike's secret objections to opening the casket was the knowledge that Grandmamma's unflushed, untreated bowels would by now be a squirming mass of putrefaction, and so they were. The onlookers drew back as the stench began escaping from Grandmamma's tightly packed dress into the air, and the lid was hastily reaffixed and screwed down. Pike refused to rejoin the mourners until the casket was once again in the grave; even from a distance he had heard their comments as they fanned the air beneath their nostrils. He stiffly released the ritual handful of earth, then stepped back. Phoebe and her mother remained by the hearse, would not contribute further to the proceedings. Kansas sod was shovelled back into the hole from which it had been spaded, and when the final pat was given to the mound Pike strode to the hearse and drove away, as rigid on the seat as a carven king enthroned. Phoebe and Jessica were driven back to town by Willard Croft and his wife. No one spoke.

Pike stayed down in the stable for the rest of the day, washing the hearse, currying the horses, reliving his humiliation and that of Beatrice. The onlookers would not readily forget the unholy stink when the Fisk had been opened, would assume his professional abilities were substandard; if he couldn't keep his own mother from smelling like a sack of dead cats just three days after her demise, how could he possibly do better for mere customers? They might have understood, had he explained his reluctance to violate his mother's rectum with hose and nozzle, but such things were not for public discussion. The damage was done. Poor Mother, to have been manhandled so; it made his blood run hot, and forced a tear, isolated and bitter, from his eye.

Phoebe made mint tea for her mother. Jessica seemed quite recovered from her fainting fit, was even smiling absently at the kitchen wall. She watched Phoebe pouring the tea into china cups used exclusively for this beverage, decided she could share her secret. "It was my little green lizard," she said.

"Oh, yes?" Phoebe experienced a familiar sensation of dread.

"He came in under the door and climbed up on her bed and on to the pillow and whispered a magic word in her ear . . . and she died." Jessica found this so delightfully appropriate she concluded with a giggle.

Phoebe set down the tea-cups. She had no intention of dissuading her mother from this nonsense; if it made her happy to think a little green lizard had removed Snapdragon from their lives, then so be it.

"Let it cool a little," she said.

CHAPTER THIRTY-EIGHT

Grandmamma would not die. Jessica felt her presence often, sometimes as an invisible malignance brushing the edge of her thoughts with causeless fears, more often as a scuttling spider, blackly furred, darting across the periphery of her vision; always, when she turned, it was gone, but of one thing Jessica was sure—the spider was growing. When she first noticed its furtive maraudings into her awareness it had been no bigger than a dime, had stayed that way for a short while, then grown to the size of a pocket watch. Jessica knew spiders have six eyes, had seen a drawing of one in a book, knew they have cruel pincers in their jaws with which to seize their prey in a grip of iron before gobbling it down, the six eyes gleaming like polished onyx doorknobs. Her spider grew and grew as the weeks passed; soon its body alone was the size of a pincushion, and its legs became so long and heavy they produced a muffled staccato tapping as the creature dashed across floor and walls in an effort to evade detection, efforts deliberately mocking in their failure; Jessica *knew* it was there, knew the spider was teasing her with these brief glimpses.

She dreaded darkness, for the spider's fur became one with the blackness of night. It could be lurking anywhere: in the corners of floor and ceiling, on any surface she might touch, in the outhouse waiting for her flesh to be bared (she claimed Grandmamma's chamber pot for her own, never again went outside at night); the spider could be hiding beneath her bed, silent but never still, for even when its legs were not scrabbling and tapping and waving, its body palpitated in a loathsome little dance, up and down, up and

618

down, like a black heart nestled among eight black springs, a quivering velvet pouch of venom biding its time, the six unblinking eyes ever watchful, waiting, waiting for the moment of its vengeance against the living.

Jessica's body shed weight with alarming swiftness. She had no appetite for food, seldom slept for more than a few minutes at a time, her catnappings always terminated by a sudden spasm of fear that catapulted her back into the life she perceived as reality, a life so fraught with terror she would not sit on a chair unless its legs were set in cans of molasses; if the spider attempted to climb the chair-legs it would be drowned in viscous syrup. She insisted also upon sitting beneath an umbrella while ensconced on her "safe" chair, in case the spider sought to drop on to her shoulder from the ceiling; that prospect reduced Jessica to nervous tremors whenever she considered it. But her precautions were in vain, for the spider demonstrated its ability to *leap* from walls and floors, from anywhere; it could spring at Jessica at any moment, scorning her umbrella and cans of molasses, could sink its pincers into her without warning. Only one defence was possible against so sprightly and devious a foe; she began wearing a bee-keeper's veil and gloves, never allowed her head to be without a hat to suspend the mesh from, never exposed her hands to the air, tucked her skirts into inelegant rubber boots, secured the hemline stretching between her boot-tops with clothes pegs that knocked and clicked like castanets whenever she moved. These were necessary measures, the only available precautions, for the little green lizard was gone for ever.

Pike viewed his wife's madness with what amounted to equanimity; since the death of his mother his mood had been so subdued as to be almost imperturbable. So long as Jessica did not make any noise and avoided the public eye he made no comment, ceased even to notice her outlandish spiderproof garb. Tucked safely away in contingency's pocket was the option of committing her to an asylum if her peculiarities became loud or intrusive; until then, he was tolerant beyond caring, lived in a solitary world filled (like Jessica's) with the memory of Grandmamma.

Her parents' differing yet concomitant disintegration was observed by Phoebe with a coolness and detachment which surprised even her. She knew her interior self was proofed against hurt, had been made hard, if not invulnerable, by the very business of living in the Pike home; but now, watching, listening to these two from whose bodies she had come, she found herself unable to feel any emotion other than a sense of inevitability, a feeling that whatever she might do, the future was advancing backwards (so to speak) with measured and unswerving steps, drawing closer minute by elongated minute. And so she did nothing, waited for that future time to enter the house and shatter this false quiet which filled the rooms like mist. She, too, brooded on the absence of Grandmamma, a departure so abrupt the very air seemed not to have invaded the emptiness left behind; the bed-throne seemed occupied still by a formless vacuum, a nothingness that repelled. Three human lives revolved around this nothingness, three planets in helpless orbit around a dark star; Phoebe waited to see which would be drawn into that maw of blackness for ever, and which would not.

She went one day to the ridge, but Joe was not there, was in Topeka selling another of the Buffalo tribe. The people of Valley Forge knew of his new trade, had seen him loading the first wooden Indian aboard a train, and the second, and Phoebe wished to see one of these creations for herself. She sat on the porch with Calvin and discussed the falling leaves that littered the yard, rustling among the heavier detritus of Joe's woodparings. Calvin informed her that Joe's next Indian would be carved indoors, out of the wind; the seldom-used parlour with its three windows was to become a "stoodio", a place Calvin figured must be kind of like a carpenter's workshop. Joe had already purchased a piano trolley for moving the next section of treetrunk across the porch, through the front door and along the hall to the parlour-that-was. Joe always figured stuff out ahead of time, real smart-like. Calvin provided bitter coffee to accompany his conversation, and when Phoebe had had enough of both she departed, smiling and waving at Calvin as a reward for his efforts.

As she retraced her steps along the ridge trail Phoebe's eye was caught by movement to her right, a glimpse of trailing skirt disappearing behind a tree. She stopped, waited for the entity to reappear. When it did not, Phoebe left the trail and went among the trees. "Is someone there?" But no one was. She went further, positive her eyes had not been playing tricks, came eventually to the ridge's crest and was drawn to the blackberry patch by the siren-call of Joe's Aeolian harps. And what was that, a stained-glass window? How on earth had such a thing come to be here? Without sunlight the white wolf and its sucklings were not seen to best advantage; nevertheless, Phoebe stood before the window until she grew cold, then went in search of the melodious and plaintive sound wafting around her on the wind. She located two long boxes high in the trees, failed to notice the third, would have found none had the season not stripped the boughs of foliage. She returned to the window, her glimpse of the mysterious woman quite forgotten in the light of this magical discovery. The place seemed to her almost pagan in its appeal to the senses, a pantheistic temple open to the elements; she half-expected to see goatlegged fauns prancing around the blackberry patch. Joe Cobden never failed to surprise her; he had said nothing of this to her on his occasional trips to the store, and Calvin presumably had been made too shy by her presence to remember its existence. Enchanting, was her conclusion and, having savoured as much of the magic as she could, Phoebe walked back down the slope to the trail, and home.

Fall surrendered Kansas to winter. No mail came to the ridge; Joe asked at the post office at least once a week. The postmaster would smirk, happy to deliver the news that Noah Puckett had yet to pen a single letter. The townspeople had taken a perverse pride in Noah's departure, judged it was their combined ill-will that had driven the boy out, felt justified and somehow more secure now that he had gone, as though Noah might at some future date have delivered into their midst a disease of some kind, one whose chief characteristic may have been a restlessness and dissatisfaction with their lot. It was better that he be exiled to shake his leper's bell elsewhere.

Calvin bore his disappointment well. Joe had expected tantrums and glowering silences, not this quiet stoicism, and considered Calvin's attitude, for all its unworldliness, to be nothing less than philosophic. "Wonder where the boy's at," Calvin would say. It was a rhetorical question but Joe always responded, felt bound to do so by his own sense of guilt for not having raised Noah to be a youth worthier of his efforts. "Oh, he'll be somewhere warm, down south probably. He's no fool." Calvin would nod, absorbing this information, refusing to see it as conjecture. "Reckon he'll be back soon?" was the next question in the ritual. "Not in this weather. Maybe in the spring." And both men fell silent, stared at the fire and imagined the thousand and one accidents which could have befallen the wanderer, who might be oiling locomotive wheels for a living in the next town down the line, or sharing mussels and sealmeat with the natives of Tierra del Fuego. Joe wished he had never mentioned spring; Calvin would be anxious all winter long, and be doubly dismayed if the thaw brought no clumping of wayfarer's footfalls to the porch. Live in hope; that was the motto he employed on Calvin's behalf. He did not tell Calvin the motto; Calvin would only have forgotten it, had been forgetting a great many small things of late.

Calvin had not told Joe of Phoebe's visit during his absence, and when Joe next visited the store without making mention of it to Phoebe she assumed he did not wish to encourage visitors. She was hurt but said nothing, gave Joe his change and watched him leave. For many months now her thoughts had been disjointed, as though perception, before reaching the brain, had first to be filtered through a distorting lens, fragmented by some malign prism into shapes unfamiliar, dream-like. Everyday objects seemed charged with invisible force, subtly altered in ways indefinable to rational analysis, were indisputably *different*. The very goods on the shelves seemed to stare at her; they sought anonymity behind the bland mask of their inanimate commonness, but Phoebe was not deceived—she knew they watched. Whenever she caught herself thinking in this fashion she was quietly appalled at her foolishness; she must *not* allow her mind, her only weapon, to be eroded by despair until it became nothing but an unquestioning receptor, monitoring fantasies of its own devising. The worst moments were those when she permitted herself to wonder if Jessica's madness had been transferred by way of blood to her own veins, had begun stealthily to eat away the mortar of sanity's walls. No, it could *not* be true. Phoebe knew herself to be tired, unhappy, sleepless, without a confidante to whom she might unburden herself; misery, in conjunction with winter, would sap the resources of anyone, she assured herself, and smiled at the customers whose pinched faces paraded before her day after dreary day.

Towards the year's end, while snow fell silently against the windows, Jessica suddenly flung herself into a corner of the living room and crouched, trembling, veiled face hidden further by her gloves. Phoebe found her in this same position one hour later, gently prised her hands away, was eventually able to learn that "she" was still growing, was bigger, blacker and more densely furred than ever, had taken to deliberately attacking Jessica by making gigantic leaps at her face. Even at night she was unsafe, had to risk suffocation by tucking the blankets firmly over her head to prevent those hairy legs, those awful fangs from touching her. The spider was now large as a hatbox.

Long after dusk Phoebe left the house. The streets of Valley Forge were deserted, corridors of emptiness aswirl with drifting powder. She tramped west along Decatur, flesh numbed by cold, heart deadened by the task ahead of her. Twice she wandered from the road before arriving at the cemetery; already the picket fence was half buried beneath snowfall, the dunes of pristine white punctured by arrow-headed boards, their tips thrusting at hidden stars. Grand-mamma's plot lay hidden among the rest, blanketed by snow, distinguishable only by its marker. Phoebe stood with rime crusting her eyelashes and brows, preparing herself. She had once made the dead woman a promise, one to be fulfilled when Beatrice Pike was consumed by worms; the time had come to make good that vow. Phoebe lifted her skirts and danced across the grave, turned and danced back, danced again to and fro, clumsily, body leaning against the wind, elbows outstretched for balance like some flightless bird; back and forth she danced, back and forth until the snow was kicked aside, the frozen mound, subsided after these many months, revealed. She was not content even then, but continued the awkward ritual until her heels met in mid-air with an audible click, as promised. And even that was not enough; Phoebe stamped the length of the grave time and again, gouging with heel and toe, leaving her in-delible mark. Finally she spat upon the marker, leaning close to ensure her spittle found its target.

"Take your spider with you!"

It was done, but her homeward path was no less difficult to follow, her heart unrewarded by the warmth of accomplishment.

A life can swing around a pivot set in its path by accident or design and assume a new direction; an old direction can be rediscovered by this same blind conjunction of influence and impetus. Staring out the living room window one morning in January, Calvin thought, for no particular rea-son, of the skeleton he had dug up more than eighteen months before, and there came bursting into his mind the notion that the skeleton was Alma. It had been a number of years since he had thought of her, but the notion sprang fully fledged from his brain and brushed the inside of his skull with madly beating wingtips; from its throat came a harsh scream, and out of the scream came these words: Joe killed her.

Calvin remembered a letter now; someone had shown him a letter from Alma, and Alma had said Joe hurt her, had . . . *done* it to her! And then she'd gone, but she hadn't run off the way folks said; nossir. Joe had killed her and buried her so she wouldn't talk about the awful thing he did, had killed her so Calvin wouldn't find out! Calvin didn't ask himself how a murdered woman could possibly have written a letter accusing Joe Cobden of rape, a letter allegedly mailed many years after her disappearance. There was a letter, there was a skeleton; only a blind man couldn't see the two were linked. Calvin had dug up his own wife by accident all that time ago, and Joe had acted like he didn't know who it was down in the hole, acted like it was no one at all, when he'd all along known for sure it was Alma, murdered and buried by him. Well, now Calvin knew, too, by God! He began lifting and lowering himself on the balls of his feet, wondering what action to take, still staring from the window. The ice crystals inches from his eyes scintillated with light pouring from a cloudless sky, dazzled him. Joe had killed Alma then buried her. Who would ever have guessed it if Calvin hadn't found out? Probably no one, no one at all, and Joe would have gotten away with his awful deed, but that wasn't going to happen now, nossir.

And then, marching through a forgotten back door, came the legions of doubt. Maybe it wasn't Alma after all. And hadn't he already confronted Joe about this, accused him of molesting his wife and driving her away? What had the outcome been? He could not recall. And hadn't Noah somehow been involved in that distant confrontation? Calvin's recollection of that day's events was a ragged spiral of unbearable emotions terminating in darkness. And now that he thought about it, Calvin had not personally witnessed Noah's departure last summer; he only had Joe's word the boy had saddled up and gone. Maybe Joe had murdered him, too! Maybe Noah was also buried under a tree on the ridge . . . but what about Noah's horse? That was gone, too. Joe couldn't have killed and buried the horse as well; digging a hole that big would've taken all day. Maybe he'd just let it loose to run off. But a horse will always return to the stable. . . . It was all too confusing. Calvin doubted his own ability to extract threads of actuality from the wildly twisted cloth of imagination.

First things first; he needed to find that skeleton again, and he needed to know if it was a woman. If it was, it would be what they called *proof,* and he would turn Joe over to the sheriff to get hanged. He wouldn't say anything to Joe about what he'd figured out, wouldn't breathe a word, not like last time with the letter; he wasn't exactly sure what had happened then, but Joe must somehow have sweet-talked his way out of things, else he wouldn't be alive right now. He could hear the tap tap, tap tap of Joe's chisel and mallet from the parlour. Wouldn't Joe be scared to learn that Calvin had finally seen the light and figured out what Joe had gone and done. You bet he would. Well, he'd learn in good time, when Calvin had the proof. Meantime, Calvin would keep a tight rein on his lip. He felt mighty proud of himself for not falling down with excitement the way he knew he did sometimes, and the expression forming on his face was ugly with craft and guile.

He walked to town, asked directions to Dr. Whaley's surgery, entered and sat waiting while the doctor attended to a woman and child. Calvin tried to overhear their conversation in the next room, but could make little sense of it through the door. When they left, both looked miserable; Calvin was unable to tell which had been the patient. Whaley sat at his desk, invited Calvin to say where it hurt.

"I ain't sick."

"No?"

"I come for to ask you somethin'."

"Yes?"

Calvin nodded. "That's right." It was gratifying to know the doctor understood.

"Ask me what, Mr. Puckett?"

"About bones. Which is which."

"Which is *what?*"

"Which is men's and which is ladies'."

"Are you referring to any particular bones?"

Should he tell? No, not yet. "I reckon not."

"You want to know if there are basic differences between the male and female skeleton, is that it?"

"Yessir."

"There are indeed, notably in the pelvic region. . . ."

"So if you seen the bones you'd know right off if it's a woman!"

"If the relevant bones were there, and in fair condition, yes, I believe so. May I ask the purpose behind this enquiry?"

"Just wonderin'," said Calvin, delighted with his own caginess. He wasn't talking yet; oh, no, not till he got Alma dug up again, and then wouldn't Dr. Whaley and the whole damn town sit up and take notice, you bet! "Just wonderin' is all."

He stood and left. Whaley was incurious; fools asked foolish questions. A patient knocked and entered. Whaley had forgotten the incident long before Calvin reached the ridge.

A week without further snow allowed Calvin to pursue his plan. He dug wherever he had dug before, worked at a frantic pace, exhausting himself. The soil in these diggings of yesteday had settled again; the topmost layers, frozen, required the pick before the shovel could be employed. "After that pot of gold again?" asked Joe, but Calvin only lifted his lip in what he hoped was a knowing smile.

"No I ain't. Somethin' else."

"Such as?"

"You'll see."

And he worked on.

Joe saw that Calvin had a secret he was unwilling to share, did not like the way Calvin had been looking sideways at him these last few days, wondered if perhaps Calvin's brain was experiencing some kind of flurry preparatory to another full-blown storm; he hoped not. Life was good for Joe at the moment; he did not want trouble or interruption of any kind. The parlour floor was littered with chips of elm, and in its centre stood an emerging Buffalo chief. Of particularly forbidding aspect, this latest warrior virtually insisted the observer partake of the proffered tobacco or risk being assaulted with the tomahawk held in readiness across his chest. He was the best yet, the equal, Joe was sure, of the $200 Indian in Topeka; his last effort had fetched eighty dollars less than that amount. Joe's aim was one day to produce a $300 Indian. His mallet and chisels and paints were instruments of salvation; while he worked he thought of nothing but the wood before him, of its texture and grain and smell, of the figure trapped inside being granted tortuously slow release. Tap tap tapping, intent on his work, Joe forgot the various tribulations of his past, even forgot his warped spine, moved steadily towards a benign future. Why had he not done this before? Why had he become a buffalo-hunter and woodcutter when this ability to shape and reveal had been within him, awaiting the opportunity to flower? It was yet another example of the stupidity he knew himself capable of, but his self-chastisement was mild; since the past and its foolish choices were long behind him, why beat his breast over them? The present occupied him fully, and Joe was content to be who and what he was. He had been chiselled from the realm of possibility by the circumstances of his life as surely as the Buffalo chiefs were chiselled from elm by Joe. Creating cigar store Indians was balm to a flayed soul, and safe within the soothing arms of his art Joe allowed himself to be lulled by what was before his nose, ignored what was behind his back.

The digging was hard work, but Calvin was not deterred from his duty; ravished innocence had to be avenged. The proof he needed was awaiting rediscovery under one of these darn trees he'd dug beneath before, maybe the one he was working on right now, by hokey! Wouldn't Joe get the surprise of his life when the skeleton was presented to him again. Calvin couldn't wait to see the look on his face. He expected Joe would be pretty impressed by the dogged way in which Calvin had unearthed the truth and accused him; he'd probably confess on the spot and be led away to gaol unresisting, and everyone in town would figure Calvin Puckett was a whole lot smarter than they ever reckoned, and Joe would be hanged for murder, and Calvin would be left all alone in the house on the ridge. . . . Alone? That wasn't what he wanted at all. He stopped shovelling. Maybe he should wait until Noah got back before turning Joe in, then father and son could live happily together without anyone coming between them. For the sake of this rosy vision Calvin expunged any lingering suspicions that Joe had also murdered Noah; that would have been intolerable, for it meant Calvin would be obliged to continue sharing the ridge with Joe rather than face his remaining years in solitary contemplation of the cruel twists fate worked upon decent folks, especially himself. He had to wait for Noah to come home, definitely. But that didn't mean he couldn't continue digging for Alma's bones; if he found them before the boy returned, why, then, he'd just mark the tree for future recognition and fill the hole in again and keep his mouth shut until the time was right, until Noah walked in the door with a million stories about where he'd been all this time. That was the smart thing to do, and Calvin proceeded to do it.

Joe suspected nothing. These two men—one thinking of nothing but wooden Indians, the other thinking of nothing but a dead woman's bones and revenge—coexisted without rancour, were careful not to infringe upon the other's silences, were generally too tired from their respective labours to have any inclination towards conversation that might have revealed the true state of things.

But Calvin's buoyant expectations, unsupported by concrete findings, could not last; by February's end he had grown angry at his failure to locate the elusive bones, and the thought of having to dig up every one of the hundred-plus holes to find them drove him into a rage. He was working at the ridge's crest when this black wave swept aside his usual veneration for the spot. Calvin clambered from his latest pit and strode fifty yards to the stained-glass window.

It was the work of seconds to demolish it completely; his pick sank into the white wolf's flank with a brittle *crash!* and the twins and brambles followed the wolf in a welter of coloured shards; *smash! crash!* and the window was no more. Every section had been knocked with ridiculous ease from its lead mooring, lay in brilliant scatterings upon the snow. Within the metal frame's circumference snaking lines of lead joined others in an erratic jigsaw, cracks on an invisible plate, blackened capillaries in an empty eye. Even as Calvin stared, the frame leaned away from him, the weight of the glass no longer securing it in its perch between the trees, and fell with an apologetic crunch among the fragments it had embraced so gloriously.

Now he was appalled by his act, and began trembling, literally shaking in his boots. Even the Aeolian harps seemed to register disapproval of his destructive impulse; they droned harshly above his head, their dissonant mutterings (several of their strings had snapped in the cold) striking a response within his skull.

He knew which tree to dig by. The knowledge came to him without effort, without appeal. He did not question it, collected his shovel, walked several hundred yards back towards the house until the tree in his head matched the tree in his eyes, then set to with the pick. Alma lay buried beneath him; his mind told him so, and Calvin did not doubt the soundless whispering for a moment. He worked like a machine, coaxed by the vision for the first three feet, goaded by it when the task became harder. His body ached, every muscle begged for rest, sweat poured from him, soaked his clothing with a fetid brine the heat of his labouring could not dissipate. Calvin was possessed; smashing the window had somehow, he knew, turned a key in his memory, led him directly to the place he sought.

He scooped out the loosened soil, eager for evidence of Joe's perfidy. Noah would hate Joe when he learned what Joe had done to Alma, would run to Calvin and apologise for ever having preferred Joe to his own father, would call him "Dad" or "Pop", would stand alongside Calvin when they saw Joe dropped at the end of a rope, would return home with him and make of the ridge a happy place. Maybe one day Noah would bring home a bride! That would be good—Noah and his wife and their children, with Calvin at the head of the table, loved by them all. That wasn't too much to ask for; he bet he could have had it a long time ago if Joe Cobden hadn't come along and murdered his wife and . . . and burned down his church! The memory came swooping from the past like a vengeful bat, flapped about his ears, twittering an incomprehensible idiot babble, snagging its claws in his hair; Joe had burned down the church, the church that stood so proud and tall and white! How could Calvin have forgotten about that? Joe's crimes seemingly were endless. What else had he done that might have slipped from Calvin's mind over the years? Had he sent Noah away last summer, threatened him somehow? It was darn likely! A church-burner and wife-murderer wouldn't think twice about telling an innocent boy he'd better head for the hills if he knew what was best for him. By jiminy, but Joe had a wagonload of wrongdoing to answer for! Hanging would be too good for him, the goddamn . . . *humpback!* How could Calvin have been so blind? Well, it would all end right quick; just as soon as he found Alma's bones (he was over five feet down now) he'd go fetch the doctor and the sheriff and get Joe Cobden out of the house and into gaol where he belonged. No he wouldn't; he'd wait till Noah got back home, that was the plan. Or was it? Serpentine coils were looped about his brain, squeezing, *squeezing*. . . . He remembered now—he didn't want to be alone in the house after Joe got taken away, so he had to wait for Noah's return. But how could he keep on living under the same roof as Joe, knowing what he knew? Calvin was aware of his own faults—the strain of deception would be too great; he'd go and blurt out everything he knew in a fit of anger and Joe would most likely kill Calvin too, and then burn down the house, just like that time a lot of years back when he'd tried to burn it down after the church was already a heap of coals. That had been Joe, hadn't it? Who else would have tried to set the house on fire? Nobody, that's who. Maybe he'd better fetch the sheriff after all, and get Joe Cobden under lock and key before he caused any more damage or bloodshed on the ridge. He wouldn't wait for Noah after all; that wouldn't be smart.

The shovel struck bones. Calvin dropped to his knees like a pilgrim before St. Peter's nailparings, reverently brushed aside the earth. Lots of bones were grouped together; rib bones, real little rib bones . . . and a backbone, and a long skull with pointy teeth. . . . Calvin's vision had led him to the burial place of his nameless dog! He stared at the bones, slowly comprehending the enormity of this latest outrage; Joe had done this, had switched one skeleton for the other just to make Calvin sweat. It wasn't fair! A thin scream rose from his belly, the keening wail of total betrayal, but was cut off before achieving volume or duration by an obstacle in Calvin's throat. He could not breathe, felt himself lifted from the hole by invisible hands, then slammed back down into it. This was repeated several times. There was no escaping those hands, big and powerful, the hands of God; they picked him up and slammed him down and flung him around the hole like a pea in a can. God had obviously made a mistake; God thought Calvin was Joe, was punishing him for all those bad things he had done. But it was the wrong man—the wrong bones and the wrong man! Calvin told God of his error, but God would not admit to it, kept taking Calvin by the scruff of the neck, flinging him again and again at the cold dirt walls until his eyes were blinded by grit and his matted hair stiff with soil. Then God told him he could go to sleep at the bottom of the well the hole had all of a sudden become, a deep well with no bones and not even any water at the bottom, just blackness. Calvin was very, very tired, and did as he was told.

Supper on the ridge was by tradition informal, unrelated to the position of clock hands. Joe did not begin to worry until it was almost dark, then went out to the yard and called Calvin's name. Ten minutes later he was dashing among the trees with a lighted lamp, yelling, pleading, breaking the silence of trees and snow. He came eventually to the crystalline jungle of the blackberry patch, found at its edge the window's sorry remnants, knew now that Calvin had not simply wandered out of earshot or ignored the approach of night.

"Calvin! Calviiiiiiin!"

Something bad had happened; it was in the air, on the wind, drifted down from laden boughs, dancing motes of mocking white settling on Joe's shoulders and hat and hump with an awful weight. Two hours of frantic searching yielded Calvin's body at the bottom of a hole cruelly close to the house. Joe jumped down, felt his boots crunch against dog bones. Calvin was huddled against one wall in a foetal crouch. Joe could not determine whether life still pulsed beneath the grubby clothing. Calvin was lifted, boosted over the lip, carried to the house and placed on the sofa. Every available blanket was laid over him. Joe threw more wood on the fire, then rode for Dr. Whaley.

Calvin was frostbitten and feverish. During his thrashing about in the hole his left mitten had come off; the three outer fingers of that hand were frozen, as were the lobe and rim of his left ear, exposed by his crushed and crooked hat. Whaley was inclined to trim these extremities before Calvin regained consciousness, but Joe refused permission. "The blood'll get back into them," he insisted. The doctor thought not. "The affected areas will turn gangrenous within twenty-four hours. It would be a kindness to perform the operation now." But Joe would not allow it. Calvin was undressed and put to bed. Dr. Whaley promised to return the following afternoon, left Joe at Calvin's bedside. Joe felt empty, drained of all response. He looked at Calvin, looked at the walls and ceiling, told himself it was not his fault Calvin had thrown a fit (if that was what had caused this—it could hardly have been anything else) and lain in a hole for hours while Joe blithely chiselled and gouged in the warmth of the parlour. He fell asleep in a chair.

Whaley was proved right; by the time he returned, the flesh on Calvin's fingers and ear was beginning to blacken.

Calvin had still not opened his eyes; his throat produced a bubbling sound. "Pneumonia," said Whaley. Joe reluctantly granted permission for the minor amputations. The operation was performed with very little loss of blood. Joe went outside and was sick, returned and asked what chance Calvin had for survival. "Very little," said Whaley, who had never in his professional or personal life expressed sorrow over the demise (imminent or accomplished) of the mentally retarded. He knew very well that Calvin's epilepsy and his backwardness were two separate things, a double burden; the doctor had never bothered to explain this, and Joe believed the fits were a part of Calvin's general malaise. Dr. Whaley wished medical science would perfect a method for the recognition and weeding out of the subnormal or afflicted immediately following birth, in order that they might be humanely gassed or strangled to avoid a lifetime's trouble and expense to parents and asylums. These views did not conflict with or refute his Hippocratic oath; the doctor was seventy years old, had seen too much of what is not pleasant to look upon. He planned to retire within a year, already felt himself removed from the endless woes of his patients. Nothing more could be done for Calvin Puckett— what's more, nothing should. "I'm sorry," he said. It was a lacklustre attempt at a bedside manner, and Joe did not respond.

Calvin lingered for two days more. Joe waited for the flickering of an eyelid, a few seconds of awareness, was not granted his wish, was not even in the room when Calvin died. When Joe discovered he was alone he covered Calvin's bandaged head and went to wait in the living room for the doctor's regular afternoon visit.

Joe bought one of Joshua Pike's cheapest coffins. He meant no disrespect by this, nor was he parsimonious by nature; he simply found the custom of burying a hundred dollars' worth of wood and silk and metal along with the dead a ludicrous waste. He refused Pike's offer to embalm the deceased at a bargain price. Why delay the inevitable? Calvin was not there any more, and his decaying body was no hallowed shrine to be maintained with chemical vigilance against his return. Pike found Joe's attitude morally offensive and financially unrewarding.

A grave was dug by the blackberry patch; Joe did not want Calvin buried in the cemetery alongside the citizens of Valley Forge. He lowered the coffin singlehandedly; at the last moment Joe's foot slipped and the ropes were released involuntarily. The coffin fell several feet, landed on its side. Swearing, Joe climbed down into the grave to set it squarely on its back. He hoped Calvin had not been left in some ungainly position as a result of the accident; the coffin was large, Calvin small—there was room to move about in there. Joe thought of returning to the house to fetch back a claw hammer, wrenching the lid off to ensure Calvin was not preparing for eternity in some ungainly pose, knuckles jammed up against the side of his face, for example, or a hand resting on his crotch. He decided against it; that kind of fussing was as pathetic as a Christian's dreams of life everlasting among the clouds. Calvin was dead meat. Bury him. Joe did it. He then unfastened the harps from their bleak perches, flung them to the ground; they twanged resentfully on impact, and when all three had been dislodged he smashed them to pieces, then set the pieces alight. This was a funeral pyre of sorts, the only ceremony Joe could think of. He had been denied Calvin's company, so the ridge must be denied its eerie wind-song; such sounds were somehow inappropriate without the stained-glass window in any case.

Calvin had been buried at noon. At two a horseman approached the house; for the first time since his daughter had aborted here, the Reverend Dr. Lyman Wilkes had chosen to visit the ridge. Joe went out on to the porch as Wilkes reined in, not to greet him but to prevent him from reaching the front door, from which position Joe would have felt more or less obliged to allow him in. He knew the purpose of Wilkes' visit, did not want him even to dismount.

"Good afternoon to you, Mr. Cobden." Wilkes had in recent years grown his beard to biblical length; Joe thought the result a little too knowingly apostolic. He nodded, willing his visitor to go away.

"May I express my condolences. Mr. Puckett was a good man."

Joe's gorge began to rise. How dared this pulpit-pounder assume he knew the least thing about Calvin, the pious prick! Joe would share nothing of Calvin with him. "Was there a reason for your coming all the way out here?"

"Neither Mr. Pike nor the editor of the *Courier* has been given details of the service for Mr. Puckett."

"There isn't going to be one. He's already under the sod."

"Mr. Cobden, you have done a dead man a great wrong."

"Horseshit. I put him above the water-table, and that's as much as any dead man can ask."

"I appreciate your wish that Mr. Puckett be buried up here, but if I could just be allowed to read a lesson over the grave—nothing elaborate—with just yourself standing by. . . ."

Wilkes began to dismount.

"Don't get down!"

Wilkes hesitated, one leg suspended over his horse's rump. Joe's hands were thrust deep inside his pockets, but might just as well have been aiming a gun. "I'm telling you, stay on that horse."

"You're not behaving in a reasonable manner, Mr. Cobden."

"Get out of here, and if I ever catch you snooping around trying to find where he's buried so you can spout Godbabble over him I'll put a bullet in you."

Wilkes retreated. Joe went inside.

That was a Tuesday. On Wednesday, Sheriff Lafferty rode up to the porch, dismounted and knocked on the door. Joe answered, barred his entry to the hallway.

"Got a bone to pick with you, Indian."

Joe said nothing, knew he must say as little as possible if trouble was not to erupt.

"Reverend Wilkes says you threatened him. Did you?"

"I told him to mind his own business."

"Dead men *are* his business. Unless you're born in a te-pee you don't go burying a dead man without a little religion to go along with it."

"I disagree."

"You can be disagreeable as you please, but that white man whose house you've been living in all these years, he deserves something better than what you gave him. Here's how it'll be, Indian: you apologise to the Reverend and let him speak his piece and everyone'll be happy. If you don't, I'll make your life a misery, understand? I don't like you, Cobden, and seeing as you're living in a house that isn't yours I figure it wouldn't take too much legalising to throw you out of it."

"The house is Noah's. He'd want me to stay—at least, until he gets back."

"That could be anytime from now till kingdom come. I'm going to get the Reverend back up here and you're going to apologise nice and clear and then show us where Puckett's been planted so Wilkes can do what he's paid to do. That's a good way to do things, don't you think? Being in public office you need to know folks approve; makes you feel good about doing your job, makes it all worthwhile, know what I mean?"

"One of these days I'll spit on the sidewalk," said Joe, "then you can hang me."

Perce Lafferty looked at him for a long while, employing the famous stare he used on drunks and potential trouble-makers in town, the one known as "Perce's pissed-off puss". Annoyingly, it appeared to have no intimidating effect on Joe. "I could squash you so easy, Cobden, just grind you under like a bug for that smart lip of yours. Reason I don't is because you're pitiful. I wouldn't want to squash a hump-back. Folks might say I took advantage, and I don't want that. But don't you ever give me backtalk again or I'll do it anyway, understand?"

Joe knew a nod would not be enough, and silence would

be suicidal. "Yes," he said, barely able to push the word through a throat congested with rage. Blood hummed in his ears. If Lafferty made the least move towards him, Joe would not hesitate, would knock him down, big though he was, and throttle the life from him. His fingers squirmed with repressed longing to encircle Perce's neck and squeeze. . . .

Lafferty went to his horse, mounted. "Back soon, Hump," he said casually, and rode off. No one had called Joe by that name since his youth. Only half-aware of what he was doing, Joe went to his room, loaded his Sharpe's, then sat on the porch to await the sheriff's return. He was going to put a bullet in Perce Lafferty's head the moment he entered the yard. Joe did not think of the consequences, thought only of the fierce pleasure it would give him to see Perce's head explode like a dropped pumpkin. He warmed himself before this image for half an hour, then admitted his folly. He selected a knothole in a distant tree as representative of Perce's eye-socket, aimed the Sharpe's and had the satisfaction of seeing the knothole disappear. Then he hurriedly did what he should have done half an hour before.

Lafferty and Wilkes returned in the afternoon. Joe guided them to the site of the dog's grave. He had refilled the hole, arranged the dirt on top into an oblong mound, bound two sticks to form a cross. Lafferty sank a speculative toecap into the loose earth.

"This it?"

"This is it." Joe removed his hat, obliging the sheriff to do the same. Perce felt he was being mocked somehow.

"Let's hear that apology before we get started."

Joe turned to Wilkes. "How's your daughter? In good health, I hope, not like a certain occasion a few years back when she couldn't keep anything inside her."

"No apology is necessary," said Wilkes. "I would like to proceed."

Perce shrugged, irritated that Joe was to be spared this added humiliation, and by Joe's enquiry about Sadie Wilkes. What the hell right did an Indian have to ask about the girl like that, and why hadn't Wilkes chewed him out over it? If Joe had made reference to one of Perce's daughters throwing up, Perce would straighten his hump for him in around half a minute. He supposed this was an example of Christian cheek-turning; it made him want to throw up himself, and he decided Wilkes wasn't half the man people reckoned he was. Perce brooded over the insult while Wilkes did what he had come for. There was a smirk on Joe Cobden's face Perce didn't like. God *damn* Wilkes for not wanting that apology! The Indian wouldn't have smirked any after having to eat crow. Perce had expected a full measure of satisfaction from this business, and had been drastically shortchanged.

He refused to talk to Wilkes on the way back to town. Somehow Joe Cobden had made fools of them, he was sure of it, but could not quite fathom how it had been done. One day he and the Indian would come face to face over something, and Perce knew who the smirker would be when it happened. He looked forward to it the way a child anticipates Christmas.

On the ridge, Joe tore the makeshift cross apart and set about getting drunk.

CHAPTER THIRTY-NINE

On a Sunday in April, a day bright with sunlight, Phoebe walked away from the town. Her steps took her south, past several farms, and out to the open prairie. She walked for almost two hours before tiring. Around her lay nothing but grass, green with recent rains; the sky had been washed by breezes to a cerulean hue along the horizon, deepening to azure directly above her head, a blue so intense as to be depthless, without a scrap of cloud lending scale to its immensity. Phoebe threw back her head, felt herself absorbed in turn by an emptiness so vast it exuded a tangible presence, within and without her. She stretched her arms, spun several times, induced the delightful giddiness familiar to children who whirl like dervishes for the excitation it brings to their senses, felt the rushing of blood, the thrill of life sent tingling to her very fingertips. She fell down, dizzy beyond standing, laughed at the swirling sky, felt nauseous momentarily as her brain seemed to shift within her skull. She gripped the earth for equilibrium, sank her fingers into the spinning grassy plate at whose centre she lay spreadeagled.

Her heart calmed at last, Phoebe closed her eyes, basked in sunlight and tranquillity. Above her a hawk wheeled in endless circles. It pleased her to imagine herself in the vastness of some uninhabited continent; nothing lay over the low rises surrounding her but more grass, more sky, an ever-receding horizon. She would walk for ever below a sun that never set, her body requiring neither sustenance nor sleep; she would revel in her aloneness, rejoice in simple freedom. But what a joke that was; Phoebe knew herself to be tangled still in the phantom umbilical cord linking her to Jessica; her wanderings would be confined, as always, to the same dreary yard, the cramped boundaries of the house on Decatur Street. She had accustomed herself to this life of circumscribed rote, learned to savour those few moments of release (as on this occasion) from the bondage of the heart. Accustomed, but not reconciled. Considering all this, her mood became one of numbness, a smearing and blurring of expectations, a refutation of those dreams common to all people, dreams of happiness and fulfilment; circumstance dictated that these things were not for Phoebe, not until changes of a radical nature occurred, changes beyond Phoebe's ability to instigate. I'm a prisoner, she thought, a prisoner whose crime was to be born inside a prison.

Warmed by the sun, she slept, was awakened late in the afternoon by an oppressive stillness. The air seemed thick, damp, as though drawing oily sweat from the ground, and moved not at all. The zephyr breeze that had accompanied Phoebe's stroll on to the prairie had died away to a stillness and silence so profound it drew the ear's attention. Phoebe stood awkwardly, stiff after lying so long. The back of her left hand was corrugated with the overlapping imprint of grass stems. She fingered her stippled flesh, felt the blood drain sluggishly from her head; she had risen too quickly, had to pause and take several deep breaths before looking around her. She must be dreaming, for the sky was pale green! Had some trick of the light caused grass to be reflected in the air? But the sun was gone; at the hem of Phoebe's skirt no shadow lay. Where was the sun? She turned. The sky behind her to the south-west had been swallowed by darkness, a turgid inkstain spreading even as she stared, unbreathing, awed by the threatening might of the thing. Its advancing edges were no roiling mass of thunderheads, no black anvil discharging lightning and reverberation—there was instead a seeping, creeping efflorescence silently, greedily consuming the pale green sky, a vast shadow stealing across a viridian field. Phoebe felt her eardrums flex; a vague throbbing had established itself in the centre of her forehead, and for one nonsensical moment she believed she was about to sprout the horn of a unicorn, or a third eye. She realised she was afraid, but could not move; her legs were very far away, helplessly swathed in the heavy cloth of her skirts. Be sensible, she told herself; if it rains, you have nowhere to shelter in any case. She stayed rooted to the faint impression her body had left in the prairie grass, and waited.

Now that it was passing overhead, the amorphous mass revealed details of itself, vague puckerings and swirlings and tumblings, a cauldron of quietness, drawn like a blanket across the world. Standing in the twilight of its shadow Phoebe shivered, felt the skin of her entire body dimple, whether from fear or sudden cold she could not say. Her eyes roamed the underbelly of cloud, searched its shifting fluidity. Where was the lightning? But there was not the least flicker of light, and still no sound. Thinking herself deaf, Phoebe clapped her hands once, clumsily; the noise produced by her striking palms came to her as if from a distance, muffled by the very air between. She was drenched in sweat, her legs trembling.

And now came a different kind of movement from the darkness overhead, a great swirling, a gradual lowering of a part of its bulk, seemingly many miles distant; the thing was giving birth, stretching to reach the earth, and its spawn was a gyrating part of itself, rushing in circles beneath its cloudy parent, a thrashing funnel of air descending with magisterial gravity, lengthening, becoming a finger that strained to touch the land, and there came to Phoebe the sound of *power* as its tip neared the ground—a ragged droning, the voice of a billion bees, a many-throated voice, louder now, humming, snarling, grinding in terrible unison. Earth and sky were linked. Instantly the spinning tube sucked into its howling intestine dust and debris, darkened its coiling, undulating silhouette with matter. Its voice grew to a banshee wail, declared itself the god Tornado, whose twin dominions, above and below, support its one mighty reaching arm. The hollow fingertip began to scrawl its heedless signature of destruction. Sustained by onward momentum, thickening, becoming darker and more distinct by the moment as tons of soil were sucked up and whirled skyward, the god aimed itself at Phoebe Pike.

She knew the thing was bound to kill her, was somehow not alarmed; to become a part of the tornado's airborne plunder seemed to her natural, a necessary offering to the vortex, the unknowable void. A voice within her screamed Run! Hide! and was ignored, supplanted by a deeper, calmer dictate: Yield. Phoebe's fright scattered in all directions, left a tight smile upon her face—If it touches me I die; if not, I'll live for ever. Her skirts fluttered and stirred as the air around her was drawn to the screaming perpendicularity of dust and darkness, feeding it, augmenting it on its wayward passage across Kansas. Phoebe set her feet firmly apart, held her arms at her sides, and the trip-hammer rhythm of her heartbeat accelerated beyond excitement, vibrated with the ground beneath her, lent its insignificant drumming to the ten thousand steam whistles blasting from the twisting, rearing tube. It loomed above her, a mile-high serpent, head hidden by cloud. She pulled off her flapping bonnet, tossed it to the wind, saw it sail and fall and roll along the ground, strings flailing as it was drawn to the roaring snout (close by now; she could see the path of its hungry orifice moving speedily down the slope of a rise half a mile distant), a swirling spiral that dredged a shallow channel in the earth one hundred yards across.

Phoebe's hair flung out its pins and streamed forward across her cheeks and brow, became a snapping pennant before her face; she could see nothing through the long, whipping hanks, felt herself drawn in the direction of their reaching—one step, two steps, three. . . . And she fell, was pulled from her feet and thrown to the ground, face down in supplication to force beyond imagining, deafened by its fury. The hem of her skirt was whisked along her spine to flap about her ears; particles of dust stung the backs of her naked legs, scoured her white skin. Phoebe waited for deliverance, waited for that irresistible hand to snatch her away.

But the willing sacrifice was refused, for this whirlwind

did not exact tribute in human life, deviated from its seemingly preordained path and swerved to the east. It would continue across two counties more before collapsing like a broken column, tearing itself apart, spilling its centrifugal energies into the surrounding air, becoming a thing of rotation without an axis, without any hold in earth or sky, fated to spin itself out of existence, leaving nothing but a twisted veil of dust suspended in the evening air.

Phoebe lay where she had been thrown for many minutes after the tornado passed her by, face hidden by tumbled hair, listening with quiet amazement to the beating of her own heart, questioning her survival—or was this place of rough earth and grass she clung to the far side of the Vale? Would she, when finally mustering the courage to open her eyes, see Kansas or some other, ethereal landscape? Phoebe raised her head, blinked, greeted the familiar rolling rises with a wan smile, reminded herself she did not believe in an afterlife. She stood, pushed the skirt from her shoulders, felt the stinging of tiny lacerations across her calves. Alive. She felt wondrously calm, stood for several minutes more, experiencing the sensations concordant with inhabiting a physical body.

The tornado was a great distance off already, its voice a thin sighing. The ceiling of cloud parted and the sun reappeared, a little begrimed, its splendour dimmed by hovering particles of dust. Phoebe found her bonnet but did not put it on, allowed her tangled mane to fall where it would. She imagined this must be how Robinson Crusoe felt after being washed ashore; delivered from death, wordlessly grateful. Had she truly wished herself gone—dead? Viewed through retrospective eyes her defiance of the wind (which had somehow become surrender) had been nothing short of suicidal. Where on earth had such feelings sprung from? Phoebe knew she would never willingly give up her life; even the miserable existence she endured in Valley Forge was a precious thing when compared to the incomprehensible nothingness of death. Her behaviour had been disturbingly atypical, but her exultation at having lived proved too strong for the intrusion of darker thoughts.

She inspected the tornado's path, a broad swathe of mangled growth; in some areas the soil had been sucked from around tenacious grass roots, left them exposed like mangroves in a swamp. Phoebe imagined herself stripped in similar fashion, not of clothing and flesh, but pared by her unhappiness to a knotty, fibrous inner self, a thing of endurance and pride, a limpet clinging steadfastly, stubbornly to a wave-battered rock. She had no cause to doubt her own strength; it was there, inside, a sturdy taproot of courage. It had always been there; like herself, it was impatiently waiting to unfurl its hidden colours.

Phoebe told her tale to no one, relived her encounter with the tornado many times over in the privacy of her room, congratulated herself on having drawn from it a very secret kind of strength. She nursed the experience thus for a week or so, then found she wished to share it with someone; to find a rare and lovely shell on a beach is all very fine but, having admired it, the finder's next thought is to show the thing to others in order to confirm what is already known: that it is beautiful.

There was only one person who would understand. She went to the house on the ridge, knocked and was admitted. "I should like to see one of your wooden Indians, please." Joe led her to the parlour, where she walked several times around the newest chief. "My opinion is inexpert," she said, "but I believe you have a great talent for proportion and drama. Even standing still he appears ready to attack anyone refusing a cigar."

"Thank you."

He made coffee; they sat and drank. Phoebe expressed her sorrow over Calvin. Joe thanked her again. A silence fell between them. Now or never, she thought, and told him all, haltingly, self-consciously. Joe did not know what to say. He appreciated the candour with which she had revealed a very private part of herself, but could not help wondering if she had done so with the expectation of hearing similar revelations from him in return. She would not get them; he would confine his conversation to the general, avoid the particular. "Everyone has latent strength and . . . uh . . . fortitude in them. It takes an act of will, or maybe something like what happened to you, to make them aware of it."

He stumbled over his tongue, felt a fool, but what else could he have said? He did not want to be told things of a confidential nature, would have preferred that Phoebe discuss other matters. He understood her turmoil and its strange resolution perfectly, but did not want to hear more; let her keep herself to herself—any further divulgence from her and she would expect reciprocal confessions from him (to Joe, talk of one's private life was a confession, that is, an admission of *weakness* rather than any Catholic sense of sin or wrongdoing) and he was not prepared to co-operate.

"Have you ever undergone anything of the like, Joe?"

This was the moment he had dreaded; she wanted him to tell her that being a hunchback had blighted his life until he reached grimly inside to that deep well of endurance, dabbled his soul in springs of resolution and intrepidity, survived to reveal all before a suitable audience, the one before him now. Joe felt a chill take hold of him; she wanted to *know,* and by knowing to possess. In fact Phoebe wanted nothing of the sort, wished only to share her singular experience. Like many a man unacquainted with women, Joe regarded her as a spiritual predator, lulling him with personal confidences in order to suck his blood. For all that he liked her, even admired her, Joe could not allow himself to forget she was a woman, a thing for ever denied him. He knew she did not want his twisted body, was convinced she needed, in her loneliness, somehow to acquaint herself with Joe's innermost feelings. Well, he wasn't giving anything away, not today, not ever. Once he told her everything (as he once had to Peter Winstanley) she would lose respect for him, think him a weakling for having admitted to past unhappiness, and Joe would lose respect for himself. Phoebe Pike was Circe, urging him to quaff the cup of intimacy before reducing him to swinedom. He would not do it.

"No."

The curtness of his reply shamed him. He could see she was offended and confused, but he would not weaken; if he gave an ounce of himself to this woman, he would be compelled to present her with all one hundred and fifty-seven pounds on a silver platter. Look at me. I'm an ugly cripple no woman ever wanted. I howl for love that will never come, therefore I howl even louder to drive it away. But now you, *you* have breached my defences, torn down the ramparts built a little higher with every passing year of my miserable life. Let me pull apart my chest, show you my valiantly beating heart, the heart *you* want to hold in your hand. I want you to have it. Take it! Take all of me, every pathetic, squirming, secret humiliation, every quaking fear, every moment of swallowed pride. Soothe my trembling limbs, assure me you understand, tell me I'm a man despite all. *Make me stop hurting!* And I'll fall at your feet like a grateful dog and fawn and whine with gratitude, and lick your hand as the collar is fastened around my neck.

"No, I never did."

Phoebe reddened, felt she had been put in her place, as though she had committed some inexcusable *faux pas.* And it had been deliberate; there was no avoiding that conclusion. Joe Cobden had locked himself away behind an iron door, and all because Phoebe had offered him a chance to speak his mind before a sympathetic friend. Friend? He probably thought her nothing more than a meddling female. She was disappointed at the predictable nature of his response, this hasty raising of the masculine drawbridge to ensure no womanly eye glimpsed the crumbling keep within. She had not wished to pry, but obviously he believed she had. Perhaps she should have anticipated this from someone with Joe's unique affliction, should have couched her question in terms less open to misinterpretation. But none of this could be spoken of, for to do so would be to admit that she now understood exactly why he had shut himself away from her, and she did not want to admit to him (or to herself) that she thought of Joe as a hunchback. The impasse thus imposed upon their meeting appeared insoluble. Both sat in uncomfortable silence for some minutes. Joe felt guilty and resentful; he hadn't invited her here, hadn't asked to hear about abstract offerings to windy gods. Why should he have to listen to talk of pseudo-mystical emotions? He wanted her to go away.

Phoebe attempted further conversation on the subject of woodcarving; she thought of art as a glow-worm shedding light in the dungeon of everyday life, envied Joe his ability to create. "I'm not an artist," he said. "I make cigar-store Indians." Phoebe was thoroughly humiliated by this unmerited treatment, disappointed herself by enduring it, by not having the strength to walk out the door. Was this the same man who used to sweep his hat off to her in the store and make amusing remarks that bore the stamp of having been perfected for her alone? He sat there, lumpish and dull and uncommunicative, not even looking in her direction, wishing her gone; yes, wishing her gone.

She stood. "I must be getting back to town."

He walked her to the front door, did not offer to hitch the wagon.

"You'll tell me when Noah returns?"

"All right." He felt terrible, knew he had driven her out, did not know how he could make amends, was not even sure, in the blackness of his mood, that he wanted to. He had behaved like a churl toward this fine woman, and now it was too late to apologise; no, not too late, not while she stood before him. But he said nothing, retained his selfish and unfeeling attitude out of sheer stubbornness, fully cognisant of the nature of his crime. He knew already that he would get drunk tonight.

"Well, goodbye." She offered her hand.

He took it. "Goodbye."

Phoebe crossed the porch, descended the steps, walked across the yard to the ridge trail, and was gone. Joe had held his breath from the moment she turned away to the moment she disappeared. He resisted the urge to run after her. I've destroyed something, he thought, and indeed he had. Creative, she had called him, and he had taken her gentleness and intelligence and crushed these virtues as he would an annoying insect. He was the lowest of men. She would not be coming back, was too proud to revisit a place in which she had been snubbed so openly. Every step she took along the trail widened the gap between them; once widened beyond shouting distance it could never be closed again. He let it widen, loathing himself. He could not blame Calvin's death for his boorish behaviour, could not blame Phoebe, either. Shame was too mild a word for the demons clawing at Joe's insides; he could not bear to look at the trail, at the last place he had seen her, allowed his eyes to drift across the yard instead, unable to focus on any one thing. The weight of his body was intolerable; he had to sit on the porch steps. He stared at his boots for a long time.

On her way along the trail, Phoebe remembered the wonderful stained-glass window by the blackberry patch, and went to see it for the second and last time. In her present state of mind it struck her as appropriate that the window was gone, the Aeolian harps silenced, the ground bearing the unmistakable outline of a grave. She continued homeward, telling herself that weeping was the kind of thing a foolish woman, the kind Joe Cobden obviously thought she was, would indulge in. So she did not weep, and her tears were dammed against a future time when weeping might be considered acceptable to herself.

CHAPTER FORTY

Fifty-three weeks after his departure from Valley Forge, Noah returned, stepped down from an eastbound train on a day of blazing heat. He wore a suit and stylish derby, and the stationmaster did not recognise him. Noah strolled along Decatur, suitcase in hand, watching the faces of those approaching him along the sidewalk. Several people obviously knew who he was, but no one detained him or spoke. This did not surprise him, and the habitual sneer soon was fastened upon his face. He thrived on this kind of rejection; it reinforced his belief that he, Noah Puckett, was unwelcome here for the simple reason that these yokels were jealous of him, mistrustful of him. And why? Because not only was he different, he was *better,* a superior being altogether. And they knew it, the clodhoppers. He had been to the shores of the Pacific while the rest of the populace had been lucky if they crossed the county line. Let them ignore him to his face; he knew they stopped and turned to stare at his back after he had passed them by. That was recognition enough. He had a clutch of cigars in one pocket and a nickel-plated derringer in another, and carried himself with a confidence tending towards hubris. He was sixteen.

Noah stopped beside the rectory yard when he saw Sadie Wilkes by the front fence, weeding around the stunted rose bushes her mother had planted. Noah set down his case, lifted his hat. "Hello, Miss Wilkes. A pleasure to see your lovely face again." It was done with an aplomb that surprised even Noah. He wondered what to say next. He could not have picked a prettier girl to show off to, nor, unfortunately, a less responsive one. "Bad weather for the garden," he said, and she nodded cautiously. Two women on the opposite sidewalk had stopped to watch. Catching sight of them from the corner of his eye, Noah decided he would give them something to talk about. Stooping, he threw open his suitcase and took from it a broad, flat paper package bound in string. "This is for you," he said, thrusting it at Sadie.

She accepted it awkwardly, confused. She knew who he was, of course, but did not understand why he should have given her a gift; nor was there time to find out via pencil and paper, for Noah had snapped shut his case and was already tipping his hat. " 'Bye, Miss Wilkes." And he was off down the street again, tramping west for the ridge. Sadie watched him go, looked again at the package; even the paper was exotic, neither white nor brown, but purple! What could be inside? The two women who had observed the presentation were crossing the street; notorious gossips both, they lifted their skirts to hasten their progress, reminding Sadie of vultures flapping along the ground towards a carcass. She deliberately turned from the fence and followed the brick path to the house, went inside without a backward glance. The two ladies were outraged; one called her "Miss Stuck-up" and the other "a minx, just a spoiled minx".

The road from town was unchanged, the ridge trail also, but for the peculiar propensity of both to lengthen on a hot day. Noah's elastic-sided boots, cream coloured, chisel-toed, were layered in dust and pinching badly by the time he reached the porch and set his suitcase down. He needed to wait a little before entering, and so placed himself beside the case, mopped his brow with a lawn handkerchief. From within the house came an unfamiliar sound, a tap-tap-tapping, rather like that newfangled contraption the typewriter; Noah had seen such a device in San Francisco, had even shared the bed of the young lady, the "typist", who operated it with such nimble fingers. Noah had seen and done quite a bit that was new to him since leaving Valley Forge.

Joe heard the thump of the suitcase, thought at first it was a footstep, halted work in anticipation of a knock at the door; when it was not forthcoming he resumed chipping at the fringes on a set of leggings. He worked another ten minutes before hearing a faint sound on the porch, the sound of someone moving. Phoebe Pike, he thought. She knows I'm here, must have heard me working. Why didn't she knock and be done with it instead of waiting out there? Steeling himself, readying either an apology for his behaviour at their last meeting or an iron face, depending upon how the situation struck him, he went to the front door and opened it. Noah turned to look at him, a cigar jutting from his teeth. Joe required a few seconds before realising who this nattily dressed young man was. Noah hesitated for as long as he thought necessary to establish that he rose promptly for no man, then stood. He had grown an incredible three inches, had thickened proportionately, looked older than his years.

"How goes it, Joe?"

"All right. Coming in?"

"It has to be cooler in there. I'd forgotten what a Kansas summer is like."

They went to the kitchen. Joe began making lemonade, knew the boy watched him critically, thinking this a womanish task for a man to perform. Fuck him; it was too hot for coffee. Joe felt less nervous at this long-awaited reunion than he had thought would be the case, was not intimidated by Noah's improved appearance and fancy clothes, suspected they were intended to impress; and as for the cigar—Joe knew the stink of a ten-cent stogie masquerading as Havana when he smelled it. How to open a conversation? First rule: Don't make a fuss. The little bastard wasn't going to get any red carpet treatment hereabouts, not after skulking off that way. But recriminations could wait until later, when Joe could really work up his anger and say exactly what he thought. Such a confrontation must not be rushed into. He squeezed lemons with murderous intensity.

"No horse?"

"Sold him in Denver pretty soon after I left. You don't need a horse to get around this country any more. Sold the

Remington as well; too bulky. A pistol's handier, or a good knife.''

"My, we must have been moving in dangerous circles this past year."

"You might say that."

Noah had tried his hand at mining in Denver, quit after two days, bought a ticket to San Francisco; there he had been in turn a printer's apprentice (one week) freight-loader (four days) newspaper-vendor (the *Bulletin*— three weeks) newspaper copy-boy (the *Bulletin*—again—the typewriter, the typist, not a bad job until Noah insisted he be promoted to cub reporter, an impulsive act resulting in instant dismissal; time on the job—two months) and then three tough months with the fishing fleet. He quit when his accumulated wages allowed it, loafed around the docks, tried to rekindle a friendship with the typist (thirty-two years old; she had thought him "too cute to resist" but lost interest once she had taken his virginity; besides, one of the reporters was sharing her bed on a regular basis now) and when Noah's hopes in that direction ran out at around the same time as his cash he found employment again, the worst job of all, in a fish-market. There he consoled himself with Daisy (seventeen; she thought he might be persuaded to marry her so she could quit the market and live on what he earned). Noah encouraged this wild fantasy until his pocket was again filled with hard-earned money, quit when Daisy informed him she was pregnant. The market job had lasted almost three months, and Noah was more than ready to wash the smell of fish from his hair and clothing for ever.

He exchanged that odour for a blend of dung, canvas, straw and greasepaint, joined a carnival working the Salinas and San Joaquin valleys, attempted to ingratiate himself with the trick rider (Angelica; aptly named, uninterested in youths with close-set eyes) and having been rebuffed, made overtures to the Fat Lady (Wilma—three hundred and thirty-four pounds, interested only in food). Noah's penis was forever hard or semi-tumescent, a divining rod directing him towards this female, then that, begging admission.

In desperation he again pestered Angelica, was soundly thrashed by her father (the lion tamer) and took his revenge on the night he left by opening the lions' cage. (The beasts, three in number, replete with a recent meal of raw beef, left their dwelling and strolled around the carnival site for a short while before falling asleep together beneath a tree to dream of Africa; they were driven sulkily back to their cage the following morning.) Noah returned to San Francisco, decided it was time, after a year away, to revisit Valley Forge, catch up on the local news (that was a joke—ha, ha!) then head east to see what that half of the country had to offer.

Joe listened to this story with mounting resentment. He was jealous. The boy had led a life of adventure, crammed a hefty slice of living into twelve short months, had not been seriously hurt or made unhappy while so doing. And, above all, he had slept with women, with *two* women! Joe had had a few adventures of his own at Noah's age, but had not experienced that ultimate sensation, never would. Jealousy, plain and simple, too obvious to be denied. He swallowed his vexation, slammed a pitcher of lemonade on the table. "Drink up. You must be thirsty after all that excitement."

"Where's the old man?"

"Dead. The glasses are on the shelf."

"Dead?"

"You heard me."

"How . . . how'd he die?"

Joe told him everything, from Calvin's non-appearance at suppertime to the building of the fake burial-mound. He fetched glasses himself. He'd put a lot of muscle into that lemonade; it wasn't to be wasted. Noah stared at the pitcher, unseeing. Joe hoped he felt guilty. He drank two glasses; it needed more sugar, but he did not want to appear fussy at a time like this.

"I wish . . . I wish I had've been here."

"Do you, now? Do you really?"

"I mean it. I just . . . wish I'd been here."

"Well, you weren't."

"It wasn't my fault he died," said Noah.

"I'm not saying it was. Are you going to drink some of this? It won't stay cool for long."

Noah poured a glass for himself, sipped listlessly. "So the place is mine now." There was a note of abstract speculation in his voice.

"I was wondering when you'd realise that. The house and the ridge, all yours. What are you going to do, sell them?" Joe was deliberately blunt, wanted the subject out on the table before them. He did not want to leave this place, had to know what he might expect from this capricious boy who had impregnated a young girl and blithely left town, ignored his responsibilities as though the feelings of others were of no account. Joe hated to be held thus, in another's palm, subject to his whim; it was humiliating. He had wiped this selfish monster's ass times aplenty, taught him his ABC, acquainted him with certain facts—the world is a sphere, Leonidas and the Spartans defended Thermopylae against the Persians, blue and yellow make green—had been all that a father should be; and now, rather than hastening to assure Joe his tenure here was secure (if that was what Joe wanted) the little prick in his arrogance simply drained his glass, wiped his lips and said: "Maybe."

It was a calculated challenge. Joe hadn't been sufficiently impressed by Noah's tale, was downright nasty about Calvin, insinuating his death had been Noah's fault even if he hadn't the guts to say so out loud; well, he could just cool his heels a while and wait for a decision. Noah wasn't going to make things easier for him by making up his mind on the spot. Noah was calling the shots here. It was his house after all.

"What was that noise I heard before, that tapping?"

"Me. I make wooden statues nowadays."

"Statues?"

"In the parlour. See for yourself."

Noah did so, returned to the kitchen. "Did you really do that?"

"I already said so."

"What'll you do when it's finished?"

"Sell it like all the rest."

"You don't chop wood any more?"

Joe related the story of the expanded city limits and the new trade practices. "I'm glad it happened. I make more money this way."

"How much?"

"Enough. Listen, Perce Lafferty hates me. He's as good as threatened to have me thrown out of here because I don't own the place. So long as you're around he can't do anything, but when you go he's liable to try something. If you don't want to sell the place to me, at least make out some kind of legal contract that says I can stay here."

"You *want* to stay here?"

"It's where I live."

"But there's a whole world out there."

Joe took a breath, prepared himself to tell Noah he was thirty-five years old, did not want to start anew elsewhere, had invested a sizeable portion of his life in this location, did not wish to relinquish his attachment to the ridge. He was a hunchback approaching middle age, a man without roots anywhere but this place of no worldly significance.

"I like it here," he said.

Noah snorted. "You can have it."

"Literally or figuratively?"

Noah ignored this, ground out the cigar stub in his glass, a sight that made Joe wince, as Noah had known it would. We're drawing the boundaries, thought Joe, chalking the circle and getting ready to fight. I'm beholden to someone half my age, can't attack him outright. Kid gloves, that's the way. I want this place.

"I'm tired," Noah yawned. "Hope you haven't sold my bed."

"It's still there."

Noah went upstairs to sleep away the rest of the afternoon. Joe did not feel like continuing his work but did so anyway; he did not want Noah to think he was too scared of the boy to risk disturbing his sleep, and so resumed the tap-tap-tapping of his craft. Noah slept through the noise anyway.

In the evening they ate in silence, neither having much appetite. Noah went upstairs, opened his suitcase, returned with two packages done up in coloured paper. "Presents," he announced. Joe unwrapped the first, a glass ball containing a shrunken landscape of pine trees and snow. "Shake it," said Noah. Joe did so, and the whiteness around the pines swirled to life, eddied among the boughs and slowly settled. "It's got water in it," explained Noah. "It was for Calvin. This one's for you." Joe unwrapped the tapering package, found a long-stemmed, small-bowled pipe and a thumb-sized packet of something solid.

"What's this?"

"Opium. I had it a few times with some of the boys from the *Bulletin*. They knew a place in Chinatown."

"What's it like?"

"Makes you kind of . . . dreamy. You just smoke a little bit at a time."

Noah unwrapped the packet of resinous gum, pinched off a small wad, rolled it into a ball and filled the pipe bowl, offered the stem to Joe. "Here." Joe hesitated. "It's all right. You won't turn into a Chinaman." Joe placed the stem in his mouth. Noah applied a match to the bowl. The opium was at first reluctant to ignite, then began to smoulder. Joe drew the acrid smoke into his lungs in little sips, felt the inside of his mouth protest at the alien taste. It was foul, and he said so. "You'll get used to it," Noah assured him, meaning he presently would not care if it tasted like dogshit.

Joe puffed on, inhaling moderate doses of smoke, felt his scalp begin to crawl with sweat. Was that a result of the opium? It was a hot night anyway; he mustn't be nervous about this, ascribing to the drug those sensations unrelated to its ingestion. Noah was smiling at him. The boy looked almost handsome when he smiled, lost that sly, feral look. He wasn't so bad beneath it all. He'd brought home presents, hadn't he? Calvin would have loved the snowy bubble (or did he mean bauble?), would have shook it and looked at it for hours. Shook and look. Shake and lake. The water inside the glass ball was a kind of lake, wasn't it? He reached for it, arm extending like an elephant's trunk, seized the thing, raised it close to his face. It was very beautiful, the trees so real he could swear their branches moved. Canada. Arctic wastes. He shook the ball, felt his skin prickle with goosebumps as the snow whirled and flowed and sifted steadily down again. He was ignoring the pipe, puffed some more to make amends. The ball became intolerably heavy; every snowflake that settled made it fractionally weightier, until it sat in his palm like a cannonball. He eased it on to the table-top, and the ball's hardwood base met the surface with a thud. Joe wondered if it would sink through and smash upon the floor. He shifted it to what he was sure was a stronger section of the table. The positioning was important. He puffed again, felt air, disappointingly insubstantial air, flood along the stem to cool his mouth.

Noah refilled the pipe. Joe smoked on, gazing at the patterned wallpaper beside him. He had never really noticed it before; fourteen years in the place and he had never given the kitchen wallpaper a second glance. He tried to recall ever having seen wallpaper in another kitchen, but could not; steam and smoke were bad for wallpaper. Alma Puckett must have been a strange sort of woman to paper her kitchen as though it was a living room. Yes, steam had got beneath it here and there, raised wrinkles and puckers, even induced mould, by the look of it; but the patches of mould shifted as he stared, so Joe dismissed them, tried to follow every curlicue of the rambling rose pattern, found he could not keep his eye from glissading away to another part of the wall. Walls were a thing he seldom considered, a foolish oversight on his part, for they *held up the house!* Walls were important, very, very important. Without walls, the house would fall down. You couldn't put up a house without walls. He imagined putting up a roof unsupported by walls. What a ludicrous notion! He laughed somewhere in his belly, a laugh that did not reach his lips, those mobile flanges of flesh still sucking at the pipe, itself a brittle reediness in his hands; he could have snapped it so easily, like a twig.

"Feeling all right?"

A variety of responses sprang into Joe's head, and while he sorted through them, trying to find one wittier than the rest, he lost interest in delivering an answer. That was strange. Or not. Well, Noah would understand if he said nothing. They hadn't spoken much all evening. Why start now? He simply could not be bothered. Noah was removing the pipe from his hands. . . . How dare he! But he was just refilling it, not taking it away as a punishment for not being replied to. He refilled it and began himself to smoke. Joe did not resent the loss of the pipe; the boy deserved it. He wasn't a bad boy, even if he did let lions out of cages. He was practically Joe's son. Joe was practically his father. Joe looked at Noah with a fatherly eye, watched him smoking opium, thought about the two-year-old he had diapered, about the good times when Noah was learning things, then the difficult times when the boy went around as though he'd shat his britches and wasn't allowed to clean them till sundown. And the eventual departure. Joe did not want to think about that, and so did not, thought instead about the homecoming. Noah was back, bearing strange gifts. Joe sank into reverie, drifted along a corridor of many doorways, unfamiliar openings to rooms without walls or ceiling, rooms as big as all the world, filled with sunlight and shadow.

Noah left the kitchen without disturbing Joe, lit a lamp and wandered up to the ridge crest. The blackberry patch, that was where Joe had said Calvin was buried. Noah wanted to see the grave, knew he would have to search for it since Joe had left no marker there for fear of Wilkes and Lafferty finding out they'd been deceived. Joe was a clever bastard all right, Noah granted him that much. He decided he probably liked Joe after all; he hadn't when he first entered the house, had wanted to walk right out again. But things were all right now; the opium had done the trick. Joe was sitting in the kitchen, staring at nothing as though he'd seen the heavenly host come trooping out of the pantry. Joe was all right, had just needed a little Chinese ear-wax to loosen him up.

Fireflies danced around Noah, escorted him up the slope, flitting and darting through the trees, winking like stars, bobbing about the lamp, the brightest firefly of them all. A night breeze stirred the blackjack and cottonwoods, clashed their leafy boughs softly overhead, cooled the opium sweat on Noah's brow. It was a macabre business, going in darkness to visit his father's grave, and it appealed to him very much; Noah prided himself on a penchant for the unlikely, the bizarre. This was one of the moments of his life he would remember always; there were already plenty of similar moments, would be plenty more, an endless chain of memories. He would forget none of them, for their importance lay in the fact that they were linked to none other than Noah Puckett; no doubt the memories of lesser beings faded quickly, being of no importance to anyone, not even the memory-keeper. It was wonderful to feel his own uniqueness flow through him like a bracingly cold stream.

And there was the blackberry patch rising before him in the lamplight, a frozen wave of briars, a tangle of arching stems freighted with thorns, its berries long since pecked away by birds. Had he ever eaten the fruit himself? He seemed to recall trying it once, a long time ago; it had been bitter, not the way ripe berries are supposed to taste, and of course he had been nowhere near the patch since reburying Sadie Wilkes' baby under the bell in its hollow heart. How many years ago had that been? But arithmetical reckoning was beyond him.

He began searching for the grave, found it after five minutes that seemed like hours. It was a sad thing to see, just the raw, settled mound with a few small green shoots taking hold. Noah tried to feel what he thought he should feel, was aware only of the euphoric drifting of his disordered senses. Beneath his feet lay Calvin, poor mad Calvin, and Noah could not muster a single tear. Ahh, what the hell. He turned from the grave, walked face first into an idea of great daring. Why not crawl inside the blackberry patch the way he'd done when little, and see if the bell was still there? There was no reason why it should not be, but Noah wanted to be sure, wanted somehow to link himself with that other, younger Noah Puckett who used to play his secret games here. He would not dig up the baby's bones—God, no, he wasn't a ghoul—but it had suddenly become vitally necessary to confirm the bell's existence. Should he do it? Did he have the nerve? A full moon seemed to smile upon the plan.

He began at once, delighted at his own boldness, quickly located the entrance to the bramble tunnel, got down on hands and knees and thrust the lamp inside. It had not grown over, was of sufficient width to accommodate his broader shoulders. Pushing the lamp ahead of him, Noah entered the blackberry patch on his belly, grinning at the impulsive absurdity of his act. His new clothing became soiled within seconds by dirt and disintegrated charcoal; thorns snagged at his arms and back, plucking at threads and stitches. Noah felt like a Virginia coalminer worming through some forgotten crack in the earth, the weight of the world pressing down upon him, cut off from sunlight and all living things as he inched forward in search of the dark fossil.

Now the tunnel was widening, opening on to the low bower at the patch's heart; and, yes, the bell was there, gleaming with a surly dullness in the lamplight, an idol hidden by design, angry at this unwarranted disturbance. Noah rested his torso in the chamber of brambles, hips and legs still in the tunnel, thrilled that everything should have remained unchanged. The cruel walls shifted, creaked in the wind that reached even here, thorny stems communicating with sly abrasion. Noah pushed the lamp closer to the bell, wanted to see it gleam brighter, shine like an effigy of smeared metal in some temple of pain, and in the heightened glow he saw beyond the brassy dome, saw the ground littered with . . . bones! Had the baby somehow been regurgitated by the earth? It was not possible; the bones were too large in any case, too numerous for the body of an aborted foetus. What were they? A delicious thrill of fear rippled the skin across Noah's sweating back. He edged forward, craned his head around the bell, was greeted by a grinning canine skull. A dog? But what dog? Calvin's pet was buried under the false mound near the house, Joe had said, and there had been no other dogs on the ridge, before or since. And *what* a dog! Its size was massive, heavy, the skull alone of impressive bulk; those fangs had never eaten kitchen scraps, appeared capable of pulling down a horse. The thing was not a dog at all, but a wolf! Noah was positive. A wolf. And just how had it come to be here in his childhood hideaway? At school he had been told the story of the Church of the White Wolf by children who had garnered it from the conversation of their parents, and here lay the beast itself, denuded of flesh and fur by ants and tiny scavenging creatures, a wolf none the less, and right where the church had stood. How was this possible in a rational world? It was not. Noah became frightened. His distorted pupils were filled with the skull's mocking grin; I am impossible, it said, but I am here—and so are you.

He wanted to leave this place, knew that to back out would ruck his clothing around his armpits, snag him permanently in the tunnel; he must drag his body completely inside the bower, nudge the bell and bones with his elbows, haul himself across those splayed ribs, that serpentine backbone. Noah's dread was not lessened by the moan that crept from his lips, a very soft yet heartfelt moan that seemed to echo, to return through the corroded smile of the wolf. It had to be done; if it was not, Noah's bones would whiten alongside those of this mysterious interloper. Whimpering a little, he dragged himself fully inside the chamber, edged around the brazen bell, eased his body across the wolf's remains, aware of every bone that pressed with such insistence against his breast. How had he ever fitted in here with room to spare? The span of years between the child he used to be and the youth he now was had never been made more apparent than during those few tense minutes required to turn in a circle and push the lamp ahead of him back into the tunnel; and yet the distance between child and youth was diminished the moment Noah began elbowing his way back to the outer world, for the crocodile that used to lurk beneath his bed, waiting with its snapping jaws to seize him by the ankle as he bounded to safety between the sheets, now was reborn among the bones around his feet. Noah knew the wolf was reassembling itself, becoming a spectral monster, a skeletal hound of hell preparing to fasten its fangs in the tender flesh of his calf! He kicked like a drowning man, scrambled on belly and elbows as fast as he could, tore his suit on thorns, laid open his cheek in his haste to be free, squirmed frantically to escape the bramble bower and its terrible occupant.

He wriggled at last out to the open night and stars, knocked the lamp aside and scrambled several yards from the blackberry patch, stood up to assure himself he was well and truly beyond the tunnel's constriction. His heart galloped wildly, erratically. Remembering the crocodile, Noah was ashamed of his panic, regretted his cowardice. What a fool! A good thing no one had witnessed his discomposure. Despite assurances directed at himself he could not stop shaking, the tremors induced partly by opium, partly by something deeper, a primeval fear instilled when man was naked prey, cowering in darkness between the worlds of seen and unseen. Sweat cooled on his face and neck. He watched the moon slide hesitantly behind a tracery of boughs. A memory nudged itself to the forefront of his thoughts—a wolf, a wolf on the ridge. Who had seen it? Not himself, not Joe or Calvin. . . . Phoebe Pike! She had come to the door with a frightened look on her face, told of having seen a wolf; and they had not believed her (with the possible exception of Calvin, who would have believed her if she'd said it was a dragon). He laughed, a startling sound in the quietude of night, cackled until the rich irony of his find was exhausted. Phoebe Pike and that damn wolf. If he saw her while he was here in Valley Forge, he would tell her she was right. He might tell her a few other things, too; Noah, in his narcotic lightheadedness, felt he was just about ready for Phoebe Pike, not like the last time—only a year ago, seemingly a lifetime. He wouldn't be so fumble-tongued again. Noah considered himself a man of broad experience. He had entered the bodies of two females a grand total of twelve times and, did he but know it, neither of his partners had enjoyed his brief attentions

The slash on his cheek began to sting. He picked up the lamp and returned to the house, found Joe in the living room, lying on the sofa and staring at the ceiling; he had obviously fixed another pipe for himself and been unable to cope with the gossamer whimsies parading behind his eyes. Joe did not stir when Noah plucked the pipe from his fingers and went upstairs to bed. Joe was entranced with the pattern cast by curtains and moonlight across the ceiling; it was a limpid pool, a shallow sea, and he bathed in its time-less waters like a god.

CHAPTER FORTY-ONE

Every man has his limits, Pike told himself; Pike's limit had been reached. Two weeks ago Jessica had, while alone in the kitchen, pulled down her underwear, squatted in the corner and defecated. In the *kitchen!* She had not even bothered denying it, had simply looked dazed when confronted with the evidence of her crime. Phoebe had defended her, of course, said she was "unwell". Unwell! The woman was mad, utterly mad; it was as simple as that.

And yet he hesitated to take the necessary steps. She was his wife after all, and the townspeople would flap their tongues over it for ever. Commitment was an irreversible act, awesome in its finality. What would Beatrice have done? The answer was obvious; he must rid himself of the increasingly clumsy, careless and, yes, downright dirty albatross hanging from his neck, suspended on the slender thread of Pike's charity. Better to get it over and done with, surely. He asked Dr. Whaley to pay a call. The doctor spent five minutes alone with Jessica, confirmed that she was indeed mad, offered to make arrangements with the asylum in Kansas City. The responsibility of decision had been taken from Pike at last; he abdicated gladly; surrendering to the inevitable was no reflection on a man; only a fool denied the obvious, and Pike knew he was no fool.

He did not tell Phoebe of the arrangements being made for her mother, postponed the confrontation that was sure to erupt into argument; Phoebe was the kind to nurse a sick cat rather than put an end to its suffering. Practical measures had to be taken with regard to Jessica. Who knows, she might next decide to perform a similar abomination in the middle of Decatur Street! No, she must be locked away for her own good; the doctor had said so, and doctors knew best.

All the same, Pike was glad when his wife evinced further signs of mental decay just a few days later. Jessica awoke screaming in the middle of the night, babbled of giant spiders scrabbling across her bed, pulling at her hair with their furry legs. It was nonsense, insanity at its undeniable worst, and it fortified his justification for having taken the steps he had. The following day the capstone was set firmly upon Jessica's future when she took the shears from her sewing basket and snipped grey swatches of hair from her head until it resembled a badly mown meadow.

After that incident Pike waited with impatience while the formalities were arranged. His decision could not be kept secret any longer. He asked Phoebe to step into his study, revealed the plan in a few crisp sentences. Surprisingly, she made no protest, simply stared at him for a long moment, then said in the calmest of voices: "It will be for the best." Pike was flabbergasted. Where were the howls of outrage, the handwringings, the pleas for time, just a little more time during which Jessica might become well again? But there was nothing, not even the expression of loathing he had come to expect from her. He knew his only child hated him, had learned to live with the knowledge as comfortably as he could, like a sailor with a wooden leg; accepting the hatred of one's offspring can be accomplished with a kind of numb resignation, he had discovered, and was not an incapacitating condition. Cheered by Phoebe's acquiescence, he ordered her to make ready a chest of clothing for Jessica to take with her, as though preparations were being made for a sea voyage rather than incarceration in a house of stone where all wore smocks of a uniform shapelessness.

Phoebe meekly obeyed, packed not just one chest but two, dispatched them ahead of time to the Kansas City depot, then reported back to Pike for further instructions. Her compliance made him uneasy; still, it was easy to live with his doubts in a tranquil house. Phoebe took over the running of things completely during those last few days, even prepared for Pike his favourite meals! Alarm bells in his head positively clamoured for attention. His doubts hardened, became suspicions—she was poisoning his food, was prepared to murder him rather than allow her precious mother to be taken away. He could not enjoy Phoebe's culinary efforts at all, and a good many nibbled-at dishes were dumped in the alley for local mongrels with infinite intestines. Ashamed of his own fears, Pike told Phoebe he was too distraught to relish her cooking with the gusto it doubtless deserved. Phoebe said she understood. Pike lived for several days on crackers and dry bread munched secretively in the study. Then came the reason for her mollycoddling (as Pike saw it) and it seemed innocuous enough—Phoebe wished to accompany her mother on that last train ride to the asylum. Pike was vastly relieved, granted her wish with a generous wave of the hand, a king dispensing largesse. "The whole family will go," he announced, as though several generations of relatives would be chartering a special train to accommodate their swarming numbers.

The day came; coincidentally, the same day on which the afternoon eastbound train would deposit Noah Puckett on the wooden deck of the Valley Forge depot. All arrangements had been made. The house of stone a day's journey away lay waiting to receive Jessica into its labyrinthine heart. She wore her best dress, the one in which she attended church on Sundays. A bonnet hid her barren head. Pike and Phoebe escorted her, one at either elbow, to the depot for the morning train. Jessica stood on the platform and stared at nothing. Perhaps she knew where she was being taken, perhaps not; all she had truly digested was the fact that a long train ride was in store, and that would surely take her beyond the reach of the spider that had by now grown too huge to pass comfortably through doorways, but must enter and exit a room through the walls, like a black ghost. She felt little patterings of excitement in her chest when the train at last appeared on the horizon, little tumblings and twitchings behind her blouse, like a sparrow trapped in a gauzy web. The locomotive, when it rumbled to a halt and stood hissing and panting, seemed to Jessica a messenger from the gods, a living machine, huffing fiery breath, sweating steam after its exertions, patiently awaiting her dainty step aboard one of its trailing carriages. The Pikes boarded, found seats. The locomotive responded to Jessica's silent command, began straining at the rails, eager to carry its mistress to the east, away from this place of torment, and soon was snorting black breath from its nose, gathering speed with its flailing rods and pistons.

The journey was never-ending, a time of hiding behind lowered eyelids, a time of movement without apparent progress, a day in limbo. Scarcely a dozen words passed between Pike and his daughter, and none at all escaped the smiling mouth of Jessica, whose thoughts were graced with wings while those of her escorts were crippled and broken. Her snorting steed was hauling her to paradise, away, *away* from all creeping, scuttling bedevilment, away to regions unsullied by fear. She could not wait to arrive. Onward, black and clanking charger!

Topeka was reached by late afternoon. The family transferred to the Kansas Pacific line and continued east for several hours more, stepped down in Kansas City at dusk for the last leg of their benighted travelling. Phoebe stayed with Jessica while her father fetched a carriage for hire, then Pike stood at the side of his wife while Phoebe went to claim a large chest from the freight office and had it wheeled to the carriage by a porter. The cab was driven across town to a building set behind high walls. Lamps burned atop the brick pillars flanking a wrought iron gate; beyond this could be seen a gravel driveway leading to the asylum itself, squatting darkly beneath emerging stars, only a few of its many windows lighted. Pike left the vehicle, tugged nervously at a chain beside the gate. No bell rang within hearing. "Push the button," said the driver. Pike saw a small button set into the bricks; an electrical device, no less, the first he had ever seen. He set his fingertip against it with some trepidation, applied force, was still unrewarded by any kind of sound. "There's a wire goes all the way inside," explained the driver. "You can't hear nothing from here. They'll be along pretty soon. Everyone pulls that chain first off. They should take it down. It don't even have a bell on it nowadays."

Presently two figures appeared along the driveway, one carrying a lamp, the second pushing a trolley. A smaller gate within the larger was unlocked. Phoebe could not hear the muttered exchange. Pike's face appeared at the carriage window. "We will have to walk in. The gates are padlocked." Phoebe assisted Jessica from the carriage. The heavy chest was lifted down and strapped to the trolley, wheeled quickly away. Phoebe could hear its axle squealing, wheels crunching on gravel as the trolley was pushed into darkness. Jessica was led by Pike to the small gate. Phoebe remained by the carriage. "Are you not coming with us?" asked Pike. She shook her head; Phoebe suspected that once inside the asylum grounds her father would have her committed as well; no trickery was beneath him, and she still was in possession of a secret that could destroy him professionally. She would stay where she was.

"Will you kiss your mother goodbye?" His voice was coldly disapproving.

"I have already done so, in the carriage."

She had not, had been unable to do more than squeeze Jessica's hand. Jessica had not responded even to that. This is a nightmare, Phoebe told herself, and will soon be over. Pike escorted his wife through the gate, was followed by the lamp carrier. Wrought iron bars swung shut behind them; their footsteps crunched away to silence. Phoebe could not take her eyes from the gate, was hypnotised by its bars, black and twisted like licorice. This will soon be over, soon be over. Nothing about this transaction, this handing over of Jessica to the care of strangers, was real; such grotesquerie could not fully be assimilated into commonplace awareness and understanding. She stared at the wrought iron bars, heard the champing of the carriage-horse, the jingling of its harness as it shook a bothersome moth from its head. Somewhere in the grounds an owl hooted softly.

"Been out here a couple other times," said the driver. "That's how I know about the bell."

Phoebe said nothing, did not turn, had in fact not heard the man's words, assumed he was talking soothing nonsense to his horse. The driver was not offended, expected peculiar behaviour from people handing over someone in the family to the high walls and secret practices of the madhouse. He took out a tobacco-pouch and filled his pipe, smoked unconcernedly, was in the process of knocking out the dottle when Pike returned. Father and daughter entered the carriage without speaking.

"Where to, folks?"

"Any respectable hotel," said Pike, and the carriage moved away.

Jessica was given a hot bath. She enjoyed the warmth and damp of the tiled room, was not embarrassed to be naked before the muscular female attendant, found the smock handed to her after drying herself a very comfortable garment indeed. All went well until she was taken to her room and locked inside; it was not the sparse furnishings which upset her, nor the sound of the key turning in the lock, but the immediate appearance in an empty corner of her blackly furred nemesis, its hideous body pulsing up and down, up and down, the pincers opening and closing, the six onyx eyes glaring at her with predatory hatred. Her screams brought half a dozen attendants running, and Jessica was wrestled into a straitjacket, her feet and those of her keepers splashed with urine. Strangely, the leather-walled room to which she was carried seemed impervious to the spider, and she quickly fell asleep, secure at last.

Father and daughter found rooms at the Bickford Hotel. It was after midnight when Pike answered a knock at his door. Phoebe stood in the corridor.

"I must speak with you, Father."

"I would prefer to wait until morning."

"I would prefer not to."

670

She walked past him into the room. Pike was greatly annoyed by her disregard for his authority, but experience had taught him no good would come from a lecture on filial duty and obedience. He closed the door.

"What is it? Please be brief."

"I will not be returning with you to Valley Forge." Her back was to him, her voice indistinct.

"I beg your pardon?"

"I have a ticket to Chicago. My belongings are in a trunk at the depot. I will not be returning home with you."

"Are you quite mad? Are you your mother's daughter?"

She turned to him, a smile sitting crookedly on her mouth. "Perhaps I am. My mind is made up."

"I forbid it!" He could feel the expensive and tasteful carpeting shift beneath his feet. Not returning home? Not returning?

"I have saved a little money. You need not worry about me."

Not returning home with him? He would be alone, utterly alone. First it was Beatrice, then Jessica, and now. . . . "You will stop this foolishness! I am your father. I *forbid* it!" His heart was skipping, his face red with blood yet filmed with a cold sweat; even his bowels had suddenly loosened. He had not experienced these symptoms since being brought before the board of the Des Moines School of Embalming and charged with theft. He was afraid, and recognition of this fear was itself sufficient to aggravate the symptoms to the point where his entire frame began to shake. He would be alone, alone with the dead; what could be more ghastly? It must not be allowed to happen. "We will discuss this in the morning. You're upset over what has happened. I understand. We both have suffered, and now we must give support, one to the other. . . ."

He talked on—time of sorrow, misfortunes of fate, begin anew, brighter tomorrow—his voice quavering; the flesh of his jowls shook like moulded lard as the words spilled from his lips, the upper hidden by his moustache, the lower plump and moist as a slug. Phoebe could say nothing in reply to this ventriloquial yammering; her father was not quite real, not an actual human being, was a clever mannikin manipulated from within by hobgoblins. She had come to his room, had said what must be said if she was to depart without feeling a coward; if he chose to ignore her words, it was no fault of hers.

Again he instructed her on their mutual need, the wisdom of continuing to live beneath the same roof, to share their loss and plan for a newer, happier life together, the details of which could be worked out on the train ride home tomorrow. It was quite hopeless; her words had set him trembling like a tuning fork receptive only to the sound produced by itself. She almost pitied him, caught herself in time, felt the usual dull revulsion reassert itself while he blathered of impossible things.

"I'm tired, Father."

"Yes . . . yes, goodnight, then, goodnight." He beamed hugely, as though this was some occasion of great joy; sweat beaded his cheeks and brow, glowed feverishly in the lamplight.

"Goodnight, Father."

Honesty would better have been served had she said "Goodbye". Was it hypocrisy which prevented her, or simple weariness? It did not matter any more; she had come to him to say what she must, and tomorrow would do as she had planned, would be gone even before he awoke. Her course was as firmly set as an arrow in flight, would not be deflected by the feeble winds of bombast and self-deception gusting from her father. She turned away, left him, closed the door quietly but firmly. The corridor stretched before her like a road.

CHAPTER FORTY-TWO

The day was perfect for testing Noah's gift. Sadie had shown it to no one, not even the children; it was *hers* almost as much as the picture of Jesus above her bed. Sadie had seldom been indulged with toys, had, as she grew older, deliberately eschewed bright and frivolous things, was naturally ascetic. Yet when the gift lay unwrapped upon her counterpane its vivid colouring inspired in her a modest thrill of interest enhanced by bafflement, for the thing was at first beyond her comprehension.

When unfolded it was at least ten feet long, a hollow tube of finest lightweight silk some two feet in diameter, held open at one end by a pliant hoop of bamboo, tapering for the last half of its length to a finely crafted tail. It was a fish of silk in red and yellow, with painted eyes and scales and fins, a very beautiful fish, but what could one do with it? The accompanying ball of silken thread skewered on a stick gave her the answer; it was a kite, not the flat diamond of tradition or the clumsy box, but a veritable flying fish, its mouth held open by the bamboo hoop to swallow the wind. Piercing the hoop were three small, equidistant holes, and the ball of thread terminated in a cunning arrangement of three short lengths with the tiniest of sticks at their tips; grasping the concept, Sadie pushed these sticks through the holes and the fish was hooked in triplicate. She admired it for a long time, found the slits along its sides which allowed the wind to pass completely through its body, as water passes through the gills of a real fish.

There was about this piscine gift a certain exoticism, a hint of distant lands and peoples; the airy reaches above

Kansas were surely not its natural home. And the greatest puzzle of all—why had Noah Puckett presented her with such a thing? Was it a form of wooing? Should she go to him and ask? Sadie knew that most of the young men in town had, in their disappointment over her unavailability for matrimony, taken to viewing her as nothing but a beautiful idiot, an untruth easily accepted when no sound came from her mouth to deny it; in short, they despised what they could not have, a state of affairs tailored closely to Sadie's own preferences. The Nazarene was still and ever the only man to whom she willingly would give herself, and she had thrust the memory of her father's sexual predations so deeply inside her the light of conscious scrutiny never fell upon it. Sadie was a virgin and a bride of Christ, but a tiny portion of her remained unaffected by excessive spirituality, was flattered at having received so unexpected and unconventional a gift. Was Noah attempting to *win* her? She knew of his reputation as a social pariah and, while not disturbed by it (she was herself in a similar, if lesser category) felt she must let him know that the kite, intriguing though it was, could not possibly be accepted, not if the string attached to it was intended to bind her with obligations of an amorous or intimate nature. Love was not for Sadie Wilkes, not love as the word is generally understood. Her course was plain—she must return the gift before anyone learned of its existence, before awkward questions intruded upon the comfortable and self-sustaining cocoon she had spun about herself.

But before the kite was refused it must be tested, just once, just for the joy of seeing it hang in the sky. Sadie folded and gathered it into its original package, left the rectory early in the day and followed the road out past the ridge; she would release the fish to the prevailing westerly winds from the open land there, would let the thread unwind until the fish hovered above Noah's home. Then she would wind it in and go to the ridge, deposit the package on Noah's doorstep. She did not wish to see him, had always tried to avoid human contact on those occasions when she visited the stained-glass window (an accidental discovery on a day when she had simply wanted to be among trees, a kind of dreamy longing, a compulsion almost). She did not wish to complicate matters with an explanation he would never understand. Perhaps she should not even risk leaving it on the doorstep—that was too dangerous an enterprise—perhaps she should simply leave it by the blackberry patch, nowadays so empty of colour and sound (why had the window and harps disappeared?), its sole feature an unmarked grave. Yes, that was the place for it, left like an offering (was this a pagan notion?) to whatever unrequited urges had prompted Noah to hand her the package in the first place. She assumed he would find it there, sooner or later.

Sadie took up a position a quarter of a mile west of the ridge, unwrapped the kite and let it trail at arm's length. Its belly ballooned with wind in a trice; the stiff breeze set it tugging at her fingers, and Sadie had only to run a few yards before it was airborne. Quickly she turned and paid out thread, watched the fish soar, tail whipping in an ecstasy of freedom, body undulating, rippling, as though distorted by rushing torrents. The fish swam in sky, its thread invisible, swam higher, higher, steadily moving backwards to the east until it hung as planned above the ridge, itself (in Sadie's watery imaginings) resembling a whale's humped back, the vast bulk of the beast hidden beneath rolling waves, the gap among the topmost trees where the blackberry patch lay, its gaping blowhole; she imagined a geyser of spume spouting directly up from it, catching the flying fish unawares, sending it crashing, waterlogged to the ground. A part of Sadie travelled the silken thread, merged with the red and yellow kite, hummed and thrummed, ingesting windy currents as it swam against the stream, tugging and buffeting, pulling at her arms, the stick in her hands jumping as if alive. She wished herself aloft, straining, fluttering high above the wooded ridge, looking down upon the doll's house on its eastern slope; longed for higher, more windswept regions of sky. Anchored by the slenderest of chains to the figure far below, the fish bucked and plunged with the urgency of a salmon nearing its spawning ground.

And then the unthinkable happened—the thread broke, sent the kite tumbling and flapping down, down, its taut flanks crumpling, emptied of air, down and down, twisting, writhing toward the trees. Sadie's arms fell with a slap as the force exerted against them was removed in an instant, and she took a step backwards to recover her balance. The stick and thread fell unnoticed from her hands as she watched the kite dip and twist for one last moment before disappearing somewhere on the ridge.

Heart thudding, she began to run, eyes fastened on the skyline of trees, trying to detect there a flash of reddish gold. She did not question her alarm over a few yards of silk and a sliver of bamboo. These were the trappings of a greater thing—a gift—that must be returned undamaged; a single flaw and she would be obligated to Noah Puckett, for a gift damaged is a gift accepted, and she could not allow herself to be encircled that way by any male. She huffed and puffed a silent prayer for the fallen kite as she ran, imploring Jesus to save it from the ravages of branch and thorn. Her footsteps were directed by the collapsed thread which, with minor loops and tangles, pointed to the centre of the ridge; there were miles and miles of it, or so it seemed to her as she followed its barely visible path across kneehigh grass rustling dry and yellow in the wind. Please, almighty Jesus, let it be saved from harm. . . .

The snake was a diamondback rattler, thick as Sadie's arm and five feet long. It had not eaten in twenty-three days and its poison sacs were full. Sadie trod squarely upon its spine, displacing several vertebrae; up swung the blunt head, blinded by terrifying swirls of cloth that shut out the sun, and its fangs sank deep into the flesh of her calf, so deep the snake was carried along with Sadie for the several steps it took her to realise something had happened, something painful. She stumbled and fell, frightening the snake further; it bit three times more at her lower thigh and the back of her knee, saw daylight around Sadie's boots and slithered to freedom, its usually graceful undulations made awkward by the damage to its spine.

Only when she saw its tail vanish into the grass did Sadie become aware of her predicament; she had thought the sharp pains in her legs were sudden cramps, the result of all that running. Horrified, she pulled up her skirts, saw the neat punctures. Country lore stated that snakebites be slashed immediately with a clean knife, the poison sucked out before it had a chance to enter the arterial system; without these measures a victim's hopes of survival were slim. Sadie had no knife, could not contort herself sufficiently to reach the wounds with her mouth in any case. The ridge! She must go to the house on the ridge for aid. Once before she had been sick, had been nursed in that house of rumour and sadness; details of the memory were fragmented, blurred, yet bright with the hope suddenly invested in them. She must get up *now* and reach Noah's door before the poison spread; already her leg felt . . . dead! This was largely her imagination; the poison would not begin to affect her nervous system for several minutes yet. The ridge was still hundreds of yards distant.

She stood shakily, began walking, favouring the bitten leg. Sweat ran from her every pore, soaked her underclothing, began darkening her linen blouse. For the first time in many a Kansas summer Sadie Wilkes could smell herself, and this caused her almost as much distress as the creeping paralysis overtaking her body, a numbness stemming not from the leg but from her heart; her faithful pump of gristle was busily distributing the rattlesnake's toxin through miles of artery, vein and capillary. Despite her slow progress Sadie found it increasingly difficult to breathe, as though the plug of flesh in her throat not only prevented the formation and expulsion of words, but now precluded the inhalation of air itself. And her heart! How it hammered—not a one-fisted knocking but a double-handed pounding; she thought of a sailor on a sinking ship, his cabin door and porthole nailed shut, water rising about his knees, waist, chest. . . . Panic swept through her in a curiously slow wave that threatened momentarily to crest and break, yet never did, a rolling, swelling pale green wave looming higher and higher, its foaming lip, while moving still, steadily approaching stasis. It began to swamp her, slowly, lovingly, instilling a monotonously low-pitched song inside her head, a buzzing and humming having about it an almost mechanical atonality. Her armpits and belly reeked of sweat, floods of moisture, a shameful exudation offensive to the nostrils, causing her undergarments to chafe; yet these sensations were not felt by Sadie herself, were experienced by someone very close to her, someone occupying virtually the same space as she. Her legs were moving still under the dubious control of this other person, were thrust before her with the ungainly hesitation of a newborn colt or lamb, and now that attention was paid to them the legs became aware of their clumsiness, were rendered useless in their keen self-consciousness and buckled beneath her in shame. Sadie retained just sufficient control (pushed the *other* away for one half second) to ensure she fell on her side, not on her face. The breath was knocked from her on impact. The ridge was still within view, an impossible distance away, the trees appearing to lean sideways, their greenery bleeding off into the air, reconstituting the wave that now had dragged her below its skin, away from sunlight to a coolness that embraced her with its welcome chill.

Her body had quite disappeared; Sadie was no more than a pair of eyes suspended inches from the prairie soil in a forest of grass. These, then, were the trees of heaven, these tall and slender yellow trees waving slowly before her, and the toilers of the forest of heaven were armoured, six-legged, bearing the burden of their past sins before them (was this place purgatory, not the ultimate destination after all?), pale and lumpy sins tightly clasped as the forest byways were negotiated—huge sins, some of them; an endless parade of tiny black sinners displayed their burdens while marching beneath her nose. Sadie wondered what had become of her arms and legs now that they had been taken from her, wished the droning in her ears might be a little less intrusive, the faraway thudding of her heart less distracting. Sadie's world shrank, all remembrance of family and town pared from her brain like the skin of an apple; these things ceased to be, bore no relation to the fact of her dying, were surprisingly unnecessary. The yellow forest and its trail of tiny penitents occupied her attention fully as poisoned blood pushed with sluggish insistence through the tributaries and estuaries of her body.

Oddly, she thought not once of Jesus Christ, had not invoked his name since begging that the kite be spared, did not request divine intercession even when it became clear to her that this time and this place had met in mysterious conjunction, had conspired to form a unique event, the shape of which was Sadie's death; she did not anticipate seeing the Saviour on some golden shore, had expunged him from her consciousness completely. Jesus Christ had been deposed by a humble snake, itself no longer a part of her thoughts. Where the robed figure had once held sway there now existed a vacuum, neither benevolent nor malign, an implosion of emptiness, and Sadie felt her phantom self tipping toward the void. With unquestioning acceptance she fell.

Some snakebite victims recover; others survive many hours before succumbing to the poison. From the moment of her setting foot on the rattler to the last beat of her congested heart, Sadie lived for just twenty-one minutes. It had seemed even less to her.

Joe and Noah slept while Sadie lay dying on the far side of the ridge, their minds troubled by narcotic shadows. They awoke shortly after noon. Phoebe Pike at that time was halfway to St. Louis, where she would change trains for Chicago. Her father was in the bar of the Bickford Hotel, steadily downing whiskies, eyes glazed with alcohol and disbelief; he did not know if he could bear returning to Valley Forge alone, was trying to reach a decision. The Bickford had one of the longest bars in Kansas City, and the distance between drinkers at this early hour seemed immense.

Having no appetite for breakfast (or, more appropriately, lunch) Joe took himself for a walk. Noah had avoided him (or he had avoided Noah since both had risen from their beds—in Joe's case, the living room sofa). The opium had left him drained, yet curiously clearheaded; every step taken among the trees granted him a wholly alien perspective, as though he was observing familiar things for the first time, every leaf and bough, every stone and trunk, the flat sky, the very air brushing his skin—the ridge was a disturbingly different place that day. Joe's thoughts were haphazard, his plans for confrontation with Noah postponed until he felt better able to handle such a thing; for the moment, he had difficulty deciding in which direction to point his feet.

Then he saw the fish, a reddish golden fish high above him, fluttering like a pennant from the topmost branch of a post oak; and the sight, for all its fantastical element, stirred in Joe not amazement but a sudden shock of recognition. He was not concerned with its impossibility, simply wondered where he had seen this extraordinary incongruity before; a fish in a tree is a surprising thing to come upon only if one has not already seen just such an unlikely sight. But where? He would not have forgotten it, not a giant goldfish in a tree, mouth to the west, tail to the east; it was too singular a phenomenon. Could it be the residual effects of opium, making him see something that was not there, or tricking his memory into believing this was not the first time such a vision had presented itself? It *must* be an illusion (if the former) or delusion (if the latter) induced solely by the thick blood of the poppy. It was the only plausible explanation, yet he dismissed it, head still craning to keep the fish in view; it was *not* an apparition and he *had* seen it before. But conviction provided no answers. Joe's puzzlement gnawed at him, scratched irritatingly at his brainpan, shaped itself into something approximating understanding, then skittered away before he could shift his inner eye to focus upon it; the answer was there, inside him, as elusive, insubstantial and fascinating as a dragonfly, dancing and darting with provocative closeness to a net flung this way, then that, in hopeless attempts at capture.

Frustrated, annoyed at his own inability to fathom the enigma, Joe began climbing the oak. Irritation gave way to exhilaration as he clambered up the trunk and from bough to bough; he ascended with the ease of an ape, enjoying the motion of the tree and the plucking of the wind as much as any child. The last time he had climbed thus had been to remove the mutilated body of Eli Tilton from a fork, and the time before that he had climbed the elm in the Cobden's backyard, spurred by fright and guilt after attempting to release his foster-mother from her room. Moving slowly now, nearing the tree-top, Joe examined the great fish flapping and snapping in the wind mere yards away. A kite, he thought, a strange kind of kite! And the string was within reach, snagged around a branch. Joe took out his pocket-knife, carefully opened the blade, reached out from his swaying perch and cut the fish free. It backed away from the tree, crumpled in mid-air and fluttered to the ground. Joe climbed down, well pleased with his catch, gathered the fish into his arms and returned to the house. This was something he could not keep to himself.

"Where'd you find that?" The legs of Noah's tilted chair hit the porch with a thud.

"At the top of a tree. It's a kite."

"I know it's a kite. It cost a dollar fifty in Chinatown, the same place I got your pipe."

"It's yours?"

"I gave it to Sadie Wilkes yesterday."

"You gave Sadie Wilkes a *kite?*" Joe thought this as inappropriate as handing the Virgin Mary a skipping rope.

"Sure I did. Why not?"

"Well, she's lost it already."

"The string must've broken. Did you see her anywhere around, looking for it?"

"No. Want to take a look?"

"May as well."

Together they began to search. They could have shouted her name, but did not; shouting for a mute seemed improper, somehow. She would be found soon enough if she was herself looking for the kite.

"Did you plan on giving it to her when you bought it?"

"I didn't plan on giving it to anyone. I bought the pipe, headed for the door and saw the fish. I liked it, so I bought it."

"How'd you come to give it to Sadie Wilkes?"

"I saw her after I got off the train and just . . . handed it over."

"Sounds like Cupid's dart to me."

"She's not my type." He resented Joe's puerile insinuation.

"A good-looking girl like that? What's the problem, too religious for you?"

"I like to talk a while after I roll off," Noah snapped.

Joe stiffened; he did not appreciate being reminded of his own virginity, and Noah's calculated crudeness was also an insult to Sadie Wilkes' handicap, by implication an insult to Joe's own. He did not lose his temper, told himself he'd probably deserved a smartass answer for having prodded the boy, however lightheartedly. Keep a tight lip, he advised himself.

They searched for half an hour without success.

"Maybe she went home," suggested Noah.

"Could be."

They sat on a tree stump. Noah lit a cigar. Joe shifted himself upwind of the stink. Noah ignored the move, puffed from the side of his mouth. "How did you like Dr. de Quincey's patent brain medicine?"

"I'm not sure."

"You looked as if you'd been hit over the head."

"It made me . . . dreamy, the way you said. Did you disappear for a while, or was that my imagination?"

"I went for a walk."

"A little moonlight trysting with a certain young lady?"

Joe couldn't seem to help himself; the jealousy had resurfaced. Was it possible Noah could actually seduce someone as unlikely as Sadie Wilkes? Perhaps it was not such an impossible task; a few years ago someone had successfully impregnated her. The thought of Noah following in that man's footsteps filled Joe with sadness and envy. He must try to overcome these foolish emotions; it was no fault of Noah's that Joe was not a potent young man with a straight spine.

"Just a walk to nowhere in particular." Noah preferred not to think of the blackberry patch incident, resented Joe's harping on the gift to Sadie Wilkes. Noah regretted telling him, hoped Joe wasn't going to pursue the subject like a half-witted mother.

They sat in silence. Joe again sieved his brain for an answer to his rootless memory of another fish in another tree, but no answer came. Even had he been able to recall the dream that had flowered in his head while asleep in Dr. Cobden's library in 1872 Joe would probably have dismissed it as coincidence, for how can one dream of a thing eighteen years before one sees it? Puzzlement left him uneasy, troubled by misgivings of perplexing vagueness. He had quite forgotten Sadie Wilkes.

Noah ground out his cigar stub. "Want to keep looking?"

"No. She's gone. You can always take the kite back to town and give it to her again."

"Why don't *you* take it back. I couldn't give a shit."

"What's that supposed to mean?"

"It means quit hounding me like some stupid old woman!"

"I'm not hounding you about anything. . . ."

"Like hell you're not! Just don't say another word about it, all right?"

"About what?"

For a moment Joe thought Noah would hit him. He hoped so. For all Noah's added inches and pounds, Joe was confident of winning any kind of tussle. He'd broken his own rule, though, hadn't kept a tight lip. Maybe I *am* an old woman, he thought. And all anticipation of a fight left him. "Sorry," he said.

"You should be," was Noah's response. He got up and stamped away in the direction of the house, left Joe alone on the stump, anger and cigar smoke slowly dissipating in the air. Joe knocked his boots together a few times for something to do, was reminded by this casual act of his short legs; Noah would have had to lift his knees to knock his boots. Joe saw he was beginning to consider himself Noah's inferior. That must stop. He was not so very old, had little to be ashamed of in his life. Noah's sole advantage was his youth. Joe should not be jealous of something as unearned, as fleeting as that.

He stayed where he was until the moving sun drove shadows across and beyond him, exposed the stump to direct light and heat. It was now late afternoon. He may as well go home; there was nothing else to do, nowhere else to go. Leaving the stump was difficult, Joe's movements slow, a rehearsal for the old man's shuffle that would one day be his. Joe didn't care; no one was watching.

A roundabout route would delay his arrival at the house. Joe meandered to the west slope of the ridge and spent some time staring across the plains. The land here was still unbroken by the plough, the farms of Valley Forge having spread mainly to the east and south, as though the ridge was some kind of barrier between wilderness and civilisation. That suited Joe; he could see the town from the attic window, wanted the view on the other side of the ridge to remain unimpaired by fences, fields and livestock. He watched a hawk patiently circling above the grassland, looked below it to see if any wild thing could be detected— an idle exercise, he knew, since the hawk's vision was probably fifty times sharper than his own. The hawk could probably distinguish every hair on a thistle while Joe could not, at this distance, even separate thistle from grass. The only thing to catch his eye was a scrap of whiteness a few hundred yards from him. He could not identify it, became intrigued by its stillness. Had he been standing a little higher up the slope its elevation might have provided a better view, but walking downhill rather than up struck him as the more acceptable option.

When he reached Sadie it seemed to Joe that his troubled state of mind regarding the fish in the tree had been some kind of portent, an image of inevitability, fate cast in mocking, inexorable outline.

For twenty-four hours a number of townspeople assumed foul play; Noah Puckett had given to Sadie Wilkes the very thing which drew her away from the safety of her home, out to the land beyond the ridge where the lowliest of God's creatures had struck her down. It was too coincidental to be termed an accident; skulduggery was afoot, and the Puckett boy was its agent. The two women who had witnessed the kite's presentation from across the street were the first to suggest the victim's body had been ''improperly tampered with'' by ''someone living not a stone's throw'' from where ''it'' had happened. Clearly, Noah had threatened Sadie with the snake (a pet of his) before ''interfering'' with her, had then murdered her with his reptilian accomplice (Noah was accorded a power over animals worthy of St. Francis) hoping everyone would be fooled. This novel theory was laid to rest when Dr. Whaley made it known Sadie had not been sexually molested, had died alone, of snakebite only; in fact he embroidered the truth by stating she was *virgo intacta,* a lie calculated to soften the blow to Lyman Wilkes by allowing his daughter to pass into Valley Forge lore unsullied—a virgin and a viper are the stuff from which legends are woven.

Perce Lafferty was still suspicious. He *wanted* to be suspicious, but there existed no evidence to indicate an actual crime. Joe and Noah had co-operated fully with him, telling everything they knew (omitting all references to opium and portents), and he could not justifiably throw them into a cell. It was a damn shame. The kite itself lay across a corner of his desk, even in its limpness suggesting oriental perfidy and subterfuge. If Noah Puckett had not given the girl this heathen toy, she would not have gone out behind the ridge to fly it, would not have been bitten, would be alive still. Perce thought the least he could do was take the thing outside and burn it. This he attempted to do, but the silk refused to ignite; Perce knew a challenge when he met one, poured coal oil on the kite—and the flying fish was consumed by fire. But it was small compensation for having missed the bigger game.

Joe and Noah were drawn no closer together by the tragedy, were, if anything, thrust further apart. Joe pondered still the paradox of the fish in the tree, unable to dislodge his certainty that all this had somehow been foretold, preordained, in direct contradiction of his understanding that time and nature proceeded from the past to the future like an endless ribbon which, however much it might twist or bend, did not, *could* not loop back upon itself. Noah endured a kind of guilt not so far removed from Perce Lafferty's view of things—if he hadn't . . . she wouldn't . . . it wouldn't . . ., etc. He spent some time in the kitchen cleaning his derringer, then took the opium pipe upstairs for consolation.

In the evening Lyman Wilkes came to the ridge. Noah did not come down to greet him. The minister sat with Joe in the living room. Joe prepared himself for interrogation, but Wilkes' mood was not accusatory, was strangely abstracted, his voice hesitant, eyes wandering at will about the room, avoiding Joe's face.

"There are ugly rumours," he said.

"I know. Do you believe them?"

"I do not. But there is a mystery. . . ." He stopped, strangled his fingers, stared at the floor. "I find myself unable to accept that in this instance the ways of God are simply . . . unknowable. There is here a clear example of cause leading to consequence, but . . . the elements of chance and inevitability—contradictory things—are too . . . intertwined, unnaturally so. . . . Perhaps I am not expressing myself properly. . . .''

"I've had the same feeling myself."

Joe did not elaborate; even Noah had not been told of Joe's curious sense of recognition when first he saw the kite straining at the post oak. That was a puzzle he would decipher to his own satisfaction in his own time.

Wilkes mashed his knuckles between his knees. "There is the possibility that God is punishing me. . . ."

"For what?"

"For my sins, Mr. Cobden."

Joe's sympathy for the man evaporated; introducing God into the already tangled equation of circumstance and coincidence seemed to him folly of the worst kind. God had no part in this sad little death in Kansas, just as God had no part in wars, earthquakes, the collision of worlds or the manufacture of curtain rods. Wilkes might just as sensibly have wrung his hands and assumed personal blame for the sky's blueness, the roundness of the earth and the glimmering of stars—such things *were* and *would be* regardless of the Reverend Dr. Lyman Wilkes and his nonsensical agonies. Grieving for the loss of his daughter was one thing, thought Joe, but to invite the pointing (nonexistent) finger of God was nothing short of stupidity and warped conceit.

"I doubt it," was all he said.

Wilkes looked up. "You do not know my sins."

He appeared genuinely anguished, but Joe could find no words of comfort or support which would not have rung like a cracked bell in his own ears. Best be silent and let the poor bastard say what he wants, think what he feels he must, wallow in self-recrimination if that was what he required. He was curious to know what a man like Wilkes considered a sin, but was not informed. Wilkes appeared as reluctant to reveal his hidden self as was Joe; and Joe began to wonder, after fully ten minutes of silence, just why the man had bothered to make this visit at all. Wilkes sat chewing his prophet's beard and gripping his knees, brow furrowed, a picture of misery, entirely oblivious to Joe's presence. Joe felt like a spy, observing the outward signs of some inner torment while peering through a keyhole. He became embarrassed by Wilkes' restless silence, then annoyed.

"It's pointless to punish yourself," he said. "It had nothing to do with you, or with anyone else. It just happened."

He did not fully believe this himself, simply wanted the matter resolved in order that Wilkes might leave, a move the minister had no apparent intention of making. He sat with downcast head, concocting Dantesque visions of heavenly wrath, a mighty funnel aimed at *him,* down which came swooping the words INCEST! TRANSGRESSION! PUNISHMENT! and SIN! Wilkes loathed himself, found he could not mitigate his crime by way of the love he had felt for Sadie. He had broken the laws of God and man, had his precious girl taken from him in retribution. That an innocent person had died for Wilkes' sin did not strike him as unjust or nonsensical; the sin had been his, therefore the suffering that followed Sadie's death must also be his. Sadie herself was beyond suffering, was no doubt within reach of the throne while he, Wilkes, now had half a lifetime remaining to him in which to reflect upon the nature of his wrongdoing and prepare himself for damnation. Yes, the punishment was not only just, it was *perfectly* just.

After a painfully extended period of stillness Wilkes jumped like a dog startled from sleep, looked around, stared at Joe as if they had never met. "I must go home," he said, his voice made hoarse by guilt.

"So soon?"

"My wife will be worried. Thank you for. . . ." He tried to remember if Joe had done anything deserving of gratitude. "Thank you, Mr. Cobden."

"No trouble."

Wilkes departed, to be with a wife who secretly was glad Sadie had died; now she could have her husband all to herself.

Noah came downstairs. "I'm leaving," he said.

"Tonight?"

"Tomorrow."

The news was not unexpected. Joe pointed to a chair. "Take a seat."

"I'm going for a walk."

"We've got some things to discuss."

"Later."

"Noah, I'm asking you in a friendly, even a humble manner kindly to spend a few minutes over something important. Please sit down."

He waited. If Noah moved toward the door Joe intended pouncing like a tiger, and if he did so it would be hard to stop matters there; he would be compelled to strike the boy several times to teach him some manners, and he did not want to do that—not because Noah didn't deserve a brisk beating but because it would not establish the cordiality required for the business at hand. He waited.

Noah sat. "Well?"

"I want this place, the house and ridge. I'll pay cash."

"What if I don't want to sell?"

"You wouldn't want me to be unhappy, would you?"

Noah shrugged, looked at the ceiling.

Joe leaned just a few inches closer to him. "I said, you wouldn't want me to be unhappy, would you?"

"I guess not."

"That's very gratifying. Do you have any plans for settling down here?"

"No."

"I didn't think so. Can you think of a good reason not to sell?"

"Not offhand, no."

"Name a price."

"Five thousand dollars."

"I'll give you one thousand."

"Four and a half."

"Noah, I've just spent time with a man of God who doesn't know if he's Job or Jeremiah. The experience left me with a severe pain in the gut. I'm not going to haggle with you like an Afghan rug merchant. One thousand is a fair price."

"What if I don't take it?"

"I'll probably break your neck."

"You think you're mighty tough."

"I *am* mighty tough. You've seen me too many times with an apron tied around me to believe it, but if you want a demonstration I'll oblige."

They glared like tomcats in dispute, neither wavering an inch, yet Noah was already aware he had been bested. "I'll want it first thing tomorrow."

The deed of sale was made out and witnessed by the manager of Joe's bank. Joe handed over the cash, then walked with Noah to the depot for the early eastbound, the train the Pikes had taken three days before. It was running behind schedule. Both were made tense by the wait.

"This time do me the honour of dropping me a line every now and then."

"All right."

"Don't say that if you don't mean it. It's a little late to be humouring me."

"I'll write."

"And don't spend the money on women. You'll get a disease and your dick'll drop off."

"I don't need to pay for what I want."

"Bully for you. And for Christ's sake get rid of that toy gun before it lands you in trouble."

"I don't need your advice, thanks."

"Yes, you do, you just won't take it."

A smudge of smoke appeared on the horizon. No further conversation was necessary; the approaching train gave them the excuse to ignore each other, minutes later enveloped them in steam and sound, stood hissing while Noah hefted his suitcase on to a carriage platform.

Joe put out his hand. "Look after yourself."

Noah shook it. "And you."

He stepped aboard.

When finally the train had disappeared in the east Joe stood for a long while examining the sky. Then he went back home.

691

CHAPTER FORTY-THREE

Pike was absent from Valley Forge an entire week. Sadie's body had to be taken by rail to the next town for embalming. When at last he returned, Pike found himself in bad odour with the community for having abandoned his post, so to speak. His business did not suffer, however, for his was the only funeral parlour. Pike's monopoly lasted until 1892, when a rival enterprise ("Oswold Bros. Fine funerals—Bereavement Is Our Business") was established on Shawnee Street. Oswold Bros. services included the installation of tasteful markers, crosses, monuments and funerary statues in marble or stone; actual tombs and vaults were available at a reasonable price for those with an eye to posterity.

Pike's profits were drastically truncated within six months. He sought comfort in drink, chimed away his professional life with every clink of bottle neck on tumbler rim. In 1894 he tasted the dregs, found them unpalatable, unseemly, unbearable. His last meal consisted of a brass nozzle and rubber hose; he filled his stomach with embalming fluid until it rebelled, died minutes later, suffocated by vomit and the hosepipe of his patent pump. Had he simply drunk the stuff he might well have regurgitated it in its entirety and survived, but Pike preferred to administer the agent of his deliverance ("Renouard's Special Fluid—Contains no arsenic or mercury—Does not harden the body but renders it firm and preserves the natural characteristics of life—Does not injure the hands") in the traditional manner. The building on the corner of Decatur and Wyandotte was sold by public auction, remodelled into a mercantile store. The new owners lived upstairs, a normal, even dull family, untroubled by serious discord.

Phoebe never wrote a single letter home, never (like her father) visited the asylum in Kansas City, where Jessica lived in outright lunacy interspersed with periods of tranquillity until her death in 1903. Chicago was Phoebe's home for two years while she worked as a governess in the home of a wealthy meat packer. When her employer made advances to her she moved to New York City; she had not been offended by the man's sexual proposal, had been shocked instead at her own willingness to jeopardise the happiness of the family (she adored the children and their mother) by yielding to him. The only sensible recourse was flight.

In the greatest American metropolis she found work as manageress of a small restaurant. The hours were long, the work demanding, but under her supervision the business prospered. One of its regular customers was an artist, a self-professed bohemian whose canvases found no defenders among the complacent fold of critics. He imagined himself a genius surrounded by mediocrity, was aggressive, voluble, amusing. Phoebe modelled for him on several occasions, sometimes nude (surprisingly easy; no shame, no timidity), and soon became his mistress, a position as free from profit as the modelling. In fact the artist, for all his grievances and sarcasm, had not much talent, was never deserving of the acclaim he considered his due. Phoebe herself attempted several more times to compose verse but her style did not improve. Nevertheless, she was happy. She encouraged her lover to persist, paid for his canvases and oils, shared his bed and his dreams of greatness.

In 1894 she gave birth to a daughter, and in 1896 to a son, bastards both since the artist refused the conventionality of marriage. Following the second birth he began to drink, drank himself into a surly mood and raged at Phoebe, accused her of robbing him of artistic power, draining his precious gift with her petty nigglings about money and her obsession with the children when it was he, *he* who needed her most. She forgave him that outburst, and the next, but the third resulted in physical abuse. Phoebe took her children and her fractured arm to a new address, found new employment, never saw the father of her girl and boy again. She called herself Mrs. Pike to avoid possible humiliation for the children, and raised them with a love tempered only by that necessary dash of discipline. Her son, smitten by war fever, volunteered in 1918, was killed in the Argonne. Phoebe did not fully recover from the loss.

The artistic streak surfaced in Phoebe's daughter; at twenty years of age she had several stories published in literary magazines, was eventually brought to the attention of a film producer and shipped to Hollywood, where she assisted in the construction of scenarios for some of the silent era's most successful celluloid fantasies. In 1927, Phoebe purchased a ticket to Los Angeles to be with her daughter. She fully intended facing the past by stopping *en route* at Valley Forge, but neglected to study the railroad schedule; her train ran express from Topeka to Dodge. She could have gone back—to see her father, to see Noah and Joe— but did not, continued on through the southwest to her new home. The past is gone, she told herself, and interference is unwise. Perhaps it was fortunate the train did not stop; her father, at the time of Phoebe's passing through, had been dead for thirty-three years, Noah for fifteen, Joe for eleven. Phoebe died in Long Beach in 1939, just two days before Hitler invaded Poland. She was seventy-eight.

The poets have a word for Noah's condition: wanderlust. The psychological sciences refer to it as dromomania. Noah's chafing spirit took him across America a dozen times, a score of times, times beyond remembering, the steel web of a hundred different railroads taking him to every corner of the nation in his search for that thing which is nameless even to the searcher. A confirmed road-kid at seventeen, he rode the rods beneath boxcars, on their catwalks and blinds and empty interiors; he exulted in motion, a continual *going*, his journey to everywhere and nowhere a fierce and prideful thing. He was not alone. Youths by the thousand were leaving homes impoverished by the economic depression of the 1890s, a mass wandering that would not be seen again for another forty years. They left to ride the rails, to beg and steal and be thrown from moving trains by irate brakemen; they left to escape the anguish imposed on families by poverty, to remove that extra, hungry, unwanted mouth, and they left for freedom's own sake, some of them to die beneath the iron wheels that took them far from home in the company of hardened drifters and questing dreamers.

Noah carved or scrawled his name on water towers from coast to coast, border to border: Kansas Kid '92, '93, '94—and later KK (the initials, instantly identifiable, were indicative of his fame among the road-kid brethen) '95, '96, '97. Sometimes, of necessity, he left the boxcar freights to perform that abominable chore, work (Joe's thousand dollars long since gone, the derringer pawned) a few weeks here picking fruit, a few weeks there assisting with a wheat harvest. There were men who followed the agricultural seasons as a way of life, but that was not for Noah and his ilk. The lure of the rails drew them on when a few dollars had been earned; food could be snatched from open fields and the homes of unwary citizens in small towns everywhere, and hobo jungles charged no admission for the night except a contribution to the ever bubbling pot. Noah obeyed the dictates of whim that directed him here, there, across the next state line, to the far side of the mountains, first to one ocean then back to the other, across the awesome distances of America, and somehow these loopings and switchbacks and criss-crossings, if recorded on a map, would have suggested a wayward yet consistent influence exerted upon the wayfarer by one of that map's most insignificant specks, located at its centre. These annual or bi-annual reunions with Joe Cobden were brief, a few days at most, and then he was off again, restless, steam-driven, his soul stretched along a million miles of railroad, a crosstie walker beneath a sickle moon.

In 1898, four years after Phoebe Pike was delivered of her firstborn, Noah hit the grit (jumped from a slow-moving train) on the outskirts of a town in Michigan and walked until he came to the main street, prepared to seek out those people soft enough of heart to dip into their pockets for a nickel or dime. Having secured and spent the price of a meal Noah lounged in the public park, toying with the idea of returning to the railyard to catch an outbound (north, south, east, west—who cared?) when a girl walked by. She was very nearly as lovely as Sadie Wilkes, and Noah did not hesitate, but followed her like a sleepwalker to her home, watched her disappear inside. For several hours thereafter he wandered the streets of that town, wrestling with the most difficult decision he had faced since leaving home. He was twenty-four years old and realisation had dawned—he was wasting his life. Noah wanted that girl. He had never encountered love at first sight outside the pages of a novel, did not even think in such trite terms of the thunderbolt that had struck him; he was positive his aggravated emotional state was unique, knew it would not go away. He would have to marry her.

Noah worked in the railyard for a month, loading and unloading boxcars; when enough dollars had been saved he bought a suit of clothes, found employment with a storekeeper, impressed the owner with his intelligence and ability. Noah despised the work, but used the mind so much admired by his employer to almost double the store's profits within twelve months by offering cut-price inducements to customers, a marketing technique apparently unknown in that part of Michigan (or anywhere else, for all Noah knew)—only the first of a long string of inspirations. He reorganised the store from top to bottom, added new lines of stock, expanded the premises, had coupons printed in the local newspapers, to be cut out and credited for a dollar on any purchase over ten dollars, anticipated the twentieth century with this and other practices, all equally laughable in his eyes, fared so well he was made a partner after just two years and given complete control of the new, even larger store (Noah insisted it be called an emporium) across town. He prospered, and the mainspring behind his drive to succeed was the Botticelli face on Sycamore Street.

Her name, he had discovered by circumspect enquiry, was Constance Croker, and by the time Noah was ready to woo her the siren of Sycamore was entering her nineteenth year. He attended the same church as the young lady (Joe would have fainted—church!) and made sure he tipped his hat to her every Sunday until she became familiar enough with his face to smile or nod in return. He spied on her home until Constance one afternoon went for a walk chaperoned only by her terrier. Noah introduced himself at one end of a long and shady lane, and by the time man, girl and dog emerged into sunlight he knew she would not object should he call upon her parents. This he duly did, and they, like their daughter, found him charming, witty, altogether an impressive young fellow, and so very go-ahead. Why, the whole town knew what he'd done with Quakenbusch's store.

Their engagement was brief, the marriage held in September 1900. Joe was not informed, Kansas forgotten. Constance's parents provided a home. By 1905, Noah had fathered two girls. For seven years more he ran the new store (both stores after Mr. Quakenbusch suffered a mild heart attack in '06) and the Puckett family lacked for nothing. Then, on a summer evening, Noah went for a walk through town. People greeted him from swing seats on front porches and he returned their small talk and smiles. His steps took Noah to the railyard, where he watched a boxcar being uncoupled from a freight; this operation completed, the train moved out, and when the engineer sounded the whistle its mournful wailing opened Noah's heart like a scythe.

For three days he heard no conversation directed at him, stared at familiar faces as if they belonged to strangers, gazed at walls as though divining in brick and plaster the elusive line of forgotten horizons. He loved his wife, loved his children, yet felt nothing whatever for them during those three dream-like days; really, they'd be better off without him. He employed the coward's goodbye—a letter on the mantelshelf; it expressed his regret, his shame, left every cent in his bank account to Constance. He was many miles away, clinging to the catwalk on a westbound freight, when the letter was found. The dawn sky bathed him in glory, the wind forced down his throat was wet with dew, his pockets were unburdened by a single reminder of what he left behind, not photograph or coin. Noah thrilled at his freedom, trembled at his baseness, howled at the sky. Kansas Kid, aged thirty-eight, was loose upon the face of the nation again.

The market for wooden Indians continued to thrive; the advent of the cigarette increased tobacco consumption among the populace, and no dispensary of the weed was complete without a swarthy redskin by the door. Joe's artistry continued to develop; the $200 Indian had been achieved by '92, superseded by the $300 model in '94, which in turn was replaced by the $500 Big Chief in '98. He made seven or eight each year, sold them by way of a Kansas City dealer who retailed the statues at $650 each in every midwestern State, an arrangement satisfactory to both men. The Big Chief was worth every cent, a magnificent specimen of native American, carved nowadays from imported redwood or mahogany. In 1899, Joe received his first private commission; a Rhode Island millionaire who had seen one of Joe's Indians while in Chicago required a figurehead for his yacht *Medusa*, and Joe tackled the task with an energy somewhat lacking in his approach to the latest Big Chiefs. He produced a masterpiece of the grotesque—a demon-woman, snakes writhing from her scalp, tumbling and coiling in a thick mass down across her shoulders and breast, mouth open in a frozen scream, the whole thing hideous enough to turn the waves to troughs of stone. The customer was greatly satisfied, commissioned a second figurehead for *Medusa's* sister yacht *Minotaur*. This creature had about it a little of the artist—humped back, bull neck, an expression of rage and suffering. Laying aside his chisel after the final paring had been eased from the beast's knotted brow, Joe doubted that he would ever again draw satisfaction from a mere wooden Indian. The Buffalo tribe had been good to him, had supported him in comfort for a decade, but their challenge had long since been met and overcome. The shape of his future needed careful pondering.

As it grew older, Joe's body began causing him pain. He consulted a medical encyclopaedia, saw that a hunchback can expect continual torment in later years; but the news was not all bad—those later years would not last long, for hunchbacks, like dwarves, were generally not blessed with longevity. So be it. When he carved the minotaur Joe was forty-four; he estimated ten or so years remained to him. What to do with them? First he needed to alleviate the pain in his spine and joints; this was achieved with the aid of Dr. Pierce's Nerve Nostrum, a cocaine-based elixir which, although it did nothing to rid him of pain, substantially blurred his perception of it. But Dr. Pierce's sovereign remedy was effective only when taken in quantity, and constant ingestion turned Joe's stomach. He turned (*re*turned) to opium. Noah's gift had lasted Joe a full year; he had not smoked often, fearing addiction, but the dreaming state induced by coagulated poppy milk soothed his mind, compensated for the things he could never have, the very things Noah would, a dozen years hence, abandon in the night. Nerve Nostrum could be purchased for a dollar in the pharmacy on Wyandotte, but for opium Joe was obliged to venture further afield. A bar in Kansas City yielded a name and address, and Joe's connection was established; until his death in 1916 he was never without his supply of opium, sent in small parcels each month, courtesy of the US Mail.

He smoked whenever the pain became too great, did not allow the habit to interfere with his work. Big Chiefs continued to leave the ridge for shipment elsewhere, but now

Joe interspersed their production with sculptures to suit his fancy. Somewhat tired of the human form, he began a series of animal studies, his first since those far-off days when he had idly whittled squirrels and elephants. He found his forte in the great cats, invested his renderings with all the grace and power his own body lacked. The finest was a snarling black panther carved from ebony, a fluid nightmare of arrested motion. Joe lost enthusiasm for his regular work after that, felt he had crowned his efforts as an artisan (he still did not consider himself an artist) and was therefore entitled to a rest, *more* than a rest—a vacation!

The automobile had been a commonplace part of American life for several years before Joe thought to buy one for himself. He went to Topeka, paid $475 for a four-cylinder Babcock and drove it home, exhilarated by the mad dash across Kansas at twenty miles per hour, feet sliding from the pedals as he jounced and bounced over roads made by and for horse-drawn wagons. He camped alone on the prairie twice before reaching Valley Forge. Pedestrians on Decatur scattered before him as Joe aimed for the ridge beyond town. He pulled up broadside to the front porch and switched off the motor, knew he had fallen in love at last—with a machine.

There was no holding him now. Joe drove the Babcock down to Texas, across to New Orleans, up through Mississippi on the third leg of his right-angled odyssey (in Yazoo City he stopped traffic; a hunchback in an open car was a sight none there had ever seen) through Memphis (where Joe was thrown out of a bar for daring to suggest that this proud city was named after some old Ay-rab town over there in Ee-jipt!) and on up to St. Louis, where he found Dr. Cobden's home had been torn down to make way for a newer dwelling. Making enquiries, Joe located the doctor's grave in the Episcopal churchyard, within sight of the doors outside which a foolish man had once left a baby, and another, wiser man had taken it home; altogether a surprising place to find two atheists, but there Joe was, and there, buried beside his lunatic wife, Joe's foster-father:

William Baxter Cobden
Born Feb 11, 1818
Died July 4, 1876
A friend of the poor

Presumably Dr. Hopkins and the infirmary staff had erected the stone. Joe tried to remember where he had been on July 4, 1876, the centennial of these United States; it was just before he had come to Valley Forge, so far as he could recall. A more auspicious moment could not have been found for the sloughing off of Dr. Cobden's mortality. I never wrote him a letter, thought Joe, so why should I expect Noah to write me?

Sobered, he steered for home, west through Kansas City, arrived nine weeks after his departure. The snarling panther had gathered dust. He wiped it off, oiled the wood, wondered what to do with it; wondered, too, what to do with the remaining years of his life. He packed and lit his opium pipe to consider things.

In the winter of 1912 word of the prodigal came to the ridge:

Dear Mr. Cobdin,

I am a friend of Noah Puckit. He told me about you and I am writing to you because Noah cant any more. Me and him were both of us bound for south of the border to fight with Pancho Villa, a fight justifiable on account of terible conditions down there Noah says. But he took sick in El Paso and we never did go over the border like we planned although I am leaving soon to do it now that Noah is gone, dead I mean. He died of something he et, tomane poisin the doctor says, just heaved up til he died, three days of it. The food here is not fitten for a dog. They say its worse in Mexico but I aim to go anyhow. Noah was a good man although peculier sometimes. I have also wrote to his wife & kids so no need for you to do same. I am sorry to be the bearer of bad news as they say, but you shoud now what happened.

yrs sincerly,
J D Pennebaker

Why would Noah have wanted to take part in a revolution? Was it intended to be some kind of romantic, Byronic gesture, the suffering malcontent throwing in his lot with sons of the soil? Was it a penance of some sort for his wasted intelligence and all the missing years? (Joe had neither seen nor heard from him since 1898.) Or was it merely whim, a boyish game of soldiers that had gone pathetically wrong? And how had Noah convinced the semi-literate Pennebaker to join him in the conflict, and on the side unpopular with the US government? How was it possible that such an unlikely duo could imagine their destinies linked with that of a nation in turmoil? Wife and kids? *What* wife and kids? Oh you bastard, you little bastard, you went and had a family and never told me, not a word. Nothing, nothing. . . . And now Noah was dead, had puked himself to death miles and days away from the conflict that presumably was supposed to give his life direction and meaning. Would not this mysterious family have done the same thing? No, not for rambling Noah Puckett. And unless J. D. Pennebaker survived bullets and Mexican food (he did not) Joe would be unable to trace the whereabouts of this wife, those kids. Surely a little bit of them belonged to Joe. It was too cruel; he wished the letter had been lost in transit, wished he had never learned of these people he would in all likelihood never meet, hoped (against his better judgement) that J. D. Pennebaker had thought to include Joe's address in the letter to Mrs. Puckett (he had not), wished time could be turned backwards, mistakes rectified, misunderstandings resolved, wish wish wish in one hand, piss in the other—see which fills up first. Now he truly was alone.

Joe went outside. The snowfall in recent days had been heavy. He began building a white mound in the yard, piled up every grudge and grievance, every disappointment and rebuttal, assembled, added to, patted down a hulking surrogate of snow—humped, barrel-chested, the head domed and horned, a buffalo bursting from the ground, pristine, gleaming, already slick with sunmelt. When it was prepared to his satisfaction he smashed it down again, reduced it to a formless jumble of trampled lumps.

He went to the ridge's spine, looked westwards across the prairie, an unbroken expanse of whiteness. If he squinted his eyes, squeezed his lids almost shut, he could imagine before him an endless plain of white buffalo.

WILLIAM W. JOHNSTONE
THE PREACHER SERIES